KING'S OAK

Also by Anne Rivers Siddons

PEACHTREE ROAD

HEARTBREAK HOTEL

THE HOUSE NEXT DOOR

FOX'S EARTH

HOMEPLACE

KING'S OAK

A Novel by

Anne Rivers Siddons

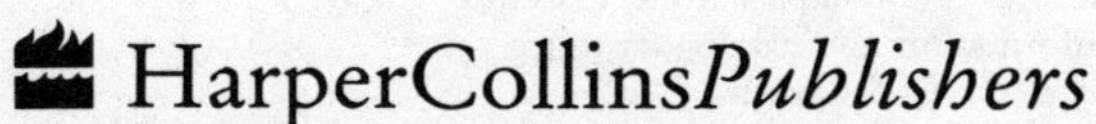

HarperCollins*Publishers*

Grateful acknowledgment is made to the following for permission to quote from copyrighted material:

"My Funny Valentine," by Richard Rodgers and Lorenz Hart. Copyright 1937 Chappel & Co. (renewed). All Rights Reserved. Used by Permission.

Helena's Prayer to the Three Magi, by Evelyn Waugh. Copyright 1950 by The Estate of Evelyn Waugh. Printed by Permission of Peters, Fraser, & Dunlop, Ltd.

The Immense Journey, by Loren Eiseley. Copyright © 1957 by Loren Eiseley. Used by Permission of Random House, Inc.

Poems of Dylan Thomas, by Dylan Thomas. Copyright 1945 by the Trustees for the Copyrights of Dylan Thomas. Reprinted by Permission of New Directions Publishing Corporation. U.S. rights; for Canadian and British rights, refer to: David Higham Associates Ltd, 5-8 Lower John Street, Golden Square, London W1R 4HA England.

A Child's Christmas in Wales, by Dylan Thomas. Copyright 1953 by New Directions Publishing Corporation. Reprinted by Permission of New Directions Publishing Corporation. U.S. rights; for Canadian and British rights, refer to: David Higham Associates Ltd, 5-8 Lower John Street, Golden Square, London W1R 4HA England.

"Song from the Moulin Rouge," by William Engvick and Georges Auric. Copyright 1953, renewed 1983, by SCREEN GEMS-EMI MUSIC INC. All Rights Reserved. International Copyright Secured. Used by Permission.

"Easy to Love," by Cole Porter. Copyright 1936 Chappel & Co. (renewed). All Rights Reserved. Used by Permission.

"Moon River," by Johnny Mercer and Henry Mancini. Copyright © 1961 by Famous Music Corporation.

Designed by Alma Orenstein

Library of Congress Cataloging-in-Publication Data

Siddons, Anne Rivers.
King's oak : a novel / by Anne Rivers Siddons.—1st ed.
p. cm.
ISBN 0-06-016248-1
I. Title.
PS3569.I28K56 1990 89-46116
813'.54—dc20

To HEYWARD

My huckleberry friend

I am become Death, the destroyer of worlds.

—*from the* Bhagavad Gita, *as quoted by*
J. ROBERT OPPENHEIMER,
upon first seeing a nuclear explosion

Moon River, wider than a mile,
I'm crossing you in style someday . . .
Dream maker, you heart breaker,
Wherever you're going, I'm going your way . . .
Two drifters, off to see the world,
There's such a lot of world to see . . .
We're after the same rainbow's end,
Waiting 'round the bend,
My huckleberry friend,
Moon River . . . and me.

—JOHNNY MERCER
HENRY MANCINI

KING'S OAK

CHAPTER ONE

Early in the last decade of the century, the earth began to die in earnest, though few of us noticed, and as in all times of unperceived cataclysm, the very air shuddered with myths, legends, and wondrous occurrences. Goat Creek lit up for the first time, for instance, on the very day that I came to Pemberton. Tom Dabney told me that, only much later. I might have thought that he spoke allegorically, since by then I knew that he saw signs and omens everywhere. Tom saw portent in the fact that he woke up in the morning.

But then, only days later, Scratch Purvis told me the same thing.

"Lit right up like there was light bulbs way down in it, blue ones," he said in his ruined wheeze. "I could see it shinin' all the way down to where it runs into the Big Silver. I knowed then that something considerable was comin', and sho nuff, that very afternoon, there you was."

So I believed it then, this story of the shining, smoking creek. Scratch, who did have a kind of blinded and searching Sight, nevertheless did not speak of that which he was not certain. If he, too, said that Goat Creek had lit up, then light up, by God, it did. The hows and whys of it were entirely irrelevant.

Goat Creek: an unlovely and earthbound name for that beautiful and haunted finger of dark Georgia water. Still as a breath-scummed black mirror in the late summer; dreaming in the steel-blue autumn like a somnolent reptile; ice-rimmed and shut down and secret under the bled-out skies of winter; drifted with the stilled snowfall of dogwood and honeysuckle in the long, magical spring, Goat Creek loops and laces its way some twenty-odd miles from its source, a hidden spring somewhere in the trackless river swamp that covers much of Baines County in southwest Georgia, to the place where it gives up its life to the Big Silver River.

In some places along its course, Goat Creek runs shallow and sunstruck through deep grasses and reeds, through open fields and clearings in the vast woods around the Big Silver. Its life there is clear and open, the province of busy waterfowl and industrious raccoons and bees and turtles and snakes and, I have been told, an occasional small, undistinguished alligator. I have never seen a gator, though I have seen the deadly roiling of the black water as one took a baby wild pig, and heard the terrible snortings, and the thin screams of the piglet, and I saw the black water redden with the piglet's blood. So I know that the gators are there.

Deer by the hundreds come to drink at the muddy verges of these shallows. It is possible to see the mishmash left by their delicate cloven hooves almost any morning. Wild pigs chuff there, too, feral and stupid. And in season, the trees around the open fields bloom with the ugly flora of wooden and metal stands, refuge of camouflaged hunters with rifles and compound bows and an astonishing array of devices to lure, by smell and sound, the slender white-tailed deer of the Big Silver.

But mostly Goat Creek runs in secret, in an eternal semitwilight of black-green trees and hanging moss and undergrowth so dense that it is like blood or darkness, a separate element. Its life here is a secret life in all ways, as secret as the place where it begins. I have never seen the spring that is its birthplace, but I have come to know much of its secret darkness and many of its sunny interstices, and I have slept and eaten and loved in one of those, and I have never forgotten, since the first day I saw it, that Goat Creek is a finger that points to Pemberton.

I came to Pemberton chasing banality like a hound a rabbit and found instead a lush, slow beauty so insistent and particular that it frightened me. After my initial visit to Tish, to scout the lay of the land and attend the interviews Charlie had arranged for me, I think I would have backed out of the whole thing because of the unease that beauty caused me, except that by that time Tish had found a place for Hilary and me to live, and had even paid the deposit on it.

"You have to come now," she said in her rich neigh. "I've told everybody you would, and you'll make me out a liar, and in Pemberton that's worse than letting your roots show. The ones in your hair, I mean. It's perfectly okay if the others do. In fact, they'd better, or nobody will ask you to their party."

"I don't have any of either kind," I said.

"Nonsense," she said. "There's not a thing wrong with your roots. After all, you're a Calhoun. That name around here is like Cabot in Boston."

"You know perfectly well I'm not a Calhoun. Christopher is a Calhoun. I'm an Andropoulis. You got any Cabotopoulises around here?"

"Don't be stupid, Andy," she said evenly, in her best Student Government voice. "It's the right thing to do, for you and Hilary both. You've got to get that child settled down before school starts. And you've got to settle, too."

It wasn't so much the argument as the weight of her presence, her sheer, easy authority, that decided me. Tish was neither a fool nor a bully, and she had been a loving friend for over twenty years. Her enveloping presence had always had an enervating, soporific effect on me, and I was tired with fifteen years' worth of corrosive fatigue. It was not only the last terrible five years with Chris, but all those that went before, beginning in the small white frame house in southeast Atlanta that my mother had so insistently called a bungalow (which in fact it was, but her tone was that of the Newporters who so astoundingly called their vast summer homes "cottages," and I hated it). The years before my father finally died and left us in a frozen and furious peace.

Tish Griffin, who was my roommate the entire four years we spent at Emory University in Atlanta, and a psychology major, always held that I lived, moved, and had my being, as the Book of Common Prayer puts it, in flight from my father. He was a taurine man, a squat, roaring black Greek who kept a small grocery store in the blue-collar section of Atlanta where we lived, and from long before my birth to the day he died, he drank liquor and embarrassed my mother and me. Or at least my mother said that he did, and by the time that I was six or seven and had started elementary school, she had said it enough times so that I believed her. Certainly by then his stumbling, bellowing homecomings from the Kirkwood Café on the corner, late most nights except Sundays, and his erratic outbursts at the store and mumbling, lurching progress home to lunch every day were sufficient to mortify a pious conventional woman, which my mother was, and a timid, conventional child, which I was. And I do remember the stiff back and hot cheeks of youthful anguish that his behavior, and the chants and snickers of my schoolmates, caused me.

But I remember loving him, too; remember distinctly the powerful, knee-weakening wash of pure contentment, of utter safety, that I felt at the smell of his soft, sun-dried undershirts and his spicy-sweet aftershave, and the helpless fits of giggles that his loud, clumsy, Greek-laced foolishness caused to bubble up from my chest when he picked me up and held me over his head. He was a strong man, deep-chested and long-muscled despite his short stature, and I felt a sly, proprietary pride in all that maleness and strength that was near sexual. *My* father: this modern Daedalus, this minotaur among us, was *mine,* property of otherwise insignificant *me*. I might be so incorporeal as to be invisible in my small society most of the time, but in the great, black-furred arms of Pano Andropoulis I was as luminously visible as Venus in a winter sky.

So if, by the time I was old enough to recognize his behavior as aberrant, outrageous, beyond the pale, and to be, with my mother, seared and shamed by it, my pain went deeper than hers, it was because under there was that hopeless, helpless love, while under her pain there was not, I think, anything but a cold anger and more pain. I cannot remember ever having a sense that my mother loved my father.

"It's a classic escape mechanism," Tish said to me one

April night during our sophomore year, when we sat on our twin beds in the mimosa wash from the open windows, rehashing our double date. I had, for a few months, been going out exclusively with her boyfriend's roommate, like him a junior at Emory Medical School. Tish had been going with Charlie Coulter so long that their wedding, planned for the day after he got his M.D., was as fixed and unremarkable in her firmament and mine as our familiar stars. But I had only met Chris Calhoun when Charlie's old roommate, Shoe, flunked out and Chris moved into the scabrous little apartment off Ponce de Leon Avenue. I had, that spring evening, after three or four unaccustomed beers at Moe's and Joe's, announced to Tish that I'd marry Chris Calhoun in three seconds flat if he asked me, and if he didn't, I'd live in sin with him anywhere he chose, even the vast basement apartment of his parents' great gray stone house on Habersham Road.

It was a mark of my degree of abandonment to Christopher Sibley Calhoun and the beer, that statement, especially the part about sin; it was, after all, only the beginning of the freewheeling seventies in the Deep South, and we were, at Emory, still a safe remove from burning bras and the sexual revolution. And Habersham Road was worlds, galaxies, a universe away from Hardin Street in Kirkwood, even if only four miles in actuality. I had visited Chris's home once, at a large party his parents had given earlier in the spring, but so far as I knew, my mother had never been west of Peachtree Road, or north of the Medical Arts Building downtown, and she went there on a bus. It was, for both of us, a distance measured in more than miles.

"Escape mechanism," Tish said around a mouthful of Milk Duds. "Get away from Daddy as fast and far as you can. Make him eat your dust. And what's further away than Chris Calhoun and Habersham Road?"

I was silent for a moment, wondering, as I often did with Tish, whether or not she might be right. Aside from her veneer of sophomore psychology, which was ephemeral at best, Tish had, when it came to me, the prescience that comes with real affection. She both knew and loved me, something few other people in my experience had done. We had been closer than most sisters for two years. There was a marked sameness to us when it came to clothes, hair, makeup, ambitions, and bents of the heart. We were both bright, liberal-leaning, clever, and worldly in the smart-mouthed manner of the time but ludicrously innocent beneath the banter, self-deprecating in the quasi-modest way of well-brought-up Southern girls, and ironically and ignorantly scornful of anything less than total commitment to our bruised sixties ideals of peace, love, and service to society. But there was a great and basic difference in us. Under my seventies shell was a vast, empty abyss where no perceivable self dwelled. Under Tish's shell lived more of Tish, solid down to her core. Tish had a large, rooted, privileged family in Macon, Georgia, and spoke out of generations of cheerful love and a given self-worth. The authority of sureness rang in even her most absurd statements.

"I think you're full of crap," I said finally, tasting my words. Tish would have said "shit" as naturally as she said her name. "Why do I have to be running away from my father? Why can't I just be running *to* Chris? Any woman who wasn't brain dead would be."

"Bullshit," she said. "I wouldn't. You wouldn't, either, if you didn't want to escape from Daddy so bad. Chris Calhoun is a jerk, Andy. You can do better than that. You know I've always thought you could."

And she had. When Charlie had brought him around to the Tri Delt house the year before, Tish had taken one look at his open child's face and sweet, three-cornered smile and gone uncharacteristically silent. By the time the evening was nearly over and we were driving back to the house in Chris's green Mustang convertible, she was positively arctic in her silence, and Charlie was glaring at her. Chris, to whom such disapprobation must have been as rare as a pimple on his faultless tanned skin, was outdoing himself with wit and charm, and I was laughing with pleasure and infatuation. Chris has always been a funny and endearing man, and he was never more so than that night. It would have taken a real misanthrope to fail to respond, and warm, generous Tish was the opposite of that. But she was not moved, then or ever.

"He's not worth you," she said that first night. "He's too pretty. He's too rich. He's like a corrupted elf or something; he's too sure of himself. It's more than just being a doctor; they all have that kind of arrogance. It's something that goes under that. I think he's just your basic prick, and I wish Charlie had never met him. He's just as stupid over him as you are."

But she had said very little else about him one way or another through the following year, while we were double-dating every night Chris and Charlie could get free and I was falling in love with Chris and he was falling into whatever it was he had with me. That silence was undoubtedly another mark of her love for me. Tish saw Chris plain, but she also saw that my heart even early on had irrevocably gone over to him. Quite simply, I thought he was a miracle made flesh.

I honestly never knew what Chris saw in me, and still do not; even then, at what might be called my very best, I was small and dark as the Greek I am, not at all well-dressed, and round as an apple to boot, and he had long known what my family was. I had never taken him home, much less spoken of them to him, but he knew. Charlie told him, no doubt. It seemed almost beyond belief to me that he, a prince of the city in the most literal sense, moving in a world of private clubs and prep schools and family fortunes and huge old houses and long-legged, willow-waisted, drawling girls, should choose to spend all the time he had, after his medical studies, with me. But only almost beyond belief. Somehow I never really questioned it. Perhaps I did not dare to. And my dear, loyal Tish held her tongue, at what cost I shall never know.

So that night a year later, when she accused me of using Chris to escape from my father, I did hesitate for a fraction of a moment before I snapped back at her. And then I said, "Anyway, how do you know it's not my mother I'm trying to escape?" and knew in that instant that it was true. And that it always had been.

Oh, my mother. My mother, Agnes Farr Andropoulis, spinner of dreams and killer of possibilities. Reality never sufficed for her, and her fantasies never nourished her. To others, they were lethal, or nearly so. My mother was a flower of old Mobile society, according to her earliest bedtime stories, caught young in a brutalizing marriage to a virile Greek god gone, early and inexplicably, to seed and to pot. Her life was a tragedy out of Aeschylus, out of Grimm.

He was never a Greek god, of course, my father; even when she met and married him, he was what he always had been and would be: second-generation son of a southern Greek grocery store owner, pigheaded and largehearted and full of a wild, fierce exuberance that was as natural and good as the scent of wild thyme on the hillsides outside Athens, but overdrawn, excessive, threatening in the stiflingly conventional, marginally poor neighborhood of Atlanta in the 1950s where his father, Dion, had his store. But my mother needed a god to mate with; nothing else would have sufficed for a princess in disguise as a lonely young schoolteacher in a strange city. And my father, by his very heritage, coveted a princess. By the time I was on the way, she realized that her god was in actuality the commonest of clay and impervious to molding and he realized that his princess was a blighted and pious pretender to the throne. Neither ever forgave the other, or ceased in their punishing. My father sailed his outrage through the streets of our neighborhood on a flood of bourbon. My mother moved far away from him inside her phantasmagoric mind and took me with her. From my earliest memory it was as if they had a kind of mad joint custody of me; I lived half the time in his careening tenure, loving him, and half in her kingdom of cobwebs, adoring her. Both damaged me, I have come to see, but she perhaps most of all. He frightened me sometimes. But my mother made me afraid.

To this day she will not see it. For a short period of time, on the advice of an earnest young therapist who could have no more imagined my mother than he could have conceived of a griffin or a pterodactyl, I confronted her with it, seeking catharsis and insight.

"You overprotected me to the point that I thought I wasn't capable of simply living in the world," I said, trembling with the enormity of speaking so to her, but determined to seek some sort of salvation. "You made me feel like there was nothing I could do by myself, without you. Remember? You'd never let me go barefoot. You never let me play with most of the children on the street. I couldn't stay after school and play softball or volleyball. I couldn't date neighborhood boys. I couldn't ride in cars or eat spicy food; I couldn't walk to the movies or stay out after ten o'clock. It was always: 'Don't do that; you'll get hurt.' 'You can't do that by yourself; let me do it for you.' 'Wait till I help you with that.' You made me stay a child, Mama. Listen: I'm still calling you Mama. Not even Mother, Mama. I know you never intended to harm me; nobody could have loved me more than you have. But all that . . . smothering, that hovering . . . Mama, it makes me do things I shouldn't do, or not do things I should, just to feel *safe*. Or to be . . . oh, I don't know: *respectable*. Safe and respectable are the last things on earth I ought to be thinking about."

I was crying by then, silently, at the harsh sound of the traitorous words and the effort of speaking them to her.

"Oh, toot," she said gaily. It was what she said whenever she wished to flick reality away like a fly. Oh, toot. "I gave you the only kind of upbringing that matters in this world, the kind that makes you appreciate the finer things in life. The kind that makes you a lady. What should I have done—let you grow up knowing nothing but drunkenness and coarseness and common people and cheap things around you? Life is only beautiful when we make it beautiful. Where would you be now if I'd let you run wild with all those little hooligans and hang around that filthy store? Where would you be if I'd raised you to marry some—some mechanic out at the Ford plant? If my only sin has been making you wear shoes and stay out of trees, well, maybe the Lord will forgive me. If you still feel like a child, maybe it's because you still act like one. Running whining and crying to some *psychiatrist* because you feel like a little orphan baby girl, when you've got everything in the world a woman could want. You can be very sure that Mr. Christopher Calhoun would never have looked at you if I let you grow up the way you say you wanted to, missy."

By then she had lost the gaiety and retreated into the

aggrieved tears that had always smitten me with the full sense of my monstrous ingratitude. I dropped the confrontations and a week or so later the therapist. I had long realized that she was no longer my most powerful amulet against danger: was indeed, in a way, a danger herself; but I was still powerless to act on that knowledge. I did, and do, love my mother. And I suppose the reality of no amulet at all against the great, killing wounds of life was simply too awful for me to deal with. I have come to see that insight by itself doesn't mean, as we say in the South, doodly squat. By the time I could act on mine, my mother had, indirectly, almost killed me and my daughter.

All her life she has been a beautiful woman, frail and shining, and people who meet her only casually, without a context, always feel a protectiveness toward her fragility that excuses her eccentricity, of the sort one might feel toward a wildly ornate Bavarian china cup found in a garbage dump. It is only later, when they have attempted to get a sense of her as a living woman, that the real extent of the bizarreness becomes apparent. I let few people that close to her. By the time I reached college, I no longer took people home with me, because of both my father's grotesque cartoon progress toward total drunkenness and my mother's by-then-perfected Blanche DuBois act.

I stuck fiercely to my studies and my sorority sisters, aping slavishly each tiny detail of dress, speech, and behavior that struck me as "normal." I loved the very triteness, the small, parochial clichés, of college life. I became a perfect "normal" 1970s Southern college student. Normality was so foreign to me that it was infinitely exotic; I was in love with it. In fact I did not, for a long time, know what normality was.

I had been home with Tish to her big white house in

Macon many times, warming myself at the life-giving fire of a family that radiated wholeness and simple, lighthearted love. Indeed, the Griffins became my prime models. But Tish had met my mother only once, when Mother attended a Mother-Daughter tea in the sorority chapter room the year before. I had been mortified by her trailing polyester frills, and the arched little finger over the teacup handle, and the fluting references to our "simple little bungalow" and "the family business concerns," but my sisters and housemother found her, incredibly, "sweet." I know that more than one, Tish included, thought she was gallant and gay, this small, fragile gentlewoman who so bravely scrimped to send her daughter to one of the most expensive universities in the South. My status as a scholarship student was no secret. But the fact was that it was my father's huge, unsteady hand that still signed the checks that supplemented my scholastic stipends, and they alone of the checks that straggled out of the white frame house on Hardin Street were never late.

It was what drew me to Christopher, of course, my long love affair with normality and convention. But it was a subterranean pull. It never occurred to me when I met him, this mercurial sprite, this gilded, elfin son of one of the city's great houses and fortunes, that there was anything conventional about him. To me he shone like a young sun. He was everything we said we wanted, we displaced young Kennedy handmaidens: single-minded in his determination to become a great surgeon, keenly aware of the world's suffering and willing to put his and his family's money to work for it, fairly shimmering with energy and intensity. He crackled and spat with it; Chris could seldom remain still for long, and his tongue and his wit were like lightning. If he was also many of the things we said we didn't want—rich, social, grounded in generations of conservatism—well, there my seventies facade failed me. My eyes saw those things and read in them, simply and subliminally, safety. They added up to a package so perfect that sometimes, in an economics class, say, or walking across campus toward the sorority house on a mild winter day, my breath leaped in my chest with joy at the simple fact of him. I moved, in those days, in a fog of disbelief at my own good fortune. Nothing Tish said could penetrate it.

Much, much later I saw something clearly, and it frightened me, finally, enough to snatch my daughter and run. I saw that, for me, convention and normality were only seductive when they had at their core aberration and madness. I saw that there was within me an essential, if deeply buried, appetite for outrage, for dangerous excess. I saw that the thing in me that I had thought of, in my secret heart, as my "otherness," my apartness from other people, was indeed a kind of deviance, and that I had never known the difference. I thought that to be fully "myself" was to capitulate to darkness. When I finally did take flight from my ludicrous life to Pemberton and Tish and Charlie, it was partly from that dark self that I fled. I had sought normalcy and convention and found, not one monster, but two, and I was the second. It was as skewed a notion of myself as any of my earlier ones, of course, but at least it served to get me on my feet and on the road. If I had not had it, Hilary and I both would, I think, be dead now.

But in the beginning I knew nothing except that I wanted Chris and he, incredibly, wanted me, and at the end of my sophomore year and his junior he asked me if I would marry him at Saint Philip's Cathedral in Atlanta on the Saturday after Tish married Charlie in Saint Martin's in Macon, and I said yes before the words were out of his mouth. The first thing he said, after that, was: "I really thought you were going to give me some bullshit about the Peace Corps for a couple of years, or marching on the White House on our honeymoon," and the second was: "Can I for Christ sake touch you now? I've had a hard-on for a year, and I don't think I can wait another."

And so the lovemaking began, that same night, in his bedroom in the hot, stale-smelling little apartment on Ponce de Leon, while Tish and Charlie were at a movie and "Little Bitty Pretty One" pounded on the radio. I could think of no reason, any longer, not to sleep with him. Marriage would happen, now. Respect was guaranteed, and my involuntary "no" died on my lips and I got into his narrow, unmade bed with him, heart hammering as if to burst from my chest, and we did the thing that, for my generation and all the ones before me, divided time.

Chris had always respected my instinctive, soft, sharp "no"s, whenever, in heavy necking and petting, his hand found its way up under my skirt or beneath my blouse to my breasts; respected them with a shrugged indifference that at first reassured me and then made me worry that he was getting what he wanted somewhere else. I knew that he would never say and that I would not ask him, but I could not imagine that he could not have had any of the gilded Atlanta goddesses in his orbit that he wanted. It was, after all, the dawn of the seventies, and all over the country young women were taking the pill and having sex if they wished, though, this being the Deep South, my contemporaries were not talking about it much, and many of us still were not doing it, pill or no pill, and the ones who were were probably never really comfortable with it. But the times, they were a-changin', and the great, primal curse of pregnancy and disgrace had largely evaporated, and there was no longer any reason for my pulling away from Chris except the real one: fear. It was my mother's longest-lived legacy to me.

Most fears fade when their object is confronted, when the deed is done. My fear was justified. After the first great stabbing pain as Chris entered me, I was lost, gone, swallowed, drowned. I came immediately and furiously, not knowing what it was, and shrieked aloud with terror as well as release. I screamed for Chris to stop, feeling myself vanishing into pure sensation, disappearing into redness, into him. I was utterly gone in panic; surely there was no bottom to this abyss of pleasure; surely oblivion waited there. It had been this fear, then, that waited for me in my own body, not the world's fears: pregnancy, disgrace, wantonness. This one, my own, the fear of vanishing altogether from the face of the earth. The fear of becoming nothing. No one. Of simply . . . not being.

Chris did not hear me, and he did not stop. He did it to me three more times, and each time I plummeted shrieking into that exquisite death, shamed and terrified and amazed that this could be me doing these things . . . for the ways that Chris loved were ways that I never knew anywhere else; neither read nor heard about ever after. Tish and I had giggled over the *Kamasutra* many times, but I had never seen, even there, the things that Chris could do with his sleek, wiry, inexhaustible body and his searching beacon penis. The last two times, even as I bucked and spasmed and wept, I had the cool and astonished sensation of watching from a vantage point near the ceiling as perverted Chinese acrobats performed. My mother seemed to hover alongside me, shrieking, "Shame! Shame! You should be on your back with your eyes closed, like a missionary!"

When he was finished the last time, I could not move or speak, and lay there feeling like my own corpse in the tumbled bed. I wanted to lie there forever, not moving, barely breathing, with cool darkness falling on my closed lids, and not this pounding, spinning redness. My heart beat in slow, huge, dragging thuds, and I wondered if one died of this. It seemed possible.

"I guess that settles the problem of marital adjustment," Chris said, grinning down at me from one elbow. Incredibly, he did not look damp or tousled. He looked like Peter Pan, alert and cheeky and gay. I began to cry.

He was contrite and tender; held me close, said that he shouldn't have rushed me, shouldn't have been so . . . inventive.

"But I'd waited for you so long," he said. "And the way you went off . . . I thought you were loving it. I never heard you make noises like that before."

"I told you to stop," I sobbed. "I told you over and over. It was like . . . Chris, it was like *dying!*"

"I know," he said, grinning. "They say it is like that when it's the best it can be. You're lucky, Andy. We're lucky. Some people try all their lives and never get it. We hit it on the first roll."

We got dressed and went back to the Tri Delt house, stopping for a beer at Manuel's Tavern on the way. We had done that a hundred times before, but now we did it in an aura of profound and irreversible change.

"We're not the same people who started out tonight," he said, hugging me hard around my shoulders as we walked into the sorority house. "We're part of something else now, part of a whole. I don't think a marriage license could make us any closer. Can you feel it?"

"Yes," I said, tottering on rubber legs, feeling a sly, insinuating soreness begin inside me from my pubic bone to up near my spine. "I certainly can."

I wondered how the others—Tish, my mother, all the

women before and around me who had gone in an evening from one who had not done this to one who had—could live with the degree of that difference. It was a revelatory, life-altering thing. I wondered how you could do it every night and remain essentially the same person you had been before.

Tish was coming out of the shower, wrapped in a thin, grayish-white Tri Delt towel, when I walked into the room, and she knew immediately. Without either of us speaking a word, she knew that we were engaged and that I had done it with Chris. I always wondered how, though I never asked her. I knew, or assumed, that she had been sleeping with Charlie for some time, but I had not known when she began to do it. We had never talked of it.

"I assume that I'm speaking to the future Mrs. Christopher Calhoun," she said, grinning.

"You are," I said, trying to grin back. "To become so exactly one week after you and Charlie."

"So your big dream has come true."

"Yes. It really has."

"Then why have you been crying?"

"Well, you know. The proverbial tears of joy."

She went over to her dresser and picked up a cigarette and lit it. Tish was trying to quit smoking because Charlie was so insistent about it, but she lapsed in times of stress.

"And how was the proverbial first night?"

"First night?" I asked brightly.

"Come on, Andy, this is me. I know you screwed. And I can see you've been crying. Did he hurt you?"

"No," I said. "It was wonderful."

She stared at me silently through smoke.

I could feel the tears stinging up through my nose again,

and said, "It was . . . awful. Not in the way I think you think, but . . . really scary. I think it's probably me. Tish . . ."

"Hmmm?"

"Can I ask you . . . ?" I stopped.

"Andy, you surely must know that Charlie and I have been fucking like minks every chance we get since he could get samples of the pill. Don't be coy with me. Ask me anything you want to."

"Well, I just . . . is it supposed to be fabulous the first time? Am I supposed to just . . . automatically love it? I've wanted to do it with him for so long; I've thought I just couldn't wait any longer. . . ."

Tish ground out the cigarette and hugged me.

"God, no. It's almost always awful the first time," she said. "It hurts like hell and it's messy and you don't feel anything at all, and you wonder if you're frigid and he's going to leave you. . . . It's not fabulous for any of us, I'm sure of that. I think it's because your head knows it's okay to do it now, but the rest of you doesn't. It makes you feel like a slut or an impostor, or, even worse, like you're a lousy lay. It's that early training at Mama's knee. I cried for two days when we first did it. But it gets good later. It really does. It gets wonderful. Gradually you'll get to trust him and the fact that he's not going to leave you and the pill really does work . . . and then it's just marvelous. Sweet and deep and tender and . . . explosive. Yow. It makes me hot just talking about it."

I said nothing.

She looked at me intently. "Don't do it again without the pill, though, Andy. Get Chris to get you some tomorrow. They can get all they want from the lab. Or Charlie will. But don't do it anymore unless you're taking them. It's not worth it—the worry. And it's really not worth getting pregnant."

"I don't know," I said vaguely. "It seems so . . . businesslike."

"Trust me on this, Andy," she said.

I did. I think at that point that Patricia Tolliver Griffin from Macon, Georgia, was the only person in the world I did trust fully and completely. No hurt had ever come to me from Tish; only good things. Only nourishment. Only love. From the moment I had met her at freshman orientation I had loved her, and I think—I know—she did me. I've never really known why.

I literally stumbled into her, nearly blinded with early-September sweat and looking totally unremarkable, even ludicrous, in my Sears miniskirt, which wrapped my round, short, big-breasted body like a sausage casing. Stricken with shyness and wrongness and trying not to show it, I had said, "Excuse me, I'm trying to find English 301."

"It's over there under *S*." She grinned at me, a tall, angular girl with a speckled colt's face peering out from beneath a coppery mushroom of hair.

"For 'Shit,' " she added.

I stared at her for a moment and then dissolved into laughter so profound that I nearly wet my pants, and she laughed, too, a glorious, deep, rich, neighing laugh that echoes even now in my happiest dreams. When we stopped laughing we were that rarest of human couplings, intended and inseparable friends. And from then on, I lived in her blazing wake like a dark little satellite. She almost sucked me into life.

My background and family and financial status didn't bother her an iota. My all-wrong clothes and hair didn't, either. She took me home with her and made me a part of the rich, raucous, loving Griffin clan; she lent me clothes and ironed my hair and bought me pale lipstick, got me dates, and told me the secrets of her sunny heart. It seems to me now that we laughed for four straight years. She was a born leader, a magnet; every sorority on campus wanted her. She pledged Tri Delt on the condition that they bid me, too. Her mother paid my initiation fee and dues, and bought me my chaste gold trident pin, and in return I tutored Tish through four years of English and history. She wasn't stupid, or a bad student; she held a plethora of demanding campus offices and high honors, and her grades in mathematics and science were exemplary. But she is the most impatient person I have ever known, and would not study what did not come naturally. I forced excellence in the humanities on her. Thanks to me, she was Phi Beta Kappa and Dean's List. Thanks to her, I was happier in college than I had ever been. Thanks to her, indirectly, I found Chris.

So I trusted her on the matter of birth control pills and said that I would ask Chris for some. But as it turned out, I didn't have to. He brought a manila envelope full of Enovids when he came to pick me up that night, and instead of going to see *Fahrenheit 451*, as we had planned, we went back to the apartment and we did it again.

And again. And again. And again, I came hard and helplessly, honking like a goose in each moist new contortion, falling once more into that obliterating red darkness. I was barely through shuddering before I felt him begin to stiffen and probe and slide again, and felt the red tide begin to rise anew from my loins, and felt the rocking rhythm take me once more down into that dark sea. Finally, after the third time, I rolled myself into a ball on the bed and screwed my eyes shut and cried, "Stop! Chris, stop!"

"Christ, Andy, I can't stop now. . . ."

"No! Stop! I don't care! No more! You're making a bedpan or something out of me! Once is enough, Chris!"

He did not argue. There was a sweetness to Christopher then; he said only, "You call it, babe." After that, we did it only once a night. But it was almost every night, and it was always something exotic and unimaginable. It was explosive, as Tish had said; it was deep; it was even, later on, transcendent. Tish had been right; I did come to relish, even to hunger after, the feeling of Chris's body in mine. In time I came to want it so much that the very thought of the coming night and what we would say and do to each other stopped my breath and loosened my legs and arms in their sockets and made me lose my thoughts and speech and focus. But it was never sweet, or tender, or slow. And for the length of my life with Chris and beyond, I thought that I alone, of any women I knew or would ever know, did things in the night from which, in my heart, I averted my eyes.

Tish and I had long planned to do what we called ghetto work after graduation, she wherever Charlie's internship took them, I with a literacy program in the urban jungles of my own city. After that, she foresaw a private practice in juvenile psychology while Charlie set up his own ob-gyn practice; and I foresaw, modestly, highly acclaimed, thoughtful magazine journalism and perhaps a slim, sensitive novel or two. Instead, in the two years before I married Chris, I became what I believe is currently called a love slave and spent the time I was not in bed with Chris turning myself into a perfect Buckhead surgeon's wife. In fairness, he did not ask that of me, but neither did he demur when after three or four visits with his parents at their home on Habersham Road and at the Piedmont Driving Club, I cut my offensively exuberant black Greek hair and dieted my solid bottom into size eight linen from the Wood Valley Shop and bought a pair of plain patent-leather pumps with tiny heels. I even found, God knows where in that age of rampant shining nakedness, a flowered cotton bathing suit with little-boy legs for splashing in the pool behind the house on Habersham Road—the shallow end, for there had been no public swimming pools in Kirkwood when I was growing up. In all the flock of snub-nosed, long-limbed girls with their sunglasses perched on their sun-streaked heads who came on weekends to swim at Chris's house with his parents and two younger sisters, I was the only one who could not swim like a young otter. Nor could I play tennis or golf, or ride a horse.

"It's a congenital trait among my people," I told his mother, Sally. ("Call me Sally, darling! Nobody calls me Mrs. Calhoun.") "Hellenic hip displacement, it's called."

"Really," she murmured. "What a pity. Perhaps, later on, some surgery . . . ?"

"She's pulling your leg, Ma," Chris said, in obvious enjoyment. "She can't swim a lick. Sinks like a rock. Look at that butt."

"Don't be crude, Chris," Sally Calhoun said, giving me a bright, lipsticked smile, which did not reach her clear blue cheerleader's eyes. "Andy will think I've raised a barbarian."

But it was clear who was the barbarian at 2425 Habersham Road, and I don't know why I did not see it from the outset, except that by the time I got to know Chris's parents I was so far sunk into my love slavery that I could not see, as Tish said once, waspishly, the "forest for the fucking." But see it I did, one summer evening about a year after we had gotten engaged, when we sat on the Driving Club terrace having drinks before dinner with Chris's parents, and a couple of their friends whom I had never met, newly returned from a summer cruising in the Greek isles, stopped by our table to be introduced to Chris's fiancée.

"This is Andy, Chris's adorable little bride-to-be," Sally Calhoun said. "Isn't she a welcome sight in all this seven-foot blondness around here? Andy Andropoulis. From Greece, of all wonderful places to call home—or at least, her father is. The Rawsons, Andy."

"Oh, how lovely! We're just back from there," Adelaide Rawson bubbled. "Are you an exchange student? Might we have met some of your family? We met some marvelous people; Tim's firm does business with some of them. Shipping, I think. . . ."

"No, I live here. I was born here," I said, light beginning to sink through the fog in my sodden mind. "My father is—"

"In the mercantile business," Sally Calhoun said smoothly. "Andy is a Tri Delt at Emory. You know, with Lila Cunningham's girl, and Bootsie Carter's . . ."

"Andy's father has a grocery store in Kirkwood," Chris said lazily, squinting amiably at the Rawsons over his gin and tonic.

"Ah," said Adelaide Rawson. "Interesting. Well, my dear, you'll be a welcome addition to our young crowd," and she arrowed a gleaming smile at Sally Calhoun and faltered into silence.

I followed her glance. She was looking at Sally, but Sally was not looking back at her. She was looking at Chris, and there was such a murderous and anguished love, such a furious and sucking thing, in her eyes that her face might as well have been drawn into a grimace of primal passion. It was nearly erotic in its purity. I could not get my breath, or pull my eyes away; whatever I felt for Chris, I knew that it could never equal this living, burning thing that his mother felt, nor match the force of her rage at me for capturing him. How much lower those fires would have burned for a slim, blond Buckhead debutante I do not know, but I do—and did—know that they would have been hidden. Only for the conquering barbarian the full force of the victim's contempt.

Still without breathing, I looked at Chris, and saw in his own blue eyes a full and rounded, uncomplicated triumph. And saw, then, his mother seeing it, too, and knew in that moment the truth of, and the reason for, my coming marriage. Oh, the children of the South! Rooted too deeply, laden like gilded donkeys with the baggage of the past, straining like twisted, pale seedlings to escape the monstrous shadows of Mother. I understood what drove Chris even as the fact of it lanced me to the heart: was I not still in flight from a mother-monster of my own? I should have left him and his family on the spot and on the moment; of course I should have. I can see that now. Instead I forgave him and redoubled my efforts to become one of the certified, approved belles of Buckhead. By the time we married, I could pass, if one did not look too closely. Few people did, except my parents-in-law, and they had long since learned to keep their peace in order to keep their son. I knew by then that he would not let them drive me away. Chris was never one to surrender a weapon.

By the winter before my marriage I was growing haggard trying to decide how to handle the matter of my parents . . . for the Calhouns had never met them, though many meaning-to-get-together murmurs had by then been murmured. My father solved half of the problem early that spring by choking to death on vomit while passed out on the sagging glider on the front porch on Hardin Street. I mourned him truly, if distractedly, and was comforted by Tish, who had met and liked him, and by Chris, who had not. But I know that Chris was truly sorry, and I think that at least part of his sorrow was for my own, though I knew, even at the time, that part of it was at losing an advantage with his mother. Pano Andropoulis had been first-class ammunition, a veritable excalibur held in reserve. Now he would never be able to use it.

My father did me one last service from beyond his grave: he gave my mother the graceful cover of mourning in which to hide from my wedding and its attendant flurry of festivities. For she had behaved so baroquely and affectedly at the one obligatory little luncheon Sally Calhoun had given for her at the Habersham Road house—not wanting, I think, to parade her past the delicately pecking bills ranked along the marble halls of the Driving Club—that it was apparent even to her that she would not be welcome there again. Asked back, probably; Sally would never be grossly and overtly rude. But never welcome. My mother had come to lunch swathed like a bride herself in trailing flounced organdy and a hat I thought she must have rented at a costume company, and had trilled and fluted and simpered and fluttered and referred to our "cottage" and our "bungalow" and her "cutting garden" until Sally had let one of her painfully amused smiles slide into a barely audible titter, and there followed a silvery chorus of barely audible titters from Sally's guests, and even my mother in full spate can tell a titter from a smile. She finished lunch in a tight-mouthed silence that rang like a fishwife's screech, left in a huff befitting a mad empress, and announced that she would never set foot in that trashy woman's house again.

"Just tell her I'm in mourning," she said. "Even she should be able to understand that. I'll come to your wedding, but I'm not going to any reception at any Piedmont Driving-te-dah-Club."

I was utterly ashamed of my own shame at her behavior, and grateful beyond measure that she had taken refuge in umbrage. My mother kept her grudges, like a piano or a tester bed, for life.

My mother never held his mother against Chris; to her, he could do no wrong. He was, and has remained, the single best thing, the one grand achievement, of my life. Much later, after the beatings started, when she finally found out about them, the first thing she said was: "What on earth did you do to make him that mad?"

And long after that, even when a bone broke here or there, and a stitch was needed, and the crazy, shamed fear of disclosure that I lived with slid over into fear for my life, I stayed with Chris. I stayed for every reason that women do stay with such monstrousness, and thought I was staying, in part, for love of my mother. I was still, even then, so much my mother's daughter that I would have died to please her.

The good, no-nonsense shrink I found that last spring told me, when I spoke about staying with Christopher because it would kill my mother if I left him, that it was a toss-up whether I was going to die of battery or bullshit.

"You're mainly sticking it out to show her you were right," he said. "That he's as bad as you said he was, and that it's his fault and not yours. A black eye? See, Mother: it's really serious. A broken arm? You were wrong, Ma. He's a jerk. Dead? Hey, Ma! I win! . . . That's not love. That's pure hate. You need to get away from her as much as him. Neither one of them is worth dying for."

"But I do love her," I said. "At least half of her. There's half of somebody in there that I love."

"Then leave the part you hate and send letters every

week to the half you love," he said. "Do you want him to kill Hilary?"

"He wouldn't hurt Hilary," I said. "He loves Hilary. I think she's about all that he does love now."

"Andy," said the shrink, "he loves you. This is what Chris does when he loves. This is what love is to him. Can't you understand that when she manages to cross him at the wrong time or get in his way, he'll hit her, too?"

But I could not understand that, because she was what we both had wanted so desperately for so long, my beautiful and bright and enchanting Hilary; tried and tried for and tried again through eight long years while Chris ground his way through internship and surgical residency and the first years of practice, and I decorated apartments and condominiums and then the house on Blackland Road in Buckhead and learned to swim and play tennis and serve on hospital auxiliaries and charitable committees and give dinner parties. Tried with teeth-grinding earnestness night after night in bigger and bigger beds in bigger and bigger houses, while Chris grew thin and febrile and remote, and I grew brittle and apologetic and outwardly Buckhead and inwardly haunted. I went to every new fertility specialist Chris unearthed and had every experimental procedure done to my body that science and Chris could envision, and often, as I lay in that familiar position of love and failure, staring at white overhead lights and feeling hands inside me that were, by then, indistinguishable from my husband's hands, I thought that the barrenness of my womb must be a kind of punishment for the Byzantine excesses that I had allowed to be practiced upon it. I felt, in those days, as if there might be some secret pocket of decay, of corruption, deep within me, that was inimical to new life. Outwardly I gardened and lunched and committeed and fund-raised and tennised and decorated and entertained and smiled with everyone and no one in particular. Inwardly I rotted, and missed Tish with every fiber of my being.

She and Charlie had moved back to Pemberton, his home town, after a stint with the Peace Corps in Bolivia, and he took over his father's ob-gyn practice and she began their family, and I did not hear much from her anymore except the obligatory Christmas letters and an occasional phone call inviting me to visit them. Chris's social set was his workday set, a handful of personable, dynamic young surgeons with whom he had formed a group surgery practice, gifted and driven men who wielded their knives even on the tennis courts or at charity balls. He did not speak of Charlie Coulter anymore except to say, when I spoke of visiting him and Tish, "Go on yourself, why don't you? I can't take the time, and God knows time is all you've got on your hands." The empty back room in the Blackland Road house where the nursery should have been rankled Chris like a spur. It was almost six years before he agreed to a fertility test himself, and when the first one showed low sperm motility, he was white-faced and vicious-tongued, mainly to me. The summer after that test was the first time he hit me. By the time Hilary was conceived, he had done it three times, once hard enough to black my eye and bruise my cheek.

Each time it happened, he cried and begged my forgiveness and said that he was under a great deal of pressure at the office, and I knew that it was true. The entire group was booked months in advance, and operated daily, sometimes twice and even three times. It was not uncommon for Chris to spend sixteen or eighteen hours a day at the hospital. "These are the years that you make it or don't," he said when I protested. "You knew you were marrying a doctor. If you're lonely, take a night course or something. Go to Weight Watchers."

I also knew that he was taking Percodan and some sort

of amphetamines fairly often, and sometimes Quaaludes or another sedative to bring him down. It was when the sedatives failed, and he was still hectic-cheeked and talkative when he got home at night and had a martini or two before dinner, that the sudden, punishing fury would erupt. I never realized until too late what I had said or done to set him off, so it was difficult to avoid potential red flags. I determined instead to avoid the cocktail and dinner hour. I did, indeed, schedule an evening class at Emory, a course in public relations writing.

"I thought I might find myself something to do part time," I said the first evening when I got home. From the look of his flushed face, Chris had had a very long cocktail hour. The cold oven and bare table said that he had had no dinner.

"Are you saying that you're giving up on my being able to father a child?" he said mildly and precisely.

"Of course not," I said, seeing too late where this might be going. "I'm just saying that until you do—until *we* do—it would be interesting to have some real work to do. I hate not using my mind and my education."

I was on the floor of the sunroom before I knew what had happened to me, head ringing, red darkness spinning behind my closed lids. I felt no pain, but my cheekbone was numb, and I could taste an alien salt that I knew must be blood. I knew the taste of tears well by then.

"You're not going to work outside this house," he hissed. I did not know his face, or his eyes, mad and glittering and all black pupil. "You're not going to advertise to the world that I can't support you or keep you busy."

He was gone before I picked myself up, and he did not come back until late that night, but when he did, it was with a huge bouquet of pink roses and such an obviously torn and contrite heart that in another half hour we were making love, and for once it was as slow and tender and gentle as Tish had said, so long ago, it should be. Like all women before me who had grasped at straws to support the only world they knew, I accepted with a leaping heart his admission that he thought he might have a small alcohol problem, and would give up his evening cocktails . . . and he did. He made a conscious effort to get home at a decent hour in the evenings, too, and to spend more time with me. That summer Hilary was conceived and the next spring she was born, and from that time until her ninth year his daughter was, besides medicine, the other passion in his heart.

She is tall and slender, as he is, and has his fine, narrow head and quick, beautiful hands and feet, and his incredible eyes, dark-lashed and with dark-ringed irises of a blue so light that they look, often, like arctic ice. But her coloring is my own warm Mediterranean olive, and her hair my coarse mop of black curls, and the result is so striking that people have stopped to stare at her since infancy. We thanked God, laughing, when she was born that we detected no trace of either of our mothers, and I still do not. She is, or was, smart and funny and sweet-tempered, with a kind of freewheeling *joie de vivre* in which I once saw glints of my father at his best. She is as unlike Chris temperamentally as it is possible to be, but from the beginning he adored her so that he became, instead, more like her. Or as much so as it was possible for him to be. It wasn't much, and in the end, it wasn't enough.

When she started kindergarten he began to drift back into his long hours and grinding absorption, and by the time she entered Westminster Lower School he was back on the uppers and downers, and the martinis soon followed. But he was handling it better this time; he might go after me with his tongue, but he kept his fists to himself, and he did not excoriate me in front of her. I think we might have rocked along indefinitely if he had not had three or four patients in succession get into trouble on the table, and finally had one die who should not have. There was no formal inquiry, Chris being who he was, but there were—must have been—informal, private reprimands, and there was a closing of the ranks at the hospital. I knew that he was not operating for a period of time, because he did not keep surgeon's hours any longer, but I did not know that he had been urged to enter a therapeutic program for impaired physicians, and had refused to do so, until the wife of one of his partners took me to lunch to tell me how badly she felt about all of it and asked what she could do to help. I don't know if it was obvious to her that I knew nothing about it; she is a nice woman, and she pretended that it was not.

I asked him about it that evening. It was not possible to ignore it, once I knew, though my mouth was dry with fear and my heart hammered. That was the evening of the first broken bone, a collarbone, which we explained as a fender bender in my new little BMW. The next one was a wrist, and that, we said, was a tumble over Hilary's puppy, Stinker. An open kitchen cabinet door got credit for the eye and cheek laceration. An alert hospital staff or a close friend could have readily seen what was happening, of course, but there is little that can befall a human body that a surgeon cannot fix out of his bag, and by then I had stopped seeing my acquaintances—they were never friends—and though my mother knew, she thought me to blame. I was still in the I-can't-believe-this-is-happening-to-me stage. Not me; I live in Buckhead. I'm chairman of the Gift Shop Auxiliary this year. Denial, I think it is called. It seems incredible to me now, but I honestly thought that Chris would soon stop beating me, as if the battering were a phase, like stuttering or male climacteric. I actually caught myself saying one morning, after he had bruised my stomach and thighs so severely that I had slept sitting up in a chair in the den—saying aloud to myself in the kitchen as if someone sat opposite me: "I don't think any of this would have happened if I hadn't behaved from the very beginning like a whore with him."

But something in me knew that I was going down for the third time—I suppose it was the part that was caretaker to Hilary, though I was still absolutely sure that she would never be in danger from him—because when I saw a television documentary about a shelter for battered women that had opened in a downtown public housing project, I jotted down the name of the young local psychiatrist who donated his time to the facility and looked him up in the phone book. And I made an appointment to see him, and from the very beginning found that I could at least talk with him about the thing that was happening to Chris and me.

But I could not seem to take action. It was my doctor's contention all along that no improvement could occur until I left Chris, and I wasted half a year of his time and mine searching for ways to stay and change myself and my husband so that we were no longer people to whom this could happen. It was time I could ill afford to lose, but at least my therapist and I were talking, and I was beginning to listen, and who knows, eventually he might have gotten me to the point where I could accept the necessity for leaving. He came near it the day we spoke of my mother, and of Chris's harming Hilary. But I still could not see that, and I could not go.

"She doesn't even know there's anything wrong between us," I said. "Nothing about her has changed; she couldn't know. She adores her father."

"She knows," he said. "Believe me, she knows. She just doesn't let herself *see*."

And then, one evening in April toward the end of the last nightmare five years in the Buckhead house, Chris wheeled his Mercedes into the driveway on two wheels and screeched to a stop because Stinker was lying there, wriggling in the gravel, as he did, to scratch his back, and blew the horn and beat on the side of the car and screamed at the dog, and when Stinker did not move he simply ran over him. Gunned the car forward and ran over his daughter's dog as coldly and carelessly as if he had been a speed break. And knew that he did it, and knew that I saw, and, even worse—horribly, monstrously—knew that she did. We were sitting on the front steps with Coca-Colas, she and I, watching a nest of redbirds in the small willow by the creek, and we saw him look at the dog, and at us, and then run Stinker over. There was a flat thump I will hear until death seals my ears, and a high, anguished, endless scream from my daughter, and then nothing. Not a whimper from the dog. Not the opening of a car door. Nothing. Hilary stopped screaming and sat frozen, her fingers bone-white around the binoculars, staring at her father as he sat impassively in the Mercedes. I could not move my eyes from her face, and I saw the color draining from it as if a primary artery had been severed. It did not seem to me that she was breathing any longer.

We did not make a sound while he got out of the car and came around it and up to us.

"Well, Hilary, look what you made me do. Maybe now you'll learn to keep your animals out of the driveway," he said. His voice was normal; matter-of-fact; regretful, even;

but his eyes were all black, and the two familiar red spots burned on his cheekbones, and I could smell the peculiar bad breath that an amphetamine dry mouth causes, and alcohol.

Hilary was gone and up the stairs to her room before I could move, and I heard her door slam. Still I could not move.

"Well, are you going to ask me in, madam?" Chris said. He tipped an invisible hat. He smiled.

I heard my words, but I could not feel my mouth saying them.

"Get the dog out of here and bury him someplace, Chris," I said. "Do it now. And then go to the hospital or the office someplace, because if you come back here the police will be waiting for you. You can come back in two days, because we'll be gone by then. If you try to come near us after that, I'll have you put under the Fulton County Jail for the rest of your life, and if you think I can't or won't, try me. I wish you would."

He raised his fist, and then lowered it. I did not move. I knew it was not I who deterred him, but the thought of Hilary. The daughter whom he so loved and had, now, wounded past his power to heal. Past, perhaps, anyone's. He turned and went into the garage and came out with a shovel and a plastic drop cloth, and started for the car and the dog's mangled body, which was, mercifully, hidden from my sight. If he had come toward me I would have done the best that I could to kill him with my hands.

He did not. He stopped, and looked back at me, and said, "Tell Hilary I'm sorry about the dog. I'll get her another."

"No," I said. I was having trouble breathing. "You're not sorry and you won't get her another one. Not ever."

And I went into the house so that I would not have to

see him take away the body of Hilary's beloved Stinker, and I locked the door behind me. And then I locked all the others, and the windows, too. I sat beside the telephone ready to dial 911 until I heard his car leave the driveway, and then I went upstairs to do what I could for my daughter and to get her ready to leave her life, and his.

We spent a week at a small residential hotel in Buckhead, and then I took a month-to-month lease on a new, ill-built condominium in a treeless development out on the Chattahoochee River. When Hilary's school ended I did not, as we usually did, arrange camps and lessons or a vacation. We spent the days splashing alone in the condominium swimming pool and the nights watching television and seeing early-show movies. I did not hear from Chris and he did not close our joint bank account and canceled none of my credit cards, so we could live fairly comfortably, in a transient, day-to-day manner, and I did not think past that, and Hilary did not seem to. I knew, in some dim and other-feeling part of my mind, that there were things that would have to be done about our lives: school, a job, a permanent place to live, a severing from Chris, a settlement about Hilary's future. But I could not seem to keep my thoughts focused on them. The summer was hot and dry and seemingly had no features and no end, and whatever was ahead for my daughter and me seemed to belong to another country and another time.

"In the fall; that's plenty of time," I said to my dithering, accusatory mother, and to Sally Calhoun on her lone call to ask if I had taken leave of my senses and what I planned to do, and to the few women from that other life who called, or whom I ran into in the grocery store.

"When it gets cooler," I said to my shrink, who was trying to get me into gear and get me to bring Hilary in to see him. "She's okay. She's pretty quiet, and she doesn't want to leave my side very often, but what can you expect, after such an upheaval? She's really been very good about the dog. She hasn't cried once that I know of."

"And that doesn't strike you as unusual, to say the very least?" he said. "Her father deliberately kills her dog in front of her eyes and she doesn't cry? She's jerked overnight out of the only home she's ever known and her father literally falls out of her life and she's pretty quiet? You have, I assume, heard of childhood depression? What else do you think turns a happy, high-spirited, active child silent as a rock?"

"I tried to get her to come with me to see you earlier," I said. It seemed an enormous effort to talk. "She said she would when school started and everything got back to normal. I promised her we'd wait until then."

"Um hmm," he said. "And when do you think everything is going to get back to normal? As a matter of fact, Andy, just what do you consider normal?"

And I knew again, despairingly, that indeed I had never really known. But I could not seem to move myself or my child.

And then, in mid-August, two things happened: a letter came from a lawyer I did not know, on the letterhead of the city's largest and oldest firm, telling me that Chris was filing for divorce and suing for custody of Hilary, and Hilary found the letter on my desk and read it and took an entire bottle of children's Tylenol. The afternoon after I brought her home from the hospital, white and mute and listless, I called our attorney friend Bill Kimbrough's secretary and made an appointment to see him the next day in his office down in the Healy Building downtown.

And went into the coffee shop on the ground floor, to

kill the half hour that I had before the appointment, and ran into Tish Coulter.

She had it out of me in fifteen minutes, her very rumpled-linen presence and plain, caring face loosening vaults and pockets and valves of pain I had thought rusted shut for nearly fifteen years. She canceled the stockbroker's appointment that had brought her the two hundred miles from Pemberton and went to see Bill Kimbrough with me, and in another hour had out of him his grim-faced assurance that the case would never see court, and that Chris would be a lucky man if I did not choose to have him jailed for assault, battery, and mental cruelty. She took me to lunch and came back to the condominium with me and saw Hilary and told her everything was going to be all right because her Aunt Tish was going to, by God, make sure that it was, and my damaged and diminished child managed a smile and a subdued "Thank you." By late afternoon, when I drove her back to the airport, she had my promise to come the next week and at least "see" Pemberton. We did, and stayed three days, and ate and slept prodigiously, and left again, I with a job in the public relations department of Pemberton State College and a spinning head and a heart full of unease at the sheer, unsettling beauty of that most atypical small Southern town, Hilary with a light in her blue eyes I had not seen since the spring before. Pemberton has, besides uncommon beauty, many horses. It was, I think, that light that decided me.

On the Thursday afternoon before Labor Day we rolled into Pemberton, Georgia, for good and all, my child and I, in a secondhand yellow Toyota Celica station wagon that was both the last purchase of my old life and the first of my new. I had traded the BMW for it and a good amount of cash two days before, wanting nothing of Atlanta, of Buckhead, of that privileged and terrible life, to cause concentric ripples on the smooth, opaque surface ahead of me. In my packed files was a court order Bill Kimbrough had gotten forbidding Chris to contact Hilary or me until the divorce was granted and he had completed at least half a year of psychotherapy, and an uncashed check for twenty thousand dollars from Sally Calhoun. There had been no note with the check. I knew I wouldn't hear from Chris's parents again. We came into Pemberton through the inevitable strip shopping centers and car dealerships and Burger Kings that outlie every town, large or small, in the New South, in past the Kiwanis and Rotary and Chamber of Commerce signs and the Holiday Inn ads, into Pembertown itself, green and dreaming and somehow a little eerie, with its wide, quiet streets divided by flowering, tree-arched parks and lined with the huge, baroque old fantasy homes of the unimaginably rich Winter People who had come here since the closing of the last century, with their children and servants and horses, to renew themselves and play. That very beauty, so nearly perfect, so unmarred here in the heart of the historic district, smote me again with unease. I thought that I simply was not up to it. I had wanted the balm of utter banality. This sort of beauty demanded a kind of emotional reckoning from the beholder. You would have to live up to this kind of loveliness.

"It looks stuck-up," Hilary said fretfully. She was flushed and disheveled in the tepid wash of the Toyota's faltering air conditioner, and the light had gone out of her eyes. She had not spoken for nearly two hours. I felt, heavily, apprehension and a vague annoyance. This silent child, Chris's legacy to me, was after all the reason for this flight into Egypt, and it disturbed me to find that she had the same doubts I did. She had been, before, captivated.

"Well, it isn't," I said decisively. "Aunt Tish says the people are wonderfully friendly. You'll make lots of new friends."

"I don't want any friends," said Hilary, whose friends, in the end, had been sacrificed to Chris's rage.

She turned her head to read a sign, and then look at me.

"That sign back there says hunting season starts next week. Does that mean people can kill animals?"

Stinker, who had died on an April night instead, perhaps, of me or her, no less a sacrifice than the abandoned friend.

I sighed. Hunting season was one thing I could not mitigate for her. The danger at the heart of this new and perfect beauty was real.

"I guess it does, some kinds," I said.

"I hate this place," Hilary said, and for the rest of the afternoon it was all she did say.

CHAPTER TWO

Just at daybreak on our first morning in Pemberton, Hilary came stumbling and sobbing into my bedroom in Tish's guesthouse, and it was ten minutes or so, after I had taken her into my bed and held her close like a small child and brushed the silky hair off her damp face, before she was able to tell me what had frightened her.

"I heard the nightmares coming," she sobbed over and over. "I heard the nightmares coming for me right outside my window. There were lots and lots of them; I *heard* them, Mama! They . . . you know, they made that noise that isn't a whinny but it's a horse noise, and their feet sounded like . . . not like they should . . ."

"Honey, it was a bad dream; that's what a nightmare is," I soothed. I thought it was not unusual that she would wake from fearful dreams in this strange place, after all that had happened to her, but the fretful babyishness of her speech and response troubled me, and there was something inexplicably awful about her words: "I heard the nightmares coming."

"It was *not* a dream; I *heard* them, just a minute ago."

"Let's go look," I said, employing the old babyhood strategy that had always served to calm her night fears. But she would not get out of my bed. I walked down the short hall to the room she had slept in, cursing myself for giving in to her desire to sleep alone in the "fairy-tale room." It was, like the other miniature rooms in Tish's little guesthouse behind the main house, a fantasy place: deep-silled, diamond-paned windows, beamed ceilings, canopied beds, and ornate armoires. The room Hilary had chosen had a pillow-piled window seat; I knew that had charmed her past her shyness in a strange place. But I should have insisted, that first night, that she sleep with me. Hilary's wounds, buried deep, always seemed to break open in the nights.

There was nothing out her window but a bed of riotous zinnias and a section of the charming old serpentine brick wall that encircled Tish's house and garden. Several of the other houses that I had seen driving in had them; I thought of Thomas Jefferson and the University of Virginia, in Charlottesville. The wall was solid and too tall to see over; nowhere here for nightmares to gallop. I went back and told her so.

She only looked at me and lapsed back into the silence she had accorded Pemberton since yesterday.

"Hilary had a world-class nightmare last night," I said to Tish a bit later, while we lingered over coffee in the sunroom off her big, light-flooded kitchen. Outside, blue morning shadows lay over smooth emerald lawn and flowering borders and a birdbath beside a teak garden bench, nestled in a loop of the wall. Early sun brushed the tops of the dogwood and hickories and oaks, and birdsong poured like water through the screened windows. It was an exquisite, hidden, perfect place, this house, this garden; nightmares seemed as alien here, in all this sunny silence, as four lanes of traffic. I glanced into the adjacent den. Hilary sat there watching cartoons and munching toast with jam, the dream apparently forgotten.

Tish laughed when I recounted it.

"That was no nightmare, that was the real McCoy," she said. "She did hear horses. We're just a block from the training track and the stables, and lots of the people who live around there ride their horses along the street just over the wall early in the morning. The street is dirt; that's why their hooves sounded funny. God! Poor Hilary; I'll bet it did scare her to death. It would anybody who wasn't expecting horses outside their window at dawn. I should have warned you."

"I'm relieved to hear it, and she will be, too. What is it—they can't afford to pave the streets around here?" I said.

"No, they're so rich they don't have to." Tish grinned. "It's the ultimate status symbol in Pemberton, to live on one of the dirt streets. Good for the horses' feet, you know, and if it's good for the horses it's good for everybody. There aren't many of these streets, and people would poison their neighbors to get a house on one."

"What if you don't have a horse?" I asked.

"Then you secretly curse the mud and dust and stuck cars and filthy carpets and go right ahead and poison your neighbor," she said. "And you get a horse as fast as you can."

"Who did you all have to poison?" I asked, intrigued in spite of myself with this town where horses were monarchs. "You don't have a horse."

"Charlie delivered the granddaughter of the woman who

owns the big house on this property; this used to be a stable, did I tell you? That's why it rambles around so. She—the grandmother—was a Du Pont; there've been Du Ponts here ever since the winter colony was founded, in the last century. It was a tricky birth, and the girl and the baby could have died, but Charlie saved them, and you'd have thought he was Jesus Christ from then on. When the old lady moved to a retirement home in Boca Raton she gave us first choice of the property, and since we could never have afforded a fifty-five-room cottage we took the stable and did it over. The guesthouse and pool came with it. She practically gave it to us. If it hadn't been for her we'd have been on a paved street like almost everybody else except the Winter People, and I'd have had to poison somebody sure enough. I've often blessed that rich little idiot and her baby; I really love this house. I don't think I could bear to live in Pemberton and not have part of one of the big old places. Besides, Charlie does have a horse. He has a polo pony. He keeps it over at one of the stables; we'll take you over and show you, tomorrow or Sunday. It's really something to see."

I choked with glee and incredulity.

"*Charlie* plays polo? On a *horse?* In one of those shirts and those jodhpurs? With one of those mallets?" I sputtered.

Tish smiled at me, but I thought that it was not her usual full smile.

"He's over at the field right now," she said. "He's pretty good, for a busy doctor. He grew up in Pemberton, Andy; he's the fifth generation of his family to be born here. His people were some of the founders of the town. He's been on and off horses since he could walk."

"I guess I never heard him talk about them," I said hesitantly. Surely my laughter had not offended her? There had been, in the old days, nothing on earth sacred to Tish and me.

"He doesn't, except here," she said. "For some reason the people who live here or come here for the winter season don't talk much about it. It's one of the South's best-kept secrets, Pemberton is. I guess it's because the very rich have never needed anything except privacy, and there's a hideous lot of money in Pemberton, dirt roads notwithstanding. Don't knock them, by the way. Your new house is on one. I've rented you the guest cottage at Pipedream, the old Belvedere place. It's on Whimsy Road. That's the granddaddy of all the dirt roads in Pemberton. Numero uno. The skinny is that there are five times as many horses as people on Whimsy Road."

"Tish, I can't afford that kind of living; I don't want to just plonk Hilary down in the middle of that kind of world. . . ." Alarm buzzed in my temples.

"Oh, relax," she said. "The Belvederes haven't owned the place in years. One of the trainers and his family has it, and they're the dullest people on earth, and they're only here from fall to spring, anyway. The cottage isn't even visible from the big house; it's off in the woods behind the track. You'll have your own private road. You can live there in austere poverty if you want to. It's wonderful, Andy. Red board and batten, with stone fireplaces and porches all around, and diamond-pane windows like mine, and a wishing well in the front yard. And it's *cheap*—this ain't Buckhead. Surely one condominium like the one you just left was enough?"

"I guess so," I said doubtfully. "It sounds perfect. I didn't mean to complain about it, for goodness' sake. Hilary will love it. It's just that . . . Pemberton is not your ordinary little Southern town, is it?"

"No, it isn't. It never has been," she said. She looked at me keenly through the smoke from her second cigarette of the morning. "You're not awfully happy about that, are you?" she said.

I was silent for a time; how could I make her understand what I myself still perceived only dimly? That even before Chris, even when we had been lighthearted, tough-talking, long-laughing young girls together at Emory, my wry, clever, self-deprecating banter had covered an almost pathological desire for safety and seemliness. Those early years with my father had seen to that. The later ones with Chris had left me in terror and disgust at sensuality of any kind, including my own. I had come to Pemberton because I adjudged a small town the most conventional, unthreatening, and conquerable arena I could find for my child and myself. Before I saw it, Pemberton meant, to me, safety. The more banal the better. Balance, order, moderation, even boredom—they were all that I aspired to. And then to find that Pemberton was not that at all but was something else entirely, something, as Shakespeare said, rich and strange . . .

I saw it again in that long moment of my silence, saw my otherness, that thing within me that reached out for exaggeration: for wildness both physical and spiritual. It was that, of course, that I had come here in flight from. Not Chris, not the city, not my mother. Not entirely. But my own appetite for excess.

"Tish, it's not that I don't like Pemberton," I said slowly. "I do. It's lovely. It's a storybook town. Who wouldn't like it? It's just that it's . . . complicated. And to me, at least, it's . . . very exotic. And my God, it's so *rich*. It doesn't seem to me to be a—oh, I don't know—a *normal* town. I don't think it fits me. Or rather, I don't fit *it*. I don't even know what I *do* fit. I always thought I was a nurturer, a caretaker; I tried for so long with Daddy, and then with Chris, to keep things normal and level. I tried so hard to make a neat, conventional life for us all. Anybody else would have just walked out years earlier, away from both of them. And Mother, too. But not little Saint Andy. It's only just now occurring to me that I wasn't normal and level at all, but that I was a codependent, indulging my own need for . . . outrage, by proxy and proximity. Don't you see? Little Miss Normal was really some kind of secret perversion addict, or something. And so, when I came here looking for the balance and order I didn't have and found all this richness and perfection, almost excessive, really—"

"It scared the shit out of you," she finished for me, smiling. "Oh, Andy. You have had an awful time, haven't you?"

"Only a white-collar bad time," I said. "You know. Poor baby. She had to sell her Beamer."

She grinned outright, and then sobered again. "Wouldn't it have just been easier in the long run to fuck the Orkin man, or somebody?"

"Tish, you will never know how I have come to hate fucking," I said. "To me, it just means messy sheets and my foot over my ear and a black eye afterward."

"Pity," Tish said. "You've flat got the build for it. You're going to drive our collection of randy sportsmen out of what passes for their minds."

I must have paled, because she leaned over and pressed my hand and said, "I was just teasing you, babe. There's nothing here to scare you. Pemberton's rich, but it's very old, very private rich. Very comfortable and unassuming. You can't tell who is and who isn't. The most dressed up anybody ever gets is an ascot with the flannel shirt and rubber shoes and a twenty-year-old Lilly. Except for the week of the Pemberton Classic, in April, when you can't even go to the john without a white tie, and lots of us go away for that. It's such an orderly world that it's almost boring. There's nothing over here that's loud or jarring or, God forbid, new."

"Or ugly," I said. "Over here? Where's over here?"

"The historic district," Tish said. "Where we are. The part of town where all the big old cottages and the training track and stables are, and the old parts of town. It's very strictly preserved: lots of codes and rules and such. Lots of wonderful old civic buildings, and clubs and schools and churches. All on the National Register. Want to take a tour? You can't get into your house until next Monday; the Livingstons are having it painted inside, and your furniture isn't due until midweek, anyway, is it? Come on, Andy. Get Hilary and we'll do the driving tour and I'll run you by the polo field—it's too late for the track, but we'll see that and the stables tomorrow—and then we'll go to lunch at the Inn and have two Bloody Marys. Maybe three. You have to see the Inn; it's one of the best historic preservations in the country. Won some kind of award for it. And the food is really good."

"I'd love to," I said, getting up and stretching. "But I warn you, I'm pulling for at least one eyesore. Just to keep you honest."

"Sorry," Tish said. "You won't see it today."

And I didn't. From the beginning, when Tish nosed her mud-spattered Blazer out of the secret garden behind her house and into the streets of Pemberton, I was laved and lulled with charm. Even in the great flaccid, somnolent heat of late August in the wire-grass South, Pemberton dreamed in a well of deep green as cool as a secret sea. Fine old oaks, some hung with scarves of gray moss, vaulted over the quiet divided streets and lined long driveways and sheltered the many-roomed whimsies of the original Winter People. Flowers and blooming shrubbery lay like prayer rugs around the smaller homes of Old Pemberton. These latter, though dignified and graceful, were not in the same league as the great, rustic mansions of the winter colony, even though they nested among them. I remarked on the difference, and Tish nodded.

"There's no difference between us and the WPs when you look at us," she said lightly, "but it's there, all right, and wide as a barn door. We're ordinary gentry, like you'd find in any little Southern town, but they're gentry on Long Island and in Bucks County and Palm Beach and Boca and Bar Harbor. Or the first ones were, anyway, the ones who built these old places. They used to say an earthquake in Pemberton during the season would empty out boardrooms from Bangor to Bethlehem. One of our local belles back in the nineties married a Long Island polo player who owned a few steel mills here and there, and he came home to meet her folks and just happened to notice how good the climate would be for his ponies, don'tcha know, and that he could do here all year what he could only do for six months back home—and the rest, as they say, is history. He went back and told his buddies and in five years they'd lit on us like a swarm of locusts and built a baby Newport and brought enough horses and hunting dogs and servants and children—in that order of importance—to populate the entire west of England. That's the idea, I guess: we're very county around here. And they've never once, in over a hundred years, paid any attention to us. At first the locals hated the ground they walked on, mainly because it had once been their own ground. The WPs bought land like there was no tomorrow. But they paid top prices, and by the time a few townspeople had made small fortunes off them, the rest of Pemberton caught on and started hiring on as gardeners and stablemen and grooms and bartenders and mechanics, and opened shops and started services to accommodate them, and before long lots of them could afford to build fancy houses right in the middle of the colony. The two factions still don't mingle much, though that's changing some now; a few of us younger ones belong to their clubs and play a little golf and such with them. But it's still very much Old Pemberton versus Winter People over here. It's not a bad arrangement. We've benefited from their money and the first-class private schools and medical facilities and libraries and museums they built, and they've gotten the best of our land and all the privacy they could ask. And of course we all ride and hunt together. Horses are the great leveler around here. But it's still kind of nice in the summer, when they're gone."

I looked at the people I saw, driving square, muddy four-wheel-drive vehicles and weeding technicolor flower beds and going in and out of the little half-timbered, brass-plaqued shops along Palmetto Street, which appeared to be the main street. They all wore cotton skirts or khaki pants and blazers and polo shirts and low boots or the ubiquitous rubber shoes, and many of them, women included, wore canvas or poplin hats with the brims turned down against the sun. I saw no one who was not tanned, and no one in a tie or high heels. I saw no children.

"What's it like when they're here?" I asked. "The Winter People?"

"Just like this," Tish said. "Only with a few more people on the street."

She turned off Palmetto and we dipped into the green maze of streets to the west. She idled the Blazer up one shade-dappled street and down another, pointing out the elephantine shingled, gabled, and turreted cottages of the Winter People, with their old-fashioned tennis and squash courts and pools and gazebos and summerhouses and servants' quarters and stables and croquet lawns hidden behind great, dense old tree hedges or the beautiful serpentine brick walls. Each had a small cast-iron jockey at the curb, beside a hollowed marble carriage block. All had gay, frivolous nineteenth-century names: Folly, Mon Repose, Cotton Patch, Daydream, Cloud Nine, Sans Souci, Shangri-la. The streets themselves had names that would have been ludicrous anywhere else, but seemed to fit as easily here as the bridle paths and topiary gardens: Champagne Street, Gin Lane, Easy Street. We passed a dignified old white clapboard golf club, a court tennis club. ("Only four of these in the country," Tish said. "Very old, very French, very la-di-da.") A famous small private girls' school flashed by, and three private clubs, for dining, croquet, and badminton, respectively. All were clapboard or fieldstone, blurred with ivy and wisteria and age.

In the deepest heart of the maze of streets the paving gave over to soft black dirt, like the street behind Tish's house, and the forested lawns turned to forests outright. We passed a stocky, tanned, middle-aged woman on a beautiful big bay horse; she wore stained riding breeches and a faded polo shirt and the inevitable canvas hat, and she raised her crop to us as we passed. Tish waved back. A foursome of polo players jingled by, their mounts lathered and blowing, their shirts plastered to their backs with sweat. They raised their mallets in salute.

"The tracks and the stables and the polo field are back in there," Tish said. "I'll save them for tomorrow. Looks like the polo's finished for the day; let's head on over to the Inn and beat the crowd for lunch. You hungry, Hil? You were up at dawn with the nightmares."

From the back seat Hilary said, "Yes." And then, remembering, "Yes, please."

I turned to look at her, and smiled involuntarily. She had been silent all morning, and I had feared that the grandeur and strangeness of the passing vistas, coupled with the fright she had had, had intimidated her, driven her even deeper inside herself. She had not liked Pemberton the afternoon before. But she was smiling a rapt little smile, her soft mouth slightly open, and her light-blue eyes were shining. Her silky head turned to follow the horses. My heart squeezed, as it so often did, with sheer pleasure at her beauty, and with fierce, protective love. Behind the heart-squeeze came a little surge of easing warmth. Nothing so far in Pemberton, then, to fear on Hilary's behalf. I would, I knew, gladly move to Disney World to keep that look on her face. Tish glanced at her in the rearview mirror and then grinned over at me.

"I have one convert, anyway," she said. "I'll get you yet."

The Pemberton Inn was a rambling, deep-roofed clapboard structure, gleaming with white paint and skirted with stone verandas. The inevitable cast-iron jockey held a small hanging brass plaque that read: *est. 1835*. Clematis and petunias glowed in pots and on trellises, and a graveled parking lot off to the right was filling with station wagons and Cherokees and Blazers and a sprinkling of big foreign sedans. Tish pulled her Blazer in beside a low cream Jaguar and tooted her horn lightly. The Jaguar's doors opened on either side, and Charlie and another man peered out. Tish and I put our heads into the car, and I breathed deeply in involuntary pleasure. The rich smell of new leather was as sweet as the old-fashioned pink roses in beds on either side of the path to the veranda. Inside, the car was all smooth beige leather and polished, honey-colored wood.

"Lord, Charlie, this is like being inside a buttered biscuit. Not bad for a country obstetrician," I said, and he laughed and tapped my chin.

"Spoken like a true child of the seventies," he said, "except that I happen to know you've been tooling around

Buckhead in a BMW for years. Andy, this is Carter Devereaux, my intrepid polo partner and boyhood coconspirator. Carter, meet Andy Calhoun, Tish's and my oldest joint friend and Pemberton's newest inhabitant. And this pretty lady is Hilary Calhoun. They're staying in the guesthouse until Randy Livingston gets the guesthouse at Pipedream cleaned up for them. I told you about Andy, I know."

"You did, and I've been looking forward to meeting her," the second man said in a rich, low drawl that was perhaps the most beautiful voice I had ever heard. He was a pleasant-looking, unremarkable man, tall and a little heavy around the waist, as Charlie was now, with Charlie's deep tan and receding sandy hair and mild blue eyes. But his smile was direct and sweet, like a child's, and the extraordinary voice had the charm of perfect music, or birdsong. It made you want to smile with pure pleasure; it made you want to hear more.

The five of us walked into the Inn, Hilary hanging back a bit and holding on to my hand. Charlie's hand rested lightly on her head. Inside, the big, cool lounge was beamed and low-ceilinged and paneled in handsome old carved oak, and scatterings of deep leather chairs and sofas sat before a huge stone fireplace filled, now, with ferns. Hunting prints and equestrian paintings and statuary were everywhere. Copies of *Forbes* and *The Blood Horse* rested on low tables. Behind the lounge, up a shallow flight of polished wooden steps, the restaurant was filling with tables of men and women, all of whom looked like Tish and Charlie and Carter Devereaux. It was dim and rich and soothing, with dark wood and green plants and snowy damask and a fireplace wall hung with brasses and stuffed pheasants. A low murmur of voices reached out to us, and most heads turned as we entered. Charlie raised a hand to the room in general, and Tish waved, and we were shown to a table beside a deep-silled, many-paned window overlooking the Inn's back garden. A smiling black waiter materialized silently at Charlie's elbow and said, "Afternoon, Doctor. Round of the usual for you and your guests?" He looked inquiringly at me, still smiling. I had the sense that everyone else in the room was, too. I felt, suddenly, too round, too dark, too vivid, overdressed in the linen dress in which I would have lunched in Atlanta, too outside, too . . . Greek. There was not a woman in the restaurant whose hair was not sun-streaked and severely pulled back or cut in the straight, loose flip of the sixties and fastened with a barrette; whose skin was not tanned and innocent of makeup except pink lipstick; whose wrap skirt or madras slacks and polo shirt or plain oxford-cloth shirt did not reveal bare, well-muscled arms and legs. One or two of the men wore seersucker or tan poplin suits, but most, like Charlie and Carter Devereaux, wore sharply creased poplin slacks and open-collared polo shirts and madras or dark-blue summer blazers. Many seemed to have comb tracks in their damp hair, as if they had just come off some golden playing field or sunny court. They probably had, I thought. The men of Pemberton worked; of course they did. It just did not, somehow, seem to be a high priority.

"Bring us all a Bloody Mary, Alfred," Tish said. At my headshake, she said, "Oh, come on, Andy. The Inn is famous for its Bloodys. We'll go home and take a nap, and I promise not to force booze on you at lunch again. We really don't all get snockered at noon here. But this is a celebration; you'll only move to Pemberton once. I hope. Hilary, Alfred makes a mean Shirley Temple."

Hilary looked at me shyly; she hated Shirley Temples, but wanted, I knew, to be polite, to make a good impression in this uncharted new world where she would be expected to make her way.

"I think a plain Coke for Hilary," I said.

"Make that two," Carter Devereaux said. "Or rather, a Diet Coke for me. I've got a client meeting in an hour, and the old fool can smell vodka two football fields away. Thinks drinking at lunch is decadent."

"It is," Tish said. "That's why it's so much fun."

"What sort of business are you in, Mr. Devereaux?" I asked, as much to keep the beautiful voice flowing as to gain information. I felt impelled to be interested, agreeable, an asset to Tish and Charlie in this place that was so obviously one of the epicenters of their world. They had nodded to virtually every table.

"Carter, please. I'm an attorney of sorts," he answered. "Kind of a jack-of-all-trades; there's not much call for specialization in Pemberton. I do estate work mainly."

"Carter is one of the best estate planners for horse owners in the South," Tish said fondly. "As well as being one of the best polo players and best steeplechasers."

"Too old and too fat for that now," Carter said comfortably. "And I'll be too heavy for polo soon if I don't get out of the office and onto the field more. Charlie, too. Our ponies were cursing us both this morning."

"We'll walk it off soon as hunting season opens," Charlie said, and I shot an oblique look at Hilary. She looked back at me, a swift, alert look.

"Is there anything to do in Pemberton that doesn't have to do with horses?" I said quickly.

"Lots of dogs," Charlie said. "All kinds of dogs. Hunting dogs, mainly. They're finishing up the Southern Terrier Trials over at the track tomorrow. Carter's got a couple of terriers competing. One of them stands to take Best in Show."

"What kind of dogs are they?" Hilary's small silver voice startled me; she had said nothing in so long. It was like hearing a beautiful piece of porcelain suddenly speak.

Carter Devereaux smiled at her, naturally and openly.

"Jack Russells," he said. "Nice, energetic, cobby little dogs with big white grins, both of them. Lila and Homer, named for my grandparents. We've always had Jack Russells. If you'll come out to the track tomorrow and bring your mother, I'll introduce you. They'll like meeting you."

She smiled back, and looked at me. I looked at Tish, who said, "We're going out, anyway. I'll pack a tailgate lunch and we can all eat together after the trials. Carter?"

"I'd like that a lot," he said. He was looking at me. I felt my face go warm, something it had not done since my earliest days at Emory, and I raised my drink and took a deep swallow. Tish was right: it was wonderful, cold and spicy and smooth. I took another.

It was a pleasant lunch, though the sensation of strangeness, of disorientation, did not leave me; was only heightened by the unaccustomed noon alcohol. I felt as though, if I should stand up suddenly, I would somehow float gently up and off the planet. The strangeness persisted as tables of people finished their lunches and came by and spoke and were introduced, and smiled, and welcomed me and Hilary to Pemberton, and said they looked forward to seeing us soon out at the track or around the stables.

"You must come over and have a drink and a bite with us soon," several of the women said, and I smiled and said we'd love that, and the talk turned back to horses and hunting. I learned that the sign Hilary had seen as we drove into Pemberton had been right; hunting season—or at least the season for some animals—did indeed open the coming week, and apparently other seasons were soon to follow. The talk was of little else. Guns, bows, dogs, equipment, clothing . . . The down-to-earth, attractive men and women at the Pemberton Inn all seemed as acquainted with the ritual slaying of animals as they were with horses, as my contemporaries back in Buckhead were with tennis and gardening and car pools.

I hated the talk for Hilary's sake, but there was nothing I could say to her in front of these people, and so I said nothing, only watched her. She was silent again, and studied the dessert menu carefully. I could not think what I might say to her when we were alone, back in Tish's guesthouse; we had, inadvertently, ended up in country where hunting was a reigning passion and could not be disguised or discounted. She would have to learn to make some sort of peace with it. I could not build a perfect world for her.

I looked up at Tish suddenly and seemed to see a woman I had never known sitting across the table from me. She looked like Tish—or rather, what Tish should look like now, given her life—and she had been, this past day and night, no less warm and loving and generous and open than ever. But something deep and basic seemed to have shifted, changed, gone over into something else. She seemed, all at once, to be one of a piece with all the other women who stopped by the table to chat, exotic in their plainness and competence, absorbed in a wild and rich and stylized world that would, I knew, forever be alien to me. Once Tish would have seen instantly that the talk of hunting was disturbing Hilary, and changed the subject; now, like all the other women, she did not seem aware that a child sat, with eyes too large, at her table. It was as if, as I had noticed before, children were no essential part of this world.

The Inn gradually emptied, and we finished our coffee and went out into the blazing afternoon sun of the parking lot.

"You really will come to the trials tomorrow, won't you?" Carter Devereaux said to me; and to Hilary, "Make your mama come. There are some horses around the stables about your size. You look like you'd fit a horse like a glove, with those long legs of yours."

The sun came out in Hilary's eyes again, and so I nodded yes, and we parted.

"I didn't realize this was such big hunt country," I said to Tish, as she pulled out of the lot. "Even women do it, I guess."

"Oh, Lord, yes. Some of the best hunting in the world is out in the fields and woods around the Big Silver River Swamp, out to the east of us," she said. "The swamp itself, too. People come from all over the globe to hunt around Pemberton. Fox hunting, quail, deer, doves, ducks, grouse, rabbit, turkey, squirrel—you name it. Some of the world's great private hunting preserves are here. You know, the big plantations . . ."

She could see from my face that I didn't, and said, "Well, they're all through the South, really, but for some reason the granddaddies of them all are around here. Most of them were established by the Winter People; they'd come down and buy up literally hundreds of thousands of acres of woodland dirt cheap, and put up a big house or lodge—some of them really grand, like the cottages—and bunkhouses and commissaries and skinning and tanning huts, and servants' quarters, and kennels and stables and all . . . really just fiefdoms, almost. And then they'd have private groups of friends in to hunt in the season, and the rest of the year they'd timber or cultivate some kind of cash crop, so the plantations would pay for themselves. Timber around here, mostly. Nowadays most of them rent in season to rod and gun clubs, and sometimes to corporate groups, but they're still *very* private and very posh. Hardly anybody outside that orbit even knows they're here. There are three or four right around Pemberton; Charlie and Carter hunt at one of them, King's Oak, and it's owned by a Pemberton man. Clay Dabney. He's a darling; we all love Clay. It's his old family place, and he and his son have hung on to it, though they could make a fortune on the property now, if they wanted to sell. But they do all right; there are enough filthy-rich people all over the world who want to come to King's Oak and hunt so that they can keep the buildings and the big house and the hands. Clay rents part of the woods to a paper company, I think. He put in a six-thousand-foot small jet runway recently, or Chip did. His son. A hunt at one of the big plantations is something to see, Andy; you'll be invited to at least one, and you should go. It's like nothing else on this earth. Very . . . old. Very European, sort of, and privileged, and secret. Very ritualized. I'm always reminded of *The Garden of the Finzi-Continis* when I'm out at King's Oak; do you remember that movie? It's not the same thing at all, but it feels the same."

"Do all the women in Pemberton hunt as well as ride?" I said. "I never think of hunting as a woman's sport, somehow."

"A lot of them do around here. There's a saying that every other woman in town is deaf in one ear, from firing a gun so often, you know. Everybody you met today does. I don't, because I'm a rotten shot and it's apparent nobody is going to be able to teach me. And I never really liked the killing part. You certainly don't have to do it. But you'll learn an awful lot about it whether you want to or not. Either that or you won't have anything to talk about at dinner parties."

I was suddenly annoyed with her. I could not have said precisely why, except that her blithe assumption that I would slip seamlessly into the world where she moved was galling to me; Tish of all people knew how fragile we were emotionally, Hilary and I, and she knew that money was going to be very tight, and that I was going to have to work very hard at my modest job to make ends meet. There would be little time for dinner parties, and less for races and hunt meets and fox hunting. And she certainly must know that my tastes had never run to the sports of the rich, or to the killing of game. I was, as was my child, profoundly a city creature at heart.

And I was deeply, if obliquely, disturbed at the thought of those great plantations, silent and hidden and dark-forested, off in the river swamp to the east of us. Somehow it was as if something wild, primeval, old as the world, crouched in the distance, unseen but almost palpable. As if a great beast of some sort was lurking in its power and stillness just outside the warm ring of the campfire.

My anger at this unknown Tish and her bright, dangerous world simmered in silence until we pulled into her driveway, and then I said, "Your jockey has a white face."

She caught nothing in my tone, and laughed.

"Yes. Pemberton is the only place in the world it's still okay to have little black jockeys on your lawn, but we painted ours white just on principle. We're the only closet liberals in town."

It was, I think, the "closet" that did it. This was Tish, my good, ardent, largehearted friend, my fierce cochampion of the world's downtrodden, my fellow refugee from Woodstock Nation, the one of us who really did follow her heart into the Peace Corps. Speaking of closets. Speaking of painting her ornamental lawn jockey white.

"Good move," I said. "Fly your flags. The jockeys are the only blacks I've seen in Pemberton since I got here who weren't serving something. No Jews to speak of, either. Or Hispanics. Am I the only Greek?"

In an instant we were fighting. It was as if a barbed and simmering anger in her leaped like brushfire to meet and match my own. She slammed the brakes on and turned on the seat to face me.

"Okay, Andy, just how many blacks and Jews and dagos came to your house for dinner in Atlanta? How many times have you marched or sat in or made a speech? How long did you have Hilary in public school?"

"But you were going to open a storefront clinic, and counsel ghetto kids, and all that. You were going to open a clinic, you and Charlie. . . ."

"And we did! We spent two entire years in Bolivia in the Peace Corps doing just that! Remember? We did our time! I *do* do some free counseling now; Charlie treats *lots* of poverty cases! Don't you talk to me about what we did and did not do! Where were you all those years in Atlanta before Hilary came, when you weren't working? Not in the ghetto, I presume . . ."

"On my back!" I screamed. "Either fucking or bleeding from the mouth! Don't *you* dare talk about what you know nothing about!"

I took a deep breath, and stopped. We stared at each other, aghast, and then, incredibly, I saw tears in the corners of her eyes, where I had never seen tears before, and she was Tish again, Tish who had loved me all the years of her life that she had known me, who had found me my job and opened her home and her life to me and my damaged child. I have never felt such self-contempt before or since, not even during the worst of my witless subjugation to Chris, as I did in that moment. Hilary opened the back door of the Blazer and jumped out and ran into the house. I dropped my face into my hands and began to cry. I had forgotten she was there.

"I don't know what to say," I sobbed. "I'm so ashamed of myself. I'm so ashamed. You *and* Hil . . ."

She moved across the seat and put her arms around me. She smelled as she always had, of body warmth and stale cigarettes and sun in her clean, coarse hair. Of Tish. Just Tish.

"Oh, Andy, don't," she murmured, and tears were thick in her own voice. "I know . . . Jaguars and Bloody Marys and fox hunts. I ain't exactly Mother Teresa, am I? It's just so easy to lose that . . . edge of perception you have when you're young, that makes all the self-sacrifice and service possible. I'm ashamed of that, but there it is. I don't blame you. You've had a shitawful time. You're worried sick about Hilary and tired and scared. You always did get mean when you were scared. I'll do better by you tomorrow. Pemberton will do better by both of you."

And as bad as it had been that afternoon, that's how good it seemed the next morning. Perhaps I was beginning to lose the edge of perception Tish had spoken of, but what had seemed excessive and ersatz the day before seemed, that morning, charming and magical. The sun seemed, not relentless and Disneyesque, but golden and beneficent. The air seemed, not rarefied and oppressive, but clean and fragrant and near to effervescent. The grass was not technicolor green, but lush and rich and almost blue with health. The people we passed on the way to the track were not caricatures, but attractive, substantial, and dignified. Even the Jaguars and Mercedeses and inevitable Jeeps and Land Rovers were not pretentious, but altogether necessary to smooth the ruts and bumps in the yellow dirt roads. Being inside Charlie's big Jaguar was warm and soothing in the dawn chill; steam from our cups of coffee curled into the rich leather smell, and Peggy Lee poured "When The World Was Young" from the radio on the burled dashboard. Hilary, in a pair of Tish's daughter Katie's outcast jodhpurs and boots, looked highborn and horsy and lovely and knew it; and even I was secretly and cravenly pleased that I could fit into a pair of Tish's jodhpurs. The pouched thigh cloth hid my round bottom, and I pulled my unruly mop back into a ponytail and tied it with a scarf. I felt like Jackie Kennedy Onassis on the way to the hunt at Peapack. It seemed, at that moment, not only possible for us to live here, but infinitely desirable.

The three big Pemberton tracks—the training track, the mile track, and the steeplechase track—lay in the woods to the west of Palmetto Street, hemmed in by the network of dirt roads on which the largest cottages and homes and most of the town's twelve private stables and breeding farms lay. The stables were lovely in the blue early-morning light, long and low and weathered and tree-arched and smartly painted in spanking white or red or battleship gray. Their tracks and corrals and rings were neatly raked, as were their white-pebbled driveways and parking areas, and each sported a weather vane and a hanging wooden sign painted in the colors of its owner. I loved the names: Dogwood, Runaway, Hickory Branch, Handtomouth. The owners' names had the patina of legend and money: Biddle, Whitney, Du Pont, Longworth, Belvedere. Charlie drove the Jaguar through the gates of Runaway: long, low, white-painted and green-shuttered. Its green-and-peach sign said: *Belvedere*.

"We'll meet Carter here," Charlie said. "He's got part interest in one of Pat Dabney's horses. And, so the skinny goes, Pat Dabney."

"You're a worse gossip than any woman I ever met," Tish said. "Carter broke up with Pat Dabney two years ago. He said he couldn't afford her and she wouldn't keep him. His wife died of cancer five years ago, Andy, and he's never remarried, but he's way past the grieving stage, in case you were wondering."

"I wasn't," I said. "Belvedere. Dabney. Who owns

what? And where have I heard Belvedere and Dabney before?"

Tish laughed.

"Everything in Pemberton is connected in one way or another. You'll get used to it. Belvedere is the name of the people who used to own the estate where your guesthouse is. A grand old name in rubber tires and horses. Pat Dabney, who owns Runaway, is a Belvedere, the only one who still comes here. Her dad left her the stable. You heard Dabney when I was telling you about King's Oak, that big plantation out in the Big Silver Swamp. Clay Dabney and his son, Chip, own it, and Pat was married to Clay's nephew, Tom. Dabney is an old Pemberton name; they've been here forever. You'll hear it a lot, and you'll probably meet some of them today: Pat for sure, and Chip maybe. Pat's pure Belvedere; I don't know why she bothered to keep the Dabney when they divorced. Clay I don't think you'll meet; I heard he's in Atlanta on business. He owns a string of radio stations and newspapers in this neck of the woods, and some real estate in Atlanta, and he's in the state legislature. Tom you won't meet. He's our resident hermit and hardly ever comes out of the Big Silver Swamp."

"Sounds like my kind of guy," I said. "Does he live in a tree?"

"No, he's got a kind of cabin on Goat Creek, back in the swamp near the river. He lives back in there year round. I think that's one reason Pat divorced him. He wouldn't move to town with her."

"And he wouldn't quit his job and take over the stable for her," Charlie said, pulling the Jaguar up to a split-rail fence lined with whiskey barrels full of petunias. "Tom hates horses."

"I know he's my kind of guy," I said. "Can I go out into the swamp and take a look at him?"

"Oh, you'll see him, right enough," Tish said. "He teaches English at the college. Even hermits have to eat. And he's awfully popular; everybody loves Tom, even though we mostly think he's crazy, which he is."

We got out of the car into the cool morning. I breathed deeply, inhaling a wonderful mixed bouquet of fresh, damp earth and blooming flowers in beds and pine and hardwood and a kind of gamy, warm zoo smell that was not unpleasant, which I took to be horse and horse manure. The stables themselves seemed to be empty; I saw no beautiful, sculptured heads hanging over the Dutch doors of the stalls. Young men with pitchforks were cleaning out stalls and tossing forkfuls of baled hay into fenced rings, and two or three much older men, browned and wizened like walnuts, sat about on benches mending harness and oiling saddles. Against the white wooden wall of a smaller building with a sign over the door that said *Office* was a row of tiny white wooden crosses. Hilary tugged at my hand and we walked over and looked at them. On each one was a name: Toomer, Patcheye, Nellie, Rouser, Duckbutt, Belinda. There were fifteen or so in all, each with dates, each planted with an edging of zinnias.

"They're all the Belvedere stable dogs," Charlie said, coming up behind us. "From the very first one old August Belvedere had to Gideon, who died last year."

Hilary turned a stricken face to him.

"Did they get run over, or horse kicked?" she said in a small, tight voice.

I saw Charlie remember about Stinker, saw the pain in his eyes and the slight twist of his mouth. He took Hilary's hand.

"Nope. Died of old age and overfeeding, every one of them. Stable owners are as crazy about their dogs as they are about their horses, and the horses don't bother the pups.

They're a lot smarter than horses, though I'm not going to let Mrs. Dabney hear me saying that. There's a new one, Buddy, who's in training now, and a stable cat, Pickle, who's supposed to be the oldest living stable cat in America. Come on, let's go find them."

Hilary went off with him, looking like one of the photographs of Kentucky or Virginia horse country that I had seen a hundred times in *Town and Country*. Charlie looked wonderful, too, tall and massive and wellborn to a ludicrous degree in tweed and chinos and rubber shoes and a tweed cap, holding my little girl's hand. I felt a wave of love and gratitude for him that started tears in my eyes.

"He's wonderful with her," I said to Tish, who had come up to stand beside me. "She's never had a strong, gentle, nurturing man in her life. Chris loves her; he always did that, but with that god-awful, sucking intensity and scattiness. I'm going to have to be careful not to let her lean on Charlie too much. She's got to get on her own feet. I know I've overprotected her. . . ."

"You could hardly do anything else," Tish said. "And ten is a little young to worry about your own feet yet. Let her lean. Charlie has been bereft since the last of our girls went off to school. He loves having her around. I do wish she could get over the thing about dogs, though. There are thousands and thousands of them in Pemberton, and things happen to them all the time. Horse people are simply not sentimental about their dogs while they're alive. Dead is another matter," and she gestured at the little row of graves.

"Well, maybe I'll get her one, or a cat, when we get settled in our own place," I said.

"Oh, Andy, I forgot," Tish said in distress. "That's the one stipulation the Livingstons put on renting: no pets. He wouldn't mind, but she's fanatical about her flower beds and said she isn't going to have dog or cat poop in them. It was such a wonderful deal that I didn't think you'd mind that one thing."

"I don't," I said. "I really don't. She said not long ago she didn't want another dog, anyway. Maybe we'll get a canary."

Carter Devereaux came around the side of the stable just then, talking with a tall, blond woman in faded, filthy blue jeans and a striped tee shirt and scuffed boots. She was tanned to the color of good glove leather, and had light, yellow-hazel eyes, and wore her straw-colored hair slicked back and held on her forehead with black sunglasses. She had the blunt, fierce face of a peregrine: not beautiful, not even pretty, but absolutely compelling in its impersonal purity. The skin of her nose was peeling with sunburn, and her lips were bare and chapped, and her fingernails were broken and dirty, and she made every woman I had seen in Pemberton look earthbound and overdressed and fussy. Her body, under the old clothing, was glorious, slender and ripe and muscled like a jungle cat at full stretch. She was scratching her thigh with an absent forefinger and smoking a cigarette, scattering ash as she gestured with the butt, and she walked with the prowling saunter of a lioness. The words "wild," "primitive," "dangerous," were the first things that came to mind when I looked at her. The next was "aristocratic." There was not, could not be, any doubt at all that this woman was a kind of very American royalty. I knew that she must be Pat Dabney. Inside my borrowed jodhpurs I felt my buttocks swell to peasant proportions.

Carter Devereaux introduced us. She nodded coolly but pleasantly to me and studied Hilary with those startling predator's eyes. Hilary's light-blue ones stared back solemnly. Pat Dabney smiled, a sudden, powerfully attractive smile that lightened her face to a teenager's. I could see in the smile an entire history of unheeded pursuit by a veritable army of outclassed young men.

"Well, Hilary Calhoun, you're a pretty thing, aren't you?" she said. Her voice was lush and slow and careless, to match the rest of her.

"Thank you, ma'am," Hilary said. She smiled. I stared at her.

"You're very welcome. You look very nice in those jodhpurs. Do you ride? I'd be glad to take you out on one of my little mares sometime soon. You'd be a sight in the dressage ring, the two of you."

"I don't now, but I'm going to soon," Hilary said with an astounding composure. Chris's voice lay, suddenly, beneath hers. "I think horses are wonderful."

"Indeed, they are," Pat Dabney said. "Indeed they are. Well, you and your mother stick around. Some of mine are just coming in from the track. I'll introduce you around."

Her smile wrapped Hilary close and skirted over me as if I were the nanny I felt myself to be. She nodded again and strode off toward the end of the driveway, where a trio of horses and their riders were turning in from the dirt road.

"Holy cow," I said weakly. "That's called presence, I believe."

"There are other words for it," Tish said crisply. "But I'll save them for later. She does have a certain impact, I admit."

"I think she's beautiful," Hilary said. She looked levelly at me and then at Tish.

Tish laughed and ruffled her hair. "So do a lot of people, sweetie," she said. "And she thinks you're beautiful, too, so you all should get along just fine. She's a good friend to have at court, and she knows all there is to know about horses and riding and racing. If you really want to learn, she's the lady who can teach you. You're very lucky that she offered."

"Mama?" Hilary said, her eyes alight.

"Oh, Hilary . . . we'll talk about it later," I sighed. I did not like Pat Dabney and I did not understand her interest in my daughter, and I did not want Hilary to be caught up in this world of horses and stables and tracks and shows. I could not afford it, and I did not know when I ever could.

"I'd be glad to show her a little about it, too," Carter said. "I have a fat old mare stabled here, with the disposition of an angel. She'd be just the thing to start Hilary off. You, too, if you're interested. I could have you riding in a week."

His blue eyes were warm on my face, and the rich voice warmed the chill inside me that Pat Dabney's had left. He had one arm draped lightly around my shoulders, and one around Hilary's. I wondered if he knew our history, Hilary's and mine; it was likely that Tish had told him. Why on earth was he interested in me . . . for he obviously was, unless he was an actor of extraordinary skill. Me, after Pat Dabney?

"I'll pass, thanks, but I'd love to come watch while Hilary has a lesson or two. Just till school starts, though," I said.

"Done," he said, and gave my shoulder a little squeeze. Beside him, Hilary did a little dance step of joy.

The riders brought their horses down the driveway and we walked to meet them. Pat Dabney took the bridle of the largest, an enormous chestnut with seemingly endless, white-stockinged legs and a small, whipping head and a wild, white-ringed eye. He danced along, steaming and blowing, and the young girl in green and peach atop him was hard-pressed to hold him in. Pat's hand tightened on the bridle and she yanked the snakelike head down, hard and decisively, and the horse settled into a springy trot. The two horses behind the big one were ridden by young girls, too. I saw Hilary's eyes widen with enchantment, and knew that at that moment the future career as a biologist had given over to that of exercise rider at a training farm. Her entire body seemed to yearn forward toward the three horses.

Behind me, Carter Devereaux gave a sudden sharp exclamation. A small black Lab, really only a puppy, shot past us and bolted up the driveway toward the horses and Pat Dabney, heading directly for the hooves of the big chestnut. Hilary was after him in an eyeblink. I started after her, but Carter grabbed my shoulders and shoved me aside and raced past me. I heard Pat Dabney shout, "Get that damned dog and that fucking kid out of here," felt Charlie's big hands come down hard on my shoulders, and saw, in frozen terror, my child reach for the dog as it bounded directly under the hooves and the legs of the plunging, neighing horse. The world spun mightily and blackly on its axis for a moment, and when it slowed, Hilary was sitting, unhurt, on her small behind a dozen feet away and Pat Dabney was pulling the terrified horse in the opposite direction and Carter was beating the cowering, howling puppy with a crop. My child sprang for him like a small cat, and I broke free from Tish and went after her.

"Stop it, stop it, stop it," screamed Hilary, and Carter shouted, "Go back to your mother, Hilary," and I shouted, "Hilary, come here this minute," and Pat Dabney boiled into the middle of us like a tornado.

"Shut up, every one of you," she said, and her voice was glacier ice. "Carter, take that goddam dog out and shoot it, if you want to, but get it out of my sight and off my property. I won't have it around me." She rounded on me. "Take your child away from here," she said. "That was a goddam stupid thing to do. That horse could have cut her to ribbons and broken a leg to boot, and we'd have had to shoot him on the spot, and then I'd sue you for everything you ever thought about owning, and don't think I wouldn't. Don't you ever," she said to Hilary, glittering like steel, "don't you *ever* rush at a horse like that again. This horse is a grand champion in Ireland and Europe and I've spent an entire summer training him, and I won't have some no-nothing outsider's kid spooking him out of everything he's learned."

"Don't you talk to her like that," I began, red rage blurring my vision. My hands curved into claws of their own accord. For the second time in five minutes, Charlie took me by the shoulders and held me.

"She may look like a thoroughbred, but that's obviously about as deep as it goes," Pat Dabney drawled calmly and deliberately, and spun on her heel and walked away, leaving Hilary in tears of utter humiliation, and me near tears of fury, and Tish and Charlie in silence. I put my arm around Hilary and mopped her face with a Kleenex, and Carter, the whimpering puppy under his arm, came up to us.

"Andy, Hilary, I'm sorry," he said, and indeed, he did look shaken and contrite. "She has a bad temper, but she'll be over it in five minutes, and before the day is out she'll apologize. The horse is a killer; I've told her so from the beginning, and she's spent an awful lot of time and money on him. She'd never have forgiven herself if one of her horses had hurt you, and there have been some bad accidents over the years, to kids who aren't used to being around horses. To the horses, too. I'm sorry about the dog, but he's a stable dog, or she's training him to be, and sometimes you just have to hit them to make them understand. He could have been killed, and he could have made a valuable horse hurt himself. A stable dog has to behave around horses or he's no good to anybody."

Hilary turned her head into my body. Against me, she said, "You didn't have to beat him."

"I think I did," he said. "He'll remember next time. He won't do that again."

She turned her face up to him, but she did not let go of me.

"Will you shoot him?" she said. "She said for you to."

"No, of course not." He smiled at her. "She didn't mean a word of it. I'll take him back and leave him with Red, the stableboy who's training him, and he'll calm him down and give him a bone to gnaw and keep him penned up and quiet for a day or two, and she'll have forgotten about it by the time she sees him again. She's a tough lady, but she isn't a mean one."

"I don't like her," Hilary said, still sniffling but beginning to be mollified.

"Well, she meant it when she said she thought you'd make a good rider, so I hope you'll change your mind," he said.

I wanted to say, "My daughter may, but I never will," but of course I did not. I knew that I would never forgive Pat Dabney for the vicious little scene. Hilary and the puppy had done a foolhardy thing, of course, but neither had done so out of malice. The malice in that patrician voice had been swift and easy and gratuitous. Something deep within me bristled at Carter's defense of her, and that annoyed me, too. He was pleasant and attentive and kind, but he was less than nothing to me and to my child. I did not intend that he or anyone else should be more. Not now and not for a very long time, and possibly not ever again.

"Let's go over to the track and watch the last horses

working," Charlie said. "It's going to be too hot pretty soon, and Hilary really ought to see that."

"Good idea," I said neutrally, and by the time we reached the Pemberton training track, those ugly moments had been absorbed into the gold of the day almost as if they had never been. But only almost.

The mile-and-a-half training track was bordered on one side by a dirt road on which half a dozen private stables and homes lay, and on the other by the deep, shadowed coolness of the pine-and-hardwood forest that unrolled itself like a carpet through the town. The infield, of the same emerald-sapphire grass that seemed indigenous only to Pemberton, was starred at the track's far turn by a great, trailing oak. On the near side, adjacent to the road, was a low wooden bleacher and enclosure, which Charlie said was the judge's stand. A small knot of men in the Pemberton uniform—poplin pants, polo shirts, and snap-brim hats—stood at the bleacher rail, hands shading eyes against the slanting morning sun. There were no other women here besides Tish and me, and no children, besides Hilary, and no one was speaking. I had the sense that intense and momentous work was being done here and, not for the first time in Pemberton, felt rankly female and intrusive.

The horses were working in sets of twos and fours. I had seen horses racing before, of course, on television and in movies, but nothing had or could have prepared me for the sheer power and beauty of these. The morning was so quiet that you could almost hear the ground mist that lay blue against the dark-green woods, where the sun had not reached, and I heard the cool crystal song of some bird I did not know, off in the far pines. Over the liquid spill of song the soft, tearing thunder of hooves on dirt and the jangling harness and the dolphin-like blowing of the horses' breath seemed to fill the world. The sound was mesmerizing, humbling; it was like being in the presence of some elemental thing so seldom heard by human ears as to be portentous.

"Mama," Hilary breathed softly, squeezing my hand.

"I know," I said. "Imagine hearing that every day."

A set of four big bays swept by, young girls hunched far over on their necks, and directly behind them a smaller chestnut, as attenuated as a Calder mobile, flanked by a chunkier roan horse pounding determinedly along.

"That's an Appaloosa," Charlie said, softly, so as not to disturb the men at the rail. He jerked a thumb at the square little horse. "He'll never make a racer, but he's that colt's best buddy, and he calms him enough to run for time. That's what these are doing today, mainly, being timed. Most of them are two-year-olds who've never raced, and they're getting their first taste of the track and the gate and other horses here. Learning the rules. See that bay across the track with the big padded strap across his nose? They call that a shadow roll. He can't see over it, so it forces him to keep his head down and look at the track."

As the sets pounded by, the men at the rail thumbed stopwatches and made notations on pads. They exchanged a few laconic words to each other, but no one seemed particularly impressed by the running colts, whose speed and beauty seemed to me almost miraculous, a supernatural thing.

"What would it take to get a full-fledged round of applause out of these guys?" I said.

"Man O' War in a tutu," Carter said, grinning. "These are some of the best trainers in the business, Andy. Guy over there, Max Phillips, is the Whitneys' head trainer and has had more winners than any other guy in recent racing history. The others have had almost as many. They've seen the best that have ever run, and even if some of these babies turn out to be among them, it's way too early to tell. Besides, it's considered terrible form to brag on your own horse. About the best somebody will say is: 'That was nice time.' Or: 'He tends to business pretty good, doesn't he?' That bay wearing the shadow roll is this season's white hope; the way he's timing out, he could, with luck and work, make a Triple Crown winner. Or then again, he could sulk around and blow the whole thing. But he's got a lot of character, and he seems to have a great heart. He's the best of the babies here now, no doubt about it. He's one of Pat's; I wish now I'd bought a piece of him. But you can't really tell when they're this young."

"Are they all babies?" Hilary said, looking with love and hopeless yearning at the horses flashing past.

"These are," Carter said. "Pemberton's the best training track in the world for the young ones. But lots of older ones train here, too, and there are separate tracks for steeplechasers and pacers and trotters. This is a flat racing track."

"It's funny to hear you talk about character and heart," I said. "I always heard horses were stupid."

"Nope," he said. "All kidding aside, they're complicated and subtle, emotional animals. You get sweethearts and stinkers in horses just like people. I'd rather have a game, largehearted horse with a little talent than the fastest rattlesnake alive, because a game horse will work his heart out for you. That kind of willingness will win a lot of races."

Across the track, near the big oak, a handful of horses were being pulled into the slots of a great barrier gate on wheels. A clangorous alarm sounded and ten horses bolted out of the slots, returning to them again and again, to the sounds of the electronic blatting and bells and shouting and clapping. There was much plunging and rearing and nickering.

"They're learning the gate," Carter said to Hilary. "They'll go through that every morning until the season starts. By then the noise, and the close proximity of the others, and the crowds, won't spook them. Or we'll know which ones it will. It's a regulation starting gate, just like the one at Churchill Downs and the other tracks you see on TV."

"Wow," Hilary said breathlessly. "I bet it cost a million dollars."

"Pretty close to it," Charlie said. "But you have to remember that Pemberton is pretty much a one-industry town. There are more than five hundred horse operations of one kind or another here, and over five thousand horses. The gate's a kind of investment."

We stopped by several other stables that morning, and poked our heads into the shabby little wooden track kitchen, where more identical men and a few women were drinking coffee and eating doughnuts, and met several of the trainers and one or two owners and exercise riders. These were mostly young girls like the others we had seen, slender and small and tanned and somehow very lovely in jodhpurs and polo shirts and goggled helmets, and they returned Hilary's shy, adoring smile with smiles of their own, which said, "We know. We were you once."

"What is this near-mystical thing young girls have with horses?" I said. "I remember drawing endless rearing horses when I was about Hil's age, and there was a time I could name every Derby winner from first to last."

"It's purely sexual," Tish said. "Have you ever seen a horse's—"

"Tish." Carter laughed.

"Well, it's true," Tish said unrepentently. "Don't you just wish, though."

We went back to Pat Dabney's stable at noon and,

pulling the hamper Tish had packed out of the trunk of the Jaguar, spread our lunch on the soft grass under a big, low-leaning tree beside the dog's graves. They did not seem to bother Hilary now. I looked furtively about for Pat, but she was not in evidence. Just as we were starting in on our sandwiches, a stableboy came out bearing a bottle of champagne iced in a huge silver loving cup, and handed Carter a folded note. He read it and laughed and passed it to me.

"Sorry I was an asshole," it read in a black, slanted backhand. "Please accept my apologies and tell Hilary it wasn't her fault. I'd still like to teach her to ride, and if she'll come by any afternoon next week around three we'll begin. I'd join you but Doodah has colic and I think we're going to have to open him up."

It was signed with a huge, slashing *P*.

I passed the note on to Hilary without comment, and she read it and glowed up at me like a white candle. I felt a small, jealous twist inside at her incandescent face, ignited by the careless scrawl of that golden raptor, but I managed to return the smile. Hilary turned to Carter.

"Does she mean they're going to operate on a horse?" she said worriedly.

"Yep, but it's not that unusual, and not really a very big deal," he said. "Horse colic happens when a section of intestine gets twisted. Grown horses have hundreds of feet of intestines, and they can't vomit, so they can't relieve themselves when something gets stuck. The only way to do it is just go in and untangle 'em."

"Will Doodah be okay?"

"Doodah will be glomming oats again in a week," Carter assured her. "There are more good vets in Pemberton than there are doctors."

"I can well believe that," I said. "I don't know how Charlie makes a living, unless it's giving physicals to young exercise riders. I haven't seen a woman of childbearing age since I got here, Tish and I excepted."

"Charlie is a hot ticket with the new people and the Stratties," Carter said. "They reproduce at an alarming rate over there."

"I never heard so much talk about over here and over there. That's the third time in two days. Where is over there? Who are the Stratties?" I said lazily, biting into a crustless sandwich. It was wonderful: smoked salmon and thin-sliced onion and watercress. When had Tish done this? I washed it down with a flute of champagne; the flutes had arrived on the tray with the silver loving cup. The champagne was icy and so dry that it was like drinking desert air. I was so swept with sun and well-being that I hardly cared that the largess had come from Pat Dabney.

"Well . . . over *there,*" Carter said. "Across Palmetto Street and out to the east toward the river. Outside the historic district and the horse stuff. There's a whole other world in Pemberton, one that's far more normal than this one, though I'd be shot in most circles for saying so. It's where, as Tish herself says, the 'real stuff' is. Real people running real businesses and keeping real hours and driving real cars and living in real houses and condos. Nice ones, too. Country clubs, department stores, shopping centers, restaurants . . . the whole nine yards. Suburbia. Plumbers and accountants and used-car dealers and so on. That's over there, and there are enough women of childbearing age to buy Charlie another Jaguar next year. And of course, the Stratties. Stratton-Fournier. The folks what run our friendly bomb plant. There are roughly thirty thousand of them at last count."

I looked at him to see if he was teasing and saw that he was not, saw Tish frown slightly and shake her head almost imperceptibly, and then his words registered. I felt as if an immense, silent white explosion had gone off inside my head; I could feel the vibrations of impact on my mouth and in my ears. Of course. Stratton-Fournier. Civilian contractors and operators of the Big Silver River Plant. Manufacturers of components of nuclear weapons for the United States of America.

"Dear God in heaven," I said, and my words rang in my ears as from a great distance. "I forgot. I simply forgot about a nuclear weapons plant. I've known since I can remember that it was here; I've read the headlines and seen the marches and protests on television; I've even given money to Greenpeace and the Sierra Club, and gone to lectures, and read newsmagazines . . . and not once since I ran into Tish two months ago in Atlanta have I thought about it. No, longer than that! Not once since . . . I don't know when."

My voice died and I sat in the sun and looked at the bubbles in my champagne glass and felt as if I simply would sit there into the night and through it, and through the next day. . . . I had fled danger with my child and brought her, instead, into the very jaws of the place that some environmental groups deemed a greater danger than even the infamous Hanford, in Washington, or Fernald, in Ohio. Worse than Love Canal, worse than Three Mile Island . . . though there had not, yet, been any accidents. But any day, said the environmentalists. Aging equipment, mismanagement, ignorance, duplicity. The accounts of toxic waste, of toxic levels in groundwater and aquifers, and air of chilling proportions, plus details of near accidents and cover-ups, appeared in the media almost every day, followed by impassioned denials and learned theories and counter-recriminations. The Big Silver. And I had forgotten.

I looked at Tish.

"You should have said something," I said dully. "You must have known I wasn't thinking about it."

"I knew you wouldn't come if I did," Tish said, red staining her cheeks. "And I wanted to get you and Hilary to the safest place I know. And this is it. Andy, those stories . . . that's *media*. That's *hype*. Don't you think we'd know if the Big Silver was a danger to us? Don't you think we'd take our families out of here on the *instant* if we thought it was? Charlie is a *doctor*, and he'll be the first to tell you that there's been no evidence of damage to babies and children, and lots of them are born to people who've worked at the plant every day for years. No nuclear accidents, no poisoning, no two-headed babies and ten-legged cows, no hot milk or whatever. No hot water. There are ten separate government water and soil testing stations around the plant and about a hundred private ones, and they test every day of the world, and publish the results, and there's nothing in our water that hasn't always been there. Or our air. We don't even know the plant is out there. We don't go out that way. Nobody I know goes over to the part of town where the Stratties live, and they don't come over here much, and not many of them go to Saint Martin's or come to the races and steeplechases; it's a whole different world out toward the river. I know maybe three women whose husbands work at the Big Silver, and only one man, and he's the director of public information, and a nice enough guy. But they're engineers and physicists and high-tech types, and they have their own clubs and neighborhoods, and their children play with each other. . . ." She fell quiet abruptly, as if she knew she was chattering.

I continued to look at her.

"Andy, it's the truth," Charlie said. "I've lived here since I was born. I remember the day the word came out that the government was going to build a bomb plant at the Big Silver. After the first hysteria, nothing changed. I mean, maybe thirty-five thousand people poured into town, but they didn't pour into the old section, and they didn't change anything essential then, and they haven't since. I follow the daily figures on the air and water. I'm not a fool. My head isn't in the sand. There simply is not any danger. I would know if there were."

I looked at Carter, trying to glean from him, too, some balm to stop my heart from its runaway hammering. Surely Tish was right, surely Charlie would know, surely they would not have risked their girls' safety all these years. . . .

"Whatever there is in the water and the soil, I wish there was more of it," Carter said. "Pemberton has had more champions born and raised and trained here than any other town its size in the country. It's okay, Andy. It's probably true enough, the stuff that's beginning to come out about other places around the country. I read about Fernald and Hanford, and Oak Ridge, too. But I know the top brass at Stratton-Fournier; some of them are clients. I've known them for years. They just won some kind of national safety award for the most improved reactor maintenance, or something, and they've never once had test results in the danger range. Not in forty years. I follow those, too. The day that changes, I will personally move you and Hilary wherever in the country you want to go, and I'll move, too. Tish is right. You simply aren't ever going to know the Big Silver is out there."

And abruptly, I believed them all, and the brief spasm of terror was over. It may have been that my crisis quotient had long since been reached and I could not maintain any more adrenaline, but their words seemed, in that mellow, cicada-humming, late-summer noon, simply and perfectly true. Anything else was absurd. I lay back on Tish's blanket and closed my eyes and felt the sun press quietly on my eyelids and heard the voices of bobwhites and bees in red infield clover, and smelled pine and sun-warmed grass and thoroughbred musk, and felt the slow tilt of the earth, and thought of the infinitely beautiful and gracious old town around me. Tish was right. The thought that somewhere out to the east, in the great, sunless swamps of the Big Silver River crouched a plant for the manufacture of death, was simply beyond my imagining. Old Pemberton, itself unimaginable to me yesterday, was in that moment the only reality.

"Is it really okay?" Hilary whispered to me.

"Yes," I said, without opening my eyes. "It really is."

Two weeks later we moved into the little guesthouse Tish had rented for us in the forest off Whimsy Road. It was all she had said it was; from the beginning the house wrapped itself around us as if it had conjured us to it, and we slipped willingly into the spell of its rustic legerdemain. It was late Saturday evening before the big van from Atlanta bumped down our rutted, pine-needled driveway on its way home, looking like a mastodon grinding its way through the woods. It was almost dark on Sunday before we finished unpacking and putting away the essentials with which to sleep, bathe, and eat. Boxes and packing crates still lay everywhere when we stopped, but I could go no further. Hilary's school began the next morning, as did my own job at Pemberton State. I lay on my back on the floor, staring mindlessly at the massive beams—our beams now—and wondering if I could ever move again.

"If you'll tell me where the stuff was, I'll make us some sandwiches," Hilary said hesitantly, and I turned my head and smiled up at her.

"Give me two minutes and I'll do it," I said, and then I said, "Oh, shit," and sat up.

"What's the matter?" Hilary said.

"I told my new boss I'd leave a copy of my résumé on her desk so she'd have it for staff meeting in the morning, and I forgot," I said. "I'm going to have to go over to the college and do it now. There won't be time for her to read it if I don't. Come on, I'll drop you at Aunt Tish's and she'll feed you."

I left Hilary in Tish's kitchen eating a peanut butter and jelly sandwich and turned the Toyota across Palmetto Street and out the state road toward the college. It was just as Carter had said: Pemberton east of Palmetto Street was another country. Here was the small-town new South that I knew: strip shopping centers and fast-food franchises and mini-malls; every possible variety and nuance of vehicle sales and service establishment; discount stores and nail and aerobic salons and trailer parks. Between the Aramantha Baptist Tabernacle and the Happy Land Child Development Center I saw my first soil and water sampling establishment, and just past it the Atomic Transmission Shop and the Magic Mushroom Pizza Parlor, whose neon sign sported, ominously, a mushroom cloud. Apparently the populace on this side of Palmetto was as comfortable with the Big Silver plant as were their counterparts on the other. I shrugged. After the charm and beauty of Old Pemberton, these banal miles were ragged and jarring to the eye, but they had an oddly soothing effect. This was familiar ground; even though I had only been this way once before, I knew this country.

I turned off into a long driveway that snaked through a pecan grove up to the cluster of low white concrete buildings that was Pemberton State College. The cluster was small, and I had no trouble finding the lot in which I had parked when I came for my interview. The Public Relations Office was just inside.

I pulled the car up to the closed steel door and got out into the hot gray twilight. There was no other car in the lot, and no sign of another living soul. The sodium lights that ringed the lot had not yet come on, and I walked in deep shadow. The door was unlocked, and I went into a long, dim hall. Discovering no light switch, I groped in near darkness the short distance to the Public Relations Office, found it locked, and stood for a moment wondering what to do. Then I slid my résumé under the door and hurried back toward the parking lot. The empty, chalk-smelling gloom set my skin prickling and my heart beating slightly faster. My footsteps seemed to ring like gongs. For the first time I thought that coming here alone was probably no smarter than it would have been back in Atlanta.

The door was shut fast when I reached it, and I could not open it. For a moment I panicked, pushing blindly at the smooth steel, and then I hammered on it, and kicked it, and it jolted open, and I stumbled out into the dusk and virtually into the arms of a man standing on the other side of the door. I drew in my breath sharply and looked up at him, and then gave an involuntary cry of fear. I jerked away from him and backed along the cinder-block wall of the building toward my car, wondering frantically if there was anything in it, providing I could reach it, with which to defend myself. The man looked, in the still, empty twilight, truly horrifying; wild; a madman.

He was small, hardly half a head taller than I, and his hair was a straight, lightless, Indian black that fell over his eyes in a dark comma. His face was striped with bars of a substance that seemed only slightly darker than the skin of his face. He wore ragged, torn fatigues that were stiff and dappled with darkness, and on his slender waist there was a leather belt that held a sheathed knife. His small, neat feet were encased in dirty moccasins, and there was something strapped over one of his powerful shoulders that looked, incredibly, like a quiver of arrows. Under the hair his eyes gleamed light, and he smelled powerfully of dried sweat and something else, something old and rank and wild. He looked as alien and dangerous in that mundane-ugly college parking lot as a troll, or a murderous pygmy. I thought mindlessly of madmen and mutilation and headlines and Hilary, waiting at Tish's house for an arrival that would never happen, and of spinning blue lights on that enchanted dirt road, and a child's wild crying. . . .

"Get out of my way," I said, my voice high and thin and silly in my own ringing ears, and he stepped back silently to let me pass, and I saw, behind him, a mud-spattered all-terrain vehicle parked next to mine, and on the hood of it, the carcass of a deer, blood dried blackly around a small hole in its shoulder. Its open eyes were opaque and glassy, and its tongue protruded thickly from its black-rimmed mouth, and there was a beautiful rack of slender antlers on its fine head, like a crown. A hunter. This mountebank-madman was a deer hunter, and the smell and the darkness on his face and clothes was the blood of the deer. My fear was replaced in an eyeblink with fury and disgust. It did not occur to me that simply because I could classify him I had no less reason to fear him. The dead creature shocked me profoundly, there in all that pitiless dark concrete and steel and asphalt; its spilled beauty and the total, despairing deadness of it moved me deeply, nearly to helpless tears. I whipped my head back to look at the man, and he cocked his own head slightly and quizzically, and then looked at the Jeep and the deer.

"Oh, Christ, I'm sorry," he said. His voice was light and soft, like that of a singer. "I didn't think I'd run into anybody on Sunday night, or I'd have left him off home before I came. Are you going to be sick, or something?"

I wanted to strike him physically, I was so angry at him; angry at his intimidating wildness and ease in his dark skin; angry at his reeking clothes and the blood of the lovely animal on him. I was outraged at his quick assumption of my weakness.

"I'm not going to be sick, no," I snapped. "But you ought to be. I hope you are. How can you eat something so beautiful? If you *are* going to eat him . . ."

"I'm going to eat him, yes," he said, and there was a rich little hill of something—laughter?—in his voice. "I don't kill unless I am. But let me ask you something: how could you eat anything that *wasn't* beautiful?"

I only stared at him, in the now-full darkness. The sodium lights came on suddenly, and his skin turned to sallow tan and the black blood to dark red, and I could see that the light eyes were the same ice blue as Hilary's. He smiled at me, his teeth flashing white, and touched his hand lightly to his forehead as if to tip a hat, and padded with the smooth, silent gait of a wild animal into the building and out of my sight. Inside, I heard a door open and then close and saw a window bloom into light. A Haydn quartet spilled out into the thick air. I got into the Toyota and turned back toward Pemberton. I was surprised to realize, as I drove, that I was shaking.

I picked up Hilary and chatted a moment with Tish and Charlie before we went home. I had meant to tell them about the man and the deer and ask if they knew who he was, but then I did not. I knew, viscerally and with absolute certainty, that he belonged, somehow, to that wild old shadow country that lay along the verges of the Big Silver River, to the east. Out there.

For a long time that night, before I finally slid into sleep in the bedroom that was now to be my private refuge in this place, I lay with my eyes closed, seeing against the lids, as if seared there by a flash of lightning, the image of the dark face and the bloodied, stiffening deer.

CHAPTER THREE

Seventy-five miles northwest of the Georgia-Florida state line, on either side of the Big Silver River, lies the Big Silver Swamp. Nobody knows why it is called the Big Silver; except in the brief spasms of the Southern winters, when the broom-sedge fields and cattails along the marshes lie silvered with rime ice, the Big Silver is nearly all green and black—the green of pines and cypresses and pin oaks and patches of open soybean fields, the black of tree trunks and still, thick water. The beards and shawls of Spanish moss that shroud the tall, straight cypresses and oaks are the gray of pewter, without the sheen of silver. No precious metal lies beneath the black ooze that floors it. The little light that filters into the cypress aisles is green and lusterless. It had an Indian name once, lost now to memory, and perhaps that name meant Big Silver, or something like it. But the name was forgotten not so long after the last of the small coastal Indians who hunted and fished there departed. All that remains of them is a time-gentled ceremonial shell-and-earth mound deep in the swamp, which few of Pemberton's latter-day citizens have ever seen, and the swamp itself. Old, dark, silent, vast, the Big Silver endures.

At daybreak on a September Saturday a week after Hilary and I moved into our little house on Whimsy Road, I sat in a kind of tree house in the lower branches of a great oak tree on a small island in Goat Creek, in what seemed to me the very dark heart of the Big Silver Swamp, and waited for a deer to come by below. I held in my hands a small, slender rifle, its barrel cold in the warm, thick dawn, and I wore too-tight camouflage pants and shirt borrowed from Tish's older daughter, Ansley, and I sat as Clay Dabney, whose tree and stand and land these were, had told me to sit: motionless and silent and as relaxed as possible, so that my nervous perspiration would not alert any deer that moved within range. But my heart beat in a staccato stitchery of anxiety, despite myself, and my jaws were clamped with the effort to breathe silently. Even if I had been familiar with the alien, repugnant weight and coldness of the gun, I could not have made my rigid arms swing it to my shoulder, or my stiff finger pull its trigger. I was too frozen with strangeness and awkwardness, too drowned in the primitive aloneness of the swamp.

I had told Clay Dabney that as he put the little rifle into my hands, after he had helped me up the steps of the tree stand in the oak.

"Your deer are safe from me," I said, trying to laugh normally in the gray light that probed through the leaves of the oak. "I couldn't shoot them if I wanted to. I'll probably fall right out of this tree the minute you leave."

"Couldn't hit a deer with this little thing, anyway," he said, handing the rifle up after me. "Too little and too light. It's a Chipmunk, for small varmints; a boy's gun, really. I just want you to take it so you can shoot it if you get lonesome, or need help. There'll be somebody not a hundred yards away from you most of the time, and they'll come if they hear you shoot. I've told them we've got a city gal up in the King's Oak this morning. Just be sure to shoot straight down into the ground. You'd be surprised how far a little twenty-two will carry in the woods. But save it for an emergency; it's a single-shot, and you'll have to reload if you want to shoot again."

"There's not any danger of that," I said. "I'm not sure I could hit thin air."

"Nobody expects you to." He smiled, the quick white smile that made his weathered face almost as young as his son Chip's; a smile of real and generous sweetness. "If a deer wanders by, just do what I do most of the time: tell him shoo. Get his ass on down the road. You won't hear any other guns, because it's not rifle season yet; everybody here today will be bow hunting, if they're hunting at all. Most of them aren't, not seriously. This is King's Oak's big party weekend; the serious stuff comes later. So everybody in the woods will hear you if you shoot; somebody'll come get you down and bring you a Bloody Mary. Don't suffer in silence. It can get right lonesome out on these stands."

Carter Devereaux had brought me in the humid early-morning blackness to King's Oak Plantation for Clay and Chip Dabney's annual Pemberton hunt, brought me apprehensive and protesting. I had not wanted to come, and had told him so as politely as possible; we had only been out together once since the day at the training track, and I had not wanted him to think me ungrateful or condescending. I liked Carter and had enjoyed his company at the quiet midweek dinner we had had at the Inn; he was so easy to be with that I felt as if I had known him for many years, and that was comforting, soothing. I did not think I wanted to go out with anyone, even soothing, easygoing Carter, and I was certain I did not want to know any more than I did about Pemberton's second great obsession—hunting.

"You really ought to go," he said. "It's not actually a hunt; it's more like a house party, though some folks will probably do a little hunting. It's the only time during the year Clay opens King's Oak to all of us; the rest of the time it's strictly private parties, gentrified rod and gun clubs, big-shot Europeans and Arabs, stuff like that. This is about the only time during the year most women set foot on King's Oak. It's really the start of the fall social season here; Clay's been giving this hunt barbecue every September for as long as I can remember. Everybody in Pemberton you'll want to meet will be there. It's something to see; there're not many of the big private plantations left in the South now. There are people all over the world who'd trade their children for an invitation to King's Oak."

I decided I should get the matter of hunting and blood sports settled once and for all.

"Carter," I said, "it would just be wasted on me. I hate hunting and killing animals. I don't wear fur. I can't watch *Wild Kingdom* without crying. I don't eat game if I know that it *is* game—which I usually don't. I don't think there's any justification for it, and I don't see any sport to it. I also think people who feel the way I do about it are probably awful bores, so the best thing for me is to just stay away from it. I'll take the Greenpeace sticker off my bumper and I swear I won't give the finger to any hunters I meet, but beyond that I cannot go. I appreciate the invitation, though. At this point, I'm not at all sure anybody in Pemberton will think meeting me is a social triumph, anyway. But maybe I can get to know them another way."

"Sure," he said equably. "I'll give a little dinner party for you sometime soon, if you'll let me. Would you like that?"

I looked at the pleasant, sun-pinked face and the smiling blue eyes under the sandy, receding hairline, and smiled my capitulation. I had, I knew, come dangerously close to sounding boorish.

"I'd like that very much," I said. "You're kinder to me than I deserve."

"It would be my pleasure," he said. "You're very easy to be kind to. I can respect your feelings about hunting, Andy, but it's not as simple as you make it out. There's something else to it, another side from just the killing: something sort of grand, in a way. Very traditional, very ritualistic. In its own way, very beautiful. It's easy to see all that at King's Oak. If you change your mind, let me know."

And I did, for the simple reason that Tish came down on me like a duck on a June bug when she heard that I had refused Carter's invitation to the hunt.

"For God's sake, can't you bend just a little?" she said in exasperation. "Refusing the King's Oak hunt is like refusing dinner at the White House. Killing deer isn't what it's about; it's Clay Dabney's way of honoring his home town. It's his gift to all of us. It's a tradition. King's Oak is one of the great hunting plantations on earth, Andy; it's a way of life that you won't find anywhere else in the world. Clay doesn't ask anyone he doesn't value, and he specifically asked Carter to bring you; Carter told me. It's like a slap in the face to him and the rest of Pemberton if you refuse just because you don't like hunting. Half the people who go there don't like hunting. But everybody loves Clay. I wish you'd reconsider. It would be a very gracious thing to do, all the way round."

"Oh, Lord," I said, knowing I was beaten. It was that "gracious" that had done it. Tish always knew precisely which of my buttons to push. I could not stand the thought of being ungracious, of repaying kindness with curtness. I remembered too well my own first days in Chris's world.

I called Carter and asked, diffidently, if the invitation was still open.

"Of course," he said. "And I'll bet you five dollars right now that after the hunt you'll have changed your mind about hunting, just a little."

"You're on," I said. "I never give a sucker an even break."

And so I had set my alarm clock for three o'clock this morning, and he had picked me up in his Jaguar, a dark-blue twin to Charlie's, and we had dropped a sleep-numbed Hilary off at Tish's, where she would spend the day and evening by the pool with Charlie's sister's children and a teenaged chaperone, and we had driven the black predawn miles out the state highway toward the Big Silver River and King's Oak Plantation. He had brought coffee in a thermos, and I sipped it as we drove, and looked at him, unfamiliar now in crisp new fatigues and heavy lace-up boots, his face, under his camouflage cap, alien and Mongol-shadowed in the green light from the dash. A profound sense of strangeness, of disorientation, swept me. What was I doing, sitting here in this silent, luxurious car in the thick September night on a road I did not know, headed for a place I could not even imagine, with a man whom I had known only ten days sitting beside me, on the way to a great and ancient pageant of ritual murder? Loneliness and desolation swam inside me; I felt a simple, one-celled, child's homesickness for the life I had left behind me in Atlanta; yes, even that life. Even my mother. Even, almost, Chris. I felt tears of weakness and loss welling up in my eyes, and took a big swallow of coffee.

"Tell me about Clay Dabney and King's Oak," I said cheerfully, wanting to put my head back and howl like an abandoned dog.

"I guess you could call him sort of the village squire," Carter said. He did not appear to have noticed the falsity in my voice. "He's the biggest landowner in this part of the state. He has other business interests, but it's the land and the plantation that people think about when they think about the Dabneys. His—let's see—his grandfather John Thomas, I think it was, came down after he graduated from the University of Virginia and did a year at Heidelberg University, and bought up about twenty thousand acres around the Big Silver. Swamp. A lot of folks thought he was out of his gourd. But he'd done a lot of hunting and fishing in Germany, and studied some kind of woodsmanship stuff they teach there, and he built a big white columned house on one side of the river and a big log lodge just on the other, and invited some of the rich Yankees and Europeans he'd met to come down and hunt, and before long King's Oak was famous among hunters—the big rich kind, not the pickup-and-squirrel-gun kind. Thirty-thousand-dollar custom guns. All that. Old John Thomas had some fancy ideas about roughing it, no doubt about that. The hunts have gone on almost since then.

"Well, in due time he passed the land on to *his* son, Thomas, and he kept the tradition going, and then Thomas had two sons, Claude and Clay. He left Claude the land on the east side of the Big Silver, with the house, and Clay the land on the west, with the lodge. Oh, and the tree, the big old oak tree that the place is named for, King's Oak. Clay got that, even though it's on an island in the creek that divides the property. There's a legend about some ancient king who lived in an oak tree, or something; old John Thomas read about it in Heidelberg. Claude died of pneumonia back around 1960, and his widow, Caroline—Caroline Pinckney, of the Charleston Pinckneys, you understand—sold the house and land before he was in the ground, practically; sold it to the Atomic Energy Commission to use for the Big Silver facility. She moved to town and built herself a miniature Versailles over near the training track, and she still lives there with her daughter, Miggy. Margaret. Miggy never married; when you meet Miss Caroline you'll understand why. Claude and Caroline's son is Tom Dabney; who was married to Pat. Wheels within wheels. I don't think you'll have met Tom yet, unless you've run into him at the college. He doesn't come around where Pat is much, and he almost never comes to King's Oak. He doesn't speak to his mother; hasn't, if he could help it, since she sold the land and the house. He loved that place; he's a great woodsman, like his dad and granddad and great-grand."

"Oh, yes," I said. "The hermit. Tish has told me about him. It must be tough to live in Pemberton and hate horses and hunting."

"He doesn't hate hunting," Carter said. "He's probably the best hunter in Georgia. He just hates big hunting, organized hunts. He has some land in the swamp, back up on one of the creeks that feeds the Big Silver and runs parallel to it for a way. It's a kind of strip between Clay's land and the Big Silver plant's land; his father built a shack up there when Tom was little, for the two of them to stay in when they went up there hunting and fishing. Tom bought it from his mother when she sold to the AEC; sold his car and met her market price. He stays up there in the little house, and hunts his own property, or hunts leased land or forest service land like everybody else who doesn't have access to one of the big places. Clay has given him carte blanche to King's Oak; he's always treated him like his own kid, and Tom is crazy about him. But he won't go on King's Oak land except maybe to pay his respects to Clay, like at today's hunt. And he wouldn't cross the creek to spit on Chip."

"Chip," I said. "That's Mr. Dabney's son, isn't it? Tish told me a little about the family."

"Yes," Carter said. "Chip. Clay Dabney junior. Chip off the old block, see. Only he never has been. He's about Tom's age or a year or two younger, but Chip just never has gotten it together somehow. He's the apple of his Mama Daisy's eye, and Clay loves him, of course, but you can tell he's worried about Chip baby about half the time. Chip is what is commonly known around here as just plain sorry; he has been, ever since he was a little kid. I grew up with him and Tom, and they were as different as night and day, even then. I think Miss Daisy just plain spoiled Chip into sorriness, no matter how hard Clay tried to make a man of him—and he did try. But it just didn't take. Chip was scared of horses and scared of the woods, and he couldn't learn to shoot a gun. Not that that's any disgrace, but he never learned much of anything else, either. I think Clay gradually quit hunting and fishing when he saw Chip was never going to go with him; he used to take Tom whenever he went, but I guess it hurt him too bad to take his nephew where his son wouldn't or couldn't go. So he turned the lodge over to his foreman and staff and for a long spell there wasn't any hunting at King's Oak.

"Chip has always been into instant gratification. Went

to the University of Georgia law school and squeaked by, but never managed to pass the bar. Never kept any of the jobs Clay got for him, even in the family businesses—or created such havoc in them that Clay had to find another for him and clean up the mess. He always had the cars and clothes he wanted, and the girls. . . . Women fall at his feet, for some reason, and he can't keep his pants zipped for two days straight. He's been in hot water since he had his first erection. He's got just the wife and children a rich young man should have, and the house; his mama built the house for him, and she probably got Lucy for him somehow. For all I know, she pays her to stay with him; he's been caught with other men's wives so many times nobody even bothers to gossip about it anymore. But he has a sweet smile and a kind of boyish way about him, and he's always sorry if he's hurt anybody, and can't understand quite how it happened. . . . Clay's spent thirty-five years and God knows how much money getting him out of trouble. I know he loves Chip. I just don't know why. Oh, hell, of course I do. Chip's his boy. His only kid. His only shot at . . . whatever. If he wishes Tom were his son he never says so, but you can't help seeing the contrast, or the look in his eyes when Tom's around."

"What does he do now? Chip?" I asked. It was an engrossing story, and a sad one. I forgot the howling loneliness.

"Well, he's finally found something he likes, and seems to be doing okay at. Clay turned King's Oak over to him about fifteen years ago, to manage, and he's started the big hunts up again, and manages the plantation, except for the part that the lumber company leases. He's spent about half Clay's money in the process, but he's breaking even, or pretty near it—I see the figures on it; I'm a trustee—so I guess

Clay figures it's a worthwhile investment. He just kind of closes his eyes to the people Chip brings in there, and what they do. Ol' Chip always did have a taste for lowlife trash, and he brings 'em in by the planeload; he put in a private jet strip first thing, and it's almost always full in season. Big rich, those folks. Not old rich and responsible, like the horse people on the other side of Pemberton, but new and showy, most of them, a lot of them Middle Eastern and European. Eurotrash, I've heard them called across town. They have fifty-thousand-dollar guns and outfits and can't hit shit, and they snort cocaine and drink Clay's hundred-year-old booze, and sometimes they bring their women with them, the best they can buy, and it's one week-long roll in the mud after another. Lots of gambling, for really big money; so far, I guess, Chip has managed to stay out of that, or he'd be in jail. I hear he baits the fields and provides released birds for them, and I've also heard that he lets them take doe and fawns and shoot out of season, but nobody has ever proved that, and Clay doesn't seem to have heard it, so nobody pushes it. Like I said, we all love Clay Dabney. He's done a lot for Pemberton. And Chip isn't his fault; nobody ever tried harder with a kid."

"It sounds Greek, a Greek tragedy," I said. "Like the House of Atreus, or something."

"Yep. All that's missing is the deus ex machina. And so far the pissed-off Olympian, to bring it all down."

I stared at him, and he grinned sideways at me.

"I took one or two courses besides estate law," he said.

He turned the car off the highway onto a narrow, unmarked sand road that appeared to run endlessly through black woods, woods so dense that in places the trees met overhead, and it seemed that we were passing through a tunnel. The headlights picked up yellowing ferns and tall weeds and mounds of blackberry brambles on the road's edge, and more than once the blazing eyes of small wild things that shot or flowed across the road just ahead of us. Once I saw, incredibly, a fox, red and full-brushed and beautiful; it posed, a foreleg lifted as if pointing, on the weedy verge, and then melted into the deep blackness.

"Will we see a deer?" I asked, my heart still hammering at the wildness of the fox.

"Not on the road, I don't think," he said. "It's been a wet year, and they'll have all the forage and acorns they want in the swamp. Deer don't usually travel more than a mile or two outside their territory in their entire lives, unless they're hungry. These aren't."

Abruptly the darkness ahead of us gave onto a vast gray-lit clearing, and I saw the King's Oak lodge for the first time. It was enormous, with a massive two-story central structure of silvery-weathered logs and a long front veranda supported by huge timbers, flanked by two low, rambling wings. Its great windows were leaded and diamond-paned, like the big cottages back in Pemberton, and great stone chimneys broke the line of the hulking, mossy shake roof at intervals. Behind it, a cluster of lower buildings lay like sleeping animals in the thin first light, and off to the left was another, smaller two-story log building. A number of jeeps and cars and wagons were parked about on the split-railed and graveled circle in front of the lodge, but they were empty. A light burned in one of the lodge's downstairs windows, and a thin column of white smoke was drifting up from behind the outbuildings. From somewhere out of sight I heard the faraway barking of many dogs, but other than that, there was an immense and echoing silence.

"It's like a frontier settlement, a little town," I whispered, looking up at the huge bulk of the lodge.

"A city-state," Carter said. "It is. It's almost totally self-sufficient. It even has its own generator, and power plant, and wells for water. Clay could come here and sit out Armageddon. It's really a fiefdom; besides the permanent hands, there's a settlement of blacks on the property, way up the river where Goat Creek starts, that's been here for about two hundred years. The place is so big that some of the old ones have never even realized they live on a plantation. They think Mister Clay just owns a big old log house and some outbuildings way downcreek. He'd never tell them, either; he's looked after them like all the Dabneys before him: paid their taxes, and tried to get them medical attention when they need it, and let them take what fish and game they need all year round. I know, it sounds too Old Massa for words, but it works for everybody, and Clay doesn't make a big thing of it."

"Who are all the people?" I said, gesturing toward the cars.

"Most of them are hunters, already on the stands," he said. "Clay makes everybody stay put when there's a crowd. Probably some of the caterers, and some extra help from town, and I see Chip's car there, and Clay's. Most people will come in about eleven, for Bloody Marys and hors d'oeuvres. That smoke you see is from the barbecue pits; Clay's had hands tending pigs and maybe a goat back there all night. By noon there'll be tables set up on the veranda and about five hundred people gobbling barbecue and Brunswick stew and drinking free liquor. The band will be down there at one end of the veranda, and there'll be another one out by the pool, for the kids, and black women to watch them, and a lifeguard from the club in town. Whole thing will last until about midnight, when the last drunk lurches out of here, and the ones that can't Clay will put to bed in the bunkhouse, and the hands will have a breakfast for them in the morning before shooing them out. It's right out of *Gone With the Wind*. I don't know why he puts up with us, but he seems as tickled with it as a kid."

"And that's just what I am, a big kid at heart," a man's deep voice said, and Clay Dabney stepped out of the shadows of the veranda, smoke curling from the cigarette in his hand. "I've been sitting here waiting for you to get Miss Andy out here since four A.M., you sorry hound," he said. "I'm gon' take her out to the King's Oak myself, and get her set up. Don't trust you as far as I could throw you."

I looked up into dark, dancing eyes and a face as brown as a walnut, under a shock of pure silver hair. Clay Dabney was not especially tall, but he was so slender and wiry, except for the small, hard melon of his belly, that he seemed to tower over me, and the silver thatch gave his face a kind of senatorial grandeur that I associated with liberal heads of state and grand old movie stars. He stood perfectly erect in his faded camouflage cotton, and balanced a slim rifle with a scope easily in the crook of one arm, and the sheer presence of him smote the air around him almost palpably. In the darkness of his face his smile was white and somehow extremely masculine. He smelled of wood and cigarette smoke and clean cotton and a kind of graphite odor that I learned later was gun oil. It was a wonderful smell. I felt my lips curve into a smile before the impulse to do so formed itself in my mind.

"I'm Andy Calhoun, Mr. Dabney," I said. "It was nice of you to let me come. I know about as much about hunting and the woods as a geisha."

"Well, that'll do for a start," he said. "You sure look like a woodsman, or a woodslady, rather. You'll blend right into the King's Oak." His eyes took in Ansley Coulter's pants and shirt and Tish's stout boots with approval.

"It's all pure fake," I said. "I honestly never have even held a gun. I haven't even really been into the woods. I don't want you to think I know more about it than I do. I'm terrified of being a trouble to you, and I wouldn't be here at all except that Carter absolutely insisted that I come. I really don't plan to shoot at a deer or anything."

"Time for that later, if you should be interested," he said. "The first time is for looking and listening. For letting the woods talk to you."

I looked more closely at him; it was an oddly poetic turn of phrase for such a totally masculine man.

"Well, I hope they will," I said. "I'd hate to go out there and have them not speak to me."

"I have a feeling they'll have plenty to say to you," he said. "You ready? I'll run you out to the King's Oak in the jeep. Carter, you go on. I've got you down in F. In the stand at the creek fork. Good hunting."

"Good hunting, Colonel," Carter said, and turned and opened the car trunk and took something out. I drew in my breath reflexively; it was a curious kind of bow, sleek and intricately gnarled and threaded with taut crossed strings and fitted at its ends with small wheels. Long silver arrows were affixed in a cradle to its shining handle, and it looked altogether savage and awful. I could not even imagine the flight of those arrows, or what they must feel like entering the flesh of the animal struck with them. Standing in the misted dawn holding the terrible weapon, Carter was someone else, someone I did not know and could not imagine knowing. How could I know a man who could use this thing?

"New bow," Clay Dabney said. "A Hoyt-Easton?"

"Yes," Carter said. "Pro Hunter. Probably more bow than I need, but these new wheels are supposed to up your energy about a hundredfold. I can use the help."

"Hear it's the best available," Clay Dabney said. "You won't have to track very far with that baby if you get a hit. Looks like it could stop a water buffalo."

He saw my face and smiled.

"Looks fearsome, doesn't it?" he said. "But it's the most humane kind of bow for hunting deer. Got the power to drop them quickly, almost like a gun. Most of them never know what hit them, if the archer's good."

"What if he's not?" I said. My mouth was dry.

"If he's not he doesn't hunt at King's Oak," he said. "At least not when I'm here."

We got into the jeep and bumped down what appeared to be merely a sandy trail leading away from the house and into the close-pressing woods beyond the clearing. Once out of sight of the big house and the rising smoke, we seemed to have slipped a thousand miles and as many years away from civilization. It was a dark wildness that you knew, on the back of your hands and neck, had no limits, either physically or spiritually; a wildness of the soul as well as of trees and water and earth. I could feel the huge power of it, off in all directions around me, almost sleeping but not quite; pulsing gently, breathing like a giant, just-waking animal. As far as I could see, wherever I turned in the oncoming morning, aisles of black-green giants marched away from me, buried to their knees in black undergrowth and still, dark water. The very light was diffused and particulate, as if filtered through some green scrim from above. The air felt as thick as wet gauze on my face. At first just the forms of things were visible, but definition was coming fast, and the emerging textures and colors were strange and new, as if born of some awful young sun. I did not look often from side to side. I did not want to see this place clearly, and I did not want to be left alone in it. There was simply no telling what might come out of this primeval darkness, seeking this primordial light.

"It's very mysterious, isn't it?" I said, my voice almost clattering in the silence. "Like there's something old and secret back in here, that hasn't seen the light in a million years. Are you sure you aren't raising dinosaurs, maybe?"

He looked at me sidewise, a curious, appreciative look.

"Nope, but I know what you mean. These swamp woods are one of the last real mysteries we have, I guess," he said. "Not everybody feels it. I thought you might. I've always thought I wouldn't be surprised to see a unicorn or something come out of a thicket in here and drink from the river. And there're people who do think they've seen things. Of course, they've been back in here a long time and been nipping right along when they do. But if you're in the woods alone any time at all, you really can get to seeing things. That's why I brought this little gun along for you. If there's any place in these woods to see a unicorn, it's up in the King's Oak."

"I'd never shoot a unicorn," I said, as lightly as I could in this old place.

"No, you wouldn't," he said. "But you might want to kind of warn him, like, so nobody else does, either. An arrow is a swift and silent thing."

I looked back at him and saw he was not joking. He caught the look and smiled.

"Well, there're lots of myths about the woods," he said. "You ever read any of them, or studied them at school? Carter says you have an English degree."

"Not really, that I remember," I said. "I read some myths when I was small, Greek mostly. I guess I remember some bits and pieces about wood nymphs and pools and things. . . ."

"You'll find most of them in the northern myths, the Norse and Germanic ones," he said. "But all civilizations have had them. Myths and legends about the woods, and hunting. My grandfather studied a lot of that in Germany, and passed it on down to my father; I can remember sitting for hours on some stand, or up in a tree, listening to him, me and my brother Claude. Wonderful things. Mostly crap, of course, but you really can feel something in the woods sometimes, a kind of quiet, like in church. A power. My nephew knows them all; my brother was a great storyteller, and Tom has the kind of mind that keeps things like that. He's an English teacher at the college; you'll be bound to run into him. I told a few of them to old Chip, my boy, but the ones that didn't scare him, he laughed at. Well, here we are. The heart of the matter, as they say. The old oak that my grandfather named the place for."

I got stiffly out of the jeep and followed his outstretched arm with my eyes. The light was still dim, but clear enough, now, for me to see for some distance. We stood on the bank of a creek that ran wide and still and black, and so shallow that it spread up among the leaning trees on either side like a lake. In the exact middle of the spread of water there was a small island about the size of a large drawing room, covered in emerald-green moss, and in the center of the island stood the largest and oldest oak tree I had ever seen.

It was as massive and symmetrical as a monument or a fortress out of antiquity: gnarled and spreading almost the width and breadth of the island, its great branches bearing a dense canopy of green. You could not see into it; I thought that you could live on the earth beneath it and never feel the rain or the sun. Its trunk had the girth of an automobile, and it branched out low, so that one could have simply stepped up into it, instead of climbing, and disappeared. Its leaves were small and dark green, seemingly infinite, and its shawl of Spanish moss almost touched the earth, like hair from a bent head. It stopped the eye and the breath simultaneously; its age and presence were as powerful as one of those terrible Greek elementals, only this presence was unmistakably beneficent. There could be no doubt that this tree was the god of this place, the heart of this forest. Wildness flowed from it like honey.

I simply looked at Clay Dabney and smiled.

"It's something, isn't it?" he said. "Live oak. There's not another tree in the Big Silver like the King's Oak. My grandfather always said it alone was worth the price of the land, and I agree with him one hundred percent. Sometimes I just come out here and sit under it and look at it. Even in winter; Miss Daisy thinks I'm crazy as a loon. But it means the world to me. The man who owns a tree like that is a rich man."

There was a rough old ladder of silver wood disappearing up into the huge oak, and I said, "And best of all, there's a tree house up there," and he laughed.

"I told you I was a kid at heart," he said. "All hunters are. All woodsmen. Those are the steps up to the stand; that's where I'm going to put you. This is the best place for deer on the plantation. The water is shallow enough for them to wade across to the island, and somehow the King's Oak acorns are a whitetail's Cordon Bleu. They've got clear land on either side of the creek here, and good big trees for scrapes, and there's a band of oak runs right along here that keeps the acorns knee deep practically all year round. Even in a bad year you can always find deer here. It's why I don't use the King's Oak stand often; it just stacks the deck too much against them. But you won't be shooting, and I want you to see all this."

There was a small aluminum skiff tied up practically

under the creekbank, and he helped me into it and poled across to the island. The splashing of the pole seemed loud in the misted stillness.

"You could wade it here in hip boots this time of year, but this is a little quieter," he said. "And you don't want to sit up there all morning in heavy wet pants. Deer can smell wet human, for some reason, a mile away. You wearing perfume or anything?"

"No," I said. "Should I be? Eau de Whitetail?"

"Nope. A deer's sense of smell is one of his greatest weapons; he can smell something that shouldn't be in the woods half an hour before he sees it, if he's downwind of it. Lots of hunters use sprays; you can get them in any scent from acorns—drives whitetails wild—to skunk. I'm not kidding. I'd rather be caught with the real McCoy than be penned up on a stand with a fool wearing skunk spray. But it masks the smell of man. A lot of hunters will go to all kinds of trouble not to smell like men; they'll bathe three and four times in scalding-hot water, and get their wives to wash their hunting clothes without soap and hang 'em in the woods to dry, and they'll take a can up in the stand with them instead of peeing off it . . . excuse me. You know. I don't like all that business, and I hate the sprays. People who know me don't use them at King's Oak; they dishonor both the animal and the man who wears them. They dishonor the woods."

"I don't see much difference between spraying acorn juice on yourself and hiding in a tree to shoot," I said. I felt that I could say anything to Clay Dabney.

"Well, see, the tree is real. It's a part of the woods. It's natural. The deer hide; I hide. The deer don't spray skunk juice on themselves."

"They don't carry rifles, either."

"No. They don't," Clay Dabney said. "They can outsneak and outsmell and outrun and outhide a man any day of the week, but they can't shoot back at him. Come right down to it, hunting isn't fair. What you want to do is make the process of it, the hunt itself, as equal as possible. That's where the animal has the chance. That's the sense of the hunt. The killing is the finish; you have to have it to make it a hunt. But it isn't the point."

He helped me up the ladder and into the stand, which was no more than a platform up in the branches, railed on two sides and open on the ladder side. The fourth side nestled snugly against the tree. Once up on it, I was sitting in a perfect, small green room, a fairy-tale chamber of leaves and moss and dappled light, and I was surprised at how well I could see the earth beneath the oak and the banks of the river through the leaves. I felt certain I could not be seen from below. It was oddly charming and almost comfortable, and I settled myself cross-legged on the platform and leaned back against the trunk. He handed the rifle up to me, standing halfway up the ladder. I thought suddenly that he looked like the spirit of the tree or some sort of forest god, the bottom half of his body buried in green, his chest and shoulders dappled in forest colors, his face the stain of wood, of nuts.

"Just remember that one shot will bring somebody in five minutes flat," he said. "And I'll send one of the boys for you around eleven. I'll have a Bloody Mary waiting. Good hunting, Miss Andy."

"Good hunting, Mr. Dabney," I said.

He touched his hand to the silver hair and was gone. I was alone with the morning sun and the silence of the Big Silver.

At first I was fairly comfortable up in the stand; the

sheer novelty of it was engaging, and the sense of all that green aloneness outside my hidden chamber was titillating. I sat as still as I could, balancing the gun across my knees. I would have liked to put it down on the platform beside me, but I took Clay Dabney literally when he said to stay as motionless as possible. It was somehow very important to me that I see a deer.

I felt like a child left alone in a totally unfamiliar place but assured by the adults that they would soon be back for it: faintly apprehensive but important, too, at being adjudged old enough to be by itself. I listened as hard as I could for any sound that might be deer walking through the forest, and I did hear a few sounds: tiny dry rustles; the little liquid plops of small amphibians entering the water; the faint stirring of leaves in the hot, thick air; the occasional call of a bird. But it seemed to me, as the sun grew higher and the morning wore on, that sound began to cease; the birdsongs dwindled and stopped, and I heard no more splashes, and even the stirring of the leaves stopped as the wind dropped. It was close in the leaf chamber, and sweat broke out at my hairline and on my upper lip, and a midge droned in my ear. I reached up and brushed it away, slowly, and carefully laid the little rifle down beside me on the plank floor. I looked at my watch. It had stopped.

That's when the strangeness began. My heart gave a small spasm, like a suddenly caged bird, when I realized that I did not know what time it was, and despite my telling myself it could not possibly matter, my heart did not slow its sparrow-like thrashing. I looked up into the leaf canopy over my head, and then down onto the ground and along the creek, but I could not tell if the angle of the sun had changed. A sound began in my ears that I knew with my mind must be my own blood, thrumming in the silence:

a tiny, pulsing hum that gradually increased to a waterfall roar, so that it seemed to fill the world. And yet it did not, somehow, disturb the great, empty silence. I thought suddenly that anything would be better than to make a noise.

I felt the panic coming like a wave rolling toward me, but I could not seem to move to avoid it. It broke over me like a cold salt sea and carried me down. It had no bottom and no top, but in its black depths there waited despair. I sat with my head on my knees, wrapped in my arms, and felt the utter terror and awfulness of everything: of my weakness and inability to care for myself and my child; of my broken marriage and beaten flesh and shattered daughter; of the secret darkness within me that had warped my life and would inevitably continue to do so; of love that wounded and killed and life that hung over an abyss and death that waited at the end of it all. Of years and years of fear still to come, and of loss, and of aloneness. That was it: aloneness. Aloneness lay outside and beyond me, wild and total and empty and endless; aloneness sprang from inside me like a spring. I was both its source and its victim. I would carry it with me wherever I ran, and it would carry me away with it forever and for all time.

I lurched to my knees in a blind panic, sweat pouring off my face, and started to scramble down the ladder. I would run; I would run through the woods to where the other hunters were; I would run back to the house and find someone to take me back to my daughter.

"Hilary, Hilary," I whispered over and over, under my breath. "I'm coming, baby. I'm coming!"

Then I realized that I had no idea on earth which direction to take, and in any case, I could not run back to the house because it lay miles away, through forest so dense that no road or path could penetrate it. The road had ended long before we had come to the creek; Clay Dabney had driven the jeep through underbrush to reach the water. I stayed there, motionless on my knees, and lifted my hands to my mouth to call out, and then lowered them again. I knew that I would not make a sound, would not shoot the rifle. In all that wild, empty greenness, the sound would escalate until it filled the sky and touched the edge of the earth. There was nothing out there to stop it. I sagged back down onto the platform and rolled over onto my side and cried.

I cried aloud; I moaned and sobbed and for a time I think I screamed in grief and terror. I cried as I had not after Chris's beatings, after the death of the puppy, after the divorce. I cried out all the rage and hopelessness and sorrow I had not allowed to surface; I cried for hope and help and pity, and knew that none would come.

"I want my mother," I remember wailing. And then, "I want somebody's mother."

And knew that that, too, was forever closed to me.

I thought then that I must have cried for an hour, though no one ever does, of course. When I finally stopped, as much from sheer fatigue as anything else, a small wind had sprung up and fingered its way through the oak leaves. I felt that wind on my tight, hot face and lifted my face gratefully, and scrubbed my swollen eyes with my fists, and looked down at the creek below to focus them. It was sun-dappled and still as eternity, even though the little wind played in the treetops above it, and empty. And then it wasn't.

He came silently and without a ripple, wading downstream toward the island and the oak, and the canoe behind him seemed to glide on the black water without sound or motion. I could see the water break around his legs and swirl silver around the bow of the canoe, but I could hear no sound.

He might have been an apparition born of the emptiness and silence, born of the woods, born of timelessness. He was slender and lithe and dark; his head was down and his black hair hung wild over his face, and he was naked in the sun that struck the exact center of the creek. In the boat behind him was a large taupe-brown deer, a buck, its head hanging over the side so that its white-bleached antlers dragged in the water, leaving small eddies in the opaque green where the sun fell. In the stern of the canoe, on the seat, lay a bow; not a bow like the one Carter had taken from the trunk of his car that morning, but a simple wooden bow with a sweet, polished curve and a taut string. A quiver of arrows lay beside it. I could see no blood on the deer; it looked as if it might be resting in the canoe, except that its dark eye, the one that I could see, was filmed and silvered in death.

The man pulled the boat to the shore of the island and stepped out of the water onto the moss. I watched in a dreamlike calm. It did not occur to me that he might see me in the tree above him. It never did. His body was compact and brown and polished, dripping dark water, fluid and beautiful. Muscles slid long and smooth in his arms and shoulders as he pulled the buck out of the boat by its antlers and dragged it to rest directly beneath the tree. Sound still did not seem to penetrate the dense, enchanted air; I thought I might have conjured him up out of fear and intensity. But the dark body was unquestionably real. The buttocks clenched and unclenched as he positioned the buck on its side and tipped its head back, so that the white throat shone and the dead black eyes looked directly up at me. The buck lay formally and in symmetry and dignity. I breathed shallowly through closed lips and sat motionless, but I knew that the man would not look up. I sensed that in his own mind and heart he was totally alone with the animal.

He went on silent feet to the canoe and took a squat, hooked knife from the floor and unsheathed it, and walked back to the body of the deer. His genitals were full and perfect, and he was powerfully, fully erect. I could not look away from him. He stooped and murmured something into the dead ear, and took an oak leaf from the ground and laid it in the open mouth, atop the lolling tongue. Then he drew the knife slowly across the deer's throat.

Blood leaped and fountained, and he was still for a long moment in his crouch, the blood spraying across his knees. A long, hard shudder ran through his body, and then, slowly, he reached down to the pumping throat and brought his red hand up and striped the blood of the deer across his face, chest, thighs, and genitals. He leaned over the deer's open black mouth and kissed it lightly, delicately, with his own. It was a reverent kiss, a sacrament. Still he crouched, as his lips formed words, and the fickle wind tossed them clearly up to me in all the ringing stillness: "Thank you." He stood then, and brushed back the dark hair, and I saw what I had known all along: that he was the man I had seen the week before in the dark college parking lot, and that in his eyes there stood tears.

Something slow and warm and enormous turned in my groin, and I felt swimming and weak in knees and wrists, and thought that I might weep once again, or faint. It was a powerful feeling, old and totally frightening, but with something entirely new beneath it. I could not get my breath. I closed my eyes against the sight of his body, gleaming in the dappled shade like a ritual sculpture daubed in living blood, against the sight of his tears. I sat that way for a long time. I heard nothing else, but when I finally opened my eyes he was gone. Only the deer lay beneath the tree, still and beautiful and somehow without need of my pity.

I sat motionless in the waning morning, waiting for Clay Dabney's man to come and take me back to the barbecue at King's Oak. I knew that I should tell Clay about the man and the deer, and knew, too, that I would not. Twice now I had seen him, in emptiness and silence, and twice said nothing. I thought of the great, slow warmth in my groin. I had been right to be afraid in the Big Silver Swamp.

By noon I was back on the steps of the King's Oak veranda and in the world of ordinary human beings, insofar as Pembertonians could achieve ordinariness. But the grip of the past morning in the swamp was strong on me, and it must have showed. Carter, who was standing in clean madras with Tish and Clay Dabney at the top of the steps, said, "You must have seen some kind of deer out there, Andy. You don't look like the city gal I dropped off this morning."

"Deer, my foot," Tish said, peering at me. "Ghost is more like it. You're white as a sheet. And your face is all swollen; have you been crying?"

"No," I said crisply. "I've been sweating. And swatting mosquitoes the size of helicopters. No deer, no ghost, and no tears."

Clay Dabney lifted a Bloody Mary off the tray carried by a passing black waiter in a white cotton coat and handed it to me.

"I'm surprised you didn't see something from the King's Oak," he said, looking into my face. "I've seen tracks back in there almost every morning. I would have bet you would."

"Nothing to speak of," I said, looking straight into his

brown eyes. They crinkled, white lines fanning out into the brown skin at their corners. The white grin followed.

"I read you," he said.

"I brought you some fresh clothes," Tish said. "Charlie has never come out of the swamp in September that he wasn't soaked with sweat. Just like you. Come on; they're upstairs."

I followed her through the great, open hall of King's Oak and up the shallow curving pine stair to the second floor. Inside, all was cool and shadowy and shining with polish and age; faded Orientals glowed on the wide, peg-studded boards of the floors, and huge old leather and chintz furniture loomed like islands. On the paneled walls the crowned heads of generations of kingly whitetail deer stared down, looking only slightly less monarchical than the assorted oil-and-canvas Dabneys. There were as many paintings of spotted hounds as there were of people, and in the main, I thought, they were artistically superior. After the glare and babble of the crowded veranda and lawn, the big, silent lodge was as seductive as a sea cavern.

I took a quick shower in a surprisingly efficient white cave of a bathroom off a high-ceilinged bedroom obviously designed for, but seldom used by, a woman. The great tester bed and the diamond-paned windows were hung with faded chintz and the graceful pine furniture was buffed to a soft glow, but no clothes hung in the armoire except my own, which Tish had brought, and there was no scent of living flesh. I dropped my damp pants and shirt and the hot, heavy boots into the plastic bag provided by Tish and slipped into clean white linen slacks and a melon-colored tee shirt. It was too tight across my breasts, and stretch it as I might, it still clung.

"I'm going to look like a hooker at a day care center,"

I said to Tish, who was sitting in a slipper chair sipping her drink and looking at me.

"No, more like Sophia Loren at a PTA meeting," she said. "Which is precisely what I had in mind when I saw that shirt. Okay, Andy, all kidding aside. Did something happen with Carter, or scare you out in the woods, or something? You looked awful when you came back in. I've always thought that perfectly nice, civilized guys get crazy as hell when they get out in those woods with their guns and bows and things. Revert right back to the cave. Nobody made a pass or anything, did they?"

"Oh, God, no," I said in exasperation. "I just didn't like it out there. It was . . . wilder than I realized it would be. Too quiet, too . . . oh, impersonal and old, somehow. And then the idea of sitting up there in a tree waiting to kill something just sort of got to me. . . . Don't fuss, Tish. I don't have to do it again."

"Well, just so that's all," she said.

"That's all."

I reached for my purse, on top of a bureau, and knocked a small booklet off onto the rag rug. I picked it up and looked at it. It was entitled "Emergency Public Information for Big Silver River Plant Neighbors." A subhead read: "Emergency information for those within a 10-mile radius of each Big Silver Plant production reactor."

I turned around, holding it between my thumb and forefinger, and looked at Tish. She nodded.

"I know," she said. "There's one in every guest bedroom. Charlie says they're down in the bunkhouse, too."

"This'll bring you back to reality right quick," I said, my spine crawling. "If there's so little danger, why has Clay Dabney got them all over his house? Are we that close to those . . . what are they: reactors?"

"He's got them because the government requires it if you're within a certain range. The plant is pretty close; the Big Silver property starts just on the other side of the creek and river. You were probably looking at Big Silver land this morning. Did it look like a scorched wasteland to you? It's just as clean and wild and unspoiled as any land around here; they even open it for deer hunting later on in the season. The plant's way up in the middle of all those woods. It's like the emergency information on airplanes; they have to have it there, but nobody reads it. Hurry up. Charlie and the rest of the hunters should be in now, and I'm starved."

Downstairs, there was a queue at the shaded buffet tables, and about half of the round white-clothed tables were filled with people eating. A banjo-and-guitar band on a small stand at one end of the veranda was thumping out "Down Yonder," and a large crowd of handsome people identical to the ones I had seen at the training track, except that here they wore hunting khakis and boots and caps, was milling about and laughing and talking and drinking Clay Dabney's liquor. Children darted about shrieking and crowing and dogs capered and barked, and from behind one of the vast wings I could hear splashing from the pool and thumping percussion from another band. It all looked festive and prosperous and as beguiling as an American primitive, and I found that I was suddenly ravenous.

Charlie called from a big table at the far end of the veranda under a great, gnarled wisteria vine, and Tish and I went to join him. My heart sank. Pat Dabney, unkempt and raffish and as elegant as a bedouin princess in faded blue jeans and a too-big man's white shirt and bare feet, slouched opposite Carter, smoking and drinking bourbon. On her left were two men I did not know.

"Oh, crud. It's Hippolyta," I said under my breath.

"And boiled, to boot. Must be your lucky day," Tish rejoined. I smiled a wide, stretched, totally false smile as we sat down. The hunger fled, to be replaced by fatigue and irritation and a simple desire to get up and walk away from Pat Dabney and everyone else I did not know.

"Hello, Pat," I said.

"Miz Calhoun," she drawled, lifting her bourbon glass. Some of it slopped over and splashed onto the front of her shirt, joining a small colony of drying stains.

"Heard you had an unproductive morning out at the King's Oak," she said. Her rich, slow voice had thickened since I heard it last. "You must smell powerfully like the city. I've never been out there that deer didn't climb right up that ladder into my lap."

"I guess I do at that," I said, wanting to smack her brown hawk's face. "Are you a hunter as well as a rider?"

"Pat is a better hunter than almost any man in a thousand-mile radius," one of the unfamiliar men said. He was small and going to fat and had a soft, unformed baby's mouth, curved up in a sweet smile. His thin blond hair lay in a shining, just-washed drift across his round forehead, pink scalp peeping through, and there was a small, white-blond mustache perched atop his moist upper lip. His blue eyes were round and sparkling with good spirits, and his smile was quick and sunny. He wore perfectly pressed khakis and handsome new boots and, incredibly in the wet noon heat, an expensive down vest. Sweat beads dewed his forehead and neck. His chin was slight and rounded to a point. I knew that smile and those eyes.

"I'm Chip Dabney," he said. "Dad told me he was taking the pretty new schoolmarm down to the King's Oak this morning. I'd hoped we could give you a better show than apparently you had."

His voice was light and somehow insinuating; he made the words "pretty new schoolmarm" sound like something sly and suggestive.

"Maybe next time," I said.

"Next time I'll take you myself and we'll do a whole lot better," he said, still smiling, and this time there was no missing the insinuation under the words.

"I've got the next dance, Chip," Carter said, his good voice level.

"Okay, good buddy," Chip Dabney said. "No sweat. Miss Andy, this is Francis Millican. He's the top operating man at the Big Silver. I've been showing him how the other half lives in Pemberton. Lived here and run the plant for fifteen years and never been on a King's Oak hunt."

"I hope your morning went better than mine, Mr. Millican," I said. "That is, if you were looking for deer."

"I'm afraid not, no," Francis Millican said. He was tall and thin almost to gauntness, and had a gray crew cut atop a large pale face, and flat gray eyes behind wire-rimmed glasses. He looked so ludicrously like the stereotype of a scientist that I almost laughed aloud. He was the man you would have chosen to play the cold, passionless nuclear genius in a second-rate made-for-TV movie. His hand, as he took mine, was as damp and pale as a cooked mushroom. He smiled, but it was more spasm than greeting. His teeth and Adam's apple were prominent. He wore a gray gabardine suit that was as jarring on Clay Dabney's cool old veranda as a white lab coat would have been. There was a Kiwanis button in his lapel, and his shoes were brown and thick with pale dust. The thought of him in a tree, peeping down at a deer, made my throat ache with glee.

"Nobody took one today," Chip Dabney said. "Charlie thought he got a glimpse of one on D, but no dice. That's a thousand dollars going begging. This'll be the first year nobody's won it. I don't know where the bastards are. Frank, are you sure you guys aren't feeding them strontium 90 over there?"

Everyone turned to look at Francis Millican. The flat eyes did not change.

"Our runoff and groundwater are cleaner than any facility in the network," he said. "If you tested the Big Silver right now you'd find it clean enough to bathe a baby in. From any of our wastes, at any rate. What you people in town put into it is another matter, and out of our hands, I'm afraid."

"Don't you live in town, Mr. Millican?" Pat Dabney said.

"Not on the side you do, Mrs. Dabney," he said.

"No." She smiled lazily. "I don't suppose you do."

"How are the boys, Pat?" Tish said quickly, and Pat Dabney turned the smile to her.

"Fine. With their grandma in Nantucket right now, but coming home next week. They should be going straight on to school, but their father has promised them a week out at that goddamned shack on the creek, and they've threatened to run away if I don't let them go. Oh, well. Better him than me. Cal is into wet dreams now, I hear."

"Speaking of Tom, is he here today?" Charlie said. "I didn't see him at the bunkhouse. He's usually here for the first hunt."

"And I'm usually not. Today I am, so you probably won't be seeing him," Pat Dabney said, pushing her pale straw hair off her neck. Her eyes were hooded and heavy with alcohol. "He's scared I'll tell on him."

"Tell what? There's nothing to tell," Chip Dabney said, smiling widely. "Everybody in town knows cousin Tom is a fornicator and a liar and a dancing, singing romantic fool. Tom doesn't bother to hide anything he does. Only thing wrong with him that I can see is that he keeps marrying women. Married women will get you in trouble, I'm here to tell you."

"Tell just how he's crazy," Pat snapped. Her yellow-green eyes were not quite focused. "Tell what he does back in those woods. Tell what he thinks is back there."

"If he says it's back there, it is, whatever it is," Charlie said. There was annoyance in his voice. "Nobody knows the woods like Tom does. Not even you, Pat."

Her head came up and the falcon's eyes blazed.

"He goes too far," she said. "He just can't leave it alone. He's not able to behave like a decent man. He loves that fucking swamp more than anything, more than Tyler and Cal, I think. I'm not going to have them turned into what he is. . . ."

"Speak of the devil," Tish said.

We all turned our heads to follow her eyes. He was there, the man of my morning, across the lawn, slamming the door of the mud-spattered pickup I had last seen in the college parking lot and swinging a big twelve-string guitar across his shoulder. He was wearing faded blue jeans and a white tee shirt that said *#10 Downing Street* on the front, and dirty unlaced Nikes, and the black hair was damp and combed back off his dark face. The face was as I remembered it, angled and planed like that of an archaic statue; not handsome, not ugly, but arresting, and somehow pure. He was grinning in response to something someone on the edge of the crowd had said to him, but despite the grin it was a wild face. The uncanny blue eyes burned in it like live embers. It seemed simply beyond possibility that they could so recently have held tears, and that the wide mouth could have formed a whisper of reverence to a new-slain animal. The tee shirt and blue jeans outlined his body as if they had been skin, and I swallowed and looked down at the table. I was not in the least surprised that this was the fabled Tom Dabney; something in me had known it from the beginning.

He was surrounded almost before the truck door closed. Men went up to him and clapped his shoulders and knuckled his arms; women preened and bridled before him. A pale woman with her dark-red hair in a chignon whispered something in his ear, and he laughed aloud and hugged her, cupping her buttocks energetically in his hands as he released her. Another, an older, stouter woman in hunting pants and shirt, reached out and shied an imaginary blow at his crotch, and he grabbed her and bent her back and kissed her neck, and then straightened up and pulled the guitar around and struck off a little riff of chords, doing an exuberant, intricate little dance step with his quick, neat feet. The crowd around him laughed and clapped, and he bowed deeply and shouldered the guitar again and made his way straight toward us. My face flamed with a complicated rush of aversion and embarrassment; I wanted to jump up and run. Instead, I picked up Tish's half-finished drink and drained it.

Charlie went out and returned with him, his arm draped around the hard-muscled shoulders that I had seen, not two hours before, straining under the weight of the deer.

"I want you to meet our resident crazy," he said. "Andy, this is Tom Dabney. The wild man of Goat Creek. Tom, this is Andy Calhoun. She's your new little schoolmate, so don't try to rape her for a week or two. Give her a chance to get used to us first."

"Mrs. Calhoun and I have already met," Tom Dabney

said, and his voice was the light, musical one that I remembered. "I scared her to death with a dead deer."

My head came up and I could feel heat flooding my face. I could also feel Pat Dabney's eyes on me, like coals or magnets. Surely he could not have seen me in the tree. . . .

"I ran into her in the parking lot at school the other night, with a deer on my hood," he said. "I hadn't seen her since, so I thought sure she'd quit and gone back to civilization."

"You didn't say you'd met," Tish said, looking at me.

"We weren't introduced on that occasion," I said. My breath fluttered in my throat. "I thought he was an escaped lunatic at the very least."

Tom Dabney grinned again.

"I think I'll call you Andrea," he said. "I don't like nicknames for women, and you don't look like an Andy."

Rage stilled the struggling of my breath in an instant. How dared he, this man who walked naked in the woods and put his hands on every woman he met? Who bore his erection through the forest like a chalice?

"It isn't Andrea; it's Diana," I said coldly. "And no matter whether you like it or not, it's Andy or nothing. I don't answer to Diana."

He was silent for so long that I thought I had offended him, and then he laughed, a great, joyous whoop.

"Ah, God," he said. "Is it really Diana? Are you kidding me?"

"I wouldn't for the world," I said. "Does Diana bother you?"

"No," he said, still laughing. "Diana's great. It's wonderful. It's perfect. You're perfect. You even look right . . . like the Willendorf Venus."

I blushed deeper, hating the allusion. I knew that in the too-tight tee shirt I must, indeed, look very like that squat, primal little fertility goddess. I thought of Pat Dabney's golden feline body, thought that his brown hands must still recall in their very skin the feeling of that body under them. . . .

"I'm delighted that you approve," I said, as icily as I could.

I sound just as stupid as I think I do, I thought.

"Approve? Hell, I approve, all right. In fact, I guess I'm going to have to marry you. No help for it."

"I'd as soon marry a goat," I said, and my voice trembled traitorously.

His laughter redoubled. "And you will, you will," he said. Still laughing, he flipped a hand at us and walked away into the crowd. There was silence at the table.

At the edge of the veranda, he turned and looked back at me.

"Take care of yourself, Diana," he called.

I knew then. *He knows I saw him naked in the woods, covered with blood and kissing a dead deer.* My mortification was complete. It flamed down into my neck and shoulders. I could even feel the heat of it on my stomach. *He knew it all along. I don't know how, but he knew.*

The slow, thick turning warmed my groin once again.

"Well," Pat Dabney said, "I know what Tom will be doing with himself this year. Providing, of course, that Andy is partial to poison ivy and deer ticks on her butt. You could do worse, Andy. He's crazy as a loon, of course, but he's the best fuck I've ever had. And I've had a lot."

I had had enough of the Dabneys on this day.

"I'll just bet you have, Pat," I said. "I thought when I met you, Now there's a woman who likes a good—"

"I have to pee," Pat Dabney said, and rose from the table and lurched away in the direction of the house. We watched her silently, as we had watched Tom. I wanted, wearily, simply to get Hilary and go home.

"Want to call it an afternoon?" Carter said, seeming to pick up the thought. "That line is all the way to the pool by now, and it'll be four o'clock by the time we can get to the barbecue. Both of us got up too early."

"Yes," I said. "I think I do."

On the way home in the Jaguar I sat in silence, aching with fatigue and the residue of the meeting just past and the strange, racking terror that had visited me like a great eagle out in the Big Silver. I felt drained and slackened and flattened and on the verge of tears again, except that I did not think I had any left.

Carter took my hand.

"Pemberton en masse can get a little much sometimes," he said. "Not to mention Pat when she's had too much to drink, and Tom almost anytime. Don't take it personally. Neither one of them meant anything by it. Tell you what: let's get Hilary and go home and take huge naps and then I'll come over and bring the biggest pizza I can find and we'll watch *Murder, She Wrote*. How does that sound?"

I squeezed his hand gratefully, the weak tears welling under my lashes.

"Nothing on earth ever sounded better," I said.

CHAPTER FOUR

If I had wanted banality in Pemberton, I found it in my job at Pemberton State College.

Everything about it, from my beige cinder-block cell and scarred electric typewriter to the tepid, plastic-wrapped fast food in the cafeteria/snack bar to my work as editor of the alumni newsletter, was monochromatic and soporific. I did not care in the least. The college represented my first step toward securing Hilary's and my world. It's very mundanity was reassuring. As nervous as I was about performing in the first job I had ever had, I knew from the outset that I could handle it.

The public relations office in a small exurban university in the wire-grass South frequently finds itself with a dearth of public to relate to, and so there was ample time, that autumn, for me to explore the parameters of my workaday world and meet its denizens. My boss, a looming, clumping maiden lady twenty-five years my senior with, as Tish said, a face like an outfielder's mitt, insisted that I do so.

"Public relations is about people," Miss Deborah Fain said frequently. "If you make friends with people and understand them, you'll never lack for news. The number one rule in this office is to be good to your sources and protect them."

"She makes it sound like the city room of the *Washington Post*," I told Tish during my first week on the job. "Anybody from the janitor to President Syms could be Deep Throat."

"Miss Deborah had a weekly column in the *Albany Herald* for years," Tish said grinning. " 'Debbie's Dixie,' it was called, if memory serves. Homespun wisdom and how her clematis was doing. Very big in these parts with ladies of a certain age, as the French say. Charlie always called it 'Debbie Does Dixie,' but not to her face. You want to sort of watch yourself around her, though. She still writes a column occasionally for Bo Turner at the *Standard*, and she's taken some pretty nasty shots in it at people she doesn't like. All saccharine sweet, of course, and full of righteous regret and so forth. It's a petty little misuse of petty little power."

"Tish, do you think anything Miss Deborah Fain could write about me in a small-town newspaper could hurt me after Chris?" I said.

"I wasn't thinking about you," Tish said.

After that I was careful what I said around Deborah Fain, and I did not complain, even when she made me rewrite virtually every story I did for the newsletter two and three times. Hilary's nightmares had not abated, and she had lapsed partially back into her earlier wounded silence, and I would have done anything to spare her further hurt.

Miss Fain urged me to meet the faculty and staff of Pemberton State. I did, and found that, on the main, I liked them. Very few of them would have cracked the academic fortress of the Ivy League or even Emory, but they were largely pleasant and articulate—"and a lot more literate than the horse people over here," Charlie said—and they accepted me readily and cheerfully as one of them. None of us, I supposed, were under any illusions about our careers and our credentials for them, and none of us made enough money. Eating lunch with them was oddly like being on a cut-rate cruise; not bad, if you didn't yearn for the *QE2*.

For a long time after that day at King's Oak, I did not see Tom Dabney. I went to great pains not to look for him.

In the weeks before the Winter People returned with their servants and horses, Pemberton hummed with energy and purpose, seeming to gather itself together for the fall and winter. On our side of town, shopkeepers painted trim and put up new awnings and polished brass plaques and refilled summer-weary window boxes. New shipments of antiques and bibelots appeared in windows, and the shops along Palmetto set out Maud Frizon shoes and Hermès bags and scarves and Godiva chocolates. Clarion wools and tweeds appeared, brave banners in the swaddling heat of September, and leather like fresh-poured molasses, like cask-aged whiskey, gleamed behind polished plate glass. Catering firms and restaurants put elaborate new menus in their windows, and sun-dried tomatoes and squid packed in its own ink materialized in the little fancy-food shops far down Palmetto. Arugula returned to the produce markets.

The great cottages and clubs swarmed with workers, painting and mowing and planting and airing, and long, smartly painted vans and trailers lumbered into the dusty parking lots of the stables around the training track each day, laden with shining, jostling cargo as valuable, pound for pound, as gold. Goldenrod and Queen Anne's lace blanketed fields and fringed roadsides, and in the deep woods the hickories and maples were beginning to flicker with the first flames of the great wildfire that would consume them in a month or so. On Whimsy Road the dust lay motionless in the thick air in strata, as if suspended in amber, and the sun at noon was as fierce as August, but back in the woods where our little house stood, mornings and evenings were cool and blue with autumn, and once, on a night of mist and rain, I lit the logs that Carter had laid in our fireplace, and Hilary and I had our supper before it. It was a magical night, and envisioning fall and winter nights ahead of us in the leaping firelight, I was very nearly happy. I thought it a good thing, after all, that we had come to Pemberton. I could, I felt, make for us a life of peace and substance here.

I said as much to Tish in midmonth, when she and I took Hilary to the French Creek Mall on the other side of town to look for school shoes. Tish had not wanted to come, saying that the mall was hot and crowded on Saturdays, and I could get better shoes at The Children's Hour on Palmetto. But she had not argued when I said that I was not going to buy designer shoes for a child who would outgrow them in a month, and anyway, the children at Hilary's school wore nothing but Nikes. And so we went, and were indeed jostled and elbowed and menaced by boom boxes and pantsuited fat women and flocks of faintly ominous teenagers, black and white, and Tish did not even protest when Hilary asked for a stop at McDonald's on the way home. But she drew the line at going inside to eat. We sat in the air-conditioned Blazer and ate our french fries and drank our Diet Cokes, and when Hilary went to the rest room to wash the chocolate milkshake off her new tee shirt I savored the moment of closeness and normalcy, and told Tish that I thought Hilary and I could make it work here.

"Well, I should hope so," she said. "But I think you're going to have to do it on Pemberton's terms, and not yours," she said.

"What do you mean?" I said. "What's the matter with my terms? I thought making it on my own terms was the whole point of this great new adventure in living."

"The matter is that you won't give an inch to the town," she said. "You live right in the very epicenter of Old Pemberton, and the oldest gentry we've got, including some of the WPs, are your neighbors, and you still act like you're hookworm poor. You don't wear your pretty clothes, and you put Hilary in public school and let her ride the bus when Pemberton Day is not three blocks away from your front door, and you won't let her take riding lessons, and you won't take them yourself, and you act like the club and the golf course and tennis courts aren't there. You won't even meet anybody else. Andy, this is what we do; it's how we live. It's not . . . not pretentious, or excessive; it's us. And you live right in the middle of us. Forgive us our money and don't judge us too harshly. You're never going to be a part of Pemberton if you keep on pretending it doesn't exist, and neither is Hilary. Maybe you don't care, but the day will come when she does."

"You know I can't afford Pemberton Day and the club and tennis and riding lessons and all that," I said, stung. She did know, or should have. "You know what I make. You know how much rent I pay. We may not be hookworm poor, Tish, but we sure as hell are white-collar poor, and I'm not going to pretend we're not just because everybody around me is rich. I don't want a pretentious life for either of us. Hilary's doing just fine."

"Oh, shit! You've been rich all your married life," Tish snapped. "Your entire world for the last fifteen years has been as rich as anything we've got around here. Well, almost, anyway. You've already *got* your clothes, for Christ's sake; it's sheer affectation to wear the same three cotton skirts and blouses every day. Your furniture and jewelry are exquisite. And I know good and goddamned well Chris pays you enough child support to put Hilary in Pemberton Day and give her lessons in every sport there is, including martial arts. Even if he hasn't called or written. You may be doing your pride a world of good with the poor-but-proud bit, but your child needs to get to know the people she'll be growing up with right now."

"Hilary hasn't complained," I said sullenly. "She hasn't said a word about school. She doesn't even mention riding lessons anymore."

"She hasn't said a word about much of anything since you got here," Tish said, looking at me levelly over her sunglasses. "She hasn't got one single friend her own age that I know of. Not one. When she isn't in school she's with you or me. Her friends are me and Charlie and Carter Devereaux. She's turning into a little ghost of you, always at your side, pale and quiet and joined to your hip. You've told me how bright and inquisitive and outgoing she used to be, but, Andy, I just can't imagine her like that. What you're doing for her isn't protecting her; it's sucking the life and independence out of her. Pretty soon no one is going to bother to try and get to know her, because you're going to have made her afraid of literally everything. That's boring, Andy, *boring*. It's boring to have a silent, timid ten-year-old in tow every time we go out. Is that what you want for Hilary?" Bright, scalding anger flooded me and choked my reply. Under it, fear hissed like a snake. Could she be right; could Hilary be that skewed, that bent, and I blind to it? Could she be truly ill and I, out of fear, be afraid to see it? Was there something—the word itself was hideous—*wrong* with her? Should I have gotten a doctor for her, a therapist of some sort? The very thought made me flinch. I pushed it away.

By the time I could gather my wits, Hilary was coming out of the restaurant and I looked closely at her. It seemed many months since I had really done so. She was much taller and thinner than she had been at the beginning of the summer, and her features were still delicate and lovely, and her hair still the riotous mop of dark curls, but her once-luminous blue eyes were dull and too rounded, white-rimmed, and she averted them from everyone she passed. She drew herself sharply away from anyone who came within range of touching her, and when she neared the Blazer she sought my face with her eyes and broke into a trot. She carried her hands up in front of her, loosely, like a little dog begging; it had been a baby trick of hers that had enchanted us, but now it looked affected and vulnerable. She breathed through her mouth in her intensity to reach the car and me, and for a terrible moment I saw what Tish saw: Hilary looked almost retarded.

"Oh, dear God," I whispered. "Look at her. I've made her sick!"

"No, you haven't," Tish said, squeezing my hand. "Just a little too dependent on you. I've raised two girls, Andy. They're the world's quickest studies at this age. Try something you know she'd like; try the riding lessons, for a start. Carter will teach her, if you don't want Pat. He's wonderful with kids."

And so it was that Hilary began riding lessons, at first on Carter's chunky old mare, which had belonged to his dead wife, and then, later in the fall, when even I could see that she might have been born to do this one thing, with

Pat Dabney herself, through Carter's offices. I hated the thought of Hilary in the backwash of Pat's indolent carelessness, but the change in her was soon apparent, even if only in small, tentative ways, and only to me. She was still far too quiet and pale, and still clinging far too much to me, but she was soon going daily to Runaway Stables, spending hours on the small chestnut mare who was stablemate and outrider to Pat's big Irish colt, and the pale beginning of life in her eyes made my heart jolt with hope and gratitude to Tish.

"What if you hadn't made me see?" I said. "I think she really might have just faded out of the world. That's twice in a year you've saved us, Tish."

"I haven't saved her," Tish said. "She's still got a long way to go. Don't thank me. Anybody would have done it. Carter would have, if I hadn't. He was all set to talk to you."

"Were you?" I asked Carter, a couple of nights later, when we sat in front of my fireplace with a bottle of good Cabernet Sauvignon and bowls of venison chili that Charlie had made the year before and frozen. The fire was lit, though it was still too warm; to offset its heat, Carter had flicked on my air conditioner.

"Yes," he said. "I was. And with my heart in my throat, I might add, because I knew it would be hard for you to hear what I had to say, and I was scared to death you'd tell me to take a hike. That's something I don't think I could handle, Andy Panda."

He reached out and traced the line of my mouth with his finger.

I went still inside and out, and sat for a moment looking down into my chili, feeling the fire hot on my cheek and the faint throb of the old air conditioner.

"Carter, don't," I whispered finally.

I don't know why I was surprised. We had been together a great deal since we had met at lunch in the Inn; if he saw other women, I did not know it. I was almost sure he did not. I knew that he found me attractive, though he had made no overt move toward me. It was there in the turn of his head and the force of his gaze and the timbre of his fine voice when he spoke to me. He was protective without being smothering, tender in an offhand, comfortable way, attentive as much in the things he did not do as in the ones he did. He seemed genuinely and unendingly interested in my daughter, and he teased me fully as much as he complimented me. In my turn I felt stretched and warmed and soothed in the very steadiness of him, the *thereness* of him, buoyed by the attraction I knew underlay his manner toward me. I had, I realized, begun to think of him as a given in my life. But the small statement of need and the naked little touch disturbed me swiftly and viscerally. More than disturbed, frightened.

I looked up at him. He was watching me, the tanned, pleasant face tranquil but the blue eyes intent.

"I scared you, didn't I?" he said. "I'm sorry, Andy. It's the last thing in the world I meant to do. Don't worry. I'm not going to put the move on you. Not until you give me the green light, and not ever, if that's the way you want it. I know what you've just been through, both of you; Tish told me right after you came. I'd be a bloody murderous fool to stampede you after that."

I felt my face flame.

"Tish had no right to do that," I said, wondering just what she had told him, how far she had gone. Not, surely, about the darkness I hid inside me . . .

"She had the highest right there is," he said. "She loves

you very much. She doesn't intend for you to be hurt again. She let me know in so many words that if I disturbed a hair on your head she'd cut my heart out."

"She might have told me she did," I said. "I feel naked in front of you. You know all about me, and I don't know anything about you. I don't even know if you have any children. I don't even know how . . . how you . . ."

"No children," he said. "It's always been a real sadness for me. I like kids. Were you going to say, how my wife died?"

"Yes," I said. "I did ask Tish, but she said it was for you to tell me when you were ready, and so I didn't ask you. I thought it might be too hard for you to talk about . . ."

"It was hard, in the beginning," he said. "It isn't now. It's been almost six years. I don't talk about it much simply because the role of grieving widower has always embarrassed me, and because, in the end, I was glad as hell to see her go, and that still horrifies me."

I looked at him silently, wishing with all my heart I had held my tongue. Whatever he said now would cause him pain and me the burden of intimacy; that was implicit in any revelation. I felt that any more complexity, mine or someone else's, was simply beyond me.

"It was cancer, ovarian cancer," he said, and his deep voice might have been recounting an anecdote at Kiwanis. "She always had female troubles; probably it had been going on a long time. Possibly it's why we never managed to have children. It's a bad kind of cancer. It takes a very long time and it hurts all the way, or hers did. About halfway through she was crying and asking me to kill her, and by the end she was screaming most of the time she was awake. Joan was always resistant as hell to drugs, and we couldn't find anything that would kill the pain. Nothing. Anything strong enough would have killed her, too. I'd have given it to her in a minute, and she'd have taken it, but nobody would prescribe it. I went everywhere, even to Mexico, looking for something. No dice. I was set to go to Holland when she finally died. They kept saying she'd go into a coma when she got near the end, and then she'd be past the pain, but she never did. She never did."

"It must have been awful past imagining," I said, feeling tears burning in my nose.

"And beyond that," he said. "But you know the worst thing? The worst thing was that she died totally alone, because by that time I was so . . . horrified and disgusted and . . . scandalized somehow that I couldn't even respond to her. Oh, I sat there. My body was there. But my mind was a million miles away, cowering in a hole in the sand and shrieking, 'Shut up, shut up, shut up!' I hated the way she looked and her incessant demands on me, demands that I couldn't meet, and I hated that endless screaming. I hated the way she looked and smelled. And I hated myself worst of all. When people came and called and wrote and were so kind, I wanted to yell at them, 'Take your flowers and wine and casseroles and give them to somebody who deserves them! I'm not grieving! I'm not even rejoicing! I'm as dead as she is! She embarrassed me out of my life!' "

I reached out and put my hand over his large, warm, freckled one. I could feel the calluses on his palm, from the polo mallet. I squeezed, and in a moment, he squeezed back.

"And so the thing that's been most important in my life since then has been just not to make waves," he said. "To lead as normal and pleasant and uneventful a life as I could devise for myself, on as even a keel as I could keep it, and attract as little attention as possible. I'm tired to death with excess; I don't want any more extremes. I don't care if

I'm bored for the rest of my life. Cancer is an outrage and a scandal, Andy; I used up my tolerance for it in the last year of Joan's life. It's not an admirable state of existence, not by a long shot, but I need to be honest with you. I operate on low voltage now. That's why I can understand so well what you must be feeling, and why I'm determined never to push or crowd you. You're safe with me. I'd like to offer you the moon, but I can at least offer you safety. Don't worry. Let me be your good-guy, comfortable, old-shoe, always-there friend for as long as you want me to be, and we'll see where it goes. If there should be anything down the road for us, it'll be on your terms. I'll never scare you or hurt you. If I can't be gentle, I'll be gone."

"I can't imagine what's in that for you," I said. "It's wonderful for me; it's just about all I can handle right now, but you're an attractive, successful man, you're in your prime, you could have anything. Any woman would be proud to have you in her life. You must need more than I have to give you. I can't understand why in God's name you even bother with me."

He laughed and reached over and rumpled my hair. I had always hated it when Chris did that; it made me feel devalued and childlike. But there was only tenderness and a kind of cheerful absolution in Carter's hand. His touch released me from responsibility and heaviness.

"There's always polo to work off my baser impulses," he said. "Why do I bother with you? Because you're smart and nice and as cute as a chipmunk to look at, and you're trying so hard to help yourself, and you don't bitch, and because you don't wear boots and jodhpurs and hacking jackets and Indiana Jones hats. And you don't like horses and you can't shoot guns and you don't have a dog and you're not richer than me. And because—"

"Stop," I said, laughing too. "Enough. I get the picture. When I'm assimilated, as Tish puts it, into Pemberton, you won't give me a second look."

"*A,* I will always give you a second look, and *B,* you won't ever be assimilated into Pemberton," he said. "Not really. Not all the way. You'll stay you no matter what, Andy. It's the real reason I bother with you, as you put it. I can sense in you a kind of . . . aptitude for commitment. It's a powerful thing, an absolute. It feels as strong as the earth. I want to be around when you put it to use; I'd like to think it might be me you commit to. That would be worth some kind of wait."

I was moved in spite of my laughter of the moment before. I was also uneasy. He sensed it then, the dark thing, the power, but he had misread it.

"There's an absolute in me, all right, but I'm not sure it's for commitment," I said slowly. "There are things about me you don't know, Carter; there's no way you could. I'm not always like I seem. I'm not nearly as good or . . . simple as you seem to think I am. I don't want to mislead you."

"If you mean your . . . the married life you had with your husband, Tish told me about that, too, and how you think about it," he said cautiously. "How could you possibly believe any of that was your fault? A naive young girl, not even out of college yet, no experience with the world or even her own body . . . and the abuse, and the beatings later . . . That was him, Andy, not you. Him and nobody but. His craziness, not yours. I don't even think about that, except to want to run up to Atlanta some Saturday morning and shoot the son of a bitch. I could do it this week. Be back in time for dinner."

I had a dizzy red moment of hating Tish and him, too, and then felt a delicious surge of lightness and liberation. Tish should not have told him about the things I did with Chris, of course, and what I believed about them, but she had, and she had done so out of love, and now he knew and did not care and indeed seemed even to value me more. A major bridge had been dynamited long before it had to be crossed. This man would never frighten or dishonor me. He would never ask outrage or excess of me. He would not even require unseemliness. This man would keep me safe.

"Thank you," I said. "Thank you for all of this and everything else. Thank you for sharing yourself and for knowing what I needed to hear. I wish there was more I could give you, and I hope there will be. I'll work on it. Meanwhile . . . thank you."

I reached up and put my arms around his neck and kissed his cheek, and he kissed me back, on the lips, but it was a soft kiss, light and cool. His arms held me for a moment, held me hard, and then he let me go.

"Work on it, Andy," he said.

"So how is it going with you and Carter?" Tish said a day or so later, when she and I went out to Runaway Stables after school to pick up Hilary. Hilary and Pat Dabney were still working in the small ring, so we sat in the Blazer with the door open to let the late-afternoon breeze in, she smoking, me simply watching my child sitting the little mare like a mote of light in a shaft of sun.

"Just fine, thanks and no thanks to you," I said.

"I know; I shouldn't have told him," she said. "But I knew you never would, and that you'd brood and worry until you found an excuse to drop him, just so you wouldn't have to let him really get to know you. Now you're past all that. And admit it, the two of you are as matched a pair as a set of Gucci luggage, aren't you?"

"We have a lot in common, yes," I said. "But you could have found a better analogy. It's puzzling, though, Tish; he couldn't have been sitting around in a cell twiddling his thumbs for five years, and yet there he was, ready and available and willing to squire me around the second I hit town. The timing is almost too perfect. Oh, shit, now you're going to tell me he's just realized he's gay."

"No way, José," Tish grinned. "He's just—shall we say—terminated a two-year go-round with Pat Dabney, and she'd put up with a gay guy about as long as she would a black, a Jew, a Mexican, or a pauper. I have to assume he's good in bed or she'd have bounced him long since. Pat doesn't fuck around when she fucks. And she fucks lots. *Lots.*"

I felt a small, hot lick of jealousy, and looked at the distant figure of Pat Dabney in the ring, watching Hilary circling in the dusty amber sunshine on the mare. She stood hipshot, her hands in her pockets and her yellow head tilted so that the lioness's mane touched one shoulder. Even from this distance it was a splendid body, rankly female.

"Wonder why she let him slip through her clutches, then," I said. "I don't see how she could do much better than Carter, assuming I've seen Pemberton's best and brightest."

"He dumped her, finally," Tish said. "He's too polite ever to say, but Charlie isn't, and he told Charlie, and of course Charlie told me. Said he felt too much like a prize stud; it was all she ever wanted to do. And she talked too much about it, around town. And she drinks too much, and when she does she's . . . pretty primitive. He's a fastidious man, Carter is, under all that laid-back charm and sweetness. I think she finally just grossed him out. She's been going through men like a sailor on shore leave ever since she divorced Tom, and that's been seven or eight years, at least. I don't know why she doesn't go on back up to Long Island, where the rest of her family is; she could move the stable up there in a jiffy, and the pickings must be better than in Pemberton. Charlie thinks she still has a thing for Tom, and he may be right. She's sure bitter enough about him."

I thought of the dark naked body in the dappled light of the King's Oak woods again, and the blood of the deer. . . .

"What happened with them?" I said. "Was she too much for him, too?"

I could feel heat in my face and chest, and turned slightly so that Tish would not see the flush.

"I hardly think so. Tom Dabney screws as much as Pat does, when he can. He's just nicer about it. And he doesn't screw married women or women who are . . . oh, vulnerable, I guess. It's a funny thing to say, but Tom's a gentleman when he screws. He absolutely loves women; thinks they're funny and wonderful and sexy and beautiful: all women. And so, when you're around him, you feel that you are those things. All of us do, even women who've never . . . you know. I hear he's a fantastic lover. Pat said at a party once that they used to do it in his canoe all the time, and in trees. She said she used to howl like a panther; you could hear her across the swamp. Of course, she was drunk as a lord when she said all that, but I believe her. When they first married they were a real pair, both of them so alive and good-looking and vital, both of them so flamboyant. A real match.

"But then the children came, and he wouldn't leave that old place on Goat Creek, and he wouldn't give up his job at the college and manage the stable for her, and he wouldn't stop going off in the Big Silver for days and sometimes weeks at a time, with that old black man he hangs around with. And there were other things; she hints about things that he does, or did, that sound pretty crazy, but then you have to remember that it's Pat saying them. . . . Anyway, her daddy built them a big house on the road behind the stable and turned the whole horse operation over to her, and when Tom wouldn't move with her, she left him and took the children and moved in herself. And then her daddy died and left her the stable and God knows how many millions of dollars, and she filed for divorce. And there she's been ever since, and there he's been. Whatever there is between them, it's not settled. She's forever on his case, and he doesn't see much of his children at all. Just weekends in fall and winter, and not all of those. And he stays clear of her, when he can."

"And he hasn't remarried?" I said, as carelessly as I could with heat pounding through my face and body.

"No. I guess he figures two times is out. He was married once before, to a pretty little girl he met while he was at Yale. She went to Sarah Lawrence, I think. I only saw her once, when I came home from school with Charlie for a weekend. Pale and small and no lipstick and Laura Ashley and all that, but very sweet. By the time we got back here from Bolivia, they were divorced. I don't think it lasted two years, and there weren't any children. It was pretty much the same thing, I think. The house on the creek was novel and adventurous for a year or so, but then she wanted to move back up East around her family, and her dad even had him a teaching position lined up at Choate or Groton or somewhere like that. But Tom wouldn't leave Pemberton and the house in the swamp. I don't imagine he'll marry again. For one thing, he doesn't have to. For another, I don't know a woman who'd be willing to spend her life out in that wilderness, much less raise children there. And Tom's not going to come out of the woods. If he weren't such a darling, he'd be impossible."

"I didn't find him in the least bit darling," I said.

"I could have sworn you found him interesting, at any rate," she said, grinning at me over the sunglasses, which rode far down her snub nose. "You bristled at him like a riled-up cat at Clay Dabney's barbecue. You do that when somebody intrigues you. Do you like him any better in the civilized environs of Pemberton State?"

"I haven't seen hide or hair of him," I said. "I really don't think he's been around. I've met all the faculty by now. Miss Deborah made me do that. I can't imagine where he'd hide. It ain't exactly Berkeley."

"Oh, I bet I know," Tish said. "I forgot. He takes off a couple of weeks every fall and spring and goes way back in the Big Silver and camps and hunts. He and Scratch Purvis, the old black man I told you about, and Martin Longstreet—he's one of your deans, Andy; I forget which one—and Reese Carmody. Reese is an attorney; he's about Charlie and Carter's age, but he hasn't practiced much in years. Mainly he drinks. Sometimes he does a little legal aid work. I don't know how he lives, except that he farms a little on the place his daddy left him. Anyway, the four of them hunt and fish together a lot, and they do this two-week thing every year, like clockwork. They have, ever since I can remember. Charlie calls it their walkabout. God knows what they do up in there. That's undoubtedly where he is."

"How can a professor and a dean just take off for two weeks at the beginning of fall and spring quarter?" I said. "Why does the college put up with it?"

"Where else are they going to get a Phi Beta Kappa, magna cum laude from Yale and a former Brown full professor in classics? They take the time without pay, and the school hires substitutes and counts itself lucky," Tish said. "And it is. Tom knows more about more things than anybody I ever knew. And he's a very gifted writer; I've heard him read some of his poetry. And he's a born dancer."

And he goes naked in the woods and kisses dead deer, I did not say. I did not like Tom Dabney any better after Tish's recital of his accomplishments than I had before. I was vaguely relieved to know that he was far away, back in the dark-canopied aisles of the Big Silver Swamp. I could imagine him there, a creature of air and earth and water and wildness. I could not imagine him in the stale, colorless September heat of Pemberton State College.

A few days later I left my office in midafternoon to pick up the winter concert and lecture series schedule at Whitney Hall. It was the oldest building in the college complex; indeed, the only building of any age in that warren of blue prefab steel and concrete block. It had been a huge Victorian house, a mansion even by the standard of the day and the town, built by one of the Winter People who fancied the role of gentleman farmer. The big house served him through the few years that he pursued cotton and Herefords, and after he left, to move in vast relief back to the horsy side of Pemberton, the house became the county grange hall. Then it served as a private academy for the young women of Pemberton's less fortunate, supported by the winter colony, until public education became widespread in the wire grass. After that it stood vacant, and when the state bought the property for the college, the old house was given a cursory lick of paint and two or three more bathrooms and became the School of Arts and Sciences at Pemberton State College.

It was a wonderful old pile, tall and dark-bricked and frosted with rococo millwork, looking like an offended dowager among pygmies in the bland, low jumble of the newer buildings. On this day all its long windows were open, and its massive, fanciful front door stood ajar. I knew that it had no air-conditioning, and wondered if any breeze at all could make its way through the dense ranks of old junipers and cedars that grew untrimmed around it. The thermometer outside my office, when I had left it, read 94 degrees. In the short walk from my building to this one, my skirt and blouse had pasted themselves to my body as if I had walked through water, and I had twisted my damp, heavy hair up off my neck and pinned it on top of my head.

Just outside the great deodara *allée* that led to the front veranda, I stopped. From somewhere off behind the wall of green, a voice like a bell out of eternity spoke:

"Now as I was young and easy under the apple
    boughs
About the lilting house and happy as the grass was
    green . . ."

I stood still. Dylan Thomas, certainly. "Fern Hill," wasn't it? I remembered when I had first encountered Dylan Thomas, in Contemporary Poetry at Emory, on a dark winter day in my freshman year. I had felt my heart drop into my stomach at the sheer splendor of the words, like water over clean stones, like the rush of the morning sea in my ears. Before I finished the first poem I was crying. I had gone on to read all the Thomas I could find, but I had not read him again in all the arid years of my marriage. The tender anguish and innocence of that long-ago day swept me like a tide, and I sank down on a chipped stone bench beside the path to listen.

"In the sun that is young once only,
    Time let me play and be
Golden in the mercy of his means . . ."

But dear God, whose was that voice? It poured out those liquid words of hope and greenness with a caroling beauty that was so alive and immediate that I felt the tears of twenty years before rise in my throat again. The torpid breath of the exhausted little wind in the trees, the sound of traffic far away down on the highway, the crunch of gravel out of sight on the path as people passed by, all faded away, and the voice sang in my ears, the voice and it only.

> "And honoured among foxes and pheasants by the
> gay house
> Under the new made clouds and happy as the
> heart was long,
> In the sun born over and over,
> I ran my heedless ways . . ."

The voice sang of youngness, swelling and flaming and altogether glorious and then gone, and I sat on my bench and wept silently for the country of my youth, that green place where all things had seemed possible, forever lost to me now. Tears ran down my face.

> "Time held me green and dying
> Though I sang in my chains like the sea."

I got up from the bench and went blindly through the hedge of cedars to find the voice. My eyes were still streaming, and I stumbled as I came out into the little glade behind the hedge. The voice stopped, and there was a little sighing sound, and then a click, and silence.

"What did I tell you about Dylan Thomas?" Tom Dabney's voice said. "Didn't I say he could sing the very mermaids out of the sea and the nymphs out of the woods? Here's one in the flesh. The very considerable flesh, I might add."

He sat on the grass outside an open window, cross-legged, the guitar I had seen the day of the barbecue across his knees. A small circle of students sat around him. There were sweating cans of soft drinks beside most of them, and in the middle of their circle was a battered old portable record player. An extension cord ran from the open window to the machine.

"I'm sorry, I didn't realize . . . ," I began. "I heard . . . ?"

"We're honored," Tom Dabney said. There was laughter in his voice, but his dark face was smooth and polite. He looked like some satanic tailor, there on the seared autumn grass.

"I've always had a theory that Thomas should be heard and not read the first time," he said, "so I play this old recording of him reading his work when we get to him in the moderns. It was hotter than a Moslem's hell in there today, so we decided to do Dylan outside. He goes well al fresco, don't you think?"

"He has a wonderful voice," I said, trying to erase with briskness the tears on my face. "Nobody else ought to be allowed to read him aloud. Please go on; I didn't mean to intrude. I was on my way to the office to get the winter activities schedule and I . . ."

I stopped. The students were looking at me with interest. I felt the damp clothing drying in wrinkles against me, and the sopping tendrils of my hair on my cheeks and neck. The tracks of my tears felt like acid on my face. I must look like a Victorian madwoman, I thought. The treacherous heat flamed up from my chest, and I turned to go back through the cedar hedge.

"Diana, wait," Tom Dabney said. "Come back. Hear the rest of this."

I turned and looked at him. The laughter was gone out of his eyes. His voice was gentler.

"Don't be embarrassed that he made you cry," he said. "I throw anybody who doesn't cry when they first hear him right out of my class with an F for the quarter. I still sit out in the swamp and play his records and howl like a banshee. These benighted children all have had the grace to weep, so they can stay. They're not going to laugh at you."

He grinned, the quick white grin that I remembered from the veranda at King's Oak. His uncle's grin. The students all smiled, too, and I saw that there were indeed tear tracks on some of the unformed young faces. I felt my own mouth move, of its own volition, into a smile.

"I'd love to, for a minute," I said. "And then I'll just slip off and let you all go on. Miss Deborah will turn me in to the journalistic ethics committee if I'm not back soon."

"May Miss Deborah spend eternity listening to Robert Service read from his own unpublished work," Tom Dabney said. "Except she'd never know it was punishment. This is Diana Calhoun, you guys. She's new in the Public Relations Office, so she deserves all the grace and sympathy you can muster."

I sank down on the grass at the edge of the circle. He nodded and flicked on the record player.

"Here we go," he said.

It was *A Child's Christmas in Wales* this time, that richest, funniest, and tenderest hymn to childhood, and I closed my eyes and let the magical tenor of the dead bard take me off on its wings. There was none of Thomas's elegiac darkness here; whatever furious anguish he had drowned, along with his life, at the White Horse Tavern had not had its roots in this childhood. It was a very bad record; at intervals it hissed and skipped and burred, and once Tom Dabney had to reach over and lift the arm of the record player past a milky patch.

"That's Irish coffee from four or five Christmas Eves

ago," he said. "It's my Christmas ritual, Irish coffee and this. An absolutely holy thing. Hell on records, though."

I thought of him, sitting in his little house out in the winter swamp, drinking Irish coffee and listening to these wild-honey words pouring into the tender night. In my mind's eye he was alone, in a huge leather chair, by a wood fire, his dark head bent over the hot whiskey, but then I remembered what Tish had said and immediately the naked body of a woman materialized in the big leather chair beside him. His head was bent over hers, but the taut-muscled slenderness was unmistakably Pat Dabney's. I opened my eyes, and man, woman, and chair disappeared. He was looking at me intently. I looked away.

The Irish voice chimed on, through the expedition to snowball the polar cats, the fire in Mr. Protheroe's cottage, the fluting voice of Miss Protheroe to the tall, shining fireman ("she said the right thing, always: Would you like something to read?"), the dead robin by the swings, "all but one of his fires out."

When the voice reached the part that read, "Long ago, when there were wolves in Wales, and birds like red flannel petticoats whisked past the harp-shaped hills," Tom Dabney picked up the guitar and began to finger it softly, almost absently. Under the words, the chords swelled and died and swelled again; began to drift together; wove themselves into patterns. At first they seemed random, and then I recognized the melody: Bach's "Jesu, Joy of Man's Desiring." Played on the twelve-string Martin, so softly that the words shone through it like stars through cloud, the old hymn was infinitely moving and beautiful, its intricacy seeming as simple to the thin, dark fingers as a child's first piano exercises. How could he do that? It must be difficult beyond imagining on the guitar. I darted a look at his face; it appeared rapt and lost, and his eyes were closed. He segued from the rippling Bach into "Scarlet Ribbons" and "Streets of Laredo," and the music of a rawer, newer world flowed just as sweetly under the waterfall voice as the Bach had. Toward the end of the record, he drifted into something that sounded familiar and yet not, and I simply drifted with it until I realized that he was playing "The Wreck of the Old 97," very slowly and in the same measure as the Bach. I smiled and looked around at the students; none of them seemed to have noticed. They were staring as if hypnotized at the dark hands moving over the Martin.

"I said some words into the close and holy darkness," Dylan Thomas said. "And then I slept."

There was a long silence, in which a class bell blatted rudely, and then Tom Dabney played "Shave and a haircut, two bits," and put the guitar aside.

The students broke into spontaneous applause, whether for the dead poet, the living man, or the music, I could not tell. It did not matter. Something extraordinary had happened here on the matted ghost of the summer's grass, behind the hedge of cedars. The dimmest of them knew it.

Tom Dabney leaped to his feet and pulled one of the students, a fat, moon-faced girl in skin-tight blue jeans, off the grass and into his arms. He whirled her around on the grass in a mad polka, his feet flying nimbly, hers clumping, both their hair streaming out behind them. He tipped his head far back and gave a wild, exuberant wordless shout, "Yeeeeooooowwwww!" He finished up with a flourish, kissed her hard on her gaping mouth, and dropped her back on the grass. She goggled at him in panting adoration.

"Awww*right!*" one of the young men said.

"Author, author," another cried.

He bowed all round the circle and grinned, and straightened up and looked at me. His face dripped sweat and his chest heaved. I did not think I had ever seen another man as pleased with himself. The magic of the words and music vanished and annoyance flooded back, hot and prickling.

"Do you always do a vaudeville act when you read poetry?" I said. "What do you do when you get to Yeats or Rilke? Strip?"

I blushed again at my own words, furiously. His grin widened.

"Sacrifice a virgin," he said. "And when we do Ginsberg the rites are unspeakable. What, you don't think Dylan Thomas is at least worth a little song and dance? How would *you* thank him?"

I felt humbled and rebuked. It suddenly seemed to me that the mere receiving of beauty was not, indeed, enough. This unbridled, offensive man was onto something, did, indeed, have something to teach me. I was damned if I would stay around to receive it.

"Thanks for the Thomas and the floor show," I said, getting up and brushing my skirt. "Come by the office and dance for Miss Deborah sometime. She'll be fascinated."

"Thanks, but I only perform for those who're able to appreciate it," he said. "Miss Deborah would be on the phone to the board of regents before my dust had settled. Tell them I was an enemy of order and seemliness."

"And aren't you?" I said, parting the cedar boughs to take my leave.

"Of course. But I work underground. If the word gets out, my days are numbered, and then what would these poor, blighted wretches do? Who would feed them?"

"Who, indeed," I said, and stepped through the hedge and back onto the path. As I went up the steps of Whitney Hall I heard him picking out "Oh, Diana" on the guitar, and heard the laughter of the students. I slammed the door behind me.

After that, he seemed to be everywhere. I saw him in the snack bar at noon with a portly bald man of spectacular dignity who proved to be Martin Longstreet, dean of the Division of Arts and Sciences and his ludicrously unlikely partner on the walkabout Tish had spoken of. I saw him in the library, in one of the farthest-back carrels, head bent over a pile of books. I saw him walking on the dusty cement paths connecting one building with another, surrounded by chattering students, and in the sun-blasted parking lot, climbing into the disreputable truck. I saw him hugging a giggling young instructor of romance languages in the faculty lounge, and kissing the neck of a middle-aged physical education instructor, leaving her homely face the dark red of baked brick. I saw him in the hardware store on Palmetto Street one Saturday morning, and in the café next to the laundromat in the little shopping center nearest the college, with a thin, towheaded man about his age who wore horn-rimmed glasses mended with tape and an old black man so stooped and age-stained that his skin seemed dusted with a fine layer of ash. They were drinking coffee and laughing so hard at something that everyone in the café turned to watch them, smiling. I saw him driving down Palmetto Street with the black man in the cab of the truck, heading out of town, and once I saw his truck pulled up in the parking lot at Runaway.

We did not speak again after that first day. We did not get close enough. I did not know if it was by accident or design. I had not consciously tried to avoid him, but on some level I was aware that I searched crowds for his dark head wherever I went. When we saw each other, he gave me a little mock salute, and once he lifted a forefinger as if it had been a gun, and shot me, his lips forming the word "bang."

I did not salute him when I saw him, though I usually waved back.

On a Friday afternoon in mid-October the nurse at Hilary's school called me at the office and said that Hilary had been violently sick in the rest room and then locked herself into the stall and would not come out. She was, the nurse said, crying hysterically. I muttered something to a tight-mouthed Miss Deborah and ran for the Toyota, my heart hammering in my throat. I tried to keep my mind empty and unfocused as I drove, so that I would not wreck the car, but my wrists and temples buzzed with fear, and under it there was, no matter how hard I tried to push it down, anger.

Chris, you son of a bitch, you wrecked her and you don't even have to stay around and try to put the pieces back together, I thought, but I knew, cringing at the knowledge, that it was Hilary I was angry at. At the hysterics, the damning silences, the fragile, hard-won advances and the easy retreats back into frailness and woundedness. At the sucking dependence, the fussy infantilism, the stubborn refusal to be healed. Over the anger rode searing shame and self-loathing. Hilary was not a cosseted adult but a wounded and vulnerable ten-year-old child. If I had anger, let me direct it at myself, for daring to be angry with her. For my failure to protect her.

But when I thought of my child, snuffling and cowering in a locked toilet, with busy adults trying to lure her out, the tiny, dull anger persisted.

There was no one else in the rest room but Hilary's teacher and the school nurse when I arrived. A tight-faced young woman teacher stood guard at the door, and a small crowd of slack-faced, curious children lingered in the fluorescent-lit hall outside. I thought, irrelevantly, that this grammar school smelled remarkably like Pemberton State, and like every other school I had ever been in, of chalk and some kind of industrial disinfectant, and the ghostly musk of many young bodies.

At first I could not get her to open the stall door. She was not crying by now, but I recognized the self-absorbed sniffles of the very small child she became in the aftermath of one of her terrors, and knew that they signaled a kind of mindless fussiness, a fugue of irrationalism that I could not reach with argument or cajolery. Neither of the teachers or the nurse could say what had set her off, and none of the other children seemed to know, or would say. The nurse did not think it was a physical illness; one child had said that she saw Hilary earlier in the center of a small crowd of children who were laughing and jeering at her, and that she had been crying then, but that child had melted away and none of the others could be coaxed to say anything but "Idonknow." Hilary had been in the stall almost an hour, and I could read the crawling minutes in the set faces of the three adults still present.

I took a deep breath, knowing how I was going to sound, and said, as firmly as I could, "Hilary, if you don't open that door and come out right now, the riding lessons are over. For good, and I don't mean maybe. Do you want that?"

"No," Hilary snuffled.

"Then come on out now."

"No."

"All right, I'm going to count to ten. You can come out or not; it's up to you. But when I get to ten, if you're not out of there, you can kiss that horse goodbye."

Silence.

"Okay. I'm counting. One. Two. Three. Four. Five. Six. Seven."

At eight I heard her slip the bolt back in the lock, and

on nine she was outside, looking obliquely up at me. My heart stopped, ice-locked. She looked ghastly, as if she had been drowned, as if she had been in water for days. Her face was mottled and swollen with tears, and her red, tight-swollen eyes were deeply circled with shadow. The front of her Madonna tee shirt was as wet as if she had splashed it with water, and the jodhpurs and boots she had insisted on wearing that morning were sodden. Her hair was pasted to her narrow head. She could not breathe through her congested nose, and drew ragged, sighing breaths through her open mouth. The stale, thin odor of a child's vomit lingered around her.

"What happened to you, baby? Are you sick?" I said, putting my palm to her forehead. It was clammy and cold. The skin of her arms, when I grasped them with my hands, was cold, too, and damp. She felt like a small corpse.

"I want to go home," Hilary whispered. "I want to go home."

"We're going home," I said. "Just let me wash your face and hands here—"

"Noooooooo!"

It was a shriek of pure terror; I had never heard her make such a sound before. It was an adult sound, undiluted and full; there was nothing in it of childhood. I stared at her, aghast.

She backed back into the stall, screaming, her eyes shut tight, her hands beating the air in front of her.

"No water," she screamed. "No water!"

"Hilary . . ."

"No water!"

"All right, no water," I said, my voice shaking.

She let me lead her out of the building and settle her into the car, but she would not speak again. She stared in front of her at nothing as we drove home, and it was only when I had her upstairs in her bedroom in the little house and was stripping the wet clothes off her, and said, as gently as I could, "You know, if you won't talk to me, I'm going to have to take you to the doctor," that she broke her silence.

"They said there was something in the water that came from the bomb plant," she whispered, turning her face away from me. "They said it got into your blood and dried it up and rotted your bones and you died in awful pain, and you screamed, and screamed, and you got all black and blue all over. They said it made the water catch on fire and smoke, and it used to be just over where the nig—where the black people live, way up in the woods near where the bomb plant is, but now it's coming under the ground over to where the rich people and the horses are. Where we are. They said that. They said it burns horses up and turns children to skeletons; it eats them up, but it doesn't hurt grownups, so nobody believes it and will stop it. They said I already had it in me; we had a movie in geography this morning, and when they turned the lights off they said I lit up like a neon sign, and they could see my bones shining through my skin, and my teeth grinning in my head like a skeleton. They said the bomb plant knows about it, but they lie about it, and the people out there say anybody who's seen the creek and the river light up is crazy or drunk, and so nobody believes them because it's the government saying it. . . . And then they threw water all over me."

She was crying again. I hugged her to me.

"Hilary, baby, that's all wrong; that's not the way it is," I said. I was outraged and horrified. No wonder she was frightened. "The stuff that makes bones show through: that's called radiation; it's what's in an x-ray. You know, like when the dentist takes pictures of your teeth. Like when Pat's horse hurt his leg and they took a picture of it and put a splint on it, remember? It won't hurt you; it *helps* you. They make things out at the Big Silver plant that have radiation in them, but they have all kinds of safeguards and fail-safe plans and things so that the radiation can't get out and hurt people. It's worked for years and years and it'll keep on working. You don't think the government would hurt its own people, do you? They were *teasing* you, sugar, whoever they are."

"They said you'd say that," Hilary said. Her voice was lifeless. Her eyes were dead. "They said no grownup would believe me if I told them. They said some of them—you know, kids like them and me—had seen the water burning and smoking, and all of them had died right after. Before they did, their bones shone through their skin like mine did this morning. Blood came out of their mouths. They said they had blue places on them, like these."

She turned her slender arm over and I saw a small scattering of old bruises on the inside of it, going saffron and green.

"Darling, those are just plain, ordinary old bruises. You have those all the time. You could have gotten them any way in the world; you probably got them on Pittypat. Look, I have them on my shin, where I bump it getting into the car all the time."

"I don't ever remember having them before," Hilary said in the dead old voice. "They said you'd say that."

"Who in God's name are 'they'?" I cried. "I'm going to call their parents and tell them if their kids ever open their mouths to you again—"

"No, no, no, no!" Hilary flapped her hands helplessly. "No, Mama! They said if you told, they'd get some of the old people up there to send the Duppies for me, and they'd take me out to where the creek lights up and hold me under it, and I'd burn up."

"Who, Hilary, *who?*" I held her fiercely against me. "I won't call, then, I promise, but you have to tell me who said those dumb, stupid things to you."

"The black children, the ones who come on the bus from out by the bomb plant. The ones who live in those little houses up in the woods, and that little town. Everybody's scared of 'em, Mama, because they can send the Duppies. They have blue doors on their houses so the Duppies won't get them, but they can send them for other people, and they know about the water because they've *seen* it. . . . Mama, they said I was a rich horse-riding kid because I wore my boots and jodhpurs, and that it was us over here that the water was coming to. It comes under the ground."

"Hilary," I said, "look at me. No, look. Those children are poor and ignorant, and that makes them jealous and mean. They saw your boots and they thought you were rich and they wanted to scare and hurt you, because you have things they don't. Or they think you do. You should feel sorry for them, not be afraid of them. There are no such things as Duppies. The water can't hurt you. Not here and not anywhere in the United States. Do you think I would bring you to a place that wasn't safe?"

"No, ma'am," she mumbled. Her eyes slid away and she fidgeted under my touch.

"Well, then, let me run you a hot bath and then we'll put some clean clothes on and go get a pizza," I said.

She finally let me put her into the bath, but she scrambled right out again, and she did not want pizza. She ate half of the bowl of soup I heated for her and then climbed into her bed with her old bear that she had put away, and the next day, Saturday, she did not want to go and ride Pittypat. She stayed on the screened porch reading and swinging herself in the porch swing, and when I held out the promise of a movie and ice cream afterward, she said she didn't want to go. She was very quiet and very pale, and she slept a lot off and on through the day and evening.

I told Carter about it that night. We sat on the porch with drinks before eating the gumbo I had made, listening to the last of the tree frogs before winter and feeling on our faces a little wind with the steel of autumn in its depths. Carter was silent until I had finished, and then he grimaced.

"God," he said. "I don't blame her for locking herself in the john. It makes me want to hide in the crapper, too. Shining bones and rotting blood and Duppies . . ."

"What's a Duppy?" I said. "She talked about them a good bit."

"It's a particularly nasty kind of Caribbean haunt, or something," he said. "It's supposed to hide up in trees and drop down on people and ride them to death, for what reason I'm not sure. Sheer bad temper, probably. She's right; there's a whole little colony of blacks who still live way up Goat Creek in an old settlement, though I didn't know there were still children up there. Most of the younger ones have moved their families to New Morganton, about five miles this side of the plant. They're Gullah blacks, or the descendants of African Gullahs, who came from the Caribbean as slaves to the sea islands and the Low Country when the English settled them, and brought their ha'nts with them. Some of the old ones still cling to the old ways. I've heard about the Duppies, and I've seen the blue doors, on some of the shacks we pass when we hunt in the Big Silver or at King's Oak. I don't know what the business about the water shining is, but I know the runoff water from the reactors steams sometimes. It's very hot, almost boiling, when it leaves the reactors and runs into the effluent sluices, and the same water goes into small streams that eventually run down into Goat Creek and the river. I've seen it steaming myself, and it does look scary, and I've driven through the Big Silver on Route 35, the road that cuts through the property on the way to Tallahassee, and the water in the ditches beside the road was smoking like a river in hell. But it's just hot. I mean in the ordinary sense of the word. Just plain hot water. Like I told you, that water's tested six ways to Sunday every day of the week and has been for thirty-five years. Not just by the plant people, either; there are all kinds of independent testing outfits here, and the EPA and the Department of Energy bring engineers in to do their own sampling regularly. Not to mention every environmental group under the sun, from lunatic fringe to blue-ribbon scientific commission.

"There's a permanent colony of protesters and Big Silver watchers and watchdog committees in these parts who track the plant twenty-four hours a day, under the Freedom of Information Act. They can get all the records from every plant, and they do. Some of what they've found is appalling. You've read the stories. But the bottom line is, for all its faults and lapses, the air around it and the water coming out of it are clean. There are, as you know if you watch the news and read the papers, bad problems with some of the other nuclear facilities around the country: horrendous problems with near meltdowns and leaking toxic waste; lies and cover-ups; the whole sad, sorry ball of wax. Hanford in Washington State and Fernald in Ohio are particularly rotten, and there's a criminal investigation for waste mismanagement and cover-up going on at Rocky Flats right now. But the Big Silver has just never had those problems. Oh, it's old, and its waste-disposal methods are as antediluvian as any of the others', and half of its reactors are shut down because they just aren't safe. But the point is, Big Silver *knows* their waste system is outmoded and they're working to correct it, and they've cleaned it up where it's worst, and they shut their own reactors down themselves when they got past the safety point. And they've never hidden anything. The Big Silver is the most publicly poked and prodded and examined nuclear facility the government has. They're noted for their openness. Stratton-Fournier has always made a point of that. Anybody can have a plant tour, if they call the public information office first; there's a three-day wait. We really ought to take Hilary on one. That should put the problem to rest for good and all."

"It's not a bad idea," I said, somehow hating it. "I'll ask her in the morning if she'd like to do it. But it's not just this business, bad as it is, Carter. It's the whole . . . ethos; somehow Hilary just isn't thriving here. The only time she shows any of her old life and animation is when she's over at Pat's on a horse. She can't live for horses. I just can't have that. She's got to heal in every area. All of her has got to get hardier and stronger. She simply cannot grow up a victim. I don't know; Pemberton seemed so perfect at first, almost like a fairy-tale place. I thought there could be nothing in a place like this to harm her. Something's still wrong, and I can't put my finger on it."

"There's no place without harm, Andy," he said softly. "But I'd venture to say there's less in Pemberton than most places you could have taken her. She's still very young. She's lost a great deal. Give her time; you've only been here a little over six weeks."

I was silent. What he said made sense, but he had not known Hilary as she had been, Hilary before the night of the puppy's death. He could not know how enormous a gap yawned between that child and the one who slept upstairs.

"It's not my place to advise you about this, but if I were you I'd take her out of that school and put her in

Pemberton Day," he said presently. "I know you don't want to make a little elitist out of her, but from what I can see, she hasn't got much in common with kids who believe in Duppies and burning water and rotting blood. She's innately beyond that. She belongs in a world of books and music and thinking people. Notice I didn't say money. I didn't mean money. I meant cultivation. Hilary has an aptitude for it, and she's had a head start on it. To keep her away from that kind of world is to stunt her, Andy. She can't bring those other children up to her level, try though she might, but they can drag her down to theirs. You saw that yesterday. If she were an older child, maybe, or a much tougher one . . ."

He lapsed into silence and took my hand and held it in both his larger ones, and for a space of time we sat without talking, swinging gently back and forth. Then he said, "I'd be more than honored to pay her tuition at Pemberton Day, if that's a problem."

"It's not that," I said slowly. "Her father would pay for a private school. He wants and expects her to be in one. It's just that . . . somehow I didn't want her totally swallowed up in this Pemberton thing."

"But she's a part of this Pemberton thing," he said gently, echoing Tish's earlier words. "She already is, whether or not you want her to be. Doesn't it make more sense to let her feel a *real* part of it—to feel, oh, integrated and really belonging, I guess—than to try to live with a foot on one side of Pemberton and a foot on the other? Andy, the kids she'll be growing up with are already at Pemberton Day. She isn't going to go on dates and slumber parties and to proms with the kids from up Goat Creek. She may with black kids, but not *those* black kids, don't you see? The only thing I can see that this public school business is doing is keeping her off base. Unsettled all the time. No wonder she's susceptible to teasing and horror stories. She doesn't have the armor of the familiar."

I didn't reply and he said, "You have every right in the world to tell me to mind my own business."

"I hope we are your business, Hilary and I," I said slowly. "I'll think about it, Carter. I promise that. I'll think about it, and meanwhile I'll see if she wouldn't like to take a tour of the plant, providing you'll go with us."

"Say when," he said. "I'll call Frank Millican Monday morning. Might as well start at the top."

But Hilary was adamant about not going into the Big Silver plant, so I settled for taking her on an expedition out Route 35 the next day, Sunday, as far as the gate.

"Once you see how ordinary it is, and how ordinary all the little neighborhoods and towns around it are, you'll have a better picture of it in your head, and it won't scare you," I said. "You'll see. It's nothing but a big place where people like anybody else work, and live nearby. It's probably not any bigger than the Ford plant at home, and not much harder to get into."

"Okay," she said in a small, tight voice. "But I'm not going in, and I want you to promise you won't slow down at the gate."

"I promise," I sighed. "I'm not going to hijack you."

We rode out the next morning around eleven, with the bells of St. Martin's singing out through the warm, still woods and the crack and thunder from the polo field muted by humidity. The sky was gray and low, and the air was a scum on our skin. Off to the west the grayness was shading into slate.

"Summer weather," Carter said. "We're due about one more frog-strangler before cool weather. I hope this is it. I'm ready for some fall."

He had been on the polo field earlier, and still wore his jodhpurs and boots, although his blue polo shirt was clean, and his thinning blond hair had damp comb tracks in it. His forehead and nose were still peeling as they had been when I first met him, and his eyes were very blue in his tan face. He looked solid and comfortable and yet somehow exotic; I did not suppose I would ever get used to polo clothes casually worn. I wondered what the Pembertonians on my side of town would look like in the dead of winter, when their tans had faded, and decided that somehow, over here, they simply never did. I'd have bet that melanoma was not allowed in Old Pemberton, either. I made a mental note to ask Carter. Even Hilary, whose skin was Chris's luminous bisque, was honeyed with sun on her face and arms. I, the swarthy outlander, looked for once in keeping with my society. It was on the other side of town, at the college, that I stood out as an alien now.

Carter drifted the Jaguar through the tunnels of live oaks over the divided streets and across Palmetto, waving at church-bound Mercedeses and Jaguars, and turned right on Route 35, which led south and west toward Tallahassee. I had never been on this road; the college was in the opposite direction, northwest, on the road coming in from Atlanta. There had been no occasion, so far, for me to cross Palmetto. It was another country, a different world. Two months ago it would not have seemed alien to me; Atlanta is ringed with such trivial suburbs like a mammoth with pygmy spear hunters. But now, after my few weeks in the historic district, it was as jarring as an alien culture. My eyes, used to mellowness and symmetry and richness, blinked reflexively at the harshness and rawness of it.

"I've been here too long," I said. "A little while ago this wouldn't have bothered me a bit. Now it looks almost ugly."

"It is ugly," Carter said. "This stretch of Pemberton would make Scranton and Secaucus look good. There are some classy new subdivisions, houses as expensive as the ones back there, but you can't see them from here."

"It's not ugly, really," I said. "It's just ordinary. You don't realize how spoiled you are, living where you do. Us, too."

"It is too ugly," Hilary said. "I hate it over here."

There was something in her tone I did not care for, something full and smug. I had not heard it before.

"It's not one bit worse than Buckhead," I said. "And you used to think Buckhead was the most beautiful place on earth."

"I did not. I hated it, too," Hilary said.

"Well, you're just full of hate today, aren't you?" I said crisply, and then fell silent. Better this, perhaps, than whimpering, than fear. Or perhaps not. I would talk with her when we got home; I was not going to nurture a fledgling snob. But I did not want to upset her any more than she already was. She had wakened headachy and lethargic and cross, and had tried to beg off the trip out to the Big Silver. I had insisted that she come. I wanted her to have a human-scale face for the thing that menaced her. Time enough after she had laid this ghost to tackle the far more insidious one of elitism.

Route 35 ran through an enclave of small white frame houses and mustardy brick bungalows, where grass straggled in yards too darkly shaded with twisted old trees and older-model cars sat in driveways and at curbs. Then it was out into New South country, that kudzu of tedious, jerry-built conformity that is slowly strangling the richness and particularity out of the South: thickets of fast-food stores, strip shopping centers, discount malls, cut-rate "travelers" motels. What had been vast stands of pine and hardwood forests now were treeless plains upon which rank after rank of ill-built, pretentious condominiums slumped like an army of weary Visigoths. Satellite dishes and Trans Ams and RVs took the place of shrubbery and lawn furniture. Trailer parks and Baptist churches sported faded American flags. A sign in the parking lot of the Damascus Baptist Church read: *America, Love It or Leave It.* Across from the church, at the Happy Land Child Development Center, a thin woman in pink plastic curlers and shorts so short her sad little buttocks were showing was switching a screaming, dancing child with a limber green switch of privet.

"All is not happy in Happy Land," Carter said, grimacing.

"Should we try to stop that, or something?" I said, flinching with the child.

"God, no," Carter said. "Over here it's not child abuse unless it's a two-by-four." He glanced at me and said, "Sorry, Andy. I didn't mean to be flip about it."

"That's okay," I said. "Could you explain to me why there are seven—no, eight—automobile businesses right in a row? I've seen transmissions, tires, upholstery, parts, washes, waxes, and accessories in a half-mile strip. All of them open on Sunday."

"The automobile is to East Pemberton as the horse is to West." Carter grinned. "By that I mean the half-ton pickup, the van, the four-wheel all-terrain, and the panel truck. Not to mention the motorcycle, the dirt bike, and the trail bike."

"Does anybody drive a plain old car?" I said.

"Nope. If you can't sleep in it, it won't go."

"Why would they want to sleep in them?" Hilary said.

"For hunting," Carter said. "Most people don't have access to places like King's Oak. So they go off back in the woods so far they don't want to have to drive home, especially after they've been drinking and telling lies all night. So they just park their trucks and vans and sleep in them, and bring home their game in them."

"Where do they eat and take baths? Where do they go to the bathroom?" Hilary said.

"They bring stuff from McDonald's and they go to the bathroom in the woods, and they don't take baths." Carter smiled over at her. "You don't want to get downwind of a bunch of old boys coming home off a hunt. Turn you to stone."

"That's gross," Hilary sniffed.

"As a matter of fact, it is," he said. "But it's not without its attractions."

We bowled on through the dim morning, passing signs that extolled branches of savings and loan institutions, aerobics classes, tanning and nail salons, flea markets and "country antiques" and Kiwanis, Lions, Jaycees, Sertoma. *Rent a Fuzzbuster for $1.50 a Day*, one sign trumpeted. *God is the biggest blast there is,* said another, on the lawn of a concrete-block Church of God. Under the words there was a mushroom cloud. I poked Carter in the ribs and pointed. He nodded.

"They're all over the place," he said. "In New Morganton, the little town that's coming up, there's an Atomic Auto Parts and a Mushroom Cloud Pizza Takeout and several others. And the high school band and cheerleaders have mushroom clouds on their uniforms. You'd think New Morganton might be a little leery of atomic energy; when they decided to build the Big Silver plant here, the Atomic Energy Commission came in and bought up literally every house and business in Morganton, as it was called then, and tore it down, and relocated the town about fifteen miles east. Almost everybody fought it; it was in all the papers, and *Life* magazine, and Movietone News. There's even a folk song about it; Tom Dabney sings it. Ask him to do it for you sometime. But of course they lost, and some of the houses were moved and some abandoned to be razed, and there was instant new town. The funny thing is, New Morganton seemed to fall in love with the bomb the minute the paint dried. Like I said, there's a mushroom cloud on every other business, practically. And several people got rich testing soil and water before that scare wore off. They're just as proud of it as if it was Disney World."

"See?" I smiled at Hilary. She did not reply.

New Morganton flashed by, as lunar and deserted as a crater on the moon, and we were out in open fields, going brown and gold in the autumn sun. Groves of pecan trees, laden with nuts, loomed up and faded, and, soon after, the dark shoulders of the distant woods began pressing closer, and the ditches along the straight, empty highway filled with still, dark water.

"These are the beginnings of the Big Silver Swamp woods," Carter said. "King's Oak is off to the left there. We went in another way, almost directly opposite, when we went to the barbecue; it's a mighty big place. Beyond it the Big Silver property starts, just around this curve."

We swept around the curve and slowed down. Ahead of us, in the far distance, was a plain white wooden gatehouse, with a black-and-white barred guardrail across the road. There were autumn flowers planted around the gatehouse and, exposed to us, a series of consecutive neat white signs. A uniformed guard sat inside, and beyond the guardrail we could see nothing but more woods and the highway, stretching off into nothingness.

The first sign we passed said: *The Big Silver River Site (Safety, Responsibility, Security).* The second said: *Serving Baines County, Georgia, and the United States of America. Jobs, Safety, Peace, and Freedom.* The third said: *Warning: All persons enter-*

ing must show valid badges and voluntary consent to search if requested. The last said, simply: *Stop.* We did.

The guard looked at us incuriously. Carter put his head out the window and said, "Just looking. We wanted to show the little girl the gate."

"Glad to have you," the guard said. He was young and black. "Sorry I can't let you pass, but you can get a visitor's permit at the Chamber of Commerce. Takes three days."

"Thanks," Carter said. "We might do that."

"Well, come to see us," the guard said, and Carter turned the Jaguar around and we headed back out 35. Hilary was silent for a few miles.

"Well, what did you think?" I said. "Nothing there to be afraid of, was there? Just some signs and flowers."

"Was that man a secret agent?" Hilary asked.

"Nope," Carter said. "That man was probably a 1989 graduate of New Morganton High School. Security out here is a private company, or the Georgia branch of one. Proxmire Security. It's like the Pinkertons, kind of."

"Did he have a gun?" Hilary said.

"I didn't see one, but I sort of doubt it. If anybody went on through, he'd probably just press an alarm and people would come and stop them. They may have some armed people further in, around the reactors, but I think they rely mostly on electronics and dogs."

"Killer dogs?" Hilary breathed, and I looked at her in exasperation. She was certainly not going to let her cherished terror go without a fight.

"Tracking dogs and good barkers, more likely," Carter said patiently. "Killer dogs are not good public relations, and the Big Silver is nothing if not publicly related. I know they have electronic scanners and radios and some high-voltage wire and a helicopter or two, and a boat for the river. And there's an army detachment here, but I think they mainly do military work, like overseeing shipping to bases, and transportation between military installations, and things like that. It's a big place, Hilary. They've spent a lot of money on it. I don't imagine there's any more security here than you'd get at a big private plant where they make expensive things. In essence, that's just what it is, a business. A manufacturing business. You could see for yourself if you'd let us take you on the plant tour."

"No," Hilary said. "I don't need to do that."

"You aren't still scared of it, are you?" I said. "You can see that it's just a place where people come to work."

"Yeah," she said. I could read nothing in her face and voice but boredom and the beginning fractiousness that always spelled the lifting of one of her terrors.

"In that case, what do you say to lunch at the Track and Field Club?" Carter said.

"Okay," Hilary said, smiling at him, a small smile of capitulation. "And then can I go over to the stable? I haven't been out on Pittypat for ages."

"I don't see why not," I said, stretching in relief.

"And then can we go to the movies?"

"Don't push it," I said. "You missed an afternoon of school Friday. You need to find out if there was any homework and make it up."

"I don't care if there was," Hilary said, preening herself in renewed good spirits, cutting her blue eyes at Carter. "I hate that stupid school. I want to go to Pemberton Day. Pat says there's nobody at my school but me and the niggers. She says—"

"I don't care what she says." I rounded on her, my face stiff and hot with anger. "I don't ever want to hear you say that word again. And I'm going to think twice about letting you ride at Runaway if that's the sort of thing Mrs. Dabney is saying to you . . ."

"*Mama* . . ." It was a wail of anguish.

"Hilary, I can't have that kind of talk—" I began.

"Look, I'll go talk to Pat," Carter said, over our rising voices. "She forgets herself sometimes, and nobody ever called her a liberal. But she doesn't mean half she says, and she wouldn't want to upset you or influence Hilary. She'll listen to me, I guarantee it. Hold off till I have, okay?"

"Mama?"

"Okay," I said, but I said it grudgingly. I liked Pat Dabney's influence on my daughter as little as I liked her politics and her racial sentiments. If the riding lessons had not been such a liberation for Hilary, I would have stopped them then and there.

But she had been badly frightened on Friday, and had sunk so far back into silence and illness that I had been really afraid I would not get her back, and so I did not stop them. The lessons had been an instrument of healing, and I thought the trip out to the Big Silver plant had been a good idea, too. Hilary on the drive back was Hilary restored, or as much as she could reasonably be, and apparently the specter of the burning water had melted away like ground fog. On the drive back it was I, not she, who carried in my mind the habitat of the nuclear plant, like an old and unseen enemy for whom I now had a name and a lair.

CHAPTER FIVE

The great rain that had hung in the west on that Sunday did, indeed, bring autumn with it, and I surrendered the last of my resistance to Pemberton and slid into its spell like sleep. October and November in Pemberton, Georgia, are without equal in the world. Many people favor the ruffled, riotous spring here, but I find the relentless cannonade of azaleas, dogwood, wild honeysuckle, and technicolor gardens of the spring almost intimidating. And the April frenzy of races and hunts and cocktail parties and dinners and balls only adds to the Venetian excess. For me, that first slow, misted bronze-and-yellow autumn of the wire grass and the swamp forests was inexpressibly beautiful, infinitely seductive. The light that poured down onto the woods and fields and town was like syrup, like smoke; the sky was a tender Madonna's-robe blue, not the struck-steel cobalt of the north. Instead of sharpening and quickening, as they had done in Atlanta in the fall, my heart and senses seemed to deepen and expand. I felt all of autumn in my veins, but it ran like honey, not like wildfire. No matter how many seasons I spend in Pemberton, I will always love the autumn best.

Old Pemberton burst into its autumn social watercourse like a river in spate, and I relaxed the fierce knot of resistance inside me almost by an act of physical will and let Tish and Carter lead me into its shallows. Carter did indeed have the small dinner party for me that he had mentioned earlier, with four other couples whom I had not met and whom I liked, at least on this turf. I could not tell if I would have liked them in Atlanta. They were old Pembertonians as he was, and they rode and hunted as the rest of Pemberton over here seemed to, but not as militantly as the people I had met before. There were an insurance man, a realtor, the general manager of Clay Dabney's flagship radio-television station, and a retired general. Their wives did not have careers but did vast and seemingly efficient amounts of volunteer work. One had just helped found a new shelter for abused women and children over there, and another was a long-standing member of the city council. They were not trivial women.

After that, as if I had been tacitly stamped Approved, at least provisionally, I went with Carter to a series of small dinner parties in a series of charming private homes, and found that I enjoyed them all to one degree or another. There was more talk of horses and hunting and shooting and dogs than I would have preferred, but I kept quiet and smiled a lot, and actually began to learn small things that it amused me to know. Steeplechasers and flat racers have a natural antipathy for each other. Terrier owners are as fussily partisan as Southern religious denominations: the Jack Russell owner will not lie down with the Norwich, and so on. Fox hunters speak only to God. Peggy Corning had a shooting tower on her farm that had been a forest ranger's fire tower; her doting fourth husband, Tommy, had had it fitted with a hydraulic system, so she could practice shooting various denizens of earth and air from all heights and angles. By now she virtually never missed. Bertie and Bill Whisenant had won the North American Coaching trophy two years back and coached, on occasion, with the British royals.

"I assume you don't mean soccer," I said archly to Bertie Whisenant when she mentioned it, knowing the moment the words passed my lips they were a mistake.

"No," Bertie said.

I did fairly well in Pemberton society, I suppose, so long as I listened appreciatively and did not allude to anything that smacked of a personal history. I knew instinctively that I was welcome, in the homes and clubs where Carter and Tish took me, as a creature of the moment and place: Tish and Charlie Coulter's nice old friend who had the pretty little girl; Carter Devereaux's date this season. So nice for poor Carter. Such a pleasant thing for Tish, to have her college roommate close by in the Belvedere cottage. But I suspected that to have insisted on being acknowledged fully as what I was—city dweller, daughter of a second-generation Greek grocery store owner and drunk, divorced abused wife, underpaid clerk in a second-rate community college—would have tempered the enthusiasm of the smiles and cheek kisses and hugs with which I was greeted now. When I said as much to Tish, she said, "You're being way too sensitive. Not nearly as many people as you imagine are thinking about you one way or another." And I laughed.

"Well, you know what I mean," she said. "You're new in town, so you think people are looking you over critically, and you feel you have to act this way, or that. I know how it is. I've been there."

"Tish," I said, "you've never been a newcomer anywhere in your life."

"What the hell do you think I was in Bolivia?" she asked.

"I was speaking metaphorically," I said.

"You were speaking crap," she returned. "Be yourself. You'll see nobody is going to cut you dead."

And so at the next party, a huge cocktail buffet in late October at the great, beetling, brown board and batten cottage of Phipps and Gwen Carrington, deep-rooted Winter People whose annual nod to *égalité* and *fraternité* the party was, I was as fully myself as I could be.

Tish and Charlie and Carter and I were standing in the vast, somber library chatting with the square and flamboyantly Lilly'd Gwen Carrington and a group of women similar in attire and proportion—with the exception of Pat Dabney, who slouched against a great Biedermeier desk in rumpled black satin cut to her waist front and back. A frail, dark, exquisitely beautiful older woman was complaining languidly that her Annie had given notice and planned to go to Pemberton State and get a degree in hotel and motel management, "and her forty-five if she's a day. And what's even worse, I heard her out in the kitchen telling Ida she ought to do it, too. I'd have fired her on the spot if she hadn't already quit. Have you ever heard of such a thing?"

"After all you've done for her, too, Caroline," one of the other women put in, and the dark woman gave a little wave of dismissal with a slender hand.

"Oh, shoot, no more than we all have, for all of them. But it just goes to show you, doesn't it? They make too much money these days. They don't want to work."

"Well, George Bush is the right man to get us back on track," still another woman said. She was younger than the others, dark and very thin and sharp-faced. Something about her was oddly familiar; in a moment I saw that she was obviously the daughter of the older woman whose Annie had deserted her. Their features were identical. But none of her mother's fretful, exotic beauty lit her face. She wore, instead of the ubiquitous Lilly, a ruffled organdy Cullinane blouse and matching taffeta skirt, with opaque white stockings and black satin flats. She might have been a Peachtree Road debutante, except that she was past the age by two decades. I thought she must be about my age.

"Ronald Reagan would have done it, too, if he'd had time. He was getting to it," Gwen Carrington boomed. "I know what you mean, Caroline. Pretty soon nobody's going to be able to give a decent party, because there won't be anybody to serve or clean up."

I looked at Tish and she rolled her eyes. I said, "Maybe you could hire some of the hotel and motel management students at Pemberton State. Our students do nice work. You might even ask for your maid back," and I smiled brilliantly at the dark woman. "Just for the evening, of course. And at minimum wage."

She looked at me as if I had suggested she do a bump and grind, then decided I was joking, albeit untastefully, and said, "Well, that's a cute idea, isn't it, Miggy?"

"Mm hmm," her daughter said, looking narrowly at me.

"That's right, I forgot." Pat Dabney smiled ferally, blowing smoke into our faces. "You work out there, don't you? At the college? It's good to hear they're actually trying to amount to something. Not wasting our tax money."

I gave her back a brilliant smile. Gwen Carrington turned to me. "Did you go hear Mr. Bush when he was in Atlanta, my dear? We had reservations at the Ritz-Carlton, but then we had to cancel at the last minute. I was terribly disappointed. Such a solid man. Such a dear woman."

"No, I'm afraid I didn't," I said. "I voted for Jesse Jackson. So I felt the evening would be a little rich for my blood."

"Ah. Interesting. Well, my dears, there's Clay and Daisy Dabney; do excuse me, will you?" And Gwen Carrington was gone into a flock of Lillys, vanishing like a butterfly in a rose garden. The other women were close behind her. There was a little space of time in which the silence boomed like thunder, and then I turned to Tish, half expecting to see laughter on her face, or at least in her eyes. But I saw, instead, a blank, careful opacity. Carter and Charlie held up empty glasses and moved away toward the fireplace, where a bar had been set up. Tish and I looked at each other.

"I guess I shouldn't have said that," I said. I tried to sound contrite, but failed. Surely Tish had been as offended and amused as I had by the ridiculous little exchange.

"I guess you shouldn't," she said.

"Sometimes I don't know you," I said softly, feeling my eyes sting with sudden tears.

"Andy, it isn't that I don't think Gwen Carrington and Caroline Dabney are perfect assholes sometimes," she said slowly. "I do. And it isn't that I'm afraid I won't be asked to any more parties if I speak my mind. I'm not. I go to too many parties as it is. But this is Pemberton; it's very small and it's very old and it's all we have. When someone is unpleasant, we all feel the ripples. And when someone embarrasses Carter, we all feel it. I think you did embarrass him. He's a very old-fashioned man in many ways, and he was raised to be an excruciating gentleman. He can't help it. He doesn't blast foolish old ladies even when they need it. He's too kind. It upsets him when other people do it, even though he'll never say. He'd mow me down, or Charlie, or one of his own crowd, in a minute, if he thought we needed it, but not poor, dumb old Gwen Carrington and poor, poisonous old Caroline Dabney. Not to mention poor, wretched Miggy. I know it probably sounds hypocritical to you, but it's Pemberton's way, and so it's our way, too, when we're here. Because Pemberton is all the home we have, and we have to live here. It's a kind of admission you pay."

I felt my face flame. I had done a cheap and showy thing, and it had backfired. I wanted to go home and cry.

"I'm sorry," I muttered. "I apologize. I'll apologize to Carter, too. But do you think I ought to do it to those women?"

"What, and ruin their evening?" Tish said, and I looked up, to see her old grin. "They'll talk about you at every bridge table and hunt breakfast this fall. Pretty soon it'll be all over town that you were married to a black man at high noon in Saint Philip's Cathedral. Did you really vote for Jesse Jackson, or was that just the worst thing you could think of to say?"

"I really did," I said.

She grinned wider. "So did I. But if you tell a living soul, I'll deny you thrice. Not even Charlie knows it."

"Was that by any chance Tom Dabney's mother and sister I blasted?" I asked, when I had stopped laughing.

"The very same," Tish said.

"God. No wonder he lives in the woods."

"You don't know the half of it," Tish said. "All three

of his furies were here tonight. Chip, too, come to think of it. Tom's probably a hundred miles up the swamp, as far away from them all as he can get. Sometimes I think Clay and Tom are the only decent Dabneys in all that clan."

"Mmm," I said. I did not want to pursue this.

Carter demurred when I apologized later that evening for my behavior.

"Don't think a thing about it," he said. "You have the excuse of being a normal well-adjusted outsider. The only thing is, I'm afraid you just did yourself out of the Pemberton Dames."

"What ominous thing is that?" I said.

"Pemberton's most exclusive woman's thing," he said, grinning. "Small, old, select, boring as hell, probably. Learned papers and formal morning coffees and good works. By invitation only, WPs and OPs. Caroline Dabney was president last year. Gwen Carrington was the year before. This year it's Tish. I know she was going to nominate you for membership, but I do believe you have just scuttled your craft."

"Oh, Lord," I said. "I wish she'd said. I seem to have screwed up just about everybody tonight."

"Not me," he said, kissing me lightly on the temple. "I'd rather have you with me than the ladies of the club."

"I'd better call her and apologize, anyway," I said. "Again."

But when I did, a couple of days later, she surprised me by saying, "Well, as a matter of fact, I was just talking to Gwen and Pat Dabney, and both of them would be absolutely delighted if you'd accept a membership. Don't ask me why. You'll get a formal invitation sometime this week, from the secretary."

"I gather I'd better accept with what grace I can muster, right?" I said.

"Fucking aye," Tish said.

And so I became a member of that most sacrosanct of Pemberton's covens, the Pemberton Dames, and to my great surprise, enjoyed it. There were never more than thirty members, most much older than I; Tish and I and Miggy and Pat Dabney were the youngest Dames by far, and as such were treated casually and fondly, like precocious children. Miggy and Pat were legacies, daughters and granddaughters of members, and Tish was the daughter-in-law of a late member. Only I seemed to have virtually no reason to be included, except the group's obvious affection for Tish. But they treated me warmly nonetheless, and were indulgent with my lack of time, that first year, to present a paper and host a coffee.

"Oh, shoot," Gwen Carrington said. "You won't be working forever. Do it next year. It's a treat for us just to have your good mind and your fresh opinions. We've been sliding into a rut for years, us old women; most of us have known each other since we were in our cradles, and we're even beginning to look alike. We need to be reminded that there's something else in life besides dogs and horses and gardens and genealogy."

I smiled at her. They were graceful and kind words from one whose party I had nearly sabotaged, and I felt shabbily grateful for her graciousness. I had misjudged her; most of the other women, too. They were, indeed, preoccupied with their horses and dogs and flowers and ancestors, and they did, indeed, spend a lot of time talking about people and times past and out of my experience. And their opinions and values reflected an older, narrower, and far more privileged world than mine; I could neither share nor change them. But they were tough and world-seasoned women, too, who had seen trouble and sorrow and prevailed, and they had contributed vastly to the well-being of their town and region. And the papers that they gave were awe-inspiring in their erudition and execution. I was learning—slowly, it seemed—not to jump to conclusions about this town and its people.

It wasn't a totally thornless bouquet, of course. I knew instantly and viscerally, when I encountered them again, that Caroline and Miggy Dabney were not going to forgive me Jesse Jackson or much else. They were polite enough, of course; both were flawless examples of that increasingly *rara avis,* the Southern Lady. Their smiles and drawls and small talk were faultless. But they watched me out of narrow dark eyes, and talked only to whatever group was around me, never directly to me alone. And despite Tish's words to the contrary, Pat Dabney did not even speak. If I had not seen her yellow-green eyes watching, watching, I would have thought her unaware of my presence.

"I think you lied through your teeth when you told me Pat Dabney wanted me in the club," I said to Tish after a couple of meetings. "She hasn't spoken to me in two weeks."

"Who knows what Her Inscrutability is thinking?" Tish said. "She doesn't speak to many people. But I wasn't lying. If it hadn't been for her, you probably wouldn't be in the club. Caroline and Miggy Dabney started pecking you delicately apart when I nominated you, and Pat spoke up and said, 'I want her in here,' and that was that."

"Just like that?"

"Just like that. Her grandmother was founder and first president. She doesn't much care what we do, but when she does, she gets her way."

"Well, whatever their mysterious reasons, the three Dabney damsels have stared holes through me since I joined," I said. "You must have noticed. Are they waiting for me to invite Jesse for coffee, do you think?"

"Who knows why they do anything," Tish said. "Maybe they think you're going to run off with Tom. Pat was there at King's Oak when he came on to you, remember. Andy, you're simply going to have to do something about that blushing. Biofeedback, or something. I can't believe you still blush after Chris and everything. Don't tell me you're harboring a thing for Tom Dabney!"

"Don't be an utter ass," I said fiercely. "Tom Dabney is a boor and a bore. I'm not harboring anything. Why in God's name should they care if I did run off with him, anyway? From what you've told me, all three of them have kicked him out at one time or another."

"You don't know those women," Tish said. "What's theirs is theirs. You're right; his mother cut him loose in effect when she sold the old house and her half of King's Oak to the bomb plant out from under him, and Pat dumped him later, when he wouldn't knuckle. Only Miggy still yearns for her big brother, but it doesn't do any good. He and Caroline can't stay in the same room without fighting. But there's a kind of Southern woman who won't let go of a man even when she doesn't want him anymore, and it seems to be a dominant Dabney gene that rubbed off on Pat somehow. I bet you anything that if you and Tom started something, that trio would be after you with their claws out. Pat ran his last lady friend all the way back to Tallahassee with a tongue-lashing at the Pemberton Cup trials. Not that I blame her. The woman was a fool."

"Well, I guess I'm safe, then," I said. "I don't want what he's peddling. I've got enough troubles as it is."

And I did. Hilary simply could not seem to get a grip on health. For a while it seemed that she had; when she started back riding with Pat Dabney, after our trip to reassure her about the Big Silver plant, she had lost most of her sulkiness and begun to talk about horses and riding again, and about Pat Dabney herself, with something of her old animation. I didn't care for the constant "Pat says" and "That's not how Pat does it," but I said nothing. If it took Pat Dabney to make my daughter strong, then so be it. Only occasionally did I feel I had to pull her up short, once when she said "nigger" again, and once when she announced imperiously that Pat was starting her on show jumping and hunting in another year.

"I'm thinking about Saint Catherine's in Virginia," she said. "They have the best equestrian courses in this part of the country. Pat said she'd pay my tuition for a quarter, to see if I liked it. After that, she said maybe you and Carter could work something out."

"Listen up, Hilary, because I have a news flash for you," I said, anger hot behind my eyes. "*A.* No jumping and no hunting. Absolutely not. I won't have you killing yourself or some innocent animal. You used to hate that as much as I do; if you're getting to where watching dogs tear a fox apart is your idea of sport, you're in serious trouble, my dear. And *B,* I and I alone am paying for your tuition at wherever you land, and it is not going to be an equestrian college in Virginia. This business is about one inch from going too far, and this horse business *and* the association with Mrs. Dabney will stop if I hear any more about any of it. *Comprende?*"

"Pat said you wouldn't let me," Hilary said tightly, her skin mottling with temper. "She said we'd have to find another way. So we will. Whether you like it or not. It's no sweat."

And with that I sent her to her room for the rest of the evening and grounded her through the weekend. My conscience smote me and my heart hurt me, but I forced myself to honor my own edict. My instinctive fear of having Hilary fall into Pat Dabney's hands was a living, virulent thing. After that, I heard no more about jumping and hunting, or about school in Virginia. But she was silent and remote for a long time, and the chill weight that was Hilary was never off my heart.

"Let her pout," Tish said. "It's the start of that hideous time when she'll be engaged in all-out warfare with you, and there's just not a lot you can do about it. It happens to the best-adjusted of them. It's better than the little ghost who came down here with you. It would be unusual if she didn't act out at some point. Put her in Pemberton Day if she absolutely hates school; I've thought you should do that all along. It'll be enough novelty to distract her, you'll see."

And so, reluctantly, I capitulated and told Hilary that if we could get her in on such short notice, she could start Pemberton Day School at the beginning of the winter quarter. After that, she was almost herself again, sleeping more soundly and smiling more often, if still timid. She also avoided water when she could, and would not go with us when Carter offered an October picnic on the banks of the Big Silver, but it seemed a manageable neurosis. I had given up the idea, finally, of having Hilary perfectly healed. We would measure progress in degrees.

And then, in early November, Pat Dabney had her over to her house on Merrycricket Road with her young exercise riders and stable hands for an annual barbecue, and Hilary came face-to-face unexpectedly with a truly terrible thing in Pat's library, a sort of shawl made entirely of the stitched-together, mangled masks of foxes taken in the hunts in which generations of Belvederes had ridden over the years. Some of them were still dark with blood, and they all grinned in hideous rictuses of agony and fear. Hilary had gone white and nearly fainted, and had begun to tremble and then to cry, and Pat had snapped at her, casually and brutally and in front of all Hilary's cool-eyed young heroes, "For God's sake, Hilary, call your mother and get her to come and get you and stop that sniveling. This house is no place for crybabies. If you can't stand the heat, stay out of the kitchen. I guess I was wrong; you'll never make a hunter."

I got the story out of Hilary only after an afternoon of hysterics and prostration; she was mortally ashamed of herself for disappointing her idol in front of the regal young riders, and her shame made her ill. She ran a high fever for several days, and when it broke, the nightmares and the pinched white silences began again. Once again, Carter stopped me from confronting Pat Dabney.

"No. Let it be," he said. "It's Hilary's affair, not yours. I've seen that thing; the old man had it made up. It was cruel of Pat, but it's her way, and Hilary will either have to find a way to stand up to her or drop the lessons on her own. If you keep running interference for her and fighting her battles, she'll still be crying and hiding when she's twenty. Pat's world is tough, Andy. The whole horse world is. If Hilary wants to live in it, she'll have to accept the terms."

And so Hilary did not go back to Pat Dabney's stable, and I did not interfere. But the weight on my heart grew until it all but brought me to my knees. I could not see anything ahead for my wounded child.

Just before Thanksgiving, Carter asked Hilary and me to an afternoon party at Tom Dabney's house out on Goat Creek. Neither of us wanted to go, Hilary because she did not seem to want to go anywhere except where I was, and then without the company of others, and I because I was tired and frightened for her and did not want to see anyone except Carter and Tish and Charlie. That dancing jackanapes Tom Dabney was the last person in the universe I wished to spend time with.

"I didn't think hermits had parties," I said when Carter tried to persuade me.

"He's not a hermit," Charlie said. "He just lives in the woods. Actually it's a charming place. Very unusual. I've never seen anything quite like it. And he does indeed give parties, great ones; he gives one every season. They're not like anything else around here, either. You never know who you'll see there. I've gone to several, though not in a while. Not since I took up with Pat. I guess he invited me this time because he knows I don't see her anymore. He specifically asked me to bring you and Hilary."

"What on earth for?" I said rudely. "I didn't know he knew Hilary existed. I'm sure he's really terribly eager to have a sullen, disturbed child at his annual autumn gala."

"As a matter of fact, I think he is. He said a funny thing. He said to be sure and bring the little girl; he'd heard Pat had done a number on her and he thought Goat Creek could fix her up again."

"How on earth would he have heard about that business?" I snapped. "He doesn't exactly run with the in crowd, does he?" I knew I was being ungracious, but I did not care at the moment. Was there no limit to this dark swamp man's reach?

"Everybody probably knows about it," Carter said. "Everybody always knows everything about everybody in Pemberton. You and Hilary are fair game; you're new and visible. And Pat Dabney is always prime fodder for talk. Hilary is the latest and youngest victim of her infamous tongue, but everybody knows about the others. I can assure you that sympathy will be running strongly with Hilary.

Tom probably heard about it from Scratch Purvis, the old black guy he goes around with. Scratch's daughter Ruby works for Pat sometimes, when she gives a party."

"Well, I'm not going to drag Hilary out to the boondocks just so he can get off on playing good guy to his ex-wife's bad guy," I said. "You know how she's been lately. You know she's got that thing about water back again."

"I don't think he wants to get off on anything," Carter said mildly. He simply would not let my rudeness offend him. "He seemed quite concerned about her. 'Tell Diana to please give Goat Creek just one day. I've seen it heal terrible wounds,' is what he said. Diana, huh?"

"It's but one of his many affectations," I said. "Did he really say that, about healing? Did he use that word?"

"He did. Hil won't be the only child; there are usually several around. She may already know some of them. And if nothing else, she might like to see the goats and the other animals. He has quite a menagerie out there, almost a miniature wildlife refuge. A pet raccoon, and an almost-pet otter, and a flock of wild ducks so tame they walk in and out of the house like children or chickens. And the clearing where the house is is one of the prettiest places I've ever seen. Tom doesn't exactly live in squalor, though it admittedly isn't the Ritz-Carlton, either."

"Well, fancy, both a deerslayer and a Dr. Dolittle," I said. I regretted the sarcasm in the words, almost before they were out. What, after all, had Tom Dabney done to me that was so offensive? He had startled me once and frightened me once, both times unintentionally, and complimented me once and played wonderful poetry for me once. Not, surely, the stuff of outrage. And it was odd, almost eerie, that he would use the word "heal" in regard to Hilary; it was the one I most often thought when I thought of her. How could he know she was troubled to that extent? Perhaps the kind concern for her was just that: kind.

"If I didn't know you better I'd almost think you were afraid of him," Carter said. "Don't be. There's not a warmer, more generous man alive than Tom, half nuts though he may be. Come on and go. You and Hilary both need a break. And you need to see some of Pemberton that isn't mired in horse shit."

"Okay," I said. "For a little while. I'm sorry I was being grumpy. It's nice that he's concerned about her. I've been unfair to him, I guess. It's just that he comes on so strong. You wonder if he ever just goes over the edge."

"All the time. And worse than that, according to Pat," Carter said comfortably. "But that's the charm of him. He does what the rest of us only think about doing in our secret hearts. He's our lightning rod, kind of. But it's entirely a benevolent madness."

And so we came to Goat Creek for the first time, Hilary and I, on a day in autumn so blue and gold and bittersweet and tender that simply being alive in it was like being half drunk. The morning had been crisp, but the noon sun was warm on our faces through the tinted glass of the Jaguar's windshield. Outside, far away and high over the brown stubble of the soybean fields that stretched away from the road, a large bird soared and looped and circled, seeming at times to hang motionless in the soft sky.

"Redtail hawk," Carter said, following Hilary's eyes. "He's riding the thermals that rise up from the ground. They're warmer than the air, so he can actually sit on them. He'll lounge around up there until he sees his lunch, and then he'll dive like a rocket. Nice way to make a living, huh?"

Hilary didn't answer. She buried her head under my

arm as it lay loosely around her, and I smoothed the thick hair off her forehead. She had agreed to come only on the condition that I not go off and leave her with anybody she did not know, especially strange children. I had agreed. It seemed better to give in and have her go and possibly receive some sort of stimulation than to argue and risk tears and an obdurate refusal. I knew that she was manipulating me as well as suffering, but it did not make the suffering any less real. I had decided to ask Tish on Monday to recommend a competent therapist for Hilary. We could not go on as we were. I did not know where I was going to find the money.

We passed the entrance to King's Oak, and about two miles farther on, Carter slowed the car and swung it onto a rutted dirt road marked only with a rusted tin mailbox riding drunkenly atop a rotting wooden post. Abruptly we were in woods as dense and silent and seemingly primal as those we had driven through to reach King's Oak. I said as much to Carter.

"It's part of the same land," he said, not taking his eyes off the rutted road. "Tom kept just a strip that runs down the middle of the plantation, between Clay's land and the half of King's Oak that belongs to the Big Silver plant now," Carter went on. "It's a long strip; it must go twenty miles up the river. But it's not much more than eight or nine miles wide at any point. He's a sandwich between Clay and the plant. Or rather, a hot dog, I guess."

"Are we going where the bomb plant is?" Hilary breathed.

"No, sugar," Carter said. "We're going to be right on Goat Creek, and that runs parallel to the river, and it's on the *other* side of the river that the plant property starts. But the actual buildings and things are miles and miles on the other side of that."

"A creek and a river . . . ," she began, in the tight, high singsong that meant one of the terrors was not too far off.

"Hilary, you do not have to go anywhere near water," I said as firmly as I could. "You don't even have to drink it. But I hope you won't feel that you have to point out to Mr. Dabney that his water bothers you. He was very kind to ask you to his party and to see his animals, and I expect you to be polite to him."

"Don't want to," she murmured. It was a very small child's whine; an ill child's. I did not think she was even aware of the sense of her words. I felt tears of despair behind my lashes.

We lurched out of the forest and into a large, sunlit clearing, and there was Tom Dabney's little house, sprawling atop a small rise on the creekbank and rambling down it to extend, somehow, out into the green, sun-dappled water itself. I gave a little gasp of pure pleasure, and felt myself smile. It was an enchanted house, a drawing out of an Arthur Rackham children's book, a page from an English fairy tale. I felt Hilary lift her head from my shoulder and turn it toward the house.

"Is this where we're going? Is the party here?" she said.

"Right here," Carter said. "How about it? Isn't it something?"

"Yes," said Hilary.

The house was small, but it was so low and flung out along the brow of the rise and down its slope that it seemed much larger. It was made of wide random boards that had weathered a lovely, shaggy silver, and its roof was tin that had rusted a deep, rich magenta. It glowed in the sun like a pomegranate, like a plum. It was completely surrounded by a deep-roofed porch, so wide that it almost doubled the bulk of the house, and I could see, from the groupings of sagging old furniture placed at intervals on it, that the porch was used as much for living as the house probably was. From the car I could see easy chairs, an old-fashioned porch swing, a rope hammock, a twig table and dining chairs, a battered rolltop desk, and what looked to be a great old Welsh dresser. I thought that only a full-scale gale could blow rain in far enough to reach the furniture. Some kind of vivid scarlet vine grew over portions of the porch, screening it, and at one end a gnarled old wisteria vine made a deep little cave.

Down beyond the house I could see a fringe of small willows trailing bleached fronds into the slow-moving water, and stands of reeds and aquatic plants the color of a lion's coat. Beyond them the wide creek ran slowly, slowly; the only way you could tell it was moving at all was that an occasional branch or plume of red foliage would drift by, spinning languidly. On the other side of the creek more golden reeds stood, and a thicket of underbrush, and then the bulk of the glowing woods began again. I saw the end of a weathered old dock, a gray finger out into the water, with a silver canoe bumping gently against it. I had seen that canoe before, with the beautiful body of a dead deer lying in it. I moved my eyes back to the cluster of cars that were pulled up on the gray sand verge of the browning grass. I saw no people.

"Where is everybody?" I asked, as I had done when we had arrived at King's Oak.

"Probably around back on the porch overlooking the creek," Carter said. "Tom usually sets up there for parties. It's wider than this part. I can smell the barbecue pit from here."

Hilary and I stepped out of the car and I could smell it, too, a rich, dense, wonderful odor borne on pungent smoke, which brought tears of hunger to my eyes. We had not been eating much, Hilary and I. But out here, in this clear, strange light, in the warm, dense, woods-smelling air, I felt suddenly ravenous.

Tom Dabney came around the side of the house wearing blue jeans and a faded flannel shirt and moccasins without socks. He made no noise as he came, seeming to materialize out of the lambent light, and came up to us smiling broadly. In the strong sunlight I saw that there were creases between his dark, straight eyebrows and a webbing of fine lines at the corners of his narrow, deep-set blue eyes. Except for their color, they were his mother's eyes, Miggy's eyes. But the expression in them was far different. These eyes danced with a merriment that was near madness. He was slightly out of breath; the thought that he had just been dancing flickered through my mind. There was a dark shadow of beard on his strong, pointed chin, and on his dark hair he wore a wreath woven of some sort of small, pointed, shiny leaves. Wonderfully, magically, on his shoulder sat a large raccoon, black button eyes gleaming out of its bandit mask, clinging to his hair with small, clever dark hands.

Hilary smiled, a tentative, wondering smile.

"The glamorous Calhoun women," Tom Dabney said. "I'm awfully glad you came to my Thanksgiving party. Give this place a lot of class, you two will. Carter, old buddy. Thanks for bringing them."

He leaned over and kissed my cheek, a grave, chaste peck. I realized I was holding my breath, and let it out slowly. He reached out and picked up Hilary's hand and bent over it and kissed it, and murmured, "Mademoiselle, I am *enchanté*. You honor me."

Hilary giggled, a tiny, incredible sound. Tom Dabney

held her hand in his, his arm straight, and turned his head and murmured something to the raccoon. It waddled down his arm and onto Hilary's shoulder, and nestled itself into her hair. She flinched and hunched her shoulders, looking up at me, and then, ever so slowly, turned her head so that her cheek lay against the raccoon's dense brindle fur. The small smile reappeared and grew larger, and she put her hand up, gingerly, and touched the furry neck. The raccoon chirred and reached out with the small hands and patted her face.

"Is it okay?" I said to Tom Dabney. I was smiling, too, scarcely daring to let myself feel the smile.

"Oh, sure," he said. "I've had old Earl since he was a baby. Found him out in the woods under a tree, crying. Some asshole had shot his mama. He doesn't know he's a raccoon. But he's very particular about who he bums rides with. You should be flattered, Hilary."

We moved around to the back of the house, where a group of about thirty people stood and sat around on a vast, weathered porch. This one was unroofed, like a patio or deck, open to the wild-honey sun and extending out over the creek. It must have sat on pilings, for the dark water flowed directly under it. I could see it through the cracks in the wide boards. At the far end of the house, part of the porch was screened; I could not see into it. The woods and water would be as much a part of living in this sorcerer's lair as wallpaper and carpet in a normal house, I thought. I imagined that ordinary walls and roofs must soon pall to, even constrict, someone who lived in a house like this. I thought I could understand why Tom Dabney did not like to come out of his woods.

"It would be hard to leave this," I said.

"It's at its optimum in fall and spring," he said. "You're

seeing it the best it ever is. In the middle of August you can't get a deep breath and the mosquitoes carry sawed-off shotguns, and in February it's like living in a refrigerator full of mushrooms. I curse myself for a fool every summer and winter. But then fall comes, or spring, and I congratulate myself for a genius. I'm glad you like it. I hope you're not just being polite."

He was looking at me closely, the blue eyes seeming almost preternaturally focused.

"I'm not. It's really magical," I said. "It's like . . . something out of a book, out of a myth, or a fairy tale."

He grinned. "Yes. Isn't it."

He took us among his guests and introduced us, Hilary still bearing Earl on her shoulder like a talisman. There was a smattering of Old Pemberton people I had met before, Tish and Charlie among them, sitting in rump-sprung deck chairs, drinking beer and grinning lazily at us. Gwen and Phipps Carrington waved from the porch rail, looking ridiculously elegant, even in pants and boots, in all the rusticity. One of Carter's law partners whom I had met before and his wife were there, and Arne Wolfe, who operated the Pemberton Inn. There was the old black man I had seen Tom Dabney with on several occasions before, drinking something in a paper cup and nodding tranquilly like an old turtle in the sunlight: obviously he was a guest, and not the hired hand I had assumed him to be. The thin lawyer with the mended glasses was there, smiling sweetly, eyes closed, sipping steadily, and Martin Longstreet, the dean of the Division of Arts and Sciences at Pemberton State, drinking a tall drink with a lime in it and managing to look like an English don even in wildly incongruous camouflage pants and shirt and wizened old boots. The last three wore rakish wreaths, like Tom Dabney's. There was no one else from the college and no one else I had met or seen before. Tom introduced me to men and women who proved to be the owners of Betty's Beauty Box in New Morganton, an assistant librarian at the Ernest P. Fortnum Middle School, a mechanic, a drywall man with a construction company, a soybean farmer, the owner of a chain of coin-operated laundromats, the proprietor of the gunshop on Palmetto Street, a young Catholic curate from Tallahassee, and a bearded young man who operated the Greenpeace office in Albany. They might have been denizens of the training track, in their khakis and camouflage pants and plaid shirts and down vests and rubber shoes, and they were smiling and languid, as if the sun and the punch from a new galvanized-tin washtub in a corner had bewitched them into a kind of semihibernation, and all of them were friendly and easy with Hilary and me. Carter seemed to know many of them.

Off at the water's edge, on a small point screened by willows, children laughed and shouted, accompanied by the happy woof of big dogs and the *quonk* of many ducks. From somewhere behind the house the soprano bleat of goats sounded. I stretched in the sun, watching my child and the raccoon, thinking that unlike the Other Side of Pemberton, there were no hidden shoals and reefs and undercurrents here. It was possible, on this silver-gray porch above Goat Creek, in this autumn afternoon, simply to sit in the sun and *be*.

"Would you like to see the rest of the house?" Tom Dabney said.

"Yes," I said. "I really would."

"Come along, then. Hilary, bring Earl. It's more his house than mine."

We trooped behind him through a screened door off

the deck, and were in a great, low-ceilinged room, beamed with rough undressed cypress logs and walled only in screening. An enormous central fireplace of stone dominated it, and standing bookshelves spilling books out onto the tables and the floor made walls of sorts. Before the fireplace sat a shabby old sofa that had obviously been good, flanked by two old-fashioned morris chairs and ottomans. Above the mantel was the head of a magnificent twelve-point buck, wearing, around his great neck, a garland of autumn leaves. His antlers were intertwined with ivy, and there were ropes and garlands of leaves and ivy along the tops of the bookshelves. Stubs of candles sat in holders along the rough mantel beneath the buck's head, and kerosene lanterns were set on tables and shelves. Two or three guitars lay about the room. Off in a corner was another rolltop desk, twin to the one I had seen on the porch, and on it sat a personal computer and printer.

"I knew there had to be a serpent in Eden," I said.

"I gave up quill pens by firelight long ago," he said.

"What are the leaves and things for?" Hilary said, looking from his head to the buck's head on the fireplace.

"Thanksgiving decorations," he said. "Why should Christmas have all the fun?"

He led us around the freestanding fireplace and I saw that the other side of it lay in what must be his bedroom, or sleeping area. This was the screened room I had seen at the end of the porch; like it, the room stood on pilings over the creek, and I saw that he had positioned his bed so that when he lay in it, all he could see was the dark water and the trees of the Big Silver forest. Around the room were the components of an intricate sound system, with speakers mounted in the beams of the ceiling, and on the stone chimney hung an array of hunting weapons—a small, simple, seemingly old rifle, a larger, equally antique double-barreled shotgun, two or three beautiful bows like the one I had seen in his canoe that morning at King's Oak, an array of glittering, sharp-honed knives in various sizes. The chimney wore another wreath of foliage.

But it was the bed that dominated the room; it was enormous, larger even than a king-size, but obviously very old and very fine. It was a tester of mahogany that seemed to glow from within with age and polish, and it was completely shrouded in a canopy of gauzy fabric. It was beautiful, intricately carved, a bed for an aristocrat. It should have been a jarring note in all the rustic simplicity, but somehow it wasn't. On it lay a huge throw of what appeared to be very superior mink. I thought of what I had heard about Tom Dabney and the women who came to Goat Creek, and I blushed scarlet and turned away from the bed. The mental images it evoked were specific and very nearly pornographic.

He grinned again, not missing my discomfort.

"A sybarite's bed, obviously," he said. "It ought to be in Hugh Hefner's bedroom. But I came by it honestly. It was made in England for my great-grandfather Pinckney and shipped to Charleston by sail vessel; my mother gave it up gladly because it always embarrassed her. And the mink throw was an anniversary present from my second wife. She of the forked tongue. It was about the only thing I wouldn't let her have when she took off. It gets cold as hell out here in winter, and besides, you just have no idea how that thing feels on bare skin."

The grin widened.

"What do you do in winter?" I asked hastily. I saw no evidence of walls of any sort, other than screening.

"I have canvas awning things all around, that I keep

rolled up until it gets really cold," he said, and I saw them then, long rolls with leather laces, stowed neatly up against the tin roof.

"And I keep the fires going. And I stay in bed a lot. There's a very efficient electric blanket under there. Sometimes I pull the mattress in front of the fire in the living area, and just hole up in there for a month or two. Or I stay in the hot tub until my skin begins to slough off."

"Hot tub," I said. "Of course."

We walked around on the other side of the sleeping area and there it was, a large hot tub mounted on the deck out over Goat Creek, steaming gently. Behind a luminous Coromandel screen was a toilet, washbasin, and shower. Farther on on that stretch of porch stood a huge old cast-iron stove, a refrigerator, and an efficient double aluminum sink in a terra-cotta tile counter. The big Welsh breakfront I had seen from the car held dishes, linens, and cooking utensils. From the stove's oven drifted the unmistakable smell of roasting turkey, and a huge spatterware kettle bubbled softly on its top. I smelled bread baking, and the savory smell of onions, and other things, elusive and exotic and wonderful. Off this section of porch, in the soft earth of the creekbank, a great haunch of meat sizzled on a spit turned by small children, and ribs dripped slowly from an iron rack over a pit.

I looked at him. In the deep shade of the interior, with none of the lamps lit, only his light eyes and teeth gleamed, and the lopsided crown of leaves.

"Did you build it specifically for yourself?" I asked. "I can't imagine something like this just . . . happening."

"My father built the core of it years ago, when I was small and we still owned all the land along the creek and on the other side of the river," he said. His voice was noncommittal. "We used it for a hunting lodge; he and I used to come back up here in these woods and stay for days at a time, a week or two sometimes. I managed to hang on to it when my mother sold the property, and I did a little to it. Added the porches, got water and electricity brought in here, rounded up some furniture."

"And you've lived here since . . . when?"

"Since I graduated from Yale," he said. "Through thick and thin and storm and fair weather and two wives. Women love it at first: it's kind of a Rousseau noble-savage place, I guess. Romantic. But when the first frost hits, or the first heat wave, they don't tend to stick around. I don't know that I blame them."

"I would," Hilary said. "I would stay forever and ever. I wouldn't ever leave."

"I bet you wouldn't, at that, Princess," he said. He smiled down at her. "It would be nice to have a woods princess out here. Just what the spirits ordered."

"Spirits?" Hilary looked at him, and then at me. But she did not seem afraid, only interested.

"The spirits of the trees, and the animals, and the water," he said, smiling. "The oldest inhabitants of this place, or any place; the ones who make it all hang together and work. Good guys, all of them, but very definite about needing a princess. Keep after me all the time."

"Can you see them?" she said seriously. I looked narrowly at him. Fancy was one thing; this magical place seemed to call for a measure of it. But enough was enough.

"Nope," he said. "They don't mess with me much. I think maybe they only talk to princesses. But I sure do know they're around. They give me general hell when I don't do it right, show enough respect. Like to run me out with rainstorms and floods and lightning and thunder and bugs and stuff."

She smiled, slowly, faintly.

"They're just a . . . fig of your imagination, aren't they?"

"Well, you know, it all depends on your point of view," he said. "What's real and what's not. What's real out here might not be real in town. It's a matter of context."

But she was not listening. She had gone over to an easel standing in the shadows and drawn away the cloth that covered it.

"Gee," she said. "This is pretty. Who did this?"

I walked over to look at it. He followed us. When I was close enough to see in the gloom, I made a small sound of surprise and delight. It was a watercolor of a deer, very like the one I had seen in his canoe, and the one on the hood of his truck. And it was simply and exquisitely beautiful.

He had roughed in line and mass with what appeared to be a nearly dry brush, and laid on form and shadow with broad, simple washes of pure colors that seemed to have come directly out of the earth. There was little detail, but the slender body and legs and delicate head were so alive that I could almost see them move, and the white tail and belly seemed to flicker. The sensation of movement and life was enormous and almost palpable on the creamy, rough paper. It was primitive and sophisticated at once, and the degree of skill and mastery was extraordinary. It reminded me of something: elusive familiarity niggled in my mind. And then I had it: it could have come right off the walls of the great caves at Lascaux, in France.

"You did this, didn't you?" I said, knowing somehow that he had.

"Yes," he said. "Everything I kill, before I eat it, I try to paint it. You learn an enormous lot that way. And it sort of . . . keeps the animal alive."

"Well, it's a lovely thing," I said. "You're very talented. But wouldn't it be simpler just to let the animal live in the first place?"

"Well, you see, then I wouldn't have him," he said.

"Will you paint my horse?" Hilary said. "He isn't really mine, but I ride him more than anybody. Or "—and I could see her remember the ugly little scene with Pat Dabney, and her voice dropped—"I used to."

"I don't do horses," Tom Dabney said. "Too ordinary. Too . . . tame. Tell you what, though. After supper we'll go see the goats and you can pick one out and I'll paint him for you. A goat, now, is worthy of a good tube of paint. Very complicated and smart and useful animal, a goat is."

"Is Goat Creek named for your goats?" she said. Hilary had talked more to this man since we had been here than to anyone in days and days. I was both delighted and, obscurely, annoyed.

"No," he said. "Nobody knows why it's called Goat Creek. I brought the goats out so there'd be goats at Goat Creek. It seemed the right thing to do for the creek."

Carter called to us from the porch then, and by the time we got back outside, Clay Dabney was there with a small, pretty, prattling white-haired woman whom Tom introduced to us as his Aunt Daisy. She was an engaging little woman, but her patter and archness seemed somehow ill-fitted to the old-lion's dignity of her husband, as if he had somehow married beneath him.

"Sorry we're late," Clay said to his nephew, accepting a glass of the punch. "Whew. Good batch, Tom. Chip has got him a live one in town looking the place over with an eye to bringing a group in to do some hunting. Says he's some kind of German prince, some Hohenzollern or something. Looks like one, a little green suit with knickers and a Perugini-Visini custom job look like it must have cost him around twenty thousand dollars. Chip wanted me to take him around King's Oak because he was interested in the history of the place, and Chip don't know crap about that."

"Well, I hope you land him," Tom said. "Sounds like a prince could drop a little change."

"Chip says he thought he could get him to go a couple of hundred thousand," Clay Dabney said. "It's a big group he wants to bring. I don't know if they're Germans like him, or Yankees. I think the prince lives in New York City now. But I ain't betting on it. When I left them, His Royal Pain in the Ass was asking if there wasn't someplace wilder he could look at. Chip was practically wetting his pants."

"I bet." Tom Dabney grinned.

We sat down in deck chairs, and Tom brought Carter and me glasses of the punch from the washtub. It was potent and strange, with a wild, sweet, smoky taste and a slight viscosity, like thin honey. I did not think I liked it, and then I did. I looked at Tom questioningly.

"It's mead," he said. "Or as close as we can come to it nowadays. Martin learned how to make it in Greece, and we make up a batch every now and then. Watch it. It's got a kick like a mule."

"What's in it?" I said, licking my lips.

"Oh, honey from up the creek, that Scratch brings. Herbs and stuff that he gets back in the swamp. This and that. The base is pure grain alcohol, because we don't really know what made the original so potent. I don't recommend it over good bourbon, but it's kind of a Thanksgiving tradition," Tom said.

I was still sipping on my cup when three people rounded the house and came up onto the porch.

"Christ," I heard Tom Dabney murmur under his breath, and turned to look at the newcomers. Chip Dabney was there, in an astonishing outfit of poisonous loden green, with a short jacket, knickers, heavy cabled socks, and great, shining new cobbled boots. On his thinning blond hair he wore a green Alpine hat with a grouse feather in its band, and a chamois tag. The afternoon sun glinted on his feathery mustache, and smoke curled from a carved pipe in his hand, and he looked altogether like a toy burgher on a Swiss clock. His face was ruddy with sun and alcohol; I could smell the gusts of bourbon that blew before him before he came up to me. With him was Francis Millican, the dour potentate of the Big Silver plant, whom I had met at the King's Oak barbecue, looking as incongruous as Chip did, in stiff, creased new blue jeans and a raw, blaring plaid shirt and orange down vest. The third man in the party was, had to be, the captive prince from Germany.

He was dressed in an outfit identical to Chip Dabney's, but his was obviously better cut and well worn, and his cobbled boots were polished to a soft shine. He was short and solid and had a snub face and very short white-blond hair and eyebrows, and his cheekbones were so high that they gave his face a Mongol look. I would have bet that there was Hungarian or some other Eastern European blood there: Austro-Hungarian Empire, perhaps, if the prince really was a prince. He looked cold and mean, despite the crinkling blue eyes and snub nose. He, too, might have been a figure on a clock, but a much more expensive clock. His hands were soft and pink and dimpled over the knuckles, not the hands of a hunter or an outdoorsman. He was smiling hugely.

Chip swaggered forward and presented him to Tom and his guests as Prince Wilhelm Wentz-Graf of Germany.

"But you can call him Willi," Chip said. "He sure doesn't

act like a prince, if you know what I mean. He's an investment banker in New York."

"Chip, Frank," Tom Dabney said, affably enough, but there was something under his voice like a reef in warm water.

"Willi," he said, holding out his hand to the prince.

He did not say Welcome.

"I am charmed," Prince Willi said, bowing over Tom's hand. His voice was harsh and low, but his smile was brilliant. "I hope you do not mind our intruding ourselves. My friend Chip says you have a wonnerful place what is wild and natural. I have come South looking for such a place for my party to hunt. We haf hunted all over the world, and now we look for some novel place what is not spoilt, where we can shoot the wild pig and your white-tailed deer. Chip says there are many in your woods. I would like to guarantee my party many trophies."

Tom and Clay Dabney both turned to look at Chip, who smiled blandly. But I noticed that he could not keep his feet still under the twin blue gazes.

"I know, you don't lease your land, Tom," he said heartily. "But what the hell, Willi here can pay you enough for a week's shooting so you can take a year's leave of absence. I thought you might change your mind this once. Hell, of course I'd like to sell him on King's Oak, but if he wants really wild, well, there ain't no wilder than this, hardly. Be nice to have a prince on family land."

Clay Dabney looked silently at his son. There was something like shame in his blue eyes. Tom did not change his expression.

"This is not family land, Chip," he said levelly. "It's my land. And I don't lease it. Not even"—and he smiled perfunctorily at the looming Willi—"to princes."

"I just thought this once . . . ," Chip began.

"You didn't think at all," Tom Dabney said. "Or you wouldn't have bothered to come out. Or maybe you did think. I'd be interested in knowing what you thought, Chip."

"You might at least be polite," Chip said, his pink face flaming scarlet. "Willi has come a long way."

"Looks to me like you're the one who needs a little etiquette lesson, Chip," Clay Dabney said mildly. But his eyes on his son had darkened with something nearer anguish than shame. "I don't recall that Tom invited you and your company to his house."

"Well, I knew you and Mother were coming, and I thought as long as it was family . . . ," Chip muttered sullenly. Frank Millican was looking off into the distance across the creek in obvious distaste, staring at the place where, I thought, Tom's woods became his. Prince Willi did not seem to suffer from Millican's distaste or embarrassment. He turned his burred yellow head from one Dabney to another, watching and listening with interest.

"This is a wonnerful place, this house and this creek," he said. "It is just what my people are looking for. They are Europeans, like me, far from home and accustomed to shooting in the wild places in Europe and Asia. This is more like what we know than anything I haf seen, lovely though Chip's King's Oak is. If you could guarantee me game I will buy it from you. Or I can even stock it myself. I would be very generous."

"Goat Creek is not for sale," Tom Dabney said. He had not changed his tone, but it was suddenly ice and iron. "And I don't bait fields and woods."

Willi's big face reddened, and Chip's flush turned nearly purple. Tom had a ring of white around his mouth, but his face was still and composed. Clay Dabney rose from his seat and ambled toward his son. He put his hand on Chip's shoulder.

"You said you had some folks coming in out to the airstrip at three, Chip," he said in his deep drawl. "It's past that now. And Tom's got a mob to feed. Why don't you get Frank to take you back in the Big Silver's woods and see what the prince thinks of them? They're virtually the same as these, except for the house. And Tom's little old place wouldn't sleep but three or four, anyway."

"I would see to extra sleeping accommodations," Prince Willi said, his equilibrium restored. "It would be simple to build them. It is a great pity Mr. Dabney does not want to sell; his house is most charming. Most . . . old world. But I will respect his wishes. How about it, Mr. Millican? Perhaps we go and look at your woods? If you can assure me, of course, that you haf not poisoned the air and water with your bombs, so that all we would haf to shoot was six-legged deer and other monsters."

He laughed loudly. Frank Millican gave him a flat gray stare.

"Our plant is as clean as a restaurant kitchen, Prince," he said. "No monsters. No six-legged deer. I'd be pleased to show you the woods. We lease our land to hunters from time to time."

"Well, then, let us go and leave Mr. Dabney and his guests to their dinner," Prince Willi said, grinning all around the circle of staring faces. He bowed again, lowly and stiffly. "It smells most excellent. Perhaps, Mr. Dabney, you will come and be the cook for my group when we return?"

"Perhaps I will, Prince Willi," Tom Dabney said. "I am nothing if not creative."

Clay Dabney tightened his grip on his son's shoulder

and walked him around the corner of the house. The prince and Frank Millican trailed away in their wake.

"If that guy is a prince, I'm the grand vizier of all the Russias," Charlie said, half amused, half angry. "I'll bet his name is Willie Graft from Secaucus, and he rented his little suit from a costume place. But where do you suppose Chip got his?"

"You ought to fumigate the place, Tom," Phipps Carrington said from his post at the rail. "'I'll stock it myself,' my ass. I bet he's never hunted a field in his life that wasn't baited."

"Oh, I'll clean the place, all right," Tom Dabney said, his smile easy. But the white ring remained around his mouth. "Clean and sanctify it good and proper. Pity Uncle Clay can't do the same to King's Oak."

"I go give King's Oak a good cleaning terreckly," the old black man, Scratch Purvis, said. His voice was rusted and ruined, a gentle wheeze. He had not spoken since we had arrived. I looked curiously at him, and he smiled. It was a singularly sweet smile, white and full, and I smiled back.

"Yeah, Scratch has got a formula that'll detoxify any place," Tom Dabney said, grinning again. "Get rid of anything from Prince Willi to vampires. Anybody got any vampires they want run off their place, Scratch is the man to do it."

We all laughed, including Scratch, and suddenly the afternoon was all right again. Clay Dabney, coming back around the house, said, briefly, "Sorry, Tom. I didn't think he'd bring that asshole out here. I told him not to. I don't think he'll do it again."

"It's okay, Uncle Clay," Tom said, smiling at him. "It really is. Prince Willi will give us something to dine out on all winter long."

We all laughed again, and then it was time to eat.

The absent children came running in from the creek-bank, and we all filed past the laden buffet table and filled our plates, Hilary keeping close to Carter and me but looking at Tom Dabney out of the corner of her eyes. Earl had plopped down from her shoulder, finally, and ambled off the porch and disappeared.

"He has a lady friend under there," Tom said. "They've been living together for three years now, but she won't marry him. He's too big a slob. Her name's Raquel the Unwell; when I first spotted her, she was so languid and pale that I thought she was sick, but it turned out she was pregnant. She's had a litter every spring since she took up with Earl, and still won't tie the knot."

Hilary giggled and we sat down to eat. It was a proper feast, venison ribs and chili and haunch, and wild turkey that Scratch had shot way up Goat Creek, and cornbread dressing that was Martin Longstreet's specialty, and some kind of wild greens seasoned with meat and herbs that was smoky and delicious, which the lawyer Reese Carmody had prepared.

"Watercress," he said, smiling through his fog of alcohol. "From my creek. Makes a nice mess of greens, doesn't it?"

Tom brought out chilled white wine and soft drinks for the children, and we had a toast to the season, and then, before we ate, he bowed his dark head and said, simply, "Thank you for these woods and this water, and for their bounty, which we partake of again at this Thanksgiving feast. Bless those of us who have gathered to celebrate and share them, and give us a good winter and another spring."

I shot a look at his dark face while he said the words. It was a strange and formal and old-fashioned sort of blessing, and I had not, somehow, expected him to give one.

But it was oddly touching, there in all that wildness, in the sunlit silence. When he finished, Martin Longstreet and Reese Carmody and Scratch Purvis murmured, with him, "Amen."

We ate until we could eat no more. I do not think I have ever eaten such a good meal. The air was like wine, and the wine itself, and the mead before it, relaxed me to the point that hunger took over from worry, and I ate with a relish I had not felt in many months, not since before Hilary and I had come to Pemberton, before the ugly night that spelled the end of my marriage. I looked over at Hilary, who was busily munching, too, surreptitiously tossing scraps to Earl, who had come up from the creek to station himself under her chair. When we finished, and were sitting about groaning contentedly and drinking rich hot coffee with a wild liqueur that was "like retsina, but not quite; Martin makes it," the shadows were growing long and blue, and the air was cooling fast.

"We need to be getting back," Tish said lazily. "Tom, I wish you'd play something for us before we go. The end to an absolutely perfect day."

He went in and got the big Martin, and brought something small and bright from the living room, and tossed it to Martin Longstreet. I saw that it was a flute.

"Will you do me the honors, Doctor?" Tom said.

"Be happy to," said the dean in his rich bass.

As if they had decided on it beforehand, Tom and Martin Longstreet began to play. It was a strange, minor tune, almost a monotone, with a wildness in it, a kind of wailing that would have, if there had been words, been a chant. It sounded very old, and almost Oriental, but there was an Indian note to it, too, that of one of the High Plains Indians of the Americas. There was a lot of repetition, and almost no major chords. Into the third repetition, Tom Dabney began to sing, but the words were not English, or any language that I had ever heard. As they had been on the day he played Dylan Thomas for me, his eyes were closed and his face was rapt. He sang softly, in the strange old language, and on the last repetition Reese Carmody joined in, in a pure, high tenor, and Scratch Purvis, in a surprisingly true bass. When they finished, there was a long, brimming pause, in which the last plangent notes of flute and guitar seemed to hang, thrilling. Tish broke the silence, at last.

"Tom, that was beautiful," she said. "What was it? I've never heard anything like it."

"Martin learned it up East," Tom said. "He taught it to us. It's an Eskimo chant of thanksgiving for a good hunting season, and a blessing for the coming winter. Appropriate for today, don't you think?"

"Very," Tish said. "Where did you learn it, Dr. Longstreet?"

"I got to know Joe Campbell when he was teaching at Sarah Lawrence," Martin Longstreet said. "He was about the greatest folklorist and mythologist we've had. Had some wonderful stuff on tape. That was one of them."

The children, restive with the grownup talk and the music, dashed back down to the creek edge to play, calling to Hilary to come with them, but she shrank back, eyes large, and said nothing.

"Come on in the living room, Hil," Tish said. "I hear Tom's silly ducks in there. You ought to meet them. They think they're his children."

Hilary got up and put her hand in Tish's, and they disappeared into the house. Tom Dabney looked over at me.

"Something frightened her," he said. "What was it? Is she afraid of water?"

"Some of the children who live way up the creek, who

are in her class at school, told her an awful thing about the creek water lighting up and burning, and turning her blood black, and rotting her bones," I said. "It was just children's talk, you know, trying to make the new kid squirm. But it came at a bad time for her; she's not really been well since . . . since we came to Pemberton. And it just hit her wrong. She's been absolutely terrified of water ever since. I can't seem to make her see that it was all just a tall tale."

Tom looked at me for a moment, then over at Scratch Purvis. The old man looked back tranquilly.

"I've seed that," he said. "I've seed that creek light up. Don't know about no bones rotting, but it ain't no tall tale."

"Yeah, and you know it's swamp gas," Tom Dabney said impatiently. "What the old folks used to call a jack-o'-the-swamp, or will-o'-the-wisp. Marsh gas. Every country has it, and every culture has myths about it. It doesn't mean anything, except that somewhere down in the mud at the edge of the swamp, something's rotting that's producing methane. That's what those kids saw."

"Might do be," Scratch said. "But there it is, just the same. It mean somethin', too; it mean somethin' coming. But I don' know what. I ain't seed it before."

"You're an ignorant old goat," Tom Dabney said, fondly and in exasperation. "Bet your door's as blue as a dead mackerel. I'll take her out and show her swamp gas and where it comes from one day, Diana, if you'll let me."

"Let it be for a while," I said. "She's been better today than she's been in a long time. It's the animals, I think. I'm very grateful to you for that. Don't let's push it."

"Okay," he said. "But when you think she's ready. It's a shame to live in Pemberton and be afraid of the water."

The talk drifted and waned, and one by one, people got up and made their farewells and drove away into the fast-falling twilight. Carter got to his feet and held his hand out to me, and Tom said, "I wish you all would stay for a little while. There's going to be one of the year's great sunsets tonight, and an early moonrise. It's something to see this time of year."

And because I simply did not feel like moving out of the chair and the soft blue air, I said, drowsily, "Okay, if Carter can. Hilary's never really seen a Pemberton sunset, I don't think."

"Okay by me," Carter said.

Tom went into the house and brought sweaters for me and Carter, and wrapped Hilary in a soft woolen afghan. He brought the Martin, too, and leaned it against his chair. Earl came and sat on Hilary's shoulder again, chirring softly. We were still on the porch as the afternoon grayed out, and then, as suddenly as if someone had thrown a switch, the world went crimson and magenta and gold, and the sky over the creek flamed into unearthly beauty. I have never seen anything quite like it; it looked like I have always thought the aurora borealis might look. Great streamers of gold and red and pink and purple spread across the sky, and above it, in the last unearthly blue of the day, the white ghost of a full moon rose.

I felt tears of joy come into my eyes, and looked at my daughter. Her eyes were as round as saucers, and she sat perfectly still, cheek buried in the raccoon's fur, lips slightly parted, staring at the sky. Tom Dabney smiled, as if at a welcome old friend. No one spoke. I scarcely breathed.

As suddenly as it had come, the sunset flared out and it was night. The low moon swelled into translucent whiteness, hanging huge and magical just over the treetops, and the world turned the black and silver of a photographic negative. Goat Creek burned with a cold radiance; the water and the air and the fringing reeds were pure silver, alive and flaming. Hilary made a little sound: was this what the children had meant?

Tom looked at her thoughtfully, and picked up the Martin and began to play and sing, softly. He sang an old 1960s song that I had always loved:

Moon River, wider than a mile,
I'm crossing you in style someday. . . .
Dream maker, you heart breaker,
Wherever you're going, I'm going your way. . . .
Two drifters, off to see the world,
There's such a lot of world to see. . . .
We're after the same rainbow's end,
Waiting 'round the bend,
My huckleberry friend,
Moon River . . . and me.

Hilary looked at him, and at the moon-burning creek. She smiled, very slightly, and he smiled back. He reprised it, a little run of chords as silver as the moonlight, and the smile widened into a grin.

"How about it, Hilary Calhoun?" he said. "Our song."

Her smile widened, too.

From beneath the porch, another raccoon appeared and made its stately way across the silver grass to the water's edge, and waddled into it, paddling in the shallows like a child. Earl jumped down from Hilary's shoulder and made off after it, and soon they were playing together like two children in the sparkling shallows. It was an enchanting sight. I smiled, and Hilary laughed aloud, her fears forgotten.

"That's Raquel, Earl's lady," Tom said. "They'll play awhile before they settle down to fishing for their supper. What say, Hilary? Want to go down and join them?"

She looked at him mutely, her eyes black in the moonlight, longing and fear so plainly intermingled on her face that I wanted to shout at him.

He leaned over and took her shoulders in his hands.

"Hilary," he said, "you don't ever have to be afraid here. There are a lot of things in the world you're right to be afraid of, but they are not here. Never here. I was never afraid here, and my boys never have been, and you don't have to be, either. Goat Creek is a special place. It makes you well; it doesn't hurt you. Goat Creek will never hurt you. That's a promise. Come on. I'll take you down."

Slowly he got to his feet, still with his hands on her shoulders, and just as slowly she rose, and together they walked down the wooden steps onto the burning silver grass and across the yard toward the place in the willow fringe where the raccoons played.

"No," I said under my breath, and started to rise and go after them. What did this fool think he was doing with my daughter?

"No," Carter said, just as softly. "Wait." He put his hand on my arm, and I sank back into my chair.

At the edge of the creek, Tom Dabney leaned down and whispered something to Hilary, and she nodded, and they both bent and took off their shoes and socks and rolled up the cuffs of their pants. Tom Dabney threw back his head and began to sing. Standing there with the silver radiance pouring down over him, he sang, "'By the light . . . of the silvery moon . . . I want to spoon . . . with my honey I'll croon . . . love's tune . . .'" Then he sang, "'Shine on, shine on, harvest moon . . . ,'" and then he began to dance. In the pouring moonlight, like something out of antiquity, like a lissome god of night and wild places, he sang and danced on the banks of Goat Creek, sang in a pure, rollicking tenor, full of laughter and joy, danced a merry and intricate and exuberant little dance.

Hilary joined him. She took a few small, stumbling steps with her bare feet, and then, throwing back her head, began to sing along with him, and dance like the animated elf she used to be, like a leaf born aloft on an eddy of silver, like a feather caught and whirled in pure light.

He took her hands and twirled her around, and they sang and sang and sang, the dark, silver-stained man and my silver-dipped child: "'By the light of the silvery moon.'" "'Shine on, harvest moon . . .'" They danced and whirled and sang, and they laughed.

When they finished the song they ran without pause straight into the shallow water of Goat Creek, and capered and splashed and cavorted in the flying silver, stooping now and then to splash great handfuls of water on each other, drowned and dripping and haloed in silver. Around them the two raccoons capered and pranced like dogs. Above them the great moon rode higher into the sky, and their voices rode with it: "'*Shine* on, *shine* on . . .'"

Carter did not move and he did not speak, and afterward I never could say, could not have said, how long I sat on that moonburned porch with tears running down my face, watching my daughter dance and sing in the moonlight in the silver water of Goat Creek.

CHAPTER SIX

"So what do you think now?" Tish said, pouring herself a second margarita from the pitcher Charlie had left on the sideboard. It was the Sunday after Thanksgiving, and Carter and I had gone over to their house for huevos rancheros about noon. Hilary had gone, almost reluctantly, out to Pat Dabney's stable. It had been many days since she had taken Pittypat out. Since the night on Goat Creek she had been begging to go back and choose her own personal goat, as Tom had promised. But I had been reluctant to take her.

"Well," I said, rolling the tart-sweet drink around on my tongue and stretching my legs out toward the fire, "it's nice. It really is. More than nice; you know that. Everybody's been wonderful to Hilary and me, you and Charlie most of all. And it's certainly never boring. I haven't spent a night at home in weeks. And it's peaceful. Lord, after Atlanta it's like living in Eden."

"But," Tish said.

"But . . . well, it really is the Lilly and Laura Ashley and Cullinane capital of the world, isn't it?"

"Not a jot or a tittle more than Buckhead," Tish said comfortably. "I didn't mean Pemberton. I meant Tom's party. All that."

"It was okay," I said. "It was nice, too."

Carter stared at me over the salt-encrusted rim of his glass. He did not say anything. He had been very quiet since he'd brought Hilary and me home from Goat Creek.

I knew I was going to have to talk with him about that night. It was too potent, too altogether extraordinary, to leave to silence. It hung, full and finished, in the air between us. And I knew that he would not mention it; it was for me to broach. As badly as I wanted to wrap it in silence and keep if for myself, he deserved its sharing. He had been a part of it, witness to the moment. Without his staying hand on my arm, it would not have happened.

I asked him in for coffee when we got home from Tish and Charlie's, and he came, and settled into the place on the sofa in front of the fireplace that had become his. He looked around the room almost as if he had never seen it before, his blue eyes lingering on this object and that, his hands shoved deep into the pockets of his corduroy pants. Once he smiled faintly, at a jumble of photographs in a copper bowl on the coffee table, which I had not gotten around to mounting in an album yet. Most of them were of him and me and Hilary, taken at the track and the stables and on a picnic out at the nearby Indian mounds, and at the Baines County Fair back in October. Three months of Carter and Andy and Hilary, caught laughing in time, a mini-epoch in a copper bowl, a microcosmic world, like a terrarium.

I put on an album of Ella Fitzgerald singing Cole Porter, and that incredible voice, like old gilt overlaid with smoke, curled into the room. We sat in silence for a time, listening.

"'. . . so carefree together that it does seem a shame, that you can't see your future with me,'" Ella sang. "' 'Cause you'd be oh, so easy to love.'"

Carter looked up at me and grinned. It was a sweet grin, and under it there was pain. I felt the pain in my own heart.

"It does seem a shame," he said.

"What?" I said, dreading what was coming. "What seems a shame?"

"You know. That you can't see your future with me."

"Don't be silly," I said, my heart beginning to pound. "Who said I couldn't? Carter, you know we said we weren't going to push this until I thought I could handle it."

"Sorry," he said. "I know we did. But I think I have to push it now, Andy. I think I have to know now. I think I lost you a week ago out at Goat Creek. I think I know just when it happened."

"No," I said. "No. Something did happen, you're right, but it wasn't your losing me. It wasn't me it happened to. . . ."

He looked at me levelly.

"But you're going out there again, aren't you?" he said.

"Yes," I said, knowing only then that I was. "Of course I am. Of course we are. You saw her, Carter. You know what happened to her. Carter, I'd go down into hell with

Adolph Eichmann to keep her the way she's been since then. To keep it happening. So would you, if she was yours."

"I know," he said. "Sometimes it seems as if she is mine. I just . . . Andy, don't go away from me."

His wonderful voice was low and washed in hurt. He seemed to speak out of an old and bottomless gulf of pain. The quietness of his words was worse than a keen of anguish.

My heart turned over with the heaviness of his pain. I could actually feel it, like a fish or an aquatic creature flip-flopping in my chest. I felt tears rise behind my eyes, followed by a swift surge of fear that was near panic. Suddenly I wanted the safety and familiarity of his hard freckled arms, wanted to lose the throbbing sense I had of Goat Creek and the moon-silvered wildness of it, and the silver madman dancing in its shallows.

I slid across the sofa and pressed myself against him, scrubbing my face into the hollow of his neck and shutting my eyes tight against all the dancing black and silver. He put his arms around me and held me close, and rested his chin on the top of my head.

"I won't go away from you. I won't," I said fiercely. "I want to be close to you, I want to get closer. . . . Carter, please make love to me."

And he did. There on the sofa before my rented fireplace, in the enchanted cottage in the bewitched bronze woods of Pemberton, the good, big man who had been my rock and my anchor for three careening months became also my lover. I had known almost since we met that he would be, and had been afraid of that time, afraid with all the fear and horror and disgust that Chris had left as his legacy, afraid also of the ravenous darkness within me. But he had scarcely entered me before I knew that it would be all right.

He was slow and gentle, almost as a father might be, putting a small daughter to bed. He took my clothing from me piece by piece and kissed the cool bareness that it left, murmuring softly in his good voice, and whispering words of ineffable sweetness. His big hands seemed to value me, and his hardness slipping into me was slow and careful, so that his very manhood seemed to cherish me. I relaxed and rode with him, finding the deep rhythm, settling my legs around him, rocking in a dreamlike fugue of sweetness and tenderness, eyes closed, mind empty. After what seemed a very long time I felt him quicken and swell, and his warmth inside me become almost scalding; heard the soft words become urgent and breath-torn; felt the slow sliding become faster and more insistent. I quickened my own hips and tightened my thighs and lifted myself up beneath him, waiting for the great arc of heat and fire, and the helpless chain explosion, and the swift slide into blackness and wildness. I waited for my own atonal wail of abandonment and loss. None came. I heard his cry and felt his climax, but I felt only the lightening of his weight upon me, and the intrusive coolness of the air on my nakedness, where he had lain. It was over and I had not lost myself. I felt a surge of relief that was near joy. Nothing would be asked of me with this man, then. I would not have to pay for this love.

He pulled me over on top of him, and we lay for a time, my eyes closed in contentment, his breathing slowing.

"I love you, Andy," he said presently.

"Carter, dear love . . . ," I began. I felt rather than saw the grin on his face; the muscles of his cheek moved against mine.

"You don't have to repay me in my own coin," he said.

"I don't want to hear 'I love you' from you right now; you wouldn't mean it. But I would like to know that you care for me."

"I do. I do care," I said gratefully and fullheartedly. "That was wonderful for me. You'll have to take my word that it was."

But far down within me, as faint and far away as a ghost of an echo on a thunderous night, something cried out, some emptiness wailed: "Fill me!"

"This calls for a celebration," I said, so as not to hear it. "I have apple brandy and one ancient can of Moosehead. Take your pick."

And we dressed and he built up the fire and we drank a toast to this autumn beginning, and I would not hear the voice, not look into the place where the image of that cold radiance out on Goat Creek burned, burned. From that instant I redoubled my efforts to live completely in the meager reality of my job in the Public Relations Office at Pemberton State College. I strove with all my being to become more completely a citizen of Carter's Pemberton world over here. I went out of my way to avoid Tom Dabney at school, and I did not see him in the town. I kept Hilary so busy with play dates and holiday crafts and riding that she did not seem to miss her newfound love. For almost two weeks it worked astonishingly well.

But of course, in the end we went back. The pull of Goat Creek was too deep and tidal in Hilary to keep her away; she had, after all, been reborn there. And she had fallen in love with Tom Dabney, with all the shy, savage, single-minded passion of a lonely child, and after the renewed flash flood of enthusiasm for horses and riding had topped out and found its channel, she began to beg for another visit. She nagged me until I found her a recording of Henry Mancini's "Moon River," and she played it for hours, day in and day out, until I begged for surcease.

"You're going to make me sick of that song, and it's a wonderful song," I said. "Aren't you just the slightest bit weary of it by now?"

"No," she said. "It's my song. Mine and Tom's. I'll never get tired of it."

I could not name the hot little pinprick of something that stabbed me at the childish words. But the complacency of them annoyed me. Irritation flared at Tom Dabney for so carelessly and easily capturing my daughter's heart.

"Lord, Hilary, he's not a movie star. He's just a man," I said tartly.

"No, he's not," she said. "You know what he is, Mama? He's the dream maker. You know, in 'Moon River'? That's Tom. The dream maker."

And I smiled, reluctantly. Because, in a way, he was.

But I did not give in to her begging until Tom passed us in his truck on the sidewalk outside the movie theater and shouted, "Hey, Hilary, there's a little brown goat waiting for you out at the creek." Then the brief hiatus of normalcy was over, and I knew it. I sought him out between classes the next day and said, almost formally, "When would be a good time for us to come out?" and he said, "How about after school today?" and I said, "Thank you very much. We'll see you then." And knew, as I closed the door on my side of the Toyota outside Hilary's school that afternoon, that I was driving toward something as huge in our lives as a birth . . . or a death.

He was nowhere in evidence when I parked the car on the turnaround in front of the house, but the old truck was there, and smoke drifted up from the big central fireplace. The day was warm again, and mellow with Indian summer, and the golds and reds and bronzes of the trees along and beyond the creek were muted, like old metal. The sky above the steep roof of the house was the soft, washed blue of the wire-grass autumn. I stood there beside the car, reluctant either to enter the house or to call out, Hilary tugging impatiently at my hand.

"He may be off in the woods somewhere, Hil," I said. "Why don't we wait in the car for a little while?"

But just then his voice called to us from the house.

"Come on in. I need some help holding this lady."

We found him inside in front of the fire, kneeling before a small, struggling form wrapped in an outsize scarlet terry towel. The bleating that emerged from the towel was so ridiculously young and distressed that I smiled involuntarily: Disney's magic might have fabricated it. The room was shadowy and close with the great fire going, and I saw that Tom Dabney was stripped to the waist, and that his smooth brown chest and shoulders dripped with water or sweat, and his blue jeans were mottled with moisture. His old boat shoes were sodden, and his hair was plastered to his narrow skull. From the back of the sofa Earl chattered and scolded, bobbing up and down on his hind legs like a fat old comic working a crowd.

"Thank God! The cavalry! Just in time." Tom Dabney grinned. His teeth were as white as a wolf's in the dark, pointed face, and his eyes gleamed blue. I thought again how essentially wild a face it was, despite the humor in it and the genuine gladness at our presence. He had the unselfconscious ease of manner of a wild animal in its habitat, totally focused outside itself.

"What's in the towel?" Hilary asked shyly, looking at

him obliquely from under her long, feathery lashes. The coquetry was as natural and spontaneous as his lush spirits, and I saw for an instant the woman she would be, looking at a man she found pleasing. For some reason the sight shocked me as profoundly as an electrical current might have. I looked away from her face toward his.

"Somebody who thought you were never coming," he said to her, and opened the towel. A very small goat stood there, yellow eyes wild, ears laid back in fear, silky taupe body racked with shudders and tremors. It had a white-striped face of great sweetness and charm, and white on the insides of its delicate, splayed legs. As we watched, it gave another despairing bleat, and Hilary caught her breath in a sigh of pure enchantment.

"Is it mine?" she said on a little wind of disbelief and joy.

"All nineteen pounds of her," Tom Dabney said. "She's a sweetheart, she is. Right now she's a little spooked because she's had a bath and gotten her hooves trimmed for the first time, and she doesn't like it a bit. But ordinarily she's got a disposition like a good bird dog, and there's nothing sweeter. In fact, she thinks she *is* a dog: follows you around and wags her tail and tries to sleep with you. So don't tell her she's a goat. It'll break her heart."

"What shall I tell her she is?" Hilary giggled. It was nearly her old giggle.

"Well, I've been telling her she is a princess," Tom said. "And in a way she is. Her daddy was a veritable king among goats. I've been calling her Artemis, after another princess who lived in the woods, but you can call her anything you want to. You can call her Modine Gunch if you'd rather."

Hilary put her finger out and the little goat ceased its struggling and looked at her with its yellow eyes. It seemed to me that a real and living perception leaped in them. It extended its white face and nibbled at the end of Hilary's finger with its rubbery black lips. Hilary laughed outright, and Tom Dabney did, too. His laugh sounded as young as hers.

"I'm going to call her Missy," she said. "For Artemis. Maybe when she's bigger I'll use her big name. How old is she?"

"She's about a month old," he said. "It's unusual for a kid to be born in the fall; most of them are born in the spring. But her mama and papa were never much for the rules, so here she is, six months later than she should be. That's one reason I brought her into the house; it was chilly when she was born, and the six-month-olds were jostling her pretty roughly. So now she has to live here with me, because if you bring a baby goat in that early, you've pretty much got to hand-raise her till she's a teenager. I take her out to her mama for meals, but she mostly lives in here with me and old Earl, and she sleeps with me under that fur throw. Those little hooves are murder, I can tell you."

"Where is her daddy?" Hilary said.

"He's dead," Tom Dabney said, as naturally as if he'd said, "Out in the barn."

Hilary looked at him with her ice-blue eyes.

"What killed him?" she said in a frail voice.

Tom Dabney looked back at her speculatively.

"It was just his time to die," he said.

"Was he old?"

"No. But he was ready," Tom Dabney said. I knew then that he had, in some way and for some reason, killed the goat himself. I could not have said how I knew. I rose from the ottoman where I had been sitting and put my hand on Hilary's shoulder. Her eyes had the old white ring around them.

"I hear the ducks down by the creek," I said. "Let's walk down and see what they're up to."

"No, wait," Tom said. He wrapped the towel back around the little goat and plopped her into Hilary's lap. The animal nestled against Hilary, butting her silky head into her shoulder.

"He had a good goat's death, Hilary," Tom said. "It was quick, it was painless, it was without fear, and it was necessary. And it brought honor to him. Death is different for animals. They're not like us; they don't worry about it beforehand. They're not afraid of it. For them, a good death is just another part of life, the last part. The important thing is that we try to give them a good life. That guy had a great life."

She did not say anything else, and turned her attention to the little goat in her arms. Strangeness prickled along my forearms, but I knew she felt none of it. By now I could read the signs in her like tracks in wet cement.

We headed around the house and down to the water's edge where the goathouse was, beyond a clump of showering yellow willows. Hilary ran ahead toward the silvery bleating, the little goat trotting behind her. Earl leaped to Tom Dabney's naked shoulder and rode there, chirring sleepily. I felt Tom's eyes on me, but I did not turn my head to look at him.

"You're bothered about the goat dying," he said.

"I won't have her upset, Tom," I said. "She's still too fragile to handle death and dying. You may mean well, but you can't possibly know what's best for her."

"I know that it isn't the truth that will hurt her," he said. "You can't stop her from being upset, Diana. Living in the world will, by its very nature, upset her sooner or later. Probably sooner. You can only try to make sure the wrong things don't upset her. A natural death shouldn't be one of them."

"Was it natural?" I turned to look at him.

"It was," he said matter-of-factly. "For him it was entirely natural."

"Okay," I said. "All right. But no more talk about it today. Can we at least agree on that?"

"Okay," he said. "But I'm not going to lie to her. I won't ever do that, Diana."

"Can't you manage to call me Andy?" I said in exasperation.

"No," he said.

The goathouse was a long, low structure of weathered gray board, like the house itself, with a gently sloping roof and a long skylight. A tangle of vivid red bushes grew up around it, and the late-afternoon sun gave the rough boards a mellow winesap glow. Inside, the floors were packed earth under deep chopped straw. The straw smelled warm and rich and musky, but pleasant, and the light filtering in was golden. There were perhaps six goats jostling about in stalls that gave onto wooden troughs, their heads protruding through the stall bars. All were munching quietly and busily on a fragrant grain mixture. The sweet smell of sun-dried hay mingled with that of clean, warm animal. I saw Hilary take a deep breath, and smile.

The goats all looked alike to me, but the little goat ran to one of them, bleating, and Tom Dabney let her into the stall, where she nuzzled at the bursting bag of the big brown doe and settled into a noisy sucking. The doe gave her a perfunctory swipe with her tongue and went back to her own dinner.

"Obviously, that's mama," Tom said. "Not exactly the maternal type, is Aphrodite here. But Artemis—Missy—is her first baby, so I'm hoping she'll improve with time. She's still a teenager herself, but she's one of the best milkers I've ever had. I've unloaded so much milk and cheese on all and sundry that people slam their doors when they see me coming."

"You make cheese?" Hilary said.

"Yep. Goat cheese is a great delicacy among the cognoscenti, of whom you will undoubtedly be one, Miss Hil. Better start early with it; it's an acquired taste. I make some of the best chèvre going, if I do say so myself. Full of all kinds of arcane herbs Scratch brings me. I draw the line at sun-dried tomatoes, though."

"What do the goats eat?" Hilary said. "Do they eat . . . chevy?"

"Never touch the stuff." He grinned. "No; they eat a great deal of the finest alfalfa hay going, raised by my friend and counsel, Reese Carmody, just for them. Spoiled ladies, the lot of them. And then I—we—make this grain mixture ourselves. You can buy goat feed, but mine seem to do better on this. It's got all kinds of things in it that are good for goats; Martin Longstreet worked the formula out for me, and Reese and Scratch raise it. Scratch comes and feeds for me if I have to be away. These gals are really a joint venture. Goat feeding is an exotic and delicate science; what they like is usually not what they should have. You have to think about things like nitrogen and ash and cobalt, and they need at least five different kinds of grains, in addition to good clover hay, and proteins, and then salt . . . and weeds. Some weeds are great for them, and all goats love all weeds, but some will just flat kill them, like lamb's-quarter and pigweed. Also a change in diet. A radical change from what they're used to means a sick goat. All kinds of things to think about . . . Scratch likes to add a little comfrey, and some other things that don't even have names, that he grows or gets out of the swamp, and Martin Longstreet has a bed of herbs he says goats in antiquity used to eat."

"Lord," I said. "I wonder you have time to do anything else."

"Well, I think goats are important," he said. "It means a lot to me to have goats at Goat Creek. And if you're going to do it, you might as well do it right. And like I said, I have a lot of help."

"They're an unlikely group of goat fanciers," I said.

"What they are is interested in everything," Tom Dabney said. "They make time for the things that interest them most. It's why I like them. The goats are a priority for all of us."

"They're practically royalty." I grinned, watching the goats dig into their food. They were beautiful animals, sleek and subtly colored and sweet-faced.

"They're Toggenburgs," he said. "They are royalty of sorts. They're the oldest breed we have. And by far the best milkers. These gals can give twelve thousand pounds of milk a year combined, if they put their hearts into it. Aphrodite is the only fresh doe I have now, because the others have just been bred and they won't freshen till near spring, when they kid. But Ditey alone will keep me and Missy in milk and cheese for the winter."

"Are they all girls?" Hilary asked. "Where are the boys?"

"I don't keep many of them," he said briefly. I shot him a glance. He caught it, and pointed to a separate stall down at the end of the barn, where the light from the skylight did not reach. In the blue shadows I saw the outline of a massive head thrust through the bars of a stall, munching placidly. The dark ears were forward, and a magnificent beard trailed into the grain.

"Virbius is this year's big bopper," he said. "A ten-month-old buck, one of the best I ever saw. I usually keep two, one for backup, but when old Virbius came out, I knew I had another king, so I only kept him. Not even his first birthday, and he's already got all the girls but one in the family way. When kidding season comes around, we'll really know what he's made of."

"Is he going to die, too?" Hilary said suddenly.

"Probably not for a long time," Tom Dabney said equably.

She did not pursue it further. We went back into the house, its windows like a lightship in the lowering November dark, the little goat pattering behind Hilary, Earl waddling off in search of Raquel and supper and bed.

"Stay for supper," Tom said. "I've got vegetable soup and cornbread and persimmon pie that Scratch's daughter sent me, from an old tree up Goat Creek that's over a hundred and fifty years old. Very few people in the world have eaten persimmon pie. I'll give you a drink while I cook, and Hilary can have a nap, if she likes."

His blue eyes took in her drooping lids.

"We really should be getting on back," I began.

"Mama, please," Hilary said urgently. "I want to see Missy asleep under the fur throw."

"Yes, please," he said. "There's something I want to show you after the moon rises. I won't keep you late."

"Are we going to dance again?" Hilary asked sleepily.

"Better than that. We're going to march."

"Mama . . . ," she said.

Suddenly my prowling spirits lightened and my heart lifted. I felt what she must feel, a simple, breath-held joy at the anticipation of what wonderful thing might come next, here in this magician's keep.

"Okay, sure," I said. "First persimmon pie, and then we march."

We tucked Hilary and the little goat into the deep bed, pulled the corrupt and beautiful mink throw over them, watched as goat and child wriggled and curled their way into sleep, and went back into the living area. Tom pulled a blue velour crewneck over his head and brushed his black hair out of his eyes and put Solti conducting Beethoven on the stereo. The music belled out, pure and huge. He built up the fire and brought me the Scotch I asked for, and made himself a dry martini on the rocks. He conducted Beethoven as he moved about in front of the big kitchen range, stirring and tasting and talking to himself or to me, I was not sure which.

"Tarragon? I think so, and maybe just a dab of basil, and lemon juice, and another good shot of sherry . . . there . . . da *dah* da, da *dah* da, da da da da da da. . . . God, that's beautiful, that's just so beautiful; imagine having that in your head."

"Are you talking to me?" I called lazily from in front of the fire, where he had given me one of his buttery old morris chairs and a soft, heathery old cardigan against the chill of the night.

"To you or whoever will listen, or no one," he said. "It's one of the perks of solitude, talking to yourself. A vastly underrated form of therapy. And a sure hedge against boredom. You never know who'll answer. . . . There. This should just about do it. You want to wake Hil, or let her sleep?"

"Let her sleep," I said. "She won't be hungry when she wakes; she never is. I'll give her something when we get home, if she wants it. She's into cereal and milk for supper these days."

"You're a good mother, aren't you, Diana?" he said seriously. "Maybe you hover a little much, but you really care about your child."

"Of course I do," I said, surprised. "Doesn't everybody who has one? No, of course they don't; that was a stupid thing to say. But . . . yes. I do care about her. Far, far more than anything."

"Then you are in grave danger of having your heart broken," he said, and I looked at him to see if he was speaking lightly. He was not; the blue eyes were very dark.

"Then so is every other parent who ever loved a child," I said. "What are you saying? That I should try to love her less?"

"No," he said. "That you should have something else you love as much, or nearly."

"I can't imagine loving anyone else like I do Hilary," I said stiffly. He was skirting very close to something entirely too tender for a new acquaintance.

"I didn't say someone," he said. "I said something."

"So what do you love as much as you love your boys?" I said. "Music, teaching, what?"

"The woods," he said simply. "I love the woods."

"That much?"

"Yes."

We were quiet as we ate the vegetable soup and the persimmon pie and drank a snapping dry white wine. Both the soup and the pie were as good as he had said. I had two helpings of both, and by the time he had made espresso on a belching old machine and brought it to me in front of the fire, it was full dark, and the creek and woods outside were beginning to whiten with the light of the rising moon. I turned my head to look at the track of it, creeping across the black water of Goat Creek. It was fully as wild and magical as it had been on that earlier night. I thought that living each night with the prospect of that must be a richness beyond imagining.

When Solti and the Ninth came crashing to a conclusion, Tom stretched and got to his feet.

"Ready to march?" he said.

"Well . . . are you really serious?" I said. It was getting toward nine o'clock. If we left at that moment, it would still be ten before I had Hilary bathed and in bed, and tomorrow was a school day for both of us. Larks in the night woods suddenly seemed less than magical.

"I am," he said. "It isn't far, and the moon's light enough so we can walk safely. I really want you to see this. It only happens in the fall and after dark, and maybe once or twice in any lifetime. If Hilary is too sleepy to walk I'll carry her, but I want her to come with us. She ought to know this is out here."

"I don't want her going back in the water, Tom . . . ," I began.

"Jesus, Diana, do you think I'm your local day-care child abuser? I'm not going to hurt Hilary. I've raised children. . . ."

"I want to go with you," Hilary said from the doorway, knuckling her eyes. I knew from her fretful tone that she was still sleepy, but I was suddenly tired of the fuss of my own voice, aware that I must sound like a doting fool of a mother in a television sitcom.

"Be my guest," I said dryly. "If Mr. Dabney feels like lugging all seventy pounds of you through the woods in the dark, that's his business."

"It will be my pleasure," Tom said.

"I can walk by myself," Hilary said with dignity.

Tom Dabney took a short, hooked knife matter-of-factly off the stone chimney and thrust it into his belt, pulled one of his sweatshirts over Hilary's thin Garfield tee, and led us out into the radiant night. Hilary stared at the knife and I raised my eyebrows at it, and he said, "For undergrowth. All the snakes have gone to bed for the winter, and I don't do alligators."

"By the way," I said, "where is it we're going?"

"To the river," he said. "I thought it was time you two met the Big Silver."

Moving more quietly than I could have imagined in the soft moccasins he had changed into, he walked out of the clearing and paused at the edge of the trees along Goat Creek to wait for us. I looked back for Hilary, and when I turned my head again he had vanished. I stared stupidly at the line of trees. The moonlight was almost as bright as day; I should have been able to see him. But I did not.

There was a slight movement, as if the shadows had reassembled themselves, and he was there again, where I had last seen him.

"How did you do that?" Hilary asked.

"I've watched deer do it all my life," he said. "It's a matter of moving very slowly, almost in slow motion, and sort of thinking your feet into the next step. You focus your mind on the woods and the trees and the ground, and try to feel like a part of them, made of the same stuff, and somehow you do become a part of them. It's not magic. Most good trackers can do it. Scratch does it better than anybody I ever saw."

"Could I learn to do it?" Hilary asked.

"I expect you could, if you could sort of get outside yourself in your mind and into the woods. I think you might be good at it one day."

"Could Mama?"

"She could," he said. "I don't know if she ever will."

We crossed the creek on a sturdy log footbridge and moved east.

Once we were out of the clearing, the huge hardwoods closed over our heads in a canopy, so that in high summer the moonlight could not have filtered through. But with most of the leaves down, enough light dappled the spongy ground so that, following Tom Dabney's silent feet, we could walk with relative ease. There was little undergrowth. The earth was felted with a thick layer of damp matter; leaves, mostly, I thought, but I could feel the crunch of countless acorns beneath my sneakers, too, and the wet paleness of dead fern bracken brushed my ankles. Beside me, her hand in mine, Hilary trudged determinedly, looking about her with the single-minded absorption of the curious child. I wondered if she was at all afraid. I felt no tension of fear in her fingers. My own nape and forearms crawled with wildness and the rustlings and ploppings of I knew not what, but I felt no outright alarm. That, I thought, was odd. I had never been comfortable in the woods.

Ahead of us, not breaking the silken padding of his stride, Tom Dabney talked softly.

"The Big Silver Swamp isn't more than five miles wide at any point, but it runs half the length of the state," he said. "It's part of the Mississippi alluvial plain. There were twenty-four million acres of it once. Now there are less than five million left. It's been lumbered out, or like here around Pemberton, it's been drained for soybeans. But what's left is some of the oldest woodland in the world. Some of the plants and animals, like the tupelos, the salamanders and garfish and alligators, are living fossils. They haven't changed to speak of in millions of years. And a few of the world's rarest creatures still hang out back in here. I've seen cougars, and a red wolf, and I think maybe I saw an ivory-billed woodpecker once, though the conventional wisdom is that I couldn't have. But I still think I did. You can't find any wilder woods anywhere in the world than these around the Big Silver, though that's changing fast."

At my side, Hilary said, "Are there any—you know—big animals?"

"Like what? Like tigers?" Tom Dabney's voice, amused, drifted back.

"I know there aren't any tigers here. I meant like bears," Hilary said primly.

"Not on the floodplain," Tom said. "About the biggest thing would be a bobcat, and you just don't see those guys anymore. I've only seen four or five in my life, and that was a long time ago. My dad was still alive then. What you'll see here is deer, gray foxes, maybe a river otter, squirrels, swamp rabbits, and about four million of old Earl's relatives. And the gators, of course. And some runty little wild pigs. You don't want to run into those guys in a dark alley, but you won't see them at night. Lots of kinds of birds and ducks and geese, too. Professor Longstreet told me that more than four million wood ducks and two million mallards winter in the alluvial wetlands. I think the wood ducks are the most beautiful big bird we have; one day next fall when they're coming in I'll take you up on Pinchgut Pond to see 'em, Hil. And wild turkeys; that was wild turkey you had for Thanksgiving. And ruby-crowned kinglets and goldfinches and purple finches and about a million kinds of warblers. . . ."

"Were there ever any wild horses in here?" Hilary said. "You know, like on Cumberland Island?"

"No horses," he said. "The skinny goes that Hippolytus, who was a kind of king of a sacred grove of trees in ancient Greece, was dragged to death in his chariot by horses, and ever since, the horse has been persona non grata in the deep woods. So no, you won't see any horses sneaking around in here like the whitetails. Which is not, I don't think, a great loss."

"You don't like horses, do you?" Hilary said.

"No." His voice floated back to us. "Not much, I don't."

We walked in silence for a while. As we drew nearer the river, the little dry sloughs and circular ponds we had been skirting gave over to flatter ground, and the forest floor became thicker and softer and deeper. The great, arching hardwoods gave way gradually to the phantasmagorical, monolithic shapes of the huge water tupelos and bald cypresses, with their huge buttresses and fantastic gnarled knees. The darkness was almost palpable here; dense and impenetrable. Only stray shafts of silver radiance cut down into the still, thick black water in which the trees stood. We were walking along a small ridge that rose a scant foot above the water, and looking down into it, I felt a cold revulsion. It looked secret and primeval and somehow sly, as if it were a living element, possessed of some ancient and unspeakable knowledge, some vast and awful secret it kept from men. I thought that I would die of horror and disgust if I should fall into that water. It spread out among the trees like a black mirror lake, stretching as far as I could see.

"Is it much further?" Hilary said. Her voice and steps were flagging.

"We're there now," Tom Dabney said. "Only around here the river is so shallow and spread out that you can't tell where it begins in earnest. This part of the woods is flooded almost ninety percent of the year. This time of the fall is about the only time you can come in this far, and then very seldom; the place I'm taking you to see is underwater all the time except after a very dry summer and fall like we've had this year. I don't know when you'll be able to see this again."

His voice was nearly a whisper, but it rang in the thick silence like the cry of a night bird. I realized then that the old silence had been pressing down on me with the same great and terrible weight as it had the morning I had sat alone up in the King's Oak and wept in terror and despair, and that, like that silence, it was not really a silence at all but a kind of tapestry of unheard sounds, a shroud of wild forest noises. None were familiar to me. That same old, cold fear began to uncoil in my chest, and I felt cold sweat start at my hairline. I wanted, as I had wanted then, to turn and run wildly for light and air and safety.

Instead I squeezed Hilary's hand and said briskly, "We need to wrap this up, Tom. It must be past ten now."

I saw the whites of his eyes flash as he turned his head back toward me.

"We're almost there," he said, and I thought there was laughter in his voice. "It's just beyond that canebrake." He pointed ahead to a dense wall of river cane that blocked our route; it seemed to tower half the height of the trees, and looked as massive and solid as a stone wall.

He stepped up to that wall of cane and, as before at the edge of the forest, simply vanished into it. I halted before it with Hilary and stared into a thicket of stems that must have been two and three inches in diameter. I had never seen such cane before.

"Okay, open up," I called. My voice sounded high and silly in my own ears. Without his presence, the woods swelled into a giant's maze, empty and enormous.

The cane parted and he stood there holding the stems aside to make a path for us. We preceded him through and stopped. I drew in my breath sharply, and beside me Hilary gave a little cry.

Below us lay the bed of what appeared to be a large, shallow empty lake. In the stark black and silver of the moonlight I could not judge depths and dimensions accurately, but I thought it must be about fifteen feet deep, and the size of a couple of football fields laid end to end. Black water, giving back the white moon, covered its bottom, but I knew that the depth must be only a few inches. It was the trees that stopped the eye and heart.

They marched along the lake bottom in ranks, as if planted by some titan's hand eons ago, black, moss-bearded cypresses and tupelos as tall as the hardwoods we had passed under earlier, a hundred feet and more. And their huge, black, steeple-like knees, like the flying buttresses of a medieval cathedral, soared ten and twelve feet into the air over the shallow black water. They would have dwarfed a man. They looked, in the cold white radiance, like prehistoric monuments to an unimaginable god. There was nothing there in all that lunar whiteness and soulless ebony that could or would speak to the heart of a man. The place seemed inimical to life.

Tom motioned for us to sit down, and we did, dropping straight down onto the soft earth of the ridge, the canebrake at our backs, and simply looked down into the big backwater slough. I thought that he must speak, that he must sense that without his voice to make sense of it, the cypress slough was dangerous to us, was simply too alien, too removed from our ken.

Presently he did. It was the same soft whisper he had used before.

"You'll never see those knees until we've had a dry enough spell for the water to recede," he said. "Normally the water is ten feet deep in here, so what you'd be seeing would be just plain, two-foot cypress knees in water, like you do everywhere else. This is only the third time I've ever seen it like this, and I come back in here three or four times a year. I've been tracking this all fall, thinking this might be the year for it. And it is. Sit still, now, and watch. The show isn't over yet."

We sat. We did not speak. Once again the silence swelled and boomed and pulsed around me, and the utter wildness and strangeness burned behind my eyes like salt water, and I felt as weightless and without context as if I sat on a chip of a star in a different galaxy. I thought of sensory deprivation tanks, but this was not deprivation; it was its opposite. It was sensory overload of a sort totally alien to me. I wondered if Hilary felt fear, but apparently she did not. Her small weight against me was soft and loose, and her breathing was easy and quiet. She simply sat in the old moonlight between me and Tom Dabney with a child's undissipated patience, waiting to be filled with wonder.

It was almost a half hour later, thirty minutes of silence and burning whiteness and creeping chill, when the deer came. At first they were not there, and then, all of a sudden and at once, they were. A band of perhaps eighty deer, large and small, forming themselves out of the darkness as Tom Dabney had, on the far lip of the slough, ghosting down its steep sides and onto its floor in loose double lines, as if they were being sung by unheard pipes. You could see the shape of them, deep-shouldered and delicate-legged, and see the white of their flags and bellies and the faint dapple of the adolescent fawns, and see the great crowns of the lone buck's rack as he brought up the rear of the two lines. You could see the shining spatter of the water as they walked through it, ankle deep, and see the frost of their warm breaths on the sharp night. But you could hear nothing . . . or I could not. It was as if the shades of a herd out of another time, long dead and yet still living, came down into the great sunken forest of cypress knees and passed through them to the other side. They did not look to the right or left, and they did not pause or stumble or forage. They simply . . . crossed over. It must have taken them ten minutes to pass before our eyes and fade into the woods on the opposite side of the slough, and in all that time we did not make a sound, and I did not hear one.

When the last one, the great, many-branched buck, had disappeared, Hilary said, simply, "It makes me cry."

"I should hope it does," Tom Dabney said. I did not turn my head to look at him. I knew that if I did, I would see again on his face the silver tracks of tears.

"What is it?" I said, forcing normalcy into my voice. "Why do they go like that, in lines? Is it some kind of annual migration?"

"I don't know what it is," he said. "I've seen it the three times I've seen the slough dry, but I've never seen it anywhere else. Maybe they do it every year, and I just don't see it . . . maybe they just swim across. I'll check and see next fall, when the Wolf Moon comes back. But I don't have any idea where they go, or why. Usually deer travel in small bands, a buck with a few does and fawns, and never more than a mile or two from home base. The buck will send the girls and babies ahead like he did this time, and he brings up the rear. But it's never more than five or six to a buck. Maybe this one is a master animal."

"What's that?" Hilary said.

"In most of the hunting mythologies, men believed in a master animal, a super animal, kind of the guiding spirit of the animals they hunted," he said. "A master animal had great powers, and a soul like a man, and so when it was necessary to hunt and kill, say, a bear, or a buffalo, or whatever, the hunters would do elaborate rituals, and after they had killed their quarry they would do others to propitiate the soul, the spirit, of the master animal, so they wouldn't be punished for it. All cultures had some version of it. All our Indians had them."

Like putting an oak leaf into a dead deer's mouth? I did not say. Like painting yourself with its blood?

"You really must be into myths," I said. "That's the second one you've mentioned tonight."

"Sometimes I think myths are the only real truths we have," he said, looking into the space where the deer had been. His voice sounded detached, distant. "I think myths are the way we harmonize ourselves with reality, get in touch with the real experience of being alive. I think myths help us know, not only where in the world we are, but what. Who. We've killed off most of our myths in this enlightened century, and you can see the results in every ghetto and alcoholic and drug ward and every crack house and every poisoned stream on this planet. Without myths, we have nothing to honor. Mythic thinking is a way of seeing everything as a *thou*. Without it, all of life becomes just . . . an *it*. You might think twice about dishonoring a *thou*, but who cares about an *it*?"

He paused, and then grinned. I could see the white of his smile. "Thus spake the madman of Goat Creek," he said.

"But a fine madness," I said, moved. I knew that I might agree with him about the madman in the clear light of my office in the morning, but there, in that silent wood, with the phantasmagoric deer still burned on my retinas and heart, I felt the sense and truth of what he said in my viscera. I hoped Hilary was listening. Stated with elegant spareness, it was the kind of thing I wanted her to grow up knowing. But when I looked down, I saw that her lashes were feathered on her cheeks, and knew that she had fallen asleep where she sat.

I thought of the hour, and the long drive home, and knew that we should go, but I put it off, pushed it away.

"You really do love all this, don't you?" I said.

"I really do," he said. "The woods are the greatest *thou*s there are. The animals are. I guess . . . the woods are everything to me."

He looked over at me.

"I don't mean that there's nothing else in my life," he said. "I love my life. I have a life full of things I love and want. I just mean that this is where everything comes from. This is the source. The . . . patterns, the order, the natural flow and rhythm of all life, the first and oldest impulse and response, are here. It's all here, in wildness. The wild is the highest and purest order we have. When we lose it, we've lost the heart and core of us."

"People say that about God," I said. "People worship that."

He smiled again. "You could call it worship, I guess. It doesn't need a name. It just needs recognition."

"So," I said. "Is this what you worship? The . . . what: the wildness? Like a druid?"

"Nope. I'm not a druid," he said. "Don't romanticize me. I'm just a guy who likes the woods better than anyplace else. You could worship it, though. People did, once, in all cultures, and got on very well, all told. With the occasional lapse, of course. I guess some still do. If not worship, at least live by its rules, which may be the same thing. Maybe I'm one of the latter. I know I find my *thou*s out here."

"Has it ever occurred to you that you really might be crazy?" I said, lightly, and then tasted the ridiculousness of the words on my mouth.

"Not really." He laughed. "But it sure as hell has occurred to a lot of other people. Just ask my ex-wives. What about you, Diana? Do you think I'm crazy?"

I hesitated. I thought that under the lightness he was serious.

"No," I said. "Just single-minded. What the Japanese call one-pointed. I think that scares me worse than crazy."

"Don't be afraid of me," he said softly. "I would never hurt you. I—or rather, what I know—might even heal you."

"You keep talking about healing. You think I need healing?" I said.

"Why else would you come here?" he said simply. "Why else would you bring your daughter back here?"

Hilary stirred then, and cried out softly, and I got to my feet and pulled her to hers.

"We've really got to go," I said. "It must be after midnight."

"Here," he said. "Let me."

He bent and swung Hilary to his shoulder, and she put her head into the angle of his neck and shoulder and sighed, and slid back into sleep. Her long, light colt's legs and arms hung loosely over his dark chest and arms, and he rested his pointed chin on the crown of her head. Holding her easily, he led the way back into the canebrake. By the time we fetched up at the house, the Wolf Moon had sailed small and high into the sky, and its light was once again the ordinary white of an early-winter night, all enchantment burned away.

"Does the plant being out there bother you?" I said, as he was putting Hilary into the Toyota. "The Big Silver?"

"No," he said. "It's not my problem."

The words were so unlike him that I stopped and looked into his face.

"I just mean that there are people to take care of matters at the plant, people like Greenpeace and Energy Research, to keep tabs on them, monitor for funny stuff, keep them honest. That's their job. My job is to tend to all this. To look out for the woods. For the animals."

I did not know what he meant, not precisely. Did he fancy himself some sort of gamekeeper? A tender of the forest?

"But you kill," I said. "You hunt yourself."

"One day I'll tell you about that," he said. "When there's a lot more time. When it's time. I'd like you to know about . . . the killing."

"I could never do it," I said. "I might one day understand why you do, but I could never do it."

"That's okay," Tom Dabney said. "It's enough for you to know about the woods. I'll show you. I'll teach you. We can start whenever you like."

"Not now," I said. "Not yet. I think I'd like to know. But . . . not yet."

"Just let me know," Tom Dabney said.

CHAPTER SEVEN

The week after the night of the Wolf Moon, the weather turned cold and wet and wild, and a high crooning wind prowled through the tops of the trees and sent the last leaves eddying to earth. It was too stormy to think of forays into the Big Silver Swamp, and I persuaded Hilary to postpone our next visit until it cleared. But she was restless and cross, and teased to go see Tom and Missy. Finally, on a Saturday afternoon when she and Carter and I had spent hours before the fire in the cottage, listening to the rain tick against the diamond panes and playing Parcheesi, the teasing turned into a small explosion.

"Why don't you let me drive you over to the stable and you can ride Pittypat in the indoor ring?" Carter said, with more forbearance than I could have mustered. "I saw

Pat the other day and she said it's been over two weeks since she's seen you. Pittypat misses you, and you don't want to get behind. Big dressage doings coming up in the spring."

"I don't want to ride," Hilary said. "I'm tired of horses. I want to go back out to Tom's. I want to see Missy, and Earl. I can do that in the house. I wouldn't have to get wet."

"Well, Tom may just have a few better things to do besides entertaining you," I said shortly. Though I found it charming and moving when I was with them, her attachment to Tom Dabney irritated and troubled me in some obscure fashion when we were not in his presence. I sensed an enormous potential for commitment in Hilary; felt as if in my own body the great abyss where her father no longer was. Whoever moved into that space would own her, heart and soul. I wondered that it had not been Carter, long before. But though she liked and trusted him, I knew that she had kept that door closed.

"He doesn't have anything better to do," she flared at me. "He'd like to have me anytime. He told me. It's you who won't take me out there. I don't think you like him. I think you're scared of Goat Creek. I think the deer and the big trees that night scared you to death!"

"*No más,* Hilary," Carter said. "You certainly don't have to go ride Pittypat if you don't want to. But you do have to stop sassing your ma."

"Says who?" Hilary glared at him.

"Says me," he said levelly.

"You're not my father!" she cried. "You don't own me! I don't have to do anything you say!"

She burst into tears and ran for her room, and I half rose to go after her, my palm fairly itching to smack her bottom. He stayed me with a hand on my arm.

"Let it be," he said. "It's high time she showed me some of her temper. We can't ever have a real relationship until she does. It's bothered me that she's been so polite to me. I crowded into her space, and she let me know it."

"The hell with her space," I said, my face burning. "That was sheer brattiness, and I'm not going to have it. She's been running wild because nobody has had the heart to discipline her while she was so fragile, and now that she's better, she's going to have to play by the rules again."

"Whose rules?" he said mildly.

"Mine," I snapped.

"Well, she *is* better, no doubt about that," Carter said. "Goat Creek must be working its well-advertised magic. What's this about the deer and the trees?"

I started to brush it off, and then, because there seemed no reason not to, I told him about our trip to the dry slough, and the fantastic, soaring cypress buttresses, and the eerie passing of the silent deer. I deliberately shortened and flattened it in the telling, feeling strangely resentful that he had asked for the story.

"God," he said, when I had finished. "What a beautiful thing that must have been. Why didn't you tell me about it?"

"I suppose I simply forgot about it," I said, knowing he would not believe me. One would as soon forget an earthquake, or a tidal wave.

"Is Hilary right?" Carter said, looking seriously at me. "Are you afraid of Goat Creek . . . or something out there?"

"No," I said crossly. "Not of Goat Creek, not of the woods, not of the water, and not of Tom Dabney, if that's what you mean. And I think it is."

"It's exactly what I mean." Carter smiled. "And I don't know if I'm glad about that, or sorry."

"Carter," I said in exasperation, "I don't care about Tom Dabney one way or another, except to be glad that his little Walden out there seems to be so good for Hilary. As long as it is, I will continue to take her out there, and as long as I do, I will continue to think of Tom Dabney just as I do at this minute—as a nice, harmless, crazy man who is being kind to my daughter. Period. End of story. We've been over this. I'm getting exquisitely bored with it. I don't want to talk about it anymore. I just want to go on working and raising my daughter and being with you. I want things to stay just as they are right now. I want us to . . . just keep on being us. And I want you to let that happen and leave Tom Dabney out there in his woods."

He reached over and hugged me and said, "I'm sorry, Andy. I never did do the adolescent jealousy number very well. We'll do exactly that—just keep on being us. Those are the sweetest words I've heard in a long time."

We were together every day for a week or so after that, together in a way we had not been before. He came directly to the cottage after work every day, and I had the fire lit and the drinks glasses iced, and we cooked together, big, sloppy, savory messes of stew and gumbo and soup and ragout, things I never ate in other Pemberton homes, things I had never made back in Atlanta. Often, if I was late getting home—and that happened with increasing frequency, for Miss Deborah seemed determined to find more and more things that would keep me in the office—he had dinner started when I came in out of the raw twilight. Often I would sit in my car for a moment in front of the little cottage, and look through the frost of its windows into the lighted windows of home, and watch them moving about inside by leaping firelight, my daughter and my friend and lover, the one a dark flame, the other a golden bear of a man, and tears would knot in my chest and burn my nose. She would be chattering like a squirrel, and he would be smiling and stirring something and cocking his head to listen. A rush of fierce gratitude would take me then; what more could I possibly want in the world than this? What more could any woman want? It was like looking into a crystal ball and seeing the rest of your life, and finding it good almost to magical.

I almost never, in those days, heard the voice crying helplessly in the middle of me, "Fill me!" Not during our evenings together and with Tish and Charlie and other couples, not on our blissfully mundane, errand-filled weekends, not at the movies or the grocery store or the training track or the Pemberton Inn. Not in the thick, chill dark of my bedroom, under the great drifting goose-down comforter he had ordered for me from Orvis, where, almost every night now, he took me in his gentle love. Almost never. Almost.

"I either have to marry you or give up and move my clothes over here," he said one morning in the sharp darkness before dawn, as he got up to go home and dress for the day. "Tongues will be wagging from here to Waycross."

"What do you care?" I said. "A middle-aged schoolteacher and a ten-year-old child, after all those years of fleshly excess with the nubile and inventive Mrs. Dabney? We must bore them into a coma after that."

"I don't care," Carter said. "I thought you might. I wouldn't want Hilary to take any crap on my account. Kids can be vicious, as you and she both well know. Some grownups, too. Miss Deborah isn't going to suffer an arrangement in silence, especially if it's a happy one."

I stretched so hard that my knees and shoulders crackled like crushed tinfoil. The down floated so lightly on my naked body that I wanted to laugh aloud with pleasure.

And yet I had dreamed one night that week that it was the wild, secret weight of fur that pressed into my stomach and breasts.

"I can't imagine anyone being anything but glad that Hilary has a man in her life who loves and cherishes her," I said. "And as for the kids in her school, almost half of them have 'uncles' who stay over nights with old mum. And as for Miss Deborah, get serious, Carter. What on earth could she do to me? If she tried to get me fired for living with you, they'd have to fire half the faculty."

"Don't underestimate her," he said. "She's scuttled a lot of innocent ships in her day."

"Are people talking about Carter and me?" I asked Tish on the way home from a Pemberton Dames meeting the next Saturday.

"Hardly at all," she said. "You and Carter are tame stuff. Pat Dabney on her idlest day is better gossip than you and Carter. I've heard a buzz or two about you and Tom Dabney, though."

I stared at her. She did not turn to look at me, but she grinned widely, the freckles across her nose and cheeks running together like spilled molasses.

"I've been out there exactly one time," I said indignantly. "One day after school, and that was two weeks ago. Hilary's been a couple of times, but Tom has picked her up after school and brought her back in time for dinner, and he doesn't even come in. He just drops her off and toots the horn and goes on. He's given her a little goat that he keeps for her out there. . . . Really, Tish! You made that up."

"Nope," she said. "Heard all about it. It may have been just one time after school, but you came in after midnight, and I have it from reliable sources that there were mud and grass stains all over the seat of your pants. It was the talk of the Pemberton Dry Cleaners."

"Tish . . ." I stared, red rage building in my chest. "We went out in the woods to look at some deer, my God; Hilary was with us the entire time."

"Lighten up." She smiled. "I sat in some red wine Charlie spilled at a dinner party one night, and the next day it was all over town that I'd had a miscarriage. This is a very small town. Nobody cares, really. It's just fun to talk about who's seeing who."

"I am not seeing Tom Dabney. . . ."

"I know. It's just that he's by way of being Pemberton's favorite son. Everybody would like to see him with a good woman again, especially after the grim lady lawyer from Tallahassee. To get back to your original question, is there something to talk about you and Carter? Besides the fact that he's apparently moved in, which we all assumed he would sooner or later, anyway. I'd love to be the first to know."

"You will be, if there ever is," I said. "Right now I'm just happy with things the way they are."

"Don't get too happy," Tish said. "Nature abhors a vacuum."

The week before Christmas, my school and Hilary's closed for the long holiday, and the season in Pemberton moved into high gear. I went to coffees, brunches, teas, open houses, dinner parties, cotillions, balls. I pulled out the plastic-shrouded formal clothes that had been my winter-evening uniforms in the days of Chris and Buckhead and wore them, feeling elegant and equal to my peers at last, but somehow traitorous too, as if, by donning my splendor, I had betrayed the fragile beginnings of something new and precious. The silks and satins and velvets felt both familiar, brushing my legs, and alien. I was not sure who it was who nodded and smiled to accept the compliments of Pemberton. Carter, beside me in perfect, conservative evening clothes, smiled proudly. People clucked and fussed over us. It was as if each of the parties had been held in honor of us. One evening as we were dropping Hilary off at Marjorie's glowing, child-spilling house, she said, "I remember when you used to go out looking like that before. At home. You smelled the same way. But you come home laughing now. You used to come home and you'd been crying. I'd cry, too, after you'd kissed me good night and turned off the light. It used to scare me when you went out."

My heart stabbed me briefly.

"No tears now, sugarbaby," I said. "Just smiles. And that's the way it's going to stay. You aren't scared when I go now, are you?"

"No," she said, my healing child. "That was when I was little."

On the twenty-first of December, Pat Dabney had her annual eggnog party at the miniature brick Malmaison her father had built for her and Tom, and I went with Carter, wearing the short white silk jersey dinner dress that had always been my Christmas favorite. It was cut in a deep V front and back, and was clasped under my breasts with an ivory-and-gold knot, Grecian style. From there it flowed loose to a scalloped hem. It had not been fashionable for several years, but it was becoming to me, and when I first bought it I had thought how totally and archaically Greek I looked in it, with my strong face and thick, unruly dark curls. On impulse I had bought a gold-and-white fillet of artificial leaves for my hair, like a laurel wreath, and wore it to my mother-in-law's hallowed Christmas Eve party. I could read the effect on her face and on the faces of her willowy blond friends when I walked into the house on Habersham Road. They smiled brilliantly and recoiled, imperceptibly but as surely as virgins encountering a vampire. "Pagan" fairly rang in the air around me.

"Great dress," Chris had said to me, grinning lazily. After that, he insisted that I wear it to every one of his mother's Christmas Eve parties. I don't know what made me pull it out on the night of Pat Dabney's party, but it felt right. I felt as if I were walking into the arena clothed in armor against the lions. Or the lioness.

Everyone I had ever met in Pemberton and many I had not were there in Pat's exquisite drawing and dining rooms, drinking eggnog out of the largest Sheffield silver punch bowl I had ever seen and taking ham and beaten biscuits and slices of melting tenderloin in tiny dinner rolls from trays passed by black men in white coats. Through the swinging door into the kitchen I caught a glimpse of black women in white aprons, and thought again of my outburst at the Carringtons' party earlier, and of what I had said to Tom Dabney's mother and sister about their maids. Fat lot of good that did me, I thought. Dinah's still out there in the kitchen. One of the women had a narrow caramel face of great distinction, so familiar to me that I stared, until it came to me that Tom had told me Scratch Purvis's daughter sometimes worked for Pat. There was no doubt that the woman was the daughter. It gave me a small, unpleasant jolt to see her working in a white kitchen, when her father routinely sat as a guest in the house of another white. I wondered if she hated that, and thought that she probably did not, especially. I could not imagine Scratch's daughter doing anything she hated. Pat Dabney probably paid top dollar; no one would willingly encounter that tongue otherwise.

We passed through the crowd toward the bar in the vaulted and paneled den. The guests were kissing cheeks and being kissed, smiling, nodding, calling out good-natured insults and insincere compliments, as people do anywhere who know each other well. I did not feel uneasy in Pemberton company now. I felt comfortable and almost mindlessly soothed. I was not one of them yet, but I knew that if I followed the rules I would be. And I knew the rules now. It was like . . . it was like that exhilarating quarter when Tish and I had pledged Tri Delt at Emory, and waited to be initiated into full membership after Christmas, and knew that we would pass our pledge tests and make our grades. The supreme joys of full acceptance lay just ahead of us, and the anticipation was sweet.

Pat Dabney came up to us, looking so utterly spectacular that I felt my silk turn to polyester on my body, and my hair tangle itself into a mass of spitting snakes. The little tinsel folly of the laurel crown must look, I thought, like a Halloween ornament beside the smooth gold chignon into which Pat had pulled her tawny mane, and the white Greek dress like a bad rental costume. She wore a great waterfall of chiffon printed in the molten bronzes and blacks of a Bengal tiger, and one magnificent leg, sheathed in bronze silk, shone from a thigh-high slit in the cascade of ruffles. Her strong, beautiful shoulders were bare, as was half her deep bosom, and a legally blind man could have seen that she wore no brassiere. Her hard nipples brushed the thin, silky stuff; you could see a brown mole on one of her breasts through the fabric. Her hair was lacquered back and high up on her narrow head and caught with a canary diamond clasp, and other great chunks of canary glittered at her ears and wrists. She wore smooth honey makeup and topaz shadow and dark mascara on her yellow lioness's eyes, and a slash of terra-cotta on her mouth. It was not possible to look away from her. Pat in her slapdash everyday persona drew the eye like a magnet; Pat in full battle dress was the stuff of *Vogue, Town & Country, Palm Beach Life.*

"Pat, you look absolutely gorgeous," I said spontaneously.

She smiled lazily, and looked me up and down. She let the silence spin out almost until it became an insult, but not quite. Voices dropped, and heads turned to look at us.

"Thank you, sweetie," she said in her rich voice. "You look mightily fetching, too, all dressed up in your native costume. When is the sacrifice?"

I caught my breath, and Carter inhaled deeply, and a little light wind of breath passed through the crowd.

Pat laughed and hugged me lightly. "Just a joke, darling, and a bad one," she said. "Simmer down, Carter. Forgive me, both of you. You look pretty as a picture, Andy. You're just the breath of fresh air this hidebound little burg needs; I thought if I saw one more twenty-year-old de la Renta tonight I'd scream. Come have some eggnog and let me show you off."

She took me by the hand and led me through the crowd toward the punch bowl, and I had no recourse, short of pulling rudely away from her, but to follow. I felt like a float in Macy's Thanksgiving Day parade, being towed by a thoroughbred.

A knot of people stood around the punch bowl, laughing. They turned to greet us and I saw Clay and Daisy Dabney and Chip, in a ruffled shirt and a scarlet cummerbund pulled too tight around his pillowy waist, and a thin-to-bone woman with an astounding mass of blond ringlets over a child's untouched face, who proved to be Lucy Dabney, Chip's wife. Lucy Hough Dabney of the Savannah Houghs,

Tish had told me, selected and purchased by Daisy Dabney as a suitable wife for her only son, and a suitable mother for her grandchildren. She had a piping voice, like a parody of a child in a borscht belt comic routine, and a smile of real sweetness, and no discernible intelligence at all.

She took both my hands in her cold little bird's claws and said, "I've wanted to meet you for such a long time! I love Atlanta people; Atlanta is my favorite place in the world. I go up there shopping all the time, in Buckhead. I hear you lived in Buckhead; how could you bear to leave it to come to Pemberton? Not that I mean Pemberton isn't cute and wonderful, but *Atlanta* . . . Let me ask you, do you know Mr. Kevin? Of Kevin's Couture Coiffure? On Peachtree Road in Buckhead? Well, I know everybody in Atlanta does. . . . I think Kevin is wonderful; do you know, he comes down here twice a month and takes a suite at the Holiday Inn, and does all our hair on the weekends? He says he likes us much better than Atlanta women; we have an innate sense of style, and who we are. . . . He says Pemberton is one place where there's still some real blue blood left."

"I'm afraid I'm way behind on the hair scene," I said, smiling at her with real liking. Chris always said I had a weakness for nitwits. But her prattle was fresh and without guile, and it didn't take an especially astute ear to hear the loneliness under it. Who would there be, in a town full of Tish Coulters and Gwen Carringtons and Pat Dabneys, for Lucy Hough Dabney?

"Well, you let me make an appointment for the next time he comes," Lucy said. "You'd love him, and he'd love to get his hands on that hair of yours—"

"Jesus, Lucy, can it," Chip said peevishly, and she stared at him, and then clapped her hands to her mouth.

"Oh, no; oh, I just meant it's such thick, shiny, curly

hair that he could do miracles with it . . . ," she said, and then trailed off, aware that she had not yet gotten it right.

"My wife was born with a silver foot in her mouth, right along with the silver spoon," Chip Dabney said in red-faced jocularity, and I could read the annoyance struggling with the pride of pedigree in his loud voice.

"Out of the mouths of babes," Pat Dabney drawled in amusement.

Lucy Dabney's burning face mirrored my own. I squeezed her hands.

"I'd love an appointment with Mr. Kevin," I said. "It's high time I had myself updated."

The sun came out again in her face. From the back of the group an exuberant tenor sang, "Don't change a hair for me . . . not if you care for me . . ."

And Tom Dabney, in evening dress, came waltzing out of the crowd and caught me in his arms and swung me around in a whirling, perfect waltz. He swooped me down the length of Pat's polished floor, the crowd parting to make a path for us, and fetched me up in a bay-windowed alcove in the library, at the opposite end of the room from the bar, the only light a fire of apple logs in the great stone fireplace near the bay. I stood, letting my skirts settle around me and my wits drift back to earth, struggling to fit this elegant dark whip of a man into the wild tangle of the Big Silver Swamp forest, feeling still the pressure of his arms at my waist and back. It had been like being blown by a strong spring wind, wild and sweet and effortless. That's what it is to dance, I thought.

"Well, don't you look splendid," I said. He did. The tuxedo fitted him perfectly, and the dark face and gleaming animal's pelt of hair and coal-fire blue eyes were a disconcerting contrast to the formal black and white. I felt shy and stupid. He was someone I had never met, at home in drawing rooms in New Haven and Pemberton and anywhere else he might care to go.

He grinned and bowed over my hand, and kissed it. The blue eyes never left me; they slid from my hair to my face to my breasts and legs and back again, and he nodded as if in agreement.

"So do you. So do you, Miss Diana. And you really are Diana tonight. You can't know how wonderful you look to me. Don't you dare let Mr. Kevin get ahold of you. Or my ex-wife, though I suppose it's too much to hope that she hasn't already."

"She asked when the sacrifice was," I said dryly, and he threw his head back and whooped so loudly that heads turned to us again. I found myself laughing with him. Pat Dabney's thrust struck me, suddenly, as funny as it did him. The night was, in an eyeblink, light and bright and scented and young and gay and full of the spangled promise that Christmas had once had for me, when I was very small.

"What a stupid woman she is," Tom Dabney said joyously. "And how very little she knows, and how much she thinks she does. Come on over here under this mistletoe, Diana Andropoulis Calhoun, because I am going to kiss you, and then I'm going to pour eggnog down you until your eyes roll, and then I'm going to do my damnedest to steal you out from under Carter's nose and take you out to the swamp and make love to you."

And before I could draw a breath to protest, he waltzed me once more across the floor, to where a scarlet-tied kissing ball hung in an archway, and, in front of virtually everyone over age twenty-one I had met so far in Old Pemberton, bent me back over his arm like Rhett Butler and kissed me until I lost my breath and stumbled backward, and only his arms prevented me from falling on my rear.

It was a hard kiss, and a long one, but I remember thinking how soft his mouth was, and somehow cherishing. Almost any other man kissing a woman in a show of lechery at a party would have ground his mouth against hers, probed with his tongue. When he raised his head and pulled me upright at last, I could not focus on his face, and only dimly heard the cheers and claps and whistles from the other guests. I turned my blinded face toward the noise and saw Carter, standing still at the edge of the group with Pat Dabney at his side. Instantly their faces sprang into a kind of swimming hyperfocus. Pat's was white beneath the makeup, and hectic red circles burned in her cheeks. Her eyes were narrowed, and glittered like the yellow diamonds she wore. Her smile was savage. Carter's face was flushed nearly purple, and somehow fuller than I had ever seen it, as if it had been inflated with helium. He was smiling, too, but his eyes were white ice. Both of them, I could plainly see, were furiously angry, and an answering anger leaped along my veins and burned in my cheeks. Their anger spoke of ownership, of both Tom Dabney and me; how dare they?

I looked back at Tom. His face was nearly on a level with mine, and the blue eyes glittered with glee. He winked.

I tipped my head far back, and let myself go limp in his arms, and closed my eyes.

"Please, sir, may I have some more?" I piped in as good a British child's voice as I could manage. *Oliver Twist* had just finished a month-long, SRO run at the Community Playhouse; the crowd exploded in laughter and applause.

Tom Dabney crowed exultantly and kissed me again.

After that he laughed and hugged me around the shoulders, lightly, and moved off into the crowd, and I went back to Carter's side, and the ice went out of his eyes, and he said only, smiling, "Just see that you don't develop a taste for that," and we moved on to the eggnog table and the hors d'oeuvres. But his face was still pink and swollen, and he did not speak directly to me often. I felt vaguely repentant, but only vaguely. Mostly I felt prickly and perverse. It was the first time Carter had ever been angry with me, and I was not a little dismayed to find that his anger lit an answering fire in me. Before I had seen, beside his happiness, only his pain, and that had hurt me in my heart. Pat Dabney, laughing with Chip, looked through me as if I did not exist. In the main, I was grateful.

In Pat's Venetian powder room Tish said to me, "I don't have to ask if that was as yummy as it looked. You were red down to your navel."

"I might as well be hung for a goat as a sheep," I said. "But Lord, you'd think we were doing it right on the floor, from the way Carter and Pat acted. They really pissed me off, Tish. Carter is very dear, but he doesn't own me, and he's got a thing about Tom that just isn't funny. And it's been years since Pat has had any claims on Tom. So far as I know."

"Well, it looked as if you *were* about to do it on the floor," she said. "And don't think every woman here didn't want to be in your shoes. Go easy on Carter; he's a very old-fashioned man under all that laid-back charm. Carter doesn't like his woman kissing other men. And especially not enjoying it like that. This is not Buckhead, Andy. As for Pat, most of us think she still has the hots for Tom, in some strange way or other. You may well pay for that little smooch. And Tom most certainly will."

"What could she do to Tom now?" I said.

"Probably not let him take the boys out to the creek. They're home from school for the holidays, and it's sort of a tradition that Tom takes them camping out there at Christmas. I'd be willing to bet she won't let them go. That's what she could do; he's crazy about his boys. He wouldn't be within ten miles of this house if he wasn't. It's the only time he comes here, but he always comes to her Christmas party. He doesn't want to spoil their Christmas by fighting with their mother."

My anger, simmering quietly under the skin of the evening, leaped and sparked again.

"That's really rotten; that's just bitch stuff," I said.

"I rest my case," Tish said.

And Tom did pay, of course, though not the way Tish had thought he might. I paid, too. Near the end of the evening, as people were beginning to collect coats and drift toward the front door, Tom came up with a beautiful gray topcoat over his arm to say good night to Pat. Carter and I, our own coats over our shoulders, stood in the group, along with Chip and Lucy Dabney, and Chip's father and mother. Tish and Charlie were there, too.

"Thanks, Pat. It was a terrific party, as always," Tom said pleasantly to his ex-wife. "Tell the boys I'll be by about noon tomorrow to pick them up." He smiled around at us. "Christmas shopping spree. Caveat emptor."

"You'd better dig deep, sweetie," Pat drawled, and I saw that she rocked slightly in her high-heeled bronze sandals. "Your number one son is expecting that little Purdy Vic Talbot is holding for you at the gunshop. I've already had him engrave the stock; I knew you'd forget. And number two boy thinks he's ready now for his own hunter. I took care of that, too. He's coming in tomorrow from Camden; Phil Parham over at Tailend found him for me. Beautiful animal. But I warn you, you'd better seek additional employment immediately."

Dull red flooded Tom Dabney's dark face, but other than that it did not change. The blue eyes went cold and flat.

"You know I can't handle that kind of thing, Pat," he

said mildly. "The boys don't expect that from me. That's more your league. I'll talk to 'em in the morning."

"What a shame," she drawled. "I've already told them what they're getting from you. You did say anything within reason. . . ."

"My reason, Pat. Not yours," he said. "Never mind, I'll handle it with them. 'Night, everybody, and Merry Christmas."

And he turned and walked lightly toward the door.

"Wait, Tom," she called, and he stopped and turned.

"I've got a great idea," she said. As they had earlier, heads turned at the sound of her voice, and eyes fastened on her and Tom as they faced each other across the floor of the beautiful house where he would never live.

"There's a new nudie club opened up in Waycross." She grinned. "Chip told me about it. I think he's been every night. He says they feature coed acts. And he does mean *acts*. Why don't you and Andy take that little bump and grind of yours on the road? With her tits and your dick, you'd probably make enough in a week to pay for—"

There was an explosion of laughter, and I saw, through the haze of rage that scrimmed my eyes, Chip and Carter collapse against each other, bellowing their glee.

Tom nodded affably and went out through the door into the night, and Pat smiled brilliantly and turned away to another group of departing guests. I stood breathless with anger, watching Carter and Chip Dabney gasp and mop their streaming eyes and pound each other's shoulders. I looked around the circle of faces. Tish and Charlie were slack-faced with shock, and Daisy and Lucy Dabney looked merely confused, smiling politely as if at some masculine foolishness they did not understand. Clay Dabney's face was a mask.

I must have looked rather terrible, for Tish said, in a low voice, "Andy . . . ," and Charlie made a move toward me, as if to touch my arm.

"Don't wait for me, Carter," I said, and went out of the house after Tom Dabney.

He was sitting in the cab of his truck, his dark head back against the seat, looking straight ahead of him. The truck was running, and icy white clouds of exhaust chuffed out into the cold air. He did not look angry; he merely looked as if he were resting there, waiting. I heard the faint spill of piano notes from the truck's radio.

I hesitated beside the truck, and he turned his head and saw me and smiled. He leaned over and opened the door on the passenger side.

"I thought you'd probably be along," he said. His voice was as it always was, easy and quirky, as if laughter bubbled just below its surface. "Hop in. I've got the heater going for you."

I got into the truck. It smelled like him, of soft leather and warming wool, and somehow of the cold night woods. The cab was pleasantly warm, and the Chopin from the radio swam in the darkness like molten silver.

"Tom, listen . . . ," I began. My ears were ringing mightily, and I did not know what I was going to say.

"No," he said. "It doesn't matter. It was stupid, and it just doesn't matter. At least, it shouldn't. Don't spoil the rest of the night by talking about it."

He reached behind the seat and pulled something from the back and tucked it around me. It was the mink throw from his bed at Goat Creek, deep and warm over my lap and legs.

"It's going to be chilly by the time we get there," he said.

"Get where?" I said. The heat of the cab and the music and the fading adrenaline from the scene at the door and the backwash of my own impulse made me physically dizzy. I thought that I might faint; it was not an unpleasant thought.

"King's Oak," he said. "Even before I left home, I thought that we would go to the King's Oak tonight, you and I. Does that really surprise you?"

"No," I said.

The night was dark and breathed frost, and the skies over the empty winter fields were dusted with stars like silver pepper. I cracked my window to try and clear my head, and the air that rushed in smelled wild and cold. There was a musk of wood smoke in it, a rich and comforting smell, speaking of light and warmth and rooms closed against the night. Tom Dabney did not speak again until we had reached the narrow, rutted turnoff to King's Oak, but somewhere on the drive he reached over and picked up my hand, and held it in his own, warmly and firmly. I did not pull it away.

We bumped down the long, overgrown drive that I remembered from another time in the dark, that time with Carter, and when we pulled into the open clearing where the great dark house lay, he did not stop but drove past it and down the track that led through the open soybean fields toward the dark line of the Big Silver Swamp forest. Tom spoke then.

"The moon won't rise for a while, so I'll drive us in. It's too dark to walk, and you aren't dressed for it. But some night I want to bring you on a stalk up the creek to the King's Oak, Diana. It's not a thing you'll forget. And don't worry about my Uncle Clay or anybody disturbing us. Clay doesn't come into the woods on this night, and he doesn't let anyone else, either."

"What night is this?" I said through lips numb with something I could not name.

"It's the winter solstice," he said. "The holiest of all nights. We get Christmas from it. I come here every year on this night. Clay knows that. He used to come, too. So did my dad. You aren't afraid, are you?"

"Yes, I am," I said, knowing then the feeling that numbed my mouth for what it was.

"Do you want me to take you back? I will," he said.

"No," I said.

The silence, when we got out of the truck at the little clearing on the creekbank, was old and clean and immense, greater even than on the morning it had so terrified me, for now there was no sound of wind or birds or insects or moving water; only the crunch of our feet on the ice-rimmed brown grass, and the sound of our breathing. He put his arm under my elbow and helped me down the bank to where the skiff lay motionless against the dark bank, gripping it when I tottered on my high silver heels. He carried the mink throw over his other arm. I thought, crazily, that we might have been going on a midnight wiener roast, except for the extravagant spill of fur, and laughter pressed into my throat. But I did not dare let it free. The glass bubble of unreality held.

He poled us across to the island with a few deep, sure thrusts, and leaped out into the dark, shallow water and pulled the skiff up onto the bank under the great canopy of the King's Oak. Even in the dead of winter it was shawled with moss, and fully leafed, and I remembered that Clay Dabney had said that it was a live oak and did not drop its leaves in the fall. I stepped out onto the moss under it, into the deeper darkness that lay here. I looked up into the gnarled, dense branches. It was like being in a great, low-ceilinged house, a pagan cathedral. I could not see into the branches, but I remembered that on that other day I had been able to look down through them. I remembered, too, what I had seen then. The old, slow, traitorous warmth curled into my groin and stomach.

I stood still and simply looked at Tom Dabney.

He smiled at me, a slash of white in the dark, and pulled a cigarette lighter from his pocket and reached down and flicked it, and a wood fire leaped into life. The logs had been neatly piled, waiting. The shadows played wildly off the arching canopy of branches, and beyond them the black skin of the creek water gave the flames back. In the firelight Tom looked totally alien to me, as sure and easy in this wild place as a fox or a wolf . . . or something older and wilder, even. Something made of air and cold and green and silence. He spread the mink throw on the earth beside the fire and straightened up and held his hand out to me. I took it. Holding his hand, I stepped out of my earth-smeared sandals and onto the throw. My feet sank into it, warmed with fur and firelight.

"I came out this afternoon and laid the fire," he said. "I do it every year. I come out here every winter solstice and make a fire and stay till dawn. It's my one Christmas tradition. I've brought Scratch and Martin and Reese, once or twice, but no one else has ever come with me. You're the first . . . other one I've brought. One day I'll bring the boys out, and I'd love to have Hilary here eventually. But this time it's for you."

I still did not say anything. It occurred to me, dimly, that he really might be unbalanced, but the thought did not bother me. On another, deeper level I knew that he was not. It was not that that I was afraid of.

And I was afraid. My mouth was dry with fear, my

heart hammered with it, my legs and arms and fingers trembled imperceptibly. I do not think I could have gotten my breath to speak. He did not seem to notice anything unusual.

"Come here, Diana, and let me tell you something," he said, and sank down on the throw beside the fire, in his tuxedo, holding his hand out to me. I took it, and he pulled me gently down beside him. We sat in the shimmer and leap of the firelight, and I was not aware of being cold, although, in only my thin silk jersey, I must have been. He looked at me intently, but he did not touch me.

"In the days before recorded history, even, there used to be groves in certain forests that had at their heart one enormous tree. Mostly it was an oak. Those groves were sacred to the goddess Diana, who was the goddess of fertility, as well as a goddess of the hunt. They were guarded by a king who was also a priest, and he stayed on watch in the grove and defended it against all comers and served Diana until another man came who was able to fight and kill him. Then he in turn became king. They called him the King of the Sacred Grove, or the King of the Wood. Almost every culture had a grove and a king who served the goddess and died to make way for another king, though they might not have called the goddess Diana.

"And because she was the goddess of fertility, as well as of the hunt, it's said that the king, who was a mortal, was able to take her as a consort and make love to her, and that from that union the sacred grove and the sacred tree drew their blessing for the next year. That union blessed the forest and the animals in it, and kept them safe."

I began to shake my head, back and forth, no, no, without even knowing that I did it. He smiled and reached over and touched my cheek. It was a gentle touch. I stopped shaking my head, but I still stared at him out of eyes that I knew must be wild.

"Didn't you know?" he said softly. "Didn't you know when you first came to the King's Oak, and saw me bring the deer to it? I know you were there; I know you saw me. I felt you there. And didn't you know when we met, later that day, and you told me your name was Diana, and I laughed so? And tonight, when you came to the place where I was in your white Greek dress and your laurel crown, on the very night of the winter solstice . . . didn't you know?"

"Know what?" I whispered. "Didn't I know what? Tom, you scare me. I don't know what you want. . . ."

But I did know. My knees knew. The warm pit in my groin knew. I tried to draw a deep breath, but I could not.

"Stand up, Diana," he said. "If at any time you want to leave, all you have to do is say the word. I'll take you home. But stand up now. Let me look at you."

He held out his hands and I took them and let him raise me slowly to my feet. I let my arms fall loosely down to my sides, and simply looked into his face. He studied me for a long while, and then he came to me and took my face in his hands and kissed me again. It was, again, a soft kiss, but it burned my mouth like fire.

"You are very beautiful, and you honor this place," he said.

And then he reached slowly around me with both hands and found the zipper of the white dress and slid it down, and it puddled down around my feet and I let it lie while he unhooked the strapless bra and tossed it slowly aside, and gently rolled the panty hose down to my ankles. I said nothing. My heart nearly bucked through my rib cage. He hooked the waist of my panties with his thumbs and slid them down, and I stepped out of them as simply as a child being readied for a bath. I was naked before him now, in the vast black woods, in the leaping firelight, in the still of the midwinter night. I was aware of the cold air moving on my skin, but I did not feel it. I could not seem to move. I thought that surely I was frozen in the most vivid dream of my life, surely would waken soon. But I did not want to waken. . . .

From the safety of my dream I watched as he undressed, tossing his formal clothes aside on the throw, his eyes never leaving my face, my body. There was not a trace of self-consciousness about him. When he stood, in his dark, firelit nakedness, before me, the beauty of his slender body made me close my eyes once again, as I had on that earlier day, and swallow hard. I felt, rather than saw, him come to me and put his hands on me. I did not open my eyes.

"I always thought it must have happened something like this," he said, his voice close to my ear. It was soft, and his breath was warm against my cheek.

"I think he must have just wanted to touch her all over for a while, to worship her with his hands," he whispered, and I felt his hands, warm and hard and dry, slide down my cheeks and neck to my shoulders and arms, and then to my waist and along my hips and thighs. I felt the breath catch in my throat, and the fine trembling begin again.

"I think he touched her here," he said, and his fingers moved lightly in a circular movement around my nipples, slid around my breasts, cupped them, raised them to his mouth. I felt him take them one after the other into his mouth, and flick his tongue across them as lightly as a butterfly. I could feel them harden in his mouth.

"Yes," I said, my voice hoarse and low. I did not open my eyes.

"And then I think he touched her here," he said, and

I felt him kneel before me, and his hands part my thighs gently, and his warm fingers go lightly, lightly up between them into the warmth there, and linger, and seek, and find the center of me. My knees loosened until I would have fallen, except that his hands now cupped my buttocks and held me.

"And I think that then he was brave enough to kiss her there, right in the secret heart of her, right in the heart of the mystery," he said. "Here."

"Yes," I said, the great fire running through me and scalding me under his mouth with its heat. I felt him part my legs further, felt his tongue, felt the rising of the treacherous red tide in the center of me, felt the answering leap of my own fear. He must not find the darkness at the core of me.

"Tom, no, wait, I'm afraid . . . ," I whispered, but then he took my hands and guided them to the warm hardness of him, that pressed into me, and the great flood took me under at last, and I felt myself fall backward to the fur throw and pull him down hard on top of me, and felt my frantic hands pull the hardness into the emptiness there that cried aloud, and felt the beginning of that slow, terrible, old rhythm that would surely, this time, blot me out of the world for all eternity.

Even as I heard my own cries—"Yes, yes, go on, now, yes"—I heard also the intermingled sobbing: "I'm afraid, I'm afraid!"

And heard him, soothing, soothing: "Don't be afraid. I'll never hurt you, never. . . ."

And I cried out as loudly as I could, "It's me I'm afraid of!"

He lifted himself above me on his stiffened arms and rocked, rocked, looking down at me. His face was serene. "Let it go, Diana," he said, and thrust.

"No!"

"Let it go. Let me have it. Let me take it." Thrust.

"No!"

"You can't hurt me with it, I can hold it, I was born to take it and hold it." Thrust.

"No, Tom, no . . ."

"You can let go of it now, because now I'm here to take it from you. I'm here." Thrust.

And I knew, finally, in that thirty-ninth year of my life and twentieth year of my loving, that I had found the vessel that could catch and hold and transmute the explosive red darkness within me, and could pour it back into my body in fire and lightness, and I did let it go, and felt the earth and sky and woods and water fly apart, laughing, with the force of our coming.

It was nearly dawn before we stopped making love, and I laughed for most of that time. Tom Dabney laughed, too. We slept a little, wrapped in the deep fur and each other's arms, and when we woke and dressed and he stooped to pick up the mink throw, he began to laugh again.

"What?" I said, poking him lazily with my cold bare foot as I put on my shoes.

"I was just thinking what Pat would say if she could see where her famous mink throw ended up," he said. "She said when she left for me to keep it, that every time I screwed under it I'd have to think about her, whether or not I wanted to."

"And did you?" I said.

"Not for a New York minute," he said.

CHAPTER EIGHT

Sometime well after dawn I drifted out of sleep and thought, clearly and roundly, *What I did last night was so terrible that I will not think of it again,* and let the thick, warm tide of sleep take me back under. I believe I would have slept the day through, except that a great hammering on the cottage door wakened me, finally, about midafternoon. From the angle of the sun on the white stucco walls of my bedroom, I knew it must be past three. I wrapped my robe around me and stumbled barefoot to the front door, the soreness in my body and the trail of strewn underclothes on the floor registering not at all on the thick white opacity in my mind. I remembered nothing and felt nothing. There was nothing in the free-floating bubble I had built around me but the noise of the knocking. I went toward it as a cat might toward the sound of the kitchen can opener.

Carter and Hilary stood there, and I looked at them stupidly. Carter's face was stretched full, as it had been the night before, and the skin on his cheeks was mottled red and white. Hilary had been crying; the scum of her tears was still on her face. We stared at each other in the clarion blue afternoon.

"May we come in?" Carter said finally, in a flat, tight voice. "I think Hilary would like to change her clothes. And she's probably hungry."

I stepped aside and they walked into the house. Hilary gave me an oblique look and pattered silently down the hall toward her room. I could hear her give a great, rattling sniff. Carter looked at my strewn clothes and then at me. I could hear the whistle of breath in his nostrils.

"I apologize for disturbing you," he said precisely. "But when you didn't pick Hilary up by ten, Marjorie started calling you. When it got past noon, she started calling me. I've been out ever since, looking for you. We've been very worried. Hilary has been crying for quite a while. You might give Marjorie a ring. She missed church, and she and Charlie and Tish are ready to call the police."

All that I had pushed away crashed down on me like a tidal wave. Guilt flooded me, cold and awful. Revulsion at myself and what I had done almost made me gag. And yet, under it, far below, tiny and frail, anger flickered, too. I hated the stretched, smug balloon of Carter's face. I hated the dry, whiplash voice. But Hilary. How could I have forgotten that I was to pick up Hilary at Marjorie and Wynn Chapin's before they left for eleven o'clock services at Saint Thomas's? How could I have forgotten Hilary at all?

"I'm so sorry," I whispered through my puffed, dry

lips. I wondered if he could read the night's stigmata on them, or smell the musk of love about me. I could feel the tangle of my hair on my neck. The soreness between my legs smote me then, punishing and hateful.

"You should be sorry," he said, the flatness leaving his voice. It climbed like red mercury in a thermometer. "Never mind where you went or what you did with Dabney; you scared your little girl to death. You worried me and your best friends terribly. Half of Pemberton is calling around trying to find you."

"I've been right here," I said. I could not force strength into my voice. "I've been here since . . . you've been calling. I guess I just didn't hear the phone."

"I guess you didn't," he said. "I guess Dabney didn't, either. I didn't get an answer from him for four hours. Finally I went out there. I've just gotten back. He said you'd be here."

"You went out to Goat Creek. . . ." Heat began crawling from my breasts to my throat and cheeks and forehead.

"Yeah, I went to Goat Creek. And if you think that didn't cost me more than I can ever tell you, think again. I was really looking forward to the prospect of finding you out there in the fastest bed in the South."

The heat reached my brain and seared the fuzziness out of it. Anger spurted up to match his.

"I wasn't ever at Goat Creek last night," I said. "But if you want to know where I was, I'll tell you. I went out to the King's Oak with Tom and we built a fire and we talked."

"You talked," he said. "You talked until four-thirty this morning?"

"I . . . How did you know when I got home?" I said.

"I know because I asked Dabney. I know you weren't

home before then because I tried to call you from midnight on."

"And Tom said . . ." I could not look at him. I looked at the floor. My piled clothes there seemed to have scarlet *A*'s worked into the very warp and woof of them.

"Tom said just what you said. That you hadn't been to the house at all; that you'd gone out to the old oak and built a fire. He said it was up to you to tell me what you did there. So suppose you just do that thing, Andy. Suppose you tell me what you did with Tom Dabney out in the god-damned woods until four-thirty in the morning. . . ."

"Oh, for Christ's sake, Carter, we practiced unspeakable rites! It was the winter solstice; what else would we be doing?" I shouted, aware that I was attempting to mislead him with the truth. Shame backed the bile up into my throat. It felt so ghastly awful that I shouted at him again: "This is about Tom Dabney, it isn't about Hilary or being worried about me! It's about Tom Dabney and your fucking god-damned pride!"

"How could you sleep through six hours of a ringing telephone?" he bellowed at me. The veins in his neck stood out, and his cheeks and forehead were nearly purple. "What did you do out there that wore you out that much?"

"Did it ever occur to you that that awful exhibition you and Chip Dabney put on last night upset me so much that it wore me out?" I screamed. "I wish I could sleep forever; I wish I could sleep until the sound of your obscene laughter died right out of my mind! But it never will! Carter, how *could* you. . . ."

He was silent for a long time. I could not look at him. Finally I did; his face was no longer full, but slack and very tired. "I don't know," he said. "It did occur to me, yes. That's why I called you at midnight, and all those other times: to apologize. That's one reason I went out to Goat Creek: to apologize to Tom. I didn't really think I'd find you there. I shouldn't have laughed; I don't know why I did."

His voice was so soft and miserable and my own guilt and self-loathing were so complete that I began to cry, hopelessly, and wretchedly I stood in my living room in the crystal sunlight of December and wept, eyes shut tight, arms hanging uselessly at my sides. At that moment I thought that I had wrecked beyond repair everything in the world that was dear to me with my own corruption. If I could have transported myself back to my beautiful, terrible house in Buckhead at that moment, I would have done so. Whatever it might hold for me had no terror now. After what I had done, nothing else could possibly matter.

After a long time he came to me and put his arms around me and rested his chin on the top of my snarled head.

"Let's go back," he said thickly. "Let's move the clock back to before that goddamned party and just wipe it out; let's pick up from seven o'clock last night. Let's don't ever go near Pat Dabney again; let's boycott every Dabney in south Georgia. Andy, if you can try to forgive me, I swear I'll never mention him again to you; I'll never doubt you again. . . ."

Incredibly, I felt warm, wet drops falling onto the top of my head.

"Don't, don't, don't," I wept, clutching him so fiercely that I heard the breath go out of him in a little rush. "You don't have anything to forgive. Don't be nice to me, Carter; I don't deserve it."

"Shhh," he whispered. "Hush. Of course you deserve it; who more? Go talk to Hilary now, and I'll make us an omelet. I bet you haven't eaten since last night. I don't think she has, either. We'll just forget it ever happened. I promise."

I trudged blearily down the hall to try and make my peace with Hilary, only to find her serenely curled up on her bed munching something and watching the little Sony Carter had gotten for her room. She looked up at me and smiled. It was a bit watery, but a real smile, for all that.

"Hi," I said. "What are you eating?"

"Bran muffin," she said, her mouth full. "Mrs. Chapin gave it to me. Want some?"

I shook my head. "I'm awfully sorry about last night, Punkin," I said. "I just plain overslept and didn't hear the phone. It's no excuse, but if you'll forgive me I promise I won't ever do it again."

"No sweat," Hilary said. "You were with Tom, weren't you?"

"Yes," I said. "How did you know?" The heat flooded into my face again. What could she have overheard from Marjorie and Wynn and Carter?

"I heard you tell Carter you were. I listened," she said matter-of-factly. "I was scared at first when we couldn't find you, but I won't be again. I'll know you're with him. Did you see any more deer?"

"Not a one," I said. "But listen, Hil, there's not going to be a next time. I'm not going off like that again, not with Tom or anybody. Not even with Carter."

"Well, but I don't care if you do," she said. "If it's with Tom. Only I want to go with you when you go again. Can we do it tomorrow? It's the holidays. You said we could when the weather cleared."

"Oh, Hil . . . ," I began.

"You said," she said. The smile left her face. "You promised."

I would have done anything, at that moment, rather than kill another promise to her.

"I'll call him tonight," I said. I could hardly hear my own words for the pounding of the blood in my temples. I knew that I would make the call. I knew that I had to try and negate, erase, the thing that had happened between us. I knew I could not live in Pemberton anymore until I had. I could not imagine what he would say, or do.

I took a long shower and washed my body and hair. The hot water soothed the ache in my legs and arms, but it did not touch the warm, pulsing point of pain deep within me. Every time I felt it, I winced inwardly with shame. Had I been utterly deranged, doing the things I had done with Tom Dabney by the fire in the forest, saying the things to him I had said? I could only vaguely recall them now, could not feel the shape of the words in my mouth. Was he utterly crazy, saying the things he had said to me? Doing those things with me, shouting aloud, laughing aloud on that pagan fur blanket? Did he believe the things he had said to me about the King of the Sacred Grove, and the huntress-goddess, and the winter solstice? I could not imagine that he did.

"But it got your pants off and your legs apart pretty fast, didn't it?" I said aloud to myself, water running down my face but not cooling it. "It got you fucking like a wild thing in heat, so many times your twat is raw," I said. "It got you screaming like one of Pat Dabney's mares." The deliberately coarse words made me sick: I spat into the water running down the drain. But my traitorous nipples remembered, and prickled themselves erect, and the warmth in my groin turned over again. I got out of the shower and scrubbed myself with a towel until I thought my skin would bleed.

We ate our omelets in front of the fire, and talked of many things, small and of no import. Carter laughed a lot, and so did I, tinnily. Every time we met each other's eyes I flushed, and he dropped his. Hilary went back to her room to watch TV and he helped me with the dishes, as he had a hundred times, and by nine o'clock he was at the door, his jacket in his hand, saying that he thought we all three needed an early night.

Before he left, he kissed me briefly on the cheek, and said, "I apologize, one last time, Andy. I think it was just that . . . you'd always been so perfect up to now. So nearly exactly what I've always dreamed about. It couldn't have been fair to you, thinking of you like that. It's going to do me good to see that you're human like the rest of us, that a little irresponsibility isn't totally beyond you. It makes you even dearer to me."

"Well, I hope so," I said, kissing his cheek in return. But underneath the contrition, the clear voice said: "Irresponsibility? One time in my entire life I forgot Hilary, one time, and I'm irresponsible?" Even more clearly, the voice said: "Yes, that's just what you were."

"Will I see you tomorrow?" I said, over the crystal words.

"There's that thing of the Carringtons'," he said. "Do you still want to go? I think we should, to sort of scuttle the gossip before it starts."

"I guess so," I said, thinking, *Damn the gossip.* But I knew he was right. Our appearing together as if nothing had happened would effectively douse the small brushfire that must be rippling through Pemberton. And fully ninety-five percent of me yearned for the return of the comforting normalcy, the lulling banality, of the rounds of small-town holiday parties. Of my day-to-day life with Carter, before

Tom Dabney had pierced my skin and let wildness in. The other five percent was buried under a slag heap of guilt.

When he turned to go, he ruffled my damp hair, but he did not kiss me on my mouth. I stood for a long moment staring at the closed door, and then I went into my bedroom and shut the door and locked it and pulled out the telephone directory and found the number, and called Tom Dabney at Goat Creek. I have never done anything in my life remotely so difficult before or since.

"We have to find a way to forget last night ever happened," I said without preamble, when he answered. My voice was high and silly, but it did not occur to me he would not know who I was.

He knew.

"Not forget," he said. "I can't, and neither can you. But we can act as if we have, if that's the way you want it."

"Tom, I don't know what in the world . . . ," I began.

"Sure you do," he said. There was laughter in his voice, but it was not mocking. "You know as well as I do. But it's okay. I expected this call; I've been waiting for it. We can be friends or lovers or business associates or enemies or anything you want; you call the shot. I'll honor it."

"Just like that?" I said, relief flooding me.

"Just like that," he said. "It's dealer's choice, and you're the dealer. You make the rules. The only thing I hope is that you won't quit coming out here. I promise, if you won't, and if you'll let Hilary keep coming, that I won't mention last night again, until you do. And I won't lay a hand on you."

"Really? Tom, can I count on that? Can we still come . . . strictly as friends?"

"You can count on it," he said. "Friends it will be. The only stipulation is that you spare me any of the anguish and the breast-beating and the 'I can't imagine what got into me's.' Not a word of it. You lay off that and I'll lay off you. Until you say otherwise. I won't like it, and it won't change anything, but I'll do it. Is that a deal? Not a word?"

"Not a word," I said, giddy with sudden lightness. "It's a deal." The guilt flew away like a cloud of stinging gnats. I could do it, then; I could have Carter for my lover and Tom for my friend. One would not have to be sacrificed for the other. I could keep them both and make it work.

"Good," he said. "Then come on out tomorrow or the next day. I've got presents for you and Hilary."

"Oh, Lord, I haven't gotten anything for you . . . ," I began, then stopped. I knew I did not need to talk to Tom Dabney this way.

"Thanks," I said. "That's awfully nice of you. But neither of us should be spending much money just now."

"They're homemade." He laughed. "You'll see just how homemade. Tomorrow? Come for lunch, so we'll have some time in the woods. It's lesson time. But I think you'd better be home before dark from now on."

"You don't know the half of it," I said, laughing, too. "You really don't. Okay, then. Tomorrow. See you around noon."

"See you," Tom Dabney said.

He was waiting for us on the porch the next afternoon, sitting with his back against the railing and his legs stretched out before him, the pale sun striking mahogany glints in his dusky hair. The day was clear and chilly, but out of the wind, in the lee of the house, the sun had a spurious surface warmth, and he sat in a pool of it, jacketless. Earl sat on his shoulder, eating something like a hot dog with his two clever hands. He tossed it away and Tom handed him another of whatever it was, and he took it and began to gnaw greedily. Tom smiled up at us, shading his eyes against the sun, and held out his hand. Hilary took it as naturally as if it had been mine, and he pulled her down beside him on the rough planks of the porch and drew her against him, in the circle of his arm. I found I could not speak around the Sahara-like aridity in my mouth.

"Long time, good buddy," he said to Hilary. "Too long. Earl almost forgot your name, had to ask me a couple of times. And Missy is in a real snit."

"Mama's been awfully busy going to parties, and then it rained," Hilary said, scrubbing her face into his shirt. Earl chirred and patted her hair and face, and then settled into her lap, and Hilary hugged him.

"The belle of Pemberton," Tom said, his wolf's grin widening. He looked up at me. "I'm honored to have her in my humble hovel. What could I offer her, do you think, that could compete with the glittering salons of Pemberton?"

"You could take her out in the woods and show her stuff," Hilary said without guile. All the same, I looked at her sharply, and Tom Dabney laughed aloud. I felt my color rise, and looked swiftly away from him.

"So I could and so I will," he said. "And you, too. Beginning this very day. Come on in first, though. I have a Christmas present for you."

He pulled Hilary to her feet and walked her into the house, his arm still around her. I hesitated for a moment, my heart still rocketing around in my rib cage as it had been doing since we left the house that morning, my face still hot with his voice and words. You have to stop this idiocy, I said to myself, ducking my head under his low lintel and entering the dimness of the big room. You're acting like a twelve-year-old. Nothing's going to happen. You've both agreed to that. It's all spelled out and clear. You laid down the terms yourself. He's honoring them perfectly.

I heard Hilary give a soft gasp, and then I could see why. A great pine Christmas tree stood beside the hearth, its drying needles giving back a wonderful wild, sweet smell in the heat of the leaping flames. It was decorated entirely in the largess of the woods and water: vivid red berries, white lichens, pine cones and seed pods and huge, shining acorns, dried Queen Anne's lace and other flowers, the bleached carapaces of tiny creek and river creatures, great, fairly-like drifts of silvery moss. Tiny white candles flickered on it, the flames like fireflies in the dimness. Underneath it, the mink throw was coiled in rich folds and wrapped packages were piled. In the midst of them, curled into the deep nest of the fur, Missy slept. A big aluminum pail of water stood beside the tree.

"Insurance," Tom said. "I once set the tree on fire with those damned candles. Well, how about it, ladies? Do you like my tree?"

"Oh, it's beautiful," Hilary breathed, her blue eyes misted with enchantment. "It's the prettiest tree I ever saw."

Her voice negated the years of glittering Buckhead decorator trees, and the dozens of holiday confections she had seen this year in Pemberton. They no longer existed. She was right. There in that unbelievable house beside that dark creek, in the deepest woods I had ever seen, the tree was incomparable, a perfection, a miracle. It drank the light of the winter woods and threw it back into the dimness, aflame with living wildness.

"It really is," I said. "It's like something out of a Norse fairy tale. A wild, magic tree . . ."

"Exactly," he said. "It's where we get them, you know. Out of northern antiquity, old as time; older, even. Your average Southern Baptist Christmas tree is as pagan as a human sacrifice. It's a thought I've always cherished."

Hilary knelt to pet Missy, and the little goat lurched awake and stumbled, bleating, into her arms. She nuzzled Hilary's neck with her rubbery black lips.

"She knows me!" Hilary crowed. "She's not mad at me!"

"Nope. All is forgiven. Sweet-tempered animals, goats. Not at all like their reputations," Tom said. "If you really want to clinch it, take her in the kitchen and give her that dish up on the counter. Scratch has got her on a new mixture, and she's crazy about it. This week, anyway."

Hilary scampered out into the kitchen, the little goat pattering behind her on the wide old boards. Her hooves looked as shining and perfect as if they had been freshly cast of metal. She had grown in the days since we had been to Goat Creek. The sweet white face was on a level with Hilary's waist now, and the soprano bleat had a mellow note down in it. She shone all over as if she had just been shampooed.

We stood beside the tree in silence, Tom and I, in the light of the fire. It snickered softly behind its screen, and over it I became aware of the high, pure sound of young boys' voices singing something dissonant and old and lovely, not Christmas music precisely, but something that rang of ancient winters, and the sacred. Outside, the still creek was the blue of steel under the thin sun, and the air that eddied into the room under the laced canvas was fresh and cold and wild. Pemberton and its drawing rooms and laden buffets, its traffic-choked streets and overheated, wreathed-and-ribboned shops, seemed very far away. But the star-chipped night and the silent woods and the firelit edifice of the great King's Oak seemed near to the very touching. I swallowed past the dryness in my throat and looked interestedly at the tree and the creek and the fire and the big ceiling-mounted twin speakers. But not at Tom.

"Well," I said. "So here we are again."

"Here we are," Tom said.

"It's really a lovely tree," I said chattily. "What an unusual idea, using the wild things. Did you do it just for Hilary?"

"No, my boys have always liked it," he said agreeably. "And I like doing it. I do it as much for me as anyone. Some years, I'm the only person besides Scratch and Reese and sometimes Martin who sees it. But I always put it up."

"You really could win a prize for it in any Christmas decorating contest," I went on. I was miserably aware that I sounded like a fool, but I could not stop my tongue. Something inexorable waited to come into any silence between Tom Dabney and me.

"God forbid," he said.

"Oh, no, you could," I said. "It's so fresh and wholesome and uncommercial. . . ."

I lapsed into silence at last, mute under the sheer awfulness of my own blather.

Tom came across the room and put his hands on my shoulders and gave them a small shake. A surge of something, not quite shame and past disbelief, swept me so hard that I closed my eyes against it. Dear God, I thought, those hands were all over me night before last. There is not a square inch of my skin that that mouth hasn't tasted.

"Diana, stop squinching your eyes shut and look at me. You look like a bat in daylight."

His blue eyes were very near mine, and I read in them only amusement. Nothing dangerous. Nothing insinuating. Nothing else at all.

"Listen," he said. "I thought we settled this. I thought we agreed to act as if Saturday night never happened. Your preference, sweet thing, not mine. I happen to consider it bullshit and unnecessary to boot, but . . . we agreed. So let's do it. Stop looking at me out of the corner of your eye like I'm going to jump your bones when you're not looking. Stop prattling about decorating contests and my wholesome Christmas tree. You don't care about my Christmas tree. You're just scared I'm going to think you're a vile scarlet woman because of what we did. Well, I think what we did was absolutely fucking wonderful, and I think you're absolutely fucking wonderful, and vice versa, and I always will, but I'm going to treat you like the only thing we ever did together was admire this fresh, wholesome, uncommercial Christmas tree. Period. Forever, until you tell me to stop. Now: you stow the Junior League stuff and we're in business. Consider yourself unscrewed."

I erupted into laughter and he gave me a little hug, and abruptly the day was radiant and careless and festive, an endless ribbon of time, just as the day before Christmas Eve should be. We called Hilary back in from the kitchen and settled before the fire for our presents.

He was suddenly almost shy. I had never seen such diffidence in him.

"I thought it was a good idea at the time," he said. "Now I'm not at all sure you're not both going to hate them. They're not at all grand. . . ."

"It's the thought that counts, as they say," I smiled. "We don't need or want grand, Tom. We had grand, in Atlanta."

"It doesn't matter as long as it's a present," Hilary said, practically. "Hurry up, Tom. I can't wait."

"Well, as long as you've been warned," he said, and

went back into the sleeping area. In a moment he returned, holding his hands behind his back.

"Close your eyes," he said. We did.

"Merry Christmas, Diana and Hilary," he said, and we opened our eyes. He stood before us, grinning, holding in his hands two slender bows and two quivers of small, slim arrows. Even in that first eyeblink I could tell that they were not modern bows but were made in a manner that had passed out of use before books had been written and printed to tell of them. I knew that he had made them himself. They were very simple, and very beautiful.

But . . . bows and arrows? For me; for my ten-year-old daughter, city creatures, both of us? Implements for killing, for us? I did not know what to say.

Hilary knew.

"Oh, Tom, oh, they're perfect, oh, they're beautiful," she cried. "Are they actually mine? Did you make them? Will you teach me to shoot them? Can I take them to school and show everybody? Nobody has a bow and arrows. . . ."

"They're really yours," he said, his tentative smile widening. "And I did make them, just for you, and I will indeed teach you to shoot them, starting this very day, if you like. But I'd rather you kept them out here, Hil. This is serious stuff; this is not for show-and-tell. I don't know many kids besides you I'd trust to understand and treat a bow and arrows with respect. They belong in the woods. They're something for you to know and use out here only. They're like . . . a secret we know, that belongs only at Goat Creek. Nobody else should be a part of it but us out here. Is that okay with you?"

"Yes," she said, looking at him seriously. "It is. I see what you mean."

I looked at the two of them, there in the light of the fire and the pagan Christmas tree. My scalp crept slightly. I knew that she did understand what he was saying, both the words and the sense of them, and I knew also that I did not.

He looked at me.

"Do you like yours, Diana?" he said, almost formally. "They should fit you, but ideally you ought to fit them exactly to arm lengths, and I had to estimate there. I can make you another if this one doesn't fit."

"They're really beautiful," I said slowly. "It's gorgeous craftsmanship; it must have taken you months. I never saw anything like them before. It's just that I'm a complete klutz when it comes to things that require aim and control, and . . . I don't think I could ever shoot anything with them."

"I'd never expect you to, unless you wanted to," he said. "It's very satisfying just to be good at target shooting. You might surprise yourself there. I have a feeling I can teach you to shoot very well indeed. And then, who knows, you might want to do more with it. But whatever, I just wanted to make them for you. I wanted you to have them. I've been imagining you standing in my woods, holding a bow that I made for you. . . ."

"Then I love them, and I'll love trying to learn," I said, feeling a rush of tenderness for him that I might for a small boy. There was nothing in that moment of man and woman. "Just so you're not disappointed when I can't hit anything but the creek. And so I don't have to kill anything."

"No to both," he said, and put the bow and arrows into my hands, and gave Hilary hers.

My bow was light and satiny to the touch, but it felt sweetly substantial in my hands, and my palm fitted around it perfectly. The wood was a pale ash color, and glowed like a piece of good old furniture. It was simple in shape, just the curved wooden bow and the clean, sharp string. The bowstring was taut, and gave a silvery ping when I flicked it. It was not of plastic or any substance I had seen on a tennis racket; I did not know what it was. The tips were tightly wrapped with more of the string substance, and they flared a bit, symmetrically and beautifully. This bow was as different from the intricate, vicious weapon I had seen in the back of Carter's car the morning of the hunt at King's Oak as a swallow from a peacock. But looking at its clear, ruthless arc and the absolute line of the string, I thought that it would be just as deadly. Somehow, with the living satin of the wood under my fingers, that thought did not appall me as it might have.

"It's perfect, a perfect fit, or at least it feels perfect," I said. "And it's utterly beautiful. What's the wood?"

"Willow," Tom said. "Some people think chokecherry or serviceberry makes a better bow, but I like the idea of willow; it was sacred to the water gods in most cultures. And you'd have to go all the way to the high plains out West to find serviceberry, but there's willow all over the Big Silver Swamp. This willow came from way up Goat Creek, near the spring where it starts. It was a sapling that had been hit by lightning; fire-cured willow is the best there is. But you don't find it often in the swamp. Too wet. So when I came across this one, four or five years ago, I brought the whole thing home and kept it. It just seemed to me that it had the kiss of all the gods on it. It would almost have been a sacrilege *not* to make bows from it."

"Are they hard to make?" I said. "They look so simple, but every inch looks right. How do you know where to curve it, and when to stop, and all that?"

"I learned from my father," he said. "He and my Uncle Clay learned from my grandfather, who learned from his father: my great-grandfather. *He* learned while he was at the University of Heidelberg; in Germany, to get a hunting license, you have to take a very rigorous, formal course of instruction in woodsmanship and survival skills and weaponry. You come out as knowledgeable as a forest ranger, or you don't get your license. Waldmeisters, they called them. Still do, I think. I think it's a great idea; nobody who isn't that good in the woods, or who doesn't know and respect the wild that much, ought to be allowed in them with weapons. I don't let anybody who isn't on my land."

"But everybody in Pemberton hunts," I said. "Everybody in the entire South hunts, it seems like. How many of them are that good?"

"About one in every three million," he said. "I've come to hate the fall and winter. It seems like every murderous jackass who can lift a gun or a bow is loose in the woods. It's a great relief to me when I hear that some of them have shot each other in the butt, or worse. I think, *There's a bird or a deer safe for a while longer.*"

I simply looked at him. We had had this conversation before. He was a hunter himself, and yet he spoke of keeping the deer safe, and the birds.

"I'm the one in three million," he said matter-of-factly, reading my thoughts. "I'm that good. I shoot nothing that isn't necessary, and nothing that I don't mean to shoot. And I don't miss. And I shoot with respect. With love, even. If you learn from me, you'll shoot that way, too. I'm not bragging; it took me an awfully long time to get as good as I am, and I worked very hard at it, and I had two of the world's great teachers in my dad and Uncle Clay. It's not time to talk about the killing yet, Andy, but we *will* talk about it, and you'll understand better by then."

" I want to hear about it," Hilary said suddenly, looking up at him. She stood holding her smaller bow, loosely and delicately in the palm of her hand. She held it as if she had been accustomed to its weight and heft since birth.

I frowned slightly at her, and then at Tom Dabney. I had not brought Hilary here in order that she might learn to kill.

"Not yet," Tom said to her, smiling slightly. "But soon. I don't think I'll have to tell you very much, Hil. I think there's an awful lot your heart and bones and muscles know that your mind doesn't yet."

"Could I learn to make a bow like this?" she said.

"Sure, if you want to. I can teach you how to make practically anything you'd need to survive in the wild. I can teach you to find and make shelters and beds and tools and utensils and even clothing, from hides and plant fibers. I can teach you to make fires with nothing but that bow, a stick, and a rock. I could even teach you to make knives and spears, and work stone; but in the Southern river swamps you'd never need that. A bow is enough. I can teach you to find water, too, but again, that's not a problem in the Big Silver. I can teach you to find and harvest and cook plants that will keep you alive and even taste pretty good, and plants that will heal you, and how to avoid the ones that will kill you. And I can teach you to call almost any animal in the Big Silver, and to stalk them and shoot them and dress them and cook them. Even to tan their skins and make shelters and clothing from them, and utensils from their bones. Nothing should be wasted in the woods. I can teach you as much of that as you want to know. I can teach both of you."

"Why?" Hilary said, her blue eyes curious on his.

"Because for one thing, it beats reruns of *Star Trek*," he

said, reaching out to brush her silky hair away from her eyes. "And for another, because its old and valuable and it's a true thing about men and animals and the woods. There have to be people who learn it so it can stay alive. I thought you might be one of the ones who'd like to."

"I would," she said. "I'd like to learn all of it."

"Then you shall," he said.

They walked together out of the dark house and into the cold flare of the noon sun. His arm was around her shoulder, and her dark head was tipped up to his; they were talking. Like the little goat, Hilary had grown when I had not been looking. Her neck and arms had lengthened, her slender legs in the baggy stone-washed jeans were longer, and there was the very beginning of definition at her waist and hips. The top of her head reached almost to his shoulder now. Both their glossy pelts gleamed chestnut in the sun, and she had fit her light, tripping stride to his quick, soft one. They could have been father and daughter, there in the winter light. She resembled Tom Dabney far more than she did me, or ever had Chris. The enigmatic warmth began again in my groin, slow and insinuating, and I clenched my teeth against it, and thought of every annoying thing I had ever felt about Tom Dabney, and every endearing thing I felt for Carter. I would not suffer this treacherous warmth; I would not. My arrangements had been made.

At the edge of the creek, where the land was clear and the water ran shallow and sunstruck—the place, I knew, where he and Hilary had danced together in the silver moonlight—he had set up a target. I saw with a small shock of anger that it was the silhouette of a deer, black on square white. The animal stood in profile; on its shoulder area was a large black circle. On the ground next to it lay another target, with silhouettes of the animal from the front, behind, and at oblique angles. Each had its black circles.

I stopped, feeling dull anger.

"Just wait a minute, Tom," I said. "We've had enough about death and killing for one day. I have no objection to target shooting, but I'm not going to shoot at pictures of deer, and I'm not going to have Hilary doing it, either."

He looked at me mildly for a moment, and then he said, "Fair enough. I've got an old bull's-eye target in the goatshed you can use. I think Hilary has the right to pick her own target, though."

I opened my mouth to rebuke him, and then stopped. My whole often-despairing purpose this year had been to get Hilary into the habit of making her own decisions, at least about the things she was qualified to choose. I could not go on making them for her.

"Fine," I said tightly. "By all means, let Hilary choose."

"I choose the deer," she said promptly, looking sidewise at me, and though I knew she had chosen the animal only to please Tom, I nodded as calmly as I could, and turned my attention to the bow and arrows in my hand. Perhaps we could talk about this later, she and I. I did not want her waking up in sweating nightmares, stricken over the slaying of paper deer.

"Okay. About the bow and arrows . . . ," Tom Dabney said, sitting down cross-legged on the grass beside the creek. Hilary and the kid and Earl sprawled around him, and I, too, sat down to listen. He took Hilary's bow and balanced it lightly in his hand.

"This is called a recurve bow," he said. "It's the original hunting bow. Cupid had one. The Turks used it, too, and the Romans got it from them. It was replaced by the English longbow, though God knows why; a clumsier, more inaccurate weapon has seldom been known throughout history. These came back to fashion sometime in the thirties, and they in turn have largely given way to compound bows, that use a system of pulleys to reduce energy and store draw power. Those are the ferocious things with knots and knobs and sights and quivers and God knows what crawling all over them that you saw out at King's Oak back in September, Andy. They're so easy and accurate that almost any idiot can learn to use one, in time. That's the problem. Some fool who can hit a target in his backyard at fifty yards with his compound and his broadheads gets out in the woods and gutshoots a deer and then doesn't bother to track him, or isn't good enough to, and it takes the deer days and days to die, very bad days. An arrow doesn't kill by shock like a bullet does; it kills by hemorrhaging. If you don't hit a vital spot the first time, the animal will die of weakness and infection and starvation and sheer pain and fear. I don't use anything but handmade recurves, and I don't use sights. And I don't teach them. You'll learn the oldest and hardest way there is, but when you learn you'll be good enough to give the animal every sporting chance in the book, and you'll hit him the first time.

"You'll also learn to shoot from above, in trees, and below, and to sneak, and stalk, and track, in order to get close enough for a fair shot. An archer has to go about twice as close as a rifle hunter. When I'm done with you you'll be able to find a big buck and drop him from fifty yards away, whether you ever choose to or not. You'll learn field and target arrows, and then you'll start all over again with broadheads, and in a year or two you can hit anything from a squirrel to a deer or a wild pig, including fish. You'll never need to take a gun into the woods. I only have mine for snakes and intruders. And for mercy killing. Euthanasia.

"These particular bows were made, like I said, from fire-cured willow. I made them without a knife, with a piece of flint for shaping, and I heated the tips in fire and recurved them over a rock, and I strung them with strings made of deer sinew, and wrapped the tips in more sinew. I oiled them with deer fat and rubbed them for days, until I got the finish I wanted. You can make a bow in two days, if you need to, but most prehistoric hunters were real artisans, and took weeks on their weapons, and made beautiful ones, just for the joy of it. I guess there wasn't all that much to do in winter. I spent three weeks apiece on these, and got a kick out of every minute."

"You must have started on them even before you met me," Hilary said wonderingly. "How'd you know mine would fit me?"

"I started on yours right after Thanksgiving, so I'd already met you, but only just," he said. "I was nearly done with your mother's by then."

"Wow," Hilary said.

"Wow, indeed." He grinned. "All right, Miss Hilary. Here are six words you're going to come to hate over the next few weeks: stance, draw, anchor, aim, release, and follow-through. Repeat them to me, and then come over here and I'll show you what they mean."

All through the afternoon they practiced, my child and Tom Dabney.

He positioned her about twenty yards from the target, and stood behind her, and put her into proper shooting position with the bow and arrow. On her forearm he strapped a leather arrow guard, and he slipped his own Atlanta Braves cap on her, against the sun. At the end of one hour she hit the silhouetted deer in the middle of its rump. After three hours she hit it cleanly in the middle of the black spot on its chest. She was not very far away when she did it, and she did not do it again, but neither did she miss it very far. She stood tall and straight and slim as an arrow herself, her pure, serious profile serene above the full-drawn arrow, her back slightly arched, left arm straight and still, right drawn back until the fingertips holding the fletch of the arrow just brushed her round chin. As naturally as if she had been doing it all her life, she stood, when he told her to, at full draw, for what seemed to me an impossibly long time, and the bow did not tremble or jump in her hand. At his soft word she released the arrow, and it flew like a trained bird, to sit on the deer's shoulder. Still she did not move. She looked, suddenly, like a young pagan deity, focused and impersonal and totally gone from me. My breath caught behind my breastbone. I wanted to snatch away the archaic bow and grab her and run. Only when she saw that she had hit the deer did she drop the bow and remove the cap and brush the silky sheaf of hair out of her eyes, and smile up at Tom, and then over at me.

"That feels really good," she said. "That feels like something I already knew how to do."

"And looked like it," Tom Dabney said, smiling at her. It was, I thought, a rather odd smile, small and knowing, and very proud.

"I never saw anybody, kid or grownup, man or woman, do what you did the first time out. You looked like a young Hippolyta. I'd have said Diana, but your ma's got dibs on her. In about two months, you're going to be better than I was when I was twice your age. I really wish my dad could see you. Maybe my Uncle Clay can, sometime. Both of them always told me that there were a few rare women who could outshoot any man in shoe leather with a recurve bow, but that they didn't come along often."

"Did you see, Mama?" Hilary was a young girl again, pink with pride and pleasure. The forest goddess–child was gone. I breathed easily again.

"Boy, did I," I said. "That was really something. I couldn't do that in a million years."

"Let's see you try, Mama," she cried. "Come on, it's your turn now. Let's see you try and beat me!"

I knew that it was pure and simple reluctance to be shown up by my own daughter in front of Tom Dabney that made me say, "Not this afternoon, Punkin. It's getting late; the sun's going down. I'll take my turn next time we come." I felt cross with her, with him, with myself, and when she protested and he backed her up, I snapped to her, "Go inside and get your sweater and wash your hands and face," and to him, "It was you, after all, who suggested I be home from here before dark." And then, remembering what had prompted the advice, reddened furiously from chest to hairline. He laughed.

When she had gone inside he said, "Don't lean on her too hard about the archery, Diana. She's the best natural shot I ever saw, and if she isn't squeamish about aiming at animals, it would be a shame to make her be. She isn't a carbon of you. Her fears can be different from yours; it's all right."

The fact of his perception, and the sympathy behind it, angered me even more. I waited until I was sure she was out of earshot, and then I sat down on the top step in the steely pink sunset and looked at him levelly. I was very cold without my jacket, but I did not want to admit that I was. He stood as naturally in the rising night wind as a deep-furred animal, hands in his pockets, rocking a little in his soft old moccasins. His eyes sparked fire-blue under the dark wing of hair.

"I really don't like her learning to kill things," I said. "In fact, I think it's barbaric. She's only ten years old, whatever you say, and I *am* her mother, and think I'd like the hunting lessons to stop now."

He rocked for a space of time in silence, and then he said, "She needs to know how to take care of herself, Andy."

"Oh, for God's sake, Tom, when is she ever going to need to know how to shoot somebody with a bow and arrow?" I said in exasperation.

"No, I put that wrong," he said. "I should have said, she needs to care for herself. About herself. Respect herself, feel easy with her own company. Honor herself, if you will. I don't think she does; how could she, after her father? Listen, Diana, proficiency is all. It means you can take care of yourself. It means having all your senses honed. Using all of yourself. Knowing that you have almost infinite dimensions and facets, and that you can focus and use all of them. The woods are the best for learning that. The woods use everything. There's nothing that even remotely approaches them for that."

"You'd turn her into a wild thing if I let you," I said.

"No. I'd love to give her back her wildness, though," he said. "You and her father and the city . . . all of you've civilized it right out of her. She has enough civilization to last her lifetime. But she needs her wild side. You do, too, Diana, come to that. How can you control it if you've never even met it? How can you use it if you refuse to admit it's there? And it is there. In her and in you. In all of us. I'd like her to meet her own wildness, and learn not to be afraid of it. You've met yours, but you're still scared to death of it."

The heat washed me again, and under the chill wind sweat sprang out lightly on my face and body. I felt his hands again, and his mouth, and dancing fireheat on my bare skin. . . .

"I suppose you use all your . . . facets and dimensions all the time," I said angrily. "Unlike most of us mere mortals, who have a regrettable tendency to fritter and waste time and lollygag and all those bad things. Don't you ever just . . . live in bed and eat Fritos and read junk? Or watch Vanna White, or work the crossword puzzle in *TV Guide?* Are you committed and sensitive and honest and involved in mankind every waking moment?"

"Not Vanna White, no," he said. His face was shadowed and grave, over its lupine angles, and his voice was thoughtful. "I do, however, lie in bed and drink bourbon and encourage wet dreams about squatty little Greek ladies in the altogether. And I read Henry Miller and jerk off, and I watch everything I can find of Jamie Lee Curtis, because she's got the biggest hooters I ever saw next to yours."

"Tom . . . ," I cried, hot to my waist, and furiously, blindly red.

"Did I touch 'em?" he said. "Did I? But I never said I wasn't going to look at them. Are we adding that to the deal? You ask a lot, my dear."

I stared at him in mute fury, and he stared back impassively, and then waggled his eyebrows up and down and said, "Wanna buy a duck?"

I began to laugh, helplessly, hopelessly, and I was still laughing when we pulled out of the rutted lane that led to Goat Creek and turned the Toyota west, on the darkening road toward Pemberton.

On Christmas morning Carter gave Hilary a complete formal riding habit, from boots and crop to jodhpurs, jacket, stock, and derby.

"For the dressage trials," he said. "But we're going to have to put a book on your head to keep you from growing out of them. Go put them on, Punkin; I want to see how you'll look when they give you the blue ribbon."

Hilary trotted off to her room and came back in the habit, looking years older, slender and severe and somehow rich. The formal black and white suited her blue eyes and crow's wing hair, and the faint rose flush that the day in the woods had stained into her cheeks was enchanting. I smiled involuntarily; somehow I never grew accustomed to the sheer beauty of her.

"You'll certainly win the best-dressed, if nothing else," I said.

"You look absolutely beautiful," Carter said. There was a glint of moisture in his eyes. Somehow, that smote my heart.

Hilary gave him a hug, and wore the habit all that morning, but my parental antennae told me early on that she did not especially like the gift. When she took it off before we left for Tish and Charlie's for Christmas dinner, explaining that she did not want to spill anything on it, Carter caught on, too.

"Is there something else you'd rather have, love?" he said.

"No, it's perfect. I like it so much," she said, and kissed his cheek, and he said no more. But I knew that he was troubled, and a little hurt. That night, as I tucked her into bed, I said, "Don't you like your habit, Hil? Carter spent a great deal of time and money on it."

"I do like it," she mumbled, turning her head into the pillow. "I guess I just like my bow and arrows better."

"Hil, you won't be disloyal to Tom if you like Carter's present," I said, disturbed. "There's no . . . competition between them. You can like both of them, and both their presents. It's two different things, you see: Carter is special to you in one way, almost like a father, and Tom is in another. Like . . . a very special friend."

"I wish it was the other way around," she said. Her voice was muffled in the pillow.

"Well, it isn't," I said very firmly. "And it isn't going to be. You mustn't start thinking that will change. You'll only end up with your heart broken."

"You could change it if you wanted to," she said, so softly that I almost did not hear her.

I stared at the back of her dark head, exasperation and a kind of dread pounding at my tight temples.

"Well, I'm not going to, so get used to it," I said finally, and flicked off her bedside lamp and closed her door behind me. Through it I thought I heard her say, "Bet you do, too," and started to go back in and reprimand her, and then, after all, did not. The headache that had worried at my neck and temples like a malevolent terrier all afternoon and evening was bearing down with steel jaws. I went back down the hall in search of aspirin and serenity. There had been none of either at Tish and Charlie's.

Christmas Day had been wet and mild, as winter holidays should never be and often are in the South, and a restless wind smelling of dank water and swamp decay puffed and gusted around the Coulters' dining room windows. Something in the wind seemed to get into the people in the house; Tish and Charlie's daughters, Katie and Ansley, were home from college but did not seem to wish to be, sighing long sighs over the delayed dinner and dashing off to their rooms to telephone distant friends. Charlie made the predinner old-fashioneds far too stiff and we all drank far too many of them. Tish burned her hand rather badly on the cast-iron griddle and I had to finish dinner for her, squinting through bourbon fog at her old grease-smeared cookbooks and tattered recipe clippings. By the time I got dinner on the table, Katie and Ansley were remote and elaborately polite, Hilary was wan and yangy with hunger, Tish and Charlie and Carter were drunk and wailing Christmas carols, and I was rigid with headache and annoyance at them. When at last I got Hilary home and into bed and returned to my tree- and fire-lit living room, I felt the warm wind still prowling in my veins. My skin prickled and itched, and the sight of Carter sprawled bonelessly on my sofa, tie and shoes off and fond smile bent on me, made me want to grind my teeth. I knew he wanted to make love to me; it had been evident in the way he looked at me all evening, and the number of times he touched me, as if casually. We had not made love since the night before Pat Dabney's party. By all signs and portents, tonight—this night of love and largess and celebration—should have been the night I went to him and made the healing of our rift complete.

But I did not want to. Wind, headache, hangover, annoyance, and something else—some longing for cold, clean darkness and the sharp smell of winter woods, which I would not look at or name—coursed in my blood like a virus. I pulled aside the skirts of the beautiful dark-green velvet robe he had given me and sat down, not beside him, but on a hassock in front of the fire he had built. I tired to smile across the room at him, but I felt pain and perversity pull the smile sideways.

"Come over here and let me take that thing off you, very slowly," Carter said, holding out his arms. "It's the main reason I gave it to you, so I could."

"Carter, I just can't. Not tonight. I feel like my skull is going to split into two halves, like a walnut," I said.

He was silent for a moment, and then he laughed. It was his old laugh, rich and warm.

"Are we having our first Not-tonight-dear-I-have-a-headache?" He grinned.

"I really have," I said. "A killer of one. Rain check? Till tomorrow?"

He got up off the couch and came and kissed me softly on the forehead.

"Of course. I'm grateful we're close enough so you feel free to tell me when you don't feel like it. You had to put up with far too many jackasses today, for far too long. Rain check it is."

When he left, he was still smiling. I damped the fire and unplugged the tree and went to bed and cried. I did not know for what. Or whom.

Christmas Day was on a Wednesday. The long holiday weekend crept by in a steady drizzle of tepid, enervating rain. Hilary begged to go to Goat Creek, but I knew that Tom had his sons that weekend, or planned to, and made her wait.

"Holidays are for families," I said for perhaps the tenth time, on Saturday. "Why don't we see if Carter will take us down to the Okefenokee Museum in Waycross?"

"I don't want to go to Waycross. I want to go to Goat Creek. Tom is as much family as Carter," Hilary said, cutting her eyes at me, knowing full well she was annoying me.

"Well, then, want shall be your master," I said, determined not to raise my voice at her. "Tom's boys are with him, and he doesn't need strangers to entertain when he has them."

I had not meant to hurt her, but I saw her blue eyes fill with tears.

"I'm not a stranger," she said around the lump in her throat.

"No, sugar, but you're not his child, either," I said. "Wait until Monday and we'll go."

After that she stayed in her room and watched television, and I puttered restlessly at cleaning closets, and both of us were obscurely and faintly unhappy. When Carter called to tell me what time he would pick me up for the Laidlaws' cocktail buffet that evening, I suddenly felt I could not go to another party. I simply could not pull out sheer, cobwebby panty hose and glittery pumps one more time, or put on party makeup, or kiss another cheek or be kissed on mine, or drink another too-sweet cocktail or eat another too-rich hors d'oeuvre. I could not spend another four hours smiling, and I already had had enough invitations to make either dozens of small parties or one monster reciprocal mandatory in the near future. The thought of that made me weak-kneed with weariness.

"Is it absolutely written in blood that we have to go to this one?" I said. "Are they your oldest clients, or anything? Because I think I'll sit down and howl like a wolf at the sight of one more chicken liver and water chestnut wrapped in bacon."

"They're not clients at all," Carter said. "Cliff Laidlaw is so conservative he thinks George Bush is Leon Trotsky. He's been trying to draft Jesse Helms for President for years. The day he heard I'd voted for Walter Mondale was the day he took his business to Atlanta, to Hamilton and Crane. You want to skip it?"

"With all my heart. Please. Did you really vote for Mondale?"

"I may be a Republican, but I have my limits," he said.

"We'll stay in and eat red beans and rice, and I'll collect my rain check."

And we did both. After our dinner, which he cooked while I lay on the sofa before the fire and listened to my old college album of *Lo, How a Rose,* we settled Hilary in bed and had brandy and then, after Hilary slept, we stripped off our clothes and laid them in a pile beside the sofa and made the love that I had abjured on Christmas night. This time it was not good.

We started slowly, tenderly, as it always was with us, the soft love that had, since we had been together, so lulled and comforted me. The love that had healed my darkness. But then, nearing his climax, Carter quickened his rhythm past anything he had done with me before, and went deeper and harder, and shouted out things I had not ever thought to hear from his lips, and finished in me with such a grunting, driving intensity that my head snapped on my neck, and I was crying aloud with fright and pain. He lay still atop me for a full two minutes and I turned my head aside, into the sofa pillow, and tried to stop the weak, foolish tears of fear and loss. But I could not; they ran into my ears and matted my hair. I had been wrong, then. This was not, after all, the gentle love I had thought would carry me, soothed and level, through my life. There would, after all, be a price for this love.

Carter was stricken; he cried himself, and held me and stroked my hair, and begged my forgiveness over and over until I finally put my hand over his mouth and managed a smile.

"Anybody listening through the keyhole would think you'd been flogging me with a cat-o'-nine-tails," I said.

"I might as well have," he said. "I was just that brutal. I know what you went through with your husband; I know what you've been afraid of all these years. And yet I practically raped you. Forced you. Andy, before God, I don't know what got into me."

"Forget it, Carter," I said, distressed by his pain. "If a little excess of passion is the worst thing we ever have to go through, we're lucky. I overreacted. I should apologize to you. It just . . . took me by surprise."

"I should imagine it did. I treated you like a whore. You must have thought I was a closet sadist all along, like that murderous jerk Calhoun. I absolutely promise you it will never happen again. You were never made for that kind of . . . excess."

I remembered a night of cold and stars and firelight, of laughing, shouting love on a bed of fur under a primordial tree, of unashamed nakedness and absolutely nothing possible to bone, blood, and muscle held back. I thought I would weep again, this time for two losses, and I pushed the memory away as far and as deep as it would go. I had my agenda, and that fire-leaping wildness had no place in it. I would banish it completely; I could do that. I could and I would.

The next day Carter was scheduled to fly to Atlanta for two days of depositions. He spoke of canceling, of rescheduling, but I would not let him do that.

"I'm absolutely sick to death of parties, and nobody will expect me to come without you," I said. "And I need to spend some time with Hilary by myself. Go on, and we'll have New Year's Eve to look forward to. The break will do us both good."

"It won't do me good," he said miserably. "Every day I want more and more to spend the rest of my life with you, and lately I seem to be doing my dead-level best to drive you away. I don't like to leave you with this sorry night hanging over us."

"This sorry night never happened," I said, pushing him

out the door. "It is nothing. Zero, zip, *nada*. Go on and make some money. I never had in mind hooking up with a pauper."

Even lightly, I could not make myself say the word "marry."

CHAPTER NINE

Hilary's school did not start again until the Monday after New Year's, and the college did not reopen until two weeks after that. For the first time since we came to Pemberton, my daughter and I had an unblemished stretch of free time together, lying before us like a clean snowfall. I spoke of shopping for school clothes, visiting museums, atttending concerts and galleries, taking Hilary back to the stables to catch up on her dressage classes and ride Pittypat.

"Goat Creek. You said." Hilary did not even look up from the book on archery she had checked out of the Pemberton library.

We went.

"Did you guys have a good Christmas?" Tom said,

kissing Hilary's cheek and giving my shoulder a casual squeeze. He wore Earl like a fur piece around his neck; the weather had brightened again, and turned cold. Missy pattered bleating behind him, and broke into her rocking-horse scamper when she saw Hilary. Frost-white breath puffed from her patent-leather nose.

"Very good, yes," I said.

"No. I missed you," Hilary said. "What did you do? Did you have turkey? Did you and your sons shoot bows and arrows?"

Did you shoot *my* bow and arrows? hung unsaid in the hard, bright air.

"I did indeed have turkey, wild turkey," Tom said. "But the boys couldn't make it after all. So Scratch and Mr. Carmody and I ate up all their turkey and had a fine time."

"I'm sorry, Tom," I said, red anger at Pat Dabney thumping in my chest.

"Me, too," he said. "But I went in and saw them for a while Christmas night. And I took them to the airport in Atlanta, to catch their plane back to school. They hated missing the woods as much as I did; Pat is essentially a stupid woman. When they're old enough to choose, they'll come here as often as they can. I can wait. She's going to be a lonely old woman."

"Meanwhile there's me," Hilary said.

"Meanwhile and always, there's you, Princess Hilary," Tom said, hugging her hard around her thin shoulders.

"Okay. Go in the house and get those fatigue jackets on the back of the sofa. The Dabney floating school of woodcraft begins now."

We went back to Goat Creek every morning that week, and each day he taught us new things about the woods and waters of the Big Silver. Mornings were for field trips; on one of them, he taught us how to identify and gather and cook plants that would sustain life in the wild, and how to make rope and utensils and even clothing from their fibers. We built a pit for steaming and roasted amaranth, wild asparagus, bulrush bulbs and stalks; burdock roots; cattails.

"You could just about survive in the wild with a good stand of cattails," Tom said. "You can eat the roots, shoots, seed heads, and pollen. The leaves are great for weaving, and the down from the head makes good insulation for blankets and sleeping bags. It's the perfect survival plant for the river swamps."

We had tea from wild rose hips and pemmican from Tom's pockets. Made of dried venison and berries pounded together, it had a not unpleasant dark, wild taste, and was surprisingly satisfying. We gathered the plants that, he said, were the swamp's medicine chest: burdock roots, for salves and wound washes; mullein, whose burned leaves relieved lung congestion; nettles for a tea that stopped diarrhea; wild onion for insect repellent; yarrow for stopping bleeding and healing inflammation, and for toothaches.

"There are lots of others that do heavy-duty healing; Scratch claims he can cure pneumonia and bad septic infections and even cancer, if he can catch it soon enough. He's pulled the goats through some godawful, messy sicknesses. But I leave that to him; he's one of the few old-timers who know what they are and where to find them. In another time Scratch would have been a great medicine man."

One morning, he taught us the rudiments of calling the wild creatures of the Big Silver swamp. He told us of the prehistoric origins of tracking and calling game animals, of the methods of attracting them in past and present times: sounds, scents, decoys, baiting, tracking. He taught us the "talk" of the Southern swamp animals, and the emotions that came into play in the calling: hunger; fear; sexual arousal; the simple and universal need among animals for companionship and safety; the powerful maternal instinct; anger. He taught us to recognize the signs that the animal we wished to call was near, and he taught us the myriad ways to conceal ourselves and our movements, in order to attract and get within range. He taught us to use the wind, and the angle of the sun, and the time of day and year, and the features of the terrain, and the masking of our scents, and he taught us the habits of the animals themselves.

"All that, just so we can get near enough to kill them," I said bitterly. It seemed to me that possessing all that knowledge was somehow indecent, a sadly loaded deck.

"Even with all that, on your best day, on mine, every animal out there is quicker, quieter, sneakier, smarter, and more intuitive than we are," Tom retorted. "It's not all that uneven a contest. And it's why I don't let hunters with guns on my land. If you can get close enough with a bow to shoot accurately, you've earned your turkey or your deer. Besides, there was a time, and not so long ago, that your very life would have depended on knowing those things."

"That was then," I said.

"It's not impossible that it could happen now," he said briefly. "Things happen in the woods that don't anywhere else. Times change. It's stupid as well as sloppy to go into them not knowing all you can."

"Does all that really work?" Hilary said, her eyes shining. "Can you really call an animal and he'll come?"

"Well, let's see," Tom Dabney said.

We were sitting in a pool of sun at the edge of the great river swamp on the other side of Goat Creek. It loomed over us, an impenetrable wall of green even in the dead of winter, stretching off to surround and encompass the Big

Silver River and sweep on for miles on its other side. Our backs were against the trunks of leafless pin oaks, and the ground just in front of us was felted with fallen leaves and the pale gold of dead bracken, but not ten yards away the forest started in earnest. The morning was windless and quiet; I had not noticed any birdsong or squirrel chatter for some time. Even Earl, usually vibrating like a fine wire in the forest, had curled up in a brindle circle at Hilary's side and gone to sleep in the sun. From the angle of the light, I thought it must be about noon.

Tom looked into the woods for a small space of time, and then put his hands to his mouth and called. It was a strange sound, not at all human; it was an old sound, something near to "Chalk-chalk-chalk." It was, for some reason, an anxious sound. He waited a few minutes and then made the sound again. And then he fell silent and folded his hands and shut his eyes, seeming to doze in the sun. When Hilary stirred restlessly, turning toward him, he lifted one hand and motioned her to be still and quiet. We sat there, waiting.

I was just about to stop the charade and suggest lunch when an enormous bronze turkey, the biggest I had ever seen, seemed to materialize in the wood's edge, just inside the first line of trees, and stood looking at us. It cocked its head this way and that. Then it turned and strutted lazily away into the deeper trees and was lost to sight. It was so silent that it might have been a mirage.

"Oh, Tom, oh, *neat!*" Hilary cried. "Oh, Mama, did you *see* him?"

"I surely did," I said, entranced despite myself. "He was a monster. Tom, I just can't believe it works that well."

"It doesn't, all the time. I happened to know there were several gobbler groups along the creek there, and that they were young guys. Saw 'em this weekend. Young ones tend to get lost pretty often; that was the 'lost' sound I made. You wouldn't necessarily use it on an old hand. Or on a hen. You'd use a kind of 'perk' sound for a hen, and that usually in fall. In spring you'd want a different hen sound, a kind of 'Come and get me, big boy,' sound. For babies it would be 'Kee-kee-keee.' "

"Why didn't you gobble?" Hilary said.

"Because they only gobble in spring, when sex rears its ugly head." He grinned at her. "Gobble any other time and you'd run him clear out of the woods. You would if you went 'Putt-putt,' too. That's universal turkey for 'Let's get the hell out of here.' "

"Did you do that with just your mouth?" she said. "Can I do it?"

"Sure, if you practice. There are literally hundreds of devices to call turkeys, but I don't think they work very well. Each turkey has its own individual voice; using a commercial caller is like trying to call a Yankee turkey with a Southern accent. Sometimes he's so insulted and pissed off he just won't answer. I'd rather get to know my birds and tailor the call to them."

"What about deer? Call me a deer," Hilary said.

"You can't really call deer; they don't make many sounds," he said. "They grunt, and cough, and huff and puff, and make scraping noises on trees, and the fawns bleat, but they don't talk per se. What you want to do, in deer season, is rattle them up. Hunting season is rutting and fighting season, too, and the sound of antlers rattling is irresistible to some big bucks. Makes them think some upstarts are nearby, fighting and getting ready to move in on their ladies. It'll often bring them at full charge. For that you need a set of dried antlers, or at the very least a good set of dried and oiled sticks. No, the only way for deer is to hide and wait. Or to stalk. To sneak. And that's another thing altogether. That's an advanced course."

"When can we do that?"

"Soon. In about a week, if you get good enough with that bow."

I looked at him.

"No hunting, Tom. That's absolutely out. No shooting at living things with that bow and arrow."

"No. I didn't mean for hunting. I just have a rule that I don't take anybody tracking unless they're good enough with the bow and arrow. Very infrequently there are other things that may need to be shot."

"Snakes?" My neck prickled.

"Sometimes, though not this time of year, I don't think. But other things. Feral pigs, sometimes. Hurt or dying animals. You can't leave an animal to suffer. If you don't have a weapon, you have to do it with a rock or stick or your hands, and I can assure you that's something you don't forget."

Hilary's eyes were dark and large, and I shook my head slightly at him. He started to speak, and Hilary said, "No, Mama, Tom's right. That would be awful, just to walk away."

I dropped it and we went in to lunch.

In the afternoons we practiced archery, and by the end of that week Hilary was so proficient that Tom did not stand behind her anymore but sat on the ground equidistant between her and the target and simply watched. Often he nodded, and occasionally he smiled. I did not fare so well; I had largely gotten over my embarrassment of being a very poor second to my ten-year-old child, but I could not seem to get the hang of it, could not force with will and muscle the delicately calibrated confluence of factors and variables that met in Hilary and made her a natural archer, seemingly without conscious thought. I was impatient and self-conscious, and after several days had such a vicious collection of magenta and saffron bruises on my left forearm, despite the leather arrow guard, that Tom made me stop for a while. I protested, but secretly I was glad.

"You're knotted up like a cypress stump," he said from behind me at my last lesson, his hands moving lightly over my neck and shoulders, holding firm at my waist, trying to turn my body into position. "If you could just let go and let your muscles loosen, you'd do a lot better. It might help to open your eyes, too."

I could feel the faint tickle of his breath on my nape as he spoke, and smell the warm smell of him, wood smoke and sweat and body-warm leather and sun trapped in the thick, clean dark hair. I was, indeed, rigid as a piece of petrified wood; the very nearness of him turned me stiff and still, and his touch threatened to loosen my arms and knees from their sockets. I fought against taking heavy, deep breaths, with the result that my breath came high and light and shallow, and consequently I felt light-headed. My palms and armpits were wet despite the chill of the falling twilight, and there was heat again in my groin.

"I'd do a lot better if you didn't hover," I said in a high, silly voice, and I felt as well as heard his soft chuckle.

"We probably both would," he said, and I knew then that he felt the thin silver knife blade of tension, too.

"It's time we were going in," I said, moving away from him. "Hilary doesn't even have her jacket on."

"Why do I have to put on my jacket every time you get cold?" she said mildly, but she came into the house without protest. Hilary and I both loved the early evenings we spent at Goat Creek.

Tom would light the fire and pour drinks for himself and me and cider for Hilary, and would start the big stereo and go into the kitchen to begin supper. He would never let me help; we ate soups and stews and smoked game that he had prepared and frozen himself, and sometimes biscuits or cornbread, but rarely anything more complicated than that. He talked to us as he cooked, over the music, talked more of the woods and the animals, or told us strange hunting myths and forest legends that I had never encountered before, even in *The Golden Bough*.

"Where did you hear those things?" I said once, after a particularly grisly tale of a desecrated tree that snared and devoured its violator.

"Oh, here and there. Some from books of Martin's. Some from Gullah tales Scratch heard as a kid. Some that my great-grandfather brought home from Heidelberg. Some from other woodsmen. All woodsmen have a store of them. You should hear what goes on around a campfire after a hunt at King's Oak, or the other big plantations around here. Guys go to bed afraid to close their eyes. It's a good thing most of 'em sleep in community bunkhouses."

"Little boys at camp," I said. "But God, all that . . . retribution."

"It's the main bone in all the myths I've ever heard," he said. "I guess living by tooth and claw and blood was a fact of life for all those centuries. It was what our ancestors feared most. The retribution of the gods. The retribution of the animals they killed. The retribution of the very world around them. It's why we have all the rituals of propitiation that are done after killing an animal. A few of them are still being used."

I thought of an oak leaf in the mouth of a dead deer, and a kiss on its dead lips.

"So why kill them if you have to turn right around and propitiate them?" I said. "Isn't that the same as admitting the killing is wrong?"

"Well, the rituals come down from prehistory," he said, looking at me thoughtfully. "You didn't have much choice about killing in those days. You starved if you didn't. But the animal, or the master animal, was a god, remember, and had great power over you, because without him you would surely starve. So you did him all the honor you could, and hoped he wouldn't be insulted and keep his little brothers away from the hunting grounds the next season."

"You don't have to kill them to stay alive now," I said. "It may have been true then, but it's not now. Now you can stalk your dinner in a supermarket and bring it home. Don't tell me you propitiate the carrots and the coffee and the ice cream?"

"I do it now because it keeps me in touch with the men who did it of necessity then," he said. He was not smiling. "I kill and propitiate because they did, and because they were the only whole, perfectly alive men I've ever known about, and because it keeps me, at least in part, one of them. And for other reasons that you aren't ready to hear yet. Let's make a deal, Diana: I won't force my ideas about this on you, and you don't natter at them."

"I'm sorry. I didn't think I nattered," I said, my eyes burning with sudden tears of hurt. He had never spoken to me so before.

"Not often, but some," he said.

Sometimes, after dinner, he would bring out the big Martin and play for us, strange, fluting atonal songs such as he had sung at Thanksgiving. Sometimes he just played American folk songs or the popular things that Hilary liked. And always, at least once, "Moon River." He seemed to have a repertoire almost as endless and catholic as his record and tape collection, as the thousands of books spilling off his shelves. Once or twice Scratch came by after dinner, with some tidbit for the goats in a wrinkled brown paper sack, and Tom would coax him to come and sit by the fire and listen to the music for a time. He would not, on these nights, join in, but sat with his papery old eyelids down over his eyes like a turtle, his hands clasped over his slack belly, listening and smiling. He looked thinner than I remembered, and walked with a pronounced shuffle, and he had a deep, rasping cough that hurt me to hear.

"Are you taking care of that?" Tom asked him once, after a spell that bent him over and fetched him up wet-eyed.

"Got some stuff up to home," Scratch said. "Made it up just this day. It do the trick."

"Well, stay the hell out of the creek," Tom said shortly. "You're too old to be wading around in December. You know better than that."

"Does Scratch swim in the creek in the wintertime?" Hilary asked, wide-eyed, after he had gone.

"Scratch thinks he sees something in the water that ought not be there, and he goes slogging around looking for it," Tom said. "He thinks he sees lights in it. He's been making mead again up there, is what I think."

"Lights . . ." I heard the fear in Hilary's voice, and saw Tom remember her terror of the flaming creekwater.

"Seeing pinpricks of light is the first sign of an eye disease called glaucoma, Hil," he said. "It's very serious, and I worry a lot about Scratch getting it. His father and grandfather had it. It can blind you if you don't treat it. Scratch doesn't hold with doctors, but there are limits to what his medicine can do."

"Oh," she said. "I see."

One night, as we were unwinding ourselves reluctantly from the throws and blankets with which he had wrapped us in preparation for going back to Pemberton, Tom said, "Tomorrow's supposed to be clear and windy. A good wind out of the east; everything in the swamp will be upwind of us. I think it might be the day for a stalk. What do you think?"

"Oh, yes!" Hilary cried. "Oh, yes!"

"Diana?" he said.

"Well . . . I guess so." Somehow I did not want to go back into the Big Silver woods with him again. Somehow I was afraid.

"I have to be back home early, though," I said. "There's a thing at Tish and Charlie's I can't miss. And . . . Carter will be back."

I did not know why I said that, and blushed.

"I know he will," Tom said evenly. "Don't worry. I won't keep you . . . in the woods."

His voice was low and soft, and I turned to look at him. His eyes held mine, very blue. He did not smile. I could not look away. I felt my knees soften as though they were tallow held to flame. My heart began a slow, dragging hammer, and my mouth went dry. My eyelids drooped of themselves. The woods . . . Tom . . .

It wasn't until we were home and I was unloading the dishwasher, after Hilary was asleep, that my heart finally stopped its treacherous deep tattoo. For the first time since I had left Atlanta and Chris, I took a Dalmane. White sleep sandbagged me and took me down before I turned over. When I woke it was morning, and the stiffness of my legs and arms told me I had not moved at all in the night.

We set out up Goat Creek about eight, with the winter

sun still hidden behind the dark columns of the trees. We wore fatigue jackets, and thick, soft moccasins he had produced the night before. Over two pairs of thick wool socks they fit perfectly.

"Did you make them, too?" Hilary said.

"Nope. I'm no masochist," he said. "Orvis made them, and Federal Express brought them. Ordinarily you'd wear boots for deer hunting, but since this is strictly stalking, and we're not going far today, I thought you'd like to try the moccasins. There's nothing quieter in the woods."

We crossed Goat Creek about a half mile into the river swamp, at a place I had not seen before, where a fallen log made a bridge over the slow, shallow water. Without the kiss of the sun it looked opaque almost to blackness, and there was no swift, silvery darting in its depths, as there was in warm weather.

"Where do the fishes go when it's cold? Where are the frogs and things?" Hilary said.

"Water creatures are cold-blooded, so they don't really feel cold," Tom said. "But they get very sleepy, and slow up almost to hibernation. Some of them burrow into the mud till spring. Others just hang around the edge of the creek, sluggish and dim-witted and bad-tempered. This is not the time of year you'd want to meet a gator."

"I would," Hilary said, patting her bow. "I'd like to see one. Do you think we will?"

"I never have, this late," Tom said. "Mostly they don't come out till spring, when they're good and hungry."

We cut diagonally through the undergrowth toward the Big Silver River, Tom ahead of us, walking loosely and easily in his silent moccasins, a small rifle held loosely over his forearm. Hilary and I had our bows and quivers strapped over our shoulders. Where we walked the trees were tall and straight and met overhead in a canopy, but because so many of them were hardwoods, shafts of nacreous December light slanted down to the leaf-carpeted forest floor, like columns. Undergrowth was sparse. It was cold and fresh and damp, but after half an hour of walking, a light sweat sprang up on my forehead and neck, and the steady little wind at my back felt better. There seemed at first to be no color in this day but that of the wet black tree trunks and the damp no-color of the fallen leaves under our feet. But a belt of copper beeches glowed an exquisite, muted gilt off toward the river, and the dead bracken shone golden. Lichens on tree trunks and stumps were a startling, acid green. Pewter moss cobwebbed many of the live oaks and cypress. It was a subtler landscape than I had seen before, but beautiful in its own melancholy way. Except for the rattling of dead leaves in the wind, the morning was silent. No birds sang.

Nearing the edge of the river, where a canebrake loomed black-green, Tom suddenly made a small motion with his hand and stopped. We halted behind him.

"What?" Hilary whispered.

"Deer," he said quietly, not looking back, but staring into the cane.

"I don't see anything," she said. Neither did I; to me the cane looked symmetrical and open and innocent of deer or anything else alive.

"No, but they're around here somewhere," he said. "Probably just across the river, through that cane."

"How do you know? How can you see that far?" she said.

"I can't. I just . . . feel them over there. I just know that they are. It's where I'd be, if I were a deer. You get to thinking like them after a while."

"Do they really think?" Hilary asked.

"You bet they do. They think about deer things better than you or I ever can."

"Are they going to come over here?" Hilary said.

"No," Tom said. "We're going to go over there. This is where you learn to stalk. It's fairly simple, really. What you do is just get the wind in front of you, if you can, so that they can't smell you, and then you . . . move like a deer. You think like a deer doing whatever it is he's doing at the moment, and you do that. This deer, or these, are probably eating this time of day. It's not mating season, so none of them will be fighting. You wouldn't have any trouble hearing that. And they won't be on the move, because any given herd won't move more than a mile or two from its territory unless food is awfully scarce, which it isn't this year. And there won't be fawns yet to bleat. And it's not quite the time of day that they bed down. So what they'll most likely be doing is eating, and that's the best time to stalk them. When a deer eats, he'll graze for about ten seconds, and then he'll raise his head and look and listen and smell. And then he'll eat again, for ten seconds. You can almost count on the ten seconds. So what you do is, you only move when his head is down, and you walk in very slow motion, and you set your feet down very quietly. No scuffing, no sudden movements; come down on the ball of your foot and roll back on your heel. If you do it the other way, you can lose your balance. Count one-Mississippi-two-Mississippi-three-Mississippi . . . and on to ten, and then stop, and count the ten seconds again. Be perfectly still while you're stopped. Don't blink an eyelash, don't move a muscle, don't cough or sneeze. A deer's eyesight isn't up to yours on immobile objects, but for movement in the woods, it's phenomenal. Then go on like that until you've got him in range."

"But what if you can't see him? I mean, you have to

get close enough to be able to see him before you can tell when to move and when to stop, don't you?" I said. "If you're moving while he's looking around, and not eating, won't you just scare him away?"

"That's where your woods sense comes in," Tom said. "That's something I can't teach you; you're born with the gift, and you sharpen it in the woods. But it can't be taught. I suspect Hil has it. You may, too, but it'll probably take longer to uncover. Children seem to have quicker access to it. But I can teach you some signs that deer are near. One is a rub. Bucks make those when they polish their antlers on bushes or saplings. You'll see small branches broken off, and bark scrubbed off the tree trunks. There were a couple of those back there a way. An even better sign is a scrape. Those mark the boundaries of the buck's territory, and it's also the sign of a buck in rut. He'll paw the ground somewhere where there's relatively little undergrowth, and where there's an overhanging branch. He'll make his scrape and then urinate on it, and reach up and rake his antler tips on the branch, and nuzzle it with his mouth and nose."

"What for?" Hilary giggled.

"So if there are ladies around they'll know he's at home and raring to go," Tom said. "And so other bucks won't come poaching on his territory. One of the best ways to call a buck in rutting season is to rattle him up with antlers where you see a scrape. If he's in the neighborhood he'll come running with blood in his eye and fire in his belly. It's almost foolproof; it's so certain I don't use it."

"Why not?" Hilary said.

"Remember what I said about the *it*s and the *thou*s?" he said. "That night when we saw the deer down in the cypress bottom? You looked like you were asleep, but I think you heard."

"I did," Hilary said.

"Well, I don't think rattling up a buck, or fooling him, is a very *thou* thing to do. I think it's more an *it*. I think the *thou* thing would be to get so good at tracking that you can find him that way. It evens things out. *Thou* thinking is mostly about keeping things even. That's honor, when you think about it."

"Are there scrapes around here?" Hilary said.

He nodded. "A couple, back about a quarter of a mile. I'll show you when we go back. Now let's see if I'm right about the deer. Be very, very quiet and wait for me to signal you, and then do just what I do."

He moved ahead of us to the edge of the canebrake. In an eyeblink he turned into a total creature of the Big Silver. His lithe body seemed to settle lower to earth and lean forward, as if he might at any moment drop silently to all fours. Even the musculature of his back and shoulders seemed to play in a different way, tauter, smoother. He took crouching steps of a slowness and deliberation that would have seemed absurd any other place, and at intervals he stopped and simply froze into the leaf shadow. Incredibly, his feet seemed to make no sound at all. He motioned without turning, and Hilary and I moved forward, she seeming to fall into the ancient rhythm of the stalk as if she had taken her first steps so, I feeling clumsy and ludicrous and heavy.

I took my eyes off him for an instant, to look at my own rebellious feet, and when I looked up again he was gone, and I could see only Hilary, frozen in midstep on the trail, looking back at me uncertainly.

"Where is he?" she whispered. I shook my head. I could see only the dapple of early sun through the cane stalks, and beyond it the black fortresses of the cypress and tupelo that fringed the edge of the Big Silver River. I remembered that he had done this the night of the marching deer, too, disappeared in the wild air of the woods and reassembled himself just as silently from its elements. I was glad that someone else had seen it.

Tom reappeared. First he was not there, and then he was. He looked back and pointed to Hilary and made the sign of antlers on his head with his fingers. We both started forward, and he shook his head at me and smiled. Hilary looked back, and I smiled, too, and nodded. But it felt obscurely left out, rejected, unchosen. I stood still and watched my daughter go forward. It was, after all, for her that we had come into Tom Dabney's woods. It was, wasn't it?

When she had almost reached the spot where Tom stood, Hilary stumbled and nearly fell. She righted herself instantly, and froze, but the damage had been done. A buck, seeming to me enormous and frighteningly close, broke from just inside the farthest line of cane and crashed off toward the river, his white flag of a tail high and waving back and forth, the breath chuffing in his nostrils. He was so close I could see the bits of earth and leaf debris spurting up from his hoofs, and smell the wild smell of him. I watched him out of sight, the delicate legs carrying the big, barrel-shaped taupe body in unbelievable bounds, the great crown of antlers gleaming white in the sun. I had, for an instant, seen his dark, liquid eyes and handsome, professorial face plain; I had somehow felt his alarm, and something near to anger. I had not felt fear. I did not realize, until he was out of sight, that I had been holding my breath.

Hilary gave a wail of disappointment, and threw her bow to the ground. "I scared him!" She was near to tears, I could tell. "I fell over my own stupid feet and I scared him off! I'm so *stupid;* I *hate* myself!"

Tom walked to her and sat her down smartly on the earth, his hands firm on her shoulders. "If you have a tantrum every time you spook a deer in the woods, you'll be screaming a good bit of your life," he said, and his voice was cool and crisp.

"Lesson number one about stalking: It takes more patience and less temperament than you ever thought there were in the world. The hunter who stopped to stomp his feet when he scared his quarry was apt to be dead of starvation by winter. When you've been doing it about three years straight, and if you're exceedingly lucky as well as naturally good, which I think you are, you may get close enough for a bow shot. *Maybe.* Just how long do you think I've been doing it?"

She would not look at him, and he went on, "Rule two: There is no competition in the woods. Not even with the animal you're tracking. It's a dance, or a ritual, or a sacrament, or even a game, but it is not a contest. You don't win it or lose it. Neither does he. It's a thing you do together. So there's no need for beating up on yourself if you scare your quarry. I don't bring type A's, as with Goat Creek; not even ten-year-old ones. Learn from this. Remember what you did wrong, and how you came to do it. Remember how he looked, like a clipper ship under full sail, and enjoy the memory. Keep it."

She did look at him then. "Is there time to try again?"

"Nope. Not and get you all home in time for your mama to get dressed up for her party," he said, grinning narrowly at me. "But that brings up rule three: In the woods there's no such thing as time. Everything is right now, this minute. And the only place is right now, in this place. Nothing else should be in your head. That's what wild is. The total here-and-now. If you live in that, you can't ever be early or late, and you can't ever be lost. Where you are at that moment is the only place there is."

"I'm sorry I yelled," Hilary said meekly.

"That's okay. I bet you don't yell next time."

"I bet I don't, either."

We stopped for an early lunch at a bend in Goat Creek about a mile from the house, on a clear, sunny bank fringed with cattails and reeds, which sloped gently into the water. The creek there was still and wide and looked deep, almost like a small lake. Water plants and cypress stumps pierced its black mirror surface, and you could not see into it. It was sheltered from the wind, which had, in any case, dropped as the sun rose, and we peeled off our jackets and lolled on the soft earth, using them like blankets beneath us. The sun was warm on our heads and shoulders, and after we ate the sandwiches Tom had brought in his pocket, we lay back in the quiet breath of the woods, tired from the morning and lulled by the green silence. Tom had stowed the rifle against a sapling at the edge of the forest, and Hilary's and my bows and arrows lay beside us on the earth. For the space of perhaps ten minutes none of us had spoken. I know that I was near to sleep.

There was a great scurrying rush from the reeds on the bank that brought me half to my feet, heart pounding. Whatever it was crashed through the green stalks with incredible speed and weight, and then we heard a terrible, high, thin screaming, a kind of continuous, piping squeal. The reeds crashed again and then something went into the water with a huge hollow black-and-silver splash, and the water at the edge of the creek churned and roiled. The screaming continued. I was on my feet staring into the white confusion of the water, but I could see nothing, only the frenzied splashing. And then I could see. A small black piglet, a feral one, struggled and squealed in a frenzy of pain and terror at the very edge of the water, one thrashing leg caught in the gnarled root of a great oak some ten yards away up the bank. Something huge and dark and terrible under the water pulled at it, tugging with such force that it seemed the tiny leg would simply come away from its socket. But it did not, and the awful shrieking continued. I heard a twin to it from the bank: Hilary; and Tom's shouting, "Get back, Hilary! Get away from the bank! It's a gator!"

The dark water reddened in a sudden, vicious swirl, and the shrieking went a notch higher. My hands were clapped to my ears; I did not think I could bear this another instant, but would simply die of the awfulness, here in the sun. Hilary and the piglet screamed on and on.

Tom leaped to his feet and ran for his rifle. Before he could even reach the tree where it stood, Hilary fitted an arrow into her bow and shot. It was all one smooth motion, like the soft surge of the sea: the reach for the arrow and quiver, the fitting of the nock onto the string, the draw and release. The arrow flew silently home and the screaming stopped. The piglet sank swiftly into the dark water and the gator took it under and both were gone.

We three simply stood where we were, looking at the water until the concentric ripples had almost died away. Then Hilary tossed the bow away from her and began to cry and ran, not to me, but to Tom Dabney. He closed his arms around her and sank to the ground with her and rocked her, and rocked, her face pressed into his shoulder, his chin on the dark crown of her head. He murmured something, over and over, but I could not hear what he said. Shock made my mind slack and simple, and the screaming still rang in my ears. I thought I would always hear it.

I started for Hilary, but his face over her head implored me to let her be, and so I did. My knees gave way then, and I sat down hard on the ground and put my face on my crossed arms, and let the earth spin down into stillness. The casual, sunlit savagery of the attack was beyond anything I had ever seen, but the arrow that flew to stop it from my daughter's hands was even beyond that. I could not find a context into which to put it, so I simply let my mind drift and sat in the sun with my eyes closed.

I felt rather than heard her stop crying, and when I lifted my head, she was sitting beside Tom on the bank and his arm was around her. Neither was speaking. Then he did. His words were not for me, but I heard them very clearly.

"That was a very brave thing you did, Hil," he said. "It was just exactly the right and good thing to do, and you did it perfectly. It was a *thou* thing to do. I'm very proud of you."

"I wanted to save it, then I saw I couldn't," she said. Her voice was low and rasped with tears, but there was no hysteria in it. "I thought I would go and scare the gator into letting it go, but then I could see that he was . . . eating it alive."

"Nobody could have saved the pig," Tom said. "I was going to get my gun to shoot it, not try and save it. I couldn't have done it any better than you did, and I sure didn't do it as soon. You have, as they say, the right stuff, Miss Hilary Calhoun."

Hilary looked at me then. It was a shy look, questioning, almost the look of a young stranger. I knew that I must say something. I did not know what it should be. Her actions were bold and sure beyond my comprehension; I knew that I could not have done what she had. But to praise her, as he had, for the act of killing . . . Suddenly I wanted nothing so much in the world as shopping malls, traffic, fast-food places, microwaves, plastic holiday decorations, nail polish, rock music, cocktail banter. I wanted to be quit and gone from the wildness of these woods and these animals and this death and this man who lived so naturally with it all. All of it frightened and angered and appalled me. Most frightening of all was the changeling daughter who had just killed an animal with a bow and arrow and now stood looking silently at me, waiting for me to validate what she had done.

"I'm sorry you had to do that, sweetie," I said.

It was not enough, I could see that, but I could summon nothing else. Tom laid his arm around her shoulder and walked her over to me, and said mildly, "How about a big hand for the little lady, Diana? She did the only right thing that could be done. I'm not sure I could have done it at her age. I'm fairly sure you couldn't do it now."

"You're right, I couldn't," I said. "I'll bet you could have done it when you were two years old, however. I can't imagine a time when you weren't totally at home with killing and death. Thanks to you, Hilary's going to catch up with you in no time."

"Hilary," he said, not taking his eyes from my face. "Get my rifle for me and collect the jackets and mosey on up ahead of us. There's a path just up there that leads straight to the house. I need to get some things straight with your mom."

"Okay," she said, looking at me out of the corner of her eye. Still, she hesitated. I knew she was hung on the moment, still needing my validation, yet wanting to be away from me. My heart wrung with pity and shame.

"Go on, sweetie," I said. "It's okay. Tom needs to fuss at me a little and I need to hear it. You did wonderfully well, and it was a kind thing to do, and I'm proud to death of you."

She ran for the rifle then, lighter, a child known to me once more.

"Okay," I said wearily. "Shoot. Just don't linger over my sins, please. Let's make this fast and merciful."

He grinned and put his arm around me and started us off down the creekbank behind Hilary. My stride fit itself to his, and our shoulders rubbed companionably. I wanted to lay my head on his shoulder and just walk in the sun, letting the noise and anguish and blood run out of my mind like water.

"She has to learn about death, you know," he said. "Or she does if she's going to spend much time out here with me. Life in the woods is half death; there's no getting around that. It's what she learns about it that's important. That it isn't kind or merciful in itself, nor is it cruel or unfair. Death just *is*. But a good death is always humane and fast and necessary. We can't prevent it but we must, to the best of our ability, make it those things. Mainly it must be necessary."

"Then how can you hunt for sport?" I said drearily. I was as tired of this fugue as he was, but I could not let this go unchallenged. I despaired of ever understanding it.

"Do you still think I hunt for sport?" he said.

"Do you think you hunt for necessity?" I replied.

"Yes. Just, perhaps, not in the new way. Not a modern necessity. In the old way."

"Oh, God, Tom, it's just so much trouble to learn all your rules," I said. "Why can't you live by just a few of the rest of the world's?"

"Well, I do," he said. "The world's oldest and most universal rules. They've never changed. The natural world hasn't changed. But people did. We did."

He paused. Then he said, "Do you think that teaching her sentimentality and artificiality is helping her to be good? What is good, Diana? I cull male kids when they're born; I have to, or in three years I'd be up to my ass in bucks. I do it quickly and before they've even drawn a full breath. It's a necessity. They don't suffer. Why is it good to be up to your ass in billy goats? Why would it be good to let that piglet die the way it was going to die? Order and balance. The balance is all. I think man was put here alongside the animals to see to the balance. When we let it get out of whack . . . that's sin. I really think it is."

I was too tired to argue, and I wanted too much to go home and take a bubble bath and wrap myself in the deliberate urbanity of my life in Pemberton. There was a ring of realness, of heft, in what he said, but I did not want to examine it any further. I looked at Hilary, walking ahead of us on the path. Her bow dangled loosely from her curled fingers, and her back was straight and slender, and her hair was a blue-black dazzle in the sun, and she was no child I knew at all. I thought, wearily, that she would surely have a nightmare this night about the death of the piglet, but she did not, and for all the remaining nights of her life, so far as I knew, she never did.

Carter was at the house when we got back, stretched out on the sofa watching a football game. He hugged us both hard and swung Hilary around and took our camouflage jackets and hung them up without comment. He did not speak of the mud on our moccasins, either, but I saw his eyes take in the woods-stained clothing and shoes, and our tangled hair, and the pink stain of the wild in our cheeks. I thought we must look like gypsies to him, there in my orderly little storybook house. He wore a beautiful, creamy blue cashmere sweater I had not seen before, and he looked thinner, and tired.

"God, I missed you both," he said, into my hair. "I missed you so much. From now on I go nowhere that you don't come with me."

"We missed you, too," I said into his neck. And at that moment I knew that I had; had missed the massive normality of him, the comforting consistency, the utter, cherishing safety. I burrowed against him and let the warmth of his arms leach the chill of strangeness and wildness and the piglet's death out of me. In my house I was, once more, Andy Calhoun, and Hilary, skipping down the hall to take her bath, was my daughter again, and not a wild, implacable forest creature who killed with a bow.

"Oh, Lordy, I really did miss you," I said.

"I'm glad to hear it," Carter said. "I sort of thought you might have lost me in the woods."

Later that afternoon he took Hilary, scrubbed and sweatsuited and chattering, over to Marjorie's, to spend the night with her brood. When he returned I was coming out of the shower, grateful to have sluiced away the last of the morning's musky wildness with scalding Pemberton water, and he wrapped me in a bath sheet and took me over to my bed and made love to me, and I shut my eyes and let the warmth of him wash me as the water had. He was slow and gentle and careful, and though it was without the urgency that had frightened me the last time we had been together, I believe that, for him, it was deep and good. He fell asleep beside me in the damp bed, smiling. Later, I slept, too. The last thing I thought, before sliding into blackness, was: *This is good. We're back on track now. I don't have to be afraid.*

As before with Carter, I had reached no discernible climax, but rather a kind of generalized loosening, a simple bodily peace. It was, at that sleep-safe moment, all I could imagine ever wanting.

At Tish and Charlie's party that night, people were as glad to see us as if we had been absent from their midst for months, instead of barely a week.

"Where on earth have you been?" Tish said, hugging me. "I've been calling you for days. I wish to hell you'd return your calls."

"Oh, out," I said. "Around. I've been doing things with Hil. I thought I'd give everybody a break from having to worry about whether to invite me without Carter, and all that crap. I'm not used to this kind of partying."

"I kind of thought you might have been playing in the woods," Pat Dabney said, leaning out of the crowd around the buffet table to snare a fat shrimp on a toothpick. She popped the whole thing in her mouth and chewed with relish. There was cocktail sauce on the front of her black satin shirt and her chin; it looked as if she had been drinking blood. The stains in no way diminished her essential raffish splendor.

"Have you been out there spying again?" I said lightly, determined not to let Pat Dabney be the author of another cocktail party scene.

"Let's just say I know the signs," she said lazily. "There's a certain stiffness. A little bit of rump-spring, like maybe you'd been up a tree doing—"

"Whatever I've been doing to spring my rump happened a lot closer to home than the woods," I said sweetly, smiling up at Carter. There was a little gasp of appreciation and laughter from the crowd at the table, and Pat Dabney grinned and gave me a small salute with her toothpick. My face burned, as much from my own words as at hers. Carter's face was red, too, but he gave me a quick squeeze.

"Good for you. That was match point," he said. "Sorry

you had to get so . . . basic with her, but it's all she respects."

"Don't be sorry. I enjoyed every word of it," I said, knowing only then that I had. I knew, too, that I really should be more careful with Carter. He was far from being a prude, but women in his world did not habitually make such allusions in public. Pat Dabney, and, to an extent, Tish, were the exceptions that proved the rule.

"I'll do better if I can just avoid Pat," I said. "She brings out the doxy in me every time."

"I like the doxy, only just for me," he said. "I'm glad you're not intimidated by her. She doesn't really have a bad heart, but she needs to be jerked up like that every time she sticks you. I don't care if she was right; it was a bad thing to say."

"I haven't heard her say many good ones," I said, looking sidewise at him. "Carter, I think it bothers you that I might have been out to Goat Creek this week. And I have been, every day. You wouldn't believe what Hilary's learning. When we get home I'll tell you what she did today; or she will. It was incredible."

He was silent, and then he said, "I'm glad. I just wish I could make that kind of difference to her. But if it's helping her that much, you're right to go."

"But you mind that we do," I said.

"Yes," he said. "But I'm not going to ask you not to."

"Please don't," I said. "Just look at her."

"Look at you," he said.

He went to the office on New Year's morning, to catch up on the week's worth of backlogged work, and left me stretching luxuriously under the comforter, drinking the coffee he had brought me. I piled pillows behind my head and thought of the empty day ahead of me with delectation. I would spend the morning reading by the fire, as I seldom had a chance to do, and then would take a leisurely bath and make chili and a platter of nachos for the bowl games in the afternoon. We had refused the Adairs' enormous New Year's Day brunch.

"I want to start this year with just you two," Carter had said, leaving. "Just the way I hope I end it."

But at ten Hilary came briskly into my bedroom in her camouflage clothes and the moccasins.

"Why aren't you up?" she said. "We're hours late already."

"Late for where?" I said, knowing.

"To go out to Tom's," she said impatiently. "Come on, Mama. It's almost the last day I'll be able to go."

She tugged at my covers. I grasped her arm and pulled her down on the bed with me, and into the circle of my arm.

"We can't go out there every day, Doodle," I said. "It's got to be just sometimes, like for special occasions. We can't monopolize Tom's time like that, and we can't just . . . go live in the woods. Our real life is over here, in Pemberton. It's school, and work, and your friends. This week was special because it was a holiday, but it can't be an everyday thing."

"You mean we went this week because Carter wasn't here," Hilary said, her blue eyes filling with tears. "I know that's why we went. I knew you wouldn't when he came back. What friends are you talking about in Pemberton? Those creeps I go to school with? I don't have any friends. Tom is my friend. Missy is. Earl is."

There was rising anguish in her voice, and I thought with alarm that perhaps, by taking her to Goat Creek, I had only helped her swap one obsession for another. Hilary did not have the capacity for light love; I should have remembered that.

She did not let a tantrum take her, though. She might have, only weeks before.

"Well, since this is practically the last day, couldn't we just go out and say goodbye to everybody and see if Tom will let me bring my bow back? I could practice in the backyard, and then, if we could go on weekends, I could show him how I've improved."

"We could do that, sure," I said, hugging her gratefully for the aborted tantrum. Her effort at self-control touched me deeply. I left Carter a note: "Back before kickoff," and we turned the Toyota once more toward the Big Silver woods.

But when we got there, it was to find a cold, closed house and a note on the door.

"D and H," it read. "I've gone upriver with Scratch for a while. Call you when I get back. Missy and Earl are with Reese C. and he's feeding the ducks and goats. Go get anything you want from the house; it's not locked." It was signed with a sharp black *T*.

Hilary gave a little cry of disappointment, and looked up at me. Ridiculously, emptiness flooded me. I felt that I wanted to cry, like a child who got there and found the party over. We looked at each other, my daughter and I.

"I wish he'd taken me," Hilary said desolately.

"Taken you out in the woods for one whole week, or two?" I said, more sharply than I had intended. "You know Aunt Tish says he goes out there and stays that long sometimes. Get serious, Hil; you know your school starts Monday, but he's got another two weeks before ours does. There's no reason why he shouldn't do some things on his own, with his friends."

"I *am* his friend. I'm good in the woods. He said so. You saw. . . ."

"You're also ten years old and a city kid at heart," I said. "Come on, let's get your bow and whatever else you want and get on back before the games start. Would you like to ask Susan and Erica to come have nachos with us?"

"No," she said, and went into the house ahead of me. Her back was very straight, and she walked in a hip-slung pad that was a small, absurd copy of Tom Dabney's. I followed her in, found the dark, cold room too empty and echoing and lifeless to bear, and went back outside to wait in the sun until she came out. It wasn't long.

"It's awful in there without Tom," she said. "It feels like he's dead, or something. It feels like it's been empty for a hundred years."

"Well, he'll be back before you know it," I said. "We'll come out as soon as he calls us."

But a week went by, and a day, and another day, and he did not call. Hilary wanted to go out and see if he had come back, but I would not permit that. Soon she stopped asking if he had called while she was at school, and took to spending all her afternoons, until the winter light failed, in the backyard, where Carter had set up a target for her, shooting her arrows over and over, like a silent little automaton. It was a new bull's-eye target, which he had driven all the way to Waycross to get; she had thanked him, but when he was not about she tacked over it a crude silhouette of a deer. Once he came home unexpectedly and found her shooting at the deer target, but he said only, "You're a born deadeye, Punkin. Lord help us if you take to hunting."

I looked at him and then at her. She ducked her chin away from me. She had not, then, told him about the incident with the piglet. Somehow I could not, until she did.

But the savage vignette hung swollen among the three of us, a hurtful and untold secret. Hilary went back to her archery, and Carter and I walked into the house. It was cold in the twilight, and there was a thick, wet quality to it like unshed tears, or snow.

It did snow in the night, a rare, respectable little three-inch snow, and in the way of the Deep South, schools closed and a larky kind of hysteria took over. Hilary, who had loved Atlanta's meager snowfalls, was not charmed with this one. She stayed inside on the window seat, drawing pictures on the breath-frosted panes and looking, looking.

"Want to go sledding?" Carter said in the afternoon. "I don't have a sled, but I think your mama's pizza pan would get you down a hill right smartly."

"I don't think so, thanks," she said politely. Later, in the twilight, she came into the kitchen, where I was chopping onions, and said, "Mama, do you think Tom will be all right out in the woods in the snow?"

"Oh, for pity's sake, Hilary, of course he will. Go finish your homework," I said, more sharply than I might have, for I knew that Carter, on the sofa reading briefs, could easily have heard her. I think she knew it, too.

He did.

"Robin Hood is a hard act to follow," he said, coming out to stand behind me with his arms around my waist and his chin on my head.

"I'm sorry you heard that," I said. "It means less than nothing. It's not even a crush; it's just some kind of . . . thing. Infatuation. She gets them. All children do, at that age. You remember how she was about horses and riding, and how long that lasted."

"I can't help worrying a little," he said. "We had a really good thing going, she and I. I don't think I'm mistaken about that. And then . . . I don't know. I wonder if you realize how much she's changed in the last month or so."

"And she'll change again, about a hundred times before she's through," I said. "Let her be, and give it time. I promise you she'll be through it before the winter is out."

"I hope so," he said. "Because by then I'm going to have asked you to set a date, and I don't know if I can manage a child who's in love with another man."

"Carter, it's been less than half a year. Ask me in the spring. I'll give you a date then."

"Before the year is out, Andy?"

"Yes. Before then," I said. My head was spinning. I felt as if I were stepping out off the edge of the earth.

"I love you," he said. "I'll always take care of you."

"I know that," I said.

We made love every night during those days before the college started up again. Afterward we lay, gentled and unhurried, in my bed and talked before we fell asleep. Everything was level, suspended, lulling, warm. I have never felt safer in my life than on those nights, not before or since.

Once I said, "Is it enough for you? Us together, I mean? It's not exactly lights and bells, I know. I'm certainly no firecracker in the sack. We could try some different things, if you wanted to."

"It's enough. It's all I want," he said, kissing my hairline. "For me now, it's a perfect love. I've had the wildnesses, Andy. Even while I was doing it, something about it . . . appalled me. I need a friendly love. A proper love, if you like. You suit me perfectly; I can take this love all the way with me. You'd scare me to death if you started shouting in Sanskrit, or something."

"No Sanskrit," I said, slamming the small interior door behind which something cried aloud.

After a few minutes, when I was almost gone in sleep, he said, "I just hope it's enough for *you*."

"It is," I muttered. "Always. Go to sleep."

The second weekend in January, Clay and Daisy Dabney had a formal dinner dance out at King's Oak, to mark Chip's birthday. It was, Carter told me as we drove the night miles out to the plantation once again, the semiofficial end of Pemberton's holiday season.

"Clay hasn't missed this party since the year after Chip was born," he said. "Our parents all used to go; I can remember my mother coming in to say good night, all dressed up in black or white, and I'd think how funny it was for grownups to go to a kid's birthday party. It's always the same: both men and women in black and white, and an orchestra from Atlanta, and tons of flowers and a thousand lit candles and a midnight supper cooked by the King's Oak staff—quail and venison roast and wild rice and watercress from the Big Silver and about a million pies and cakes and little napoleons. It's the same menu every year; so far as I know, Clay has never hired a caterer. And enough champagne to float a submarine. It truly is elegant. As different from the September barbecue as night from day. It's King's Oak at its best, I think, the way the big hunting places used to be a hundred years ago. Maybe they still are, in Europe. It must cost Clay as much as buying a small country."

"All that to celebrate the fact of Chip," I said dryly.

"Well, to each his own." Carter grinned. "I'd guess Clay would be the first to see the irony in it, but to stop having it would be to admit Chip was sorry as a yard dog. And he'll never do that. Though I'm sure he knows. It used to be a joint party with Clay and Mr. Claude Dabney, Tom's father. Tom and Chip both have January birthdays. But that stopped when Mr. Claude died, when Tom and I were in our early teens, and Miss Caroline didn't seem to want to have any more to do with King's Oak after she sold to the Big Silver and moved to town. Just as well, I guess. There were some bad feelings there about her selling off the property to the government. She comes to Clay's party now, and Miggy does, but it was a long time before they did."

"Does Tom come? I wouldn't think he would, the way he seems to feel about his mother and sister, and Chip," I said. I thought that in this context, it was a perfectly natural question to ask, but he looked sideways at me.

"No," he said. "Not since I've been going."

King's Oak was utterly splendid that night, a blazing, shimmering, candlelit, flower-fragrant Xanadu; a mirage, a myth, a fairy tale, a crystalline winter palace. I will always remember it. As fine an affair as the autumn barbecue had been, this midwinter gala was, I thought, the real essence of the plantation, the secret at its heart, the flame at its core, just as the big oak was the secret at the heart of the surrounding forest. No matter that it was worked and hunted and lumbered in sunlight, by machines and men, and had been for more than a hundred years; this one magical crystal night was surely the motive power that kept it humming through the rest of the year. This night would burn for many months.

As before, almost everyone I had ever met in Pemberton and some I had not were there, passing down the receiving line where Clay and Daisy and beruffled little Lucy Hough Dabney and Chip, who was nodding like a helium-filled Disney balloon, stood shaking hands and kissing cheeks. They flowed out into the two huge front drawing rooms, which had been opened together to make a ballroom, and many couples were already whirling on the polished floor, from which the dim old rugs that I remembered had been removed. I suppose there must have been electric lights in that flickering vastness, but you noticed only the shimmer of what seemed a hundred thousand candles. In their phantasmagoric light, the walls and beamed ceilings of King's Oak seemed to retreat into distance and shadow, and flowers swam like something in a coral sea, and men and women looked transformed and wonderful, like actors, like specters, like kings.

"My God, it looks like the ball scene in *Gone With the Wind*," I said, waiting in line to greet Clay and Daisy. "Or maybe *The Masque of the Red Death*. Either way, it's something I'll never forget. It's hard to believe this really exists in the twentieth century, much less that it happens every year."

"It's something, isn't it?" Carter said, as proudly as if he had arranged it all, down to the last flower petal, for me. "Every time I get disgusted and fed up with the South, and feel like just turning my back on it and getting the hell out of all the decay and the dimness, I think of this night at King's Oak. It's what the best of the South is and was. I don't think we'll ever equal it again, no matter what fiberglass wonderments the Sunbelt brings us."

We moved through the line, where Clay and Chip kissed me warmly and Daisy and Lucy exclaimed over my strapless black satin ("Jailbait, sho nuff," Chip whispered wetly into my ear, following his words with a snakelike flicker of tongue), and then we moved out onto the dance floor. The band was playing the theme from *Moulin Rouge*, and Carter caught me up into the music. Charlie and Tish whirled by, waving, and Marjorie and Wynn Chapin, and perhaps a dozen more of the Pemberton crowd that we had partied with all that incandescent month. Beyond them were other people, forming other parties; there must have been, by that time, two hundred people on the floor, and what looked to be another hundred waited to siphon through the receiving line.

I thought of that September day scarcely four months before, when I had stood in this same room, curtained and dim and furnished then with old family pieces, and felt empty, nearly sick with the dread of going out onto the bright veranda that was filled with faces I did not know. I thought of Clay Dabney's kindness, and Tish's, and the swift, casual warmth of the people to whom I was introduced that day. Now they were my friends, or at least my acquaintances; before this year was out, they would, in effect, be my people. Time seemed to telescope out, shimmering like the candlelight; I was dizzy with the music and dancing, and the sense of swooping time. I thought then of Tom Dabney on that earlier day, and of his dark face laughing, and his voice saying, "Ah, God. Is it really Diana?" and the warmth of his hands on mine as he took them in greeting. And I thought of him earlier that morning, beneath the King's Oak. Naked and dark in the dappled light, kneeling before his deer.

My heart gave one single, great leap, like that of a just-snared hawk, and then I thrust the thought of Tom Dabney into the forbidden cache at the center of me, where I had kept it since New Year's Day. I had buried it deep under the weight of Carter; every time we made love, I felt another layer go thick and tight over the spot beneath which the cache lay. Soon it would be past any excavation; by spring it would be gone. By the end of the year it would be as if it had never existed. I put both arms around Carter's neck, as had been the fashion when Tish and I were at Emory, and he pulled me closer and kissed my temple.

" 'Whenever we kiss, I worry and wonder,' " sang the

soprano from Atlanta. " 'Your lips may be near, but where is your heart?' "

I drank a great deal of champagne, and danced every dance, with Carter and whoever asked me, and I laughed a great deal, and flirted as I had not since before I had met Chris Calhoun, all those years ago. Sometimes I sang along with the band. Eyes and smiles followed Carter and me around the room.

"You're high as a kite"—he smiled—"and I don't think it's all champagne. What's with you tonight?"

"I'm happy," I said. "I think I look pretty. I think everybody here is wonderful. I think this is the most elegant party I ever went to. I think you look like the ambassador to Monaco in that tux. I think I want another glass of champagne."

He snared one for me off a passing tray.

"One more and then it's ginger ale for you, my huckleberry friend," he said. "You're going to have a head like the Goodyear blimp."

" 'There's no tomorrow,' " I sang. " 'There's just tonight.' "

"Don't you wish," Carter said, smiling indulgently at me, but looking just a trifle worried. "Go on upstairs and fix your lipstick, Andy. You look like you've been in the back of the bus necking with the entire football team."

"Don't I wish," I said, and went across the dance floor and up the stairs to the second-floor bedroom that I remembered from that earlier time, when Tish had brought clean clothes for me. I smiled and was smiled at all along the way; I greeted and was greeted. I turned for a moment, on the landing, and looked back down into the merry-go-round swirl of the crowd, and thought, not without a degree of champagne-induced maudlinity, *These are my people.*

The big bedroom was dim and chintz-draped, as I remembered, but this time the great tester bed, as dark as a Viking ship in the soft rose light of the little crystal lamps on the dressing table, was piled high with overcoats and furs and beaded bags. The nuclear warning sign was gone from the bureau. The room was empty and very quiet after the laughter and music downstairs. My heels clicked loudly and perhaps a bit unsteadily on the softly shining pine floor. The grave eyes of generations of dark Dabneys looked down on me, as they had that other day, and I gave the bodice of my dress an involuntary twitch. All that varnished seemliness made me feel, suddenly, self-conscious and chastened, and very young. I went into the bathroom and looked into the wavering, underwater old mirror. A stranger looked back at me, hectic with rouge and liquor and smeared lipstick, eyes glittering and black like winter glare ice. A feral woman. My hair was a wild tousle around my face, and the dress had, indeed, crept too low on my breasts.

I reached up and touched the face of the woman in the mirror, and then held the finger to my own cheek. It was flaming hot. I turned the age-speckled taps, and cold water thundered softly into the porcelain basin. When it was full I cupped my hands and lowered my face and splashed water on it, again and again.

When I had groped for the hand towel and patted my face dry, I opened my eyes and looked into the mirror. Tom Dabney looked back at me, seeming caught in the wavy depths like someone drowned under ice. He did not move. I did not, either. I took a long, slow, deep breath, and turned around very slowly. He was still there.

"Clay told me you were up here," he said. His voice was odd; flat and somehow diminished, as if he had been running for a long time, but he was not breathing deeply. I still did not say anything. I simply looked at him. He was dressed in camouflage clothes so dirty that I could not tell where the pattern left off and the grime began, and he had the black peppering of a beard on his pointed chin. There were half-healed scratches on his hands and face, and I could smell the days of sweat and wood smoke on him. His black hair was as wild as mine, and there were bits of bark caught in it. He looked thinner than I had ever seen him, and very tired, and the deep lines between his nose and mouth cut more sharply than I remembered.

His eyes were fatigue-shadowed, and haunted. There was no other word for them.

"Tell me what's wrong," I said simply. I did not take my eyes from his. I did not realize until later that I had reached out to take his face in my two hands, and that he had put his over them.

"I don't know," he said dully. "Nothing. Something. I don't know. I've been up the creek and over the river with Scratch for nearly two weeks now; he thinks there's something wrong in the woods. Something bad. And I can't find it, but I think he's right. There's something . . . out of balance. But I couldn't find it. We looked and looked."

It was almost a child's voice, uncomprehending, fatigued.

"You're tired," I said. "You're terribly tired. I never saw you look like this. You have to rest now. When you have, you'll see that there's nothing wrong out there. Everything is all right. But you have to have a bath, and eat, and then you have to sleep."

"I thought I would call you in the morning, and you'd come, and we could talk, and you could make me see I was being a damned fool," he said, rubbing my fingers with his cold ones, looking at me, looking, looking. "I know I get a little crazy when I've been off in the woods too long. But then I passed the cutoff to King's Oak from the creek, and I saw the glow from the lights through the woods, and I remembered what night it was, and I knew you'd be up here. So . . . I came. All of a sudden I couldn't wait. I wanted you," he said simply. He stopped, and looked at me, and then down at his shirt and pants and filthy moccasins.

"I must look like a madman," he said. "I wonder the hands let me in the back door."

He looked up and grinned; it was a maimed grin, painful. I felt something in my stomach turn over with a huge, old, slow, sliding weight that pressed down into my groin and reached up to fill my chest and throat. It felt as massive and wet and warm as a dolphin in a tropical sea. My heart began to jolt and my breath caught in my throat. I thought, simply, that if I could not take his body into mine that instant I would die of it; I thought that and nothing else at all. Nothing else.

"Take off those awful clothes," I said hoarsely. "And then help me get out of this damned thing. I want you to make love to me right now, Tom, before one more second goes by. You said tell you if I changed my mind, tell you when I wanted things different; well, they've changed, it's different, and I want you now. . . . I want you now."

I could hear my voice and I could see my hands pulling at his clothes and I could feel his body as he came up against me, pinning me back against the washbasin, feel the hardness leaping against me, feel his hands at the back of my dress, searching for the zipper. But I had an odd sense that I had moved out of my body, and only sensation remained; that the thinking part of me, the recording part, the Andy part, hovered somewhere near the ceiling watching a woman in a black satin evening dress and a man in dirty, torn hunting clothes begin the act of love, standing up against a washbasin in a large, old-fashioned bathroom. I reached around him and shoved the bathroom door shut and he reached back with one hand and turned the lock, and then he put his mouth down to mine and his hands on my body and for a long time I did not think. He kicked my dress and underclothes aside with his own and lifted me up and knelt to go into me, and just before he did, and the world exploded again in fire and heat, and the great, sweet, wild singing in the blood began, he said, "I couldn't get to you fast enough. I thought I would die out there in the goddamned woods before I got here."

"You're here now," I whispered. "You're here now . . . now . . ."

"Ah, God, yes *now*. . . ."

After we were dressed again, he slumped down on the toilet seat and grinned at me. He looked a good five years younger than when he had come into the room, but still very tired.

"You coming out to the creek tonight, or what?" he said.

"No," I said. "You have to sleep. You really do. And I have to . . . I'm going to have to tell Carter."

"Yeah. You are. I gather it's going to be a worse mess than I thought."

"Yes. I told him this week I'd marry him by the end of the year. It's a rotten thing I'm going to do now. I can't put it off."

"No. I wish . . . God, Diana, I wish this hadn't had to happen like this. I wish it could have been simpler. I wish I could have made you see . . ."

"Well, you couldn't have," I said. "Things didn't change

until . . . they changed. I couldn't have hurried that. I couldn't have made that happen any sooner than it did. I guess it took your going away."

"Want me to be with you when you tell him?" he said.

"No. Save him some face. I'm not going to tell him I screwed you standing up in the john, for God's sake. I'm just going to tell him it was a mistake, all my fault, nothing to do with another man, with you. All me. He's going to know different, but at least he doesn't have to admit that he does till he's ready. If the lying bothers you, I'm sorry, but this is one lie I'm going to tell or die trying."

"Are you coming out tomorrow, then? Or anytime soon? I do want to talk to you. Just this once without Hil. This is not for her ears."

"There really is something wrong, then," I said.

"It's more that something just isn't right," he said. "I need to make sense of it. I need to tell it to somebody who doesn't already have ideas about it. It may turn out to be nothing, like I said. In any case, I'm going to want to do this again as soon as I've slept twelve hours, so if you could see your way clear to just come crawl straight in bed . . ."

I laughed. I was suddenly very happy, even with shame and the enormity of what I must now do to Carter hanging heavy over me.

"Did anybody see you come up here?" I said as he reached to unlock the door. "It will simplify things considerably if it doesn't get back to Carter that you came up to the upstairs bathroom after me. Who knows you're here, besides the kitchen crew?"

"Only Clay, I think," he said. "I had him called out to the kitchen when I got here, and came up the other stairs, at the end of the gallery. I don't think anybody else saw me, and he sure won't mention it."

"Good," I said, holding my face up to his kiss. The wiry whiskers felt like rough-grade sandpaper. "I hope this is the last time I have to act like the upstairs maid with a traveling salesman."

"You got it," he said. "Next time we fuck, we'll do it in the street and scare the horses. That would give me no end of pleasure."

He opened the door and took a step into the bedroom and stopped. I hesitated, and then moved around him so I could see. Pat Dabney sat slouched in the slipper chair before the dressing table, her taffeta skirts hiked up and her slim ankles crossed before her. She was smoking and filing her nails, and she had a heelless evening pump in her lap.

"Evening, folks," she said, smiling her slow, thick smile. "I'm relieved to see you're okay. I was just about to call mine host. It sounded like the Bates Motel in there."

"What are you doing up here?" I said. It was, among all the stupid things I have ever said, possibly the stupidest.

"Waiting to tinkle, like a little girl must at times," she said, wrinkling her nose winsomely. "I thought I was going to have to do it in my shoe. You all have really been in there the longest time."

I went around her toward the bedroom door.

"If you're looking for Carter, I spec' he gone on," Pat Dabney said serenely. "He came up here with me, to help me fix this here broken heel on my slipper, don'tcha know, and when he heard all the commotion in the john he just took off out the door. A proper gentleman, is Carter. It's too bad, really." She stretched and smiled.

I stared at her in disbelief. Tom made a low sound of disgust in his throat.

"Somebody is going to kill you one day, Pat," he said. His voice was as neutral and uninflected as if he had commented on the weather. "I hope I'm somewhere else at the time with ten people, because the police will sure as hell think it was me. And I wish it had been . . . back when it still mattered to me."

I turned and went out the bedroom door and started toward the stairs. He walked softly behind me.

"I've heard better than that at hog-killing time," Pat Dabney called after him. "I've *done* better than that at hog-killing time." Her voice sounded thin and shrill.

"Not on your best day, you haven't," he said, and followed me down the stairs. On the landing he touched my elbow and I stopped.

"I'll borrow a car from Clay and take you home," he said. "I don't want you to have to mess with all this. There's no telling how many people she's told."

"No," I said. "Tish and Charlie will take me. Please, Tom. The rest of this is between Carter and me."

"Take care of yourself," he said, and touched my hair, and went back up the stairs and along the gallery to the stairs at the opposite end. I went down into the crowd in search of Charlie and Tish.

They were waiting for me by the bar, looking worried. No one else seemed to take any notice of me, so I assumed that Pat had, as of that moment, held her tongue. It did not matter, in any event; the damage had been done.

"Carter said he felt rotten and thought he'd go on home, and asked us to give you a lift when you came down," Tish said. "He looked awful, too. Did you two have a fight?"

"No," I said. "I'm ready to go when you are."

We got our coats and went out onto the veranda and waited until Clay Dabney's man brought the Jaguar around. The cold air felt good on my stiff, hot face. Aside from that, and a dull, hammering fatigue, I felt nothing at all.

Tish and Charlie did not speak until we got to my front

door, and then it was Charlie, offering to come in with me. Carter's Jaguar was not there.

"No," I said. "Thanks. It was sweet of you to give me a ride."

"Call me tomorrow?" Tish called from the car.

"Right," I said. "I will. Good night, now."

Even without his car, I halfway expected to see Carter there, waiting for me. The wound of the night's betrayal seemed to demand at the very least the salt of confrontation. But the living room was empty, as we had left it. His old briefcase was gone from the coffee table, though, and the stack of briefs, and his shearling coat was no longer hanging on the peg by the kitchen door. I walked down the hall to my bedroom and opened the big closet. His space was empty. I walked into the bathroom. His terry robe was gone from its hook, and his shaving things from the sink. I went back to the living room and looked at my answering machine. The red light was blinking. I pressed the button and sank down on the wing chair to listen. I knew whose message it would be.

It was very brief, and he did not sound particularly angry, or even sad. Just . . . older. Much, much older, and tired.

"I won't call again," Carter said. "But if you need me, or want to talk, give me a call. I won't expect one, but I want you to do it if you need to. I love you, Andy. Take care of yourself."

I realized then that they were the same words Tom Dabney had said to me when he left me, and that seemed, somehow, past endurance. I sat in the wing chair and wept until half-past three, and then, out of tears at last, I went to bed and slept, for the first time in many nights, alone.

CHAPTER TEN

A couple of weeks after that, Tish went to Atlanta for gum surgery and I went with her, to drive her back in case she didn't feel up to it. I parked Hilary with the Chapins and took a day of my precious sick leave, and we drove up on Thursday afternoon and she had her surgery on Friday morning, and by Saturday night she felt well enough to go out to dinner. I spent the days shopping for Hilary and myself and driving the Toyota around the clotted and honking Buckhead streets where I had so recently whisked in my BMW.

I drove past our former house, and Chris's parents' great pile on Habersham Road; both were closed and shuttered, and there were no cars in either driveway. I felt nothing at all except alien. Strangeness rang in my ears and hammered at my temples. By the time I met Tish in the café at the Ritz-Carlton in Buckhead, I was anxious and disoriented, like a tourist after a hard day in a foreign city that was vaguely familiar from some long-past visit. The city stank in my nostrils and howled in my ears; I felt an ache of longing that was actually physical for the clean, stinging coldness of the winter woods. My hands and arms hurt with the wanting of Tom.

Tish was sitting in a banquette, sipping a martini, her swollen jaw nestled into the folds of a cashmere turtleneck. There was another martini at my place, pale as moonlight in an ice-fogged stem glass. I took a grateful swallow, and then another.

"Thanks," I said, grimacing at the acrid bite of the gin. "I needed that."

"Bad day among the fleshpots?" Tish said.

"Yes, sort of. I felt like an alien from another planet. It's like I never lived here at all. And worse than that, I feel like I don't live in Pemberton, either, and never did. Tish, it's all of a sudden like I don't live anywhere at all. Like I'm just free-floating in space. It's a hateful feeling; so *strange*."

"Well, I'm not surprised. You haven't exactly been Muffy Middle America lately," she said. "You're a hot ticket in checkout lines and the beauty shop."

"Are people talking about me?" I asked. I don't know why I was surprised. Of course they were; how not?

"Can you doubt it?" Tish said. "Carter Devereaux is everybody's darling. What's good for Carter is good for Pemberton, and so on. And you didn't exactly pick a discrete way to break up with him. Getting caught in the act in the upstairs bathroom at King's Oak with the whole town downstairs? Jesus, Andy, couldn't you just have written him a Dear John, or something?"

A great, bland weariness settled over me. I could have stretched out on the banquette and slept for hours, days.

"And then Carter's back with Pat, or so I hear, and that's going to be good for another two months of talk," Tish said, picking the olive from my martini and popping it into one side of her mouth. "Shit, that smarts. I hear he took her to the Bar Association meeting at Sea Island; they're down there now. Everybody's wondering what you're going to say about that, though of course nobody ever sees you anymore, so there's no way of knowing. My phone's going to start ringing the minute I walk in the house. I guess you don't want to tell me about it, do you? You know I won't repeat it."

"I just can't talk about Carter now, Tish." I felt afresh the shabby pain and guilt of what I had done to him. "I do wish other people wouldn't talk about him, though," I said. "It was none of his doing. And he mortally hates gossip. As for me, I really wonder why anybody cares what I do. I'm not one of you. Not really."

"Well," Tish said, "you almost were. You were going to be. And as for why they talk . . . are you serious? Think about it. You really have been doing an awful lot of fucking, Andy. First in town, and then all over the swamp. It's just . . . not what we do in Pemberton. Not that most of us wouldn't like to; we just don't. Not even us old marrieds. *Especially* not even us old marrieds. When somebody essentially *like* us does it all over the place with not one but two guys—we talk."

"Pat Dabney does it. Nobody cares about that; everybody seems to expect it," I said.

"She isn't one of us. She's her own law. And she's Winter People. You were going to be Old Pemberton. It was all arranged; it was a fact of our collective life. You and

Carter. Cemented into the grid. Small towns run on their routines and rituals. If you and Carter could break up over a . . . a wild man, then it could happen to any of us. Not that every woman in town hasn't dreamed of doing it with Tom Dabney in a tree or something; we have. Even the grand dames; even his mother and sister probably, they're so fucked up. Doing it, though—that's maverick. That's outside the herd. I heard that Caroline Dabney said, 'And she looked like such a nice, settled little matron.' Among *many* other things. I'm a little worried for you, to tell you the truth. And I'm surprised that you're surprised."

"They know precious little about me, to be so hell-bent on judging me," I said sharply. "You can't just reduce all a person is to *fucking*. I'm the least likely Jezebel in the world; you know that."

"Yes, I do," she said. "But remember, all they really know about you is that one way or another, you've been screwing almost every night since you got to Pemberton. In a town that size, that's pretty spectacular."

I lapsed into silence, knowing underneath the thin skin of anger and injury that she was right. I, who had come so to hate the mocking act of love that I had fled a city and a life to avoid it, had spent almost the entirety of my new life either thinking about it or doing it. First with Carter. And now, almost daily, almost constantly, with Tom Dabney.

And such love . . . I had not known its like existed. Excess I knew, and debauchery, and near depravity; knew it from Chris, from my very initiation into physical love. Delicacy and gentleness I knew from Carter. From Tom Dabney I knew all those things at once, with the added leavening of laughter. Out at Goat Creek, in Tom's firelit, winter-girt house; in his bed and on his floor and in his woods on the fur throw and beneath his trees on just the carpet of the leaves and pine needles; in his hot tub and in his kitchen and in his canoe and once, even, on the broad, low limb of a great magnolia, we made fast, silent love, or slow, shouting love, or every shade and experience of love in between, in sunlight and darkness and even rain, and always I learned a new and shuddering dimension of sensation, and almost always, we laughed. To make love with Tom Dabney was to dive down, to sink, to drown, and to rise again in joy. In those weeks since I had been going every day to Goat Creek, I had become a creature of flesh and wildness; he had only to touch my arm and look at me, and my knees went slack and I rose and went to him; I had only to say his name, "Tom," and he stopped what he was doing and came to where I was, and wherever it was, there we came together. We tried to be circumspect around Hilary, but during that time I came to notice that she went earlier and earlier into the small room Tom had built for her, and stayed outside with Missy and Earl whenever possible. I was greatly touched by her delicacy, her child's enabling. We tried not to exploit her intuitive tact. But it was, simply, hard for us to keep our hands off each other.

"Do we do this too much?" I asked him once, lying with my leg flung loosely over his, listening to rain pelt the canvas curtains. It was a Saturday, and Hilary had gone, reluctantly, on a field trip to a folk museum in Albany with her class.

Tom traced a circle around my nipple with a forefinger, leaving a wake of goose bumps. "Do we breathe too much?"

"It's just that . . . sometimes we're so vocal about it," I said, remembering. "We sound like a couple of hyenas."

"Next time we'll do it like a couple of Calvinist missionaries, and we'll pray silently and flog ourselves afterward," he said. "Come on, Diana. You don't censure yourself for eating or drinking or singing or laughing, do you?"

"It's not the same thing."

"It's exactly the same thing."

"Maybe it's all the laughing," I said. "I always thought there was supposed to be a tremulous rapture and reverent, solemn ecstasy. I remember a movie that made a great impression on me, *The Fountainhead*. . . ."

"I saw it, too," he said. "It should have been called *The Marble Maidenhead*. What a pair of tight-asses. I bet it set a generation of American kids on the road to onanism."

"It's just that . . . you can't always laugh."

"No, you can't. But you can and should until you have to cry. Would you like me better the way I was that night at King's Oak? And right after that?" he said.

"No, but I could almost understand you better that way. I've never seen you vulnerable or hurt before. It was almost a humanizing thing."

"Well, I can gladly do without hurt," he said. "Especially when I have you to heal me. And you did. That's what you did for me. You, and this."

It was true to an extent; he had been near distraction, almost haunted, when we had begun to come to Goat Creek every day, after the night at King's Oak. His conviction that there was something amiss in the woods was strong, and it hagrode him. I could not understand the depths of his unease, and he could not, or did not, explain it to me. He stood or sat for hours, staring at the dark water of the creek or into the trees, silent, his blue eyes opaque. He paced, and he slept badly, and he drank a good bit more than I had ever seen him drink. He did not go into the woods, either alone or with Scratch or Martin Longstreet or Reese Carmody, and they did not come to the house on Goat Creek.

He did not play the Martin for Hilary and me anymore after dinner, even though he did play records almost constantly. It was dark music, funereal, elegiac. And though he oversaw Hilary's archery lessons, and taught her about fishing and the making of lures and hooks, he did it almost as if by rote, and without the keenly focused attention that she was used to.

"Is Tom mad at me?" she asked me once, miserably, on the way home to Pemberton.

"No," I said. "He's worried that there's something wrong out in the woods, maybe with the plants or animals, and he can't find out what it is, and he's thinking a lot about it. It's time now to be as still and quiet as we can, and just let him work through this."

"But what do you *think* is wrong?" I would ask him, over and over. "If it's nothing you can see or hear or smell or taste, what do you think it is?"

"I don't know," he said. "It's really more Scratch than me; he's convinced. Absolutely convinced. Says he feels it, says he dreams about it. That's the clincher, for him. Scratch isn't wrong about the woods; he just isn't. But he can't get his hands on it, either. And there *is* something, Diana; you can feel it out there sometimes. . . . I'll get it. It'll come to me. I'll find it."

"Would you rather we didn't come for a while?" I asked.

"God, no. You and Hilary are the only clean, warm, solid things in this miserable winter," he said. "Don't stop coming, for God's sake. You're my sanity. You're my balance."

So we did not stop the visits. We came every afternoon after school, and stayed until about ten. On weekends we came in the mornings and stayed late. Soon it was as I told Tish: I came to feel that I lived nowhere, or rather, in air, like a bird; my home was no longer Pemberton, nor was it Goat Creek. I kept industriously at my toiling for Miss Deborah, and Hilary applied herself with remarkably little grumbling to her dim school routine, and Tom kept his class schedules running meticulously, if unwarmed by his old élan. I saw him occasionally on campus, between classes; he would lift a careless hand to me, and I would wave back, but he did not seek me out, and we did not leave the parking lot together. The only difference in Tom then and Tom in the days before we had become lovers was that in those days, when I saw him walking with his entourage of students and faculty, he was seldom laughing. And he did not sing, and I never saw him dance. He was a reflection of himself. The love we made in those early days of the relationship had more of the urgency of necessity about it than any I can remember, except one other and altogether terrible time. In those first days we had little of Tom, Hilary and I, except his presence.

But then, in early February, when a spell of wet, warm days came to the swamp and set the catkins greening and the first tender ferns uncurling, and the steely sky over the trees softened into the milkiness of false spring, he seemed to slip the dark burden of the woods off his shoulders like a cloak and was soon almost himself again, the point of living flame that we had so missed. He went into the swamp once more with Scratch and Reese Carmody and Martin Longstreet and was gone overnight, and when he returned he was fully Tom, though very tired, and the love and the laughing started in earnest.

"What on earth happened out there?" I asked him the night he returned, after we had met and made love riotously, joyously, on the dock.

"Nothing," he said. "Everything. We just . . . tended to some things, and looked around. The swamp is greening up just as it should. We heard peepers. It always makes me high, to see spring come back to the Big Silver. Even false spring, like this."

"Well," I said to Tish in Atlanta, days after that night. "People will just have to talk. I'm not about to ask the gentry of Pemberton to change their inimitable lives on my account, and I don't expect them to ask that of me. Is it just barely possible that a few of them might by happy for Tom and me and Hil?"

"They will, in time," Tish said. "If this is what truly makes the three of you happy. We're not ogres, you know. It's just that we were already so happy for you and Carter. It's been a long time since he had any luck in his life. And then, it's just plain asking too much to expect small-town people to put benevolence above world-class gossip!"

We finished our drinks in silence and ordered dinner, and then Tish said, "There's something else I'm starting to hear, something I like a whole lot less than gossip about screwing in the woods. It's all Pat, of course, and very few people are going to give it any credence, but they will listen. And they'll repeat it. I wasn't even going to mention it; it's just too silly for words, but then I thought maybe I should. It could very possibly affect Hil."

"For God's sake, Tish, what?" I said.

"Well, I've heard a little stuff about . . . things you all do out there. Not the sex stuff; other things. Really kinky, unsavory things like . . . oh, rituals. Black magic or something. You know, all the hoopla there is these days about satanism and devil worship. . . ."

"Dear God, do you mean to tell me people are saying that Tom and Hilary and I are out in the Big Silver worshiping the devil?" My voice cracked with utter incredulity; laughter bubbled just under it.

"No, nothing that specific," she said, looking down at

her plate. "Nothing you can really get your hands on to refute . . . Like I said, I've only heard it from a couple of people, and they got it straight from Pat, and she was drunk when she said it, and they didn't believe her, of course. Just said that she dropped hints about strange rites and . . . oh, blood sacrifices, and teaching Hilary things."

"I will kill that poisonous bitch. I will, with my bare hands," I said, cold rage almost choking me. "She's jealous of me and Tom; I've always seen that; a fool could see it. But to say that he's turning Hilary into . . . Who told you that? Who?"

"I'm not going to tell you," Tish said. "They didn't believe Pat any more than I do, or anybody else will. Of course it's jealousy; we all know she still wants him. The best thing you could do by far is just let her hang herself with her tongue. When she sees nobody credits what she's saying, when she sees it turns people off—and it does, my God—she'll stop. She always does. I'm sorry I even mentioned it."

She looked so miserable that I put my hand over hers and said, "Don't be. I know why you did. I'll leave it lie, and watch for signs that Hilary's heard anything, and head it off if she does. It's . . . Lord, it's grotesque. What a dangerous, *bad* thing to say about anybody."

"That's our Pat," Tish said wryly. "Underneath that tough exterior is a heart of pure basalt."

It bothered me badly, though, that the seductive old lore of the woods and the strange, haunting myths and legends Tom was teaching Hilary and me could be transmuted into such base metal. I hated it, that something as clean and beautiful and absolute as the flight of one of Hilary's arrows, or the uncanny calling of the big bronze gobbler, or the terrible and wonderful march of the deer in the dry cypress slough, could become, in the mouth of Pat Dabney, dark and clotted and corrupt. I thought about it all that weekend, and on Monday night, when I saw Tom again, I told him about it. I told him of the gossip about him and me first. He laughed at that.

"Well, then, we've made an entire town happy, as well as ourselves," he said. "Did you think they wouldn't talk? Does it bother you?"

"I don't think so, if it doesn't affect Hil," I said. "But maybe it wouldn't be a bad thing if she and I didn't spend so much time out here. If we spent a couple afternoons and nights a week, at least, in town, doing . . . oh, town things. With other people we know. And you could come in and see us there, go to the movies, have dinner at the club or somewhere. You know, so people could see us doing . . . ordinary couple things."

"I don't belong in town doing town things," he said. "We're not an ordinary couple. I'll take you to the movies if you like, or to dinner, but I'm not going to like the reason you want me to do it. We belong out here, Diana, the three of us. This is our place."

"But, Tom . . . Hilary and I can't just move to the woods forever, for good and all," I said. "We can't just . . . chuck our lives and live out here."

"Why not?" he said. "It's what I see for us. It's working so far, isn't it? All you aren't doing is spending the nights, and I can't for the life of me see why you balk at that. Hasn't this been what you wanted?"

"Yes, oh, yes, but . . . I mean to *live?* I . . . Tom, I have all those dresses and high heels and things, and I really like them, and I like to shop and go to the theater and eat out, and Hilary will have friends, and soon she'll want to go on dates and things. . . ."

"Dearest Diana," he said, laughing, rolling me over in his arms on the rug in front of the fire, where we were lying. "I'm not asking you to become a cannibal or a hermit. I'll take you to a hundred concerts; I have my very own tuxedo, remember? I go to New York several times a year, just like real people, and stay at the Yale Club, and once I even went to Lutèce and they didn't throw me out for eating with my fingers. What's this really about?"

"It's about the fact that Pat is telling people we worship the devil out here, or intimating something like that, and that we're teaching it all to Hilary," I said, and told him what Tish had told me. When I was finished, he smiled and shook his head. I was oddly annoyed; I had, I realized, expected rage, and vows of vengeance and protection for me and my daughter. "She doesn't give up," he said. "It's not the first time she's trotted out the unnatural-acts business."

"What did you do that time?" I said.

"Just what I'm going to do this time," he said. "And what I'm going to ask you to do. Ignore her. Jesus, you don't think anybody believes that shit, do you?"

"What if Hilary hears it?"

"Hilary is the last person who's going to be bothered by it," he said. "Hilary of all people understands . . . about the woods, and reverence for them. But if it starts to get to her, then I'll handle it with Pat."

"But, Tom . . . why would she say such things? Why would she even think people might believe her?"

He looked at me for a long time, and then he sighed.

"I can see why she might," he said. "I think you'd better see, too. For yourself."

He got up from the rug and padded to the telephone. The firelight flowed on his bare brown skin like lava, on the smooth play of muscles in his back. I thought again what a beautiful body he had, dark and perfect and wild.

"Who are you calling?" I asked.

"My accomplices in the black arts," he said. "My sorcerer's apprentices. Reese and Martin and Scratch. It's time for you to learn . . . some other things."

He spoke into the phone and came back to where I lay on the fur throw before the fire.

"What other things?" I said. There was a prickle along my arms, as if the firelight had a touch.

"What the four of us are to each other," he said. "What we are to the woods. And a little of what you are to us. I'd thought spring would be the time for it, but my esteemed former wife isn't going to give me the luxury of time. Better you see, anyway. 'Ye shall know the truth, and the truth shall set you free.' "

"I'm not liking the sound of this," I said. "What is it you want me to do?"

"I want you to come out later tomorrow, after dark. Around eight. Leave Hilary with Tish and Charlie or somebody; this isn't for her until you know about it. And you might be late getting back, so arrange for her to stay over, if you can. When you come, bring some red wine and a loaf of bread and some salt with you. And come on around the porch and down to the creek, beside the dock. I won't be at the house, but I'll be with Scratch and Martin and Reese down there. We'll have a fire going; you'll see it."

"Tom . . . what's going to happen?"

"Nothing you need to be afraid of," he said. "In fact, I should think you might enjoy it. I wouldn't hurt you, you know that, or let anybody else do it."

"What should I wear?" I said, stupidly. "What kind of wine? What should I . . . carry the stuff in?"

"Wear anything you like, or nothing, which I'd like." He grinned. "Mogen David if you must. Carry the stuff in a brown paper sack, if you want to. It doesn't matter. This is not witchcraft, Diana."

Hilary started to protest the next evening when I told her she could not come with me to Goat Creek, and then she did not.

"Okay," she said. "If that's what Tom said. I can finish my Egypt project for geography and then we can spend both days out there this weekend."

"Hilary is a different child," Tish said to me, after she and I had settled her on the sofa in the Coulters' den, in front of a card table. Hilary had set out her water colors and paper and scissors and gone serenely to work, after giving Tish and Charlie hugs and smiles, and had only flipped a nonchalant hand at me when I left the room. "Tell Tom hey," she called after me.

"It's like she went from . . . almost infancy, a frail infancy, to where she is now in a matter of weeks," Tish said. "I never saw a child change so. If that's what's happening to her out there at Goat Creek, Tom ought to be on morning talk shows. He'd make a million."

"You don't know the half of it," I said, seeing in my mind's eye my tall child standing on a creekbank, killing a screaming piglet with an arrow.

"Aren't you pleased?" Tish said.

"Of course," I said. "I wouldn't let her set foot out there if I weren't."

"Well," she said, "don't hurry home. I'll take her to school in the morning, if you'd like to . . . sleep in."

"I'll pick her up, thanks just the same," I said. "Don't leer, Tish. I don't stay the night out there. I never have."

"Pity," she said, and pushed me gently out the door

and closed it. I drove away toward Goat Creek in the winter darkness, my purchases in a canvas tote on the back seat, my heart thumping briskly in the vicinity of my throat.

I saw the leaping chiaroscuro of the fire in the trees before I came to a stop in front of the dark house, and I sat in the car for a long moment before I turned the motor off. The night felt close and cold and enormous with some import I could not fathom, and did not wish to. Pemberton and its lights and traffic and commerce and blessed, trivial ordinariness seemed many miles and hundreds of years away. I had come to an old place in an old silence; I wanted to ram the car into reverse and back away from there. The efficient little heater was going full blast, and I wore sweat clothes under a down vest, but still I shivered. I waited a moment more to see if something would happen, if anyone would come, but no one did. Finally I got out of the car and picked up my tote and went around the porch and across the brown grass toward the creek.

To the left of Tom's house there is a place where Goat Creek narrows to a black ribbon about four feet wide, choked waist-high and thick on either verge with reeds and water plants and, in winter, watercress. Just beyond, it flares out into the broad, lakelike expanse where the dock stands and the boats are tethered; where, those many nights before, Hilary and Tom had danced in the moonlight on its banks. But where it is narrow it is also shallow and swift, and you can wade it in two or three long steps. It was where we habitually cross, and where the goats do, and the ducks. On the near bank now, two great fires leaped and snapped and whispered, and across the creek, Reese Carmody and Martin Longstreet and Tom stood, shoulder to shoulder. Behind them, a little way up the opposite bank, Scratch Purvis stood alone. All four stood with their arms straight at their sides, looking at me. They were dressed sensibly, in what any sane man in the February night swamp would wear—khaki pants, rubber boots or waders, down vests and hunting jackets—but on their heads each wore a crown of oak leaves, such as they had worn on Thanksgiving. I had thought then that they wore them as jokes, in fun. Beside Reese Carmody a small skin drum sat on the ground, and Martin Longstreet held in his hand his small silver flute. Tom and Scratch had nothing with them. I stopped still, my tote bumping against my leg. My heart vaulted into my throat. I stared, mute. Despite the boots and vests, they did not belong to this night and this world, but to some measureless time before history, some wild place of fire and drums. My muscles clenched for flight.

"Diana," Tom said mildly. "It's okay. It's all right. It's just us."

He smiled, and motioned me forward. I took a couple of steps and stopped again. I looked from Martin Longstreet to Reese Carmody to Scratch, and then back to Tom. They all smiled, small, easy smiles. Some of the strangeness fled.

"What are we up to this fine night?" I said. I began jauntily, but my voice fell into the darkness like a wounded bird.

"We're welcoming you to the woods," Tom said. "We're making you a part of us. This is more for us than it is for you, so if you find some of it hard to swallow, that's okay. But I hope you'll go along with us without questions for a little while. If you will, we'll have dinner after and tell you about it. If it's still a little too much, I'll walk you to the car and there's no harm done. But now's the time to decide. Okay?"

"Okay," I said, after a moment. My voice was small and high. "What do you want me to do?"

"Walk between the two fires and put the things on the ground exactly between them," he said. "Then come to the edge of the creek and wait. I'll come get you."

He made a motion with his head toward the others, and Reese Carmody stooped and picked up the little drum and began to brush a small, steady rhythm on it with his fingertips. Martin Longstreet put the silver flute to his mouth and began to play. The tune he played was like the one he had played for us before, on the porch: atonal, wailing, skirling, hypnotic. Behind him, Scratch closed his eyes and lifted his head and sang something, softly, in a thin, cracked old voice. Neither the tune nor the words had any sense for me. The great, firelit black bowl of the river swamp seemed to lean down, close around me. Time flew backward like a spool of film unreeling.

I came down to where the fires burned, and stooped to let my tote drop to the earth between them. Then I walked on between them, down to the edge of the creek, and stopped. Tom parted the waist-high water plants and reeds on the opposite bank and came down to the very edge of the creek. He put his hand out to me. Where he had parted the vegetation, I saw that something had been built there, among the cattails and bulrushes, a kind of freestanding tunnel of oak and pine boughs, thatched with living green boughs of live oak and moss. It stood about as high as Tom's waist, and looked to be about five feet long.

"Diana, if you will, we want you to come across the creek and through the tunnel," he said. "There's nothing on the inside but fresh pine and oak limbs. I cut them myself this morning. You might have to stoop, or go on your hands and knees, but it's nothing, I promise you. I'd show you, but it's . . . not allowed. But I promise there's nothing there to hurt you."

"I know," I said. I had to swallow before I could speak.

"Good," he said. "Come on, now."

The flute and drum spiraled up, and Scratch raised his song higher, and I walked into the water of Goat Creek and out again on the opposite bank. I did not feel the icy sogginess of my crew socks and moccasins. I looked at Tom; he stood at the other end of the green tunnel, and nodded, smiling. I took a deep breath and ducked down and entered it.

It was just as he had said; inside the structure there was nothing but the wet black earth where he had cleared it of reeds, and the close, overarching curve of limb and twig and needle and leaf and bough. I took a great, deep breath and smelled cold, fresh oak and new-split wood; I closed my eyes; I was through the tunnel and standing upright again. Tom stood before me and held his hand out. I took it.

He led me between Reese and Martin Longstreet and stopped with me before Scratch Purvis, then stepped back. Scratch bent stiffly to the earth and picked up a small earthenware bowl and dipped his hand into it. With his forefinger, he traced something on my forehead. It was cold and wet; I closed my eyes. I did not want to see the color of the liquid on his dark fingers. When I opened them, it was to see Tom lifting a crown of oak leaves identical to theirs, to put on my head. He set it in place and smiled and kissed me on both cheeks, and then Scratch leaned over and kissed my cheek, too, and then Reese, and lastly Martin. Scratch closed his eyes once more and chanted a short sort of one-note, one-level incantation, and then it was over. They broke their ranks and seemed to stretch and jostle a bit like men after a prayer at a football game, and everyone looked at Tom.

"That's it," he said. "Welcome to the woods, Diana Calhoun."

"Welcome, Diana," Martin Longstreet said, and the others followed with their mumbled welcomes.

"I . . . thank you," I said, weakly. "I feel like Maid Marion. Will somebody please tell me what it was we just did?"

"Yep," Tom Dabney said. "But first, dinner. I don't know about you guys, but I'm hungry as hell. I haven't eaten since dinner last night."

"You sound like you're bucking for canonization," Reese Carmody said. "Nobody else has, either, asshole. Much less had anything to drink, which is cruel and unusual in the extreme."

They laughed: men after the game was over, going off to drink beer.

"Then what are we waiting for?" Tom said.

It was perhaps a measure of his personal power, as well as the power of the night and the fire and the oblique old ritual, that when I asked him why he had bade me set the wine and bread and salt down between the two fires and he said, "For purification," I merely said, "Oh," and followed him into the house.

Inside, Tom built up the fire and put Gerry Mulligan on the stereo and went into the kitchen. Martin Longstreet poured Scotch for all of us but Scratch, who smiled and shook his head and closed his eyes, nodding in his deep chair by the fire and tapping his foot in time to the music. From the kitchen the rich smell of roasting meat began to curl, and I realized that I was as hungry as a timberwolf. I took off my wet socks and shoes and held my bare feet to the fire and let the well-being that Goat Creek always engendered in me wash the skewedness out of the night. We might have been four old friends, gathered to eat and drink and laugh in the home of a fifth. In effect, we were that, though of course, over and under it we were something else now, something completely outside the parameters of my ken.

But in that moment I felt only ease and content and simple physical appetite. The Scotch was smoky in my mouth and warm in my blood. The utter strangeness of what we had just done in the Big Silver Swamp crouched off at the edge of consciousness; it did not come into the circle of the firelight. I knew that I would have to assess it soon; would have to find a place in the grid of my experience to try and fit it . . . but not yet. Out here, this night was a natural one. It was only back in Pemberton, back in the world, that it would become bizarre.

I lifted my glass to the three men by the fire.

"*L'chaim*, or whatever," I said. "Let the games begin. Who's going to tell me about it?"

"I suppose I will, my dear," Martin Longstreet said. "I can't seem to shed my academic mantle even in the woods. Unless Tom had rather?"

"Go ahead, Marty," Tom said from the kitchen. "Your credibility is miles higher than mine. She already thinks I'm nuts, but she'll have to at least listen to you. If she sasses you, you can get her fired."

Martin Longstreet smiled broadly; for the first time I saw that he was an attractive man and had once been very handsome. I thought of the talk I had heard around school of his homosexuality; none of it had been malicious, only matter-of-fact. He was greatly respected at the college, and his academic demeanor was austere and punctilious. Now I could see that a living, laughing man of substance and appetite lived within him, or once had. I hoped, suddenly, that he had had a good life.

"I'd hardly do that," he said. "Diana probably has more clout than I do now."

"Will somebody please tell me *something?*" I said.

"Yes. All right," Martin Longstreet said. He took a deep breath that came out in a sigh.

"What we did tonight, Diana, was a very old ritual of purification and welcome. It comes basically from the Hindu, who believed that a person is—shall we say—contaminated by contact with the outside world, possibly infected with its ills and evils, and must be born again into purity and innocence before he can be brought into the group, or before a king. So an image was made of the usual female channel of birth, either from gold or from the sacred yoni, and the stranger, or the uninitiated one, had to pass through this birth canal to be regenerated. We find it difficult to get our hands on either gold or yoni, so we make our edifice of oak, which we believe is sacred to the woods. When you came through it you were cleansed, as it were, of the world outside and made new to receive the mysteries of the woods. And you were made safe for contact with our shaman, who in this case is Scratch."

He nodded at Scratch, who nodded back and smiled, though he did not open his eyes. I simply looked at Martin Longstreet.

"The fire ritual we borrowed from one practiced to protect the Tartar Khan in the Middle Ages. The fires burn away any magical influence attached to the gifts brought to the Khan by his visitors. The passing through water and the anointing comes from a purification ritual of the Bashilange in the Congo Basin. We modified it a bit for you; ordinarily women to be purified bathed naked for two days in a sacred stream, and stood naked before the priest-chief to be anointed on forehead and breast. We thought that was a bit much for February in the woods, and besides, Scratch is mortified by the thought of naked ladies. But basically that's it. It means that you are now one of us and one with the woods. You can do anything you wish with it, or nothing. We hope you'll wish to . . . practice with us."

He stopped and looked at me serenely. The other two looked, too. I could not hear Tom moving about in the kitchen; the room was silent except for the fire and Gerry Mulligan.

"Practice with you," I parroted. I knew that I sounded as slow and thick as I felt. What was he saying?

"We have a number of rituals that we do in order to keep the Big Silver River and the woods and swamp around it clean and pure and safe from harm," he said simply. "We believe that this is possible, and that the ways we have developed over the years are the best ways to do it. We don't always succeed, but our record is quite creditable. For certain very good reasons, we believe that you have gifts we would like to add to our arsenal, if you will."

"Gifts," I said. "What gifts?"

"I think Tom will be the one to tell you that," he said gently. "We are mainly here for the purification ceremony, which calls for all of us, and to tell you that if you decide to become one of us you will be very welcome indeed."

I stared at him, and at Reese Carmody, and at Scratch Purvis. I could not look in the direction of the kitchen. A huge, diffuse grief was building in me; I struggled to keep it at bay. He was simply mad, then, the beautiful, dark man who laughed and danced and loved me into life, and lived in an enchanted house in the woods. He was not brushed with magic, but only mad. They were all mad. They were mad, and I had not known.

"You—all of you—worship the woods, then," I said. "You believe you have powers that can protect them. You do rituals and things out here. . . ."

"We do rituals, yes," Martin said mildly, his eyes holding mine. I knew that he saw my disbelief and grief. "We don't worship the woods per se; that's an oversimplification and an arrogant assumption we would never make. We live, or try to live, sacredly, is perhaps a better way of putting it. We think it is important to live with reverence at the core of our beings, and we find nothing so worthy of reverence as the wild—as the river and the woods and the animals here. We don't believe it is we who have the power, but the rituals themselves, or rather, that which they evoke. They are the embodiment of the great hunting and forest myths of the world since it began, and it is these myths that have the true power. It is these myths that speak of a knowledge and power that our minds can't know . . . but our hearts can. And our bodies. We think the world has great need of this good and true power, and that all other methods we know of have failed to tap it, including the orthodox religions. And so we use what we think is the realest and truest power in the world to protect what we think is the most important thing in the world—wildness. The wilderness. The woods. It's not such an antiquated concept. Somebody—I think it was Jung—held that the woods are a metaphor for the most immutable goodness and truth we know, the unconscious. Of course, he called it God, too. So in that sense, perhaps we do worship it. But not, I think, in the blind and single-minded sense that I think you mean. We simply feel that it is the only sacred way to live."

He smiled at me.

"We hoped by having all of us here when you . . . learned some of this, it would go better for all of us. We thought maybe you'd have a harder time thinking four of us were nuts in precisely the same way."

I looked up toward the kitchen then. Tom stood leaning against the peeled log that supported the entrance to it, sipping on his Scotch and looking at me. His face was relaxed and tranquil, but he did not smile. He simply looked. And then he winked.

"Ah, God," I said in defeat, and dropped my face into my hands. I knew then that he was hopelessly sane and so was I and so were they, these others. Hopelessly sane and doomed to stay that way. I would simply have to find a way to fit all this into what I knew of the world, and to mend my life around the hole it made; to believe, in effect, the unbelievable. The promissory fatigue of that almost paralyzed me where I sat.

I raised my head and looked at Tom then. He was smiling now.

"How did you all get together?" I said. "How did you come . . . to be a team like this?"

"I've told you about my dad, and how he learned from his dad, and he learned from his—my great-grandfather—who learned it in Germany. From the great woodmasters, I suppose. Hermann Göring was one, to my great shame. I guess the most . . . mythic aspects of it, the rituals and such came from reading and listening to my dad and my Uncle Clay tell stories—the Norse and Greek and Scandinavian myths. And then I found Sir James Frazer and read how the same woods and hunting and animal myths essentially pervaded all cultures during all times of history, and before. And then I met Marty and he introduced me to Joseph Campbell's work, and one day we were talking and found out that Reese had been reading and doing this stuff for years on his own, and then I always knew Scratch had more instinctive knowledge and power in the woods than any man I ever knew; he used to hunt and stalk with my dad, and Dad would tell me what a woodsman he was.

And Scratch knew the African and Gullah and Caribbean myths from the stories he heard all his life. . . . I don't know. We just all came together and made a kind of moral fabric of it. It wasn't planned; it just evolved over time. But we knew it was right; it felt more natural to us than anything before or since in our lives. It's an intuitive way of living, largely. It reconciles your brain to the natural things. Your mind has a way of going off on tangents, but your body knows the truth. That's what mythic living is about."

"Living by the *thous*," I said.

"Exactly," he said.

"How many of you are there?" I said diffidently. I was fully aware of the lunatic sound of my words, though I had no sense of it.

"I don't know," he said. "A good many, scattered around the world, I'd say. From what we read and know, there always have been, and now, with the planet in the shape it's in, when nothing our science and technology can come up with seems to work anymore, I'd say there were more of us than ever who are going back to the old meaning of wild. Doing it the old way. Around here? I'd say only us four. We'd know if there were more. We'd have found each other. Most people who go to the woods, the rich ones and the yuppies who go on the big hunts and shoot off their big Purdys and wipe deer blood on their faces and brag around the campfire while they're getting drunk on fifty-dollar Scotch—they don't have a clue. They think they know something about the woods, and men in groups, and ritual, and the old ways, but they don't know shit. They have beaters and dogs and gun carriers and Land Rovers and ten-thousand-dollar outfits; they might buy out Orvis and L. L. Bean, but out in the woods on their own overnight they'd panic, and they'd die in a week. Most of them would shoot some farmer's old goat and bring it in on their hood, if you didn't stop them."

"But you go on some of those hunts," I said. "You said yourself you go on a few of your Uncle Clay's hunts. Some of those men are your friends, or at least people you grew up with."

"Well, some of them are instinctive woodsmen," he said. "Some of them sense . . . the shape and mystery of it, but they haven't learned anything. They're okay. They're naturals. It's good to hunt with them. They'd understand if you taught them. But most of them never would. For most, the ones who come from the cities twice a year and grow beards and shoot anything that's moving, and get drunk and stink and tell lies, it's for an entirely different thing. It's a macho thing. It's saying to the city and the neckties and most of all to the women, 'Screw you. I don't need you. I'm king out here. Out here I only have to lift my arm and something falls dead.' "

"Is that so bad?" I said. "Not the killing, but the other. For city boys to play macho in the woods."

"It's not bad in itself. It just isn't what the woods are about; it isn't what being wild means."

"I don't think I'm ever going to understand this," I said hopelessly. "I don't think I can ever learn this."

Reese Carmody spoke up for the first time. He had a nice voice, low and dry and only slightly slurred with Scotch. He had a nice smile, too, beneath the tape-mended glasses.

"Maybe you won't," he said. "It probably doesn't really matter. What matters is that you understand why *we* need it. Why it has to exist. Why somebody has to keep it going. I think you'll come to see that, in time. It's an absolute, the last absolute thing we have left. We aren't accustomed to dealing with absolutes, so it's hard at first. But we all think you'll come to it. From the very first, we've seen what Tom told us you had: a quality of absoluteness yourself. A potential for enormous commitment."

"Then why can't I feel it?" I said desolately, looking around at their faces. "I don't feel any of those things."

"You git there," Scratch said, eyes still closed. His smile was ineffably sweet, though he seemed very tired. "You git there when you stop being afraid. It only the fear that be in your way. We gon' he'p you."

"Does anybody else around here know that . . . you believe all this? That you do these things?" I said.

"No. Not all of it. Not nearly so much as you know now," Tom said. "Although Clay probably has an idea. He knows about what we know, but he never practiced. Why bother people with it? They'd just think we were crazy. I mean really crazy, not just nuts, like most of them think I am now. And then our freedom to come and go would be in jeopardy. Pat already knows some of it, and she's taken the boys away from me. It's a weapon she holds over my head, like the sword of Damocles. I made a bad mistake with her; I thought she was one of the ones who would . . . see. I think she'd have me locked up, if she could. There are probably lots of other people who would, too, if they really knew what was what. So I have another life, one that passes in the 'real' world. It's not a fake. I enjoy the hell out of it. I've told you that. I love literature. I love the South. I love teaching. I love my friends and like almost everybody else. I love fucking and eating and drinking and telling stories and reading and listening to music; I love all the things my body can do and my mind and heart can understand. And some things and people I hate, and some I sorrow for, and that's good, too. All that's satisfying and right. I think I pass for ordinary as well as the next guy. I think we all do."

There was a low, rasping chuckle from Scratch. Tom

turned to him and said, "What's so funny about that, you old coot?"

"Keep wonderin' what Miss Pat and Miss Cah'line and Miss Miggy think do they see us out in the woods, nekkid as jaybirds, all stripey with blood, a-dancin' around a dead deer," Scratch wheezed.

"They'd have all our asses under the jail." Tom grinned hugely.

"Do 'em good, and he'p 'em, too, to see that," Scratch said serenely. "I don't spec' we looks as funny as they does runnin' up and down the road in them shallow pants."

"Scratch might understand the deepest and most mystic aspects of the woods, but jogging will forever elude him," Tom said.

"If Scratch is the . . . the shaman, what are the rest of you?" I said. "Are you foot soldiers?"

"I am," Tom said. "That's exactly what I am. Somebody has to sweep up after the caravan has gone by."

"Tom will most likely be our next shaman," Reese Carmody said in his dry, soft voice. "None of the rest of us has his quality of vision. We wish we did, but there it is. It's a gift; it can't be learned. Martin is our historian, I guess you might say. Our parliamentarian. He makes sure we're doing it right; he's our source of highest authority on form and etiquette and academic knowledge. An invaluable man."

"And what are you?" I asked, abstractly aware once more of the utter insanity of my words, but feeling only intense curiosity.

"I guess I'm the *consigliere,*" he said. "I'm the bridge with the real world. I make sure we live by its laws when we can, and I use what legal knowledge I have when we need real clubs to go after the world out there. Robert Duval did it better in *The Godfather*, but essentially I'm the go-between."

"Who would you need to go after out there? I guess I mean, who are you protecting the woods and water and things from? Hunters? Poachers?"

"Sometimes," Reese said. "But mostly the Big Silver plant. Our friendly neighborhood bombmakers. Poachers don't mess with these woods much anymore, but the Big Silver is a clear and present danger."

The dark, complex old fear that I had felt the day of our picnic at Pat Dabney's stables came flooding back, scalding in my throat. Furious, one-celled fear for Hilary was the dominant note, but in its depths were rage and betrayal and a kind of hopeless recognition. I could almost hear my mother's voice in the noise of the fear: There is no safety. Fear everything.

"They told me it was safe," I said in a cold, tight voice. "Everybody in this town I trusted told me that. Tish and Charlie, Carter . . . they sat in the sun and smiled at Hilary and me and said it wasn't dangerous. 'You won't even know it's there,' they said."

"I don't know that it *is* dangerous," Reese said. "My best guess right now is that it isn't. All the tests that I know of are negative. But the potential for harm is enormous if it's mismanaged, and virtually every facility in the country except the Big Silver has been, grotesquely and flagrantly and for a very long time. Since the Freedom of Information Act took the locks off the DOE's and the civilian contractors' closed files, the stuff that has come to light is just horrendous. Accidents that were never reported, gross negligence and even criminal mishandling of waste in several cases, low- and intermediate-level waste buried in open, unlined pits or leaking containers, contaminations of air and groundwater the rule rather than the exception, evasions and outright cover-ups . . . Rocky Flats, in Denver, is under criminal investigation by the FBI right now. And several reactors and whole plants have simply been shut down, they're in such bad shape. You know about Three Mile Island and Love Canal, but there's stuff just as bad and worse that no one has known about until recently, not even the Department of Energy. God knows what we still don't know. There are parts of the country so badly contaminated that they can never be used again; some of the toxic waste elements have half-lives of thousands and thousands of years. They've been officially designated sacrifice zones and closed. Sacrifice Zone. It's the ugliest term I've ever heard."

"That's insupportable." I could hardly breathe.

"One of those zones is in the Big Silver Swamp," Reese continued grimly. "It's been closed till the end of time, for all practical purposes. No man in history will ever be able to set foot on it again. Nobody's been able to get in there to see about the wildlife or the water."

I looked sharply up at Tom. He shook his head.

"Not me. I'm too fond of my hide and my working equipment to risk getting it fried with strontium 90," he said.

"Nobody told me about that," I said.

"It's a good twenty miles from here, way to the south and virtually in the middle of the swamp," Reese said. "One of the waste areas is there, the one that used to handle some of the heaviest stuff. I don't think there's any way it could touch us. And apparently it's not used anymore. A good bit of the Big Silver's bad stuff is shipped out of state now. Has been, for years. What's left is buried in underground carbon-steel tanks, and the rest is low-level stuff. Not supposed to hurt us."

"But is that the truth?" I said. "Could they be lying; could they be keeping some of the . . . bad stuff on the site in other kinds of containers and not telling anybody? Could anything be leaking?"

"I really don't think so," he said. "I have the same access to the daily air and soil and water test results as anybody else around here, and I monitor them every morning. I've also got a mole, and according to him, there's nothing all that hot on the property that isn't way underground. He'd be all too ready to blow the whistle if there was. I call him every day."

"Who is he?" I said.

"I can't tell you that." Reese smiled. "But I can tell you he's a senior physicist with enough clout so that if Stratton-Fournier was burying hot stuff or discharging hot water from inside the facility, he'd know. He stays there just to be a watchdog for our side; he'd dearly love to be out of there. He's spent his career there; he could have been Nobel material in private research. When he finally retires, or can't take it any longer, I'm going to give him the damnedest party the wiregrass has ever seen. We're going to stay drunk for three weeks."

"But what about that low-level waste on the property?" I prodded.

"It's been adjudged safe, or at least not harmful, to human beings or animals except in astronomical, impossible amounts. The thing that bothers me is the matter of those safe levels: they're government standards, and you couldn't exactly call the government a disinterested party. And then there've never been any official studies of medical or physical effects on areas surrounding the plants, not big, long-term ones. So, though you hear all the horror stories about cancer clusters and miscarriages and birth defects and mutated animals and plant life, there's no official hard data to back it up, and no studies to compare."

"That's just unbelievable," I said. "Why haven't there been any studies? They should have started testing the day the first plant opened."

"Who'd do the testing?" He smiled bleakly. "The government? Get serious. The AMA? You're got to be kidding; they're still arguing about fluoride. Scientific groups? Most of them depend on government grants to operate. Private citizens? No official clout. There are some studies under way now, since all the shit has hit the fan, but that's been in the last two years, and what we need to know is the cumulative, long-term effect of the low-level stuff. Everybody knows a meltdown or an explosion can blow you to hell or cook you, but nobody knows what twenty-five, or fifteen, or even ten years of strontium or tritium or plutonium or cesium could do."

"Where do they put it? The waste?" I said. "Can people go and see it? Could I?"

"I don't know if you could," Reese said. "I'm not even sure if I could. But people do, with the right kind of clearance. I've seen photos of the waste areas. There's been a good documentary movie made about the plant, and the cameras got in there. . . . They aren't top secret, or hidden. Just hard to get to. There's an area called the burial ground, where solid low-level waste is buried in trenches. That doesn't thrill me; they're unlined. Just raw earth. And there are open basins where contaminated heavy metal and equipment are sunk to settle. And tank farms, where the heavy stuff, the sludge, is buried; my mole says there've been more than fifty million gallons of it generated at the Big Silver. Even with most of it shipped off site, that leaves a lot of hot shit. And then there are the discharges of reactor coolant; my guy says that stuff comes out of there hot enough to boil a frog, and he doesn't think it's all too good for the fish around there, either. The effluent streams run into creeks that feed the Big Silver River in four places, and there's a network of shallow aquifers under the entire acreage that I worry about. And a deeper one, the Tuscumbia Aquifer, that supplies drinking water from here to Atlanta and Tallahassee. And yet none of them tests over the acceptable limit. I swear, I don't see how. According to what we're hearing now, every other plant in the country is cooking the air and water every day. But the Big Silver is still clean. We're not the only people watching it, you know. There's everybody from Greenpeace to little old ladies with witch hazel water wands camped around here."

"If it does—if it did—get in the water or the air or the soil, what would the effects be?" I said. "How would we know it?"

"I have no idea," he said. "That's the problem. It takes years, maybe a generation, for low-level effects to show up—you know: breast cancer, leukemia, thyroid, bone cancer. You'd have to know how long the stuff had been getting through, and in what amounts, and there just aren't any figures. There are some independent studies around other sites, that say there are double the numbers of certain kinds of cancers in areas near the facilities, and you hear of whole families and communities with awfully high incidences of it, way too high for coincidence. But they're isolated, and not official. If the stuff is altering genetic patterns, you wouldn't know for years. I've heard that the vulnerable areas in humans are the thyroid, lungs, breast, stomach, colon, and bone marrow. So far as I know, Pemberton hasn't had any unusual incidence of those; who's to say whether or when we'll ever reach critical mass with the stuff that's stored around here? I know that there've been a few aberrations around the swamp; Scratch found a nine-legged frog way upcreek last spring. And I saw a photo of a mutant sponge growing from a crack in a barrel of nuclear waste dumped into the ocean just off San Francisco. It would make you throw up, it's such a monstrosity. The article said the seabed sediment around the barrels is heavy with plutonium. And then there's the famous turtle caper: Stratton-Fournier went public a year or so ago with the astonishing news that it was rounding up and capturing all the turtles that had wandered into the site. Seems a lot of them are just too hot to go trundling around outside the reservation. I thought it was a major breakthrough. The Stratties' one visible effort at damage control in twenty-five years: the celebrated hot turtle roundup."

I could only laugh, painfully, helplessly. It was too awful for anything else. I thought of Hannah Arendt's "banality of evil." Surely she was right; the most pervasive evils must have an element of leavening ludicrousness. Monstrosity must masquerade behind disarming ineptitude. The devil must go about in burglar's clothes. It could not exist otherwise. Mankind would not suffer the naked witch to live.

"So you patrol the woods, then. You keep watch."

"Tom does, mainly," Martin Longstreet said. "Scratch takes the territory way upriver, where Goat Creek makes up. Tom does Goat Creek the rest of the way down, and the river to about twenty miles south of here, and the perimeters of the Big Silver site."

I looked over at Tom.

"It was my father's land," he said, by way of clarification. "It would have been mine. It was my mother who . . . sold it. I feel I should be the one who looks out for it."

There was no bitterness in his voice, but there was a flatness that was not good to hear.

"That's what you do when you're gone into the woods those times," I said. It was not a question.

"Partly," he said. "Sometimes I go to do a purification, to clean. Or I look for things that need taking care of: sick or hurt animals, fish kills, things like that. I just do my own land, up and down the creek and the river. Scratch does King's Oak; I don't go on that. And I don't go on Big Silver land."

"Sometimes I think you're caught out here between Scylla and Charybdis," Martin Longstreet said. "You don't go on King's Oak and you don't go on the Big Silver. You're stuck between them, like a slice of ham in a sandwich."

"S'prised them fences don't drive you crazy," Scratch said. "That one up there to where the lumber comp'ny is, on King's Oak . . . make me sick to look at that fence. I pees over it every chanct I gets, but I ain' gon' touch it."

"I don't care about those fences," Tom said. "I know every inch of both of those properties, anyway. They aren't keeping me out."

"Something is," Martin said.

"Yes, but it's not the fences," Tom said. "It's the stink. One of them stinks like a pulpmill and L. L. Bean. The other one stinks like death. Come on, folks. Dinner is served, and it's a nice little spread if I do say so myself. I slaved in a hot kitchen for hours over it."

After they left, we sat in front of the fire and drank brandy and looked at each other in silence. He did not touch me, and I did not move close to him. There was speculation in his eyes; I could not have said what he saw in mine.

"Are you going to have a hard time with this?" he asked finally.

"I honestly don't know," I said. "Before it happened, I'd have said I'd be calling the police about now, or a good psychiatrist. But I'm a part of it, too, now, and I don't feel crazy. Just . . . overwhelmed."

"Yeah, well, it's a fairly massive thing to have to deal

with. We came to it slowly, but you got the whole nine yards at once. We know it's going to be tough on you. When you're back in Pemberton you'll probably be in the 'nuts' camp, but out here it won't seem so strange. We think if you'll just give it a chance, it will come to be . . . acceptable to you. We're not going to ask that you believe. Not until you do. We know that may be never."

"I think it would be impossible for me to accept if you all weren't so damned credible," I said. "But all of you are . . . extraordinary in some way. People I'd love knowing anywhere, anytime. Educated people. Scratch is the only one of you who doesn't have a Ph.D., I'll bet."

"Scratch is the best of us," he said. "He knows more intuitively than the rest of us ever will. In another time he would have been a king. There's no doubt about that."

"You'll be the next shaman, though," I said. The word embarrassed me, but I could think of no other.

"Only by default. The field isn't very big. The really natural ones, like Scratch, come along about once a century. Hilary could be one, I think."

"Tom, get this clear right now," I said, leaning forward. "Hilary will not be touched by this. I will not have one word, not one iota, of this told to her. If I find that it has been, we're gone that minute. I'm one thing, but she's another. I have to have your promise on that."

"You have it," he said soberly. "I wouldn't have brought her into it without your permission, anyway. But I think you're going to find that nobody has to tell her. I don't think you're going to be able to keep her away from it."

"When I see that happening, I'll take her away and we won't be back," I said stiffly.

"Ah, Diana. You make this so hard," he said tiredly.

We were silent for a moment, and then I said, by way of propitiation, "You never told my why we ate the bread and salt and wine I brought."

"Well, they're sacred symbols of the early Christians, meant to bless a new house or a new undertaking. They probably go back a lot further than that, though."

"You cover all the bases, don't you?" I smiled.

"Why take any chances?" He smiled back.

"How did you find Scratch?" I said. "Did he work for your family, or what?"

"Scratch never worked for anybody a day in his life. Probably never worked, period. He's always lived off the woods; he can go out in the swamp and be gone for days, without taking anything with him, and live as well as if he had a supermarket and a motel next door. I'd always heard my dad and my Uncle Clay talk about him, when I was small and they began to teach things to me, almost like a legend himself, but I never met him until I was about ten, when Dad built this house out here. Scratch just appeared out of the swamp one morning and announced that he'd come to look after the house and the woods while we weren't there, and in return he wanted to sit in on our . . . learning sessions."

"How did he know you were having them?"

"He just knew. I told you, we find each other. . . . So anyway," Tom continued, "that's what happened. He'd sit quietly and listen while my father or Uncle Clay talked, with that sweet, sort of humble look he gets. He soaked up the best knowledge they had like a sponge, along with me and Chip at first. We must have been a sight, two tall men and two little kids and an old black man squatting in the woods. He seemed old to me, even then. But there were things he knew that none of us did, or ever came to know. My father really loved him, and more than that, he was in awe of him. And when Dad died, Scratch just . . . stayed on.

" 'After I'm gone, and Clay is . . . or before, if it works out that way,' Dad told me once, about a year before he died, 'Scratch should be your leader. Listen to everything he says, and don't let that little prick Chip boss him around. He's a great shaman, Scratch is. Maybe one day you will be, too, but you'll never see his like again. I can teach you the whats, but Scratch knows the whys.' "

"You must have loved your father very much," I said.

"He was the best thing in my life, he and the woods," Tom said simply. "He was the best man I ever knew. I thought I would die, too, when he did. And when Mother sold our half of this—of King's Oak—and to the bombmakers, at that, I really wanted to. I wrote my mother off that day. I still see her occasionally; it's not possible to avoid her in a place this small. But I divorced her on that day."

"I'm sorry you lost him," I said, knowing how inadequate my words were.

"I didn't." Tom smiled. "I still have him. He's as alive in those woods as he was on the last day I saw him."

"What you said about Scratch knowing the whys—that's what defeats me," I said. "I can learn the . . . the myths and the rituals and the woods knowledge, in time. But, Tom, I don't think I'm ever going to understand why it's important. I don't think it's ever going to be real to me."

He crossed his legs tailor fashion on the fur throw and regarded me over the rim of his brandy snifter. It was thin and old and exquisite; I wondered if it had come from his provenance, or Pat's.

"It's a matter of kinship," he said. "Literal kinship, with the trees and the animals and the living water of the creeks and rivers. With the undisturbed rhythms of nature and the seasons. Because of that kinship, every stone and tree and mountain and river and beast and man and woman is a *thou,* a creature of sensibility and awareness, to be honored and celebrated. People say that what we're all looking for is the meaning of life. I don't think that's really it. I think what we ache for is the experience of being alive, so that our life experiences on a purely physical plane will have resonance and reality in our innermost beings. So that we actually feel the rapture of being alive. I find that in the woods. I feel it in the old wood myths and legends and rituals. I taste it in the blood and flesh of the deer."

"Is it a matter of belief, like a religion?" I struggled so hard to comprehend that I could feel sweat dewing my hairline.

"No," he said. "It's a matter of consciousness. Just that. Pure consciousness. A consciousness not in your head but in your body, your flesh. In everything. The whole living world is informed by consciousness when you live by *thou*s. I think consciousness and energy are the same thing. Where you see life energy, there you see consciousness. Certainly plants are conscious, trees, growing things. Animals are, of course. And when you live naturally in the woods, you can see all these different elements relating to each other. That's what it means to live wild, to know the experience of wildness. That's what Thoreau was talking about when he said he went to the woods because he wished to live deliberately. It means you're a part of everything in creation, and it of you, and all of you are aware of each other."

"So you think you understand the deer you kill, or the birds, or that you can communicate with the water and the trees?"

"It's more than that," he said. "It's that somehow I *become* them. It's what I mean when I say you have to think like a deer. I mean you have to become the deer. It can be done; it happens. I watched a gator take a wood duck one day, and I could literally feel the . . . storm of feathers and fear in my mouth; I felt my jaw muscles clamping down hard. When I track, I sometimes know not only where a deer is heading or coming from but why. Scratch always knew that."

"How can you kill something you can understand like that?" I said drearily, back to the thing that stopped me, back to the wall.

"Because that's the way of the wild. And because hunters always have, or it wouldn't be hunting. And because then I take his . . . beauty and wildness and strength, his whole persona, into me, and they become mine."

"And so you . . . wipe blood on yourself, and put oak leaves in his mouth, and say whatever you say to him to ask his forgiveness, to get off the hook, so to speak?"

"It's more than that. It's to make his death sacred, to make him know that I honor him and that his death is meaningful in the highest sense, not senseless, not useless."

We were silent for a long time, the dying fire snapping and whispering, a night wind coming up outside. It was very late. I was tired with a tiredness of heart and mind and imagination, as well as flesh and bone. I did not know what I was going to do with the knowledge of this night. I wanted with all my heart for it to be one day earlier, before I knew of this, wished to be in Tom's arms then, sliding into sleep.

"Does it absolutely appall you that you are loved by a lunatic?" Tom said presently. When I looked up at him he was smiling. It was a tender smile, the smile of a caretaker as well as a lover. Something essential in me unrolled itself from the cold knot of self and flowed swiftly out toward him, like honey, like water.

"No," I said. "It should, but it doesn't. It pleases me very much."

The smile split into a grin and he leaped to his feet, lithe and beautiful, energy snapping around him like heat lightning.

"Come on, lady," he said, moving his moccasined feet in an antic caper. "Let's dance."

"Tom . . . it's two o'clock in the morning. How can you want to dance?" I said incredulously. "I feel like I've been in a wreck."

"Because I'm grateful," he said joyously. "I could have blown it; I could have scared you clean away with all this. But you're still here, beside my fire. It makes me happy; I need to give thanks. I do that best by dancing."

"Oh, Lord," I said wearily. "Another ritual. *Who* do you thank, Tom? What is it you're giving thanks to? These elaborate rituals . . . they seem so restrictive, somehow. Like the pagans having to appease an endless pantheon every time they go out the door . . ."

He stopped his capering and looked at me.

"Restrictive?" he said. "You miss the point entirely, Diana. It's pure gratitude, or appreciation, rather. What my dad used to call the gift of a grateful heart. It was what he said he hoped I'd come to have above all other things, and I've worked hard to cultivate it. As to what I thank . . . does it matter? I thank this. All of this. This night and the firelight and the good dinner, and you here. The deer in the woods and the swamp in the moonlight, and the way the ferns uncurl in the spring, and . . . oh, your beautiful breasts and ugly toes and my balls and chimpanzee's nose, and all the years I've got left to live. That woodpecker out there, that wakes me up every morning. Conrad Aiken and Horace Ray's Brunswick stew. The *wonderfulness* of everything, the fact of it. Sometimes, when I go out on the creek in the dawn, the ground mist looks so good that I just do a dance to it, and then a Carolina warbler starts up and he sounds so good that I do one for him, and then a gator'll break the water and start rings of rainbows spreading out, and . . . oh, well. You know. It takes me nearly until full light to get everybody thanked. You don't want to leave anybody out. But it's always because I want to. When I don't feel it, I don't do it. On a bad morning I just yell a blanket 'fuck you' to cover it all. And I don't do it in front of people, obviously, or I'd have been up at Milledgeville these many years."

"Why do you do it in front of me?" I said, tears I could not ken stinging my eyes.

"I'm trying to get you to take off your clothes and come dance with me," he said.

"Well, then, Tom Dabney," I said, getting to my feet and skinning the sweatshirt over my head, "let's dance."

CHAPTER ELEVEN

After that night we were together most of the time. There simply did not seem to be any reason for us not to be. We went out in the afternoons, and we stayed until eight or nine. On weekends we got there early in the mornings and stayed late. The only thing I would not do was stay the nights.

"I can't understand why you won't," Tom said, more than once. "We belong together, the three of us; we're a unit. This is our place. You can't look at Hilary and not know that this is a place where she'll thrive and be happy. You're happy; you could never fool me about that. There's room for your things, and you wouldn't have that long, dark drive home every night, and you'd save a bundle of money. What is it, Diana? Are you afraid people will talk about you? You must know, you do know, that they already do. Are you . . . is it that you think we ought to be married?"

"No," I said, so vehemently and spontaneously that he grinned. "I can't get married again; I don't know when I ever can. It's more that . . . oh, it's that by staying in my own place there's still a part of me—of Hilary and me—that's our own. We're our own separate people; we order our own existence. When we come out here to you, it's a choice that we make. I wouldn't feel that we had one if this was where we lived."

"You're still fighting the woods," he said soberly. "You're afraid they'll swallow you up, that you'll become like me. Like the four of us who believe . . . what we do. You'll come into the woods, but only so far. I don't guess I blame you. In a way you're right. When you really live in them, they fill your world. They *become* your world. The one out there, in Pemberton, will be the one that seems unreal. You have good intuition about that. I won't push you on it."

He was right about Hilary. She was as happy a child as I ever saw her in those late-winter days and evenings. I saw her happy again after that, of course, but not ever again as the child she was then. Then, she seemed inexhaustible and new-made, vibrating with joy and curiosity, and in her shimmering presence, all things seemed possible. I was happy, too; he had been right about both of us. It was impossible to look at the living flame that was my daughter and not feel her joy, especially since the dark weight and shape of what she had been still haunted me. Despite the great green overshadowing of the woods, and my ambivalence about them, I laughed a great deal, and sang in the evenings when Tom brought out the Martin before the fire, and sometimes, when he and Hilary danced, I joined them. Once or twice, when she fell asleep, I even danced the dark old dances with him. Each time I did I felt freer, less apprehensive, less bound in myself.

I learned in those days as never before. I laughed more. We made love more often. And each time we did, each time I laughed at something totally outrageous that he said or did, each time I took into myself some new kernel of wild lore, some new myth, I felt the tendrils of the river swamp reach out from its dark body and wrap me closer. He taught me to stalk and fish and, finally, to shoot the bow and arrow creditably well, and I became quite accurate with the slim little Ruger he gave me. I began to be able to read the woods as I could the streets of a city, and to feel less and less the total, howling, deathly solitude in them that I had felt the first morning I had gone into them and wept alone up in the branches of the King's Oak. I sensed, if I did not always see, the animals. I began to know the woods in all their times and aspects: the morning woods and the noon ones, the twilight woods and the midnight ones, were different countries, and after a while I was not a stranger in them any longer. I knew, on some level, that though I would never be of them as Tom was, I was beginning to test the nature of his world as a way to live myself. The quiet spell of the river swamp began to set up a frail colony within me. I did not understand all that the wild was to him and never would, but I did see that there was, indeed, more in the woods than I had ever dreamed.

And oh, Hilary! In a matter of days, it seemed, she was a creature of dappled light and green silence, as natural in the woods as a young doe, or a wood bird, and to me as beautiful. She would have spent all her daylight hours inside the envelope of the Big Silver Swamp if I had let her, but I would not allow her to go into the woods alone any farther than I could see her. She chafed at that, but Tom backed me up, and she began to spend some of the time that she was not out with him in the goat barn and corral. Missy stayed a precise step behind her heels wherever she went, and before long wherever you saw Hilary, down by the creek or out in the sunny glade just downcreek where the goats and ducks sunned, or heading in and out of the goathouse, you saw a mannerly line of Toggenburg does, many of them pregnant, trotting or ambling behind her. Even lordly Virbius bleated his joy when she came near him.

I had to laugh, each time I saw her with her tatterdemalion fan club strung out behind her, but a deeper part of me went cool with a kind of awe. She looked like some contemporary Pan, in blue jeans instead of laurel leaves. Martin Longstreet had given her a little willow flute that he had made, and she took it with her almost everywhere she went, and when she sat in the sun in a circle of yellow-eyed acolytes and played it, there was nothing about her but the faded denim that spoke of the present.

"Yow," Reese Carmody said the first time he saw her thus. "That's almost frightening."

"Look might pretty to me," Scratch said. He had come with Reese to bring fresh food for the goats—lamb's-quarter, early timothy, and comfrey—and stood in the brave sun, smiling at my daughter. He stood hunched slightly, with his arms crossed over his stomach, as if cold or in pain, and I thought again how much frailer he seemed this winter than in the fall, when I had first met him. The deep coughing had stopped, but he was thinner, and when he ate dinner with us, he hardly ever finished his meal.

"You not feeling up to snuff, Scratch?" Tom would say, looking keenly at him.

"Feelin' fine," he would say. "It mighty good, but I had somethin' up to home before I come."

But when Hilary would raise her head and see him, and jump up and run to him, he would straighten up and square his thin shoulders, and hold out his arms to her as naturally as if he had been a young father greeting a small daughter. And she would run into them, and sometimes he would lift her and swing her around before setting her down again.

For Hilary had fallen in love with Scratch with every inch of her young body and new-made heart, and as often as she went out into the river swamp with Tom, even more often did she go with Scratch Purvis. They went almost every evening in the cold, lengthening twilights, and at least once a weekend they spent most of the day out, with a lunch that I packed them, and Hilary with her bow and her pipe. At first I had been apprehensive, both for what the old black man might be teaching her off in his magical woods and for the fact of his physical frailty. But Tom set my mind to rest on the first count, and Hilary herself did on the second.

"I talked to him before he started taking her out," Tom said, "and told him he wasn't to be teaching her anything but woodcraft and skills. None of our other business. He said that was fine; he doubted he'd have much to teach her in that respect, anyway. And I know he won't."

And Hilary frequently came home so tired that sleep overtook her almost before she finished her homework.

"Mama, I think Scratch could walk all day and not even breathe hard," she said once, on coming in. "He may look like he doesn't feel good, but out in the woods he's like he's Tom's age."

"Scratch, do you think you go too far and fast for her?"

I said one evening, when he had brought an exhausted Hilary in, his arm supporting her.

"She look might' pert to me, Miss Diana," he said. I could not make him drop the "Miss." "Don't you worry none about Miss Hilary. I ain't gon' do nothin' would hurt this child."

And Hilary did look good. She looked wonderful. She had grown a bit taller, and the bleached thinness of arm and leg had turned to long, lithe muscle. Her skin was faintly gilded with early sun. Her hair gleamed blue black with health, and her eyes spilled over with the fullness of a child who knew herself to be the center of the known universe. It was a look I had never seen there, even in the best days back in Atlanta. I thought that for the first time in her young life, my daughter was not afraid of anything or anyone in her world.

"Finding Scratch has been one of the great things in her life," I said to Tom on a Sunday morning at the end of winter, watching Hilary fade into the hem of the forest with Scratch precisely as I had seen Tom do: first she was there, and then she simply was not. "I wonder if it's because he's a grandfather figure to her. There's no doubt that she sees you as a father, but she's never really known a grandfather. Chris's father was more like a CEO than a relative, and of course my dad was gone long before I was married. He'd have loved Hilary. He had the same kind of gentleness and patience with me that Scratch has with her. All the drinking never changed that."

"I don't know what it is with Scratch," Tom said. "He has uncounted numbers of grandchildren of his own, and so far as I know they bore him out into the woods for days at a time. Hilary has hit a chord, no doubt about it. For which I thank God. As much as I love her, I love being able to do a few other things even more."

"Like what?"

He walked me over to the fur throw before the fresh morning fire, unbuttoning my shirt as we walked.

"Like this."

"Yeah? And what else?"

"This."

"Oh, yes. That. And then maybe even . . . ?"

"Maybe even . . . this, and this, and this."

"That! Oh, yes, most definitely that. Oh, yes, that."

"Lord God, what a noise for a little woman like you to make," he said as we lay in the noon sun much later, sweating lightly in the heat of the dying fire. "Some wandering yuppie up on the highway probably heard you and called 911 on his car phone, and Harold Turbidy will be out here to see what's wrong, and he'll go back and tell everybody in town. And then what will they say about you at the country club, me proud vixen?"

"Just what they're saying already," I said comfortably into the sweet saltiness of the side of his throat. The pulse there was only now slowing. "That I come out here and screw you in the woods and yell like a banshee. Well, I don't know about the banshee part, but they sure as hell don't think I'm pressing flowers into my memory book out here, you can bet on that."

"Is that something you think or something you know?"

"Both. I mean, my God, if they think we're practicing the black arts out here, it's no stretch of the imagination to add coitus *au naturel* to that. And then Tish told me there's some gossip. Did you think there wouldn't be?"

"No. I knew there would. It's just a matter of degree. Is it bad; is it stuff you mind?" he said. I knew he meant: Is it run-of-the-mill gossip, or Pat's kind of vitriol?

"No. Not so far," I said. And it wasn't. Tish had said only, "I heard at the beauty shop that you were, and I quote,

'Letting your child run wild in the woods with an old Negro and an old fag and a drunk while you do God knows what with Tom Dabney.' The consensus seemed to be that the old Negro was worse than the fag and the drunk and Tom Dabney put together. I told everybody it was okay because y'all had painted Scratch blue."

I laughed until the tears stung my eyes.

"I'll have to tell Tom that. He told me the other day that certain early Celts did paint themselves blue. Woad, they called it. Scratch might look fetching as a Celt, at that."

She grinned, too, but then she said, "I sort of wish you'd be careful, though. You just could lose more than your reputation, about which I sense that you care exactly zilch."

"What? You mean my job?" I said incredulously. "For God's sake, Tish, the dean of the college is one of that crowd of blackguards I hang around with. Who in this day and age cares where I spend my time?"

"You know who, and I don't mean Carter," Tish said. "He cares, I know, but he isn't a threat to you. You know who is. You watch out for her, Andy."

I saw very little of Carter in those days, but I did run into him now and then, in the car driving to school or doing hasty Saturday-morning errands before heading out to Goat Creek. When I did, he smiled naturally and gave me a small, easy wave of his hand, and once, at a traffic light, he motioned for me to roll down my window, and when I did, he called out, cheerfully, "Did you hear the one about the nearsighted snake? He raped a rope," and grinned widely and drove on. I smiled after him, but my eyes stung. I could not see his pain, but I was not fool enough to think that my leaving had not left him badly wounded. I did not think that anyone would see Carter's pain again. Pat Dabney had been with him three times that I had seen him; she had not smiled, only looked levelly, assessingly at me, and then away.

I thought of him more often than I might have, those days at Tom's house, and whenever I did, my grief and pain surprised me. I did not speak of it, but Tom knew.

"I'm sorry about Carter," he said once. "I really am. He's a good man. I know you're sorry, too. What I don't know is how sorry."

"Enough," I said. "Not sorry I'm here; not sorry about you and me. But very sorry about how I got here. I never wanted to hurt Carter."

"No," he said. "But from the very beginning, you were bound to. What I'm sorriest about is Pat."

"What's to be sorry about her?" I said. "She seems as content as a cat in a butchershop to me."

"No," he said. "She's not content. She's never content, and especially now. You'll see."

And I did. On a booming, early-March afternoon of cold, fresh wind and warm, fickle sun, I found Tish waiting for me at my car in the college parking lot. I had changed clothes in the faculty lounge and wore a camouflage jacket over sweats; we had planned to go with Tom over to the soybean fields on the edge of the King's Oak property that afternoon, to learn to find and call bobwhite quail. He would go back later alone and shoot enough for a quail dinner; Scratch had professed himself hungry for a bobwhite supper, and I was still adamant about Tom not teaching Hilary to kill.

Tish wore a beautiful tweed jacket and skirt and polished boots, and I whistled. She was usually in blue jeans or slacks this time of day. I started to tease her about *Town & Country* covers, and then fell silent. The base of her nose was bone white and her eyes glittered, and even from a distance I could see that she was struggling to control her breathing.

"What is it?" I said, suddenly cold. "Has something happened to Hilary?"

"No," she said. "Hil's fine. Listen, can we go somewhere and get a cup of coffee? I need to tell you something."

I knew by her tone that it was not going to be anything I wanted to hear, so I was silent as I pulled the Toyota out of the parking lot. I fetched us up at a Wendy's down the block from the college, and we sat in the car and opened the dripping paper cups and drank our coffee, watching the steam frost the windshield.

"So tell me, Tish," I said. "Whatever it is, it's not as bad as waiting to hear it."

"It's just that I'm always the bearer of bad news for you," she said. "I hate it. I'd like just once to tell you something wonderful."

"Tish . . ."

"Oh, all right. Andy, I've just come from an executive committee meeting of the Pemberton Dames. A motion came up out of the blue to . . . to ask you to resign. I don't know who made it; it was typed and in a sealed envelope and lying on my lectern when I got there. I could probably find out, but it doesn't matter who did the typing; we both know if we went far back enough we'd come to Pat Dabney. Constitutionally, I had to put it before the committee. I was almost laughing when I did, I was so sure that it would be thrown out. But . . . it got its two required ayes right away. And then it went to vote, and . . . it passed. As president, it's my duty to notify you. But I also want you to know that my resignation is effective as of this minute. Andy . . . I've never been so angry in my life as I was at that bunch of spineless women. And I can't tell you how much I hate this."

"Oh, Tish, sweetie, love . . . don't resign on account of me," I cried softly, reaching out to her. "I don't give a flying flip if I'm drummed out of the goddamned Pemberton Dames, but I care a lot that I've cost you that association; I care horribly! . . . Those are your lifelong friends! It isn't worth it. I refuse to be such an expensive friend to have."

"It isn't you," she said, her face reddening. "I mean, it is; I'm not belonging to any group that wouldn't be proud to have you as a member. They're fools, all of them. But it's more than that. It's that I will not kowtow to Pat Dabney. She's a vicious, spiteful, jealous, foul-tongued bitch, and I don't care if everybody else in town is afraid of her! I'd turn down heaven if I thought she was there."

"So who were my two . . . ratifiers? Is that the right word?" I said. I found, somewhat to my surprise, that I was neither surprised nor particularly disturbed at being booted out of the Pemberton Dames. A month or so before, I would have cared desperately. I would have cared for Carter's sake.

"Tom's mother and his sister," Tish said, smiling bitterly. "The two women who ought to be on their knees in gratitude to you, for making him happy. The same two women who were the most righteously and poisonously disapproving of Pat while Tom was married to her. Oh, that malicious dim-witted old woman; that poor, starved vindictive old maid . . ."

"Ah," I said. "Done out of the Pemberton Dames by the Dabney Dames. What an alliance. Macbeth would have recognized them instantly. What was the charge, by the way?"

Her flush deepened and she averted her eyes.

"This is the bad part, Andy. It was . . . contributing to the delinquency of a minor, or the Pemberton equivalent thereof. The motion said something about you and Tom using Hilary out at Goat Creek for . . . immoral and occult and bestial practices, and when I said that was pure bullshit, everyone there said they'd heard some version of it. That's Pat, of course."

I felt the color drain out of my face and my hands go clumsy with ice and rage. I turned on the ignition and jammed the car into gear. The tray on the window bucked wildly.

"Wait . . . what are you doing? Don't do anything foolish; it'll just come back on Hilary." Tish reached for the keys and pulled them out of the ignition. The car sputtered and died.

"I'm going in to the police station and swear out a warrant on Pat Dabney for slander," I said. "And then I'm going to find a lawyer and sue the bejesus out of her. And then I'm going over there and pull every bleached hair out of her skull. If that bothers you, I'll drop you off first. But I'm going to do it. Do you think I'm going to let that kind of talk about Hilary just . . . go on?"

Tish took a deep breath and let it out. "Andy," she said carefully, "if you want to absolutely *insure* that the talk goes on and eventually gets back to Hil, if you want to just plain *guarantee* that it does, do just that. Do. You won't hear the end of it in your lifetime. But if you want it to stop in the shortest possible amount of time, and reach the fewest possible number of people . . . let it alone. Don't do anything. Try to pretend you never heard anything about it, and stay out of her way as much as you can, and hunker down. I know from long and bitter experience that the only way to defuse Pat is to ignore her. Nothing else works. Nothing."

"Just let her get away with it, then. Just let her . . . win," I said furiously.

"She's only getting away with it when she sees you hurt by it," Tish said. "Ignoring her not only stops her, it defeats her. She can't outrage anyone who refuses to be outraged. Those stupid women don't believe that awful shit even if they really did hear it . . . and they probably did. It's fear of Pat Dabney wagging every one of them. Pat and her old money and name. I don't blame you, by the way. I'd like to pull out her eyelashes and nails after you were done with her hair, and hold her down while somebody tattooed gargoyles on her boobs. . . ."

I dropped my face into my hands. Unwilling laughter spurted between my fingers.

"Ah, Christ," I said. "You're right. I know you are. But . . . oh, Tish. Do you mind about the Dames?"

"I only mind that they're fools and toadies," Tish said. "I thought better of most of them. I'd have resigned no matter who they said this about. This is me, Andy. I'm not going to let people say that kind of stuff about you or Hilary, while I've got breath left."

"I love you," I said, feeling tears start. "You've saved my ass and my heart and my soul so many times. . . ."

"And if I do it another fifty times, it still won't pay you back for getting me through English lit," she said. "Come on. Let's go back to my house and have a real drink."

"Oh, Tish . . . I can't. I promised Tom and Hilary that we'd start learning about quail today."

She looked at me for a long time in silence. "The only thing I really worry about is that I'm going to lose you to the swamp," she finally said. Her face was serious. "It takes people sometimes. It's taken Tom. He used to be one of us; we really loved him. . . . Don't go overboard out there, Andy. Keep one foot in the world. Don't shut us out. Keep your balance. Oh, hell . . . don't listen to me. Where did balance ever get you?"

"I'm not ever going away from you and Charlie," I said. "Don't worry about any of this. It's less than nothing to me, if it doesn't matter to you. I probably won't even tell Tom about it."

And I did not. I was not sure why. I think it was because to speak the words would have given them some credence, summoned some grotesque reality, as the naming of a demon was thought to do in savage antiquity. I did not want the ugliness of it to soil the swamp. And I did not want to appear to be seeking his protection. Tom was proud of the beginnings of courage in me. I was simply too vain to risk the image.

I sat tight and waited for the ripples to die away, and for a while I thought they had. We lived much as we had, though I lived, often, with held breath. If the talk still hummed through Pemberton, I did not hear it. And then, about two weeks later, Miss Deborah called me into her office and closed the door and told me, face pulled tight with suppressed pleasure, that certain information about my after-work activities had come to her attention, and that while ordinarily she was the most liberal of women, there were certain things that she simply could not countenance, for the sake of the college.

"I certainly don't care who . . . cohabits with whom, Diana,"she said, with the ferociously jaunty air of an outraged nun attempting to be modern. She alone of all Pemberton, except Tom, did not call me Andy. "You may cavort in the swamp with half the town, for all I know or care. But there is talk going around of a very particular and damaging ugliness, and it cannot be allowed to touch the college in any way. I should hate to have to tell you what it is, but if you aren't aware, it's my duty to do so."

Her expression said that she was quivering with joy at the prospect of telling me.

"I've heard the talk, Miss Deborah," I said coldly. I was not going to elaborate or explain to this vicious old woman, with her antennae vibrating at the nearness of dung.

"Then you know that it cannot be permitted to go on," she said. "I will trust you to do whatever is necessary to stop it. Understand that I do not accuse you of anything. I simply point out that where—"

"—there's smoke there's fire," I finished for her. "You can rest your mind about me, Miss Deborah. Professor Dabney and I are not forcing my daughter into unholy rites with goats and pigs; I haven't gotten a single whiff of brimstone in all the Big Silver. Which is more than I can say for this office, right now."

"You watch your tongue, missy," she spat, as vicious, suddenly, as a cornered pig. "I hired you in good faith to implement the fine reputation of this school, and I can have you removed in an instant, if it is adjudged you are damaging it."

I was so angry that I could not speak, and I knew that was a very good thing indeed.

Miss Deborah took my silence for capitulation, and said, "I know you'll understand the wisdom of what I say, and the reasons for it. It's for your good, as well as the school's, Diana dear. Let's not speak of it again. I trust we shan't have to. It will remain strictly between us, of course."

The shit it will, I thought, getting up and leaving her office. *You'll be on the phone before I've sat down at my desk again. You'll dine out on this for months, like a hyena on an elephant's carcass.*

I went straight from her office to Martin Longstreet's across the campus, and told him what had happened before he even offered me a chair. As angry with Miss Deborah as I was, I knew, clearly and coldly, I could not lose this job. I would not allow Tom to support Hilary and me; the woods must be a choice for us, not a refuge. I would go back to Atlanta before I let that happen. And I could not go back to Atlanta.

"So I came straight to you," I said, in conclusion, to Martin. "I'd rather bite my tongue out than bother you with this kind of ugly and stupid stuff, but I have no doubt you're going to hear it from Miss Deborah before this day is out, and I wanted to ask you formally for your support with the board, if it comes to that. I know I'll have it, of course, but I so hate it that you even have to be involved in it at all—"

I stopped, because the look on his handsome, ruined face told me, incredibly, that he was not going to help me. He was already shaking his head, slightly and slowly, no, no.

"But you know that those things are lies. . . ." I could not get a deep breath. "You know that Tom and I are not doing that; you know that I would never expose my daughter to . . . to . . ."

He lifted his hand, and I fell silent. My ears were ringing.

"I care very deeply about you and your daughter, Miss Diana," he said, and his cultured voice was tired, and old.

"The life and promise you bring to the woods are life and breath to me, and it is wonderful to see how happy you have made my young friend. In another time, I would have literally laid down my life, I think, to stop that malignant old harpy from acting against you. I will die regretting that that is no longer true. I will die regretting the man I have become. But I simply stand to lose too much."

He read my look and smiled. The smile was as hard to look at as a rictus of grief.

"No, I don't mean the gay business. Everybody in Pemberton knows about that. Damned few care, as long as I don't practice it on the country club terrace. I mean . . . the other business. The business about the woods. I know you know a good bit about that now. I don't think you know the . . . extent of it. But Tom's ex-wife does, or almost. If that should get about . . . I wouldn't be teaching in any college known in this hemisphere. And I don't fancy the life of an old fag on the street. I have three years to go until retirement. I wish the redoubtable Mrs. Dabney could have waited until then.

"No. Be careful, Diana. Stay with Tom if you like, but approach Pat with care. And be circumspect about your visits to Goat Creek."

I was so tired, all of a sudden, that I could not keep the animating rage intact. I literally felt it drain out of my body. In its dull, flat aftermath I saw with perfect clarity his point. I even felt a distant, flaccid pity for him. He was, and is, a good man.

"She is a very terrible woman," I said huskily.

"Yes, she is," Martin Longstreet said. "The worst. Tom made a bad mistake with her, back when he still felt something for her, still thought she was something she was not. I can see why. She was wonderful in the woods. Wonderful in the wild, with a gun or a bow. She could kill anything; she was the best shot I ever saw. She alone of the women I had ever met until then seemed to understand, to glory in all that the woods were and meant. And so he . . . initiated her. He taught her a great deal of what we believe and do. And she did it all, and she believed, or pretended to. I never did really think she was a believer, but she was so . . . glorious to watch and listen to that I let it go. It almost didn't matter. We all thought she did those things for the love of the woods, but we were wrong. It was for power. When she realized that her role would always be that of priestess to the shaman—of accomplice, if you wish—she turned on us, on him especially, and she's never lost that furious outrage. She wanted to be our king, you see."

Not for the first time, I felt as if I were a player in some insane psychodrama, a lunatic actor saying lunatic words to another insane player.

"I just don't know what to do," I said faintly.

"I would do nothing, my dear," he said. "The best course by far is to let her tire of you, and she will, like a cat with a dead mouse. The game simply will not be worth the candle anymore. I would stay at home with my pretty daughter for a week or so if I were you, and see if things don't settle down. They almost always do. Tom will understand. To do anything now would almost surely accomplish nothing but to bring this sorry affair to the official attention of the board, who in the main would rather not deal with Mrs. Dabney. She tried long ago to have her husband fired, and did not succeed, but I don't think anyone has the strength for another such battle. I don't think you would be the winner here. And there is the very real danger that she might train her sights on your daughter. Hilary is, after all, your Achilles' heel."

"It is nearly unbearable to let her win," I said.

"Oh, she doesn't win," he said. "She has to live the rest of her life locked up in the skin of a basically despicable woman. She knows what she is; she isn't stupid. She has to live her life without the only man she has ever really wanted, and to watch him make a good life with you. And she still isn't king. Whatever she does or does not do, she doesn't win."

"I hate it that she has such a hold over you," I said.

"I like to think Patricia Dabney is my punishment for having pillaged a temple in some former existence." He smiled faintly. "Don't worry, Diana. If things get too bad, I'll get Scratch to set a Duppy on her."

I merely looked at him, and the smile widened.

"Just joshing, my dear. It's far more likely that someone will simply get enough of her and bash her head in. That, however, will not be me. I'm fonder of my old bones than to risk the slammer for the likes of her."

I left his office almost smiling, which was undoubtedly what he had intended; smiling and restored to enough perspective to realize that he and Tish had been right: the impulse to confront Pat Dabney was both selfish and self-destructive. There was Hilary to think of; and Martin Longstreet was right about something else: I had Tom and she did not, and would not have. It was enough to keep me silent; it would have to be. I picked up Hilary after school and drove to our house to change clothes and go to Goat Creek.

The letter was waiting for me.

It may be hindsight, but I think I knew in that instant what it said. For one thing, it had been slipped under the front door without a stamp; not the usual mode of travel for good or simply neutral news. And for another, it had simply been that kind of day. I knew now that the poison about us was endemic in Pemberton. Miss Deborah's may have been the fangs that delivered it, but Pat Dabney's was the poison sac. Once she had tasted blood, I did not think she would stop.

I sent Hilary to collect her outdoor things and sat down on the window seat and opened the letter. I glanced at the neat, old-fashioned black signature first: Marcus A. Livingston. The legendary retired trainer of steeplechasers. My landlord. I folded the letter blindly without reading it and looked out into the lowering green dusk. Sooner or later I would reopen it to check the date by which my daughter and I must vacate the guest cottage; I did not even want to know what excuse had been given. Presently I looked: April 1.

Two weeks. April fool.

Fear swept me there in the dim living room in the twilight. It was almost as bad as that cold tide that had taken me under out in the Big Silver Swamp, at King's Oak. The old terror came screeching and flapping back from wherever the succoring months in Pemberton had banished it: coldness, darkness, abandonment, aloneness. Nowhere to go. Nowhere to be. It was as primal as a child's night terror; I literally shook with it as if with a bad ague. I could not move. And then it was gone.

Something cold and still and inexorable took its place. It felt dreadful: heavy, breath-stopping, but at least the paralysis was broken.

No, I said silently, to myself. And then, aloud, "No. No, you won't."

"Did you say something, Mama?" Hilary said, coming into the room. She was dressed in her last year's jeans, and I thought, abstractedly, that we must shop for new ones. These were too short by three inches.

"I have to stop and see Carter for a little while before we go out to the creek," I said. I kept my face averted so she would read nothing from it. I shoved the letter into my coat pocket.

"I want you to run give Tom a call and tell him we'll be late, and not to hold supper for us. If we miss it I'll fix us a sandwich."

She looked at me levelly.

"Why do you have to see Carter?"

"I have business with him, Hilary," I said.

"What business? About what?"

"My business," I said, annoyed. "About something private. It has nothing to do with you."

"If it's anything about going back with him or something, it's my business," she said stubbornly. I could see the beginning sheen of tears in her eyes.

"It isn't about that," I said crisply. "I would tell you if it was. Go on and call now, and you needn't tell Tom why we're going to be late. Just that we are."

"I'm not going to lie to Tom."

"Hilary," I said, taking a deep breath, "there are a great many shots in this life you do not yet call, and some you never will, and this is one of them. I have not asked you to lie to Tom, and I will not do so. There is nothing to lie about. This is, as I told you, business. I want to tell him about it myself, and I'll do that if you don't get on your ten-year-old high horse and screw it up. Now go."

"Yes'm," she said sulkily, but she went.

At Carter's office, on the bottom floor of a beautiful old restored Greek Revival just off Palmetto Street, I left Hilary in the waiting room and went in search of Angie Carlisle, Carter's venerable secretary. She was not at her desk, and she was not in the tiny kitchen where the coffeepot reigned, or in the adjacent bathroom. I looked at the coat peg in the hall and saw only Carter's raincoat there, hesitated, and then knocked softly on the closed door of his private office.

"Come," he called. "And bring the coffeepot, will you?"

I got the pot and two cups from the kitchen and pushed the door open with my hip and looked around it. He sat at his desk with his back to the door, feet up on the broad windowsill, telephone to his ear. The top of his desk was covered with scattered papers and heavy books, and his polished loafers lay on their sides on the carpet by his chair. I had seen them on my own carpet just so, many times; the sight of them made me want to cry with simple loss. The sight of the back of his head and his strong shoulders under the blue-striped oxford shirt that I liked hit like a fist in my stomach. For the space of that moment I wanted more than anything else in the world to run and throw my arms around him and wail, "I was wrong; I didn't mean it; take me back and take care of me!"

He turned suddenly, as if he had sensed my presence, and the pure, unguarded happiness that flamed in his blue eyes in that instant was nearly past enduring. Then it was gone, and the bland pleasantness he had adopted with me since our breakup took its place. He motioned me to a chair and pointed to his desktop and I set the tray down on it and sat down.

"I have a visitor," Carter said into the telephone. "I'll check with Jim Starnes to see if he's heard from Atlanta and call you back after dinner tonight. Right. Goodbye." He put the phone down carefully and looked at me for a moment, and then said, "Hello, Andy. Thanks for the coffee. I thought you were Angie. Has she already gone?"

"Hello, Carter. I guess she has; I didn't see her. Was it all right to knock?" I said.

"Of course. You know it was. I like seeing you any-time at all. Is Hilary with you?"

"She's outside, reading magazines. I'll bring her in in a minute. But I wanted to talk to you first."

"Then I gather this is not a social call," he said. I could read nothing in his eyes or voice except politeness and interest. Suddenly I thought, *I have made a terrible mistake. This visit is so inappropriate it's grotesque. This should not have to touch Carter. I have to get out of here.*

I started to rise, and he rose, too, and motioned me back down into my chair.

"Don't run, Andy," he said, in his rich voice. "Whatever it is you need to talk to me about is okay. There isn't anything you can't bring to me. I told you—the last time we really talked—that if I could help you in any way, at any time, I wanted to do it, didn't I? I meant that. And I gather from the look on your face that now is one of those times."

"Yes," I said. "It is. And I have no business in the world being here; this was an awful idea. If I'd been thinking straight I never would have bothered you with it. I just panicked."

"Hush," Carter said, grinning faintly. "Take a deep breath. Now pour us a cup of coffee and take a good swallow and then tell me what's bothering you. If it makes you feel any better I'll charge you for the visit."

I did as he said, and swallowed the strong, hot coffee, and set my cup down on the edge of his desk. I laced my fingers together so tightly that the feeling began to seep out of them. And then I said, "Carter, in the last hour I've been threatened with losing my job and evicted from my house. Two weeks ago I got voted out of the Pemberton Dames. I don't care a hoot in hell about the latter, but the two former scare me to death. I can probably find an apartment or a condo or something in two weeks, but I just can't lose this job. I came to you because I can't think of anybody else who can help me about this."

I saw the shock on his face; it was unfeigned and profound. He had not heard the talk, then. I realized that Pat would not have let him hear it if it could be helped, and she was not about to repeat it to him herself. But I was very sorry that he had not. Now I was going to have to tell him myself, and tell him where the ugliness had had its genesis. He could not help me without knowing.

"What in God's name is going on?" he said, softly and fiercely. "Don't tell me Dabney has finally done something stupid or criminal, or both."

"No, no," I said, surprised at the small flare of anger I could still feel, at his assumption of Tom's culpability in my trouble. "He hasn't done anything at all, and I haven't, either, but everybody thinks we have, awful things, terrible things. . . . There's some perfectly hideous gossip going around, Carter, and it's going to just sink me and Hilary if I can't get it stopped. I'm surprised you haven't heard it."

"I've been settling an estate in Clearwater for the past two weeks," he said. "I just got back in town at noon. Don't worry. Gossip we can handle. If anybody tries to fire you over gossip, I'll have them in court before— But wait, first you better tell me what it is. And where it's coming from, of course."

"It's coming from Pat," I said miserably. "I'd rather die than tell you this; it sounds like I'm running and telling on her. But she just has to stop. She has to. And I can't think of anybody else who can stop her but you. I came to ask you . . . if you would talk to her about it, or something. Ask her . . . It would only make it worse if I tried to."

He looked at me in silence, his ruddy face seeming to transmute itself into sandstone.

"Tell me what she's saying, Andy," he said.

And I did. I was as careful and factual as I could be about it, and I honestly tried to mitigate, by inflection and understatement, some of the murderous absurdity of Pat Dabney's tongue. It was very important to me not to sound hysterical before Carter Devereaux. My dignity was the last and only gift I could think to give him. When I was finished, I simply stopped and waited. I could not look at him.

"You're sure of this, of course," he said finally. It was not a question. I would not have known his voice.

"Yes," I said. "I wouldn't be here if I had any doubt at all. But Tish can verify it, and I expect Miss Deborah can, too, if she will. I don't know about the Livingstons. Tom's mother and sister might be willing to talk to you, too."

"Does Hilary know any of it?"

"No. I'm almost sure not," I said.

"Tom?"

"I don't think so. I haven't . . . we haven't talked about it."

"He probably doesn't know," Carter said matter-of-factly. "Pat would probably be dead if he did."

I looked at him then. I had never seen him so angry; I have seldom seen any man so angry. His face did not change, but there was a terrible flame in his eyes, and his color was completely gone.

And then, even as I looked at him, the flame died and the color came creeping back. In a moment he looked only tired. Tired and almost physically repelled.

"She's not entirely responsible, you know," he said, and his voice was as slow as that of a man near death from freezing. "Something's been left out of her; she's like a motor with the governor left off. She can't stop even when she wants to. She's always surprised at the wreckage around her, and sometimes she's genuinely appalled. I don't know how she'll feel this time. But I guarantee you she'll stop. Have no more doubts on that score. She'll stop."

"Carter, I don't want to . . . spoil things between you.

I just want it stopped. I just want to keep my job, and my house, if I can," I said.

"You're not going to spoil anything," he said wearily. "It isn't as if I didn't know what she was. I've always known." He sounded almost ill. I thought again what a fastidious man he was.

"Then how can you—" It was purely spontaneous, and I stopped, appalled at myself. "I'm sorry," I said.

"Don't be." He smiled, a wintry little smile. "How can I keep seeing her? How can I even be around her? It's simple. She's what I know. I'm what she knows. There are no surprises. And she's part of Pemberton. No matter what she ever does in her life, she'll still be at the core of Pemberton. That's very important to me, Andy. You must know by now that it is."

"I know," I said softly.

I heard Hilary calling me from the waiting room then. "Mama? It's almost six. . . ."

I stood up. "I really have to get going," I said.

"Sure," he said. "I know. Me, too. I'm awfully glad you came to me. No matter what, I hope you always will. Whatever is in my power to do for you, or to fix, I'll do. Always. And this can be fixed. Let me talk to her, and then I'll know what to do about Miss Deborah and Mark Livingston. I don't think there'll be any trouble either place."

"Will you . . . What will you have to do?"

"Just talk to her." He smiled. "That's all. Just talk to her."

"You know there isn't any way I can ever thank you, or repay you, don't you?" I said. "Oh, I mean, I can pay your bill, and I insist on that, but beyond that . . . what this is really worth to me . . ."

"Be happy, Andy. You may not believe this, but it's all I ever wanted," he said simply.

I looked at him, massive in his darkening office, and I did not know what to say or how to leave him. So I just said, "Thank you, Carter. Would you like to come say hello to Hilary?"

"Is the Pope a Catholic?" Carter said.

On the way out to Goat Creek, Hilary, who had been silent, said suddenly, "Is Carter going to fix it about our house and your job?"

I snapped my head around to look at her. Her profile, in the green light from the dashboard, looked as serene and chaste as that of a young chimera on a cathedral.

"Were you listening at the door?" I said.

"Yes," she said. "I knew something was wrong when we went over there. I wanted to know what; you don't ever tell me anything."

"Well, Carter's going to fix it, yes, so you don't have to worry about that. But Hilary . . . did you hear all of it? I mean, about . . ."

"About what Pat said about me? About us? Yeah. But I knew about that before. I wasn't sure you did."

Sheer stupefaction made me thickheaded. All I could do was look at her.

"I heard it in school; some of the kids were saying things about what we did out at the creek, you know, with goats and pigs and things, and laughing, and doing dirty things around me. I was real scared at first, so I told Tom, and he told me about what people were saying, and that Pat had started it because she was jealous of you and me. He said it would be all right eventually. He told me I had to tell you I'd talked to him, but I didn't want to until I thought you felt better."

Her words moved me so deeply that I thought I would have to stop the car. This frail, wounded child, protecting me . . . but not, obviously, so frail or wounded anymore.

"What else did Tom tell you?" I said.

"That I ought to try to handle it myself," she said. "That if it got too much for me, to come and tell him, but it would be better all around if I took care of it like you were trying to take care of the things that were happening to you. He said you were being very brave, and that he was proud of you."

I felt a curl of warmth in the hollow cave of shock. He was proud of me. . . . Very few people had been, before. "So what did you do?"

"I took my bow and arrows to school, and told them at recess that there was poison on the tips and they better leave me alone. And then I put a pear from my lunch on a post way off and shot it down the middle. I know they still talk about me, but nobody does it to my face anymore."

I began to laugh and she laughed, too, and I reached over and squeezed her shoulder.

"You've grown up so much in the last month or two that I hardly know you anymore," I said. "I hope you know how proud I am of you. Tom, too, I bet. Did you tell him what you did?"

"Yes," she said. "He said he couldn't have done half as well himself. I know he was trying to make me feel good, though. Are we going to move out there now?"

"No, baby," I said. "Not if Carter can fix it about the house, and he thinks he can. One reason Tom is proud of both of us is that we're trying hard to take care of ourselves. We may not always be able to, but it's important to try. We need our own house, that we pay for and take care of ourselves. Tom ought not to have to support us."

"Will we ever move out there? Are you going to marry Tom?"

"I'm not sure anybody ought to marry Tom," I said.

"Tom is a wild thing in his heart. I don't think he needs us enough. He may never. I'd have to know that he did before I could move in with him, Hil. But I promise you that if we ever do, it will be for keeps."

"Well," she said. "Just so you don't say no for sure."

"Are you sad about Pat? About what she's done?" I asked, remembering her earlier adulation of Pat Dabney and all that surrounded her. "Do you miss the horses?"

"Well, sometimes," she said. "I thought she was just about perfect, and I do miss Pittypat. I remember how good it felt to ride her, and to know I was doing real good. But Pat acts like she owns everybody and everything, and when they don't do like she wants, she does bad things to them. Tom says you can't own people, you can only borrow them, if you're lucky. Trying to own them is an *it*, not a *thou*. I don't like her much at all now that I like me better."

Take that, you sad, sorry, empty woman, I said to myself. *Out of the mouths of babes. I don't think you'll ever frighten me again.*

Aloud I said to my daughter, "You're a smart little broad, and I'm glad I can still borrow you for a while."

"Me, too," she said.

I told Tom that night about my meeting with Carter, and about Hilary's and my conversation in the car. He nodded.

"You did good, both of you. You knew just which buttons to push. I couldn't have helped you much on this; she still holds the boys hostage. Whatever I'd have tried to do would have come back on them, as well as you and Hil. But Hil has defanged her as neatly as can be, and in Carter you found the only other person in Pemberton who could reach her."

"I can't imagine what he'll say to her that could make

any difference," I said. "He's got no more real power over her than anybody else."

"He's got Pemberton in his pocket," Tom said. "He's the darling of Old Pemberton, the best-loved native son. In a way he *is* Old Pemberton. She may be Winter People, but Pemberton is her only arena now. If he wanted to, he could set everybody in town against her with a word. Nobody really likes Pat; they're afraid of her. And then she'd be a queen without a country. Or a king, which is closer to what she wants. I'd say your job and your house are safe."

"So you knew all along," I said. "Would you have . . . done anything, or tried to, if it had gotten really bad and we hadn't been able to take care of it?"

"Yeah, I would have," he said soberly. "But it would have been clumsy and badly done and probably futile, and it would have been very costly."

I thought about his vulnerable young sons, and about Tish losing her membership in the Pemberton Dames. I wondered what else I might have cost them, which I did not and would never hear about. I knew that even when the talk died down—and I knew that it would, eventually—I would no longer be of Pemberton anymore, and though Tish and Charlie would remain as staunch and loving as ever, there would be a price to pay among their old friends for my presence in their lives. Perhaps, I thought, it would be better if I did move to Goat Creek with Hilary after all, or at least to one of the bright, shabby new condominiums over on the Other Side. But I did not want to do either. The little house in the woods was home to Hilary, even though it stood now on alien ground. The only other one she had ever known had been blown out of her life like a tornado, on the day of the puppy's death. And I was damned if I would be driven out.

"I feel like Typhoid Andy," I said to Tom as we lay in front of the fire that night. "Everybody I touch loses something or is punished in some way. I wanted to be a blessing, not a curse."

"Poor Little Nell," Tom said, grinning evilly. "Diana Btsfplk. Remember Joe, in 'Li'l Abner,' with the rain cloud over his head? I'll bet Joe couldn't do this . . . or this . . . or what about this?"

"Watch out," I gasped, breath thick in my chest, as I wriggled around under the throw to accommodate his hands and body. "Lest you be struck in midfuck . . ."

Carter was right about Miss Deborah and Marcus Livingston. The next week, another letter appeared under my door, saying that the guest cottage would not be needed, after all, and the Livingstons hoped Hilary and I had not been inconvenienced. A new lease was enclosed for my signature. Only days later, Miss Deborah called me into her office and gave me a cost-of-living raise. Her great, hanging face was suffused with the agony of having to do it, and she assured me it did not constitute a merit raise but was merely automatic . . . yet we both knew that any threat to my position at the college was in abeyance. I never knew what had transpired between them and Pat Dabney, and Carter would not tell me what he had said to Pat.

Pat herself, the first time I ran into her and Carter after that, coming out of the movie theater, said only, "Hello, Andy. Long time no see. Carter won't let me play with you anymore." And she grinned, her slow, radiant, unrepentant grin.

"I know," I said. "Isn't it awful?"

And our lives gradually stopped their spinning and we slid, with the Big Silver Swamp, into spring.

It was a time of magical beauty, that first April on Goat

Creek. The earth and water and sky went suddenly tender and milky with richness; there seemed to be a luminous mist in the woods, radiant in the sun and lambent in the dark shade, that sprang from the very wet black earth itself. The spongy ground sucked and chuckled and gurgled and smelled indescribably wonderful; the creek and river ran full and clean and light-struck; the forest greened overnight; the newly awakened creatures in it peeped and whistled and crowed and shouted and sang. Ferns uncurled and dogwood lay in radiant strata, like snow, and wild honeysuckle made each breath such a delight that you wanted to shout aloud with it. We went out into the bursting, thrumming woods early and stayed late.

"It's almost a textbook definition of the word 'life,' " I said.

"It's what everything is for," Tom said. "It's what all the rest is about."

"Are there babies now?" Hilary said. "Are there fawns?" One by one, Tom's goats had been kidding, and she was enchanted with the tiny, perfect new does. There had been bucks, but I had kept her away when I knew Tom was drowning them. She knew, though. It was not hard to read the loss on his face on one of those evenings. He had kept the best two, but she would not go near them. I thought I understood why. You cannot grieve for what you do not know.

"There are probably lots in the swamp," Tom said. "It's a good year for fawns. I haven't seen any so far, but Scratch has, and so has Reese. When they're a little older we'll go take a look. Let them get their woods legs now."

Despite the beauty of the woods, it was not a very good spring. It was almost as if the vitriol of Pat Dabney's campaign against me and Hilary had presaged a general malaise. Scratch did not come so often, and when he did he was quieter, and thinner, and more stooped, and ate almost nothing. He still took Hilary into the woods on their walkabouts, but they did not stay long on those soft, shining days, and Hilary was quiet and withdrawn when they returned. Once or twice he missed a supper when Martin and Reese were there, a thing he had never done before.

"He's sick," Tom said on one of those nights. "I've a good mind to take him bodily to the hospital. He may know a lot, but he doesn't know everything."

"He's old, is all, Tom," Reese Carmody said, looking with pity at Tom. "He was old when I first knew him, and he won't be getting any younger. If he says nothing is wrong, nothing is."

"Yes, it is," Tom said. "Sometimes it's like a light shining through him; you can almost see his bones. I don't know why he's being so stubborn about seeing a doctor."

"He told me he'd go when he was finished with his business," Hilary piped up. "But right now he's got something he's got to do. He'll go later."

"What? What is his business?" Tom said to her.

"He didn't say," she said. "But I expect he's taking care of the woods. Watching things. Isn't that what he does?"

"That's it exactly," Martin Longstreet said, smiling at her. "He watches things. Do you happen to know what he's watching, Hilary?"

"No," she said. "But he'll probably tell us when he's found it."

In the middle of the month, Scratch and Hilary found a fresh fish kill far up the creek, farther than I had ever been, and came home and told Tom about it.

"It was terrible, Tom," Hilary said. "There were stacks

and stacks of them, and their stomachs were all swollen up like balloons, and they were shining in the sun like mirrors. And the smell was awful."

She was near tears; I had not seen her this upset in many weeks.

Tom looked at Scratch. "What do you think?"

Scratch shook his head. "Don't rightly know. They awful swole up. I ain't seen it before."

"We'll have to go tend to it," Tom said to Reese and Martin. "And we'll need to do a cleansing. I don't think you ought to come, Scratch; it's just too strenuous. Takes too long. You either, Diana and Hilary. This is a two-day thing. Later I'll take you, when the . . . desecration isn't so powerful."

"I goin'," Scratch said, and nothing could dissuade him. I took Hilary home early that night; I knew that there would be some sort of ceremony in the house or around a fire outside, a ritual of song and dance and firelight and incantation, and I felt that if we were not to be a part of the whole thing, we should not intrude on the preliminaries. They were gone for two days, and when Tom returned he was moody and laconic. I knew that he hated mass dyings, and unnatural disturbances of the rhythms of life and death in the swamp.

"What caused it?" I said.

"I don't know," he said. "It happens. I hear about it fairly often, and you read about it more and more. Nothing you could ever isolate, probably. Just . . . the twentieth century. Us. All this shit."

In the last week of April, Scratch told Tom about seeing a sick deer in a small herd up by the King's Oak. That night, after Hilary had gone to her room, Tom told me that he was going to track and kill the animal that weekend.

"She's a yearling, Scratch says. I hope to God she doesn't have a fawn. Scratch didn't see one. I just can't let it go; Scratch said she looked bad sick, but he couldn't get close enough to really tell. God knows what it cost him to say that. I've never seen the deer Scratch couldn't track before."

"Did he say what he thought it might be?" I said, thinking with pity and horror of the young animal trying to keep up with the herd, and the pain, and the fear and the weakness.

"Well, not really," Tom said. "I know he thinks it has something to do with his famous lights in the water. He's still seeing them, upcreek. But he isn't talking much about them."

"I don't like the sound of that," I said. "I thought we were through with lights in the water. I hope he hasn't said anything to Hilary about it."

"No; I told him not to," Tom said. "And in any case, I don't think he would. He wouldn't scare Hil. Don't worry about it. It's marsh gas. Or jack-o'-the-swamp, according to the folks in Scratch's neck of the woods. I told you about that. There's probably more phosphorus in Goat Creek up there than in the Diamond Match factory, with the lumber camp, but you can't tell them that. They're probably sacrificing chickens, or something, as we speak."

"I hope you're right," I said. "Tom, why is it you're willing to accept, to give credence to, almost any myth you ever heard about the woods except this one about the creekwater?"

He was silent for a moment, and then he said, "I guess it's because water is the most sacred thing. Water is the mother and the redeemer. You know, in every culture and religion, it's by being washed in the water that you're born again, made new, redeemed. If I have a real and abiding terror, it's of something . . . spoiling the water. Wait a minute; there's something I want to read you."

He got to his feet and padded into the bedroom, and then returned with a handful of pages that looked to be torn from a magazine.

"Listen to this. It's something Loren Eiseley wrote in *The Immense Journey* a good while ago. I never heard it said better. He said, 'If there is magic on this planet it is contained in water. . . . Once in a lifetime, perhaps, one escapes the actual confines of the flesh. Once in a lifetime, if one is lucky, one so merges with sunlight and air and running water that whole eons, the eons that mountains and deserts know, might pass in a single afternoon without discomfort. The mind has sunk away into its beginnings among old roots and obscure tricklings and movings that stir inanimate things. Like the charmed fairy circle into which a man once stepped, and upon emergence learned that a whole century had passed in a single night, one can never quite define this secret, but it has something to do, I am sure, with common water. Its substance reaches everywhere; it touches the past and prepares the future; it moves under the poles and wanders thinly in the heights of air. It can assume forms of such exquisite perfection in a snowflake, or strip the living to a single shining bone cast up by the sea.' "

He lifted his head and looked at me.

"I see," I said simply. I did see.

"Anyway," he said, "I'm going to go up and take her Saturday early, if I can. And I'll do a cleansing ritual. I thought . . . I think it's time now for you to come with me. It will be a clean and quick and merciful death, and a necessary one; you won't have any ambivalence about that. It's a good way to start to teach you about the killing. And I'd like you to see a cleansing ritual."

I hesitated, and then I said, "I might as well do it. Everybody thinks I do arcane rituals, already. But not Hilary, Tom."

"No. This is for you," Tom said.

"Do you think . . . . could I be a part of the ritual?" I said suddenly. I had not known I was going to ask it.

"Do you believe in it, Diana?" he said soberly.

"It's more a case of wanting to believe, I guess," I said. "I'm still trying to understand what it gives you, what you feel. But I can't seem to go that way with you. I thought maybe if I did one with you I'd be closer to feeling what you feel."

"Maybe. Maybe," he said. "Essentially, it's that I want to feel what the animal feels. All of it; everything. To know. The fear of the stalk, the laboring heart, the actual impact of the arrow, the convulsion, the mortal wind that's the passing of life . . ."

"But to do that really, you'd have to die from an arrow wound yourself," I said, "and then what good would the knowledge do you?"

"It's not the knowledge so much; it's the *moment* of knowing. The split second, the mortal *now* . . ."

"You lose me, you see," I said, out of the old desolation. "You leave me behind. You go so far into this thing . . . I can't be around you if I think I'm going to lose you to it. It's too hard. What if that—wanting to feel everything—literally led you into death yourself? I can't let Hilary lose you like that."

"It isn't like that," he said gently, touching my face with his finger. "It's about life, not death. The ultimate life experience. I don't think I can tell you about it. I have to show you. That's why I want you to come with me. It's time now. I think you're ready to see."

"Well, but I'm not going to shoot, either my bow or the rifle," I said.

"That's fine. That will always be your choice," Tom said.

Over the next two days I half regretted that I had agreed to go with him. In the midst of a tussle with the inky old mimeograph machine in our office, or in front of the yogurt counter at the supermarket, I would think of what I had agreed to participate in, and the absurdity, the utter strangeness, the outrageousness of it, would flood me. But under it all, I was powerfully curious about the stalk and the cleansing ritual. I had gone deeper into wildness and the woods than I knew.

That Saturday I got to Goat Creek before sunup, shivering in the cold spring darkness. There was a voluptuous softness under the chill, though; it promised that the day would be as tender and sensuous on the skin as silk. Tom was waiting for me at the front door of the house, and I opened my mouth to speak to him, but he shook his head.

"Before a kill and a cleansing it's important to be quiet and go inside yourself and bring the animal in with you," he said. "It's not easy, but it will come. Just move quietly and slowly, and follow what I do."

"All right," I said. It was a whisper. Strangeness swept me.

Tom slipped off his faded flannel bathrobe and hung it on one of the wooden pegs that lined his bedroom wall. He moved deliberately and so quietly that I could not hear his feet on the floor. He came to me and slowly slid my sweat suit and underclothes off my body. His eyes held mine as he undressed me; they were dark with pupil and far away from me. I thought that we would make love then, but he led me out onto the deck over the black creek, where the hot tub steamed.

"We always bathe before a kill," he said in a soft, incantatory voice. "This is water from the creek, and it's been blessed with oak and pine. Scratch came and did it last night. When we go to a sacred death and a cleansing, we go as clean as water can make us."

He helped me into the tub. The water felt wonderful in the chill, hot to dizzying; silken; as receiving as a womb. I stood still and closed my eyes. Tom took up a sponge and washed me slowly all over, hair to toes, singing under his breath one of the soft, atonal chants that I had heard them sing before, he and Martin and Reese and Scratch. I could not follow the words and did not care. The water and the song washed the strangeness from the morning. The water smelled of fresh pine, and I saw that needles and oak leaves floated on its surface.

Still silent, we stepped out of the tub, and he dried me off with a great white Turkish towel. If felt and smelled absolutely new. Then he led me into the bedroom, where our camouflage clothes were laid on the great, looming, ridiculous tester bed. They were wrinkled, as if they had been washed and dried in the sun, and when I slipped mine on, I could smell the trapped sunlight, and the residual April wind in which they had hung.

"We go smelling as closely as possible of only wind and water," Tom said.

He slipped his bow and his arrow quiver over his shoulder and strapped one of the cruel, hooked hunting knives from the wall rack onto his belt. He lifted my little Ruger off the rack and handed it to me. Motioning me to follow him, he padded into the living room, where the built-up fire roared up the stone chimney.

He knelt before the fire and held his weapons out before him, until the arrow and knife tips flirted with the living flame. He indicated that I should do the same, and I did, being careful not to let the barrel of the Ruger touch flame. He tipped his head back and closed his eyes and sang, again something atonal and oddly cadenced, sounding older than memory. Looking at him, I felt the same surge of awe and near-fear that I had felt when I saw my daughter sitting in the sun, surrounded by goats, playing her willow pipe. There was nothing ridiculous about him in that moment, and nothing of the now. He was gone from me into wildness and time before time.

He sang for a long time. When he stopped, he helped me to my feet and shouldered his weapons again, and helped me to slip the Ruger over my shoulder.

"Before a sacred kill, we sing a praise song to the animal, so he will know that we honor and revere him, and will bring all glory to his memory, and to his brothers," Tom said. "We tell him that his death is a sacrament, not a diminishment, and that through it he will live forever, in our songs and our memories. We promise to hand his song down. We ask him to give us good hunting and not to keep his brothers away from us. If he is a sick animal, we promise him the ease of mercy. We dedicate our weapons only to honorable death. And we promise him a songfest when we have taken him. We sing them, too, and tell about him, and how grand he was, and how worthy of all our skill, and we dance. We don't dance before the kill; it's a celebratory thing. A thanksgiving. I'll show you the dance; it's beautiful. If this doe isn't in too bad a way, I'll bring her back and paint her before we bury and consecrate her. You know; you've seen one of the paintings. . . ."

"Yes," I said. "I've seen yours, and I've seen the ones on the cave walls at Lascaux. It's the same thing, isn't it?"

"Yes," he said.

We went out into the pearled morning. The white-silver of a late-April dawn was just flushing through the trees, with little of winter's hectic pink in it. In an hour, I knew, the light would be a pure, lambent green, like an underwater reef.

"It's really nothing but a long, quiet hike," Tom said. "We won't be stalking until we get up past the King's Oak. The herd won't have moved far from there. They should just about be getting up to graze by the time we get there. Just follow me as quietly as you can, and don't talk. When we get in range to track, I'll make a motion to you. Then you just freeze, and only step when I do, and make absolutely no move between steps. You know. I've showed you."

He moved off into the edge of the forest and was gone, and I went in behind him. Inside the wall of trees the darkness was green and pungent, sharp with new life. The morning sounds had not yet begun. For the first time, I felt the woods close around me and swallow me as I had seen them do to him. It was a matter of actually feeling it, as though by some cellular action I became part of the woods, and they of me; they entered my flesh, and throbbed there. My skin prickled with the beauty and strangeness of it; this, then, was a little of what he meant when he spoke of being wild. I felt, at that moment, that I wanted to drop to my hands and knees, to walk the woods in the way of a four-footed thing, to feel the woods sting and itch and bubble in my blood. I could have shouted aloud with the exultation of it. The feeling was gone as quickly as it had come, but I knew something had happened that would, forever after, bisect time. For a moment, I, too, had been wild.

We walked, quietly and steadily, for more than an hour. I did not have my watch with me, but I found that I could read the light with some certainty. I did not know when that skill had been born. I could hear my own feet on the spongy leaf detritus, but it was not the clumsy, random crashing I had made when I had first gone into the woods with Tom. I could not hear Tom's feet at all. I could only make out his silhouette, moving as quietly and steadily ahead of me as a phantom.

We followed Goat Creek all the way. By the time the white sky had begun to show a pale, satin blue through the new leaves overhead, we came to the island in the wide, shallow water where the King's Oak stood. It loomed monolithic and unmistakable, a totem, the heart of this darkness. Daylight in no way diminished its presence and power. When I was away from it, I would think of it and it would seem to me that my own eyes had invested it with its power, its near-living sense of person. It was, after all, only an oak tree, one of millions in that infinite old forest. But when I saw it again I knew it for what it was: the fulcrum and the source of this wild place. It was not like any other tree.

Tom stopped for a moment, and I went to him and leaned my head on his shoulder. He pulled me against him and we stood, looking up at the great oak.

"Remember, I told you the first time we came here about the King of the Sacred Grove, who married the Huntress under the sacred oak, to keep the earth and the animals safe?" he said.

"Yes. I thought at the time you were just telling me a legend that interested you," I said. "But you weren't, were you?"

"Nope," he said. I felt, rather than saw, him smile. "I figured if I couldn't make it legal I could at least make it sacred. It had to be here, Diana, the first time."

"I guess it did," I said. "It was a good thing I came

with you that night. Otherwise we'd still be necking in corners."

"We'll do it again here, after the hunt," he said. "We can't do it before. But after, we'll celebrate under there, right where it happened the first time. Good timing, too; it's almost May first. You know the old song: 'Hey, hey, first of May, outdoor screwing starts today.' "

"I can't wait," I said sarcastically, but the warmth in the pit of me, and the familiar loosening of my knees, told me that it was true. I wondered if a time would ever come when the thought of making love with Tom Dabney did not shake me like an earthquake. I could not foresee it.

Five minutes past the King's Oak, Tom suddenly froze ahead of me. He stopped so suddenly that one foot stayed suspended in midstep, above the earth. I went still and quiet, too, trembling with the effort not to move. I heard or saw nothing, but I knew that deer were near, and that he knew where they were.

In slow motion, Tom drew an arrow from his quiver and fitted it into his bow. In the same fluid motion he went into a crouch. He pulled the arrow far back, until his thin fingers lay just beside his eyes, against his temple, and held the bow at full draw for what seemed to me a trembling eternity, a breath-held millennium. The string did not quiver. I heard and saw nothing.

It was only when he began a murmured incantation that I saw them: a file of five silent deer that seemed to form itself out of greenness and ground mist and move past us, just across the creek on the opposite bank. The last one in the file, a small taupe doe, moved slowly and jerkily, her head down, white tail drooping. She did not look sick to me, but she did not move like the others, and there was a gap between her and them, as if some malignant difference about her made them keep her at a remove. I knew this was the doe Tom had come to take, and I closed my eyes. I heard the *thunk-twang* of the bowstring, and a small, solid *smack,* and a small, leafy scrambling, and then I heard her fall to the ferny floor of the forest, and the other deer stampede away through the undergrowth.

There was no other sound, and I opened my eyes. Tom had gone silently across the creek and up the bank to where the doe lay, her back to us. As I watched, he paused and stood over her, his head turned to one side, as if puzzled. He stood there without moving, and, curious, I crossed the creek and went up to his side.

He cocked his head again, as if listening for something, and then sniffed, as if searching the wind. Then he knelt and turned the little doe over on her back, so that we could see her neck and belly. I could not see his arrow. Her eyes were calm and open, still liquid, not yet opaque, and her tongue had not yet slipped from her mouth. But my eyes did not linger on her face. They moved down, and I gasped with shock and horror, and then clapped my hand to my mouth and spun away, feeling last night's dinner rise in a sour column from my stomach. For a long, ringing moment I stood there, struggling not to vomit. From Tom I heard a great, soft intake of breath that seemed to go on forever, without end.

The silvery-white belly was hideously disfigured, mottled and knotted with great, bulging tumors and blackened open sores. It was so distended that she might have been fallow, but such a belly would deliver nothing but death. The surface was as uneven as a cratered moon, distended with tumor, and in one place the flesh was eaten away so that a slick coil of blue-white entrail showed. Flies crawled and buzzed. I had never seen anything remotely so horrible before; it was outside the realm of the natural entirely. You knew that viscerally, in a split moment. This was no disease of nature.

Behind me, Tom made a sound that froze the blood in my veins. I could feel the prickling of hair along the nape of my neck and on my forearms, and I remember thinking that it was true, after all: hair did stand up in fright and horror. It was a long, wordless howl of grief and fury. It was terrible, primitive, unhearable; it climbed and skirled and ululated through the woods like a shriek of a great cat; it rang against the pale helmet of the sky. It might have come from the throat of a man without words, without language. The man who could make a sound like that could do anything: grind bones, tear and eat living flesh, pull down the world with his rage and grief. I was back across the creek and arched against the trunk of a tree, almost hissing in fear, before I realized where I was. Tom dropped his head and stood in the ringing echo of his own voice, eyes closed, fists clenched at his sides. Then he stooped and took the doe by her hind legs and dragged her away from the creekbank, back into the underbrush. As he moved I could see the glint of tears on his face, and the fear loosened its hold, and I stood up and went after him.

"No," he flung over his shoulder, not turning. "Stay there. I have to do this by myself. Wait for me." It was a strangled voice, terrible.

I sat down in a patch of sun beside a fallen tupelo to wait.

It took him a very long time, whatever he did for the deer. In all the time after, he never told me. I think he must have skinned and dressed her, for that is what he did with the others I saw him take after that, and I believe that he buried her, there in the deep swamp. He did not, as he did his other kills, bring her out. As the sun climbed overhead until I could feel it on my hair, I heard him there, moving rhythmically in the undergrowth, as if he were dancing. I thought he probably was. He chanted, too, a melancholy, one-level song that could only have been what it was: a dirge of grief, of old woe. I had little sense of the passage of time, but I knew that it was nearly noon when he came back across the creek, stopping to wash his forearms and face in the water. He was calmer, but grim and silent.

"Tom . . . ," I began.

"No. Not now. Don't talk, Diana. When we get back, maybe. But right now . . . just don't talk."

Anger spurted up in me. I knew that it was born of fright and horror, as well as his peremptory tone, but it was no less real. He had brought me into his world by the sheer force of his will, and urged me to share his rites and his myths and his passions, and now he had shut me out of this thing that had so wounded him, and he'd frightened me out of my wits, to boot. And then he had made me sit, shaken and alone, in the wild depths of the Big Silver, while he assuaged his grief and tended to the ruined doe. All in all, I had had no part in this morning's business.

"Either I'm in this with you, or I'm not," I said coldly. "It was your idea to bring me out here, not mine. I want to know what was wrong with that poor animal; I have a right to know."

He looked at me with eyes that, I thought, neither knew nor even saw me.

"Something is wrong out here," he said. "There's something in the swamp. Something is not right up here."

"Don't deer get cancer and such?" I said. "You told me they did, just like people."

"Not like that," Tom said. "Not ever like that. Not so

soon after those fish. I know; I know. It's something . . . outside of nature."

His eyes lost their long focus and fastened on my face; they seemed to suck the wits out of me. I flinched physically. But still I think he did not see me, not completely.

"It's that goddamned plant," he said slowly. "It's the Big Silver. I've known almost from the beginning that something like this would happen. I knew when they came; I knew when she sold to them. . . . I've read, we all have. We've sent away for all the dissident literature; we've been to meetings in Atlanta and Tallahassee. . . . Reese is our expert, but we all know; we've been tracking it all along. . . ."

Fear so powerful that it almost dropped me struck again in that empty green swamp. From somewhere long ago I seemed to hear Tish saying, "If you're worried about the Big Silver, forget it. We no more know it's there, except when the traffic gets bad around closing time, than Honolulu knows Diamond Head is a volcano." And my own voice, saying, "They probably said the same thing in Pompeii."

And my laugh. My own laugh.

The fear receded before a tide of anger.

"You can't be serious," I said. "That's just . . . bullshit. You can't know that. You're . . . you're having a tantrum. You can't just bury a few dead fish and shoot a sick deer and announce that the plant is poisoning . . . what? The ground? The water? You know the tests are all negative. . . ."

"The water," he said, very quietly, as if to someone else. "It would be the groundwater. They cool the waste with water; they bury hot waste in pits that leach into effluent streams, that flow into the creek and the river. . . . There are a hundred ways it could be getting in. I don't know. And they're sure as hell not going to tell us, you can bet your ass on that. They've been lying to us for years; they must be. But I'm going to find out. I can do it. I know every inch of that stinking property; it was mine once. I'll find where it's coming from. And then I'm going to stop it. I can do that, too. I *will* do it. I'll blow the fucker up, if I have to. I'd love to do that. I'll die doing it if I have to, but I'll stop it. I'd love that death; it would be a grand death. . . ."

"Tom, don't be absurd, don't talk utter craziness," I said loudly, to drown my hammering heart. "Don't do anything stupid. Think about what you're saying. You sound like a lunatic. Nobody's going to die, for God's sake. Go talk to their . . . their public relations people, or that man, the president, you know . . . or whoever, or go see your congressman, or talk to your Uncle Clay. That's the thing to do, talk to your Uncle Clay. . . . But get real! This kind of talk is just irresponsible."

"Go through channels, in other words: is that what you're saying?" he said softly. I could tell his eyes saw me now. They were narrow and mad and blue as the heart of the sun. "Work in the ways of the world, live in the real world. . . . Jesus Christ, Diana, it's the real world that's doing this to the swamp. You saw that doe; that's your precious real world; how did you like that?"

"Oh, don't talk to me about the real world," I cried. "Why are you always knocking the real world? You say you renounce it, you won't live in it, but you damned well do; you get your living from it, and your friends, and . . . and your books and music and clothes. You think you're such a goddamned purist, Tom, but you've got the best of all of it; you haven't lost anything! You haven't given up anything! You get to romp naked around Eden without a tyrannosaurus rex nipping at your ass. Big deal, Tom . . ."

"Your trouble, Diana," he said slowly and coldly, "is that you are not willing to die for anything. A lady, alas, sans passion. That scares me. Until you know what you'll die for, you can't know what's worth living for. You don't have the least idea in the world what it means to be truly outraged, to feel the pure power and rightness of passion and irrationality and total commitment: those things scare you to death. You've spent half a year running from them in me, and your whole life running from them in you. But they're down there, Diana. In your deepest heart you're just what I am, and I am a madman and a lunatic and all those things the world calls a man who is willing to live for what he believes, and to kill for it, and to die himself for it."

I knew at that moment that he spoke absolutely literally, and that he would do those things, if he thought he must: Kill. Die himself. He was, just as he seemed, a man possessed. Again, rage struggled with my fear, rage at being betrayed once more, rage that I was my own betrayer. The rage won, and exploded.

"You *are* crazy!" I screamed at him. "You're just plain *crazy*! You are insane! You scare me to death!"

"Yes," he shouted back. His face was white and his eyes black and wild. "I am crazy! That's just what I am! Don't tell me you hadn't heard! That's right, Diana! All this time you've been fucking a crazy man out here in the swamp! You weren't scared then! *You got off on it, Diana!*"

I pulled my arm back and slapped him as hard as I could.

"Don't you ever, ever, *ever* call me Diana again," I cried. "I am not your goddamned fucking hunt goddess! I did not marry you under the fucking sacred oak! I am Andy Andropoulis Calhoun, and you are a crazy goddamned *lunatic*, and if you ever call me Diana again I'll kill you!"

We looked at each other for a long moment, in the

honey-thick sun of noon, and then he wheeled on his soft moccasins and was gone into the woods. I stood still, struggling not to cry, struggling to get my breath, trying to think of nothing at all but the call of the birds in the vast, sunny silence of the Big Silver.

Then I called after him, weakly, "It's really a brave thing, Tom, leaving me alone a thousand miles from nowhere, in this swamp. You're a big man, Tom!"

There was no answer. I had known there would not be. I stood awhile longer, trying to work up a righteous charge of fear at being abandoned in the Big Silver Swamp. But in the end it was no good. I had the Ruger, and I knew that all I had to do was follow the creek. Presently, feeling as old and empty and hollow as the core of a dead planet, I picked up the little rifle and set off.

When I came wearily into the yard of the house on Goat Creek, an hour and a half later, wet with sweat and scratched by brambles, my camouflage jacket tied around my waist and my hair matted and wild, the house was closed and his truck was gone, and no smoke curled into the washed April sky.

CHAPTER TWELVE

I stood the separation for most of a week, and then I went back to Goat Creek. I had not seen him at the college, but sometimes I did not for the space of days; we had never counted on that. I waited in the afternoons and evenings for the phone to ring, and when it did not, reminded myself of the times he went into the deep woods and stayed for long periods; he never told me he was going to those times, either. His absence and silence could be accounted for in many ways, and I did not think any of them were true. I had said killing words to him. He had been offering his deepest anguish to me, and I had punished him near mortally for it. Away from those silent, dreaming spring woods and the sunny horror of the grotesque little doe, it seemed to me that I had simply and terribly overreacted to his rage and grief. He was only talking; talking out of outrage and pain and fury; he would not stalk some nonexistent source of poison, or bomb a nuclear plant. Dear God, of course he would not. He was Tom, no less but no more than that; he would not kill for the Big Silver, or die for it.

But even as I drove, I knew on some level that he would do both of those things, and under my remorse and pain, there was a cold and steady dread. I knew that I loved a man without limits, and the knowledge frightened me as badly as the love consumed me. I reexperienced the familiar helplessness and hopelessness and loss that love had brought me before. In flight from excess, I had once more run into its arms. I felt real fear. And I missed him so much that halfway to Goat Creek I began to cry.

"Please be there," I said aloud, tasting my own tears. "Please be there and let it be all right again. Please don't be crazy. I can't do without you."

But he was not there. The house was dark and, for the first time in my experience, locked, and the truck was gone. I walked down to the goat barn and peered through the windows; it was empty, but I could see the does and their kids fanned out in the sun down by the creek, grazing, and there was fresh hay in their mangers. I caught sight of Missy among them; she raised her head and looked at me across the sparkling water, but she did not come cantering up, bleating her joy, as she did to Hilary and Tom. I did not see Earl. The ducks were not about, either, though I heard their distant quacking. Someone was feeding the animals, but I knew that it was not Tom. The dark house spoke of absence, and I would have known he was gone, even if it had not. I felt the absence of him from this place in the very marrow of me. There was no note on the door for me. I had rather thought, until now, that there would be.

The next day I went to Martin Longstreet's office at the

college, but he was not there. His secretary shook her head in resignation.

"He's gone again," she said. "Third time this year, not counting holidays. Left almost a week ago and said he didn't know when he would be back. You ought to see what they've got in to substitute for him this time. I've had at least five kids by here, griping. If he weren't a genius he'd absolutely be fired. I'll tell him you came by."

"Thanks; I'll just catch him later. It wasn't anything," I said, and went down the hall of the Arts and Sciences building to Tom's office. It was dark and locked. I knew that he shared a doughy, discontented secretary with three other professors and did not want to deal with her, so I walked to his first morning classroom and looked in through the glass panel on the door. A tanklike woman in a polyester pantsuit stood at the blackboard, drawing what appeared to be pentagrams. The room was only half full. So he was really gone, then, gone far back up Goat Creek or, far more ominously, into the dark reaches of the woods across the river. Big Silver property. For days after that I lived in a sweat of apprehension, afraid almost to turn on the evening news or pick up the telephone when it rang. It seldom did.

After another week I stopped being so afraid that he had gone into the Big Silver plant woods to do harm. I would have heard if he had. But I did not see him at school, or Martin Longstreet, either, and I did not see Reese Carmody when I stopped by the café he frequented next to the coin laundry. The anxiety slid into a kind of inert heaviness, a dull stasis. I went to work. I picked Hilary up after school and came home. I shopped for groceries and cooked dinner and washed dishes and did our laundry and got the car lubricated and had the air conditioner serviced. The weather turned still and hot, and I took Hilary to swim at Tish and

Charlie's a couple of times. I knew that the pool in Marjorie and Wynn Chapin's backyard would be full of crowing, splashing children on these long, warm afternoons and weekends, but Hilary did not want to go there, and I was just as glad. Without the leavening aegis of either Carter or Tom, I knew that I was no longer a provisional member of Old Pemberton. Hilary and I would have been greeted cordially, she for herself and I for the sake of Tish and Charlie, but the easiness of my old cadet status would have been missing, and I refused to go anywhere on sufferance. It occurred to me that I had shut myself out of two of the three places here where I was truly welcome.

Hilary did not ask after Tom, only nodding when I told her he was gone into the woods. I had not told her of the plight of the doe, nor, of course, of the quarrel. But she read the trouble that clung to me even if she did not know the sense of it. She did not cry, or whine, or tease. Instead she went silent and still, and her quicksilver energy drained away. She did not want to go out. I rented endless videos and we watched them together, usually not bothering to turn on the lights after the warm darkness fell. I was reminded of those endless, featureless days in the rented condominium in Atlanta, after we had left Chris and before we came to Pemberton. The thought moved me to dull despair, but I lacked the energy to turn on the lights or stop watching videos. Hilary, I think, would still be there, eyes lightlessly following E.T. on his quest for home, if it hadn't been for Tish once more.

She came into the living room of the cottage on an evening at the end of May, and slammed the screen door behind her and marched silently around the room, turning on lights. She found the remote unit and thumbed off *The Sound of Music* and sat down in the wing chair facing Hilary and me. We were sprawled on the couch in shorts and tee shirts, drinking Diet Cokes and eating microwave popcorn. It was a late-afternoon snack that had, somehow, turned into dinner. I blinked in the light and Hilary drew herself up into a ball, arms around knees. I seemed to see her clearly for the first time in what seemed weeks; she looked as bleached and fragile as something that lived underground, in a burrow.

"I'm sick as shit of pulling you two out of your cave by the hair," Tish said loudly, without preamble. She was faintly tanned with the first of the summer sun, and newly sprinkled with copper freckles, and her mop of hair sprang cheekily into her eyes, and she looked so vivid and vital and real she almost hurt the eye. Neither Hilary nor I said anything.

Finally I said, "Then don't."

"I'm not. Nobody else is, either," Tish snapped. "I came to shove something into your cage. You can take it or leave it. I'd advise you to take it. Otherwise, Andy, you might as well go back to Atlanta or move to Birmingham or somewhere, because Pemberton isn't going to stick its hand out to you again. And, Hilary, you're going to accept what I have for you if I have to stand over you until you do it. Ten doesn't make a very attractive holy martyr."

"I'll be eleven in two weeks," Hilary said sullenly.

"Even worse. Okay, here it is. Andy, Philippa Dobbs over at Baines County Family Services is trying to get a shelter for women and children started, and she's asked me to take Tuesday and Thursday afternoons for counseling and some administrative stuff. She needs bodies. I have just volunteered yours for two nights a week and one weekend day. The hours are hideous and the pay is nonexistent. Practically every woman you know is going to help out, and everybody is glad to hear that you are, too, and if you don't, nobody's going to try with you again. It's the only chance I think you're going to get to build something in Pemberton that's yours, that doesn't have anything to do with Carter or Tom or me or somebody else."

Before I could answer she turned to Hilary.

"Mrs. Dabney is starting a junior class for next fall's dressage trials. You missed the spring ones, and this is the only other one there'll be this year. She specifically asked me to tell you that she was awfully sorry about everything, and she hoped you'd come back and work with her and Pittypat. She said you're the best she's ever seen for your age, and she thinks you can go a lot further than the Georgia competitions if you'll work. She promises it will be strictly business, and I believe her. There has to be something in your life besides Goat Creek and videos, Hilary, and the way I look at it, right now it's horses or nothing. If I were you, I'd try to be an adult about it and take the horses. You are awfully good and you used to love it, and there's not a better teacher in the South. Mrs. Dabney can be an awful jerk, but when she says she isn't going to be, she usually isn't. And she's the only game in town. I told her I'd bring you over tomorrow to see about it, and I plan to do that. If you don't go, it's a long hot summer and Julie Andrews forever, toots."

I drew a breath to protest, but Hilary looked at me and then at Tish and nodded.

"Okay," she said, and if there was little color in her voice, at least there was not, either, the whine of hysteria and regression. I closed my mouth and let the breath sigh out. Whoever this silent child was, she was not the old, wrecked Hilary. She looked at me.

"Yeah. Okay. Why not?" I said.

"Why not, indeed," Tish said. "Hilary, why don't you go see if your habit still fits. And linger over it, sugarbaby. I need to give your mother some hell."

"Okay." Hilary smiled faintly and went off down the hall. My heart hurt for the cantering grace that was not, now, in her step, but I was grateful for the smile.

"Thank you," I said to Tish. "Again. One day it's going to be you at the bottom of a well and me throwing down a rope. I really didn't realize how . . . dug in we'd gotten over here."

"What was it, a fight?" she said. "He has a manicurist stashed in Valdosta? He's taken to leering at lady goats? Men goats? What? I know it's a first-class *crise de coeur*, Andy, because with you that's always what it is. I wish to hell you'd go into a funk over abortion or the homeless or Central American rain forests, but no, it's always something about a goddamned man."

I started to flare back at her, and then lifted my hands and let them fall into my lap. I was very tired, and I had missed her badly without realizing it, and she was right.

"It was a fight," I said. "A bad one. I think I've blown it right out of the water. But . . . he scared me so badly, Tish. He isn't . . . Tom isn't what I thought he was."

"Oh, Andy," she said, and there was only sadness in her voice. "Nobody is. Charlie isn't. Chris wasn't, Carter wasn't, Tom isn't. Tom, especially; how could he possibly be what I suspect you thought he was? He's just a man."

"But this . . . this is something else than what you mean," I said.

All of a sudden I wanted so badly to tell Tish about it—about the swamp, and the four of them, and what they believed and did, and what I had done with them, and what Hilary had—that I was stuttering with it. I wanted all that primal green beauty and mystery out in the sunlight of Tish's clear eyes; I wanted to see it with her sturdy vision. I wanted to hear her easy jeering, and feel the comfort of her rich laugh. I looked at her and hesitated.

"What else?" she said, her eyes narrowing. "How different?"

I knew then that she was thinking of the twisted, dark things Pat had said about us, and finding them, for an instant, not so hard to accept after all. And I knew then also that I would never tell her all of it.

So I told her only about the doe, and Tom's anguish and fury, and what he had said about the Big Silver plant, and his threats against it; and about the terrible, burning words we had hurled at each other, and how very afraid I was of that thing in him that shimmered wild, without top or bottom or limits of any kind.

When I was finished, she did not speak for a while, and then she said, "Well, he's wrong about the plant, and he'll see that he is if he really looks into it, but I can see why it scared you. He's always been that way, Andy. Sooner or later he does something that—I don't know—just runs almost everyone away from him. Or not that so much as keeps them from ever coming really close. Everybody adores him, but nobody wants to get too near. It's just that you never know which way he's going to go. I've thought a lot about Tom. This . . . absoluteness, this one-pointed, never-stopping thing that he has . . . a person can turn it inside, against himself, make it a weapon, and then you have a drunk or a madman or a criminal. Or he can turn it outside, and use it as a . . . battering ram, I guess I mean, to break down walls and silence and stupidity, as a key to unlock doors—and then you have a saint. Nobody is ever sure which it's going to be with Tom."

"A saint," I said, tasting it.

"Yes, I think that's just what I mean," Tish said. "Tom is willing to commit any excess he thinks is necessary. Any. You said that just a minute ago. You know it's true. All of us do. That's a quality that's shared not only by saints but by madmen, criminals, and fools. Maybe they're all one and the same. So in that respect, a saint is a man who is willing to make a fool of himself to make a point to fools. And in that respect Tom is a saint."

"Jesus, Tish, I couldn't live with a saint," I said.

"Well, I think you'll either have to choose that or live with a madman or a fool—he's not a criminal yet, that I know of. Or give him up entirely. Are you ready to do that?"

"No," I said, and knew that it was true, and missed him, in that moment, with a physical longing that shook me like the chill of influenza. "But I'm still scared to death of what he's capable of. You didn't hear him, Tish. I need a merry-go-round, not a roller coaster."

"Then you're a little late finding that out," she said crisply. "You had the best one in town, and handed him over to Pat."

"Yeah," I said. "I know."

"So." She stood up and hugged me briefly. "How about it? Can I tell Philippa you'll help us out?"

"Sure," I said. "It's only fitting. The battered leading the battered. Maybe I could do chalk talks."

"Not a bad idea." She left, grinning. I cleaned up the living room and put the videos in a stack beside the front door, to take back the next day. I might not be going to Goat Creek again, but neither would I hide out in my cottage in the woods. I was as disgusted with myself as I could imagine being at that moment; I actually seemed to taste the stale sourness of my lassitude.

Making a small sound of distaste, I headed down the hall to take a murderously hot shower and put fresh sheets on our beds. I had not made them in days.

"Mama," Hilary called from her room. "These jodhpurs are way too short. Could I get some new ones?"

"You bet," I said. "And maybe a new jacket, too, if they don't cost the entire earth."

"Boots, too? My toes are all crumpled up in these."

"Boots, too," I said.

Within days Hilary was a creature of horses and habits and stables and rings and jumps again, looking, with her dark hair pulled back into sleek, severe wings and her new height and slenderness, as if many generations of Old Pemberton blood ran in her veins. She slid back into her training with Pittypat as faultlessly as if she had never left, and by the time the week was out, Pat Dabney had mounted her on a new horse, a tall, elegant bay with a wild eye and a conformation as attenuated and beautiful as Hilary's. His name was Diablo, and he spent the better part of the first day with Hilary trying methodically to throw her. By the second day he was following her about the ring as if she had bottle-fed him from birth. This I learned not from Hilary herself but from Tish, who picked her up after school and took her to her lessons. She insisted on that, and I was grateful. I conceded the wisdom of having Pat Dabney back in my daughter's life as a necessary conduit to acceptance and self-fulfillment, but I could not have brought myself to deal with her. Especially now, since Tom was not in my life.

"She's gone from baby of the class to star in one season," Tish said. "Pat spends most of the ring time with her. And she's keeping her word, Andy. I haven't heard her say one word to Hil that isn't the strictest of business. She's not contrite, or anything; that's never going to happen. But she's keeping to the teacher-student thing. I wonder what on earth Carter said to her."

"Your guess is as good as mine," I said. "According to . . . to Tom, he pulled some kind of Old Pemberton rank on her. That's your department."

"Whatever, it's working," Tish said. "How is Hil feeling about all this?"

"Who knows?" I said. "All of a sudden I've got a mystery woman on my hands. 'How's it going, Hil?' 'Fine, Mama.' 'Are you enjoying your lessons?' 'Yeah, they're neat.' 'Do you think you'll keep on with them when school's out?' 'Sure. I guess so.' 'Is there anything you'd like to talk about, Hil? Anything bothering you?' 'No, ma'am. I'm fine.' And it's not sulkiness or that awful depression she had before, either; this is a whole different thing. She seems perfectly satisfied to be riding again, and it's just fine to be taking lessons, but it's like . . . the essence of her is off somewhere else. No, it's more like she's biding her time. Keeping busy with something she likes all right while she waits for something else. It's a very . . . grownup attitude. An adult would do this. I don't know what to make of it. It almost frightens me."

"You think she's waiting for Tom and you to get back together?"

"I don't know. As far as I know, she doesn't even know we're apart. She knows he's gone to the woods, but he does that. . . . She hasn't mentioned her goat, or the raccoon. But again, she doesn't seem sad."

"She knows, count on it. She's not stupid. Meanwhile, enjoy. Maybe it's only that she really is growing up. They do, you know. A few months ago she would have been whimpering and hanging on to you like a baby monkey."

I knew that that was true, and let myself simply enjoy this strange, poised, waiting daughter as much as I could.

"What do you want to do for our birthdays? Want to go to the beach?" I said on a day in early June, on the week that her school ended for the summer. I had her enrolled in the summer session at Pemberton Day, but it would not start until mid-June. She and I both had birthdays then.

Always before, we had planned something special for the two of us to share. This year, her first away from Atlanta and without the presence of either Carter or Tom in her life, I thought I might take her down to the Florida gulf coast, where Tish and Charlie had a beach cottage. We could both, I thought, use the sun and sea and the anodyne of a new and neutral place.

"No, ma'am, I don't think so," she said matter-of-factly. "If it's okay with you, I'd just like to stay home. Maybe you could fix us lasagna and strawberry shortcake for dinner, and we could get a good video."

I looked sharply at her, to see if there were any signs of languishing, regression, illness about her. But there were none. Her face was brushed with new tan, and her eyes were clear and calm. She looked superbly healthy. It was simply that Hilary no longer shone. I sighed.

"It doesn't sound like much of a birthday, but if that's what you'd like to do, we'll do it."

"It sounds fine," she said. "Maybe something will come up."

I knew then that she meant Tom's return, and felt my heart squeeze with pain and pity for her. She was waiting for him, then. I could not just let her sit in patient anticipation for a man who was not going to come back. . . .

"Sweetie, if you mean Tom, we need to talk about that," I said.

"I don't mean Tom," she said. "And I don't want to talk about that right now."

So I let it alone, and watched my waiting daughter, and immersed myself as deeply as I could in my job at Pemberton State, which I did not enjoy, and at Philippa Dobbs's new women's shelter, which, to my surprise, I did. The plights of the women who came for refuge and stayed to be counseled both moved and irritated me; how could they let themselves be ill-used in such terrible and ignominious ways? And then I would remember that I had done so myself, and not so long ago, and felt shame and remorse at the irritation. I could not now remember the woman who had let Chris Calhoun so misuse her; I knew he had done so, of course, but it seemed that it had happened to someone else. And in a way it had. So much had happened between that time and this. I had started, however clumsily, to build a new life; I had had two loves. . . .

Pain would flood me when I reached this stage of the ruminations. I did not think I would ever be able to think of Tom again without that sick, dizzying descent into pain. Sometimes it actually doubled me over. But I was sunk safely once more into the normality of Pemberton life, and I would not, could not risk it again. Some of the sharp fear that was born in the woods on the day of the doe dulled under the wrap of safety, but the pain did not. Dullness and work and pain; dullness and pain. It is what I remember about the cusp of that spring as it slid into summer.

The week before our birthdays, Tom came back. The spring session at Pemberton State had ended, but one morning I saw his truck in the parking lot, its bed and tires spattered with dried mud. Over the slow, deep jolting of my heart I walked to the truck and looked into the cab. The right seat was piled high with textbooks and papers to be graded, as if he was taking home all the work he had let slide for the past weeks. I realized that I did not know if he was taking classes for the summer session. I walked around the truck and looked into the bed. There was a pile of dark-stained burlap on its floor, and I knew with certainty that it was the blood of some animal. It sickened me suddenly, as I stood there in the white sun of the parking lot. Wild, it was wild, and rank. . . . I went back into my office.

All that morning I waited. Every time the phone rang,

I jumped as if I had been burned. But he did not call. His truck was gone when I came out after work, and he did not call that evening, nor the next one, nor the next. By that weekend I was drowned in pain, but also secure in the certainty that he would not call, that it was, indeed, over. I knew I would not call him now. School began again, and his truck did not reappear. I did not know where he was.

Summer came. Hilary waited. She did not speak of the dream maker, but in the late nights she played his song.

On a night of thick, thunderous air and shimmering heat lightning off to the west, my doorbell rang. I almost did not get up from the sofa, where I had dropped in exhaustion after a late counseling session at the center. Hilary was asleep, and I wanted nothing in the world so much as to simply sink into lightless sleep myself, where I lay. I ached all over with the need. I was not frightened at the knock in the night; this was Pemberton, not Atlanta. But I was annoyed. Whoever was collecting for whatever charity along Whimsy Road was going to find no bounty here.

The ringing gave way to knocking, a rhythmic, mannered tapping, and finally I struggled upright and trudged crossly to the door, scrubbing my fists in my tired eyes. When I opened it a gust of sweet, fresh wind came in ahead of the storm, and Tom Dabney came in with it.

I felt nothing at all but stupid disbelief. He wore what appeared to be doublet and hose, and a striped silk tunic under which great, puffed sleeves of some satiny claret-colored fabric bloomed. He had a plumed and cockaded hat on his black head, and there was a neat, piratical mustache on his upper lip, accenting the furrow there, and a close, perfect Vandyke beard on his long, cleft chin. He held a scroll in his hand, rolled and tied with gold cord, and he looked at me solemnly. I opened my mouth and closed it again. It occurred to me that I was dreaming.

Tom grinned and swept the hat off and dipped in a deep bow.

"May I come in?" he said. The sound of his light, rich voice made a warm path from my ears into my stomach. My heart began to pound.

"You are in," I said witlessly.

"Well, it seemed like a good idea at the time," Tom said, looking ruefully down at his garish and beautiful dress. He handed me the scroll.

Still staring at him, I unrolled it. It was thick and creamy, more fabric than paper, and the words that ran in precise lines and ranks down it were exquisitely calligraphed in black ink. I had seldom seen such work except in illuminated manuscripts, in museums. I looked from the scroll back at Tom.

"I wish you'd read it," he said. "It took me hours to compose it and Martin days to calligraph it. He hasn't done any since he was a student in Florence. Bitched the whole time."

I held the scroll up to the light and read it. It said:

Sumer is i cumin in,
  Lhude sing cuccu!
Groweth sed and bloweth med,
  Andy's birthday comes a-speed.
    Sing cuccu!

Ewe bleateth after lamb,
  Loweth after Andy, Tom;
Bullock starteth, bucke farteth.
  Birthday sing, cuccu!

Cuccu, cuccu!
  Celebration's overdue
At Goat Creek when the week is new!

Sing cuccu now! Sing cuccu!
Sing cuccu! Sing cuccu now!

I looked back up at him, an unwilling smile tugging at my mouth. His grin widened under the Mephistophelian mustache.

"There's more," he said. "On the back."

I turned it over. The same exquisite cursives bade me, in perfect but atrocious Elizabethan blank verse, to attend an evening of drama, in verse, to celebrate my and Hilary's birthdays the following Monday night, at Tom's house on Goat Creek. The celebration was to last from sundown to midnight, with an Elizabethan game feast after the play: juggling, minstrel lays, mimes, dancing, and singing. There was a cast list of perhaps ten people, all of whom I knew, and credits that cited Tom as author, director, and casting director, and Martin Longstreet as costume director. Gwen Carrington and Tish were listed as seamstresses. Sets were by Tom and Reese Carmody. Game for the feast was to be provided by Scratch Purvis, and wines and meads were by Scratch and Martin Longstreet.

"I've been holed up at Reese's working on this thing for two weeks," Tom said. "I've rehearsed people until their tongues are hanging out, and nobody involved in it is speaking to me. These invitations have gone out to fifty people, and if you won't come I'm going to have to call every one of them, and then I'll cut my throat. I'm an awful asshole. It's easier for me to mount a full-fledged Elizabethan verse production than to say I'm sorry. But if you need for me to say that, I will."

I still could not speak. He had not been planning anarchy, then; he had been writing a play for me. Something luminous and fizzing, like champagne bubbles, was starting up in my chest and tickling along my veins. I felt that I wanted to laugh or cry, but I did not know which, and so I simply continued to look at him. A part of me knew the feeling for happiness, albeit frail and tentative, but another, older part refused to name it.

"Please come to your party, Andy," Tom said, as simply as a child. "I've missed you."

The champagne bubbles burst in my throat and behind my eyes, and I began to laugh and to cry at the same time. Nothing that had gone before mattered; how could it? Who could resist this half-mad forest mountebank in his beautiful, ridiculous silks, with his glinting, quicksilver mind? I did not care if this man threatened to blow up ten bomb plants. I did not even think I cared if he did so. I could not stay away from him. My body moved toward him of its own volition, and I went into his arms, my face finding its familiar nest in the warm hollow of his throat.

"I've missed you, too, you damned fool," I sobbed. "I'd love to come to my party."

It was only much later, after I lay in bed and let the galloping of my heart slow back into a livable rhythm, that I remembered that he had not called me Diana. I felt a pang of loss, but contentment swallowed it, and simple sleep drowned both. When I woke in the morning, it was to joy.

On the way out to Goat Creek on the day of the party, Hilary burned like a blue flame. She prattled nonstop, happiness pouring out of her like spring water. She tapped her feet and fiddled with the radio and sang. She wriggled on the seat until I looked over at her with annoyance and amusement. I had bought her a new dress, a blue A-line Laura Ashley, knife-pleated all around, with a scoop neck and an ankle-length skirt, and found a blue velvet headband to which I had, ineptly, sewn small white silk flowers.

She looked lovely in it, chaste and severe and of another age entirely. I thought it would be perfect for Tom's Elizabethan party.

"You're going to fidget the pleats right out of your dress," I said.

"I don't care," she said gaily. "Tom will make me another one, out of flowers and leaves."

"That'll be the day," I said. "He may be a Renaissance man, but a magician he's not."

"You know he can make clothes and stuff from fibers and leaves," she said. "He showed us how. Did you forget?"

"No. But I don't imagine his skills run to knife pleats and appliqué," I said. "Come on, Hil, he's just a person like anybody else, after all."

"Then why are you looking like that? Why do you smile all the time? You never smiled when y'all had had the fight."

"How do you know we had a fight?" I said.

"I just knew. I always know about Tom," she said. "I knew we'd be coming back to Goat Creek, too. But I didn't know when. I'm glad it was for our birthdays. I was getting tired of being nice to Pat."

I shook my head. "Ain't no flies on you, are there, missy?"

"Nope," she said matter-of-factly. And then, "Oh, Mama, I'm just so *happy*."

"I'm glad, sweetie." I smiled, but a small breath of dread clouded my mind. Don't be too happy, my little girl, I thought. That kind of happiness calls down fate. . . .

Tom was sitting on the porch steps with Earl on his shoulder, as he had been the first time we went to Goat Creek alone. He was dressed in his hose and doublet, and the puffed sleeves of the silk shirt were rolled up. It was warm for mid-June; sweat dewed his forehead, and his beard and mustache were damp with it. He was paring potatoes into a great black iron kettle, feeding occasional slices to Earl. The raccoon ate them with the resigned air of one doing an onerous favor for a friend. When they saw us, Tom's grin split the black beard in a white slash, and Earl began to chitter and chirr, and bob up and down. Tom tossed down his paring knife and held out his arms, and Hilary ran into them and hid her face in his shoulder. He hugged her to him, rocking her. Earl patted her black hair all over, and then trundled off Tom's shoulder and onto hers.

"I've missed you, Princess," he said to Hilary. "We've all missed you. Earl got so neurotic I had to threaten him with a shrink, and Missy has almost pined away. Won't eat a bite. Maybe you can get her to nibble a little now."

Hilary stood back, looking at Tom.

"You look like a picture in a history book," she said. "Your beard scratches, though. Is Missy sick?"

"Then it's off with my beard right after this party," Tom said. "I do not scratch ladies. On purpose, anyway. I don't think she's sick. Scratch can't find anything wrong with her. But she won't eat. She's gotten pretty thin. I really do think she went on a hunger strike until you got here. Why don't you run down and see her and take this clover Scratch brought?"

He handed her a basket of fresh crimson clover from the porch behind him, and she dashed off toward the goathouse, a vivid wind of blue in the still, yellow midafternoon. He looked after her, and then at me.

"She's grown in just a month. She's gotten prettier. Damn, I've missed you both so much. I don't want to miss any more of her growing up. I don't want to miss any more of you, period."

"No," I said. "Me, either."

"Then let's don't."

"No."

Hilary came back from the goathouse, walking slowly. The little goat trotted beside her, bleating and nuzzling at her hands with her pretty black mouth. I was shocked at Missy's appearance. She seemed really much thinner than I remembered, and her taupe coat looked rough and without luster. It was not that she was unkempt; her small black hooves were newly and neatly trimmed, and she had been recently washed and brushed. But there was something, a dullness, a plodding to her steps, where there had once been an airborne, pattering lightness to match Hilary's.

"Tom, are you sure she's not sick?" I said under my voice. "She really doesn't look good."

"I really think it's that she's missed Hil," he said. "Scratch is better with goats than any vet I've ever seen. He can't find anything. Or at least, anything he's seen before, and he's seen every goat disease known. I think he's right. She's perkier now than she's been for a couple of weeks. Let's see if she's eaten."

"How'd you do with the clover?" he said to Hilary.

"She ate it all and cried for some more," Hilary said. "But, Tom, she sure is skinny."

"She'll be fine now that you're here," he said. "There's some more clover in the kitchen. We'll give her some a little later. She'll be okay, you'll see."

"I'm never going to leave her again," Hilary said, hugging the little goat fiercely. "I'm never going to leave her for that stupid horse."

"I've been hearing great things about your riding," Tom said. "I'd hate to see you give that up, Hil. According to my sources, you're a shoo-in for a prize next spring."

"I don't care about it. It's stupid. I was just doing it for Mama, and to keep busy till we could come out here again," she said. "I don't want to do it anymore now. I just want to stay out here."

"I really wish you'd keep on with it," Tom said.

"No way," Hilary said. "Besides, I didn't think you liked horses."

"I don't," he said. "But that doesn't mean *you* can't. We aren't joined at the hip, Hil, thank God. I expect I'd like them fine if I was as good as you are. You keep on with that riding, and bring home all the blue ribbons you can. They'll look terrific on Missy."

"Do you really want me to?" she said.

"I really do," he said seriously. "You have to live in the world for a very long time. You can't retire to Goat Creek until you're an old lady who's had a good and full life. Not allowed. So you might as well live well in the world, rather than badly. It will make you lots happier in the long run, and that will make your mother and me happy."

"You live out here all the time," she said. "You've retired out here."

"Yeah, but I do a lot of other things, too," he said. "Besides, I'm the boss around here. I get to do what I want. When you're the boss, you can, too."

"Well," she said, "when I'm the boss, I'm going to stop riding."

"Don't you like it, really?" he said. "I don't see how you can be good at something and not like it."

"I guess I do," she said finally.

"Then go ahead with it." He smiled at her. "It's allowed to like more than one thing at a time. You need to be all you can be, all the time."

"Is Scratch here?" she said.

"He's in the kitchen, making moonshine," Tom said. "And waiting for you."

She started for the house, and then turned and looked at him from the first step.

"Virbius isn't there," she said. It was not a question.

"No," Tom said.

"Is he dead?"

"Yes, he is."

"Was it time?"

"It was time. And he did it grandly. He brought honor to himself and us," Tom said. "And he did a great thing for the woods."

For a long moment my child's blue eyes looked into the blue eyes of my lover. I thought that some unspoken covenant passed between them. For myself, coldness flirted up my spine. I could see the scene in my mind's eye: the night and the fire, and the great blackness beyond, and the lordly, shining buck being brought into the firelight, and the silver dazzle of the knife. . . .

I shut my eyes and swallowed and opened them again. I knew I had to find a way not to mind this, to accept it as naturally as Hilary did. Otherwise I would, one day, have to go away again. I could not take only a part of Tom.

"That's good," Hilary said, and went into the house.

Tom looked at me. "You want to talk about this?"

"No. Not now," I said. "I want to go see Scratch. And I'd really love a drink, if you have anything that isn't Elizabethan and cute."

"Got gin," he said. "Even got olives. Come on and I'll make you a silver bullet. Not a vampire in the county will come near you after a couple of those."

Scratch was stirring a great kettle of something that smelled wonderfully of spices and herbs. He had a steaming cup beside him, and he sipped at it from time to time. He sat on a kitchen chair, and was wrapped in a great, thick winter sweater of Tom's, despite the heat pouring from the big range. Hilary sat in his lap. Scratch's head seemed to me positively skull-like in the gloom, and it shook gently, as did his papery, white-dusted old hands. Foreboding hit me squarely. Surely that was illness, and in that dark good face, waiting death. . . .

Scratch grinned at us, around Hilary's head.

"Got me a might fine lapful," he said.

"Way too big a one," I said, thinking of her new weight, and his old legs, so weakened now that he needed a chair. "Hop down off there, Hil. Scratch can't cook with you on his lap."

"Leave her to be," Scratch said. "She right where I wants her."

At the kitchen table Martin Longstreet, magisterial in the same costume Tom wore, only several sizes larger, was just placing an apple in the mouth of a pig. The pig was hairless and horrible: grayish pink and blankly baleful of eye. There was a crown of honeysuckle on its naked head. I grimaced and Martin laughed.

"And people wonder why all the great chefs are men," he said. "Don't worry, Miss Diana. He's going straight onto the spit in a few minutes, and by midnight he's going to taste mighty good. He was a proper villain, anyway; Scratch got him way upswamp. He'd been stealing baby turtles for weeks."

"There's turkey from the A & P deli for them as can't eat something that's still looking at them, myself included," said a voice near the ceiling, and I looked up into the gloom to see Reese Carmody on a stepladder, affixing brilliant heraldic banners to the wall. Against the dark logs, in the dim light, they looked mysterious and baronial and medieval. I said as much.

"Wrong period, but right effect," Tom said, grinning. "We decided not to be purists about this. The evening sort of runs the gamut from pre-Beowulf to eighteenth-century Venice. And we've got a lot of medieval friars and nuns coming. Not everybody's legs are as exquisitely suited for doublet and hose as mine and Martin's."

"You can say that again," Reese said from the air. He was wearing carpenter's overalls over an emerald satin shirt with flowing sleeves. "Scratch won't dress up at all."

"Ain't gon' dress up like no foreign Hottentot," Scratch said serenely. "Look like to me white folks all wants to be somebody else. I has a hard enough time bein' me all the time."

I laughed and went over and hugged him. I could feel his birdlike ribs under my fingers, and his breath smelled sour and thick, like air in a sickroom.

"Take care of yourself," I said. "You're the only one of this gang of four with any sense. . . . Lord, Scratch, I can hear you breathing."

"It just a col'," he said. "Got it upcreek, fishin'."

"I'm glad to hear that's all you were doing," I said. "I had some idea you all were indulging in a little free-lance espionage up the river there a while back."

"Why, Miss Andy, how you do run on," Reese Carmody said from his perch.

"So you thought we were out blowing up the Big Silver, huh?" Tom said a while later. We were in his bedroom, and he was fastening a brilliant purple satin cape with a scarlet lining around my shoulders. On my head was a garish tiara of silver paper and rhinestones. A small cape and crown for Hilary lay on the great bed.

"Well, the thought did occur," I said. "After all, you were not exactly prudence itself in the woods that day. What were you doing up there, Tom? Or should I ask?"

"Sure," he said. "You have every right. Well, the first thing we did was have Reese check every soil and water test for that day at every station around the swamp and on the river. All miles below the danger range; absolutely nothing there. But we did a cleansing, anyway; we had to, after that doe. . . . It was the longest and most exhaustive one we've ever tried. Took three days. It just about finished Scratch, but nobody could make him stay home. He stayed in bed for days after it. God, it was tough on everybody. . . ."

"Virbius . . . ," I said.

"Yes," he said, and hesitated. Then he said, "It isn't often necessary, Andy. Very seldom, in fact. But . . . the contamination was very great. We gave him a great songfest afterward."

"I'm sure he appreciated it," I said, and then regretted my sarcasm. "Are you satisfied that it's clean now?"

"I think so. Scratch says it's clean, if it—whatever, it was—was a one-shot thing. If it's something else, that's another matter entirely."

"You said you all watched the tests every day. . . ."

"I know," he said. "We do. The water's as clean as it ever was. I guess I just went off half-cocked. But something just felt so wrong. . . . But the others think it's okay. It was a very powerful cleansing."

"And can you just leave it alone now?" I said.

"I have," he said. "We did the best we could. It's always been enough before."

At about seven, Tom's guests began to arrive. As he had said, there must have been around fifty, mostly couples, all in costumes that bespoke more enthusiasm than historical accuracy. They were all I knew of Pemberton; it had been they who had given the parties that Carter and I had attended during the holidays; theirs the charming carriage houses or great, sprawling "cottages," theirs the balls and buffets and suppers and brunches and teas and tailgate lunches and hunt breakfasts. I had seen them in the shops and movies and concerts, at the training track and the club and the beauty parlor and the dentist. They were, for better or worse, my people now. Welcome for me had been on their lips during the time of Carter, and, I knew, talk about me and Tom and Hilary had been there later. But tonight there were only smiles, and good wishes for our birthdays, and laughter at each other's finery. I felt the last of my reserve and animosity toward them slide away on the magic of the night Tom had created. How could I blame them for listening to Pat Dabney's malice? Who wouldn't, given the grotesquerie of it? But I did not think that, after all, they had given it credence; or they would not have come to celebrate with us. Apparently those who had were not present or had not been invited. None of the members of the Pemberton Dames were present, except for Gwen Carrington and Tish, her freckled bosom pushed high out of a laced satin bodice ("I ordered it from a costume shop in Atlanta. Does it or does it not look like the Old Whores' Ball?"), standing beside Charlie, who wore a sheet with gold and silver stars and moons pinned all over it.

"What are you, Nancy Reagan's astrologer?" I said.

"I'm a wizard," he said. "Merlin, to be exact. Want to drop up to my cave and see my frescoes?"

Pat and Carter were not there. "I have my limits," Tom said.

Clay and Daisy Dabney came in late, with Chip and Lucy, the former in correct modern evening dress, the latter as Pierrot and Pierrette. Lucy looked enchanting and lost in the loose harlequin suit, her downy duckling's head thrusting up out of the ruffed collar like a lily. Chip looked like a clown at a supermarket opening.

Clay Dabney kissed me on the cheek and bent over Hilary's hand.

"I've missed seeing you around, Miss Andy," he said. "I've been in Atlanta most of the winter, arguing with the FCC and trying to get the asshole legislature to pass pari-mutuel. No luck, I might add. The thought of a legitimate source of income scares the pants off of them. May I wish you and Miss Hilary the happiest of returns, and that you have many more, all in Pemberton? You bring smiles where there haven't been many in a spell."

He gave Tom's shoulder an affectionate squeeze, and Tom put his hand over his uncle's. In the twilight they might have been father and son; both of them lean and slight, both weathered from long days in the spring sun, the same blue eyes looking out from under thick eyebrows, the same long, cleft chin. Beside them, Chip was elephantine and pink and boyish and somehow disturbing to look at, like a baby endowed with powers beyond its control.

"Birthday kiss, Andy?" he said, and kissed me wetly on the mouth, the sly tongue probing. I jerked my head to the side. He stepped back and smiled, looking down my dress.

"Them Elizabethans knew how to dress a woman," he said. "Prob'ly how to undress 'em, too. Looks like you could just squeeze the waist and out they'd pop, like grapes."

"Lord God, Chip, you'd think you was raised in a barn," Clay Dabney said heartily, taking my arm and leading me away from his son, over to a table on the porch over the creek, where Tom and Martin Longstreet were opening fresh oysters and piling them high on plates with lemon and cocktail sauce. There were two spots of red on Clay's cheeks, and the laughter in his voice did not reach his eyes. I thought again what a son Tom would have made for him, and how much silent pain his own son must bring him. How much love could survive shame? Perhaps a lot; perhaps it grew stronger with the parents' desire to shield, to protect the offending child. . . . I remembered that the most love I had ever felt for Hilary was when she was behaving the worst, under the anger and embarrassment. She seemed so vulnerable then, so at risk from her own demons. Undoubtedly Clay Dabney felt the same about Chip. But I could not doubt his love for his nephew. His face lit with it whenever they were together.

Tom's eyes took in his uncle's hectic cheeks and my own flaming face, and moved to Chip, still staring after us, a smirk on his face.

"Saved the best ones for you," he said, handing Clay a plate of glistening oysters. "Got some of the cajun hot sauce you like, too, and some fresh black pepper to grind on 'em if I can find it."

"Here's a boy looking to suck up to an old man," Clay Dabney said. "What do you think, that I'm gon' leave you all my worldly goods?"

"Nah, maybe just a little old radio station or two. And I wouldn't say no to a newspaper."

"Hit me again with that hot sauce and maybe I'll go a microwave dish," Clay said, and we laughed, and the evening swung on its jeweled axis toward night.

I will never forget that night, and I don't think anyone who was present will, either. It was like certain childhood Christmases, or a special, rite-of-passage birthday: whole, luminous, whirling, shining. Many years later, those of us who came to Goat Creek that summer night will still be talking of it. It belongs in the pantheon of perfect times; they are largely accidental, and cannot be planned, and so are the rarer for it. That was probably true of this evening, too, but there was no doubt that the fire at the heart of it was Tom.

He was everywhere, laughing, teasing, singing, dancing, telling hideous jokes, kissing women, hugging men around their shoulders. There was no person there who did not feel the singular magic of his extraordinary focus. His exuberance lifted the most leaden of us out of ourselves and sent the airborne spinning even higher. Even solemn Wynn Chapin joined an impromptu chorus of "The Night They Shagged O'Reilly's Daughter." Even square, sunless Helen Chambers giggled when he kissed the nape of her leathery neck and pronounced her a sight to ravish starved eyes, and bloomed with blushes like a ruined old rose. Hilary, in her crown and cape, shone like a new young sun. I could hardly look at the joy on her face. I felt drunk with happiness, hers and his and mine.

"It don't get any better than this, does it?" Tom said to me as he whirled his Aunt Daisy past, stretching over to give my cheek a smack. It missed, and landed on my ear, tipping my crown over one eye.

"No," I said, sudden tears swelling my throat. "It don't."

Reese Carmody and Martin Longstreet passed great trays of the spiced wine and mead that Scratch had made. There was ordinary liquor and wine for anyone who wanted it, but I did not see anyone drinking it. The mead flowed like . . . mead. Before the first hour was out, a Viking-like hilarity prevailed. Baroque music poured from the huge speakers on the ceiling, alternating with nineteenth-century waltzes, and during one of these Tom crossed the floor to Hilary and bowed low over her hand and led her onto the floor.

When they reached the center, he stood for a moment, looking up over toward the big stereo, and I heard the needle lift from the Strauss and fall again, and pause, and then the plangent guitar strains I knew, by this time, viscerally:

Moon River, wider than a mile,
I'm crossing you in style someday. . . .
Dream maker, you heart breaker,
Wherever you're going, I'm going your way. . . .

Hilary's face lit into a flame of joy so beautiful that I had to look away. He held out his arms and she floated into them, and they whirled away into the music.

The crowd pulled back to watch; as if they had rehearsed it, the dark man and the child in blue circled slowly in a waltz of, and yet not of, this century, or even the last. Under the shimmering banners in the eldritch light of the long candles Tom had set about the big room, they might have been two specters swirling in a ghostly waltz finished three centuries past. Martin Longstreet took up his flute, and the silver notes of "Greensleeves" skirled up over the Mancini. Tom bowed Hilary back to her place and held out his hand to me, and I was swept in my turn out into the crystal stream of the old music, his arm at my waist so light it felt more like a displacement of the air than a living pressure. I could not feel the floor through the soles of my feet. If someone had told me, at that moment, that I was dead or dreaming, they would have had no argument from me.

"Are you having a good time?" Tom said against the hair at my temple. The light little puff on his breath tickled like a finger.

"I've never seen a night like this; I've never had such a birthday," I said. "It's pure magic. I think I'm drunk. Don't let me have any more of that stuff."

"You've been drinking apple cider." He grinned. "Scratch's special. Not a drop of booze in it. I want you sober tonight, me lovely. If you're drunk, it isn't off that."

After the dancing, Tom and Reese and Martin set the game feast out on the long trestle table on the porch over the creek, and lit the tall white candles. The sweet green night seemed to hold its breath. Tom gave the same odd, formal little blessing of the food that he had done at Thanksgiving; now I knew the sense of it. And then we ate. The pig, regal now in his crisp brownness and dressed with succulent apples and pears and nuts and with flowers shielding his dreadful eyes, looked appetizing instead of ghastly. Reese carved him expertly, and most of the guests partook of him without a qualm, Hilary included. Reese and I and a few others ate the A & P turkey. In addition there were huge bowls of potatoes and turnips, new asparagus, leeks and chestnuts, platters of tiny fried smelts, a pot of venison stew, and baskets of coarse, fragrant bread. The wine circled and circled. Candied fruits and honeyed pastries followed.

"I thought dinner would sober me up," Tish said owlishly, patting her fiercely boned waistline. "All it did was produce a flatulent drunk. But what the hell; I read someplace that farting and belching were signs of great approbation with the Elizabethans."

"I think that's the Arabs," I said, licking honey off my mouth. "The Elizabethans were into throwing bones over their shoulders, weren't they?"

"Then by all means, let's do it," she said, and tossed a gnawed-white rib bone over her shoulder and the porch railing. In an instant, bones were flying like shrapnel. Shouts and cheers rose in the still air toward the high white moon.

Tom came to stand by me. "What's Middle English for food fight?"

"What is it for swine, you mean," I said. "Your guests have regressed about twenty centuries in one night."

"Then maybe we'd better get the show on the road," he said, and walked to the middle of the porch.

"Ladies and gentlemen," he shouted, "lords and ladies. I bid you gather in the great hall and betake yourselves seats. And let the games begin!"

We found seats in a semicircle before the fireplace, some of us stumbling. Gwen Carrington was nodding on Phipps's shoulder, and Chip was frankly drunk, his eyelids at half-droop, a spoiled little smile on his pink mouth. He put his hands on Lucy's breasts and she pulled away from him, her face reddening, and he shrugged and reached over to make a try at Tish. I saw her say something to him in a low voice, her smile never fading, and he jerked his hand away. He did not stop smiling, either, but his face darkened nearly to purple. Chip had laid hands on every woman at Goat Creek that night who was not related by blood to him. I wondered if it was going to be possible to get through the evening without trouble from him. He did not seem to be able to come gracefully to the house of his cousin.

While the actors scurried into Tom's bedroom to get ready for the performance, Tom did an extraordinary juggling act with Earl. The fat old raccoon wore a gold leather collar with tassels and a small gray homburg of the kind that comes in a gift hat box, of which he seemed inordinately proud, and the crowd roared when he waddled out of the kitchen at a small whistle from Tom. He bobbed up and down as I had seen him do many times before, but tonight it seemed that he was bowing to the crowd. There was laughter, and whistles and applause. Earl scampered over and gave Hilary a palmy hug, and then went back to the center of the floor, where Tom waited with three polished red apples. Solemnly, he began to juggle them, frowning in concentration, and Earl circled him, bobbling and nodding. Every so often Tom would toss Earl one of the apples, and he would chitter and sniff it, and start to retreat with it, but when Tom whistled he would scurry up his leg to his shoulder with the apple, and down his arm, and put it in his hand, and the juggling would begin again.

It was a wonderful act, if a simple one, and by the time Tom and Earl took their bows we were all stamping our feet and clapping and cheering. Earl torqued out of the room, and Tom dropped down beside me, sweat running down his forehead into his beard.

"That was incredible," I said. "How long did it take you to teach him that?"

"About two weeks and two thousand apples," Tom said. "It worked better with cheese, but I had to stop that. He ate it."

And then the play. Unlike the juggling act, it was not simple. It was formal and faultless in form, and lavishly and painstakingly mounted, and acted with spirit and style, if not professionalism, and I will never see anything like it again. None of us who were there will. It told the story of Hilary's and my coming to Pemberton, and of my courtship by Tom, and an imagined marriage and consequent bizarre and slapstick life with the wild man of Goat Creek. It was bawdy, funny, lyrical, tender, overwhelming, a true tour de force. Hilary adored it, sitting in Scratch's lap on the floor by the fireplace, her long legs asprawl, her eyes shining, obviously understanding more of it than I might wish. Scratch himself smiled and nodded as if Elizabethan comedy were a fixed star in his firmament. I laughed and cheered and sometimes blushed, but more often I stared in simple wonder at the dark, whirling, darting man in silks who read Faulkner and slew deer ritually; who taught Conrad Aiken and Dylan Thomas and danced naked in the moonlight, smeared with blood; who wrote and mounted an original work of this magnitude and almost literally worshiped an oak tree. I could make no sense of him, nor find an orderly way in which to think about him. I realized, about halfway through, that the play was, as well as an inspired parody, a proposal of sorts. I was not surprised and I had no more doubts as to what my reply would be. But under the glittering surface of the night, apprehension waited to be noticed like a begging dog. I knew that there could be no rules for Tom Dabney, no conditions put on the loving of him, no formula for a life with him.

When the play ended, Tom and his actors lined up and took great sweeping bows. I looked around the room; all the faces there were suffused with a kind of self-forgetting alacrity, the nearest thing I had ever seen to mass joy. It was hypnotic; the applause went on and on. The cast bowed and bowed. And then the applause straggled and died.

Chip Dabney lurched to his feet and stood before the audience, in front of the ranks of actors. He held up his hands for silence. It fell. He swayed slightly on his feet, and the sly grin widened.

"I been studying Elizabethan," he said, slurring thickly, and Clay Dabney started to get to his feet and go after his son. And then he did not. He sat back down and looked at his hands. Daisy tilted her head and looked brightly at her son like a bird waiting to be fed. Lucy closed her eyes.

"Yessir, I been studying. And I got some original verses of my own for this distinguished company here. The first one goes . . . let's see," and he tilted his head back and closed his eyes, smiling. "It goes: When in silks my Andy goes/Her boobs fly up and hit her nose."

There was a silence, dead and palpable. I did not look at anyone. I felt my breasts rise and fall with painful breath, and wished I could simply will them out of existence and be, at that moment, as neuter as a mule, or a tree. Heat rose up my chest to my face.

"Got another one," Chip said, and this time his father

did rise to his feet. I felt rather than saw Tom start out of the line of actors.

"No, wait," Chip said. "This is a better one. This one goes: Oh, prithee sir, please tell me how/Tom Dabney does it with a cow."

The silence roared.

"Well, hell, Chip, you know, it's not that I really like it," Tom said in a slow, mild, dangerous voice. "It's just that I can't keep women away from me, no matter what I do."

The audience laughed, too loudly perhaps, but in obvious relief. Tom could, after all, handle Chip.

"Well, you got the right place for it." Chip's voice rose over the laughter, jocular and furious. "Got more and better tits out here on Goat Creek than anywhere in Baines County."

He took a few steps toward me, craned his neck, and pantomimed a look of astonishment and wonder at my breasts. Then he smiled beatifically at Tom.

"The goats and all, I mean," he said. "Aren't you a goat man? Seems I've heard lately that you were. . . ."

Tom turned Chip around gently by his shoulder and hit him. It was a long, smooth right to Chip's fleshy jaw, and Chip spun and flew across the floor and fetched up in his wife's lap, in a flaccid harlequin heap. He mumbled and scrambled a little, and then he lay still.

Tom stood still in the middle of the floor, looking at him.

Clay Dabney rose and walked out onto the floor and put his arm around his nephew, and faced the audience.

"I apologize for Chip," he said. "He doesn't handle his liquor well, and he'd had a little before we started out, but that's no excuse. I am ashamed for him and of him, and I will see that every one of you gets an apology from him.

Miss Andy, I can't tell you how sorry I am. He won't embarrass you again. Tom, you know how I hate this. It was a once-in-a-lifetime night, and I hope that's what you and your guests will remember. If somebody will give me a hand, we'll say good night and let you all get on with the party."

"I'm sorry, Uncle Clay," Tom said.

"Don't ever be," Clay Dabney said, and Tom and he and Charlie lifted the mumbling Chip to his feet and walked him outside. Daisy followed, clucking and fussing, and then Lucy, tears spilling over her feathery lashes.

"I'm so sorry," she said to me in a stricken whisper as she passed.

"Please don't even think of it," I said.

People stayed awhile longer after we heard Clay Dabney's Land Rover grind away outside, but of course the evening was over, its jeweled surface broken. Scratch had taken Hilary to her small room the moment Chip Dabney had risen to his feet, and he did not reappear. Tom and I stood in the doorway with Reese and Martin, saying good nights and thank yous and brushing away expressions of sympathy and concern. I was so angry with Chip Dabney that I was shaking with it, but Tom, beside me, seemed unconcerned. His smile was full and natural, and the laughter in his voice as he said goodbye to his guests was unfeigned. I looked down at his right hand; the knuckles were reddening and swelling, but he did not seem to feel it.

Tish and Charlie were the last guests out.

"It was so perfect that even the Asshole That Walks Like a Man couldn't spoil it," Tish said, hugging us both. "I hope you'll remember that."

"You have to whack Chip every now and then, but you don't have to take him seriously. Basically he's harmless. That's what's the matter with him," Tom said. "Thanks for everything, you two. It couldn't have happened without you. I love you guys."

"Love you, too," Tish said, hugging him and kissing me on the cheek. "Call me tomorrow, Andy. But not before noon, or you're dead."

They drove away, and Martin and Reese started into the kitchen to begin clearing away. Tom waved them off.

"Go on home," he said. "Nobody should have to wash dishes after a night like this. We'll do it in the morning. Or maybe we'll just throw everything in the creek. But not tonight."

They went without further protest. I knew they wanted to leave Tom and me alone.

He went into Hilary's room and came back grinning.

"Come and look at this," he said, and I went to the door of the little room. The lights were off, but the white light of the summer moon flooded in almost as bright as morning. Scratch was stretched out on top of Hilary's bed, his polished old heavy work boots placed neatly beside the bed and his eyes closed. Hilary lay in the crook of one arm, lost and boneless in sleep. Next to her, head on Hilary's shoulder like a sleeping person, the little goat lay, slender legs folded neatly, sides rising and falling quietly. Earl was curled on the pillow behind Scratch's head. My heart squeezed with love for all of them.

"I wish I had a picture of that," I whispered.

"Make one with your mind and keep it," he said, pulling me close to him and kissing the top of my head. "I will. Practically everybody and everything I love, all asleep in the same bed."

We sat down on the deep, rump-sprung sofa in front of the fireplace and he poured us a cognac. I sipped it, looking over the rim of the thin old crystal at him. In the lamplight and moonlight he looked fabulous and beautiful in his silks, wrinkled and sweat-stained now, and I knew that I wanted him with every atom in my being, both that night, on the rug, and always. I stretched luxuriously, feeling my tense muscles loosen and soften, feeling my body grow warm and open and ready for him, putting off the moment that I knew was just ahead.

"I thought for a minute you were going to kill him," I said, putting my feet into his lap. He traced the line of my leg from ankle to thigh with his forefinger. He smiled.

"Nope," he said. "Chip's not worth the slammer or the electric chair. He is infinitely unworthy of dying for. I'll die for you or Hil or the woods, but I refuse to die for an asshole. Like the man said, I may be insane but I'm not crazy."

"You sure could have fooled me out there in the woods that day," I said, reaching up to brush the hair out of his eyes.

His face stilled and sobered.

"I'm sorry about that day, Andy, but you need to know all of me," he said. "I'm not a rational man. I'm not balanced. I can be, at times, or I can try, but I'm other things, too, and one of those things is what you saw out there. That's me, just as much as the Faulkner, or the music, or the bullshit. Would you really rather I was tame?"

I thought of that great shout of pain and fury, and the utter wildness in him sometimes, and the half-hidden hint of cruelty, and the spiraling sense I often had in his presence of no boundaries, no limits. I thought of the singing and dancing and laughing and the courtliness and the foolishness, and the wild sweetness of his lovemaking. The familiar great heat started up from my stomach, and rushed down my arms and legs, and my breath grew thick and ragged in my mouth. I reached up and pulled him down onto me. My fingers fumbled with the tiny round buttons on the back of his tunic. I wanted to tear it off him, to feel the fabric part under my hands and send the buttons flying. I wanted him over me, around me, inside me.

"Oh, no, my love," I said into his ear. "I don't want you tame."

We fell asleep afterward, there on the sofa, and when I woke, the angle of the moonlight had lowered, and the night silence outside had deepened. I stirred, thinking of Hilary and the long drive home. He stirred, too.

"Will you stay, Andy?" he said sleepily, his hand reaching around me for my breast.

"Yes," I said. "I'll stay."

And he nodded, and kissed me softly, and we slid back into sleep.

Later that night, almost into morning, I had a dream. I dreamed I was watching Hilary riding in a horse show, taking jump after jump with effortless and exquisite precision. I was part of a large crowd that clapped and cheered her, and the cheering grew louder and louder as the jumps grew higher and higher. Soon they were nearly deafening, and my daughter and her horse were taking jumps so high that they seemed to be soaring into the sky. In the dream my heart began to pound with fear for her; she was going too high; she would soon fall. . . . The cheers turned to screams and then became Hilary's screams, and I struggled up through the layers of sleep and fear like a drowning person, to reach the safety of wakefulness. I sat up, my heart about to suffocate me with its slow, dragging pounding. I reached up to push the wet hair off my face.

The screaming did not stop.

I was off the couch and at the door of her room before

I even realized that I had stood up, and I could hear Tom stirring behind me. The room was empty. The milky summer paleness that presaged dawn bleached the windows. The screaming came again, from outside, from somewhere down by the creek. I stumbled through the living room and out onto the porch. Scratch was there, making his way painfully down the steps, clinging to the railing, toward where my daughter stood in the shallow water of Goat Creek, in the spot where she had danced in the healing moonlight with Tom Dabney. A long time ago, now. In the milk-light I could just see her. The water covered her ankles, and she stood in it and screamed and screamed and screamed. At her feet, the small form of the kid jerked and spasmed in a terrible convulsion, sending silver water flying. I knew even as I vaulted the steps that the convulsion was mortal.

"The fire, the fire! The water is on fire," Hilary screamed, and as I stared, I saw it: down the creek, where the willows arched black over deep darkness, a bluish glow lit the black water, a thin, steady, malignant glow, as if someone had dropped a tube of blue neon into it and it lay on the bottom, shining mindlessly on and on. A blue light in the water, and from its surface, like smoke, the thin vaporous steam of hot water.

Tom nearly knocked me down as he ran past me down the steps and down to the creekbank, but not before I had seen his face. I ran across the snake-cold grass to his side. I looked at my child, and the little goat, and the shining, smoking water, and up at Tom. His face, as he lifted the rifle to shoot the dying animal, was that of a man who had looked into hell.

CHAPTER THIRTEEN

When I was a small child and the tides of trouble in the little house in Kirkwood overwhelmed me, I used to get one of my father's undershirts out of the clothes hamper and take it into bed with me, and fall asleep feeling its much-washed softness against my cheek, smelling the deep, complicated smell of his sweat and bay rum aftershave, and the Persian-market smell of the store, and the new-hay smell of backyard sun. Those undershirts comforted me simply and profoundly for a long time, as nothing else did; they were the essence of all the constancy and towering solidity of Pano Andropoulis, without the capricious uproar of the man himself. When I had croup or a chest cold, as I often did, my mother would make a raging-yellow mustard plaster of a torn old undershirt and slap it on my chest, and I was content to lie there and let it eat nearly through my skin, knowing that now healing was on its way, borne in the chalice of my father's underwear.

I had not thought of those shirts for many years, not with my mind, but they must have lain, soft and waiting, in the deepest core of me, because two nights after the horror on the bank of Goat Creek I dreamed about them, dreamed so vividly of their cottony tenderness and solacing particularity that I woke at dawn in a cocoon of utter safety and rightness and lay there, mindless and healed, until wakefulness began to flood back. And then, before awareness had claimed me fully, I knifed myself into a fetal knot underneath the sheet and wept with a grief and fear and desolation I had not felt in all of adulthood, not even on the morning I had wept in the tree stand in the King's Oak.

It was a terrible and consuming spell of weeping, utterly beyond my ability to control, and though I was mindful of Hilary sleeping her damaged sleep just down the hall, I could not stem the tide of abandonment and hopelessness. I rolled over onto my stomach to try and stop the noise of my weeping in the pillow even if I could not stop the weeping itself. Pain bloomed inside me and pushed itself into every crevice and fissure; I literally felt my skin fill and stretch taut with the pressure of it. In the pillow I heard myself scream aloud, thinly and hopelessly.

"I want my daddy," I howled. "I want my daddy, I want my daddy!"

Presently, I do not know how much later, I felt my shoulder being shaken, shaken, and I heard Hilary keening above me like a little animal in a trap: "No, Mama, no, Mama, no, Mama, no. . . ."

The touch and cry had its own imperative; muscles other than mine seemed to lift me out of my sodden pillow and turn me over. Hilary crouched above me in her short summer nightgown, black hair wild around her white face, eyes blind with terror and spurting tears. She looked feral; she looked like a creature once beloved of and cosseted by man, but now abandoned and dying of it. Even when I turned over and looked at her, she continued to shake me, like a little automaton.

I struggled to smooth my face and get my breath, and somehow managed to sit upright and take her into my arms. She shook all over like a child in the grip of a convulsion, and her skin was icy and damp. She fought me for a moment, and then she went slack, inert. But the keening continued, wordless now. I pressed her face into my breasts so hard that it was a wonder I did not smother her, but I thought that I could not endure that awful, inhuman sound another moment.

"It was just a nightmare, darling," I said in as steady a voice as I could manage. I felt a last sob gather in my throat, and swallowed it. "I was just having a bad dream. Even grownups have bad dreams, and they can be awful. They can be a hundred times worse than anything that can really happen. . . ."

I thought of that dawn two days earlier, and stopped talking and merely held her, rocking. In Hilary's recent world, no nightmare spawned could hold a candle to reality.

She stopped the terrible quivering, but the keening slid over into a repetition of my own litany: "I want my daddy. I want my daddy. Oh, I want my daddy, I want him. . . ."

My heart twisted. He had beaten her mother and killed her puppy and crushed her heart and soul almost beyond healing, and my child wept for her father, seeing in her entire gray, howling world no one else who could or would help her. Feeling in my own arms no healing and no refuge.

But under the pain and guilt and despair I felt a small, tough, rude spike of hope. She had spoken words, made a sentence. Since I had brought her home from Goat Creek two days before, still screaming and swaddled in her wet nightclothes, Hilary had not spoken. She had not, after that storm of weeping passed, cried anymore, and she did not tremble and cling as she had once when frightened or hurt. Though she had eaten and drunk what I brought her, she stayed in her room with her door closed, and would not answer me when I called to her. Most of the time, when I eased the door open to look in on her, she was heavily asleep. I had called Tish's pediatrician and told him she had had a very bad shock at the accidental death of her pet goat and would not speak, and he had prescribed a mild tranquilizer and said that it was not particularly unusual behavior and to bring her in in a couple of days if she didn't perk up—his words—but to let her sleep as much as she could. And so I had, finding in the mindless hiatus of her unconsciousness an anodyne of my own, grateful for a space before I would have to do battle against enormities once more. But once or twice I had found her sitting up in bed writing in one of her school notebooks with a yellow pencil.

"Feeling better?" I said the first time, and she nodded, but she put her arm over the page so that I could not see it, and waited silently for me to go away. The next time I found her writing, I simply smiled and said, "Let me know when you're hungry," and closed the door again. The smile hurt my mouth and bounced off some invisible skin around Hilary like a rubber-tipped arrow. The next few times I looked in she was sleeping again. I had decided to take her in to see the doctor this morning, but now the awful dam was apparently broken, even if cruelly. Perhaps catharsis had been, after all, what was needed.

When the incantatory "I want my daddy" finally slowed and stopped, I lifted her blotched and swollen face to mine and pushed the hair off it. Where she had been clammy before, she was steaming hot now, and I thought she might be starting a cold. The water in Goat Creek had not yet warmed with summer. Her eyes were nearly stuck shut, and the breath rattled succulently in her nose. But the wildness was gone. Now she merely looked beaten and drowned.

"Would you just listen to us?" I said, pulling from somewhere a watery smile. "Both of us, sitting here like two-year-olds, hollering for our daddies? What jerks! I'm glad nobody can see us. We'd be laughed out of town before sundown."

I flinched even as I said the words; who was there, now, I could be glad did not see us? Not Carter. And not Tom Dabney. I had known even as I snatched my screaming daughter from the devil's fire in Goat Creek and run with her to the car, known without consciously thinking, but *known,* that we would not go back to that place of death and decay and smoking water. That we would not go back to Tom. And I knew that Hilary knew, too; though I could not have said how. Otherwise she would have asked for him. She would have wept, not for her father, but for him. I might as well, with my clumsy, joking words, having painted "Tom is gone" in the air between us in letters of fire.

But she managed a smile of her own, a small, ectoplasmic one, but a smile.

"You scared me," she said in a voice frail with disuse. "I knew your daddy was dead. I thought you meant you wanted to . . . be dead, too, so you could see him."

"Oh, poor sweetie," I said, holding her hand against me again. "Oh, no. Never for one single second would I want to be dead and leave you alone. It's just that when adults have nightmares, it's like the little kid they used to be takes over, and they cry for whatever or whoever they did then. It doesn't mean anything, and it's gone when they wake up. Now, when I have a bad dream, I can just wake up and know that I can take care of myself. And I can take care of you, too. You don't have to worry about that."

"You can't stop bad things from happening, though," she said in a small, dead voice.

"Not always, but sometimes I can, and I can help make it okay when they do happen, until you're grown up and can do it for yourself," I said. "You can count on that."

"But you can't stop them," she repeated. I thought of the things in Hilary's life that I had not, indeed, been able to stop: loss, fear, death. I had not been able to stop those things. And at the last, even Tom had not. Even Tom. I knew then that that was what she had meant when she wept for her father, and what I had meant, too: we had both wept for the terrible knowledge that sooner or later you cried out in terror and need and nobody was there but you. She had discovered that at far too early an age. Far too early. I did not see how a child could survive the knowledge. Even I had not fully known it until I woke screaming for my own dead father, in the fortieth year of my life. Even before, at the King's Oak, when I had thought that my own despair would kill me, I had eventually stopped crying and sat still and waited for someone to come for me.

And Tom Dabney had come.

But I could not let him come to me now, and I could not go to him.

Now there was only me. Only me, for both of us. I felt

a fresh wave of terror and abandonment start to form, and I sat still with Hilary in my arms and let it crash over me and take me down again. When the blackness rolled on past, I was still upright, and my arms were still tight around my daughter.

Okay, then, I said silently. All right. It's just a feeling. Widows must have it, orphans must know it. It's terrible beyond words and even beyond imagining, but it doesn't kill you. A feeling doesn't kill you. And even though I knew that sometimes it did, I was able to sit there with grief and death and fear old and rotten in my heart and say to Hilary, "Want to go down to the Pancake House for breakfast, or would you rather sleep some more?"

"Sleep," Hilary said drowsily, and before half an hour had passed she was gone back down into that thick, lightless sleep that had claimed her for the past few days. But this time she left her door ajar.

I had thought that we would leave Pemberton. I had it all planned; we would go at the end of summer, after Hilary's session at Pemberton Country Day had ended and my own hiatus between summer and fall quarter began. We would live quietly to ourselves until then; and then we would go and stay for a week or so at Tish and Charlie's beach house, and while we were there I would go into the bright, sun-punished, trashy little resort towns within driving range and find myself a job and an apartment or a rental house, and we would go back to Pemberton only to get our clothes and arrange to move our furniture. Somehow I never doubted that I could find the job; the town did not matter, nor did the apartment, or the school for Hilary. Whatever and wherever they were, they would be light-years away from this all-pervasive wealth and this uncanny beauty, and this death in the water. I wanted ugliness and banality as I had wanted them nearly a year before, and this time I would find them. I had even started to draft a letter of resignation for Miss Deborah, a neutral, courteous one that would not endanger my slender month's severance pay. I would tell only Tish and Charlie what we intended, and then only just before we left. I could get away without seeing them for a while yet; I did not think anyone knew what had happened out at Goat Creek after the birthday party. Perhaps they never would.

I did not know yet if I would tell the Coulters about the water.

On the way home from Goat Creek that morning I had stopped at a 7 Eleven store and bought several jugs of distilled water, and I had used them for cooking and drinking, but over here on this cloistered side of Pemberton the deadly neon creekwater was already losing power and dimension. Already the awful image was dimming in my mind. Already it had achieved the status of a fever dream. The water had been horrific, unspeakable, unthinkable, but oddly it was not vitally important. That was not the impetus to our flight into Florida. Tom was. Even though I had no actual evidence of it until later that day, when I switched on the six o'clock news, I knew without knowing what he was going to do. I think I knew even as I drove my shrieking daughter away from Goat Creek in the spreading summer dawn.

But by the time I knew what I had thought was indeed true, I knew also that we would not leave, Hilary and I. The running had to stop sometime, else we would be fugitives forever, and it had stopped that morning, when I had finally realized that I was alone and Hilary had only me. That would be true, now, wherever we went. And in simple truth I was tired with a bone-melting fatigue that seemed only one step up from death, a zombie's state. I don't think

I could have driven my child and myself to Florida. I don't even think I could have packed our suitcases.

And so for the rest of that morning and afternoon I simply sat down and waited for the news of Tom, which would not, to me, be news. When I saw him on the local station's six o'clock pickup out of Atlanta, I could have sketched in, detail for detail, the trajectory that had put him there, and the one that would follow. I learned later that I would have been right on almost all counts.

I suppose the conventional wisdom around Pemberton, that he went berserk, or nearly, was as good a way to put it as any. I never thought he did, and there were a few other people—Tish and Charlie, Reese, Martin Longstreet, Scratch—who did not think so, either. Not then. I thought, rather, that he had simply taken all that he was and had been and would be out to its farthest parameters, that he had become Tom to the ultimate degree. But that is probably the same thing as madness. Certainly few of us ever deliberately seek our own outer limits, and those who do step irrevocably outside the arena of normal human intercourse. Forever after, their consorts must be the wing-walkers, the edge-dancers, the lawless ones. So it was with Tom, after the morning on Goat Creek. When I saw his face, a banshee's mask, a Medusa's head, on the television screen that afternoon I felt no shock, but the deepest and most hopeless grief I have ever felt for another being fell onto me like a doomed queen's mantle, and until it vanished into the all-pervading white fatigue I could not move or draw a deep breath.

"Oh, my dear love, you're gone now," I said silently with my bled-out lips, and with the remote changer I destroyed him. It was days before I heard his name again. I did not think I would ever see his face.

Tom was on the sheriff's doorstep when the office opened the morning of the dying kid and shining water, demanding an investigation of the Big Silver plant and threatening violence, mayhem, catastrophe. Before the sleepy deputy could even reply, Tom got into his pickup and drove out Highway 35 to the gates of the Big Silver plant. He simply drove on past the guard and up to the administration building parking lot, and by the time the breathless security force arrived he had bulled his way into Francis Millican's office, almost tossing his secretary to the floor, shouting and raging. If Francis had not called them off him, security would have had him in handcuffs on the spot. The disgruntled secretary was already howling about lawsuits and warrants when Tom boiled out of the office and told the woman to be sure and fuck herself because nobody else would ever want to.

From there he drove back to Goat Creek and called the state patrol, the Pemberton Police Department, the county health authorities, the GBI, the Environmental Protection Agency, the Waycross and Savannah Greenpeace representatives, the county agricultural bureau, the local television and radio stations, the newspaper, his senator and congressman, and the presidents of every civic organization in Pemberton. By noon he had a gallon jug of water from Goat Creek in the truck and was on the way to a private laboratory in Atlanta with it. While he was in the city, he called the Atlanta newspapers and television and radio stations. Most ignored him, but one or two got him on tape, and one aired the segment on the six o'clock news. A paragraph in the State and National section of the *Atlanta Constitution* followed a day later. After it ran, the Pemberton television station obtained the Atlanta film and aired it. It was this that I saw. So, apparently, did everyone else in Pemberton.

By the time Tom was back from Atlanta, there was a warrant out for his arrest on charges of disturbing the peace and bodily assault. Francis Millican, whose blue lapels Tom had almost ripped from his suit, filed it on behalf of himself and the furious secretary, who had threatened Francis with OSHA action if he would not obtain the warrant. Perhaps he would have done it anyway, but I doubt it; Francis was a man who knew what was in a name, and in Pemberton, there was a great deal in the name Dabney. Before Clay Dabney could post his bail and extract from him a reluctant promise of temporary seemly behavior, Tom had spent a night in the Baines County Jail. By the next morning, the news was on everybody's lips: Tom Dabney had gone as crazy as a loon and was threatening to get the Big Silver plant closed.

If he had been anyone other than Tom, or if he had not mounted a screaming frontal attack, there might have been a substantial number, out of thousands of Pembertonians who rose up in indignant protest or shook their heads in enjoyment over their breakfasts, who gave his allegations some credence. Pemberton was not inhabited by fools; they read the papers and watched the news. They knew about Chernobyl, Three Mile Island, whole families with leukemia, dead sheep in Montana and Washington State, report after devastating report from the committees investigating allegations of mismanagement and cover-ups at the nation's nuclear plants. They were as used to the regular activists' protests at the Big Silver gates as they were to the Elks' annual barbecue, or the Jaycee's Empty Stocking drive at Christmas.

But this was the Big Silver, whose safety record was the bellwether of the entire nuclear industry, heralded and pointed to the world over as an example of how well and safely nuclear weapons and components could be produced and their wastes stored. The Big Silver, perhaps the most publicly, consistently, and frequently tested nuclear facility in the government's entire stable. There had never been a word, a whisper, a thought about the safety of waste disposal at the Big Silver plant. Everyone knew that. Everyone had known that for more than thirty years.

And besides, the Big Silver accounted for more than half the jobs and payrolls in the entire three-county area. Close the Big Silver and it was, for many, back to mowing lawns and shagging canapés for the rich people. That or welfare and food stamps. Back to a backwater Brigadoon whose businesses and services came alive only in the winter season, and then at the whim of a vastly diminished tribe of wealthy nomads whose progeny had long since found newer playgrounds.

In the space of hours after the film aired, Tom Dabney found himself a pariah. I thought of what Tish had said about saints and madmen, about a saint being a man who was willing to make a fool of himself to make a point to fools. About Tom being willing to commit any excess he deemed necessary, a quality shared by madmen, criminals, and fools as well as saints. I would have liked to call her and tell her she had been right, but the cottony fatigue smothered that and most other impulses I had, and besides, as Marlowe said, that was long ago and in another country.

When the report came back from the laboratory, showing that water Tom had taken from Goat Creek had astronomically high levels of plutonium, cesium, and strontium 90, he called Francis Millican and told him he would be out in fifteen minutes with proof of his allegations, and to call off security. Francis did. Tom walked whitely into Francis's office and threw the report on his desk, announcing in tones audible three offices away that he was going to the Environmental Protection Agency and the media in Atlanta as soon as he could gas up the truck. It was, he admitted to Reese Carmody later, the stupidest single thing he had ever done in his life. By the time the EPA representatives and the media arrived at the Big Silver the next day, the report had vanished from the face of the earth, there was no record that Tom Dabney had paid an authorized visit to the office of the plant's manager, and the lab in Atlanta disclaimed any knowledge of a man named Tom Dabney and a jar of water from Goat Creek in Pemberton, Georgia. An exhaustive and supervised search produced no paperwork or other evidence that Tom had ever been there. The word went out to every checkpoint at the Big Silver that Thomas Dabney was to be detained on the spot if he attempted to breach security. A photograph accompanied the directive.

Tom went to Clay Dabney then. He begged for coverage in the radio, television, and newspaper outlets Clay commanded. He was not comporting himself well at all by that time; he alternately raged and wept, and his hair and eyes were wild. Clay Dabney, tears in his own eyes, tried to reason with him.

"Listen, Tom," he said. "Please, just for Christ's sake listen for a minute. Without proof, I can't run a single word of what you're saying. I'd be shut down in two days. I'd be run out of business. And without proof, you're going to end up in jail again if you keep on this way. Why in God's name did you leave that report with that asshole Millican? Of course the bastard shredded it and got to the lab in Atlanta, or the government did; what did you think they'd do? Nominate you for Citizen of the Year? If you want proof that water's bad, this ain't the way to go about it. You get the government on your ass and you'll never find out anything. Stonewallin' ain't the word for it. Now let's just be calm and think this thing out and see if there's not another way to go about it."

What Clay came up with did not wholly appease Tom, but it quieted him for the moment. Clay Dabney had long known Frank Millican and the other top management at the Big Silver; if he did not like or admire them, or they him, he still thought them to be sincere in their claims that the plant was safe and clean and in violation of no public safety considerations, and they in their turn knew him to be a straightforward man firmly committed to the good of his community. Clay offered to find as good and impartial an independent engineer as he could, and propose to the Big Silver management that this man run his own check of conditions there, including open access to all plant and property areas and exhaustive air, soil, and water tests. Clay would pay the bill. And he would choose the engineer. The Big Silver would have no strings on him, purse or otherwise.

"Hell, you can even help me find the engineer, if you want to," he said. "Will you trust me to do this, Tom?" His blue eyes were still wet as he stared at the nephew he had long loved as his son. Tom looked as though he had been starved and beaten.

He eyed Clay Dabney for a long time, and then he said, "Yes. Okay. I guess so."

"Okay. It's done," Clay Dabney said. "Now go home and get some sleep, and for God's sake shut up about Goat Creek until we know what's what. If it turns out this report backs you up, then I promise you we'll go git 'em. That very minute. With all I've got and can get. But meanwhile you have to lay low and be quiet. You're making a damned fool of yourself. It would kill your daddy if he knew you were running around town looking like a wild man and yelling about poisoned water up in the woods."

Tom looked at him narrowly out of his haunted eyes.

"No, he wouldn't. He'd be doing the same thing," he said. "I saw the fish, Clay. I buried the deer. I shot that goat. I read that report. And I saw that water. Clay . . . it's the woods. The *woods*. Have you forgotten what the woods mean?"

Clay Dabney looked at him for a time, and then sighed heavily.

"I guess I have, in a way, Tom," he said. "It's a hard thing to keep alive, a hard thing to live up to. . . . But I know what you mean. You're right about your dad. And you have my promise about going after them if my man finds anything out there. I'll be right behind you. Deal?"

"Deal," Tom said, and walked out of Clay's office and went home to Goat Creek.

After that the furor subsided a bit, but Tom did not forget it. He kept his promise to Clay to keep quiet until the engineer could be found and make his tests, but it ate at him like a malignancy. He grew silent and hollow-eyed, and no longer hunted or fished or went out into the woods, and he did not come into town. He missed many of his summer classes at Pemberton State, and when he needed provisions he bought them at a meager convenience store on the road out past King's Oak. He shut himself up in the house on Goat Creek with his tapes of Beethoven and Wagner and endless books and pamphlets on nuclear waste that Reese Carmody got for him through the Savannah chapter of Physicians for Social Responsibility. His lights often burned all night. When Reese and Martin Longstreet went to Goat Creek to see him, he did not ask them in. Scratch was the only one he allowed in the house, and Scratch did not come often. Scratch was weakening by the day, and still refusing to let anyone take him to a doctor.

"I be okay as soon as I gits some business tended to," he said over and over. They did not know what that business was, but they knew that Scratch spent as much time alone in the woods as he could manage. Sometimes, his daughter told them, he was gone overnight. When he returned he could do nothing but lie in bed, gathering strength for the next time.

There were more fish kills. Reese saw them, lying along the creek. He buried them silently, but there were no more cleansing rituals in the Big Silver Swamp. Scratch was past that now, and Tom seemed oddly disinterested, abstracted. Reese and Martin did not even attempt them alone. Several of the goats were sick, too. Tom did not take them to the vet. He treated them himself, dosing them with herbs and bark potions he found in the woods and brewed himself. His hair was growing long and wild, and the once-elegant Vandyke was ragged.

All this I learned from Reese Carmody, more than a week after Tom's talk with Clay Dabney. He appeared at my door one thick, still twilight in late June, to ask me if I would go myself and see what I could do for Tom.

"It's as if he's just pulling away from the world and going all the way to the wild," he said. For the first time since I had known him, his words were more than slightly slurred, and there was the acrid odor of alcohol on his breath.

"He needs you, Andy," Reese said. "He won't let us near him, but I think he would you. He's out there starting to die of something. I don't know what it is exactly. It's the woods and the water, of course, and worry over Scratch is part of it. And I know lonesomeness must be. Lonesomeness for you and Hilary, I think. I'm afraid he's just going to . . . lose it. I know something has happened between you, but you must know what you are to him. Can't you go out there? Just to see what's going on, just this one time?"

"I can't," I said, the fatigue so great that the words came out without breath behind them. "I can't, Reese. I . . . it's dangerous out there. He's right about the water. And Tom . . . has gone beyond where I can follow. I have a child, you know. I'm not free to follow Tom off inside his head somewhere."

"Andy . . . you are one of us," he said. There were tears, the easy tears of alcohol, but of grief, too, in the mild eyes behind the mended glasses. "You did the ceremony, you know it all, you're part of the woods, too, you believe—"

I began to cry, surprising myself.

"No," I sobbed. "I don't believe. It was Tom I believed in, not the woods. Not . . . all that. It was Tom. And now he's gone . . . away from me, and the woods are sick and the water is on fire and my daughter is hurt in her heart and if she's hurt one more time she'll die from it. One more time, Reese! Reese, all he taught her, about the woods and the animals and the water, all of that—all that she learned from him to love more than anything else, that she gave up everything else in her life for, that she gave up her *childhood* for—Reese, don't you see: all that was *false!* It was all a *lie!* The woods aren't clean, the animals die, the water kills. . . ."

I stopped crying and took a deep breath and prayed silently for the blanketing fatigue to come back. It did.

"So you see why I can't go," I said. "You see why you can't ask me to do that."

"I see," Reese said. "You're wrong, Andy; it isn't the

woods and the water that are false; it's something else. . . . But I see. I won't ask you again. But if you find you can change your mind, please . . . let me just ask you one thing. Do you love Tom?"

"Yes," I said. "But it doesn't make any difference."

"If it doesn't, then nothing does," Reese said, and went away.

"Then nothing does," I said into the air of the empty living room. But I knew as I said it that that was not true. Hilary made a difference, Hilary made all the difference, and Hilary was no longer anyone I knew.

Before, when Tom and I had had the fight and I had thought myself done with him, before the birthday party, Hilary had been like a lamp with the light turned off. The illumination was gone, but still the lamp was whole. Instead of the tantrums and hysteria and regression that had marked the beginning of our time in Pemberton, she had become withdrawn and distant and preoccupied, but then she had moved through her full days dutifully if with the air of one biding time until she could take up her real life again. She had gone to school and gone back to her riding with Pat Dabney; she had been docile and pleasant and self-contained.

"Maybe she's just growing up," Tish had said. "They do, you know."

What she had been doing, of course, was waiting for her life with Tom to resume. When it had, the night of the birthday party, she had burned like a flame in the wind. The joy and beauty of her smote the eye and heart. And then had come the glowing creek and the convulsing kid, and she had watched Tom Dabney come down the steps of the house on Goat Creek and shoot her beloved Missy dead with a rifle.

And the silence had begun, ending only in terror at my terror, and tears at my tears. And ever since, Hilary had been as inert and flaccid as a puppet whose strings have been cut. She spoke when spoken to, but in as few words as possible. She would drink only the bottled water and would take only sponge baths in water that had been boiled. She ate when you put food on her plate, and drank her milk, and she went to her summer classes at Pemberton Day, but she absolutely refused to go back to the Dabney stables, or to the myriad parties and outings that occupied the young of Pemberton in the summer. She would go with me to Tish and Charlie's, but she would not swim in their pool, and went silently into their den and turned on the television set when we got there. If we came into the room with her, she did not talk with us. At home, except for mealtime, she spent her time in her room, with the door only slightly ajar. I knew that most of the time she was writing in the notebooks, writing steadily and with a concentration that was altogether adult and more than a little frightening, but she did not show me what she wrote, and I did not ask her. She never spoke Tom's name.

"I think it's called lack of affect," Tish said once during those first weeks, when she came by with an armful of rowdy zinnias and an invitation to supper. I accepted the zinnias and refused the invitation.

"I just can't make her do it, Tish," I said dully. "This lethargy thing is like quicksand. She can't seem to move. I'm just not up to a battle every time I want to take her somewhere. It's easier to stay home."

"Easier for who?" Tish said, looking narrowly at me. "You look like you've been in a dungeon for months. You look like you just got out of Auschwitz. Have you looked into a mirror lately? Do you realize that you're thinner than

I've ever seen you? *When* I see you, that is. Look, Andy, I'm not going to go on about this, but a fool can see that this business about Tom is killing both of you, and Charlie and I are at our wits' end to know what to do to help you. I don't blame you; he's been acting like an escaped lunatic, and I can't think what in the world has gotten into him, but the deepest part of me knows Tom Dabney is not crazy, and you must know that, too. You of all people. And I don't think you give a damn if people are talking about him; when did you? Maybe this—staying away from him, not seeing him—is not the way to go. Maybe if you'd go back to him, or at least go see what's going on with him, it would do you all good."

"No," I said, and something in my voice made her drop it.

"Well, then maybe one day you'll tell me what it's really all about," she said in a low, troubled voice. "Until then, I won't bug you. But I'm still going to worry. And I can't keep quiet about Hilary. I love her like my own; you'll just have to run me off if you don't want me to nag you about her. You're going to have to get some help for her. You have to get her to a good shrink. There's one in Waycross, a new guy; I hear he's absolutely marvelous with kids."

"We saw him last Tuesday," I said. "His name is Harper. Frick Harper. He wants his patients to call him Frick. I liked him. I don't know how Hil feels about him. But at least she went, and she talked to him, which is more than she does to me. I don't know what about, but he seems to think she'll eventually be okay. He has her on a new antidepressant that doesn't have many side effects, and he says once it kicks in, in about three weeks, she'll start to improve. He said the silent treatment was fairly standard for the kind of trauma she's been through in the last year, and the water thing is understandable, and the writing is actually good therapy. Let her do all she wants of it, says ol' Frick. It's one of the things he suggests for depression."

"Did you tell him everything?" Tish said cautiously. "About . . . how Tom is now, what he's saying and doing?"

Not everything, I said silently. Not about wildness and rapture and sacrifices and dancing naked. Not about arrows in bleeding piglets. Not about water that burns and kills. No, Tish. Not everything.

"I told him about Tom," I said. "He said it's especially hard for a child who's been cut loose from all her stability once before to see . . . aberrant behavior—I think was the term—in someone she has finally learned to trust. Stability and quiet are the ticket now. He suggested it would not be such a good idea for her to be around Tom. In fact, he said it would be disastrous. And I quote."

"Well, he's the doctor," she said doubtfully. "But I still don't think Tom is crazy. And nothing can convince me he's dangerous."

"Tish, he's been to jail," I said. "He goes around ranting like a madman on TV. He almost knocked Francis Millican down."

But I saw the water burn; I saw.

"Knocking Francis Millican down is crazy?" Tish grinned. "Look, I know he's *acting* crazy. I just don't think he *is* crazy. And I know how you were before, with him, you and Hil, and I see how you are now. . . . Okay. I'm finished. I'm out the door. But, Andy, if Charlie and I can help . . ."

"I know," I said, feeling a lump rise in my throat. "I love you, Tish."

I went to her and hugged her, and she hugged me silently, and was gone, shutting the burning day out behind her.

I went into Hilary's room. She was asleep on the rumpled bed, the television squalling softly and mindlessly, her notebook open on the spread beside her. In the dim green light she looked very frail and thin and almost ghostly; the fancy came to me that there was something fey about her, something that would soon fade and be gone. The words "Anne Frank" formed in my mind from nowhere. I was suddenly very cold. I reached down to touch her arm, shake her awake, and then drew back. Her breath was coming deeply and evenly, and her chest rose and fell sturdily. I looked down at the notebook; its pages were covered in her close, small hand, and I could not read what was on it. The pages were near the end of the notebook, and the notebook was thick. Gently I turned it over so that I could see the cover; many more thickly written pages riffled past as I did. On the cover Hilary had written in swooping, ornate strokes of black Magic Marker, a creditable attempt at calligraphy. *The True Story of Tom Dabney*.

I went back into the living room and lay down on the sofa and cried for a long time. It is what I remember most about that summer: endless, unstoppable tears. Tears that quenched no sorrow and eased no pain.

The engineer Clay Dabney promised duly appeared early the next week.

"I met him at the Inn," Tish reported with relish. "His name is Tim Ford, and he's a big ol' raw-boned, redheaded boy from east Tennessee with a hillbilly drawl and shoulders that would fill up my guest bathroom. His blue jeans were dirty and he had on lace-up clodhoppers and he wears a slide rule on his belt. Jesus, I haven't seen that since college; I thought they used computers now. His nose and his smile are crooked, and he looks sort of like Gary Cooper in

The Fountainhead, and I almost grabbed him and rushed him right over here to give you a little therapy. What a hunk! But then I thought he'd just be wasted on you, seeing as how you're practically in purdah, so I decided that maybe he could give me a little therapy. But then he said something about his wife over at Auburn, a little lady by the name of Earline, so I desisted. I'm not about to take on an Earline."

"He sounds more like Li'l Abner than Howard Roark," I said, smiling in spite of myself. "Thanks a lot for thinking of me. He sounds just my type."

"He's a lot like Tom, I think," she said, and she was not smiling. "Not physically, but there's something there, some kind of rightness in his skin, some kind of rock under the affability. I think Tom will trust this man."

"What are his credentials?" I asked quickly. I did not want to dwell on Tom Dabney. And I did not want to meet this redheaded stranger who reminded Tish of him.

"Oh, the best, no doubt about it," Tish said. "He's attached to some kind of water research institute that's a model for the whole country, Clay said, and he's on the civil engineering faculty at Auburn. They've pioneered a new technique for testing groundwater and aquifers and things: they inject something called tracers into the earth that holds the aquifers and it tells them what's in there, and how much, and sometimes how it got there. I *think.* It's supposed to be a whole lot more accurate than even the best we've got around here. This guy may look like Li'l Abner, but I gather he's no dummy."

"Well, more power to him," I said. "I hope to God he can clear this up. It's just a nightmare."

She peered at me. "Don't tell me you think there's really something the matter out at the plant."

I could not look at her. The burning water was dim and flat in my mind, more like an old memory now than an image. But I had seen it; I had seen . . . hadn't I? Hadn't Hilary? Hadn't a little goat sickened and convulsed, and died before our eyes? The quality of a dream was thick and heavy around me. I could not seem to fight through it to clear air.

"I don't think Tom lies," I said.

"No, but he's as prone to mistakes and imaginings and hangovers as anybody else. And it all started the morning after the party. If that wasn't a morning for hallucinations there'll never be one. Andy, I said I wouldn't pry into whatever's gone wrong between you, but I wish you'd tell me: did he say what makes him think the plant is polluting the Big Silver?"

So insistent was the dreamlike fugue state around me that I was able to look directly at Tish and say, "He never said a single word."

And he had not. Not when he shot the goat, not when I jerked my screaming daughter out of the flickering water, not when I rushed her inside and brought her back out wrapped in a blanket and thrust her into the Toyota. Not when I drove away from there in the brightening morning. Not a word.

But I had looked back. Just once. And seen the face of a man sliding over the edge of the world.

"Not a word," I repeated to Tish. "But if he thinks there's something the matter with the water, I'm going to drink bottled water until this miracle man tells me it's okay. And you should, too. You said yourself Tom wasn't crazy."

"Yes, I did. It was you who seemed to think he was. It's you who won't go near him. And now you're saying you think he might be right."

"Oh, Tish, just drop it, *please!*" I said, the tears beginning to rise up my throat again. "I just can't handle this right now."

"I'm sorry, sweetie," she said contritely. "This time tomorrow it'll all be over and things will have settled down. You'll see. I'll let you know what Li'l Abner finds. It's going to be good news, I know it is."

But by that time the next day it wasn't over. It was good news we got from Tim Ford, but the nightmare was not over. With the blessings of the Big Silver management, Tim Ford went onto the Big Silver site and stayed there twenty-four hours. He went alone; Francis Millican was showily insistent on that. Security was told to let him go wherever he wanted. He took a jeep and a dog and a Georgia Department of Natural Resources geological survey map and a field-testing kit with him and covered the entire three hundred square miles of the property. He tested the water from every spilloff creek leading out of the property into the Big Silver River and Goat Creek. He missed no sluice, rivulet, spring, pond, or creek. He took core samples from far down into the sand that held the Tuscumbia Aquifer. He even took a sample from the Big Silver River itself, though it would have been impossible for the river to be contaminated if the spill-off streams in the Big Silver were not. He found nothing.

"Clean as a baby's breath," he told Clay Dabney that night. "Or at least way below the levels the government calls acceptable. Lower than any other inactive hazardous-waste site we've tested, and we've done most of 'em over the years. I was surprised. I went through most of the plant area, too; even though I'm not a nuclear engineer, I could tell some of the equipment was held together with chewing gum and baling wire, and some of it was inoperative. I tell you, I wouldn't work in that place for a million bucks a month. But the water's clean. I went back and checked again after I saw the plant facilities."

"Thank God," Clay Dabney said simply and profoundly.

"I told you," Tish said to me on the phone that night.

"I don't believe that," Tom said, when Clay telephoned him.

"Tom, we had a deal," his uncle said in alarm.

"We had a deal and I'll honor it until I can't anymore, Uncle Clay," Tom said. "But I saw that water and those sick and dead animals, and three of my goats are sick now. I don't believe that water is clean."

"Then God help you, son, because I can't anymore," Clay Dabney said in sorrow.

"I know," Tom said. "I know you can't. I hope He can."

Tom honored his word to Clay for eight more days. On the eighth day he went out into the woods, up Goat Creek, for the first time since the night of the birthday party. Four miles upstream he found a dead six-month-old doe, so hideously deformed that it was scarcely recognizable as a whitetail, lying beside its dying mother. The older doe was covered with the same open sores and bulging tumors we had seen that morning much earlier, when I had first seen in Tom the seeds of limitlessness.

Martin Longstreet told me about it. I had not seen him all summer and thought perhaps he was off on one of his sabbaticals to Greece or Italy or some other font of classical nourishment. But he told me, when he came into my office at the end of a workday and sat down on my lone visitor's chair, that he had been at the college all summer.

"I wish you had come by sooner," I said. "I thought you were probably out of the country."

He smiled. He did not look well. He had lost weight, and his face, once pink and full, now hung in dewlaps under his chin. A silvery stubble frosted it, like rime ice on a washed gully. His eyes were tired and dark-circled.

"I wanted to come," he said. "Tom said to let you be."

"Did he tell you what happened?" I said. My mouth and throat were dry.

"About the water? Yes. Not that you had seen it, too. But I gather from your . . . absence from us that you did."

"Yes," I said. "And Hilary saw it, too. I hope you're not going to ask me to go back out there, Martin. I hope you can see why I can't."

"Yes, I can see," he said. "And no, I'm not. I don't think you should go back to Goat Creek until . . . things are settled one way or another. I should worry terribly if you did."

"Then you still think the water is dangerous?"

"Oh, yes," he said, and told me about the dead and dying deer.

"Oh, God," I said softly, thinking of that earlier, awful scene on the banks of Goat Creek, of the doe Tom had shot. "Oh, Tom . . . Martin, what is he going to do?"

He grinned widely. At that moment he did not look as badly as he had. There was a grim joy in the grin.

"He's going to mount a guerrilla campaign against the Big Silver plant," he said.

And he did. The next day teenagers and a few indigent blacks from the settlement far up Goat Creek appeared on the main streets of Pemberton, carrying picket signs saying: *Big Silver Is Killing You.* When Chief Harold Turbidy and his deputies shooed them away, they freely admitted that they had been hired by Tom Dabney.

"Well, don't let me catch you out here again," Harold said.

The next morning an entirely new platoon appeared, carrying the same signs.

When Harold Turbidy warned Tom that he would arrest the next group of protesters for unlawful assembly, Tom hired a small Cessna and a pilot from Waycross to fly over the downtown area every day at noon for the next three weeks. Its trailing banner said: *Big Silver Is Killing You*. Harold Turbidy could find no law that forbade unlawful assembly in the skies over Pemberton, and so the daily flyover persisted until the crowds that gathered to stare and point upward began to wane. Then Tom affixed the same signs to his truck and circled the downtown streets each afternoon after school. Harold could not forbid that, either, and Tom kept at it until someone let all the air out of his tires in the school parking lot one day, and took what appeared to be an ax handle to the truck's cab. But he did not abandon the campaign. He simply found new tactics. Effigies of Francis Millican and various government and Stratton-Fournier officials cropped up on the lawns of City Hall, the Episcopal church, the country club, and the Inn, each bearing a sign that said: *Big Silver Is Killing You*. No one saw them being erected; when Harold approached Tom on the matter, Tom said, "Who, me? You know my truck's out of commission. Why don't you just run 'em on in, Harold? There's always been room at your place for dummies."

Harold grew purple and the accompanying deputy buried a snicker in his hand. Tom came within a hair of being arrested for insulting an officer, but not even Harold could truly find an insult in the mild words. Reese Carmody was counseling Tom carefully; he always, through the entire campaign, stayed just a shade inside the city and county ordinances. The deputy talked, and the story of Harold Turbidy's fearless arrest of the effigies made the rounds of Pemberton, which in any case was, by now, focused to a man on the war between Tom and the Big Silver. A great many people were disturbed and not a few were very angry, and I knew that there was a group in town, headed by an outraged Francis Millican and his faithful sidekick, Chip Dabney, who were actively searching for grounds on which to have Tom arrested. But there was laughter in those days, too, and much of it was, I knew, tinged with admiration and even affection. Tom had always had a large hold on Pemberton's imagination. And there were some people whose doubts about the Big Silver had not faded away, only submerged. Tom's antic war brought them bobbling to the surface like corks. He was never without a few allies; they were simply not effectual ones, or vocal. And none were rich.

And so the effigies bearing their signs continued to appear, as fast as Harold Turbidy could get them taken down. But by midsummer Tom had begun to slide over into darkness. And the laughter slowed and stopped.

He began to patrol the boundary fence of the Big Silver where it touched his property, night after night, until dawn, wearing a strange costume of his own devising. It consisted of a camouflage hunting shirt, hunting pants, deerhide moccasins, a black band around his arm, and a garland of oak leaves on his head. He carried one of his willow bows and a quiver of arrows, and strapped to his leg was one of the wicked hooked hunting knives that habitually hung on the chimney of the house at Goat Creek. He came within inches of the boundary fence, but he never touched it. Once, a small security patrol, on foot and with dogs, came face-to-face with him in the dark, and the men stood staring at each other, frozen, until Tom gave a little salute and moved silently off into the woods. He was, the unnerved patrol said, striped and dabbled over his face and chest with what looked to be fresh blood. That story made the rounds in Pemberton as swiftly as the one about Harold Turbidy had, and this time people looked at each other uneasily. They stopped saluting Tom cheerfully on the few occasions when he came into Pemberton, and the next time he appeared after that night meeting at the boundary, they simply stared. Tom had grown gaunt, hollow-cheeked, disheveled, glittering-eyed. His hair had not been cut in weeks and fell over his forehead and ears, and his beard was nearly full.

"He looked like something out of *The Leatherstocking Tales,*" Tish said, after seeing him leaving the hardware store. "Or, no . . . you remember reading *The Devil and Daniel Webster* when you were a kid, the part about the ghosts of all the evil men coming in to sit as a jury? There was something about a frontier murderer, a man who walked like a cat, stained with blood. . . ."

"Oh, Tish, don't!" I cried spontaneously.

"That was an exaggeration," she said hastily. "But he looks awful. Everybody's talking. I'm afraid for him now, Andy."

I, too, was afraid, and appalled and overwhelmed with a kind of premonitory heaviness, a bad, dense thing that smelled and tasted of inexorability. There was something abroad in Pemberton. Something still quite far away, but unalterably focused and aimed, that seemed to be gathering speed and mass like a snowball rocketing down a hill. I had the dull and hopeless sense that it would smash my child and me along with Tom and whatever else got in its path. I went to work and Hilary went to school, but we stopped going out to the movies or for pizza or to Tish and Charlie's, and I began to do my errands at night, at one of the suburban malls that stayed open late.

"Cooler," I said to Hilary, and she nodded.

"You okay?" I said.

"Yeah," she said, and went back into her room and took up her writing again. She was on her second fat notebook now. I did not wonder. The True Story of Tom Dabney was not a simple one. I wondered if she wrote about the times up until now—the woods, the animals, what we did together, the old magic in the forest—or if she recorded the sorry and frightening present. I hoped she was relatively unaware of that; it was so that she would not have to see Tom that I had curtailed our outings, and changed my shopping hours. But avoidance was difficult. A good chunk of the world knew about Tom Dabney now.

His mountebank's war attracted the attention of the media, where his sober and heartfelt warnings had not. The Wild Man of Goat Creek and his one-man campaign against the Big Silver plant became the stuff of breakfast and evening sniggers all over the state and even out of it. In Pemberton, it was the stuff of outrage. For with the media attention had come the enforced attention of official eyes: anonymous suited-and-tied men in sober sedans from virtually every agency bearing initials—the DOE, the DNR, the NRC, the EPA, the CDC, the FBI, the GBI—came and went at the Big Silver as if through revolving doors. The usual protesters set up outside the gates and in the parks in Pemberton proper, joined by new groups from across the country. Cameras and camcorders pointed their blind eyes at official and citizen alike, and tracked Tom whenever he put his head out of his door. He never refused an interview. After inadvertently watching the first one on television, I simply stopped turning on the news. The face and voice that I had so loved were someone else's now, and that someone frightened and horrified me. He was not, I did not think, a sane man.

Rumors circulated that the Department of Energy would be closing the Big Silver in the autumn. Talk about Tom turned to uproar. I was dully unsurprised to hear, in mid-July, that he had been put on indefinite leave by the English Department, on medical grounds. I began to hear talk that a move was afoot to have him involuntarily committed to a psychiatric facility, and that Chip Dabney was spearheading the attempt, but then I heard that a grim, gray-faced Clay Dabney had told Chip he would disinherit him if he did not shut up, and gradually the commitment talk simmered down. No one could have done it, in any event, but his Uncle Clay or his mother, and I knew that the former would never do it, and the latter was too mortified and coldly appalled to attempt it. I did not know what would happen, either to Tom or to Pemberton. Or, for that matter, to Clay Dabney, who had worn himself and his welcome in the town extremely thin in his attempts to keep his nephew out of jail or a mental facility. I saw Clay once, at a distance, going into the drugstore. He looked like a man with an advanced wasting illness.

Oh, Tom, how can you possibly think it's still worth it? I said silently.

Tish told me, sorrowfully, that he had become a ghastly parody of himself, a ragged, obsessed laughingstock. He was coming into town almost every day now, walking the downtown streets, mumbling to himself on the sunny sidewalks of the city to which he had laid siege. By now, she said, all of his allies except Clay Dabney were gone. Martin Longstreet had retreated back into his Frazer and his herbal teas and his little apartment and his bleak silences, his own job said to be in jeopardy. Reese Carmody drifted gently in a Stolichnaya bottle. Tom's mother and sister would not speak of him. Scratch Purvis, Tish heard from Scratch's daughter, who was serving canapés at a League tea Tish attended, hardly ever left his bed in the cabin up Goat Creek now.

"Is there anything he needs?" Tish had asked.

"No'm, he don't need nothin' except to die. He tired. He ready to go on now. But it looks like he just ain't gon' let himself go yet; say he got somethin' left to do."

"What?" Tish asked.

"He don't say," his daughter said. "Daddy don't talk much."

I felt a dull, sick grief. Scratch had talked much and wonderfully to me, and even more to Hilary. I did not think I could bear for her to hear how ill he was. But she did not ask about Scratch. She never had.

One night, when Hilary and I had gone out to the Shop 'N Save in the shabby little mall near Pemberton State for groceries, we saw Tom. I felt rather than saw Hilary go still—actually felt her breath stop in my own chest—and looked up slowly and in profound dread. Somehow I knew that he would be there.

He stood on the other side of the low row of shelving, holding a carton of milk in his hand. He was looking at Hilary, and then he raised his eyes and looked at me. It was like looking into the eyes of a dead man come to life, or a holograph: unreal, eerie, affectless. He was thin to gauntness, and his hair and beard, though combed and clean, were close to the fabric of his shirt on his shoulders and chest. He looked like a man who had been in prison underground for a long, long time; his skin had lost its tan, and the black hair was lusterless and limp. His eyes were sunken.

And then he smiled, and the blue eyes leaped to life and were Tom's eyes and no other's, and I felt as if he had laid on me, suddenly, the warm, strong pressure of his hands and mouth.

He did not speak, but his smile widened into a grin, and he looked back at Hilary and winked. He lifted his hand and made the old symbol of "OK" with his thumb and index finger, a jaunty circle. And then he turned and padded away toward the cashier's desk with the catlike tread I felt physically in my own legs and hips. I simply stood there with Hilary's hand in mine, ears ringing, heart pounding, until I heard the automatic door open and close, and then I paid for my purchases and we got into the car and shut the doors. Only then did I look at Hilary.

Her face was white and still, and she looked straight ahead, blindly. She did not turn her face to me. I thought she looked like a mummy of a child, dry and bloodless and very, very old. Perhaps she was, in some dreadful, spiritual way. Rage at Tom burst over me and then receded, as quickly as it had come. I was simply too tired to sustain rage.

"Tom didn't look so bad at all, did he?" I said to the cold white profile.

She did not turn. "He looked awful," she said remotely. "Like he's sick. He's probably going to die."

"Oh, Hil, of course not . . . ," I began.

She turned and looked at me, and in her dead, level stare I saw, for the first time, something of Chris, something that had looked out of his eyes in the worst of the bad times.

"I'm not going to talk about this anymore," she said.

We were silent until we reached the outskirts of Pemberton, and then she said, "You forgot to get water."

"Well . . . we don't need to drink bottled water now,

do we? I mean, Mr. Ford is the best expert there is, and he tested everything twice, and said the water was absolutely fine. You know, I told you. You saw it on TV."

She looked at me with the flat, clenched gaze again, and I felt myself redden. I had seen that livid, consuming water, too. I had snatched her away from it, lifted her bodily and run with her, away from Goat Creek and virtually all of what she loved in the world. And kept her away . . . And now I was asking her to disbelieve her own senses, and the one human being who still validated them, and put her trust in those whose words denied her very eyes and ears. I fell silent. I thought, on the whole, that it was entirely honorable of her that she had said nothing about that before, and did not now. But her face said it, and her eyes. I pulled into a truck stop and bought the water.

On the way into Pemberton I stopped at Tish and Charlie's. Charlie was playing court tennis, but Tish made coffee and found half an angel food cake, and we sat at her kitchen table with it. Hilary took hers into the den. I waited until I heard the television set go on, and then I said:

"You know the other day when you said all Tom's allies had deserted him but Clay? Did you mean you and Charlie, too? He needs somebody, Tish. He needs somebody just to . . . stand with him. I didn't think so, but I do now. It could make all the difference to him. It might even help him . . . stop all this. It can't be me, but it could be you all. Just talk to him, anyway. . . ."

I watched Tish's plain, good face as the light went out of it and tears came into her eyes, and I knew she was not going to reach out to Tom. Presently she said, "I can't. I've been scared to death you'd ask me. I know it's rotten of me, but there it is. He scares the shit out of me now. I hate myself for it, but I know it's true. I always loved thinking of myself as a fierce liberal, a committed enemy of injustice, an unshakably loyal friend. I was the one who was always able to see the . . . the saintliness of Tom, to endorse every wild, outrageous thing he said or did. I thought of myself as living in his world; I thought that his kind of . . . eccentric, one-sided goodness was the only way to make a difference in the world for . . . oh, mankind. I thought he and I were kin. But as soon as goodness turns to madness it loses me, because I lose any kind of world I could make a difference in. I'm just too normal, in the last analysis. I have to have rules and a context, even if they're outrageous, scandalous rules. Tom has gone beyond rules."

And I went away knowing that she was right, and that he had. I waited for the next thing he would do as you wait for an inevitable death, one diagnosed long before. It came two mornings later, when he drove into Pemberton at first light and lovingly laid the bodies of his sick goats, which he had carefully and ritually slain, on the doorsteps of the mayor, the presidents of the Rotary, the Civitan, and the Downtown Business Association, Francis Millican, and Harold Turbidy. The result was hysterical wives and children and a public outcry that was heard to Savannah, Atlanta, Waycross, Valdosta, Jacksonville, and Tallahassee. The overjoyed media of those cities arrived just in time to film Tom Dabney, in his bizarre night patrol dress and blood-striped face, being wrestled into a Pemberton black-and-white and taken once more to jail.

CHAPTER FOURTEEN

The next night Clay Dabney and old Caroline came to see me. I answered the knock at the door expecting to see Tish, and found myself instead looking into two faces that were and were not Tom—blue-eyed, long-chinned, strong-boned. But these faces were old, one slack and stained with trouble, the other a mask of social pleasantries painted on crazed ivory porcelain. I stared mindlessly for a moment, and then opened the door to them. I knew why they had come. On some level I had been waiting for them. Or, at least, for Clay. Caroline Dabney in my house was as alien and askew as an old show peacock in a cattle pen.

They declined coffee or a drink, and settled into the chairs I indicated for them. My heart was pounding light and fast, and my hands were icy. I wondered, idiotically, what they would do if I simply said to them, "I want you to leave." Probably they would have done so. I sat on the sofa in the low light from the two flanking lamps and looked at them. Clay did not look at me at first, but at his hands, clasped loosely together on his knees as if in prayer. Caroline Dabney's avian eyes swept my living room, assessing and cataloguing furniture and bibelots as an appraiser might have. I thought that she was probably not even aware she was doing it.

She smiled at me. Red lipstick leaked crazily up the fissures around her mouth, as if she had been eating flesh. The carved hair shone like spun glass.

"You've done a lot with this dark old place," she said in her dying-flute voice. "Honey Livingston never could quite figure out how to handle it. Not surprising, of course, when you think that after all she started out as a trainer's daughter, and lived over the stable for years before . . . well, anyway. This is charming. Very modern. You young girls take such adventurous *chances* with your homes, but it's all fun and sweet, isn't it?"

I stared at her in fascination. Between us lay pain, lies, gossip, ostracism; between her and her son lay enormities of betrayal; and yet she chirped of decorating and lineages. She was so precisely like most of the older women I had known in Chris Calhoun's world, back in Atlanta, that I answered automatically out of those days: "Thank you, Miss Caroline. We like it."

Clay Dabney shot his sister-in-law a look. He cleared his throat and began, "Miss Andy, I expect you know we've come to talk to you about Tom . . . ," and I started, entirely unconsciously, to shake my head.

He held up a big walnut hand. "Please, just hear me out. After that, if you want to sling us out of here on our behinds, I'll go quietly. But please listen."

I looked over at Miss Caroline. She sat staring straight ahead, smiling, as if waiting for a passport photo to be taken. I turned back to Clay Dabney. "I'm sorry. Please go ahead." Across the miles and years to Sally Calhoun, I said silently, "You taught me well."

"He's in a bad spot," Clay Dabney said heavily. "I don't know if he can get out of it, or if anybody can get him out, but if anyone can, it's you. Harold Turbidy has a court order to get him committed for psychiatric evaluation, and he says he's not going to have any trouble at all finding a shrink who'll swear he's a danger to himself and others, and that'll mean being put away for a long, long time."

"But he's no *danger* . . . ," I began.

"Headshrinkers don't make much in these parts," Clay said grimly. "Wouldn't take a lot to find one who'd see Harold's point."

"But who would do such a horrible thing?" I said, and by the time Clay's dead smile had finished forming, I knew. Francis Millican's wintry gray face, on the day Chip had brought him and the loathsome Prince Willi out to Goat Creek, shimmered in the air before me as in a holograph.

"I see," I said.

"I hope you don't, but it don't matter," Clay Dabney said. "Harold said it was either the state hospital up at Milledgeville or jail; Tom could take his pick. He has a restraining order already signed, and if Tom so much as pokes his head past the city limits once it's served, he'll be in jail for contempt until he's too old to lift a bow. And if that don't work, Harold's got three or four women ready to swear to grievous mental harm from them dead goats, and one that says she had a heart attack, and another one that says she suffered a miscarriage."

Sickness flooded me. "Who could possibly hate him

that much?" I whispered. "Why isn't it enough just to . . . make him stop?"

Clay did not answer, and in the silence a monstrous thing was born in my mind, and grew to vivid certainty. I saw, behind the faces of Francis Millican and Prince Willi at Goat Creek, the furious, affable smile of Chip Dabney. I did not speak, but I saw Clay Dabney see his son in my eyes, and saw the anguish in his own eyes before he dropped them to his hard, speckled hands.

"Harold says he'll let him off one more time if he'll sign a statement that he'll stop. But Tom won't do that," he said. "I've told him everything Harold said. I've begged him till my voice just went. His mama has begged him. I've even thought of gettin' his boys down here to beg him, but I just can't do that kind of slimy thing to him; besides, he says he's doin' this partly for them. Says the minute Harold lets him out of there he's going home and kill the rest of the goats. Lots of 'em dyin', anyway. Says Harold and . . . the others ain't gon' know there was that many dead goats in the world."

I shut my eyes in pain and tiredness. I wished, simply, that I could get up and go into my bedroom and climb into bed and pull the spread over my head and sleep forever. I would do that, the minute these two people left my house.

"I can't help you," I said. "Tom isn't going to listen to me any more than he would to you. I can't. I can't help you."

"He said he'd talk to you," Clay Dabney said. "He didn't say he'd listen to you, but he said he'd like to talk to you. He won't see anybody else now. You're the last hope he's got. I wouldn't be here if you weren't. I know . . . you and Miss Hilary been hurt somehow. I can imagine it was pretty bad."

"Before God, I cannot do it," I said. My eyes were still

closed. If Clay Dabney said one more word, I was going to begin to scream like a madwoman.

There was a thick and terrible silence, and then, incredibly, I heard the weak, mewling sound that is weeping in the very young, or the very old. I opened my eyes and looked at Caroline Dabney. She still faced straight ahead, but her eyes were screwed shut and her mouth was open in the square, hopeless grimace of a child's uncontrollable grief. Mascara-blackened runnels scored her old cheeks like runoff from dirty snow, and her face, dead white and splotched with purple, looked as if someone had slapped it. The perfect, shining hair rode her head oddly and horribly, and I realized suddenly that it was a wig. She struggled so for breath that I thought she would die. Then she found it and drew it deeply into her lungs. I heard her chest wheeze.

She opened her eyes and looked at me. I do not think she saw me.

"He was the best little boy," she said. It was a tiny, piping singsong. The black tears flowed on. "He was always writing things. He wrote me a poem once, for Mother's Day. I had it framed; I still have it. And his merit badges. He got all the merit badges, one right after another. You ought to see his merit badges. . . ."

I felt tears start down my own face. I looked at Clay Dabney; his eyes were wet, too. I knew then that I would go. We would bleed to death of tears, we three, if I did not.

"In the morning," I said. "As soon as I can get Hilary to school. She's asleep; I can't leave her alone."

"If you would go tonight, I think Caroline would be glad to stay here with her," Clay Dabney said. "I'll take you over to the jail and wait for you. Or if you'd rather, I'll stay here with Caroline."

"You don't have any reason to trust me, I know," Caroline Dabney said, and under the tears there was a kind of strength in the frail voice. "But I've sat with more than one child in my time. And if she wakes up, I'll just tell her I'm Tom's mother. Wouldn't that ease her mind?"

I knew it would. "Let's go, then," I said to Clay. "There isn't anything on earth I'm going to be able to say to Tom, but you'll have to see that for yourselves. And then . . . please: don't ask me again. Don't do that to us."

"Not ever again," Clay Dabney said. "We'll owe you too much for that."

The Baines County Jail sat on a side street off Palmetto, and wore the same rich, age-stained bricks and discreet brass plaque as the Palmetto Street shops.

"Where's the jockey?" I said to Clay Dabney. I had willed my mind to go white and calm, and it had.

Surprisingly, he chuckled. "There was one, until Harold hired a black deputy. Then even Harold could see that it had to go. I think he took it home and put it up in his own front yard. Lord God, Miss Andy, I wish things could have worked out for you and Tom. You're the only lady I've ever seen was a match for him."

"No," I said. "I never was that."

Harold Turbidy was not at the jail. Only the night deputy, the aforementioned black man, sat at the desk, reading a video rental catalogue. He got up out of his chair when we appeared, looking as if he did not know whether to challenge us or shake our hands.

"Evening, Elwood," Clay said. "Can Mrs. Calhoun here see Tom for a minute? I know it's after hours, but she's got a child asleep at home, and this is the only time she's got. I'll explain to Harold," he went on, as the deputy hesitated.

"He asked to see her," Clay added. "I think he's entitled to one visitor at a time, isn't that right?"

"Yessir," the man said. He opened a green metal door and shouted, "Hey, Tom. You got a visitor. You ask to see anybody?"

I heard Tom's voice in reply, but I could not hear what he said. The whiteness exploded in my mind, and pain and memories dived at me, shrieking and pecking like carrion birds.

"I guess you can go on back," the black man said. "You'll see him. Ain't nobody else in here right now."

Tom sat in a cell at the end of a short, mercilessly lit, spotlessly clean corridor smelling of antiseptic and old cigarette smoke. He did not wear jail clothes, but was still in his ridiculous ritual hunting dress. There was no blood on his face and hands, though, and no oak leaf garland. He looked like a captured lunatic, but a calm and clean one. In the midst of all the wild blackness of hair and beard, the blue eyes burned clear and steady. He smiled. Some of the old antic fire leaped in the air between us.

"Come into my parlor," he said in his soft, rich drawl. I don't know why I had thought his voice would have changed. He indicated a folding metal chair in the corridor, and I pulled it up to the bars and sat down, facing him. I could not think of anything to say. I could not think of anything at all. I just looked at him.

"Wanna buy a duck?" he said.

My breath came out on a gust of anger. "You can't go on with this," I said. "It's all over for you right now unless you stop this. Clay can't get you off this time. It's either the state funny farm or the county prison farm. Either way, you'll be locked up for years. You won't see the swamp or the woods or the creek until you're an old man. You can't help the . . . the woods where they'll put you. Martin and Reese can't do it without you. Scratch is terribly, terribly sick. Who's going to look after the woods if you're locked up? What will it take to get you to stop this?"

He looked at me for a long time without speaking. I looked back at him.

Finally he said, "Do you trust that Ford? That engineer who was down here running tests? Did you believe what he said?"

"Yes," I said. "I believe him. So does Clay. So does—"

"I only care whether you do," he said.

"Yes," I said. "I did and I do. I think he's a very good man, Tom."

"How can it be true?" he said softly, more to himself than to me. "I saw the water. I saw the test results." He lifted his eyes to me. "You saw them, too. . . ."

I leaned forward and looked into his face. "I saw something shining in the water. I saw a sick goat and my child screaming. But, Tom, I've been thinking . . . I've never seen phosphorus in water. . . . Tom, it's just so confusing. We'd just waked up, and we'd had a lot to drink the night before, and Hilary was screaming. Please think very carefully. Is it just possible that . . . you could have made a mistake? Isn't it just barely possible?"

"No," he said. "It isn't. And there was the lab report. . . ."

"I never saw that," I said. I hated the saying of it. "I never did and nobody else did, either."

There was another long silence.

"Do you think I made that up?" he said.

"No. But I wonder if by then you might not have been so tired, and so upset about the water and the goat and Hilary . . ."

"I didn't make it up and I didn't hallucinate it," he said. "It was in the water, and no matter what Millican did with it, it was on that paper. It doesn't matter a shit to me whether anybody else believes that, but I still wish you did."

"I want to," I said, and found that I did. "Listen . . . could it be coming from somewhere else besides the plant? From some business or some industry or something?"

"There isn't anything else that runs into Goat Creek but the Big Silver River, and there's nothing on the river for two hundred miles but the plant," Tom said. "The creek makes up above where the river runoff comes into it. That's King's Oak land. There's nothing up there but woods. Woods and that black settlement where Scratch lives."

"Could there be anything around the settlement? Like . . . oh, sewage, or bleach, or weedkiller, or something?" I knew I sounded ridiculous. He did not smile at me, though.

"No," he said. "Not with strontium and plutonium and cesium in it. It was probably cesium that lit the water up. It does that. I've read that the water in the pits where irradiated fuel and target rods from the Big Silver are sunk shines blue. They sink them in water so they can decay; it's the energy from the spent fuel and rods that lights it up."

I shook my head hopelessly. "Tim Ford tested all the water that could possibly get off the Big Silver property and into the river and creek," I said. "He didn't find . . . what was it? Cesium? He didn't find plutonium or strontium. He's the best there is, Tom. From what I hear, there isn't anybody in the country who could have done it any better."

"Can you get him back down here?" Tom said. I looked at him.

"Can you get him to come see me out at the creek, like tomorrow night or the next? I'll sign Harold's goddamned statement if Ford will come down here. I'll tell him I'll lay off for good. I'll sign it the minute you tell me Ford's on the way. You can tell Clay I'll sign it."

I was silent.

"It's the woods, Andy," Tom said.

"I'll try," I said slowly. "I'll do my best. I'll call him tonight, when I get home. I'll tell Clay. . . ."

"Don't tell him about Ford," Tom said. "Just tell him I'll sign the paper and that I promise there won't be any more trouble about the Big Silver. Just tell him that."

"Tom," I said. "What are you going to do?"

He got up and walked to the opposite wall of his cell, where a small, high barred window gave onto the alley behind the jail. He stood looking out it, into the hot night.

"Andy, I'm asking you to do this for me with no questions asked. None," he said, without turning. "It's the last thing I'll ever ask of you. If you can't do it, tell me now."

I felt the tears begin again, warm and tired and hateful.

"I would give anything in the world to be as . . . sure and focused and committed as you are," I said bleakly. "All my life I've been . . . unsimple. Confused, on the fence, mired down in facts and politeness and all the different sides of things. I wish I had your . . . Tish called it one-pointedness once."

" 'You are my especial patrons, and the patrons of all latecomers,' " Tom said slowly, in the voice he used when he was quoting. " '. . . of all who have a tedious journey to make to the truth, of all who are confused with knowledge and speculation, of all who through politeness make themselves partners in guilt, of all who stand in danger by reason of their talents.' "

He turned around and faced me and smiled.

" 'For His sake who did not reject your curious gifts, pray always for the learned, the oblique, the delicate,' " he said. " 'Let them not quite be forgotten at the Throne of God when the simple come into their kingdom.' "

I did not say anything, and his smile widened into a grin. "It's part of something Evelyn Waugh wrote. 'Helena's Prayer to the Three Magi.' I read it in his biography, a long time ago. I've always liked it. When I met you I thought of it again."

I put my face down into my hands. A hiccuping sob erupted through my fingers.

Tom came up to the bars and put his hand through them and touched my bare arm. He did not take hold of it, simply touched it, lightly and softly, and then took his hand away.

"I never in my life meant to hurt you," he said.

I rose and turned away and started down the corridor.

"I'm going to call Tim Ford," I said, struggling to control my voice. "If he can come, I'll leave word at the desk for you. I'll just say, 'Your appointment is confirmed,' or something like that. If he can't, I'll say it's been canceled."

I was nearly to the green metal door before I heard him say, "Thank you, Andy."

He said it very softly.

When we got back to Whimsy Road, Hilary was still asleep and Caroline Dabney, restored and smiling as graciously as if she were welcoming me into her own home, rose from the sofa with my old college copy of *Tropic of Cancer* open in her hand.

"I've always wanted to read this, but I thought I'd have to sneak off to Atlanta to a pornographic parlor to buy it," she said merrily. "Goodness, it's a long way from the Penrod stories, isn't it?"

I did not feel like playing any more of Caroline Dabney's delicately vicious pecking games that evening, and Clay Dabney apparently sensed it, because he said, "We'll say good night and go on, then, Miss Andy. Come on, Caroline, I left the motor running."

And he took her by the forearm and bore her out of my living room and down the porch steps before she could bridle or bat her lashes at him.

At the bottom of the steps, he turned and said, "There isn't any way the Dabneys can thank you for what you did tonight, or repay you," and before I could answer, he had Caroline Dabney in the car, the door shut firmly on her.

"Goodness, no," she trilled from the darkness.

"I meant that," he said, opening his own door and looking up at me. "We won't forget that. None of us will."

"I may not have done anything at all," I said. "Please don't thank me yet. He may not stop, Clay."

"But now he has the chance," Clay Dabney said, and got into the car and shut the door. I went back inside and looked in on Hilary; she slept still and quiet, on her stomach with her face pressed into the pillow and her hair flung out over it. I shut her door and went into my bedroom and sat down on the bed and looked for a time at the number Tom Dabney had given me to call. I never knew where he had gotten it.

I fully expected Tim Ford to refuse out of hand, before I had even finished my request. If he did, I could not amplify it, or explain. I knew only what Tom had told me, and I told Tim Ford that.

"He said he'd pay your full fee for however long it takes," I finished. It was all I had to add.

But when I heard his wire-grass drawl say, across the miles from Alabama, "I reckon I could probably be in Pemberton by sunup," I was somehow not surprised. Tish had said that there was something in him of Tom. I fancied I could hear it, too, some sympathy, some commonality.

"I don't know my way out to this Goat Creek, though," he said. "Can't even find it on a Geological Survey map. I looked, last time I was over there."

I told him to come by my house and I'd draw him a map and give him some breakfast, and he said he'd see me about six. I hung up and called the black deputy at the jail and told him Tom's appointment for the next day was confirmed. And then I took off my shoes and slumped back on the bed and fell asleep in my shorts and tee shirt. I was still in them when I heard Tim Ford's car roll into my driveway the next morning.

I went to the door barefoot, shaking my hair out of my eyes and squinting against the light. He stood on the other side of the screen, massive as an oak, blotting out the sullen beginning of the day. It was late July, and we were in the middle of an extended spell of thick, breath-sucking heat. I was already damp from it. But he was as crisp as if he had been carved of ice, in immaculate, knife-pressed field khakis and the kind of lace-up boots I associated with old television shows like *Green Acres*. His dark-red hair was skull short and shaved over his ears, and his eyes were gray and cool and looked straight at you. The muscles of his jaw were so pronounced that they stood out in little symmetrical ridges. I would have bet my life that he chewed tobacco.

"Miz Calhoun?" he said, in the slow rural voice I remembered. "I'm Tim Ford."

"Who else?" I said, smiling at him in spite of myself. You would no more distrust this man than you would a good, big dog, or a healthy Clydesdale. Capability and strength and simplicity of the kind Tom sometimes had about him, underneath everything else that he was, flowed off Tim Ford like water.

"Come on in," I said. "I'll start the coffee. That must be a bad drive."

"I've done worse," he said.

I made breakfast for him and sat down to have a cup of coffee while he ate, and surprised myself by eating a full meal. When we had finished, he asked politely for the map, and I drew it for him, and he said he'd be getting on out to the creek.

"I saw that water myself," I said suddenly, to my own profound surprise.

He looked at me with grave, mild interest. "It would help me a good deal if you could tell me about it," he said. There was no disbelief in the gray eyes, and no surprise; I looked closely before I spoke. Just interest.

I told him what I could about the water without mentioning the dying goat, or Tom's killing of her. That was for Tom to share, if he chose.

"Hmm. Could be cesium," he said. "Not surprising, considering the state of those cooling ponds and storage pits out there. Only, if it was cesium, it would have to be just saturated. I've never seen or heard of that much in open water. If it was cesium, I just flat missed it."

"That's what he said. Tom," I said, walking with him to the door. "At least I think he said cesium. Will you be checking it again?"

"Don't see how," he said. "I got no clearance to go on plant land now. It was just for the one time, when Mr. Dabney got me over here. I don't have no idea in hell what I'm doing over here today."

"Then," I said, "do you mind telling me why did you come?"

He looked at me speculatively for a moment, and then said, "I grew up in the woods around Cade's Cove, Tennessee, before it turned into a public circus. I always thought it was like the world must have been when it was brand-new. I'd still be living out there if it hadn't changed, and I hadn't. The woods are the best thing I know of that we've got left in the world. This job I got now is the closest I can get to lookin' out for 'em and still support my family. I'm too old and too clumsy to work for Greenpeace and knock heads, or I'd be doing that. This Tom Dabney may be as crazy as everybody says he is, but I've seen him on TV and I like the way he tends to business. I'd like to meet a man who can bumfuzzle a police chief as good as he done yours."

He pronounced it "*po*lice." He sounded as if he had barely made it out of seventh grade, instead of through three college degrees, as Tish had said he had, but as he swung down the steps and got into a dusty old sedan that said on its door *Auburn University Agricultural Extension Service,* I felt again the deep aura of authority and sureness in which he moved. When he drove away, after promising to stop on his way home and fill me in, I felt, suddenly, lighter than I had in weeks, and less tired. Almost jaunty.

"Who was that you were talking to?" Hilary said thickly, coming into the kitchen scrubbing her eyes with her fists.

"Santa Claus," I said, giddily. "He's a little late coming this year, or early, depending on how you look at it. But he made it."

My fragile euphoria lasted, with some conscious nursing on my part, for the next few days. When reason prevailed, I knew I had no more cause to feel hopeful than I had before Tim Ford had come. He certainly could not alter the composition of the water in Goat Creek. He could do nothing, except perhaps ascertain if his tests had somehow been wrong and Tom was right, and I did not think he could even do that. He had, as he said, no access now to Big Silver land. And Tom would be apprehended and jailed again the instant he breached security; he knew that. Besides, I had his word. There would be no more trouble about the Big Silver plant.

But still, in those late-July days, my mood of dreaming

peace persisted. Some lightless, monolithic weight seemed to have been lifted off my shoulders. Nothing remotely resembling well-being or joy had taken its place, but I had foundered under the weight so long that its mere absence made me feel airborne. Even the fact that Hilary, who had always seemed to catch my moods like a virus, obviously did not feel the lifting and lightening of the air around us did not diminish the relief. I basked in it like warm, frail sun after a tundra winter.

I began to make plans for the first time since the spring. "How would you like to go to Disney World between quarters?" I asked Hilary. "I bet Dr. Harper would let you miss a few sessions; you're really doing very well. You could ask somebody from school to come with us."

"If *you* would," Hilary said, and went back to her writing. She was into her third notebook now.

"We might even think about going to Europe next summer. It would give us something to save our pennies for. Aunt Tish has asked us to go with them to Uncle Charlie's medical conference in England. Would you like that? Buckingham Palace? The Tower of London? We could drive around the country some, too."

"That would be nice," Hilary called from her room.

"Good," I said, finally stung. "It's not for a year yet. You should have time to wrap up your magnum opus."

This was greeted by the silence it deserved. I had no cause to be annoyed with Hilary. She was making progress with her therapist; she was doing well at her studies, even if she did not participate in any of Country Day's extracurricular and social activities; she was eating well and sleeping soundly. She still insisted on bottled water and sponge baths, but there had been none of the tears and hysteria and clinging, none of the hideous nightmares and soul-shattering terrors, that she had brought with her from Atlanta. It was just that she was not Hilary. I wanted Hilary back. The thought occurred to me, somewhere in that short, bright string of days, that I was, somehow, waiting for Tim Ford to bring my daughter back to me from Goat Creek. It was so entirely and altogether irrational a notion that I thrust it out of my mind. But while it lingered there, before it melted like a snowflake on the tongue, it had the taste of truth.

Tim Ford came back three days later, on a Saturday, at midmorning. He still looked like an oak, but now he had stubble over his jaws and chin, and the cool gray eyes were pouched and webbed and sunken, the thin skin around them stained blue with fatigue. There were long, just-healing scratches on his face and arms and hands, and the khaki field clothes, though still clean, looked as though they had been drenched, submersed, and dried outside in the wind, without ironing. His loping shamble was more pronounced that it had been before. I felt such a stab of alarm that I jerked the front door open and ran down the steps to meet him. At closer range I drew in my breath; a great red-and-purple bruise covered most of his left jaw.

And then he grinned, and some of the alarm fled. But a cold core of it remained. It was a good grin, jaunty and rueful at once, but he did not look like a man who had solved a problem or won a victory. He looked like a man who had lost, though with some grace, a fistfight.

"My God, what happened to you?" I said in dread. "Are you all right? Tom didn't . . . ?"

"Tom? Oh, this." He touched his jaw. "Naw. A cypress root did that. Honeysuckle and briers did the rest. Naw, ol' Tom wouldn't hit me. Good man, Tom Dabney. Right now he's sleepin' off a hangover that should have killed him, and that's ninety-nine percent of what's wrong with me. The rest, a cup of coffee and some scrambled eggs would fix. I've been living on venison jerky and boiled comfrey tea for three days."

I brought him into the kitchen, as I had three mornings before. Hilary, seated at the table cutting pictures of lepidoptera out of magazines for a school project, gave him a wary look, a polite nod, and melted into her room. The door shut firmly.

"I know I ain't gon' launch a thousand ships, but I ain't used to scaring children." Tim Ford grinned.

"Please excuse her. Eleven is an age I'd just as soon we could skip. It isn't you personally," I said.

"Well, I can't fault her," he said. "Tom said to steer clear of town, or your *po*lice chief would run me in just for being ugly."

"You do look kind of beat up. What did happen out there, really?" I said, pouring coffee and breaking eggs into a bowl.

"Jesus H. Christ on a sailboat, what didn't!" he said. "Sit down here with me while I eat, and I'll tell you. Or some of it. Some of it I ain't gon' tell a living soul long as I live. Not even Earline. I'd a hell of a lot rather she thought I was over here with a woman, which is prob'ly what she does think."

And that is how I learned of the incredible night raid on the cooling pools of the Big Silver Nuclear Weapon Facility by a half-starved madman and a six-foot-five redheaded civil engineer from Cade's Cove, Tennessee.

They spent the first day circling one another like dogs, sniffing and backing off and sniffing again. Tom did not tell him, at first, why he had summoned him, but by the time they had exchanged brief histories and settled down on the porch of the Goat Creek house with drinks and lunch, Tim had a pretty good idea. Or at least he thought that it had something to do with the Big Silver that would not have pleased any authorities he could think of. Tom Dabney was obviously a man without limits and at the far edges of his reason, and he had just as obviously been burning with his obsession for a long time. Even if Tim had not read the newspaper stories and seen the television coverage, he would have known that by looking at him. In the first hour Tim was there, he thought he was dealing with a lunatic. In the second he wasn't at all sure. After that, he no longer cared.

"He is one magnetic sonofabitch, isn't he?" Tim Ford said. "Lord God, but he can talk and spin a tale and sing a song and dance. . . . That fool can dance like nothin' I ever saw, and I've flat seen dancin' back in Tennessee. You ever seen him dance?"

I nodded. I could not take my eyes off Tim Ford. Singing? Dancing? What could Tom be thinking of? In my unwilling mind's eye I saw him, seal-sleek and brown and naked, dancing in the night woods, his body stained with firelight. I shook my head like a dog coming out of water.

"He's a wonderful dancer," I said.

"And that house of his, out on the creek," Tim said, in genuine awe. "Jesus, I would do anything on God's earth I had to do to have a place like that. It's just . . . magical, kind of. I didn't know anything like that existed in this century. I used to think I'd build me a cabin back in the hills one day, when the kids were grown and gone and I had a nest egg, but now that I've seen that, I'm gon' have as near to that as I can, a place right over the water, with a wild river swamp around it. Do you like that place? Have you seen it? God, I'd have to nail Earline's feet to the floor to keep her out there. . . ."

"It's a very special place," I said. Something in my voice

drew his eyes; he looked at me speculatively for a moment. But he said only, "I don't wonder he's gone off his head, if he thinks the water out there is poisoned."

"Is it?" I said bluntly, holding his eyes with mine.

He lifted his hand. "I'm comin' to that."

They had talked all afternoon, and eaten supper on the porch, and then settled in with a quart of bourbon and talked some more. By midnight he knew as much about Tom and his life and what he did and how he thought as he could take in.

"It was like he couldn't quit talkin'," he said. "Like he had to make sure I understood how he was, and what was important to him. Hell, by that time he could have been Jack the Ripper and I wouldn't have cared. He had me hypnotized like a mongoose does a snake."

Gradually Tom had stopped talking of himself and begun to talk of the woods and the river and the creek, and about the old ways of the forest, and the myths of the hunt and meanings of the wild. He had played his guitar for Tim, and sung him some of the strange, atonal songs that he had taught Hilary and me, and had brought out his bows and arrows and knives for Tim to see. By three A.M. and half the bottle of bourbon, he was telling Tim about rituals and their purpose and power. By dawn and the bottom of the bottle, he had shown him one, and more than that, Tim had participated.

Tim did not tell me this directly; he merely said, "He had me doing things nobody in their right mind would believe." But I knew. Of course I did.

Then and only then, after the ritual, Tom told Tim Ford what he wanted him to do: to go with him onto Big Silver land, in darkness and stealth, under the noses and past the devices and weapons and dogs of the entire security force, up into the very heart of the complex, where the great reactors and the cooling ponds and burial grounds for waste lay, there to test with the field kit all the water that ran from the area and the groundwater itself. And then to come back out again.

"I nearly shit my pants—scuse me, Andy," Tim Ford said. "I told him we'd never see the outside of the federal prison they'd put us in if they caught us. And he just grinned at me and said, 'You think they gon' catch us?' And I knew right then I was going to do it. Because I didn't think they were. And by God, they didn't."

They went blearily to bed as the sun was coming up, and Tom woke him as it was setting. He had laid out commando dress of his own devising for both of them: camouflage pants and shirts, soft-tanned stalking moccasins, belts to hold his hunting knife and Tim's field testing kit.

"I told him I wasn't going to take no weapons into a U.S. military atom bomb plant, and he said he wasn't, neither, that we wouldn't need 'em. The knife was only for snakes. That didn't make me feel a whole lot better, I can tell you. Then, by God, he blacks both our faces and hands and puts this wreath thing made out of oak leaves on my head and his, and I just ain't gon' tell you what we did next. I ain't gon' ever tell nobody. And then we started off, just as the last of the light left."

I nodded, waiting for him to go on. He did not have to tell me what they had done, there on the banks of Goat Creek in the last of the summer light. I had been there, I had seen it—the leap of fire, the swift silver path of the knife, the solemn and tender striping on of the fresh blood, the measured steps of the old dance, the old song . . . But I had forgotten, or thought that I had. Yet an older part of me than my mind remembered. With that part I saw them, the two of them, as clearly as if I had stood there with them.

It unrolled before me like a movie as he talked. They

crossed Goat Creek in the shallows just downstream from the house, where Tom and Hilary had danced. Where the water had burned and the little goat died. They went up the deep-wooded ridge that separated Goat Creek and the Big Silver River, and down it and across the river, wading sometimes chest deep. Tom went ahead, with Tim behind; he went in the swift, silent padding walk in which I had seen him cover miles without raising a sweat. Behind him, Tim Ford struggled in the thick dark to keep up without making noise.

"I been in the woods all my life," he said. "I could keep up with him, all right, but most of the time I couldn't see him, except for a white rag he hung on the back of his belt. That's what he put it there for. And I couldn't move anywhere near as quiet. I sounded like an elephant going through that underbrush. And when we got to the river I sounded like a hippopotamus. But that sonofabitch went across it like an otter or a good bird dog. He didn't make a splash and he didn't make a ripple."

When they came up out of the river they were on Big Silver land. Tom had stopped then, and showed Tim the strange, stylized stalking gait that he had taught Hilary and me, the step, the freeze with one foot lifted while he looked and listened, then the infinitesimally slow rolling down of the other foot, ball to heel, so that no branch or twig cracked.

"This is going to take all night," Tim had whispered to Tom.

"I got all night," Tom said.

Tom figured that, until they neared the central heart of the facility, where the three operable reactors, the solid-low-level-waste burial grounds, and the tank farms for high-level waste lay, their chief worry would be patrols with canine teams. Besides power boat and helicopter support divisions, largely ineffectual at night, and a special response team ("You don't want to fuck with those guys; they only come out for one reason"), most of the private security manpower was foot patrols with dogs and jeep patrols. Tom thought the best way to handle those was simply to move as though they were tracking something mortally dangerous and stay upwind whenever possible. The wind was out of the east; that was a great boon. And the moon was down. Tom could track by the stars like an Indian. And he had in his pocket a vial of skunk scent. "I hate the stuff, but so do dogs. If I pass it back to you, rub it on, no questions asked. It won't kill you. You'll just wish it would."

Once they neared the heart of the property and their quarry, however, the security would change from human to electronic, and not even Tom was foolhardy enough to tackle that. He had ascertained that the entire critical operating area was surrounded with a tall electrified fence topped with razor wire, guarded by men with dogs, mercilessly lit by sodium vapor, and watched over by tower-mounted scanning television cameras.

"There's probably some other kind of Star Wars stuff, too, but it doesn't matter, because in any case we're not going to try to go in there," he said. "I just want to get close enough to test some runoff and groundwater outside the fences. I've marked one place especially on your map—here. There's a little no-name creek that cuts through just to the west of the fence. It runs straight into the Big Silver River about two miles above where the river feeds over into Goat Creek. Whatever's coming out of there has to hit that creek. Whatever's seeping into the ground in there will show up in the groundwater around it. It couldn't miss Goat Creek if it tried."

And so they went into the dark heart of the Big Silver,

the slight, dark man and the big ruddy one, went silently in crouching slow motion part of the way, at a swift, padding, doggy trot part of it, and went the last miles on their stomachs. Once, early on, Tom froze and motioned for Tim Ford to do the same, and they watched as a buck, three does, and a handful of adolescent fawns passed through a canebrake not six feet ahead of them. No ear flicked, no white throat swung toward them. Not a sound broke the night. They might have been ghosts in a fantastic lunarscape of black water and swollen cypress knees and towering tupelo roots and winding sheets of moss.

Another time, Tom stopped and lay still on his stomach on a narrow deer path until Tim, frozen obediently behind him began to think Tom had fallen, incredibly, asleep, or ill. Only then did he see the great coiled root in the path ahead of them reassemble itself and slide off into the underbrush. He felt cold sweat spring out at his hairline and heard, unmistakably, soft, exultant laughter from Tom. For the first time since the afternoon before, it crossed his mind that he had placed his life and future in the hands of a madman. The sweat increased, and ran into his eyes. He did not have a prayer, he knew, of getting himself back to Goat Creek alone.

Just before they reached the edge of the enormous clearing that surrounded the reactor and storage cluster, they heard their first foot patrol. Tom heard it first, of course; and went still again. Tim, lying flat with spongy leaf detritus in his mouth and his eyes blinded with sweat, heard them a long second later. In a few moments the patrol was near enough for them to hear the steps of the men, and the fast, springy, shuffling trot of the dogs. The patrol, secure, perhaps, in the very ordinariness of the unblemished blackness around them and the impregnability of the great complex to their right, talked in normal voices that rang like gunfire of a movie they had watched on television earlier, and exchanged a few fervent opinions of Michelle Pfeiffer that made Tim, face pressed into the wet forest floor, nearly suffocate with an idiot's uncontrollable glee. The dogs did not break stride.

And then one did, and another. Men and dogs stopped. Tim felt himself growing dizzy and the blackness behind his eyes pinwheeling with exploding lights. He tried to stop his breathing and go limp and let himself "go into the woods all the way, just fade into them," as Tom had told him to do. And incredibly, fantastically, in the outmost extremity of his fear, he felt it happen—felt his flesh open and the earth pass into it, felt his veins open to receive the wildness, felt the forest and the night pour into him through his ears and closed eyes and pores. He knew in that moment that he was invisible. He knew that if he lifted his head and looked at Tom, just ahead of him, he would see nothing but earth and the roots of trees. He knew that the patrol would not see them and it would not hear them.

"I can't explain it," he said to Andy. "I just . . . melted into it. He told me I could do it. I was part of it all. I was the night and the trees and the water. . . ."

I looked at him silently, my scalp crawling, the skin on my hands and neck cold. I knew. It had happened to me, too. Only once, but it had happened. Tom had told me it would, and it did. I had become wild. I had known what it was.

"What happened then?" I said. I realized that I was whispering.

"Then we heard the sound of somebody pissing in the bushes, and a zipper, and then they went on," he said. "That's it. That's all. We got on up to where the little creek cuts through there, just about thirty yards outside the circle of the lights, and I drew my samples, and we went on back. It seemed like only half an hour or so before we were wading the river again, but by the time we came back across the creek it was first light. Tom went and got the bourbon jug and I tested the water."

I just looked at him.

"It was clean," Tim Ford said. "It didn't vary more than a hair from the first series I ran."

"And . . . what did Tom do then?" I could hardly get the words out past the vise that held my chest.

"Opened the bourbon and took a long swig and passed it to me, and said, 'I think I just bought a duck.' " Tim Ford grinned enormously at the memory. I fought tears, silently.

"I offered to test the water from Goat Creek where he saw the lights, but he just shook his head," Tim said. "Said it didn't matter what the tests said; he knew the water was poison. But he didn't sound too bent out of shape about it. Just . . . matter-of-fact. After that, we just polished off the bourbon and staggered in and went to sleep. He was still sleeping when I left. He's probably right about the water; there's been too many sick and dying animals out there for there not to be something. Could be sewage, chemical effluence, almost anything. But whatever it is, it's not the Big Silver plant. God almighty, though. What a night! I can never tell anybody about it; I'd be locked up myself. But by God, I wouldn't take anything for it. You should have seen the sonofabitch. I never saw anybody like that in the woods. It was something. It's a pity he's nuts."

"You still think he is?" I said.

"Oh, yeah," Tim Ford said. "He probably is. Not many people who know him would care, but enough would, and they're the wrong ones. If he don't stop about that plant, there ain't no way he's gon' stay out of jail or the funny farm. And a man who'd do what he did last night ain't likely to stop."

But he was wrong. Tom did stop his war against the Big Silver. He not only stopped; he seemed to drop off the face of the earth. No one saw him in the town, and Reese Carmody, calling to see if I had heard from him, said that he had not been able to raise him at the Goat Creek house for a couple of weeks. There was, the first time he went, a note saying that the animals that had not died were being boarded with the local veterinarian, who had been given leave to find homes for them if he could, and Scratch Purvis's small grandchildren came every day or so to look in on Earl. Reese thought that perhaps Tom had gone off back into the river swamp on one of his weeks-long walkabouts; he did that sometimes in the summers, Reese said, with only his bow and arrow and matches. I was not to worry. Sirius, the Dog Star, rose, and the town sagged and quieted under the weight of the dog days. Soon only the drained face of Clay Dabney and the peculiar emptiness at the core of me stood witness to the antic, awful Summer of the Dream Maker.

Those, and the further retreat of Hilary.

When Tim Ford had driven away for the second time, I stood for a long moment waiting to feel the great rush of relief and exultation I had supposed would come upon finding that the water was truly safe, and that Tom was, as he had promised, done with his craziness. I actually closed my eyes and stood with my palms up, waiting to feel it, the way you wait for the first rush of healing rain in a dry season. Nothing came. Emptiness pressed on my face and palms, and whistled in my ears.

"Not with a bang, but a whimper," I said aloud. I had,

I realized then, been subconsciously longing for that clean, healing bang all summer, thirsting for it. Closure, Hilary's shrink would call it. It was what he was trying to achieve for her.

But in truth, it was the awful, level weight of the unfinished that had the power.

I went down the hall to Hilary's room and knocked on her door. She put her head out.

"You can stop drinking bottled water and take a bath, sweetie," I said, forcing myself to smile at her. "Mr. Ford went with Tom over to the very place where all the water starts in the Big Silver plant, and they tested it right there, with Tom watching. It's clean as a whistle. And Tom's not going to do any more funny stuff. He promised."

Her expression did not change, but the very life drained out of her face before my eyes, horribly, as I imagined the blood did from the face of someone being embalmed. I could only stare at her. I thought that I might faint. By the time she finally spoke, her face was as white as snow, as milk, as paper.

"I don't believe you," she said. "I don't believe him. All of you are lying."

She slammed her door and locked it.

I stood in the hall outside for a long time, rapping on the door and calling, cajoling, even threatening. I heard nothing, no movement, no sound at all. Presently I went into my bedroom and called Frick Harper, Hilary's therapist. He called me back at the end of his hour.

"I wouldn't worry yet," he said, after I had told him what had happened. "It's not an uncommon grief reaction. In a way, it may not be a bad thing. Maybe we'll get closure now."

"Grief about what?" I said. "I thought she'd be relieved to know that the water's clean and Tom isn't going to . . . be doing those things anymore."

"Grief because her idol just died before her eyes," he said. "What was it you said she called him sometimes? The dream maker? She's just found out he was fallible, flawed, terribly wrong about something. The prince is dead and the dream maker is gone and instead there's only a nice man who's been acting like a damn fool. She's heartbroken and angry at you—the old shoot-the-messenger syndrome—and she's probably scared. A prince or a dream maker can keep you safe forever, but a mere man just doesn't have that power. No matter how much he'd like to. Let her be, and let's see what's going on tomorrow."

So I left her alone and went about my business, heart laboring with fear, one ear cocked to hear any sound she might make. I heard none all that day until after sundown, when she finally unlocked her door and came down to the kitchen for a glass of milk and a banana sandwich, which she took back to her room. Sometime that night, I suppose, she slept. It was four A.M. before I did.

In the morning, when I was collecting trash to put out for the collectors before we headed off to school and work, I found the thick, close-written notebooks bearing the True Story of Tom Dabney in her wastepaper basket. At the bottom, in jagged black shards, was her record of "Moon River." I lifted out the notebooks and put them away in my desk, unread, and locked it, and dumped the broken record in with the other trash. I was weak and cold with dread for Hilary.

Nothing much changed, outwardly, except that before, when Hilary had been closed away, she had been writing passionately in her secret notebooks, keeping her paper vigil with all the force of her being. I had been waiting to see if the writing would, as Frick Harper hoped, serve as therapy; meanwhile there had been no real problems with her, only the absence of her essence.

But now, when she closed her door, she did not write. Now I heard the television set go on, and sometimes I did not hear it go off until I was starting for bed, and beyond that. Sometimes it was the last thing in my ears before thin sleep claimed me. Now she grew listless about her schoolwork and silent in school, and her grades began to drop, and the calls from concerned teachers began. Now she stopped eating and lost weight. Now even Frick Harper began to be concerned, and started her on a new tricyclic drug, and even spoke of a possible short stay in a good psychiatric facility if she did not improve.

"Let's give the drug three weeks to a month, and then reevaluate," he said. "Sometimes you go along with little or no results, trying this one and that, and then bang, you hit the right one, and the depression just lifts like fog. If it doesn't, we'll talk about Crestwood. It's first-rate. And we're only talking about short-term."

"Oh, God," I whispered in terror. "I can't put her in a mental hospital."

"You may have to," he said, "or risk losing her."

Bizarrely, as things grew worse with Hilary, they bloomed in other areas of my life. Tish and Charlie drew close again, wrapping me and Hilary in the benison and safety of their love and their sheer physical closeness. Other friends, from whom I had not heard since the first day of Tom's siege of Pemberton, called in concern for my daughter and came by with food and flowers and with gifts for her. Carter brought a new riding habit by, exquisite and handsewn, and hugged me wordlessly and rumpled her lackluster hair before he left. Even Pat Dabney sent something, a magnificent full-color picture book of all the Kentucky Derby winners since Aristedes, in 1875.

There was also a formal little note from the corresponding secretary of the Pemberton Dames, saying only that they had missed me and would love to see me become active again in the fall, if I cared to do so. I knew it was my cold and exact payment from Caroline Dabney for seeing Tom the night she had come to my home, and crumpled the note and threw it into the wastepaper basket. The message was clear: Pemberton would take me back like a prodigal daughter, once Tom was out of the picture. I was so deeply and dully disgusted that I began to think once more about taking Hilary and moving on to Florida, as I had at the beginning of the summer.

But she was ill now, there was no question of that, and I was frightened, both by the illness itself and by the necessity for good continuing treatment for her. I could not afford to uproot us and take a chance on finding a job, of changing therapists. And then Miss Deborah Fain slipped in her bath and broke her knee and took disgruntled retirement, and the college offered me her job and salary, and I knew that, for better or worse, we would stay in Pemberton, and that my battle to heal Hilary would be waged there.

The day that her summer term ended, a letter came from Chris's lawyer in Atlanta. Chris had finished his program of therapy for impaired physicians and had been reinstated, with curtailed privileges, at his hospitals and with the surgery group. And he had recently and quietly remarried, a young woman who was a juvenile nurse practitioner in the facility in which he had been treated. Her name, according to the lawyer, was Dawn, and she was "warm and caring and experienced with troubled youngsters, and eager to get acquainted with Chris's daughter." There was no thought of seeking custody or even regular visitation rights unless I agreed, the letter went on to say. But if I could see my way clear to letting Hilary come to Atlanta and visit her father and his wife on a one-time basis, everyone would be very grateful. Chris was not the same man he had been. If I wanted to come and stay at a hotel nearby so as to chaperone Hilary, Chris had offered to pay my way.

I went over to Tish's after work and threw the letter on her table and waited while she read it. My mind was blank and white; I did not know what I thought or felt.

"What do you think?" I said when she looked up, surprised to hear that my voice was shaking.

"I'd let her go, if her shrink says she can," Tish said matter-of-factly. "What have you got to lose?"

I called Frick Harper.

"I don't think it's a bad idea at all," he said. "Providing she wants to go. And after I've talked to her father's therapist, of course. If she doesn't want to, that's the end of it. But if she isn't afraid of him now, if enough time has gone by, then it could be a very positive reinforcement for her to make that connection again. It isn't as if he'd ever abused her, or even threatened to. I don't believe in teaching children how to punish by withholding themselves."

I felt as if I had been severely reprimanded for something I had not done.

"I'll ask her, then," I said coolly, sure that Hilary would refuse. She had refused to go anywhere at all except school since the morning Tim Ford had come by.

But Hilary did not refuse. She looked at me with faint but recognizable interest, and read and reread the letter. Afterward she was silent for a long time. She closed her door again, and I heard her television start up. Just before dinnertime, she came into the living room and stood beside my chair.

"Does he still live right in the city? You know . . . Daddy?" she said. The word came past her lips with difficulty. "Right in the city, with fences and sidewalks and little tiny yards?"

"I think so," I said. "I believe I heard that he has an apartment or a town house or something right down with all the stores and big buildings near the hospital." I thought, with pain, that I knew where this was going.

"I think I'd like that," Hilary said presently.

"Then that's what we'll do," I said, the pain swelling like a tidal wave. "I'll see if we can't fly up from Waycross or Tallahassee. That might be fun."

"I think . . . I'd like to go by myself," my daughter said, not looking at me.

"All right," I said.

But my leaden heart said, even though my mind knew it was not true, "I will never see you again."

After that she was just the slightest bit better. I set the date through Chris's lawyer, and made the arrangements, and bought her ticket, and got her some new clothes and even a smart new suitcase and overnight bag. They sat open in her room, gradually filling with piles of bright, cleaned and ironed clothing. Each garment that went in was like an arrow through my heart.

"Come on," Tish said. "It's not like she was going for a year. It's just ten days. We'll do lots of stuff. Maybe we'll run down to the beach. We won't let you rest for a minute. You'll be so tired by the time she gets back, your fanny will be dragging."

"You don't have to baby-sit me," I said sulkily. "I'm not worried about me. I'm afraid for her."

"Afraid of what?" Tish said. "Frick Harper has talked to Chris's shrink for an hour. He's even talked to Chris. You said yourself he was all for it. What are you afraid of?"

"I guess . . . that he'll hurt her."

"With a child therapist in the house? Come on, Andy," Tish said. "You're scared she's going to like her father again, or even love him. But shouldn't she? Hasn't that been part of the problem all along?"

"That's not it at all," I said, knowing that, in part, it was. "I'm afraid he'll be . . . erratic. There one minute and not the next. Like he was the year before we left. She doesn't need that right now. She needs consistency and constancy. Right now I'm the only constant in her life. You know what she's lost."

"You sure it's not more like she's the only one in yours?" Tish said. "She's not the only one who's lost a lot."

I said nothing, and she came over and put her arm around me.

"Maybe you both ought to learn that the only really constant constant is yourself," she said gently. "You can lose all the others, but you can't lose that. Maybe it's time to know that now. This could be a start toward that."

"I really hate you when you get all sage and earth-motherly," I said.

"Me, too," she said equably. "Come over tonight and let's watch that movie of Kevin Costner's about the baseball player and get horny and talk dirty. It'll take fifteen years off you."

After that it was better, if only slightly. My child came a tiny way outside the dark cave of herself, if only to incline her attention infinitesimally toward the north and Atlanta, like a stunted plant reaching feebly for the light. And though that hurt me like a never-healing wound, the awful fear for her sanity began to lessen. The part of my heart that was Hilary eased a bit.

But the other part didn't. Pain and tears and flatness . . . endless, endless flatness. And more pain. And more tears. I had found neither safety, moderation, nor peace in Pemberton, and I myself had abjured ecstasy.

"This rough magic I here abjure," Prospero said in *The Tempest*. I wondered if he had felt the same colorless immensity inside him when the magic was gone, and the same certainty that none would come again.

On the afternoon before Hilary was to leave, I heard a tentative knock on the screen door and went tiredly, in my cocoon of cottony grayness, to answer it. Neither Hilary nor I had slept much the night before, or for many nights before that. The fatigue was telling on both of us.

My heart gave a convulsive clutch when I saw the man who stood there. Or leaned there. He was so skeletally thin that he resembled nothing so much as a pile of old bones loosely wrapped in ashy gray skin and propped on a walking stick made from a dried, gnarled vine of some sort, coiled around a stout pole. His head was down on his chest, and even though the thermometer beside the door read 92 degrees, he wore a voluminous, flapping old cardigan sweater, and a faded muffler around his throat, and a stocking cap on his head. I did not fear harm from him—I knew instantaneously that there could be no harm here—but I feared horror. I opened my mouth to ask his business, and then his head came up and he smiled and I saw that it was Scratch.

A powerful, tidal grief sucked my breath from my chest. Simply, he was dying. I read the fact of it in his entire body and the knowledge of it in his eyes. They were filmed and somehow very quiet, focused inward now. But when he smiled, the smile touched them. I fought for control, and smiled and held out my arms.

"Scratch," I said. And then, "Oh, I've missed you so much! I didn't even know how much!"

He thrust himself forward on the stick and put his arms

around me, and I smelled the old Scratch smell of woods and wood smoke and clean, sun-dried cloth, but under it there was something new. It was a dark, thick, sly smell, slightly fruity and sweet, slightly spoiled. I shuddered. I knew I had smelled his death waiting for him. I hoped that he did not smell it every day, while he waited for it.

We stood there quietly a moment, I holding him firmly lest he fall. Even under the layers of fabric I could feel the old bones. They were spongy, inert. Then he squeezed me softly and put me away from him.

"I come to see you and Hilary," he said. He did not sigh with the effort to speak, but the words were faint, as if there was little breath behind them. "I knowed both your schools was out, and I figured to catch you home. I heared Hilary ain't feeling good, and I heared she goin' away. I thought I better check on y'all."

"Come in," I said. "Sit down and let me get you something to drink. Would you like a bite to eat? I have some good old-fashioned lemon cheesecake; Mrs. Coulter made it."

He waved away both offers, politely, but like a man who has little time.

"I cain't stay long. My girl comin' back for me in a little while. She drop me off when she come in to the clinic with J.R. He gittin' vaccinated for school; it ain't gon' take long. I wouldn't say no to a little drop of whiskey, though."

He was still standing when I brought the glass. He took a sip and sighed, a slightly stronger sound than his words. Then he looked at me. The look was his old one, level and calm and many-layered.

"Where Hilary goin'?" he said.

"She's going to . . . spend a few days with her father," I said, clearing my throat around the words. "How did you know she was going away? Or that she'd been sick, for that matter?"

"You hears things," he said, dismissing it. "What about you, Andy? You all right? You don't look like you doin' too good, either."

"I'm all right. Of course I am." I spoke briskly, in dread that he would speak of Tom. Surely he had not come here to plead with me to go back to Tom. . . .

"Scratch, Hilary's in her room," I said. "I'll take you in a minute. She's . . . she's really not herself, but she's starting to get just the least bit better, and I don't want anything to upset her. I know you wouldn't for the world; she'll love seeing you. But, Scratch, please . . . don't talk to her about Tom. She's made some kind of peace with herself about that; she doesn't talk about him at all."

"I ain't gon' talk about Tom," he said, smiling gently at me.

"And not the woods," I said, hating this litany of don'ts, but having to say them. "I think one reason she wants to go to Atlanta is to get away from the woods."

"Andy, I ain't gon' talk to her about Tom lessen she asks," Scratch said. "But I cain't promise about the woods, not if she wants to talk about them. She's a smart little girl, and a good one. We got a lot between us, me an' her. It don't belong to anybody but us. But I will promise that I ain't gon' say nothing to hurt her. I didn't come to preach to her. I come for me. Seem to me I'm gittin' on along now. I had a fancy to see both of you before . . . winter git here."

Tears stung my throat. "We'll see lots of you before winter," I said. "You don't have to make the long trip over here to see us. We'll come . . . we'll come up to see you."

He shook his head firmly.

"No. That ain't no good, Andy. It's better we leave it

like this. The woods ain't a good place for her right now; nor you, neither. You let the woods set for a spell."

A thought struck me. "Did you come to try to talk her into not going away?" I said. I did not know why the idea alarmed me. I had had to bite my lips for days to keep from doing the same thing.

"No," he said, and his voice was rich with a kind of amusement, under the sighing weakness. It was the amusement of an adult toward a child; I had heard it in my own voice sometimes, with Hilary.

"I think she ought to go. I'm glad she goin' clear up yonder to Atlanta. How long she goin' for?"

"Ten days," I said. "She gets back the Friday before school starts."

He nodded. He looked away, into distance.

"That's good. That's long enough."

"For what?" I said.

"For somethin' I got to finish," he said. "I gittin' close. It ain't nothin' for you to fret about. But she just as good off up there for now."

He looked back at me, into my eyes. "Don't worry, Andy," he said. "She comin' back."

"How do you know?" I whispered.

He smiled. "It's one reason I come."

I took him down the hall to her room and knocked on the closed door. There was a long silence, and then she opened it and put her head out. For a second she simply stared at him, there in the gloom of the hall. And then her face lit into a ghost of the radiance that I had not seen since that long-ago June night, at our birthday party.

"Oh," she said simply. It hung on the air like a pure, silver note from a hunting horn, far away. "Oh."

And then she was in his arms, hugging him, her eyes

squeezed shut with joy, her face rapt. When she was done, she pulled him into her room.

"Please, Mama?" she said, looking over her shoulder at me.

"Sure." I nodded. "I'll make you all some lemonade."

She closed the door behind her. I stood for a moment in the hall, not trying to listen, simply letting the complex stew of sensations and emotions eddy and whirl around me. Then I went into the kitchen and made the lemonade. As I left the hall I heard her begin to talk. I had not heard her talk so much or so fast, or in that breathless, pattering tone, for months. A feeling that did not dare form itself into thankfulness swelled inside me.

When I went back down the hall with the tray of lemonade and cookies, she was still talking. This time I could hear some of her words.

". . . but I can't remember, Scratch," she was saying. There was urgency in her voice, and hopelessness, and pain. "I thought I would never forget, and I was writing down about it, but then I didn't, and now I've forgotten so much. . . ."

The loss in her voice was so vivid and so somehow focused and unchildish that I felt the tears start back into my eyes. And then I remembered. . . . I went into my bedroom and unlocked the desk drawer I had thrust her abandoned notebooks in, and got them out and put them on the tray with the food. She came to the door at my knock, to take the tray, already murmuring, "Thank you," and then she saw the notebooks and went white, and then she flushed with joy.

"Oh, Mama," she said softly. "Oh, Mama . . . "

"Tell Scratch I'll come knock when his daughter gets here," I said, turning away, the tears finally warm on my face. I would have taken her my living heart on a tray if I had thought it would make her look like that.

For another hour they talked. I sat in the living room with a magazine, reading the same inane sentence over and over. I did not consciously eavesdrop, but I could hear her voice, rising and falling in excitement and the new urgency, and sometimes I heard Scratch speak, and once or twice I heard them laugh. I heard, throughout the hour, distinctly, the riffle of pages and the furious scratch of a racing ballpoint pen. Toward the end of the time I heard Scratch singing softly, or chanting, and Hilary joining in with him, and at the very end of the hour I heard a curious, rhythmic pounding and shuffling, as if they were, incredibly, dancing. There was a long silence after that, in which I heard the rattling crunch of Scratch's daughter's old car entering my driveway, and I rose to go and knock on the door and tell him she had come.

Halfway down the hall, I heard Hilary begin to cry.

It was not the piercing weeping of hysteria, or the thin, fretful wailing of fearful dependence. This was the weeping of grief, full and mature, and heartbreaking to hear. It was a woman's weeping. I would have wept that way; I had. . . .

Scratch met me at her door and barred the way.

"Let her be for a spell, Andy," he said. "She be all right."

"What is it?" I said frantically, trying to see around him. I could not. "What did you say to her?"

"I tol' her I ain't gon' be seein' her no more after this," he said mildly, keeping his skeleton's hand firm on my arm. "Better she hear it now, from me. I don' want her hit with it terreckly, out'n the blue. She be okay."

"No," I said, almost whimpering. "No, she won't. She's lost too much; she can't stand to lose any more; she can't stand to lose you. . . ."

"Yes, she can," he said. "She sad, but she know it be all right. We talked about it. I tol' her that as long as she got the woods, she got me. I be there, in the woods. I always be there. She know that. She just got to grieve a little." He laughed, his rich old cackle. "I sho be disappointed if she don't," he said.

"Oh, my dear Scratch," I said, my own inexhaustible tears beginning to spill over my lashes and down my face.

He moved forward and put his arms around me, and I buried my face in the hideous old muffler. I could feel it going damp with my tears.

"That go for you, too, Andy," he said. "Long as you got the woods, you got me. I right out there, all the time. Always. Don't you lose the woods. Don't you let Hilary lose 'em. You don't know it, but everything you need is out there."

"But the water," I sobbed. "I saw the water. I know you saw it. . . ."

"Things pass, Andy," he said. "Things pass. But the earth abides."

I was crying so hard that I did not hear his daughter knock, and when she came hesitantly into the living room, calling out for him, he patted me gently and disengaged himself. I leaned against the wall, flooded with grief, slackened with it, drowned. I heard him make his way down the hall and through the living room, and I heard him stop at the door.

"Look inside, Andy," he called. "You find what you need in there. You got the woods inside you. Look inside."

And the screen door groaned and twanged shut, and the old car grumbled to life, and they were gone.

I clung blindly to the wall, not certain I could move without falling, thinking, as I had thought once before, that it might, after all, be possible simply to die of grief. Hilary's door opened and I felt, rather than saw, her come stumbling out, and felt her arms go around my waist, and her face press itself into the hollow under my chin where she fit now. I put my arms around her and we stood there, my daughter and I, crying for Scratch and for all things lost and gone. I had not heard her cry for a long time. I could not remember ever letting her see me weep.

It was she who stopped first. When finally I could raise my head to squint at her through my hot, swollen lids, it was to see, on her own splotched and wet face, a smile. It was small and lopsided, and her mouth trembled around it but it was fully hers, Hilary's and no one else's. For however long, my daughter was wholly present behind her pale face.

"It's all right, Mama," she said, reaching up to pat me awkwardly. "I promise it is. It's okay."

CHAPTER FIFTEEN

We did not do things together, Tish and Charlie and I. The evening before we were to go down to their beach place—two days after Hilary left for Atlanta—Tish's mother fell and broke her hip, and Tish and Charlie left immediately for Macon.

"Please go on down to the cottage," she said on the phone to me. "I'll put the key under the doormat. If things turn out better than I think, maybe we'll join you there. I'd really feel better if you went. I don't think you ought to stay in Pemberton by yourself right now."

"Why on earth not?" I said, ignoring a strange finger of something that felt very like fear probing coldly in my stomach. "This is where I live. What could happen to me here?"

"Nothing, I guess," Tish said. "You've just seemed so funny lately. Edgy and tight and . . . not here. I thought a change would be good for you."

"Rest is what will be good for me," I said. "Utter and complete quiet in an empty house, without jumping out of my skin at every sound Hilary makes. I'm going to sleep for two days, and then I'm going to clean this place from chandelier to shithouse, as the man said."

The cold tongue of fear left my stomach and reached up to caress my heart, setting it racing. I swallowed hard. What on earth was the matter with me? What was there in my own quiet house to be afraid of? What was there to fear in this visit of Hilary's? Her therapist had assured me she was safe; was, in fact, a good bit improved. And I knew this to be true. It was a fair approximation of the old Hilary I had put on the plane to Atlanta two days before. Somehow, Scratch had done that, despite her grief for him.

"Well, I'll call and check on you every day," Tish said. I could hardly hear her around the pounding of my heart in my ears.

When I had hung up the phone I sat for a moment on the side of my bed, looking blindly around the room. It appeared strange, somehow elongated and overly bright, not my familiar bedroom at all. My heart escalated its pounding, and my palms were wet. This was absurd. I got up and walked into the kitchen and looked at the wall clock; seven thirty-five. Past the time I was accustomed to getting supper for Hilary and me. And I had not, I remembered, had any lunch. Perhaps the sinking, fluttering tremors in my stomach were simple hunger. I pulled a can of soup out of the cupboard and carried it over to the stove and got out the can opener, and then put it down on the counter. My hands, I realized, were shaking. I reached up and took out my lone bottle of Scotch. A drink first, I thought. I'll have a drink and watch the news.

I took the drink into the living room and turned on the television set and settled on the sofa, and then turned the television off again and got up. I felt compelled to stay in motion, to find something to occupy my hands and legs. The strange, formless, unfocused fear grew stronger, coming at me in waves and gusts. Sweat broke out at my hairline. I took a deep swallow of the stinging Scotch and felt it burning its way into my stomach, cutting through the fear. I took another.

"Booze is the answer," I said aloud to myself, and my voice rang tinnily and terribly in the emptiness. Before I even knew what I was doing, I was at the telephone, dialing. The number I dialed was, I realized only when I heard the voice on the answering machine, Carter's. I started to hang up, and then I did not. His recorded voice was deep and caressing and warm, as I remembered it, and my hand tightened on the telephone as if clinging to the safety of the voice.

"I'm not at home right now," Carter's voice said. "If this is an emergency I can be reached at 422-7877. Otherwise I'll return your call as soon as I can."

I put the phone down. The number was, I knew, Pat Dabney's. The safety in that wonderful voice was an illusion, a chimera. I could not call Carter. He was not, now, mine to call.

I felt something huge and black and formless crouching off at the fringes of my mind, some magnification of fear so awful and inexorable that I knew, simply, that it would kill me if it reached me, and I shut my eyes and clenched my fists to keep it at bay. When the shrill summons of the telephone broke into the silence, I leaped to answer it as if someone had thrown me a lifeline in a cold and swallowing sea.

"Mama?" Hilary's voice said, across the miles from Atlanta.

I nearly wept aloud with deliverance.

"Hi, Punkin," I said, in as normal a voice as I could manage. The black mass receded slightly. "How's everything up there?"

"Okay," Hilary said. "Fine, I guess. Dawn said I should call you and let you know things are all right, so I did."

At the sound of that faceless young name on my daughter's lips, the fear crept closer. It was her idea, then, my daughter's call, this new Mrs. Christopher Calhoun.

"Well, that was nice of Dawn," I said, with my dry mouth. "Tell her I said so. Are you having a good time?"

Please don't be, my racing mind said clearly into my ears. Please be homesick and wanting to come home. I'll start now. I'll be there before midnight. . . .

"Yeah. I guess so," Hilary said. It was the voice of a child who wanted to please. I knew with a flash of the intuition that had always bound us that Hilary was indeed having a good time but did not wish to sound as if she was. The implicit loyalty in the neutral words made my heart ache.

"Hil, it's okay to have a good time," I said, sounding as mature and encouraging as possible around the implacable fear. "I want you to enjoy your trip. It's why you went. How's . . . how is your father?"

"Okay," Hilary said. "He's not as big as I thought he was. He's taking some vacation to do stuff with me. So is Dawn."

I could not read her voice.

"Well, that's great," I said heartily, feeling ridiculously

betrayed and somehow guilty, as if I had been caught lying to my child. "What all have you done?"

"Well, yesterday we went to this new place, Underground Atlanta," she said. "It was nice. It's down under the streets, all these stores and places to eat, like a hundred years ago. We rode down there on the rapid transit train. And tomorrow we're going to go to Six Flags, and the next day to see the new zoo. . . ."

Her voice picked up speed and animation as she talked, excitement creeping in in spite of herself. I tried to picture Chris at the zoo, or on a Ferris wheel or merry-go-round, and could not. Except for the hospital, I could not remember him going downtown in all our married life.

"Sounds great," I said falsely. "Be sure and thank him, and Dawn, too. They're spending a fortune on you."

And I can hardly keep you in school, I did not say. Off in the edge of the light, the dark thing in my mind growled.

"It's okay," she said. "I think Daddy's rich. He has a houseboat. We're going up to the lake this weekend and spend the night on it. And he has a house up in the mountains, and we can go there sometime. And Dawn has five Swatches. All different."

"How nice for her," I said.

"They have a dog, too," she said, and I could hear the effort she was making to keep her voice casual. "A puppy. He looks just like Stinker. He's mine, only I have to keep him up here."

Oh, Chris, you bastard, I thought hopelessly and dismally. *Kill her love and just buy it back. Couldn't you let her bring the dog home with her? Do you have to tether her to you with a puppy?*

The fear gave my stomach a great, direct, sickening blow, and I doubled over the phone with it.

"Better hang up now, Punkin," I said. "Your daddy won't be rich long if you keep on talking."

Dear God, don't let her hear this awful thing in my voice, I thought.

There was a small silence, in which I clung to the wall behind the telephone and tried to keep my mind blank and still.

"Mama?" she said finally.

"Yeah, Pooper?"

"I miss you. I'll be glad to get home."

I leaned against the wall, knees going slack, love for her flooding me.

"I'll be glad to see you," I said. "It's a lonesome old town when you're not around."

Another silence. Then, casually, "Have you seen Tom?"

The breath that had come sliding back into my lungs went out again.

"No, sweetie. I don't think I'll be seeing Tom."

"Yes, you will," she said serenely. "You will. I know. When you do, tell him I said hey. Tell him I said wait for me. Will you tell him?"

"I . . . yes. I'll tell him," I said.

"Bye, Mama. I love you," Hilary said. Hilary, eleven years old now, and whole, or almost.

"I love you, too," I said. "Hurry home."

When I hung up, it hit.

There isn't any way to describe it, that awful, sucking, idiot storm of mindless, amorphous terror. Remember any moment in which you have ever been totally and desperately afraid and magnify it tenfold, and maybe you will have some idea. . . . I could not have said what I was afraid of. I was simply inside an endless cyclone, an earthquake, of fear. I was flung, shaken, buffeted, thrown, savaged. My eyes were blind, and my muscles useless. I sank down on the floor beside the telephone table and rolled into a ball. My heart raced wildly out of control, pounding so hard that I could not breathe around it; I gasped, and shook all over, hard. Sweat poured off me. In the darkness of the maelstrom I could see no comforting face, hear no familiar voice, feel no hand reaching out for me. Hilary was gone, and Tom, and Carter, and Tish and Charlie. My mother and father were gone. I was absolutely sure that I was dying. They would have to call Chris, and he would tell Hilary that I had died. . . .

Help me, I said with my soundless voice, so weakly that I could not even move my lips. Help me.

I don't know how long it lasted. When it receded, not fully but enough so that I could struggle to my knees, it was wholly dark outside. I thought it must be near midnight. Still on the floor, I reached for the telephone and dialed Frick Harper's number. I did it unconsciously, my fingers moving of their own volition. Somehow my nerveless hands knew, even if my mind did not, that no doctor of conventional medicine could help me.

Mercifully, he was still in his office, and not with a patient.

"I think I'm dying," I whispered. "Help me, Frick. I think I'm going to die."

Slowly and calmly, as if we had been two old friends talking of nothing in particular, he coaxed the details out of me. Just listening to his flat, pleasant voice made me feel better, somehow. Out there in the night, on the end of my telephone, a strong, competent human being stood like a stone, and he would not let me die. As long as I held the telephone in my hands, I could live a little longer.

"Panic attack," he said, when I had finally stopped

gasping into the phone. "Pure and simple, classic, world class. I should have warned you you'd be a prime candidate, once Hilary left."

"Frick, it was more than just some kind of anxiety thing," I said. "It was . . . unspeakable. If it happens again it will kill me."

"No, it won't," he said. "And it may well happen again. But it won't kill you. Listen, Andy, virtually everybody who has panic disorder thinks they're dying. It's one of the clinical syndromes. It's awful; God, I know it is. But these attacks are explainable, and they're not all that uncommon. Often they're triggered by trauma, usually loss of some kind. Just think for a minute what you've lost, and in a short time: your husband, your home, your security, and now the person you've been living every second of your life for, for almost a year. . . ."

And Scratch, I thought. And Tom. And the woods.

"I haven't lost Hilary," I said.

"No," he said. "You haven't. But you thought you had, didn't you? Didn't you think, when she went to her father's, that you'd never get her back?"

"I . . . yes," I said. "I did think that. But I don't now."

"Maybe your mind doesn't. But try telling that to your subconscious. Listen, I don't think you've got a full-fledged panic disorder starting. I'd bet this was an isolated reaction to too much loss you haven't dealt with yet. We'll have to watch and see. But meanwhile let's try to get you some relief, and if it persists, I'll refer you to someone. Do you still have that Xanax I gave you for Hilary? I think you told me she'd never taken any. . . ."

"Yes," I said. "It's still here."

"Well, go take two right now, and then one every six hours or so as you need them, and call me tomorrow.

Chances are they'll do the trick. But I wish you'd let me send you to somebody and get started working on all that unresolved garbage you've been carrying all this time. Hilary needs you with all your parts working."

"Maybe later," I said, around the huge white weariness that was coming swiftly upon me, like a storm surge at the height of a hurricane. "Maybe when school starts again. I'm sorry to bother you so late, Frick. I just . . . I'm sorry."

"Don't be," he said. "It's not late. It's just eight-thirty."

I put the phone back in its cradle and went and got the Xanax out of my medicine chest and took two. I washed them down with the diluted Scotch in my tumbler. When it was gone, I had another shot of Scotch, straight. In a few moments I fell asleep on the couch, all the lamps blazing, the television set blaring. It was as thick, still, and lightless a sleep as I can remember in my life. When the pounding at the front door finally reached me, miles and fathoms deep in my Xanax tomb, I could not, for a long moment, move my paralyzed limbs or get a deep breath through my dried-out nose and mouth. And I could not force my leaden lids open. I simply lay on my sofa, listening dully to the knocking that I knew, on some deeper and simpler level than my mind, had been going on for a long time.

I struggled to a sitting position and called out, my voice thick in my throat, "Who is it?"

"It's Tom," came the light, rich voice that was under every thought and at the edge of every dream that I had had that summer. "Can I come in? I need to talk to you."

I pulled myself to my feet. I could not feel them. I ran my hands through my wild hair; I could not feel my fingers on my scalp, either. There was an awful, metallic taste in my mouth, and the acid sweetness of old liquor, and a cottony unpleasantness that I thought must be the drug. I had no idea on earth what time it was, and could not focus on my watch.

"Andy?" he called again.

"I'm coming."

I went on prickling, clumping feet to the door and unlocked it and stood looking at him through the screen. In the faint yellow light of the porch fixture, he looked as lunar and strange as if he had just come from another star. He was thin to bone, thinner even than on the night we had seen him at the convenience store, so thin that the ropes of his muscles and the long cords of the big veins stood out in his flesh like one of those plastic models that Charlie and Chris had used in med school. His thinness was shocking. But he was clean-shaven, and his black hair was cut short again, and the skin of his face and arms was its old deep walnut, the color of Clay Dabney's skin. Because of the dim light and the tan, I could not see the circles beneath his eyes, but the old eldritch blueness flashed at me out of the darkness of night and skin. There was the gleam of something wet on his face, and I thought it must be rain, but behind him, hanging low and swollen in the still, hot night, I could see the great, new-risen August moon.

He moved a little closer and I saw then that the wetness on his face was tears. My mind refused to compute, to deal with this fact. I simply stood still and stared at him. The thought occurred to me that we stood in a dream, Tom Dabney and I.

"Can I come in?" he said again, softly. His voice was thick and ragged in his throat. Silently I unhooked the screen door and stood aside, and he came into the room on his silent feet. I saw that he wore his soft, ragged old deerhide stalking moccasins, though he was dressed conventionally enough in fresh khaki pants and a faded old blue oxford cloth shirt with the sleeves rolled up. He smelled of soap and the woods, and the older, warmer, unknowable yet all-known smell of Tom.

We sat opposite each other in front of my dead fireplace, he on the edge of the chair Carter had favored, I on the rumpled sofa. I saw the half-empty Scotch bottle on the table, and the empty glass, and saw him see it, and was suddenly aware of how I must look, my face puffed and pale, my hair a snarl, my shorts and shirt corrugated like cardboard with the drenching sweat of terror.

"Are you all right?" he said, staring at me. "You look awful. Is Hilary all right? Scratch said she'd been sick."

"Hilary's fine," I said. "She's visiting her father. She'll be back in a week or so. She told me on the phone tonight to tell you hey. Did you . . . did you come to see her?"

"No," he said. "I came to see you. I . . . there wasn't anybody else who wouldn't throw me out. But if this isn't a good time for you . . ."

I shook my head to clear it. The room and Tom came into sharper focus. Some of the scum of the dream peeled away.

"I must look like I've been on a three-day drunk," I said. "But I've been asleep." The fact of his physical presence in my house hit me then, and my heart began to pound again. This time, though, it was not in fear. Not precisely.

"I think you look—" His voice thinned and broke, and he was silent, struggling for composure.

"What is it, Tom?" I said. Fear did come in then, over the other thing that had quickened my heart.

"It's Scratch," he said, and grief was heavy in his voice. I felt my own grief leap, freshening, to match his.

"Oh, God," I said. "Is he . . . ?"

"No," he said. "He's not dead. Not yet. But he's . . . Jesus, Andy, he's just eaten up. Just eaten up . . ."

I went over and sat on the arm of his chair and put my arms around him. I did it without thinking. My muscles did it, my hands and feet and arms. He pressed his head against my breast in silence, and then he sat up and took a deep breath, and I pulled away a bit, and looked at him.

"He came dragging up on the porch tonight about eight and collapsed," Tom said. "I had to carry him into the house, and put him on the sofa. I tried to call an ambulance, but he wouldn't let me. He kept trying to talk and choking, and choking, but finally he got it out that he'd come to tell me something—dragged himself all the way from upswamp to the house to tell me—and then he had a hemorrhage. I never saw so much blood. Out of his mouth, and his nose, and his . . . rectum, and oh, Christ, Andy, on his neck and head . . . the tumors, the sores, like the deer."

I saw again, sickly, yet at a remove, the terrible sores on the belly of the dead doe, and the sly, slick blue of entrails. I remembered the muffler around Scratch's throat, and the stocking cap. It had not been cold, then, but the need to spare us, Hilary and me. . . .

"Oh, Scratch," I whispered, putting my hands over my face.

"I took him to the emergency room," Tom said, heavily, over the tears. "I thought the ER staff was going to throw up. They've got him in intensive care, with tubes and a respirator and God knows what else, but it isn't going to do any good. The doctor just shook his head when I asked."

"What is it?" I whispered. "What is it?"

"Cancer," he said. "I don't know what kind. They'll probably never know where it hit him first. I'd say lymphatic system, or liver. Lungs, maybe. That's where radioactive poison gets you, usually. I should have known all along. I've been seeing those animals all summer. It's the motherfucking, murdering water, of course; Scratch never would drink city water. They've got it, up there in the settlement, but he carried his own water from Goat Creek. He even kept jugs of Goat Creek water at my house to drink. . . . Andy, I need for you to come with me now. Can you come? Can you do that? I can't ask anybody else. . . ."

"Where?" I said. "Where?"

"Back up the creek to the lumber camp on King's Oak," he said. "Andy, he told me that the . . . whatever it is in the water, that's lighting it up and killing everything, is coming from the camp. Oh, God, when I think what it must have cost him to find that out . . . He went all the way back up there from his house; it must have taken him all day. Said he got the idea to look there in some kind of dream, or trance, and sick as he is, he went. And he went through that fence. You know how he hated that wire. You know he's never touched it, not in all the years since Clay put it up, but he took wire cutters with him and cut it and went in there and saw . . . whatever it is, and then came all the way downcreek to tell me. And it's killed him. He's dying now. And so I'm going up there. Tonight. I need you to come with me. Somebody . . . sane has to see it. Nobody else would go."

He stopped and looked at me. His eyes burned blue.

"Are you telling me that it's something Clay is doing?" I whispered, my voice shaking. "Are you telling me that, Tom? Because I don't believe you! My God, Clay Dabney has practically given up his life for you this summer!"

He shook his head.

"No. I don't know. I don't think so . . . but I don't know. But can't you see, I have to find out? Don't you see that I have to go and at least try to stop it? If you're afraid, I won't blame you, but don't you see why I need somebody else, somebody who isn't . . . suspect? Andy, Martin just plain won't go, and Reese is passed out drunk and can't. And I can't wait. Andy, please . . ."

His voice broke again, and tears ran down his brown face and dropped one by one onto the collar of the blue shirt. It was sodden on both sides, just above the small pearl buttons. I could see that one of them had been crushed in the laundry. One tear trembled, perfect like a diamond, in the hollow of his throat.

My thinking mind switched off and the old thing there, the old, deep, simple thing that had once called out to Tom, and been answered by him, lurched and ground and lumbered back to life.

"Fix yourself a drink," I said. "I'll just be a minute."

I went down the hall toward my bedroom and once again I heard him say, as he had said the night I had come to him in the jail, "Thank you, Andy."

I did not answer him this time, either.

We drove through the hot, moon-thick night mostly in silence. The truck was neat and swept out, and smelled as if he might have cleaned its interior with cleaning fluid. He had closed the windows against the heavy, breathless heat, and we jolted through the near-deserted town and out the highway toward King's Oak and the turnoff to Goat Creek in a humming capsule of stale-cold breath from the air conditioner. Just before we crossed the railroad tracks that marked the boundaries of Pemberton Over There, I caught a glimpse of the lighted time-and-temperature sign on the mellow brick First National Bank of Pemberton. It said 92 degrees, 10:10 P.M. Faint surprise scratched at the bubble of Xanax and fatigue and simple shock in which I floated. I had thought it must be the middle of the night.

Tom drove intently, bent slightly forward, his face cruelly and jovially underlit by the green dash glow, like a jack-o'-lantern. He did not look at me, did not seem to realize that I was with him in the truck. An occasional tear still slid down his face and dropped onto his collar, but the tears did not seem real; they had the illusory quality of the stigmatic tears on the face of a carved saint, bizarre miracles. Whatever part of him wept for Scratch, it was not his mind. I could feel that focused powerfully and singly on that burning point up the creek, like a palpable searchlight. Incredibly, I was almost comfortable, bowling through the night with this once-beloved madman on the way into what could scarcely escape being danger of one degree or another.

Once, he turned his head to look at me, and said, "I can't tell you this is not dangerous, but I don't know yet just how dangerous it is. When we get upcreek close to the wire, I'll know better. If it looks bad I'll leave you and go in alone. If you come in with me I'll take all precautions. I'm not going to let anything happen to you."

"I'm not afraid," I said serenely, and realized that I was not. Underneath the fatigue and the drug and the unreality of this night another feeling throbbed steadily, like an artery. It was a sense of ending, of impending settlement. One way or another, when this night was over, I would know something about Tom and myself and the water in Goat Creek; the obscene terror of it would have a name, and we could speak that name and find a way to defuse it of its menace. Perhaps Tom could end it; perhaps it would, even, end Tom. Either way, there was a finish to this foulness in the sunny silence of the Big Silver Swamp. Either way, Hilary would be safe and we could go on from this night. I was content to ride in silence toward whatever finish we would find. Frick Harper would, I suppose, have called the feeling the need for closure. It was a simpler and more powerful need than any fear of danger. And besides, I simply did not believe that Tom would let me be harmed. Even this new Tom, reviled and half mad with obsession, would keep me safe.

I turned my head to look through the rear window at the unwinding silver ribbon of road behind us and saw the gleam of dark metal. I looked more closely. On the ledge behind the seat lay two rifles, his old single-shot and my slim little Ruger. I caught the scent of fresh gun oil, and saw the sheen of newly cleaned barrels. I looked over at Tom.

"You're not taking your bow?" I said. And then, catching for the first time the significance of his ordinary dress, "You haven't done any kind of . . . ceremony, have you? I thought, for something like this . . ."

"The bow and the rituals and the songs and all that jazz haven't done any of us a whole hell of a lot of good, have they?" he said briefly and flatly. The flatness was more painful to hear than bitterness would have been, or grief. Pain flared in my chest like brushfire, but dully, like pain far down under morphine. I ached with the need to give his magic back to him, but the ache was far away.

"Maybe, when we get there, we could do one," I said clumsily. "I'll help."

The smile he gave me was brief and dead.

"Thanks, but it would be a sacrilege now," he said. "I can't do that anymore. I've lost the power. Maybe I never had it; I think it must have been Scratch all along, and what I felt was just spilling off him. All of it, everything, all that we learned and believed and loved . . . It couldn't help the woods. It couldn't heal the water. It couldn't save my goats. It couldn't keep Hilary safe. It couldn't get rid of one iota of the stink and pain and death out in the swamp. And Scratch . . . I couldn't even save Scratch."

"Tom . . ."

"No. Be quiet, Andy. I'm sorry, but we can't talk about that anymore. I can still stop it. I'm as good with a gun as I ever was with a bow and arrow. Or a fucking chant."

This time the bitterness was there, dark and old as the water at the core of the earth. I felt the tears begin to slide out of my eyes, even though the bubble in which I floated still held. I prayed silently that it would, for a little while yet. Enough to get me through this night.

After a space of silence we reached the turnoff for King's Oak, and he slowed the truck and turned in. We rattled down the close-grown, black dirt ribbon noisily, at a good clip, headlights on bright. I expected him to cut the lights and slow to a creep when we approached the clearing where the great lodge stood, but he didn't. He felt my question, and said, "There's not anybody at King's Oak. Chip gives the staff the last two weeks in August off, before hunting season opens. And besides, I rode by his house in town tonight. Having a dinner party, old Chip is. Looks like half the honchos from the Big Silver are there. I counted seven top-level security stickers. We don't need to worry about anybody seeing or hearing us until we get close to the lumber camp, and maybe not then. Scratch didn't see any sign of life this afternoon."

He laughed, an ugly laugh. "No sign of life at all."

As we had on that night, seemingly eons ago now, when we had come to King's Oak at the winter solstice—oh, that night of star-chipped magic!—we drove on past the great, sweet black bulk of the house, silvered now with thickly poured moonlight, and went on down the rutted lane through the black-green soybean fields, toward the blacker line of the river swamp. Tom did not speak again until he had parked the truck in the clearing on the bank of Goat Creek where he had parked it on that night. We got out of the truck in the same silence in which we had moved then; I remembered that silence, and the crunch of my high silver heels through ice-rimed brown grass stubble, and the sound of my breathing and my heart's deep, slow pounding. He had held my arm going down the bank to where the little skiff was tied that night, and over his other arm he had carried the mink throw. Now he carried the two rifles, and he did not take my arm. Now we went down the little bank, but we did not get into the waiting skiff. I remembered that on that other night crazy laughter had bubbled into my throat, irrepressibly, like champagne. Now what pressed there was grief and pain held back, and under that, the beginning again of fear.

"How far we've come," I said to myself. "What a long, terrible black way we've come."

I did not realize I had said it aloud until he said, softly, "A long way indeed."

We stood together in the moony white night, both looking across the summer-stunted creek to the island where the King's Oak stood, its great, beautiful, dark canopy clean and monstrous against the sky. I do not know what he saw under those cathedral branches. I saw leaping firelight, and the shimmer of joined naked flesh, and heard the caroling laughter of exuberance and joy. I turned away, so that my back was to the tree. He turned with me.

"We're going upcreek from here," he said. "You've never been up as far as we're going, and I don't go up there, either. But I have, when I was much younger, with Clay. Before he leased the land to the lumber company. I know the way. It's not a hard walk. There's a little ridge that parallels the creek most of the way, and the walking is firm and there's not much undergrowth. With the moonlight, it'll almost be like walking in your backyard. About three miles upcreek, we'll cut inland, up a little branch that forks off to the left. It runs right through the lumber company's main clearing, if I remember right, and on up to where the creek makes up. When we come to the branch, then we'll stalk, or maybe even go on our stomachs. I'll know by then. But it won't be far, and I'll lead the way. If I think I need to, that's where I'll leave you, at the cutoff of that branch. If I tell you to, I want you to go on back and take the truck into town and get Clay. But I probably won't have to do that."

"Tom, I can't get back through all those woods to the truck by myself," I said, the fear sharpening. "You can't leave me up there. . . ."

"You can track almost as well as any of us, and better than Martin," he said. "I've seen you do it. All you have to do is follow the creek to the King's Oak. Andy, don't let me down now. This is the end of it, this is where we start to stop it, if it can be stopped. This is for . . . this is for Hilary. Do this for Hilary if you can't do it for me. Do it for Hilary and yourself."

"Let's go, then," I said. And then, surprising myself by smiling, "If it's half the night you gave Tim Ford, I wouldn't miss it for the world."

His answering grin flashed out in the darkness, briefly. "That was some kind of night," he said.

We walked steadily for over an hour. He moved fast and quietly, and his feet in the soft, dry earth of the ridge were sure, but he was no longer totally silent, and I did not lose him into the immensity of the swamp forest, as I had on the other occasions when I had gone out into the night woods with him. At first, despite my thick-soled Nikes, I had trouble with my footing on the spongy, detritus-strewn floor of the forest, and was certain that I could be heard for miles around us, but it did not seem to bother him. He carried both guns and went steadily ahead, not turning back to look at me, as if certain I was not lagging behind. And I did not lag; even though, at first, my breath labored in my chest and sweat drenched through my jeans and long-sleeved shirt. I tramped grimly on behind him, hearing nothing but my own heart and feet, grimacing at my own noise. Occasionally he lifted his free hand to his face, and I thought that he was still weeping silently for his friend as he walked, but I heard no sound from him.

Gradually the noise of my clumsiness seemed to settle, and then dwindle, and my laboring heart found its rhythm, and the vivid silence of the Big Silver Swamp grew in my ears and slid into my mind, a living silence that seemed enhanced, not broken, by the night noises around me. I heard the thousands of tiny rustlings and splashings and snappings and whistlings and pipings and croakings and tickings that were the night music of the Big Silver. I heard, once, the faraway bellow of a big gator, hollow and ghostly over water, and an unseen stampede that was whitetails in flight from something, and the unearthly hunting call of a drifting owl, and the silver glissando of a whippoorwill. Under it all was the susurration of cicadas, a continual rhythm like a heartbeat, and under that, even, a kind of high, pulsing, dreaming hum that seemed to come from the very earth itself. Presently I felt myself begin to move in that rhythm, to swim through the dark, thick, murmurous air of the swamp as easily and naturally as through warm water. The night became, for a time, like those other nights that I had gone out into the woods with him. I forgot, as I had then, the essential incongruity of a forty-year-old divorced college public relations worker with a child and a leased house and a Toyota doing this. I forgot pain and fear. The night woods swallowed me and were, for a small space of time, all.

The pain and fear and the incongruity flooded back soon enough. We came at last to a place where Goat Creek doubled back upon itself, forming a dark, silent elbow. We had to cross it to go on. It was in thick, moonless shadow here, and looked deep. Tom stopped, and I stopped behind him. I waited for him to go through the creek and continue on the other side, but he did not. Instead, he ranged slowly up and down until he found a place he deemed narrow enough, and he pitched the rifles softly across and leaped himself, landing surefootedly and quietly in the leafy mold of the creek verge. Then he turned and held his hands out to me.

"Jump," he said. "Be sure and get a good start. Don't let the water touch you."

I remembered, then, why we had come. The woods, which had swallowed me, spat me back into reality. Coldness prickled the hairs on my arms and the back of my neck, even in the heat. The water flowed on between us, dark, unmarked by that devil's fire, but I would rather have died than gone into it at that moment. For the first time I feared the water as my daughter had, as Tom Dabney did now. I looked at him in terror, and then I backed off and got a running start and closed my eyes and flung myself into space. He caught my outstretched hands on the other side and pulled me up the bank, and we went on upstream. We did not speak again until we came to the tiny branch that cut off to the left through the woods. I thought that it must be well after midnight by then.

Tom stopped and looked ahead into the darkness. He signaled for me to be still. He stood motionless, hands relaxed at his sides, the guns laid at his feet, simply looking into the night and listening to it. I knew that the essence of him was ranging out in the night, a part of the water and wind and trees; I knew that when he moved again he would know what he wanted to do. Presently the stillness went out of him and he turned to me.

"It's okay," he said. "I don't think there's anybody up there. If there is, we're upwind of them. We can walk naturally until we're almost to the camp. But if I signal you then, I want you to drop. We'll have to go on our stomachs then."

He handed my rifle to me. "Don't use it unless I tell you. Or unless I can't help you anymore. Then use it instantly. You know how."

This time I did not argue. The fear in my stomach was not far from breaking free.

We turned and followed the little branch away into the deep heart of the Big Silver. This was country that I knew, country of deep, thick, wet woods floors and long, dark sloughs and standing black water, country of cypress and moss and tupelo and a thousand close-pressing hardwoods. The moon thrust through here only in sly, fitful fingers, and the wet heat thickened. Insects abound, keening in ears, swarming at mouth and nose. When we lifted our feet from the forest floor, they came away with a sucking sound. The calls of furred and feathered things dwindled, and the slither and cry of gilled and webbed things rose. Along the branch, ferns and reeds were black and lush. We saw no fire in this water, either, but I kept well away from it. I thought I would never again feel on my flesh the warm sweetness of the water of Goat Creek.

We came to a place where a fence of rusted wire, five barbed strands, bisected the branch and ran off into the darkness on either side. Tom stopped.

"Beyond that it's lumber company land," he said. "I don't know where Scratch cut the fence, but I don't have time to look for it. We'll have to go under it. Follow me. I'll hold it for you when I get through."

He dropped to his stomach, holding the rifle in the crook of both elbows, and wriggled under the wire on the creekbank, going like a snake, or a commando. Halfway under, he stopped, froze. A sound came from him, a gasp, a thick snort of revulsion. Then he wriggled on under and held the wire for me. It was only after I was under and upright again that he parted the reeds on the creekbank with the barrel of the rifle and pointed at what he had seen. I leaned close, and then jumped back, my heart hammering with fear and disgust. Down at the very edge of the black water, at the roots of the ferns and the reeds, where the water kissed, a monstrous line of sickly white plants stretched, hidden in the dankness of the bank's curve. I did not know what they were, but knew in my hammering heart and heaving stomach that they were not natural. They were fleshy and pale, glowing white, damp and mottled and peeling and splotched, twisted and tumorous and altogether grotesque. They might have been mushrooms, but were not; might have been twisted tree roots, but were not. They had never pushed through the soil of any other earth in any other time; you knew that. They gave off their own light, somehow; and they were truly terrible things. The line of them stretched off into the darkness upcreek and was lost in it. I looked at Tom, unable to speak. He looked back at me, impassively. We went on, keeping well away from the creekbank.

As we moved, the ferns and reeds themselves began to look strange, blighted and whitened and malformed. Soon they died, and then there were none at all, only wet black dirt, and standing slime, and the black roots of the trees. I became aware, gradually, that the sounds of the water creatures had stopped. No owls called, and no night birds. I could scarcely breathe around the fear in my chest. It was not the mindless fear of the early night, but an altogether and eons-older thing, something atavistic, something that lifted my hair roots and drew my lips back over my teeth, just this side of a snarl. Ahead of me, Tom motioned to me to stop, and I did. Peering through the thick darkness, I could see, ahead of us in the forest, a thinning of the blackness and the faintest fitful frost of white light. We had come to a clearing, and I knew that we were at it now, the heart of the lumber camp, the dark thing we had come to find.

"Stay here," Tom whispered, and moved off toward the light. He moved quickly and soundlessly, in a running crouch. I stood hunched over, trying to will my hammering heart still, trying to think of nothing at all. Soon he had moved out of my sight.

In what seemed an eternity, but was more likely five minutes, I heard him call my name: "Andy." There was something wrong with his voice. I hesitated, and he called again. "Andy. Andy, come here."

And I broke into a trot, following the sound of his strangled voice, and ran into the clearing from the shelter of black woods.

It was large, perhaps the area of four football fields. In the middle of it, a jumble of rusted tin shacks stood, leaning in upon one another. Heavy machinery stood about, tire-deep in weeds, looking like the monstrous carapaces of prehistoric insects. There were one or two tanker trucks, tireless and obviously long useless, and a larger board shack, open on one side, where coiled wire and old tires and tools and sodden, disintegrated cardboard cartons were piled. The floor of the clearing was weed-choked white sand, and a spur rail line threaded through it, running out of sight into the trees on both sides. Only the rail line looked usable, or used; the rails were not rusted, but were the soft, buffed pewter that spoke of traffic. A staggering row of utility lights, white, so that I thought they must be mercury vapor, circled the clearing. There were no human beings in evidence, and no trace that any had been, for a long time. What tire tracks there were in the sand of the work yard had been diffused by months of rain and wind and sun.

At first I did not see Tom, and then I heard him call again and saw him, a small figure at the very end of the clearing on the far side, past the jumble of shacks and equipment, partially obscured by them. I followed the spur line to where he stood. It ended there. I saw what it ended in before I came near to it, and I could not make myself go further.

Four vast, square concrete pools lay there at the end of the spur, white-lit by another circle of work lights. Around them, the forest stretched away black and old and silent. Beyond them, the spur line picked up again and ran off into the forest to the east. Toward Goat Creek and the Big Silver River. The night was utterly still and quiet, but the pools were not. They were filled with a terrible, opaque, green-white liquid, and smoke and vapor lay so thickly over them that I could see their surfaces only intermittently. But I could make out that the surfaces were in motion of themselves; there was no wind. They writhed and bubbled and sucked. There was the sound of sibilant hissing, of boiling. When the vapors parted and the pool surfaces flashed clear for an instant, I could see that deep down, far down, the pools were an eerie, burning blue.

I went on numb, stumbling feet to where Tom stood.

"What is it?" I whispered, knowing that I was seeing horror, but unable to define it. "What in the name of God is it?"

"Seepage basins," he said. His voice was the high, eerie growl of an animal about to attack. "Seepage basins, cooling pools, whatever, for nuclear waste. I saw twenty-six others, just like them, over at the Big Silver plant last week; I've been over there for two weeks, scouting. Twenty-six just like these four, only they kept those cleaned up. They weren't . . . boiling. They weren't lit up. No wonder they test clean. This . . . this is where they put the worst of it, then. The really bad stuff. The stuff that tests out of sight with plutonium and strontium and God knows what else; the stuff that kills you. The stuff that spoils all your pretty PR. The stuff I took out of Goat Creek. They're dumping waste water up here on King's Oak, and more than water, I'll bet my life. I'll bet if we looked we'd find tank fields for sludge, and salts, and pools where they dump the radioactive hardware and tools and clothes, and maybe even the irradiated fuel and target rods. . . . Ford said that's what lights the water up blue, the rods."

He swung around to face me and I saw that his open eyes were totally mad, and blind. I knew that it was not me he saw with those eyes.

"They're not lumbering up here," he said, in the awful voice. "The spur, the turpentine trunks, the tank cars—they've been hauling it in here at night, maybe even in the daytime, for God knows how long. Look, see that second spur? That doesn't go out to the main line, you can bet your ass on it. That goes straight across the creek and the river onto the Big Silver. They can ship directly in here, in tank cars, and nobody even knows the hell they're doing it, because nobody ever comes in here. What do you want to bet there hasn't been a log or a drop of turpentine out of here in Christ knows how many years?"

He stopped, gasping for breath. A great, strangling, hopeless grief flooded me, a drowning, impotent outrage. I saw again the slender little goat, and the struggling death in the tender, perfect new morning.

"How dare they?" I said in a low, shaking voice. "Stupid, stupid, stupid . . . How *dare* they? How dare we? Look what we've all been given, and look what they've done to it, and what we've let them do. . . . Oh, how *dare* we? God should kill us all in our arrogant stupidity—"

"There isn't any God," Tom said. "We've killed sacredness, too."

We stood silent for a moment, and then he threw back his head and shouted, "They've been poisoning Goat Creek right out of King's Oak, Andy! *Right out of King's Oak!* Dear Christ in heaven . . ."

His voice rose, and rose, and I knew that I was about to hear once again that terrible, primal howl I heard the morning of the diseased deer, and that I could not, this time, bear it. I put my arms around him and held him close to me, and rocked him, or tried to. His body, under my arms, was as rigid as if in death.

"We have to go to Clay," I said. "Come on, Tom. Let's go tell Clay. Clay can help; Clay will know what to do about this."

"No," Tom said. "We don't have to go tell Clay. Clay knows." His voice was scarcely the voice of a living man. "He knows. He'd have to know. This is his land; there's no way he couldn't know. . . ."

In all my life, I will remember only snatches of the terrible, stumbling journey back to the King's Oak, and the silent, careening ride in the truck back into town, to the quiet street behind the training track in Old Pemberton where Clay Dabney had built a miniature chateau for his pretty, foolish Daisy. The big house was dark as we lumbered down the long driveway toward it, but when we pulled up to the porte cochere, I saw the glowing red tip of a cigarette from the dark front veranda and knew that Clay Dabney stood there waiting for us. I became aware only then that I had been crying, softly and monotonously, for a long time.

We went up the shallow, graceful steps and Tom stood facing his uncle. At this range I could see Clay's white hair, and the pale oval of his face, and smell the smoke from the cigarette. He wore a light seersucker robe over pajamas, and his feet were bare.

"Tom," he said. "Andy." His voice was without surprise, and colorless with exhaustion, weak. An old man's voice.

"We've just been up to the lumberyard," Tom said in the flat, inhuman voice.

Clay nodded. "Yes," he said. "I wondered when you'd get up there."

Tom's voice faded and shook with pain. "Clay," he said. "Uncle Clay, please. I just need to know why. Wasn't it enough? That you had the land, all that was left of King's Oak? Of the woods? Wasn't it enough that you had the actual King's Oak, the tree at the heart of everything? Couldn't you just have lumbered it, like you said you were doing? Shit, you didn't need the money; you've got all the money you'll ever need! Couldn't you have sold off some of it, if you needed more? Why did you have to let them pay you to poison it? Clay? Clay, did you know that some of that stuff takes four hundred thousand years to go dormant? *Four hundred thousand years, Clay!* Clay . . . you knew about the woods. You were one of us! *You desecrated sacred ground!* You know what Oppenheimer quoted when he saw the first atomic bomb explode? The *Bhagavad Gita*. He said, 'I am become death, the destroyer of worlds!' That's you, Clay. Death. The destroyer of worlds."

Clay Dabney's white face twisted. "There wasn't anything illegal about it! It was legal, a plain legal agreement; it was just as legal as anything ever was, a straight business contract. . . ." His voice trailed off.

"I think my father would kill you," Tom said softly.

"Your father was crazy as hell," Clay Dabney shouted. "And you're crazy, too! I've always thought you were! Maybe not at first, but after I grew up and out of that woods shit . . . The trouble with you and your father, Tom, is that you never grew up. Playing goddamn King of the Sacred Grove all your lives, while I went to work and made enough money to keep King's Oak in the family, what I could save of it . . . Christ, it's just *dirt!* It's just swampwater! They're just goddamned deer! They ain't gods! They're deer, with fleas and ticks and tumors and spavins! I kept the fucking taxes paid on this damned land and kept the land in this damned family! How would you like me to have made the money to do that, Tom? Sell it off piece by piece for a strip shopping center? Put a fucking ball-bearing plant on it? This way not a single tree went down, hardly. . . . I didn't know the fucking stuff was leaking out; I didn't know about groundwater, or aquifers! Stratton-Fournier built all that stuff up there; they're supposed to know. . . . I didn't know it was poison! Nobody did! Come to that, I still don't know it is."

"Clay, the reason I'm not going to kill you now is that I'd do it in anger," Tom said, and the terrible animal voice was back again, "and then it would be a personal act, a killing for *me.* It would not be a sacred act, if any such thing is still left. But I'll tell you one thing: I look forward to the chance to kill you. I will search for every chance I can to kill you so that it will be an act of vengeance, a ritual act. Get the stuff out of there starting tomorrow and bury those pools ten feet deep in clean dirt, or as I am standing here I will go to the newspapers and the television stations and then I will come back and kill you. And it will be just that—a sacred act of vengeance."

He whirled and walked away toward the pickup, stiffly, as a man might who was trying to hold himself erect despite a mortal wound. I could not move, and Clay Dabney did not. I looked up at him, on the beautiful steps of his veranda. There were tears on his face, and such an expression of anguish and hopelessness that I felt my heart start to break with it.

Tom turned then, and looked at his uncle. He looked for a long time at the twisted face, and then he said, in a barely audible whisper, "It was Chip. Wasn't it, Clay? It wasn't you, it was Chip. Chip cut a deal with . . . who: Francis Millican? And Chip got those pools put in, and that second spur line. . . . Chip. A little nest egg for ol' Chip, so he could keep his precious society hunts going, so he could pass out coke and liquor and God knows what else to every international sleazebag who bought his way into King's Oak, so he could keep the high-class whores coming, and pass out custom-made Purdys to fucking terrorists, and slaughter released birds by the thousands, and bait fields, and hunt deer out of season and at night from trucks . . . It was Chip. I should have known right away, when I saw it. You knew; of course you knew. For how many years, Clay? Ten, fifteen? But you didn't say anything. It would have been the end of ol' Chip in this part of the country, wouldn't it? The end of your only boy, Chip, the one who never could seem to make it on his own . . . Oh, no. You couldn't say anything. Never mind that it was the end of King's Oak. Of all that King's Oak is and has been . . . of all that the woods mean. And now it's the end of Scratch, because he's in the hospital dying of that water. But never mind that. Christ, what a time it must have been for you, Clay, these past few months. I hope every day was agony, and every night was hell."

He turned and stumbled back to the truck, and this time I went lurching after him. Tom turned once more then, and looked at Clay Dabney, sagging against the columns of his house, the great, moon-white, August sky pressing down upon him. I turned, too.

"I still ought to kill you, Clay," Tom said. "Chip's too sorry to kill; somebody ought to have done that when he was born. But you can tell him for me that if that stuff isn't out of there and the land cleaned up as well as it can be in a week, by God I will kill him. I will. It would be a supreme pleasure to go to jail for *that*."

He slumped against the fender of the truck and half lay there. I knew he could not drive. I took the keys from his fingers; they were flaccid and cold as death. I opened the door on the passenger side and half lifted, half pushed him into it, and got in on the driver's side, and started the engine. I had never driven the pickup before, but I knew I could do it; there in the wreckage of that terrible night I knew that I could do almost anything possible for a human being, before the great, sucking death tiredness took me, as it had him. I knew that it would soon, but I knew, too, that I could get us home.

I turned the truck off Palmetto Street on the road toward

King's Oak and Goat Creek, instead of left toward my house on Whimsy Road, and he lifted his death's head slightly from the back of the seat and looked at me.

"Don't you want to go home?" he said. There was no substance behind his voice.

"I am going home," I said, not looking at him, and he lifted his hand and touched mine, on the wheel, and then it fell away onto the front seat.

"I don't think that can be home for you now," he whispered.

"Well, it is," I said, knowing only that whether or not it was, or could be, it was where I must go now.

After that we drove in silence. The humming unreality settled closer around me, and by the time I pulled up at the house on Goat Creek, I was as light-headed with it as if I were quite drunk. Off on the other side of the bell of giddiness, ghastly fatigue and enormity bumped and mouthed, like a predator fish at the side of an aquarium. But my arms, as I helped him out of the truck and up to the wide porch, were steady, and my legs did not tremble. He had pulled the great, ridiculous carved bed out onto the part of the porch that hung over the moon-paved creek, and hung it with mosquito netting, and I parted the netting and let him sag down on the mattress. I flung off my filthy, sweat-stained clothing and climbed in with him, and wrestled the pants and shirt off him, and tossed them on the porch floor, and gathered him into my arms.

He turned his face into my breasts and lay still. I held him, feeling the weight and shape of his head on my flesh, the soft print of his mouth against my nipple, the sweet way his long chin fit into the hollow between breast and rib cage. I had held him this way a hundred times, sliding into sleep; it felt as if some amputated part of me had been, miraculously, rejoined, and I had been made whole. The light-headed calmness parted and I was swept with a surge of tenderness so simple and powerful that it literally shook me, and then the calm flooded back in and I lay still, watching the moon sink to meet the tops of the still trees across Goat Creek. Across my daughter's Moon River.

Tom lay still, too, so still that I thought he had fallen into sleep, and then he turned his head and said, in a voice so low that I had to strain to hear it, "It's all gone, Andy."

"No, it isn't," I said, tightening my arms around him. "You stopped it tonight, and now it will start to heal. Clay will get that horror cleaned up; you know he will. The plant will have to stop now. For one reason or another, it will be stopped, and then the creek will start to clean, and the woods will come back, and the animals. It will heal, Tom. You did that. You did that for Scratch and Hilary and . . . us."

"I didn't heal it," he said, sighing for breath. "I didn't even know it was there all those years, and when I found out, it was from Scratch. He knew. He found it. He's the one. . . . All this time, what I thought I had, what I thought we could do, the four of us, and my father, and his, and his—it was just crazy men mouthing crazy words. Dancing and singing in the woods like savages. Killing good animals who should have lived. Clay was right. There isn't any . . . power. There aren't any *thou*s. It's just dirt. They're just trees. The deer are just deer."

"Hush," I said. "Hush. You're tired to death, and you're half sick and half starved, and grieving for Scratch. You aren't making any sense. You'll know that when you're feeling better. There *is* power. I've seen you call it. I've seen you use it. If it isn't the power you thought it was, what difference does it make? Beauty has power. Peace and silence and wildness have power. Love has great power. Isn't that enough? You still have all those things. You have Hilary, and me. . . ."

"I don't have you," he said dully. "Not really. Not all of you, not all the way. You wanted to be part of it, you tried, but you never really could. You were always afraid. And you were right to be. And Hilary is gone. . . ."

"No, she isn't," I said. "She never was. She always believed. She still does. She wrote about you, Tom, and called it 'The True Story of Tom Dabney.' She worked on it for weeks. And when she called and told me to tell you hey the other night—last night—she said something else. She said for me to tell you to wait for her."

I felt him smile, slightly, against my breasts. " 'The True Story of Tom Dabney,' " he said softly. Then the smile was gone.

"I meant that I was gone," he said. "Some kind of thing—energy or joy or something—that I always had . . . I can feel that it's gone. I'm really afraid now, Andy. I never was before, not of much, but now I can't think of anything that I'm not afraid of. All the things that made me run, that were my . . . engines: I'm afraid of them now. I ought to make love to you. I want to make love to you. I want to do it all the rest of my life, and now I'm afraid to. I'm almost afraid to let my body touch you. I don't know what that water has done to my body. I don't know what it would do to you. I've been in that water all my life. . . . You know, Andy, I used to love my prick, glory in it, thank God for it. I mean that sincerely. It brought me joy and oneness, and I could give joy with it, and oneness. Now . . . it's been in that death water, and I can't put it into you. I'm afraid of that water. I've lived on and in and for the water all my life, and now I'm as afraid for a drop of it to touch me as a drowning kitten. I'm afraid."

I thought that I had never known what desolation meant until I heard that voice, those words.

"I'm not afraid," I said fiercely, sliding down so that my body fit into his, hollow to hollow, curve to curve. He was cold, cold. "I'm not afraid of the water. I'm not afraid of you. I'm not afraid of anything about your body. I will never be afraid. Make love to me, Tom. Please, now, right now . . . make love to me."

He rolled away from me, as violently as he could. "No," he said in a strangled voice. "I can't."

I think that he slept then. I felt the stiffness go out of his body, abruptly, and felt it loosen and slacken into the great bed. I lay still so that I would not wake him, but I did not sleep. I lay staring at the waning moonlight, misted with the thin stuff of the mosquito netting, and the dying blaze of molten silver on Goat Creek, and I wept silently in the dark for the man at my side who had been broken by the uncle he had loved and the cousin he did not, who was no longer the king of the sacred grove or even a maker of dreams, but only a tired and starved man with a shattered heart.

About half an hour later the telephone shrilled, as portentous as a banshee on the roof, and I leaped with hammering heart to answer it, knowing what it heralded.

When I came back to the bed on the porch, Tom was sitting up, looking at me. His eyes flashed blue in the darkness; the moon was down.

"Scratch," he said. It was not a question.

I could only nod. And then I found my voice. It stuck in my throat.

"Fifteen minutes ago. Very quietly, Tom. Not badly at

all, the doctor said. He . . . left you a message. He told the doctor to tell you that you did fine and he was proud of you. He said . . . you'll be good. He knew, Tom, somehow he knew."

"Good," Tom Dabney whispered. "Good. Well, he was wrong. Scratch was wrong. I won't be . . . good. Ah, God, Andy, they killed him! He's dead and I miss him! Scratch is dead and *I want him!*"

He began to cry, a child's desperate and abandoned tears, racking and rough and terrible to hear. I had never heard a man cry like that, only a child, only Hilary when she had reached the outer limits of terror and bereavement. He turned over in the bed and buried his face in the pillow and shook with spasms of grief. I got in beside him and did my best to hold him still and could not, and then simply pressed my body on top of his, the length of it, trying with all my strength and weight to contain the grief, to absorb it. Pain and loss stopped my own tears. I lay there for a long time, holding on to him, until the awful weeping and shaking gradually slowed and stopped, and only when I heard his breathing go deep and even did I let the monstrous white fatigue take me under, too. As it did, I thought, for the first time in my life, how simple, and how very seductive, it would be just not to wake up again.

I did, of course, because you always do, except once. When I did, heavy-limbed and still stupid with fatigue, the sky over the line of trees across Goat Creek was going ashen with another hot summer dawn, and the first thin, sleepy calls of the morning birds in the woods were beginning. Floated on the great bed as in a ship, and swathed in mosquito netting as in mist my emptied mind did not know where it was. But my flesh and muscles knew, and I stretched, with the deep, primitive luxury of a tired lioness, and my hand reached for Tom of its own volition, as it had many times before in this house, in this bed. Memory and his absence hit me at the same time. Galvanic grief and dread had me out of bed and running naked into the house before I had formulated a thought.

Heart hammering, I scanned the cool, silent living room and looked into the empty bathroom. I made a trotting, stiff-legged circuit of the wraparound porch. I ran back into the house and looked in his closet. His hunting clothes still hung there, and his rifle was still in the rack on the great stone fireplace, and the clothes he had worn the night before still lay in a heap beside the bed, where I had tossed them. But even before I saw that the pegs that held his bow and quiver of hunting arrows were empty, I knew that he was gone, and where. Cold and stiff with terror, weighted with foreknowledge as if with stone, I ran to the telephone and riffled clumsily through the Pemberton residential directory and found and dialed Chip Dabney's number. It would be Chip, I knew, not Clay; Tom would go for Chip first. Only then Clay, and perhaps not. But certainly Chip. I was literally whimpering and sobbing with terror as I dialed. Tom must not harm his cousin. It would be, for him and me, the end of everything.

Lucy Dabney's sleepy child's voice answered on the second ring; she had not, I thought, been asleep. I realized that I had been praying to hear Chip's sly drawl.

"It's Andy Calhoun, Lucy," I said, as briskly as I could. "Is Chip there? I have to talk to Chip."

"Hey, Andy," Lucy's fretful voice said. "What on earth are y'all doin'? First Tom and now you, and it's not even light, hardly—"

"Lucy, where is Chip?" I fairly screamed into the phone.

"Well, for goodness' sakes, you don't have to yell," she said. "He's gone out to the plantation. Tom called a while ago and said there was something out there that had to be tended to, and for Chip to meet him and make it quick. Chip left right after that. He said not to worry about breakfast; he'd get something at the Toddle House later on. He said something about Tom sounding funny. I said, When doesn't he? Really, is there no end to the trouble Tom Dabney's going to cause before he simmers down or somebody hauls him off? Chip looked awful; I told him to call his daddy and tell him where he was going; you never know with Tom."

"Did he call?" I said, unable to breathe.

"I don't know."

"Call him, Lucy, call him right now. Call Clay now!" I cried, and slammed the phone down on her aggrieved prattle. I scrambled into my damp, filthy clothes and shoes, sobbing in haste and fear, snatched my rifle from its rack on the chimney, and ran blindly out of the dim house into the brightening morning. Earl came rolling sleepily from under the steps and bobbled at me. I stopped on the bottom step and stared at him, and then ran back and dialed the Pemberton police station and told the thick-tongued deputy who answered to wake Harold Turbidy and send him out to King's Oak as fast as he could get there.

"Tell him to go on past the house down the dirt track through the soybean field, as far as he can go, and get out and come to the creekbank. He'll see a huge oak tree in the middle of the creek; he can't miss it. Tell him to hurry . . . tell him to hurry!"

"Jesus, lady, what's going on out there?" the deputy yelled.

"I don't know," I sobbed, and dropped the telephone and ran again. I did not wonder how I knew that Tom would have summoned Chip to the King's Oak, but there was no doubt in my mind that I would find them there. I could not have said what I planned to do when I got there. I could not think what I meant to do with the rifle. I only knew that I must not be too late. . . . It was not Chip Dabney I had called Harold Turbidy to save, but Tom. There was no doubt in my mind, either, what he had gone there to do.

I leaped the creek at its narrowest part and plunged into the undergrowth, heading upstream. I had been through these woods up to the King's Oak with Tom twice before, along Goat Creek, the precise route that I thought to follow now. But fear and tiredness and the sheer awfulness of the night before robbed me of wits and purpose and agility. I could not remember how long the trip took, and if at any place we had left the creekbank, and if there was, anywhere, the need to cross water. . . . I stumbled over a cypress root and fell headlong into the wet briers and undergrowth, my hands and knees sinking deep into the black slime beneath the leaf detritus, the rifle spinning down into it. I scrambled up, sobbing, shaking slime off my hands, and fell again, and got up again. I picked up the rifle and crashed on, blind and floundering, sweat already running from my hairline into my eyes, tears strangling in my nose. The rifle barrel banged against my leg, and the morning chorus of birds swelled and shrilled with alarm, and I heard the splashes of fleeing amphibians in the dark water, and farther away, on the other side of the creek, the crashing of deer put to flight by my clumsiness and the scent of my terror. I fetched up gagging and gasping beside a fallen tupelo and sank down on it and put my head in my hands and cried, because I knew that I could not, in the state I was in, get myself a mile upcreek, much less all the way to the King's Oak in time. I have never felt such a powerful sense of separateness, of otherness, from my surroundings, before or since. I had as totally and surely alienated the woods as if I had set fire to them.

I heard Scratch's voice then. There will never be any doubt in my mind that I did, and not some ghostly, disembodied voice from out of the ether or my subconscious, but a real, living, vivid, particular voice, with heft and sense and substance to it. Scratch's voice, and no other.

"That go for you, too, Andy," it said. "Long as you got the woods, you got me. I right out there, all the time." And, "Look inside, Andy. You find what you need in there. You got the woods inside you. Look inside."

A great stillness came into my laboring chest. I raised my wet, hot face and looked around. I knew I would see nothing; they were the last words he had said to me, in the living room of my house. I had brought them with me into the woods. But they were here, too; the living words had been waiting for me, in the Big Silver River swamp. Ease and looseness ran into my arms and legs, and my heart stopped its strictured struggling. I took a deep, shuddering breath of the wet, fragrant morning, and another, and got to my feet. The little rifle fit sweetly into the curve of my arm now, and my muscles felt springy and warm and powerful.

"I love you, Scratch," I said into the brightening silence, and went on upcreek. I found that I did not need to think ahead where I was going, that my feet and legs and muscles and eyes and ears and nose—all my senses but my mind—had a newfound wisdom beyond that in my head. As Tom had told Tim Ford to do, as Scratch had just bidden me, I let myself go, and went into the woods, into wildness. I became, as I never had before and never have again, not even the night just past, a creature of them, sure and silent. When I reached the bend in Goat Creek where a small clearing on the left broke the black wall of trees, the gray of dawn had turned to the bleached white-blue of a dog-day morning, and I was not even breathing hard. I straightened up from the crouch in which I had been trotting for the past miles, muscles only now beginning to cramp, and stretched, and looked to my left. If I remembered correctly, I should be able to see, perhaps a mile away, the great jumbled roofline of King's Oak over the surrounding trees. The tree was only another short mile upstream.

I saw the roof and more. I saw a great column of black smoke, boiling straight up into the deepening blue of morning.

"Scratch," I said aloud, mildly and insanely. "Look. Tom has set fire to King's Oak."

I ran the last mile and remember, now, none of it.

I came out on the bank of Goat Creek just across from the small island where the King's Oak stood. I shook the sweat from my eyes, fingers rigid around the stock of the Ruger, heart shaking my body as if in an ague, straining to see into the gloom under the great, ground-brushing branches, through the skeins of pewter moss. I saw a gleam of white and thought at first it was a probing finger of sunlight, but then watched as the shadows rearranged themselves and the whiteness built itself into the figure of a man. Squinting, I saw that it was not Chip Dabney, but his father, Clay, and that he was standing straight and still and empty-handed, and was wearing, astoundingly, nothing at all but a rough crown of oak leaves. The skiff was beached on the tan sand shelf of the little island, where Tom had beached it the night we had come to the King's Oak, but there was no sign of anything else touched by the hand of man in all the wild green morning. I could not look away from Clay Dabney, from the strong, spare, gnarled nakedness of him, from the still ruin of his face.

And then there was a sound above him, a muffled, strangled sob, like a child or an animal half-mute with terror, and I looked up into the canopy of the King's Oak. Chip Dabney was there, in the tree stand where I had sat almost precisely a year before, crouched in a tight knot on the floor of the stand, his face wrapped in his arms. I found that I could see him, though not clearly, through the screen of leaves that did not entirely hide him. I found that I was not surprised that he was there. I looked again at the motionless figure of his father, below him.

Clay could not have failed to hear me, but he did not look at me. He was staring straight across the creek at a point on the bank just opposite him, and he moved neither muscle nor eyelid. Slowly I turned to follow his gaze. Tom stood there, motionless in a hunter's crouch, about twenty yards upstream from me. In one hand he held, loosely, his bow. Like his uncle, he was naked, except for his arrow quiver, and like Clay, he wore a crown of oak leaves. I saw that his face and chest were striped, and wondered crazily what there was left alive at Goat Creek to sacrifice. Earl had certainly been fat and healthy enough. Still staring, I put my hand to my mouth, to stifle the insane laughter that bubbled there. I did not imagine that Tom could have failed to hear me, either, but I knew somehow that he was not going to look at me. The moment stopped and spun out endlessly, like a spider's web flung to the wind.

Tom lifted his head and looked up into the tree stand at Chip's cowering figure. I saw disgust and revulsion on his face as clearly as if he stood next to me, but it faded, and a peaceful, faraway, supremely focused intensity took its place. He looked back at the man beneath the oak tree. He straightened up from the crouch, slowly, slowly, and fitted an arrow into the bow, and just as slowly drew it back. He held the draw for a cold, ringing, endless moment. It was aimed at his uncle's heart.

The breath that had been stopped in my chest burst free then, and I screamed. The sound seemed to crash and carom on and on in the woods, trapped forever in a sphere of silence. Birds rose screeching from trees, snakes and turtles slid into black water. Off in the canebrake the stampeding hooves of whitetails sounded.

Tom turned slowly and looked at me. He did not lower the arrow. His face was pure and emptied, and his eyes were light and blind.

"Don't," I said. It was a whisper. I could not raise my voice. "Don't."

Tom held both the look and the arrow for another endless moment, and then he threw his head back and howled, the same eerie, wordless howl I had heard once before and would hear, now, for the rest of my life, and threw the bow and arrow aside and plunged straight into the still black water, the water that, now, he so loathed and feared, and crashed through it to the island. Spray sheeted and glistened around him in the first of the morning sun, and water ran off him onto the mossy earth; pink rivulets of water and blood or paint sluiced down from his face and shoulders. His eyes were closed and his mouth contorted with the cry, which echoed on and on, over and above mine. Clay Dabney stood under the oak like a statue. He did not move and he did not blink. Still howling, Tom reached for him, hands curved into talons, muscles knotted in his forearms. Like an automaton, I swung the rifle to my shoulder. I got Tom in my sights just as he reached his uncle and seized him in a terrible, strangling grip. In the mad, whirling moment before I tightened my finger on the trigger I thought that he meant to crush Clay to death in his arms, and then I saw that he had buried his face in his uncle's neck and was crying, huge, tearing, primitive sobs. Slowly, slowly, Clay Dabney raised his arms and embraced his nephew. Tears ran from his closed eyes.

I felt the earth heave and drop away under my feet. I threw the rifle into the underbrush and sat down hard and dropped my head into my arms. The darkness whirled and whirled; white motes and colored pinwheels arced behind my closed eyes. A crawling, hateful buzzing ran up my arms from my wrists. Nausea rose like a cold flood. I heard, over the wrenching men's grief from the island, the morning birds begin their songs once more.

I was still sitting so, and the two men, young and old, still stood in each other's arms, when the thin yowl of Harold Turbidy's patrol car whined to a stop far away, up at the big house, and I heard the faint sound of voices, and slamming doors, and running feet through the woods of King's Oak.

"Hey, Harold," I said into the filthy, salty wetness of my forearm, not opening my eyes. "Wanna buy a duck?"

EPILOGUE

It is Indian summer now. I say every season that I think spring is, after all, the best time at Goat Creek, or winter, or summer. But today, with the high, steel-blue vault of October perfect and unbroken overhead, and the water giving back the blue, and the high sun burning dry and sleepily on my face and forearms, I have to think that Goat Creek will never be any better than this. Today is the best of all of the seasons. The air is clear with the crystal clarity of winter, and the wind has the softness of spring, and the woods are afire with autumn, and the water still holds the warmth of summer. From the porch I can see Hilary in the water, up to her brown waist in it, calling for Earl and Raquel to follow her in. Earl bobs on the bank like, as Tom once said, an old borscht belt comedian, but I know that he will eventually follow her in, coming out to where she is in a resigned dog paddle. Raquel, unless her temper has vastly improved, will chirr crossly and go back to her babies under the porch. There are only two of them, I think, unless there are more and we only think we are seeing the same ones over and over. Off in the goathouse the Toggenburgs are bleating for their supper. There are four, three nice does and a conceited young buck we have named Sylvester Stallone. Reese and Martin found them for me. Goat Creek must never again be without goats.

Goat Creek is not the same, of course. It can't be, without him. I'm not a saint, and I'm probably not even crazy enough. I'm still never going to kill an animal, and I still draw the line at deer blood. But I'm trying. I've done a little dancing and a little chanting out here, on the odd occasion, and I find that I am really indecently fond of going naked in the woods. And Hilary is extraordinarily good at the old things. She has them in her manuscript, "The True Story of Tom Dabney." It was what she was writing down, all those long days back in the summer; what she remembered of the old things. What she sensed. What Scratch told her, that last day. It isn't perfect, by any means, but it'll do until Tom gets back.

He'll come out of the hospital. It won't be long. Reese says probably around Christmas. They've already said they'll release him into Clay's custody, or maybe even mine, as he asked. Of course, that was before they knew I'd quit my job at the college and moved out here. They'll probably think I'm too crazy now myself to take charge of a recovering crazy. A paranoid schizophrenic with pyromaniacal tendencies, I believe they said. So it'll probably have to be Clay, at least officially. He'll do it. He'll spend his life trying to make up to Tom for . . . all of it. Everything. He really was going to let Tom kill him that morning. He stood there, naked and wreathed, and waited for that ritual death. Tom won't care whom he's released to, he'll be so glad to get out of there. He says it's full of sociopaths and substance abusers, not a decent lunatic in the place. But it's a damned sight better than jail.

Oh, yes, he'll come out, if he doesn't die from the water. I don't think he will, not for a long time, anyway. Nobody has seen Goat Creek light up since they filled the pools. But, as he says, maybe his prick will fall off. Or maybe not. It doesn't matter to me. When he comes out we'll be here, Hilary and I. He's right; I can see that. I saw it when he walked into that awful water, knowing what it could do to him. I guess I saw it before then, really. I don't understand it, and maybe I never will, but I know that he is right. There has to be a crazy saint at Goat Creek. If there isn't, a hole in the world will open up and all the *thou*s will leak out, and the woods will die. The wild will die. It was a very near thing this time. A very near thing.

So we will stay and wait for him, and keep things in place. And I will teach my child the things she has to know about this place and the world, including the hard necessity for saints. That there are very few ever in the world, and we should honor and take care of the ones who accept the call to it, or at least, not make things harder for them. That sometimes, when we can, we have to sort of . . . stand in for them.

I can teach her all that, and she can learn. She is, after all, my daughter.

And my name, after all, is Diana.